CALIFORNIA
CAPERS

D1056088

CALIFORNIA CAPERS

THREE ROMANCE MYSTERIES

DANA MENTINK

BARBOUR
PUBLISHING

© 2008 *Trouble Up Finny's Nose* by Dana Mentink
© 2008 *Fog Over Finny's Nose* by Dana Mentink
© 2008 *Treasure Under Finny's Nose* by Dana Mentink

ISBN 978-1-60260-417-9

All rights reserved. No part of this publication may be reproduced or transmitted in any form or by any means without written permission of the publisher.

Scripture taken from the King James Version of the Bible.

Scripture taken from the HOLY BIBLE, NEW INTERNATIONAL VERSION®. NIV®. Copyright © 1973, 1978, 1984 by International Bible Society. Used by permission of Zondervan. All rights reserved.

This book is a work of fiction. Names, characters, places, and incidents are either products of the author's imagination or used fictitiously. Any similarity to actual people, organizations, and/or events is purely coincidental.

Cover thumbnails:
Design by Kirk DouPonce, DogEared Design
Illustration by Jody Williams

Published by Barbour Publishing, Inc., P.O. Box 719, Uhrichsville, OH 44683, www.barbourbooks.com

Our mission is to publish and distribute inspirational products offering exceptional value and biblical encouragement to the masses.

 Member of the
Evangelical Christian
Publishers Association

Printed in the United States of America.

TROUBLE UP FINNY'S NOSE

We grow accustomed to the Dark—
When Light is put away—
As when the Neighbor holds the Lamp
To witness her Good-bye

EMILY DICKINSON

Prologue

The view from up Finny's Nose was amazing. Breathtaking even. According to the guidebooks, it offered an "uninterrupted panoramic of the majestic Pacific Ocean and its pristine coastline."

Frederick Finny had admired the coastline for a different reason. While aiming for a secluded nook in which to unload his Canadian rum for the parched victims of Prohibition, he ran aground in the treacherous California riptide. The only hope of escape for his vessel was to empty hundreds of barrels of premium liquor into the ocean.

But even after every precious drop was dribbled into salty oblivion, the vessel remained stubbornly wedged. The ship was lost, but Finny old-timers elevated to legend the exploits of a gaggle of drunken crabs that wove their way to the beach and marched in dizzy circles for hours.

Finny slogged ashore and made the best of his misfortune, changing careers from rum smuggling to beekeeping, eventually settling at the top of the steep bluff that looked, for all the world, like a tremendous nose.

In the afternoon sun, through squinted eyes, the town of Finny was straight out of a postcard. The residents and buildings alike seemed to age gently into a condition just shy of shabby with enough quaintness sprinkled throughout to make the town a charming little stop for tourists looking for that perfect coastal escape. Not the overnight, weekend getaway, but more along the lines of a lazy morning stop on the way to the larger towns like Carmel and Monterey—places less shabby and more chic.

On this day, except for the peeling paint on the Finny Hotel and the dead man propped on his head in the Central Park fountain, the town was definitely postcard material.

Alva Hernandez walked his entire route along the foggy main street before he finally stopped to chat with the upside-down man in the fountain. Eventually, he put down his remaining newspapers and whacked on one of the protruding muddy boots. Scratching his grizzled hair, Alva removed his teeth, inserted a lemon drop, and sat down to await further developments.

1

W hat is this?" Ruth Budge stammered. "What is going on here?" Her husband, Phillip, was supposed to be writing memoirs before his sudden death, a collection of stories from the life of a country vet. What in the world was this thing? Certainly not a recounting of anything her husband had ever experienced. It couldn't be. Ruth began to read again at page one. . .for the third time.

"Oh no!"

She slammed on the brakes and skidded to a stop inches from the squad car. "I get a parking ticket for an expired meter, and this guy can park his cruiser practically in the middle of. . ." Her words trailed off as she noticed the cowboy boot sticking out from under the open car door. "Ohhh. This is not good." Ignoring the pinging of the keys-in-the-ignition warning, she slid out of the car.

The cop was facedown in the gravel, one arm stretched toward the radio, which rested just out of his reach in the dust.

"Are you all right?"

Really smart question, Ben. People commonly lie facedown on the road if they are fit and perky. Especially cops. *Trembling, she knelt down and patted his shoulder.*

"Ummmm. . .sir? Officer? Can you hear me?" She patted some more. With shaking fingers she felt for a pulse under the prickly brown hair just below his throat, recoiling at the stickiness left on her fingertips.

"Ohhh boy. Calm down. Think what to do. Get your cell. . .no!" The phone sat on her kitchen table, recharging. "Think! People used to do charitable deeds before cell phones. Okay. Radio."

As she fumbled in the gravel for the receiver, a mustard-colored sedan pulled out of the copse of trees and began backing up. Stopping about fifteen yards from where she crouched, three men got out.

She felt her body go cold as she struggled to breathe. Frantically, she pounded the prone figure on the back. "Please wake up, Mr. Officer. I think this is what you would call a situation."

She squeezed the button on the radio. In a cracking sotto voce *tone she quavered, "Help me, please! I am Benjamina Pena. I am with, er, a really big cop, and he's unconscious. There are three nasty-looking men on Old Highway One just past the breakwater. I think they're gonna kill us. Ten-four, uh, over and out, oh no!"*

Praying her message had been received by someone—a truck driver, crop duster, anyone—she peeked over the top of the driver's side door. The three men had slowed to a stop a few cautious yards from the car, peering into the windshield and under the front license plate.

"Hey, lady. What you doin' to that cop? He ain't no business of yours."

Desperately, she fumbled with the fastener on his gun belt. "Yeah? Well, I don't reckon he's any business of yours, either." That sounded pretty close to the John Wayne movies she'd seen.

They laughed. One said, "She has a streak of somethin', eh? We goin' to have fun with you."

With a jerk, the catch finally gave way. She yanked the gun out and stood up so quickly it made her dizzy.

"Okay. Now you listen up, you troglodytes. Any one of you comes a step closer and I'll drop you right where you stand."

That brought them up short. After a second of shocked silence, they relaxed. "A trogla-what?" said the skinniest one.

The tallest one with the bandanna tied like a sausage casing around his head interrupted the laughter. "Well, well. Ain't she a tough girly. I guess we got ourselves here a Jane Wayne."

Their eyes widened as she released the safety on the semiautomatic.

Aiming at what she took to be their midsections, midway between the bandannas and underwear poking out of oversized pants, she croaked, "I don't know what your problem is with this cop, but I will shoot you if you take one more step."

Later she tried to recall if they had actually stepped or just realigned their slouching, but somehow she pulled the trigger. The recoil knocked her over, slamming her shoulders into the gravel.

Lying on her back, shoving the hair out of her eyes, she watched the thin man grab his ear and howl in pain. The others hoisted him by the pants and hauled him up the road to their car. They roared away in a shower of loose gravel.

Benjamina watched the dust settle.

She flopped back onto the gravel. "I can't believe I just did that."

———

Ruth rolled the papers into a tube, clutching them to her breast. This story, this novel, whatever it was, had hit her blindside.

She had discovered the small pile of papers in the file drawer, next to the information on her funeral plot. The bizarre surprise threw her completely off balance, compelling her to read and reread before tearing the file cabinet to pieces looking for more. By the time she returned to what was left of her senses, she had missed her morning hair appointment by an hour.

By now, Felice was boarding a plane to Fiji. Ruth felt like crying.

It was not just a matter of vanity. Ruth was not, nor ever had been in her forty-six years of living, a beautiful woman. Nevertheless, she refused to be wandering around town looking like Miss Havisham. When Phillip was alive, he made a point of taking her to lunch after her monthly salon appointments.

"You look like a million bucks," he would say. Her cheeks would warm every time.

Rescheduling with another hairdresser was simply out of the question. Ruth would die with numerous sins on her conscience, but committing infidelity to her long-time hairdresser was not one of them. She would just have to endure the three weeks until Felice returned.

The striking of the clock made her start. She felt guilty, as if she had been caught reading a teenager's diary. "Oh, for goodness' sake," she muttered. "It's not like he'll catch me reading it."

Phillip had been gone for almost two years, and she still expected to see him around every corner like the Ghost of Christmas Past.

She stuffed the papers back into the crammed file drawer and sat in the chair, listening to nothing. There was only a faint rustling from her flock of handicapped seagulls and terns outside and the ticking of the clock inside to break the silence. Ruth looked around the space she had lived in for twenty years and wondered why the furnishings seemed strange to her, as if she were an insect that had just flown through the window to reconnoiter. She folded her hands to pray. "Dear God," she began. After a minute more of silence, she gave voice to the thought that grieved her most. "Where are You?" There was no answer, only that endless tick.

She looked down to see what she had put on in the middle of the night when she mistook it for morning. Faded denim stretch pants and a ragged crocheted sweater the color of a rusty scouring pad. Now that it really was Monday morning, she felt as though she hadn't slept at all the night before. She sat as the silence squeezed in on her with the inexorable pressure of a glacier, until she couldn't stand it any longer. After a quick check of her backyard gaggle, she set off.

The cold morning air left her breathless as she crested the bridge of Finny's Nose. She figured it was an enterprising sweatshirt manufacturer who spread the rumor that California was one warm sandy beach from Canada to Mexico. Though the drive along the rugged coastal cliffs bordering Highway 1 provided spectacular views of secluded beaches, the sun had to wait until the fog evaporated to make an appearance. She had sold many a photo of this amazing scenery to travel magazines. It was quaint, poetic even, and colder than a well-digger's toes. All in all, it was the kind of sleepy little town that fine postcards are made of. The kind of place that, at one time, spoke to Ruth's soul. As she plodded along, her mind replayed scenes from her late husband's. . .novel.

Lost in her own thoughts, she murmured a hello to Alva Hernandez seated on the edge of the Central Park fountain and passed by. Then it hit her. A quick double take dispelled the notion that she was hallucinating. There was definitely a pair of ragged boots protruding from behind Alva's shoulder. A few moments of closer examination convinced her that she wouldn't need her rusty CPR skills.

"Alva. Are you. . .all right?" she asked.

"Yep," he said around a mouthful of yellow candy.

"Oh. Good." She fiddled with the zipper on her jacket. "You know there is a man in the fountain, don't you?"

"Sure do." He stuck a finger deep between cheek and gum to dislodge a sticky ball.

"Well, he—he doesn't seem to be all right," she proposed gently.

"Nope. Ain't moved a bit. Never seen anyone hold their breath that long."

Marveling at the sheer ludicrousness of the situation, she suggested to Alva that perhaps they should have a go at removing the upside-down man from the lazily bubbling water.

"Sure thing. I'll get the starboard side," Alva said cheerfully.

It was as if she were watching from outside herself as they each grabbed a handful of the slippery figure. The man was heavy and uncooperatively stiff. Fighting the bile rising in her throat, Ruth clasped the slick boots, and with Alva tugging vigorously on the man's overalls, the pair hauled the body onto the grass.

The dead face seemed surprised to be looking up into the two live ones. He was cold and slimy, like celery left too long in the vegetable crisper. Ruth leaned back on her heels, nauseous, and then noticed several people hastily making their way over to the damp trio. A few chilled tourists clapped their hands over their mouths in astonishment. The slippery dead man was definitely not part of their mental postcards.

"Ewwww," cried a woman in an *I Went up Finny's Nose* sweatshirt. "Is he really dead?"

"Yep," said Alva. "Pretty much."

By this time, Bubby Dean had emerged from the nearby High Water Pub and ducked his head back inside to call for help. The small crowd grew. Two middle-aged women stood with their hands fluttering over their mouths. A well-dressed man with a speckled bald head talked on a cell phone.

Ruth sat down on the edge of the fountain, suddenly overwhelmed by the outrageous events of the day. The novel. The man in the fountain. Felice in Fiji.

Alva patted her head and said gently, "It's okay, chickie. I got somethin' here for you." He fished around in his pocket and handed her a sucker. It looked as if it had been licked a few times and rewrapped.

The police arrived to find a huddle of tourists, a sticky old man asking bystanders for change, and a middle-aged Ruth Budge, laughing until the tears ran down her chin.

2

S he passed a solitary half hour reading and rereading the posters on the police station wall later that morning. Officer Katz sat behind his desk, chin resting on his hand while he waited patiently for someone on the phone. He'd been holding for ten minutes so far.

Her head whirled at the bizarre turn her life had taken in the past twenty-four hours. Ruth Marylyn Budge was not the sort of person who happened upon secrets and found dead bodies languishing about. Excitement did not visit her often, maybe not ever, except that day in December when a deer found its way into her upstairs bathtub and destroyed two chairs and her hair dryer during its crazed rampage. Her reflection in the mirrored door reminded her that she was basically square—rectangular actually—with a wide brace of collarbones, a thick middle, and short serviceable legs. Solid, reliable, built from sturdy farm stock.

So here she was. A nice, square woman who had recently discovered a dead husband's secret novel and a corpse. She looked down at her hands to see if there were any telltale marks of her strange activities. The entry door popped opened and Maude Stone billowed through, her bun bobbing along behind her.

"He did it again!" she bellowed to no one in particular. "He does it on purpose. I want him arrested immediately." She was a tiny woman with a voice intended for a much larger vessel.

Officer Katz glanced up, covering the phone still stuck to his ear. "Good morning, Maude. Is that fog lifting any yet?"

Her eyes widened into saucers and a flush mottled her face. "I do not want to discuss the weather, Nathan Katz. I want you to arrest Alva this minute."

Nate cleared his throat. "I've told you before, Maude, we can't arrest someone for accidentally stepping on your primroses."

"Accidentally! He does it on purpose. He brings my paper to the door and intentionally ruins my flowers."

Maude lived in the second house down on Whist Street, and the children nicknamed her the Wicked Witch of Whist. Often, on her way to the beach in the wee hours of the morning, Ruth witnessed Alva delivering Maude's paper and zestfully treading on each and every flower with precision.

"Well, I am not going to let you ignore me, Officer." With that, she hiked herself onto his desk and folded her arms defiantly across her striped sweater, like the King of Siam. "I am going to stay right here until you deliver some justice."

TROUBLE UP FINNY'S NOSE

In her youth, Maude had been a contortionist in a traveling circus, so it did not surprise Ruth that she made the jump onto Officer Katz's desktop without even rustling his Post-it notes. It didn't seem to surprise the officer, either.

At that moment Nate's colleague Mary Derisi came into the office. She shot a look at the woman standing on Nate's desk. "Hi, Maude. Hi, Ruth. Nate, if you don't stop borrowing my stapler, I will be forced to glue it to my desk."

"Sorry," Nate said, reaching around Maude and handing Mary the stapler.

"So, Ruth," Mary said, flipping her short braid behind her shoulder, "I hear you had quite an experience at the fountain. How are you doing with all that?"

"Oh, well, okay, I guess."

"Good. The weird thing about dead bodies is they look so lifelike, apart from the not breathing thing." She tapped the stapler against her muscular thigh thoughtfully. "Jack is ready to see you now. I'll walk you back." She left the room without a backward glance at the woman atop the desk.

Officer Katz was still holding.

"Do you see this?" Maude yelled to Ruth. "Do you see how these people treat me?"

Ruth nodded, making a mental note to bake some cookies for Nate and Mary before her next hair appointment.

The door to Detective Denny's office opened and Alva shuffled out, a crumpled bag of M&M's in his hand. "Your turn, chickie," he croaked.

"Thank you, Alva. Do you need a ride?"

The detective spoke up. "Officer Katz will be escorting him home."

"On a motorcycle?" Alva's bushy brows zinged upward hopefully as Nate walked up behind Ruth.

"Sorry, Alva. We don't have any motorcycle cops in this department. The car is nice, though. You'll have a comfortable ride." He tried hard to hold the corners of his mouth steady. "Thank you for your time. We'll call if we need any more information."

"Right." Alva hitched up his pants and whispered to Officer Katz. "Is that crazy woman still standing on your desk?"

The officer nodded mournfully.

"She's like a fungus between your toes. You'll never get rid of her." He patted Nate on the back. "Got any change for the candy machine?"

Ruth and the detective watched him depart and settled into the mud-brown office. She noticed a neat circle of yellow M&M's on the mammoth metal desk.

"He doesn't eat the yellow ones?" she asked.

"Nope. Says they taste like, er, urine." They both chuckled. "Hello, Mrs. Budge. It has been a long time, hasn't it?"

"Please call me Ruth. Yes, we haven't spoken in quite a while. If it's all right to ask, how is your little boy?" She watched the pain settle over his handsome face like a fine dust.

"About the same." The wrinkles around his brown eyes were deep. "I forgot how long it's been since we talked last. Have you been all right?"

"Yes. Fine," she said.

Jack looked at her intently. "You're sure, Ruth? I haven't seen you around for the past few weeks. Maybe I'm not supposed to notice, but you look a little tired." He cleared his throat. "I think you'd better tell me about your morning."

She related in an absurdly matter-of-fact manner the sequence of events that had brought her to sit in this hard-backed chair, leaving out the parts pertaining to novels and Felice. "Now that I think of it, I guess we shouldn't have moved the man out of the fountain. It just seemed so wrong to see him in there. Did we ruin some evidence or something?"

Jack rubbed his hands over the dark stubble on his chin. "Don't worry about it. I think we can work around it. Did you know the victim?"

"No. Well, I know his name is, was, Crew Donnelly. He is, was, well, I know he worked as a gardener in town. I think he was employed by the gallery. He planted a beautiful display of flowers in front of the library, too."

"Ever talk to him?"

"Only a 'Good morning' now and again. He wasn't what you would consider a warm, fuzzy sort of fellow. I had a suspicion that he blamed my birds for eating the grass seed he planted at the post office. They didn't do it," she hastened to add, "but they do have beady little eyes and a shifty manner about them, I'll admit."

He laughed again. "I don't usually get such entertainment from murder investigations, but this one has definitely 'got color,' as my wife used to say." The shimmer of sadness stained his face once again. "So you were headed to the beach and just happened across a body. Talk about the wrong place and the wrong time. Alva didn't know the guy, either."

"Wait a minute." She shook her head. "Oh, actually, it's nothing pertinent. Never mind."

"What?" He put down the stained coffee mug he had raised to his lips.

"Well, I am sure this is wandering off the beaten path. I did have a short conversation with Crew Donnelly just yesterday, but I forgot all about it. Anyway, I was walking the birds down by the lake, and I took a stroll around the gardens while they bobbed. Mr. Donnelly was pushing a wheelbarrow from the greenhouse out to the back lot where the compost piles are kept. I thought it was odd because he had the most gorgeous shrubby plant in the wheelbarrow. I asked him where he was taking it."

"What did he say?"

"He said it was going to the trash heap. I couldn't believe it, a lovely plant like that, and I made some comment to that effect. He told me orders were orders. I assumed the orders came from Napoleon Prinn. Weird." Ruth toyed with the yellow circle of M&M's on the desktop.

"Is there anything else?" Jack prodded gently.

"Actually, I sort of. . .took it. The plant. After Crew left. It just seemed like such a shame to let it wither in the trash heap. Is that a felony of some sort? Discarded plant theft?"

He laughed long and loud, his tanned face looking suddenly younger. "I don't think so. Believe me, if that's the only crime you ever commit, I'd say you're doing well. And how is the plant, by the way?"

"Hmm. So-so. Rutherford managed to get hold of a branch on the way home, but I think it will recover." She noted his blank look. "He's one of my crankier gulls."

The phone on the detective's desk rang. "I'm sorry, Ruth. I'll let you go before I get knee deep in a phone conversation. Thank you for coming down, and I hope I see you around soon. Do you need a ride home?" When she declined, his dark eyes twinkled, "Are you sure I can't buy you a bag of candy or something?"

"Surely you don't think I would be tempted by a measly bag of chocolate? Now if you've got a bushel basket of M&M's in that vending machine, that's another story." The boyish smile on his face was so very like her son's that it made her heart twist.

He was still chuckling as the door closed softly behind her.

In the hallway, Ruth sagged against the scarred wall under a sudden onslaught of fatigue. She checked her watch. Ten past twelve.

"Well, Ruth," she sighed, "at least you made it to noon. After a morning like this, things could not possibly get worse."

Within hours she regretted the words.

3

By the time Ruth had returned home from the police station, she was too tired to do anything but fix herself a frozen dinner and stare mindlessly at the television. Then she sat in a near-scalding tub and tumbled into bed before the sun was fully set. She dreamed about rubbery dead men and women shooting people's ears off.

Now, on a frigid Tuesday morning, she was in the kitchen, enveloped in a cloud of sizzling steam. The heat from the oil stung her face, rousing her from a daze. It still seemed so unreal that the same hands deftly slicing mounds of white onions had quite recently hauled a corpse from the Central Park fountain. She could almost feel the slippery rubber on her fingertips.

She was jittery and irritable and she did not want to be in this kitchen at the crack of dawn, slaving over a hot stove for seven feathery ingrates. Martha and Grover were both the victims of BB guns, and the others boasted battle scars from cats, fishing lines, and lures. Phillip had adopted them all, and they got along as well as a totally selfish group of toddlers with no social skills can be expected to. He built them a small covered area where they could weather out the storms, should there be any. The only insurmountable problem was their despicable behavior with guests. The Budges tried a few backyard barbecues, but the birds flattened anyone who held, might have held, or would likely hold in the future any type of foodstuffs. Phillip swore he saw them conspiring before they tripped Pastor Henny and sent him sprawling while they quickly devoured his shrimp canapés.

It was much easier to care for the persnickety bunch with Phillip around.

It was much easier to live with Phillip around.

It was not fair, she thought, that Phillip and God had deserted her on the same awful day. The notion filled her with guilt. Was her faith really so weak? Like the mustard seed that briefly flourished until it met with scorching sunlight? Was God only in her heart when times were happy?

The doorbell caused her to jump, and she gouged her thumb. Grumbling as loudly as she dared, she put down her knife and headed for the door.

The bell clamored a second time before she opened it to Gregory, a pimpled youth sporting a Smashing Pumpkins T-shirt. She wondered if the "smashing" was a verb or an adjective. The boy looked distinctly startled.

"Hello, miss, er. . .ma'am. . .um. . .madam. I am sorry to interrupt, uh. . ."

"No problem, Gregory. I was just doing some frying. What can I do for you? Can you come in for a minute? I've got something on the stove."

His eyes were firmly fixed on his tired sneakers. "No! Er, no, ma'am. I have— it's a delivery." He hastily shoved a stiff white envelope into her hands and scurried like a frightened beetle down the gravel walk.

"Well, thank you," she yelled to his retreating back. He answered by springing onto a dilapidated bike parked at the curb and pedaling furiously toward town.

It wasn't until after she had closed the door that it came to her. She removed her apron and went upstairs to put on her pants.

On the return trip, somewhere around the seventh step, her nose caught the smell of melting kitchen. Recovering from a moment of frozen panic, she sprinted down the remainder of the stairs and plunged into the black smoke. Locating the stove more by familiarity than sight, she grabbed a sooty pot holder and turned off the heat, but not before some of the oil caught and a plume of flame leapt at her. Slamming a lid down on the boiling pot of oil, she flung open the door to the outside. The cool air felt delicious on her scalding face as she gulped in lungfuls of mist.

The shrill beeping of the smoke alarm pierced the air. There was a distinct smell of singed hair. With a finger, she explored her remaining eyebrow stubble. In the distance came the wail of a siren.

Seven pairs of fluorescent yellow eyes glowered at her.

"Well, I'm sorry," Ruth said, "but I had a kitchen fire."

The glowering continued unabated.

"You're lucky the whole house didn't go up in smoke."

More baleful looks.

"You'll need to make do with the ones I've finished, and the rest will have to wait." Fourteen bandy gray legs vied for positions on the small step.

She solemnly shouldered the platter of cold onion rings and hung two of the greasy treats on each anxious beak. As the gulls hustled off into the yard to devour their treat, the littlest one looked at her with a cocked head.

"Yes, I am all right, Herbert. Thank you for asking." She watched his wedged bottom disappear into the yard before she sat down on the step to cry.

She did not need to check the clock later when she heard the crash against the front door. Her paper was always delivered at precisely ten o'clock, long after the breaking news was no longer newsworthy. Alva was as ruthlessly reliable as zero-hour labor pains. At eighty-two, he was a fine newspaper boy, and apart from occasionally urinating in the Central Park fountain, he was an asset to the community. An odd visitor to the park would complain now and again, but his indiscretions were easily remedied with an extra squirt of chlorine. That little problem was a good deal easier to fix than the latest unwanted addition to the fountain.

"Thank you, Alva," she shouted from her blackened kitchen.

"You got it, sweet cheeks." The endearment was one he applied to everyone, from the waitress at the Rusty Pump to Finny's mayor. "It was a hoot to watch all them fire engines this morning. See ya later."

She felt the accumulated humiliation of having to explain to the fire department the events that led up to one of her neighbors, Mrs. Hodges, calling 911. She didn't think the black smoke billowing from the kitchen was all that momentous, but apparently even small kitchen fires required a code-three response. Within moments her house was filled with the eager, helmeted volunteers of the Finny Fire Department.

Even more embarrassing was the arrival of Monk, who had jogged from his catering business as soon as he heard the news. His face was lined with concern. She was not sure why she felt so jittery when he was around, but the last thing she wanted was to have him witness her kitchen disaster. He was sent away with a hug and a thank you.

Securely zipped in the white Tyvek suit borrowed from the fire department and armed with Pine Sol and a soft brush, she began scouring her kitchen from ceiling to tile. The blackened grease did not give up without a fight, and Ruth finally tumbled into a chair on her patio, too tired even to remove her green rubber boots. How in the world could she forget about a pot of boiling oil on the stove? Probably the same way she forgot about the pants.

Her husband would have said something comforting about it happening to everyone and quietly helped her clean up the mess, knowing she was thoroughly punishing herself. Then again, he consorted with a whole collection of wild folks whom she didn't even know about. Now that was ridiculous. It was a book, a story, not an affair. Then why did it feel like such a betrayal to find out her life partner, her soul mate, had a secret passion? Even if it was for something imaginary. And now there was no way to know, no way to find out. She was alone with her grief and her questions.

Alone.

The word bounced around in her head. Where was God in all this? Where was the Father who had given her a soul mate and then taken him away, leaving behind only memories and a big, fat secret? For what seemed like the millionth time, she wondered why she could not feel His presence anymore. She tried to shove down the anger, but it would not go quietly. "Why did You leave me, too?" she called to the ceiling. Her heart felt as empty as her house.

When she finally made it upstairs again, Ruth reached for her bedside lamp

TROUBLE UP FINNY'S NOSE

and found the crisp envelope that the boy had delivered before the fire, nestled innocently next to an antique hairbrush. "You'd better be something good, you lousy piece of pulp. I'll never get the grease out of that coffeemaker." She tore open the stiff envelope and read the invitation inside.

4

The residential portion of Finny proper tended to huddle along the nostril area of Finny's Nose, pockets of small dwellings clustered along narrow streets radiating outward from the center of town. The farthest-reaching clusters looked down from their precarious perch on the steep cliffs to the ocean. Ruth counted herself lucky to be farther inland when the heavy storm season hit.

As she marched upslope that afternoon, occasionally stepping over one of her bird companions, the houses gave way to fields of ornamental flowers: neat squares of geometrically precise plantings and irrigation systems, cut in between with chocolate brown soil. The palette of colors changed with the seasons, from pastel lilies and snapdragons in the warm weather to vibrant poinsettia reds in the winter.

The nurseries gradually morphed into grazing land and mom-and-pop farms, producing everything from brussels sprouts to bottles of translucent amber honey with the comb floating, fetus-like, inside. Finally, at the top of Finny's protuberance was a grassy plateau, home to the Finny Art Gallery and its outlying greenhouse. At certain opportune moments, visitors could stand on the gallery steps and enjoy a snootful of perfumey chrysanthemums, liquefied cow manure, and the pico de gallo wafting up from the town square.

When Ruth finally led the squabbling parade of birds along the gravelly path in front of the gallery at the apex of Finny's Nose, she paused to catch her breath, noting that the restorations were limping along at the proverbial snail's pace.

That must really frost Prinn's cookies, she thought with a smile.

What was it about that man that made people enjoy goading him? Perhaps it was the arrogance that coated him like a Teflon glaze. He was handsome, successful, educated, certainly. And charming. Flattery was his specialty. Absently she turned and separated two of the gulls. "No, Zachary. Let him alone."

"That is absolutely fascinating."

Ruth peered around at a young lady struggling to haul a box from an old Volkswagen van.

"Pardon?"

"Those gulls just follow you around like, like, ducklings." The redheaded woman ogled over the top of the heavy cardboard box clutched against her stomach.

"Actually, only four of them are gulls. The other three are terns. They are the

21

walking wounded, I'm afraid. None of them could fly away if they wanted to. So they've taken me on as their adopted squadron leader. If they don't get their walk, my shrubs suffer the consequences."

"Do you walk them for their exercise or yours?"

"Both, actually. I came to talk to Mr. Prinn about the gallery dedication, and I thought I'd kill two birds with one stone, so to speak."

"He's not in today. I just talked to his secretary and he won't be back until late this afternoon."

"That figures. I just walked three miles for nothing. Oh well. That's the way things have been going lately."

The woman jerked her head quickly to toss the rusty curls from her face. She let the carton slide down her legs to the ground and brushed her hands on her patched overalls to extend a palm to Ruth. "Red Finchley."

"Ruth Budge. Are you helping with the gallery restoration?"

Red squatted next to the milling birds. "What?" she said. "Oh no. I work for the Shaum Gallery in New York. Mr. Prinn purchased a few of our pieces and I'm delivering them. Good service, eh?"

"Excellent, I'd say. What type of pieces did he purchase?"

"I'm afraid I'm not at liberty to say. All that hoity-toity art secrecy stuff. I guess he wants to keep it a surprise. Do they have names? The birds, I mean?"

"Oh yes. That's Zachary, Rutherford, Grover, Teddy, Ulysses, Herbert, and Martha's the one underneath your van."

"You're kidding."

"No. My husband named them. He thought they had a presidential air. He was a veterinarian, sort of the Pied Piper of maimed birds. We had a real trend going there until Martha was given to us. She had to settle for the first lady."

"And they just follow you around?" Her freckled lips quivered in amusement.

"Well, they sort of live with me. I have a cottage. They probably just stick around for the onion rings. That and the fact that a flightless bird wouldn't last long here."

"They get to have onion rings?"

"I'm afraid that's a naughty treat I indulge them with occasionally. I'm sure their cholesterol levels can handle a little fried food."

The woman stretched out her hand to the nearest bird that inclined his head for a gentle scratch. Ruth thought she had never seen such interesting hands. Red's knuckles were knobby, nicked, and stained like the old leather coin purse Ruth's grandfather used to carry. The nails were bitten down to the quick, and a tide of freckles washed over her hands and crept upward into the dirty sleeves. Staring at them made the freckles seem to dance.

"Which one is this?"

"Ulysses. You can tell by the scar under his eye. He got tangled up in fishing net." During the explanations, three other birds sauntered over and insinuated themselves under Red's outstretched arms, poking pointy beaks into her pockets.

"Oh my." She laughed. "I think I'm surrounded."

"Yes, they are rather forward, I'm afraid, and nosy, too." Ruth pushed a pointy beak out of the cardboard box. "That's none of your business, Grover."

"That's okay. All the really good sculpture winds up sitting in a park buried under gull poop anyway."

"How did Mr. Prinn come across your gallery? I didn't know he traveled to New York."

"It's a very long, boring story, I'm afraid. I really should get this piece of rock into the museum while the getting's good. Maybe I'll see you around."

"Are you staying for a while?"

"I'll be here until the grand dedication or whatever it's called. I'm representing the gallery."

"I just received an invitation for it. You wouldn't believe the inconvenience that envelope turned out to be. Anyway, I'm sure I'll see you there."

"Great. Take care of your feathered friends, Mrs. Budge." She grunted as she heaved the box up onto a dolly and wheeled it toward the museum doors. The gulls echoed with colorful language of their own.

5

*T*he big man at her feet began to make encouragingly conscious noises. With what sounded suspiciously like an expletive, he planted calloused hands on the ground and hauled himself to his knees, drops of blood staining the gravel black.

"Oh. Hey there. I don't think you are supposed to stand up after a head trauma, are you? Officer?" Benjamina reached out a tentative hand.

He ignored her, using the car door handle to pull himself gradually to his feet. He was forty-something, she guessed, creased and weathered from the sun. He had blue eyes that she abruptly noticed were becoming unfocused and beginning to roll back in his head.

"You really need to sit. . ." The breath was squeezed out of her as he collapsed, knocking her down and pinning her shoulders to the ground with his torso. "Oh brother!" she gasped, trying to shove his head off of her shoulder. "I am so not in the mood for this!" As she struggled to free herself from underneath the deadweight, sirens began screaming up the country road.

Ruth slapped the notebook closed on the scarred library table and felt the tension gradually diminish. Her breath sounded loud in the early evening quiet of the library. It was beginning to be a familiar routine; apprehension as she found ways to put off reading the bits of manuscript, then the anxiety mounting with each page, and finally a depression settling down on her like a mist.

She took a deep breath, trying to match coherent thoughts to her feelings. It was a story, fiction. A fantasy made up to entertain the reader. Wasn't it? But how come Phillip had not told her anything about it? She had assumed the hours of typing would result in a charming collection of memories from a country vet, not a—a what? A mystery? Love story?

Ruth flashed back to the beginning of their own love story. It was a very tiny ad in the *Kansas City Gazette* newspaper that drew her to California; the chance to teach a semester of English at a picturesque high school on the coast. It couldn't have sounded more attractive to a bored woman fresh out of teaching college, desperately looking for a chance to escape the terrible sameness of life on a Midwestern farm.

So it was off to sunny California, where she promptly invested in sweatshirts and long underwear to fend off the foggy chill. Ruth was enchanted by the ever-changing quality of life on the coast; from fog to blazing sunshine, rich soil blending into rocky beaches, and most of all, the sea that seemed to perform majestic foaming undulations for her benefit alone.

Every afternoon when the school bell rang, she hopped into her grumbly Toyota and made a beeline for the beach with a bologna sandwich, a good book, and the warmest coat she could find. It was a wonderful, surreal routine until the day her empty Coke bottle bounced off of the passenger seat and wedged itself under the brake pedal, causing her to crash directly into the rear of a Ducky Diaper Service truck. The impact forced the truck up onto a curb, just enough that its contents disgorged themselves on the top of Ruth's car, burying the front end in pungent baby by-products.

Then Phillip came. He spoke calmly to her and the truck driver before clambering through the goo to release her from her smelly incarceration. She emerged, hands shaking, bleeding from a slight cut over her eye and totally smitten with her handsome rescuer.

They spent a lifetime together, and he had never changed. He loved her in the gentle, steady way that only a soul mate can love. Ruth felt she knew him better than she knew herself. She was totally certain that he would never betray her, certainly not with another woman.

She shifted uneasily in the hard wooden chair. Was that the real root of her unease? The fact that the protagonist of his book was a beautiful woman? A fictional woman, yes, but a woman nonetheless. Her own plainness hadn't ever bothered her before, even on the rare occasions when she noticed Phillip glancing at a pretty woman with admiration. But what about this woman, this lovely, brave woman on whom he had spent so much thought and attention? Maybe beauty was more important to her husband than she had realized.

Or was it that she'd really had no idea what was in his head? After twenty-five years of marriage. No idea at all.

Angrily she piled the library books she had collected into a stack. How come she had not noticed this before? Forty-six years of life and she had never noticed that something was missing. She wanted to run, run until she reached the ocean, and continue until it swallowed her up.

"I am *so* not in the mood for this garbage."

"What garbage?" The scratchy voice made her jump. Looking up, Ruth saw an old woman in a wheelchair staring at her. Bun Zimmerman. Bun's daughter Wanda was a quasi celebrity in Finny, an extremely talented artist.

"Hello, Bun. I was just, er, reading something." She covered her husband's notebook with her sweater.

The older woman directed her wheelchair closer to the table strewn with books about the care and feeding of fuchsias. "Fuchsias?" Bun's mouth drooped on one side, and her hand lay motionless in her lap.

TROUBLE UP FINNY'S NOSE

It was occasionally difficult to understand her since the stroke. "Confucius? Oh. Yes. Fuchsias. I've become interested in them lately. Do you know anything about them?"

"Knew someone who was involved with a plant freak. Even named her child after one. Ridiculous." Bun used her good hand to flip open the heavy textbook and scan a few of the pages.

Ruth laughed. "Did you meet her when you were a nurse?"

"Still am a nurse. You don't stop being who you are because your body gives up on you."

"Of course. I'm sorry."

Bun ignored the interruption. "Too many people trying to be things they're not. Gets them into trouble."

Ruth took note of the small pile of books in Bun's lap. A biography of Eva Perón and two Westerns. Idly she wondered if you could decipher a person's life by seeing a complete list of all the books they had checked out.

Wanda, Bun's daughter, was at the front door of the library. "Gotta go. Taxi's here," she said.

Ruth watched the motorized wheelchair cruise to the front door. Wanda waited until the chair had reached the threshold before she turned and held the door open for her mother.

Ellen Foots, the librarian, was the next person to materialize at Ruth's table. Ellen was the complete antithesis of the stereotypical librarian. For one thing, she was enormous, a good six-foot-four in stocking feet with the shoulders of a linebacker and the voice to match. Her black hair stood out from her head in tumbleweed fashion, and her face was angular and serious. Rumor held she had started a career as a dental hygienist, but the sight of her bearing down on patients with a hook in hand discouraged too many people from seeking their regularly scheduled dental visits.

"Hello, Ruth. Haven't seen you here in a while." She tucked her chin and looked down as if she were wearing bifocals.

Ruth felt a twinge of nervousness, reminiscent of being sent to the corner in third grade. "Oh yes, Ellen. I've been really busy lately."

"You're never too busy to read, I hope." She arched a thick eyebrow. "That's funny."

"What's funny?"

"The book you're reading here." She stabbed a finger at the fat green volume. "What about it?"

"Do you know who was the last person to check it out?"

"No."

"The late Mr. Crew Donnelly. Odd, don't you think?"

Ruth thought maybe *creepy* was a better word for it.

"Hmm. Anyway, how about making treats for the rec center show Thursday? Two dozen. No nuts."

As the librarian clopped away in her ankle boots, Ruth looked down at the open book in front of her. *"Most fuchsias will die from overwatering."*

She had a fleeting thought of Crew Donnelly in the fountain. *Overwatered people don't seem to do well with it, either.* Shuddering, she packed up her books and left.

6

Ruth often thought Wanda looked less like an artist than an upscale den mother. The pale blue silk tunic and pants cooperatively hugged her ample bust and accentuated her muscular legs. She was an almost handsome woman with a proud, pointed nose and a chin just a shade too wide, and she was constantly in motion, zinging from item to item like an enraged bee punishing itself against the blossoms.

After parking the shrunken bundle in the wheelchair inside the front door of the grocery store, Wanda swooped in, her black ponytail bobbing in her wake. She scooped apples carelessly into a wooden produce basket and careened on to the dairy case.

Ruth watched from behind a pile of onions. People-watching was one of her guilty pleasures. She found people far more entertaining than television. Besides, Wednesdays were buy-one-get-one-free on onions. How could she pass up a deal like that with her gaggle of onion ring fanatics?

Bert Penny, the young clerk who followed along behind Wanda, steadied wobbling towers of cereal boxes and perky displays of toothpaste. He stopped to say hello to the woman in the wheelchair.

"Goooood morning, Ms. Zimmerman. How are you today?" he asked loudly. The woman with the puff of white hair regarded him solemnly and nodded.

"You just let me know if you want anything," he shouted before resuming his pursuit of the other Zimmerman.

"Simmer down, Bert," said Luis, the owner of Puzan's Grocery. "Mrs. Zimmerman had a stroke—that doesn't mean she's deaf. Enough bellowing already."

"Oh, right. Sorry, Mr. Puzan."

Wanda called from the cheeses. "Bert, can you please get that wedge of Camembert? I would just about have to crawl over a mountain of cheese to grab it."

"Yes, ma'am." He gingerly reached his way to the pungent wedges at the cheese summit, balancing one foot on the metal rim of the counter and the other on a wooden crate of figs.

"Wait," Wanda said, patting him on the calf, "I think I would prefer Brie instead."

Unfortunately, her request was lost in an avalanche of cheddar, garlic feta, and a tangle of gangly adolescent limbs. Several nearby shoppers came running to aid the stricken clerk. Ruth put down her onions and grabbed the balls of mozzarella as they rolled by.

"Oh my," Wanda sighed, catching Ruth's eye. "I knew that was an accident waiting to happen. I was just telling him that is no proper way to display cheese." She reached out a toe to halt a fleeing wheel of baby Swiss.

A pair of broad shoulders appeared over the conglomeration, and two strong hands grabbed the boy's white apron, hauling him out of the rubble. "Are you all right, Bert?"

Ruth did not know why, but the sight of Monk made her want to duck behind the onions. The caterer set Bert upright.

Bert did a quick inventory of all the important parts and declared himself fit.

"Well, better get a box, son," Monk said, "and I'll help you separate the unfit for human consumption variety from the rest."

Bert trotted away, a fig firmly glued to the seat of his pants. Monk turned his attention to Wanda with barely noticeable regret. "And I suppose you are all right, Ms. Zimmerman?"

"Yes, Monk, and please call me Wanda. It was a shock, though."

He cleared his throat. "Well, er, most cheese accidents are," he said lamely, retrieving his own basket of fresh herbs and root vegetables. "I saw your mother on the way in. How is she these days?"

"Mother? Oh, you know. The same. The doctor says we can't really expect much improvement. It's been years since the stroke. I think it's only downhill from here. Have you given any thought to my offer? I think one of my seascapes would be just perfect in your shop. I would be thrilled to give you one, for a very reasonable price, of course." She tapped a porcelain nail against her front teeth.

Ruth knew Zimmerman paintings were well done, more than well done. Visitors from up and down the coast purchased her bold oils of thundering oceans and wave-battered coastlines. They sold for a hefty sum, and Napoleon Prinn's gallery often devoted an entire section of wall to her work. For a reason she could not articulate, she hoped Monk would decline the offer.

"Well, Ms. Zimmerman, the thing is, I'm an ex–navy man. From my window I can see the old gal, er, the ocean I mean, up close and personal. Having a painting of her would be like, well, like having a photo of your camera. Kind of redundant, you understand."

It sounded as if Wanda was suffering from some type of intestinal blockage until shrill peals of laughter exploded from the artist's mouth, or perhaps her nose.

"You are hilarious. But I am serious; you really should consider it. Several of my larger pieces will be on display for Mr. Prinn's gallery opening. Will you be attending?"

Monk growled his answer. "I'm doing the grub. So what's the new piece the

TROUBLE UP FINNY'S NOSE

Prinn keeps blathering on about? Is it one of yours?"

Wanda's smile dimmed like a spent bulb. "No. No. I don't know what the big secret is all about. He is very closemouthed."

It was then that Monk caught sight of Ruth hiding in the produce section. "Oh hello, Ruth. How are you?"

Her cheeks burned as she emerged from behind some eggplant. She tried to pull her bangs down over her invisible eyebrows. "Fine, thank you. How are you?"

He ran a hand through his prickly crew cut. "Swell, just swell. I was talking to Wanda." A thought stopped him. "Say, are you going to the art gallery shindig?"

"I think so. I'm not sure."

"Well, I guess I'll see you there. If you decide to go and all."

At that moment the bell on the door chimed, announcing the arrival of a shopper who needed no clanging bells to draw attention to herself. The stunning dark-haired woman picked up a shopping basket and glided into the store, carrying the gazes of all the males in the vicinity with her.

Bert emerged from the back with eyes glued to the voluptuous figure enhanced by jeans and a V-neck sweater. Mr. Puzan hastened to the woman's side. "Hello, miss. What can I help you find?"

"I was just looking for a good Teleme and a baguette. Some Perrier would be wonderful, too." She smiled at him with full wattage and gently pushed a wave of dark hair away from her eyes.

Bert's mouth fell open with an audible *plop*.

Wanda took in the woman's attributes with the subtly hostile look that an almost attractive woman reserves for a drop-dead gorgeous one. Nevertheless, she approached.

"Hello there. I'm Wanda Zimmerman. I noticed you at the gallery yesterday when I was seeing to the details of my pieces on display there. Are you visiting from out of town?"

"Yes. I have business here with Mr. Prinn. Is he a friend of yours?"

"Oh, we've been business partners for years. I am an artist, watercolors and oils. I'm sure you saw some of my pieces when you visited the gallery; they've been on display continually since the gallery opened." She raised an eyebrow before adding, "Are you an artist?"

The woman laughed. "Not exactly."

Ruth was intrigued.

Bert hastened up with a paper bag. "Here's your order, miss. Would you like service out?"

She laughed again. "Well, how about I pay for these things first and then you can carry it for me, okay?"

He escorted her to the cash register and trotted behind her to the door.

Monk nodded cordially as she went by. "Who do you suppose that was?" he said to Ruth. He winked and added in a louder voice, "Maybe she's the new *über*artist he's unveiling next week. Could be he's discovered a new talent. The next Degas, right here in Finny."

"What?" Wanda hurried over. "Did he say the artist is a woman?"

"Not that I've heard; mere speculation on my part." He smiled sweetly. "I guess we will all find out soon enough."

Wanda smoothed her hair and picked up her basket before she grabbed hold of her mother's wheelchair. "Well, I won't be holding my breath about seeing the work of a prodigy or anything, but at least I know the catering will be exquisite." Wanda pursed her lips thoughtfully. "When can I drop by and sample your wares?"

Monk looked as though he would very much like to give a superbly inappropriate answer. Instead he said good-bye to Ruth and Bun, turned on his heel, and went off in search of the sticky clerk.

7

R uth deposited the onions safely in the fridge and ate a quick lunch. Then she found herself walking up the graveled walkway to Finny Art Gallery. Sitting on the top step was a giant flowering plant wearing Birkenstocks. The shoes wiggled a bit as Ruth approached, and a round face pushed itself through a gap in the foliage.

"Hello, Dimple. I almost didn't see you there under the flora."

Dimple was Buster Dent's twenty-six-year-old daughter. Buster had raised her single-handedly since her early years when Mrs. Dent ran away with a vacationing investment banker. Buster was wealthy after selling parcels of the land he used to raise pumpkins and Christmas trees to a developer who then raised a crop of tract houses. Buster was a solitary man, with a face full of deep furrows caused by the sun or, Ruth thought, by the harsh glare of life.

Dimple was. . .different. Ruth found that talking to her was like trying to return corn syrup to the bottle; a lot of hard work for very little payoff.

"Greetings, Ruth. Isn't this a lovely specimen?"

"Sure is. What is it, anyway?"

"An upright fuchsia. Single blossoms. The common name is 'Mary Jane.' This particular variety can have red or blue blooms, but as you can see, this little sweetheart is showing off her blues."

"Er, yes." Ruth floundered for a second. "Um, I didn't know you were such a plant expert."

"Hmmm." Dimple gazed at the huge plant in her lap. She was so petite that the pot covered her entire lap.

The silence stretched into the awkward zone.

"How did you come by it?"

"Napoleon didn't want it. I was coming along the path and he carried it out to the landing. He didn't seem to like it at all. Maybe his thumbs are more black than green." She dropped her voice to a whisper. "I suspect all of the fuchsias in his greenhouse are actually fake."

Ruth was just picking up her jaw when she noticed the hint of a smile on the girl's lips and in her huge green eyes.

Whew. Humor.

"Well, that's a lovely bush. Did he grow it himself? It looks like a gorgeous plant to me," Ruth said.

Indeed, the tiny blue flowers seemed to be exploding from every branch. It was like looking at a bushful of infinitesimal bluebirds.

"It was delivered by an unknown giver. I don't know why he doesn't like it. He can be temperamental, you know." She rubbed her tiny gumball nose. "A changing temper mirrors the sadness within."

Ruth tried hard not to let her eyeballs roll back in her head. "Uh, I suppose." Why did she frequently find herself trapped in conversations with this writer of fortune cookie wisdom? How much could that pay, anyway? Did she get paid by the cookie? Good thing she had a rich father.

"How is your fortune cookie business these days?" She knew Dimple exported her fortune cookies to various Asian restaurants along the coast. The cookies were unique; multicolored and intricately twisted, much like the woman who made them.

"Very nice."

Ruth tried to inject some humor into the dying conversation. "Uh-huh. I guess there's plenty of good fortune in your line of work."

The girl blinked behind the leafy screen.

"Will you be coming to the gallery dedication?" Ruth asked desperately.

"Could be." Dimple struggled to her feet with the giant bush. "I must be off. May the road rise up to meet you."

"Right. You, too, Dimple." She watched the small woman haul the plant down the drive, her blond hair mingling with the branches.

Inside the open double doors, the gallery was undergoing a painful face-lift. The place was a buzzing hive of speckled drop cloths, paint buckets, and overalls-clad men. It smelled of new paint and sawdust. Ruth caught a glimpse of a slender dark-haired woman who vanished down the hallway with Prinn's secretary.

Napoleon stalked back and forth.

"These carpets must be protected," he articulated to no one in particular. "They will be every bit as immaculate when you are finished as on the day they were installed. Is that perfectly clear?"

The nearest set of overalls mumbled something incoherent. The curator continued his reign of terror with serrated comments to the plasterer, the carpenter, and the two Peruvian electricians.

As he stopped to refill his lungs, his harried assistant returned and waved to Ruth before she leaped into the void. "Excuse me, Mr. Prinn, but Mrs. Budge is here to see you and I just showed Ms. Sawyer to your office. I believe she is on a tight schedule today."

Napoleon stepped off the dais and strode toward Ruth with purposeful steps. His lips formed a half smile, and he extended a hand to her.

"I'm surprised to see you here, Mrs. Budge."

Actually, no one was more surprised than Ruth that she was here. She could only chalk it up to an unaccustomed feeling in her gut; a burning speck of curiosity had penetrated the ever-present sadness. She didn't want to analyze it too much in case it went away.

"I'm sorry for dropping by, Mr. Prinn. I don't want to throw a wrench in your schedule. I should have called before coming."

"I am so happy to see you, Mrs. Budge. Let's drop the formalities. Please call me Napoleon, and I'll call you Ruth, if I may. I have been meaning to call you, but as you can see, things are hectic here."

He turned to his secretary, his smile disappearing. "March, tell Ms. Sawyer that I will be tied up for another half hour or so. If she doesn't care to wait, she can make an appointment for another day when I have some free time."

March Browning's eyes widened in exasperation. "I'm finished showing her around the gallery. She has already been waiting for twenty minutes, Mr. Prinn."

"Then she obviously doesn't have anywhere else to be." There was a hint of impatience in his voice.

Ruth contemplated the curator's handsome, angular face, amazed that he could change moods so artfully. His slightly graying hair was obediently settled on his head, the forehead smooth above pale green eyes.

Napoleon must have been a hard name to grow up with, she thought. It just sort of screamed, *Beat me up, I'm different!* He was in his element at the gallery, though. Smooth, elegant, cultured.

"I see this is still very much a work in progress. Will it be ready in time?"

"It will be in peak shape by Friday if I have to complete the work with my own two hands."

One of the Peruvians eyed the manicured hands with skepticism.

"I'm sure. What is the 'new addition' you mentioned in the invitation?"

"If I told you that, it wouldn't be much of a surprise."

Napoleon rested a hand on her shoulder. His eyes sparkled, and he smelled faintly of cologne. Ruth was annoyed to feel her pulse quicken at the attention. The only man she had shared any physical contact with for the past year was her dentist, and he was protected by sturdy latex gloves.

"And you'd like me to photograph the evening for you?" she asked. She often did freelance work for newspapers and local magazines.

"Absolutely. Obviously, you will attend as a guest for the dinner, and then perhaps we can hire you to take a few shots of the new addition."

"Does it drool and spit up?"

Prinn frowned. "I'm afraid I don't. . ."

"Never mind. Just a small joke."

"Ahh. Well. Anyway, it would be a great service to the gallery if you would photograph the event for us. I know the paper will have some representative there, but I would like to hire someone to document the entire evening."

She contemplated the offer. Why not? She could use the money for the birds' next veterinary visit. Finny had finally replaced Phillip with a new doctor who came with loads of high-tech equipment and fees to match. "Yes, of course I'll do it. But, Mr. Prinn"—she noted his waggling eyebrows and started again—"Napoleon, it really would help to know the nature of the new addition so I'll be sure to select the correct film and filters."

"Sorry. You'll just have to come next Friday. Oh, actually there is one other favor. I'm working on a brochure to advertise the gallery, and I think it would be a wonderful touch to include the greenhouse. It will be in perfect form in a few days. Would you possibly be able to take a few shots? We would be happy to pay you for that, too, of course."

"You don't mind if I just take a peek in the greenhouse now, do you?" she asked.

"Of course not. Just be careful to close the door behind you. I don't want the babies to catch a cold."

She found the remark vaguely disgusting, though she wasn't sure exactly why. "Thank you. I will see you officially on Friday."

Still smiling, he opened the door for her. "I look forward to it. It will be a night to remember."

8

After walking up the low hill, Ruth yanked open the door of the greenhouse, scuttling inside before a chill could settle on the leafy infants. The air closed around her in a slippery blanket.

It took several minutes for her eyes to adjust to the brilliant colors that seemed to explode from each plant. Fuchsias crowded every conceivable inch of counter space and dangled crazily from hanging baskets overhead. The blossoms were tissuey, resembling the fragile paper lanterns that festooned the shop windows at Chinese New Year.

The lower shelves were crowded with similar pots stabbing pointy smooth leaves at the ceiling, topped with frothy crepe flowers that she recognized as some sort of iris. Each container was affixed with a tiny plaque: BLAZING SUNRISE. LILAC STITCHERY. The fuchsias were also labeled. "Gartenmeister Bonstedt. Now there's a lovely little moniker. Rolls right off the tongue."

"He shew'd me lilies for my hair, and blushing roses for my brow. He led me through his gardens fair, where all his golden pleasures grow."

She whirled around and yelped into the face of the speaker.

"I'm sorry. I didn't mean to scare you."

He was a young man, she thought at first glance. Long and lean with windblown curls. There was another impression, a sort of less pleasant aftertaste. He looked. . .scuffed. She suddenly realized he was examining her with equal interest, a look of puzzlement playing about his lips.

"Eyebrows," she sighed.

"Beg pardon?"

"Eyebrows. That's what's missing. I had a kitchen fire; they've been reduced to stubble."

He laughed. "I couldn't quite put my finger on it. Eyebrows. Of course." He chuckled some more then wiped his eyes and gestured to the gently bobbing blossoms. His fingers were long and slender.

"Well? What do you think?" He gestured vaguely. "Do you think Phoebus would approve of this garish display?"

"Umm"—she hesitated—"garish wouldn't be my first choice. It's lovely, I think. Just the thing for a poet."

"But Phoebus was not easily fooled. He could see straight to the root of things, if you'll excuse the pun. Ever see what these spring from?" He stabbed a finger at the potted irises. "Nasty things, corms or rhizomes. They look like shrunken heads. You should see Boney brooding over the bunch, peeling and chilling them. It's unnatural."

She was uncertain how to take this commentary. "Boney?"

"Could it be that you don't know the great man responsible for this wonder? Napoleon Prinn, horticulturist extraordinaire."

"Oh, well, I've never heard him referred to as Boney. Are you a friend of his?"

"Much better than that. We're brothers, twins even. Randy Prinn. Actually, it's Randolph Prinn, but I think Napoleon is pretentious enough for one family."

She could see the resemblance now. This young man seemed like a blurred photo of his brother, darker, softened around the edges, and slightly fuzzy from wear and tear.

"But enough about my family saga. Correct me if I err, but aren't you Ruth Budge, widow of the late Dr. Phillip Budge?"

He took in her surprise. "I saw your biography on the pamphlet for the Women's Photographic Society. President, aren't you?"

"Vice president, actually. Have you been here long? I haven't seen you at any gallery functions."

"Only just came. I don't really think Boney would like to have me attend too many of his galas. I'm not nearly attractive enough. I'm just here for a brief, unavoidable time. I'll be gone before the bloom is off the rose, so to speak." His voice vibrated with laughter.

"Are you vacationing in Finny?"

"No, ma'am. I'm here on business. I write for a coastal paper and I'm covering the stupendous Finny Art Gallery dedication." He took another quick look around the greenhouse and grinned. "I've got to go. All this humidity is terrible for my hair. It has been a pleasure to make your acquaintance, my dear Mrs. Budge. May your eyebrows flourish once again. I bid you farewell."

He snatched up her hand and kissed it with a delicate smack.

She watched him saunter out of the greenhouse, oblivious to the tender plants, which Ruth fancied were recoiling from the chill of the open door. She gazed after him, struggling to recall the rest of Blake's poem. *"With sweet May dews my wings were wet, and Phoebus fir'd my vocal rage. He caught me in his silken net and shut me in his golden cage."*

Blinking her way back to the gallery, she meandered back out to the front entrance and headed off down the steps. She noticed a woman unlocking an immaculate metallic blue Mercedes convertible, the same woman who was in the gallery earlier waiting for Mr. Prinn and charming Bert at the grocery store. She'd heard March grumble the name Summer Sawyer at the galley.

Summer Sawyer was the kind of woman who seemed to be unaccountable to all Newtonian laws of gravity. The top of her was curvaceously plump, accentuated by a tailored wool jacket. The jacket draped over a wool skirt that covered the top of her impossibly long legs. Ruth doubted she could approach those dimensions even standing on her head.

The woman's black hair was cut into a short, sharp bob, which set off her creamy skin. She tossed it out of her face angrily as she yanked open the driver's side door and slid inside. The car zoomed away with a squeal of tires. The lovely Summer, it seemed, had not been at all charmed by her visit to Napoleon Prinn.

9

Ruth found Monk up to his elbows in clams the next day. This was not unusual for the only caterer in Finny; everyone knew that Thursday was clam day. His name did not cause any confusion anymore, either. Everyone had long ago ceased to wonder at his apparent lack of a first name, or was it a last?

Ruth met Monk the day he became a fixture in the town when he stepped off the USS. *Providence* and left his navy career at the docks. He was famous for his divine cooking and exquisite cable knit sweaters. He had knitted several lovely specimens for Ruth over the years. He broke off from a delicate bellowing of "Spoon River" when she entered the shop and dropped the ladle with a clatter.

"Good morning, Ruth. It's good to see you. You haven't been in for a while." He wiped his hands on a floury apron and hastened to the front counter.

She put down the cardboard box she was carrying and surveyed the hodgepodge of boiling pots and bowls of half-risen fleshy dough. The hair hanging limply in her face reminded her that she had missed her appointment with Felice. Surreptitiously, she tried to pat it back into submission. "You seem awfully busy. Is business looking up?"

"That it is, Ruth. I think I told you that the little weasel hired me to cater his shindig at the museum. I've been getting a head start on the grub. You said you might go—as a guest or the official photographer?"

"Both, I think. The little w—er, Mr. Prinn asked me to photograph the event and the greenhouse. At least I know the food will be well worth the trip." She breathed deeply, trying to remember when she had eaten last. "That smells wonderful."

"At the risk of being immodest, it is. Fish chowder with potatoes and a hint of tarragon. Let me dish you up a pint. On the house." Searching for a spoon, he continued. "You know, Ruth, I've been by your house a few times to visit, but no one answered the door. You were out walking the birds, I guess."

"Well, they do need lots of exercise." The warm swirl of scents was intoxicating.

He began ladling the pungent creamy soup into a Styrofoam container. "I haven't seen you in church for a few Sundays."

Her eyes dropped to her shoes. Lately the thought of singing praises of gratitude and salvation made her feel queasy. She desperately missed the joy that used to fill her heart at service, but she did not know how to get the feeling back. "I think I've been, uh, fighting off the flu. The headaches come and go."

Monk nodded. "Well, maybe Sunday you'll be up to snuff again. I could come by and pick you up."

"Maybe." She put the box down on the floor. "Did Alva tell you about the excitement?"

"Yes, I understand you both had an interesting experience."

"You can say that again. It still seems so unreal to me. It was Crew Donnelly. Did you know him?"

"Nah. We jawed about our days in the service awhile back when he came in for some coffee, but he wasn't a real talker."

"Did he serve with you?"

"He was an army man," Monk said with a touch of condescension. The screeching coming from the box at her feet suddenly interrupted them.

"You have another commission for me, I gather?"

"Yes, I do. It is so awfully kind of you to do it for me." She knew if she took enough Dramamine, she could make the drive up the coast by herself, but for some reason she continued to ask Monk to do it for her. Was it just to have the excuse to talk to him? She shook the uncomfortable thought away. As she lifted the red towel from the box, a crooked brown neck periscoped out of the opening.

"He's a tiny one, isn't he? Where'd you get him?"

"I found him on the beach. He had a fishing lure imbedded in one wing. It's healed nicely, though. I'm sure he's ready for his own patch of coast, far away from all my crabby critters."

"All right," he sighed, "hand over the little honker." The bird straightened indignantly. "No lip from you, or you'll be tomorrow's special." The calloused hands cupped the gull's slender neck gently. His fingers overlapped hers for a moment.

She lingered for a split second before she pulled her hands away. He had been a friend for so many years, but lately another feeling began to swirl in her brain when she saw him. It was followed by a surge of guilt. "Thank you so much."

"No problemo, dear lady. Maybe you could pay me back in some of those chocolate chip cookies of yours. I haven't had any in months."

"I haven't felt like baking, I guess. Oh no! I completely forgot. I'm supposed to provide the snacks at the rec center today. Ellen hornswoggled me when I let my guard down."

"That's something you never want to do with our librarian. What's cooking over at the rec center?"

"It's a puppet show for the kids. Ellen booked a traveling puppeteer to do a performance this afternoon." She smacked a hand to her forehead. "How could I have forgotten? I've got to go, Monk. I'm supposed to be there with snacks in hand by two o'clock."

"Well, you'd better go, then," he said reluctantly. "Don't want Big Foot on your case. Come back soon, Ruth. Are you busy this weekend? Maybe we could catch a movie."

"Oh, uh, I'm not sure. I don't have my calendar with me." She turned and scurried to the door.

"What about Saturday?" he yelled to her retreating back.

She was already halfway down the sidewalk.

"Ruth! Wait! The chowder!" he called from the door.

She was too far away to hear.

⁓

The store-bought cookies could almost pass for homemade after Ruth arranged them on a plate and swathed them in plastic wrap, setting some aside for little Solomon whom she knew would stop by later. She made it to the Finny Recreation Center with five minutes to spare.

The kids were gathered in front of the makeshift stage. She recognized Paul Denny with Louella, the lady who watched him during the day, and Solomon and a few other Finny youngsters. In the back row the Solari twins sat on each side of an unusually tall preschooler.

"Hi, Alva," Ruth called, setting down the refreshments.

"Hey, sweet cheeks." Alva waved a sticky hand. "You want some candy corns?" He held up a crumpled paper bag.

"No thank you."

He nodded and returned to his conversation with the also sticky Solari boys.

Ellen swooped out from behind the shoulder-high curtain hung to conceal the puppeteer from the audience. Her face seemed unnaturally thin in the alarming explosion of coarse hair.

"There you are." She pushed up the sleeves of her Nike sweatshirt. "I was beginning to wonder. We'll keep the cookies covered until after the show so Alva doesn't get into them."

Alva looked up guiltily and shoved his baseball cap farther down on his head. Ruth couldn't hear his muttered remark, but the twins giggled wildly.

Ellen stood before the group and reminded them in stentorian tones to stay seated and quiet. She dimmed the lights and the show began.

It was a charming version of *The Three Little Pigs*. The backdrop was a simple painted canvas depicting a wooded glade, complete with whimsical forest animals and three storybook cottages. The marionettes seemed to have a life of their own as they danced and cavorted. Ruth had trouble believing they were controlled by strings and found herself sitting at the end of a row of mesmerized children, every

41

bit as enchanted as they were. When the show ended, the children made a beeline for the cookies and juice.

Seeing that the librarian had taken charge of cookie monitoring, Ruth slipped behind the curtain. The man in black was carefully hanging up the marionettes in a large trunk, securing their arms and legs with Velcro straps.

"Excuse me. I just wanted to tell you how much I enjoyed. . ." She broke off as she recognized his face. "Randy Prinn! I had no idea."

He squinted at her in the dim light. "Oh, hello, Mrs. Budge. You didn't know I had a side job, huh?" He laughed. "I don't really advertise this one much, in grown-up circles, anyway. Did you enjoy the show?"

"I enjoyed it tremendously. It was amazing. I can't believe you can get those puppets to move like that."

He looked pleased. "It's all in the controller. That's this crosspiece at the top where the strings connect. I've used rod puppets, too, but marionettes really come alive if you know what you're doing." The sarcastic demeanor was gone; he was beaming with boyish enthusiasm. "Do you want to see my best gal?"

He carefully drew a shrouded form from the back of the trunk and unwrapped it. It was a beautiful wooden marionette with curly golden hair and delicate features. She wore a shimmering silver dress and tiny glass slippers.

"Cinderella, dressed for the ball," he said proudly. "I made her myself. Most people these days use plaster molds, but she's made from balsa wood. She's got a hybrid controller that allows me to do some neat tricks." With a few graceful movements of his hand, the puppet closed her eyes and pirouetted.

"She's beautiful. Why don't you do shows full time? It seems to be your passion."

He looked down hastily, busying himself with repackaging his star puppet. "Ah well, I guess playing with puppets isn't really much of a profession, is it? I mean, unless you have the money and time to create your own theater or touring company."

"I don't know much about the business end of things, but you definitely make these marionettes come to life."

Randy chuckled, his mouth a half smile. "Yeah. I was famous on my block. The kids would come from all up and down the street to see our shows."

"Our shows?"

"You probably won't believe this, but Boney was my stage manager. He painted all the backdrops, too. As a matter of fact, the backdrop I used today is one he painted when we were kids. Amazing, isn't it?" He shook his head. "What a difference a lifetime can make."

Ellen poked her head backstage. "The cookies are gone and I'm closing up now."

"Okay by me," he said as he snapped down the lid of his trunk.

Back at home, Ruth sat thinking about Randy. He was gifted, to be sure;

able to make magic out of scraps of wood and string. It was hard to believe that once upon a time, he and his self-absorbed brother had made magic together. Napoleon had about as much whimsy as a dishwasher manual. What a difference a lifetime makes, indeed.

She had been so lost in her thoughts that she hadn't even noticed the passing time until it was almost dusk. Now the waning light brought back all the gloomy feelings again. It was not a fear of dark or strange noises that caused her to turn on every light, but rather a need to fill up all the corners of an empty house. She had spent many nights under piles of down comforters trying to understand these feelings. The only thing that had come out of her self-analysis was a dreadful realization that she was passing time, filling up days, months, years.

Maybe the void had always been there. Maybe she'd just been distracted by a marriage to a wonderful man. All her life she had been taught to look up, trust God, rely on Him. Had she done wrong by loving Phillip so deeply? Was it a sin to build your life around a person? Was God highlighting her transgression by leaving her so very much alone?

"Oh brother." She exhaled with disgust. "I have simply got to stop watching *Dr. Phil.* You're okay, Ruth. Today, you are okay."

Tomorrow was another story.

10

Napoleon sat in his office. The cool morning air whispered through his slightly open window. Buck Pinkey watched him over his thick glasses as his bald crown shone under the track lighting. Napoleon crossed, uncrossed, and crossed his legs again.

"This is a lovely office you have here. So airy. Clean." Pinkey cradled the cell phone in his hand. "You've done an outstanding job on this gallery, Mr. Prinn. And the gardens are exquisite." He gestured outside to the profusion of dusky pink and white hydrangea blossoms. "I have tried my hand at growing hydrangeas before, but mine don't show the vibrant colors you have here. Why is that?"

"It depends on the acid of your soil, and the sunlight. They appreciate sun, but not blistering heat." Napoleon shifted in his chair behind the desk. "Mr. Pinkey, may I call you Buck? Can I get you some coffee? Water?"

"Water, sure. Call me anything you want, except late for dinner." He laughed at his joke, the tire around his middle jiggling. He took the glass offered him and patted in his pockets, producing a small pillbox. Extracting a pink pill, he swallowed it with a grimace. "Dramamine. I am itching to get in some fishing while I'm here, but the water is rough." He smiled. "Do you ever fish?"

"No. I don't really care for the water."

"You live on the coast and you don't like the ocean?" He laughed. "I love the sea. You know, I caught a Chinook salmon one time; tipped the scales at one hundred three and a half pounds. Can you believe it? The thing almost killed me, but I hung on. Took three of us to lift it into the boat. Have you ever seen a Chinook? Ugly old monsters with black mouths and gums. The males get this enormous hook-like structure on their mouths when they are spawning. It's called a kype." He gazed out the window into the foggy gardens. "Does the sun ever shine here, by the way?"

"It does, but not until afternoon, typically."

Buck leaned back in his chair and folded his manicured fingers together. "I saw that woman here again, the gorgeous one with the short hair." He smiled slightly. "Who is she?"

"Just a business acquaintance."

"What kind of business?"

Napoleon cleared his throat. "I've done some work with her college, and she wants her students' work shown at my gallery. Mr. Pinkey, you are aware that we have had some trouble here. I am sure you have heard about our gardener. It was an unfortunate accident. The schedule was slightly delayed, but I am confident. . ."

Pinkey interrupted. "Do you have it?"

"I. . ."

"Do you have it?"

"No. But I can have more soon."

"Did the gardener have it?"

"I don't know."

"That's all I needed to know. Thank you." He rose. "I'll meander through the gardens before I'm off to hook the big one. Say, you know of anyone who would charter me a boat? Show me the prime spots?"

Napoleon shook his head. "I'm afraid that's not my area of expertise."

Shrugging, Pinkey left, a trail of musk following him out the door.

Ruth finished snapping a picture of the greenhouse. The newly risen sun provided a fantastic rosy backdrop, just as she'd hoped it would. She had deposited the birds at the pond, knowing they would forage happily until she finished her task. Out of the corner of her eye she saw movement in one of the gallery windows. "Wow. They start their day early," she mumbled to herself. "Maybe I'll just pop in and say hello to March."

The gallery was silent, except for the distant tap of a hammer and the mumbled voices of workers. She walked down the corridor just in time to see March enter Napoleon's office. She waited outside, trying not to listen in on the conversation that floated out the door. "Mr. Prinn, is everything all right?" she heard March say.

Through the open door, Ruth could see the curator reach out a hand toward a painting on the wall, fingers extended but not touching the canvas. "March, did you ever wonder about genius?"

"Genius?"

"Yes. Look at my hands. I have the same number of fingers, tendons, sinews, the same brushes, paints, oils, and canvases as any great painter. I could even look at the same subject one of the great masters studied, yet my paintings would be adequate only. How can that be? Where does the genius lie? It certainly doesn't reside with the desire."

"I don't know, Mr. Prinn. Maybe it's somewhere between the eyes and the hands, a deeper perception combined with a natural talent." She thought for a moment. "Matisse said it is the 'condensation of sensation' that makes a picture. Maybe it has more to do with feeling and seeing the subject than painting it."

He turned away from the painting to face her. "Hiring you was one good thing I did for this place." He pressed his fingers into his temples.

"Mr. Prinn, are you all right? Are you ill?"

TROUBLE UP FINNY'S NOSE

He did not answer for a long time as he stood gazing out the window. She repeated the question anxiously.

"Thank you for asking. Please close the door behind you." March quietly closed the door and stood in the hallway.

Ruth opened her mouth to announce her presence, but the woman was so preoccupied she did not turn around. Removing a tiny cell phone from her purse, March punched a speed dial code.

"Things are getting weird here," Ruth heard her say. "There's a man from out of town and he's got Napoleon spooked." There was a pause.

Who in the world is she talking to? Ruth wondered.

"How should I know?" March hissed into the phone. "I've never seen him before, but they know each other." Another pause. "He's from New York. Prinn is really upset. He's talking about genius and how much he appreciates me. I think he's gone around the bend. What should I do?"

She tapped a pearly fingernail. "But what if he changes the schedule? I'm just not sure we should go through with it." More tapping. "Right. Fine. I won't worry, but I need to see you now. Come right away."

She clicked off the phone and walked distractedly into her office. Picking up one of the pictures, she wiped it with the hem of her jacket. "Boy, oh boy, Dad. If you could see me now. What have I gotten myself into?"

Ruth decided now was not the time to visit with March. She turned silently and left the building.

11

Four, five, six. All right. Who's missing?" The surface of the pond was stippled by the busy water striders that stayed out of reach of the birds. She again counted the bunch that milled about her legs.

"Zachary, Martha, oh, it's Ulysses again. What on earth did I do to deserve this?" She knew he must have wandered away from the pond, and if she guessed right, he had probably headed straight for the succulent gallery gardens. With a sigh she shouldered her camera bag and retraced her steps.

Forty-five exasperated minutes later, as she stood peering under bushes, she noticed a man walking down the hill away from the Finny Art Gallery. He was in no particular hurry, strolling along examining the foliage bordering the path. When he reached the bottom of the slope, he nodded his head at her. It was the man who had upset the unflappable Napoleon Prinn and his secretary.

"Good morning. Are you looking for someone?" he asked her. He was well dressed, almost dapper even. Dapper was a shade unusual in Finny.

"Actually, I'm looking for a wayward seagull. Have you seen one around?"

"Surprisingly enough, I have. There was a crabby-looking fellow lurking around the offices behind the gallery. I thought he might be a resident of the grounds or something." He smiled, revealing dazzling white teeth.

"Thank you. I'd better find him before the curator catches him nibbling on the landscaping."

"You seem to know your way around. Could you recommend a place for rent? Near the water. I'd like something small, a bungalow perhaps."

"Are you from out of town, then?"

"Yes, how rude of me. I am Buck Pinkey. I'm just here for the healthy sea air."

If he was here for the air, she was the Queen of Sheba.

"Ruth Budge. There aren't too many rentals here in Finny. You might check farther up the coast. Half Moon Bay is lovely and has more to offer."

"I'd really like to stay in Finny. It's quaint here."

"Right out of a postcard, some would say."

"Yes. I want to do some fishing. Rent a boat, that sort of thing. I'm staying at the Finny Hotel now, but I'd like something more private. I passed a small cottage as I strolled the beach the other day, white trim and a slate walkway. Is it occupied?"

She watched him closely. "I really couldn't say."

TROUBLE UP FINNY'S NOSE

He nodded, and she could see the perfectly unmarred dome of his head, shining like a newly laid egg in the emerging sunlight. "I see. Well, thank you for your time, and I do hope you find your errant bird."

He vanished into the distance. "Why in the world," she wondered aloud, "is he so interested in Crew Donnelly's place?"

—

Feeling more than a little foolish, she returned to the gallery and skulked around the back entrance. Checking under shrubs and in flower beds, she made a thorough search for the escapee. Nothing.

Abruptly she stopped scouring the ground for feathers when she noticed one of the back doors was slightly ajar. She caught sight of a feathered behind under the umbrella stand. "Aha!" she said. Slowly pushing the door open another few inches, she crept into the room and stopped short.

Sitting on a recliner was Randy Prinn, and on his lap, March Browning. Luckily, they were facing away from Ruth. Randy was whispering something into March's ear, which made her turn pink. Her normally upswept hair was completely undone. Ruth now had a pretty good idea who was on the other end of March's cryptic phone call an hour before.

"What if something goes wrong? What if he finds out?" March said.

"He won't. He thinks I'm a moron, remember?" Randy said, kissing her on the temple.

Ruth was mortified at what she had walked in on. She felt her face burn, and she held her breath until her chest tightened. Scooping up Ulysses in a football hold under one arm, she ran outdoors like a Heisman Trophy winner sprinting toward the goal line.

—

The road snarled its way through the spiky shrubbery, grudgingly leaving a narrow crust of gravel along the margins. The sunlight felt nice on her shoulders as she walked briskly, oblivious to the crunch of rocks underfoot. She was thinking about recliners. More specifically, what Napoleon would think about the way in which this particular recliner was being utilized by his faithful secretary and estranged brother. What were those two plotting?

She was muddling through these thoughts when a slip of fluttering white just around the bend in front of her caused her to speed up. Her heart sank as she found the person attached to the fluttery white stuff.

"Oh, hello, Dimple. Are you on your way to town, too?"

The white stopped fluttering and subsided into the tiny fair-haired woman nestled in layers of floating fabric. She smelled of roses.

"Ruth. Greetings of the morning to you."

48

"Er, greetings right back at you. I was just going to town to stock up on batteries for my camera. Are you going, too?"

"Going?" She looked puzzled.

"To town. Are you going to town?" Ruth repeated.

"To town, yes. I am going to pick up some vanilla."

Ruth was relieved to find some common ground. "What are you cooking?"

"Perfume. I make all my own scents from the flowers in my garden."

So much for common ground. "Well, I guess we could walk together." She could feel her doom gathering around her like flies.

"Yes. The road traveled with a friend is always brief."

It must be punishment for a multitude of sins to be meandering with a woman who thinks in fortunes and brews her own perfumes. The silence lapsed into the intolerable zone. "So what do you think of the gallery renovations?" Ruth ventured.

"Very thorough."

"Yes, they are." The conversation faltered again, and Ruth was unsure how to kick-start it.

"I was there this morning to pick up some work. It was very unsettled," Dimple said as she bent to pick up a feather from the ground.

"Do you work for the gallery?"

The slender woman stopped to untangle her silk scarf from a spiky branch while she considered the answer. "Sometimes. Napoleon asked me to hand-letter the placards for the new addition."

Ruth wondered why everyone referred to the thing as if it were a child. She was also surprised that Dimple used Prinn's first name. "Do you do much work for him?"

"Hmm. I don't think it's very much, no."

"Oh. Well, the new addition, what's it called again?" Ruth asked innocently.

"I don't know. I haven't met the new piece yet."

"Met the new piece? You mean you haven't seen it yet."

"A piece of art is like a person. With great feelings and ideas to express. Don't you agree?"

"Sure." Ruth shoved her hands into her pockets, stifling the impulse to throttle the woman with her own scarf. Then the outer edges of her mind became aware of the sound of a roar bearing down upon them.

Ruth had only enough time to grab Dimple by the ends of her scarf and hurl her in a great fluttering ball into the shrubs. She dove down next to her as a car barreled down around the turn, skidding crazily on the loose gravel.

In a moment she raised her head out of the shrubbery. An engine idled several yards away. She had an impression of a figure looking into the rearview mirror before the car roared off again, leaving them in a shower of gravel and dust.

TROUBLE UP FINNY'S NOSE

She coughed and sat up, taking inventory of all her vitals. Her head was spinning. It had happened so quickly. Ruth had only enough time to gather a vague picture of a dark sedan. Green, gray, blue? She wasn't sure. No license number. Nothing. She tried to stand, but her legs shook so badly she sank back to a sitting position.

After a few more minutes of deep breathing and a quick check of her major parts, she extricated herself from the clawing shrubbery. With a start, she remembered her eccentric companion. Her rubbery legs finally did their job and held her up. "Where did she get to?"

She was relieved to see Dimple lying like a Christmas tree topper in a tangle of gauze and bushes.

"Are you all right?" Ruth panted.

The woman gazed at the sky, hands neatly clasped across her abdomen. Ruth wasn't sure if she was still considering the last question or applying her thoughts to this one.

"The road to adventure is uneven and perilous," she said.

Ruth plucked off a juniper berry hanging by a hair above her stubbly right eyebrow, thinking about the weird set of events that had turned her life around lately. "Ain't it the truth."

~

The sun was just beginning to set as Ruth finally hobbled in her front door. Her feet were aching and there was a definite spasm developing in the small of her back from her dive into the junipers. She concluded that when you start measuring your life in decades instead of years, that dated feeling is inevitable. Especially when you are leaping away from out-of-control vehicles.

She spent the rest of the afternoon soaking in a tub and trying to nap. Though she tried her best to put it out of her mind, the fact surfaced. She and Dimple could very easily have been killed by the crazy driver. Was it someone in a hurry? Just a moment of unfortunate carelessness? Another thought froze in her mind. Or was it someone on a mission to kill?

"Lord, help me," she breathed more out of habit than hope.

Ruth was just finishing her dinner of canned ravioli when the doorbell rang. After a moment of unreasonable panic, she gave herself a shake, assuring herself that the stove was safely asleep for the night. Who could be wanting to see her? She was very accomplished at the commando crawl to stealthily ascertain the identity of visitors without the need to open the door. Many a chicken broccoli casserole and plate of homemade cookies had been left on her doorstep in the months following the funeral.

The bell chimed again.

After a torturous minute of indecision, she yanked open the door.

12

Detective Denny was standing on the front step, hands jammed into the pockets of his brown trousers. "I'm sorry to call on you so late. I heard about your accident today and I came to check in on you."

"News travels fast. How did you hear about it?"

"Alva. He said he stopped you in town to ask how many licks it would take to get to the center of a Tootsie Roll Pop. He noticed your grubby knees and hair and figured you'd been in some sort of a scrape. How come you didn't report it?"

"I was sort of in a daze, I guess. Please come in." She led the detective into the kitchen and gestured him into a comfortable yellow chair. He gently fingered the fuchsia dangling off of the plant stand where she had plopped it.

"Is this the boasted fuchsia?"

She blushed. "It's called a Heston Blue."

"Doesn't smell?"

"Not a bit. I think it's really so odd that our gardener extraordinaire seems to have such an aversion to these plants. This is the second one I've encountered that Napoleon seems to actively loathe."

"Weird. But then, he kind of marches to a different beat."

"That is definitely true." She shook her head. "I'm sorry. I haven't had visitors in a while. I've forgotten all of my hostessing skills. Let me fix you some coffee and a muffin. I discovered them in my freezer when I decontaminated my kitchen."

"I heard about that. How are the eyebrows?"

"I'm not expecting to see them anytime soon. I think I'll have to fill them in with magic marker from now on."

"Not to worry. I couldn't tell at all."

"You're a sweet liar, Detective." She poured the coffee and served him a succulent muffin.

"Please call me Jack. We've been through enough together to drop the Detective and Mrs. stuff. Don't you think?" After what they had been through, he thought of her as more of a mother than his own flesh and blood.

She nodded. "And how is Mr. Boo-Boo these days?"

"Ecstatic as usual." Jack drifted back to their first meeting. Mr. Boo-Boo was the impetus for their introduction. He was the most unnatural collection of canine parts ever assembled. Tipping the scales at just over ninety pounds, his gangly body was covered with wiry whorls of hair, and his head was a compact bony wedge. The poor beast's only attractive feature was his eyes, one a soft green and the other a startling blue.

It was these amazing peepers that proved irresistible to Lacey Denny when the dog catapulted into the front seat of her car in the Shop and Go parking lot. He licked her face happily, forgave her for not bringing along any doggy toys, and waited patiently to be driven home. No amount of coaxing or threatening could remove that dog from the passenger seat.

Jack had never shared his wife's conviction that the dog was keenly intelligent. He watched Lacey and Paul throw endless weekly editions of the *Finny Times* and hopefully command, "Fetch!" He would never forget his astonishment when, one overcast morning, the dog trotted out to retrieve the paper. It took him forty seconds to maim the edition before trotting victoriously into the kitchen with a slippery rubber band clenched between his teeth. Mr. Boo-Boo fetched fourteen rubber bands before Lacey admitted defeat.

He remembered, too, the desperation he felt when Mr. Boo-Boo escaped two months after Lacey's death. The unlatched gate, the explosive panic. He spent two hours scouring every pungent corner for the dog and winding up completely desperate in front of Ruth's front yard. She was hacking away at some wickedly spiked bougainvillea. She said, "Are you all right, Detective?"

He could not give words to the desperate aching in his gut, the black fear that welled up inside him like a poisonous mist. He could not lose this dog, the only link to his little boy's world. "My dog. . ." was all he could manage to gasp.

She had looked at him for a long minute, reading the despair washing over his face. Jack could still remember the tiny drop of blood on her cheek where a thorn had pricked her. "Yes," she had said simply and put down her clippers. Together they walked out into the copse of trees behind her house and began whistling for the elusive dog.

Mr. Boo-Boo made his appearance shortly thereafter, climbing out from under a tangle of branches. He smelled strongly of mold, and his matted hair carried an impressive sampling of foliage. He bounded over and sent Jack sprawling in a puff of dirt.

His thoughts returned to the present. With a sigh, he put down his coffee.

"Boo-Boo is his usual slobbery self. My current undertaking is to teach him how to greet people without causing any contusions."

Ruth smiled then asked softly, "And Paul?"

"He talks to the dog. That's all. Just the dog. I can't even get him to smile. It's so frustrating. He was so happy before. . ." His voice trailed off.

Lacey, his beloved wife and the mother of their precious boy, had walked out to the mailbox while Paul watched from the window. She collapsed at the end of the driveway, dead of a brain hemorrhage.

Paul, Jack surmised, had called her and called her, but it had been a good hour before a neighbor noticed and dialed 911. By then the boy was crouched into a little ball with his hands around his knees, his face terribly white, huge Mr. Boo-Boo cradling him protectively.

Jack snapped out of his recollections with a shudder. "The psychologist says he needs to feel safe again. He needs to be sure that I'm not going to leave him, too." He shook his head. "How can I promise him that, Ruth? How can I assure him that his mother was gone in a heartbeat but I somehow will be here forever?"

She sighed. "I don't know. I still think I hear Phillip singing in the shower sometimes. I guess I am supposed to have gleaned a deep wisdom about the mysteries of life and death since I'm on the downside of forty. All I know is, time does not heal some wounds, Jack. There is just not enough of it." She stopped talking as her eyes filled with tears.

He busied himself drinking coffee while she recovered herself. "You know, Ruth, I haven't seen much of you in a year, and here is our second visit in a week. I don't know whether to be glad or alarmed." The detective wrapped his hands around the steaming mug, happy to be back on safer conversational ground. "Do you want to tell me what happened today?"

She related the events in a rough chronological order. "The strange thing is, I got the distinct impression that the car stopped down the road for a minute and then kept going. Was Dimple able to add anything else?"

He gave her a telling stare. "Not unless you count her advice about fate being kind to the penitent or something to that effect."

"How is the Donnelly investigation going?" she asked.

"Slowly. No family that we can locate. His cottage didn't really tell us anything except that he was planning to leave soon."

"I don't suppose he fell headfirst into the fountain and drowned accidentally?"

"Nope. The medical examiner says he drowned after someone clobbered him with a blunt object. He probably fell backwards into the water with or without help sometime between 11:00 p.m. and 4:00 a.m."

"It wasn't a robbery?"

"Doesn't seem to be. He had a wallet on him with a couple of bucks in it. Nothing was disturbed at his place."

Jack massaged his face with one hand then straightened up suddenly. "It's my beeper," he said, consulting the tiny screen. "I've gotta go."

At the door he paused. "Did Crew Donnelly strike you as the type who would appreciate fine art?"

She considered this. "He seemed more like the type who would appreciate a nice carburetor."

"That was my take, too. His cottage was bare bones, no embellishments at all."

She waited. He turned to face her on the darkening doorstep.

"So why do you suppose he had a Zimmerman seascape lying on top of his bed?"

13

Ruth wasn't really sure what brought her to the door of Prinn's greenhouse on Saturday morning. It seemed that curiosity had infected her like a hostile virus. She had spent the wee hours searching for Phillip's novel and worrying about things, some phantom detail niggling at her, prodding at the corners of her mind. She couldn't understand why Prinn would send away a gorgeous plant, the same plant Donnelly had trucked off to the dump just before he was murdered. The conversation with Jack only made her feel even more strongly that something was fishy in the town of Finny.

The sunlight caught the greenhouse glass, which reflected the light, sending it spinning crazily in all directions, like some great winking insect eye. She couldn't see clearly in the windows because of the opaque covering of moisture.

How odd.

The door to the precious temple of greenery was ajar. She was reaching for the handle when a missile came sailing out and smashed onto the slate stepping stones at her feet.

Rusty shards of terra-cotta pot entwined with the branches of a leggy green plant. The whole mess was dotted with exquisite white flowers edged in pink, identical to the plant she had rescued from the compost pile.

"This is intolerable!" hurled a voice on the same trajectory that the plant had taken a moment before. The curator's voice broke off as he emerged from the greenhouse and caught sight of Ruth as she stepped forward into the settling dust and fragrance.

He brushed his hands together and smoothed his tie. "Ruth. I didn't know anyone was standing there." His laugh was nervous. "Are you hurt?"

"No. You are a pretty strict disciplinarian with your plants. What did this one do? Stay out after curfew?" She bent and plucked a fragile white blossom from the crushed plant.

"Well, I am a perfectionist, I'm afraid. They must be perfect to stay in my greenhouse. I don't tolerate mediocrity." The flush was gradually receding from his cheeks. "I wouldn't want to bore you with the specifics."

"It won't bore me. Actually, I have been reading up on fuchsias lately. What is the name of this variety? I've forgotten."

The flush crept up his throat once again. "I can't recall."

"It's a man's name, isn't it? Henley, Hestor, Heston. Heston Blue. Odd name, don't you think?"

"I'll just get a broom and sweep this up. Please forgive my fit, Ruth."

"I saw your brother's show Thursday."

Napoleon looked blank.

"Randy's puppet show. At the rec center."

He was uncharacteristically silent for a moment. His lip curled in disgust. "I didn't realize he was still playing with puppets."

"Randy said you painted the backdrop when you were younger."

A strange look of confusion washed over his face. "The backdrop?"

"The country scene with the trees and the little thatched cottages."

His mouth fell slightly ajar, and she saw for the first time some genuine emotion seeping through the mask of self-assurance. "That old backdrop? He still uses it?"

"Yes. He said you could make magic on a canvas."

He blinked again and closed his mouth. "Magic. That was years ago, Ruth. I don't have time to stroll down memory lane at the moment. If you'll excuse me, I really need to get this mess cleaned up."

He walked stiffly down the path toward the gallery. As he passed her, a sweet scent whispered along with him.

"Of course." Ruth made sure the greenhouse door closed completely before she turned to go.

He stopped a few yards away. With his back still turned away, he asked over his shoulder, "Was it good?"

"Pardon?"

"The show. Was it good?"

She thought for a minute. "It was magic."

<hr>

At the corner of Whist and Main, a familiar car was parked at the curb, its shiny finish blinding Ruth momentarily as she rounded the corner. The driver's window was open. A woman sat in the front seat having a furious conversation with herself. No, not herself—she was speaking into a tiny cell phone hidden under a sheaf of hair. It was the woman Ruth had seen driving angrily away from the gallery. The angry bob of the head and the increasing pitch told her it was not a pleasant conversation.

The woman yelled, smashing the cell phone repeatedly into the dash until a piece of the black plastic broke off and sailed through the air, landing just in front of Ruth's shoe.

The woman peered out of the window. "I'm sorry. Did that thing hit you?"

"No, I'm fine." Ruth bent to retrieve the piece and walked over to the woman as she unfolded from the car. "Do you want it back?"

"Sure." She exhaled loudly as she dropped the plastic into her slim leather clutch. "I'm sorry. I guess I'm under some stress lately. Don't you have a gym or anything in this town?"

"Only the one at the high school." She felt the need to defend Finny. "Lots of people relax at the beach, running, hiking, boating, what have you."

"I prefer climate control to outdoor breezes. I don't think we've met. I'm Summer Sawyer."

"Ruth Budge. I saw you at the gallery. Are you in town on business?"

"Yes. I am the dean of the art department at Pomponio University. I came to attend the dedication."

"Why?" Ruth asked bluntly.

"Why?"

"I mean, is there a special connection between your college and the gallery?"

Summer fixed her with an intense stare. "Napoleon is the connection. He has donated generously to our art program." She turned and opened the car door. "It was nice meeting you, but I really need to go. I heard there is a salon around here. Am I getting close?"

"Sylvia's. Just keep going this direction; it's two blocks down on the left-hand side. One of the gals is on vacation in Fiji, so you may have to wait."

"Right. Thanks."

Ruth watched her drive away. It would be interesting to see what this elegant woman looked like after enduring a Sylvia hair treatment. Sylvia only knew two styles: short á la a Marine Corps buzz cut or curly as in the well-groomed poodle look. Chuckling to herself, she continued her walk home, puzzling as she went.

The town of Finny was getting stranger by the minute. A beautiful woman with some anger management issues arrived in town for the gallery dedication, only to be snubbed by the gallery owner. Prinn's behavior was a mystery, too. This self-assured, arrogant man was a painter of whimsical theater magic. What was that emotional response to news of his brother's show? Disgust? Envy?

These confusing thoughts followed her all the way back to her cottage. As she walked into her kitchen, the fuchsia seemed to wave gently at her.

Something from the encounter with Napoleon tried desperately to surface in her brain. She closed her eyes and saw the fuchsia smashing to the floor, saw Napoleon's face tight with anger as he brushed by her.

It came to her like a lightning bolt.

Fuchsias have no scent. Who, then, left the musky scent of roses on Napoleon Prinn's clothing?

It could be only one person.

Dimple Dent.

The detective had all but decided he should have stayed in bed. Working on Saturday wasn't the problem—he was used to that. It was the way the whole day started that added to his funk. While getting out of bed he stepped on a sharp Lego and skidded to the floor with a thump. Limping into the bathroom for a Band-Aid, he found a naked Paul unfurling a second roll of toilet paper and dumping it into the potty while Mr. Boo-Boo the dog panted encouragingly. Jack chastised the boy soundly until Paul galloped down the hall and hid under his bed. Jack tried apologizing and cajoling as the dog gave him a profoundly disappointed look, to no avail.

He felt a heavy sense of paternal failure as he drove to work.

Lacey was just better at kid things. She always knew how to talk to Paul without letting minor problems escalate into major productions. And how did she do that kissing thing? Ouchies were supposed to be kissed, but his lips just didn't have the same healing power hers did. Try as he might, he was not cut out to be a mother.

He wasn't sure he was great father material, either.

At the office he caught his first whiff of impending disaster when he encountered all three of his officers gathered mournfully around the deceased coffee machine, empty mugs dangling from their fingers.

Three professionals who can foil bank robberies, find missing children, and subdue armed felons—thrown into complete turmoil by a backfiring Mr. Coffee.

"Please, somebody tell me the coffee machine is not still broken."

"The coffee machine is not still broken," Nathan Katz announced. "The coffee is just a tad weak." He handed Jack a mug of barely warm water.

"Oh man."

"My sentiments exactly," said Nate.

So much for Saturday.

The library should have been the first stop for the detective, but facing Ellen Foots with no coffee in his veins caused him to procrastinate. Pulling up to the Finny Art Gallery instead, he heaved his decaffeinated body out of the car and through the front door. He heard the yelling long before he saw the five furious people in the lobby.

"What is that piece of ugly s'posed to be?" Jack recognized Buster Dent,

Dimple's father, poking his calloused finger toward a canvas-covered lump. "You call that thing art?"

A flushed, red-haired woman leaped out of her chair and confronted him. "That happens to be a Carmine, you clod! It's worth more than any Motel 6 art you've got hanging in your house."

Dent ignored her and turned on Napoleon. "I didn't pay for no cryin' lady statue, Prinn. You promised me somethin' pretty. I came to this preview expecting to see a landscape or some sunset somewhere. What is this thing?"

"Mr. Dent." Napoleon Prinn's smooth voice rose over the din. "I assure you the sculpture is a very valuable piece of art. A Carmine sells for well over five times what other marble pieces do."

"I thought you were buying a painting. And what kind of a name is that? Carmine? Don't he even have a first name? Where's he from, anyway? One of them third world countries?"

"It worked for Picasso, da Vinci, El Greco, Van Gogh, Donatello, Michelangelo." Red ticked off the names on her fingers. "Shall I go on? But you probably don't even recognize those masters. . . ."

"He is a very elusive artist. He has never been photographed, nor does he appear at any exhibitions of his work. The entire art community agrees, however, that his work is simply exquisite." Prinn moved toward the sculpture. "If you'll only look. . ."

"He must be elusive," said a black-haired woman Jack had never seen before. She sat gracefully in a chair observing the group, one shapely leg crossed over the other. "I've never heard of him, and neither have any of my colleagues."

Red stepped in front of him. "Don't even bother to educate them, Mr. Prinn. They obviously know as much about sculpture as they do about manners. I think I should take this back to the Shaum. Our curator would be horrified to see it so unappreciated."

"Now, Ms. Finchley, there is no need for. . ." Prinn was momentarily distracted. "What are you writing?"

Randy, standing next to an anxious March, looked up from his notebook and laughed. "The most interesting piece of behind-the-scenes hysteria that I've come across in years. This is really great stuff, Boney. It'll make great copy."

At that moment, several things happened simultaneously. March clasped Randy by the forearm as Napoleon grabbed him by his shirt collar, Red and Buster stepped forward reflexively, and Jack cleared his throat.

Everyone froze in a ridiculous tableau.

"Good morning, folks. Am I interrupting anything?"

After a second of shocked stillness, the gathering smoothed their collective clothing and lowered their voices several octaves. Prinn stepped forward. "Hello, Detective. To what do I owe this unexpected visit?" His mouth was crimped into a less-than-welcoming grimace.

"Just some routine questions about that gardener-in-the-fountain problem. I'm sure you have a few minutes to chat, don't you?"

"Of course, but perhaps we could talk at a later time. We were just having a strategy session before the party on Friday. You know Mr. Dent and March Browning. This is Red Finchley, from the Shaum Gallery in New York, and this"—Prinn turned, gesturing to the statuesque woman in the chair—"is Summer Sawyer, dean of art at Pomponio University."

"Pleased to meet you." Jack took Summer's slender manicured hand for a moment before turning. "And you are?" He extended a hand to the man with the notebook.

Randy jammed the chewed pencil into the curly hair behind his ear. "Randy Prinn. I write for the *Coastal Times*. I cover all the gallery openings, up-and-coming artists, new exhibits. You know, riveting stuff like that. So would you like to give an official quote about the murder?" He leaned forward eagerly.

Napoleon put his hand on Jack's shoulder. "Let's chat in my office, Detective. March, would you join us, please? I will finalize the rest of the details with you all tomorrow." He led the way to a plush room overlooking the blooming gardens. There was a tantalizing aroma of freshly brewed coffee. None was offered to the detective.

"What can I help you with, Detective?"

"It seems you have your hands full with your own problems, Mr. Prinn. Trouble among the ranks?"

"Not at all, not at all. Just a difference of opinion. Nothing a short discussion won't mend."

"The reporter—is he your brother?"

Prinn cleared his throat and clasped his hands firmly on the lacquered top of his desk. "Yes."

"I've never met him before. Does he live around these parts?"

"He doesn't live anywhere. He's a drifter." The words fell like shards of glass. "Shall we move on to your questions, Detective Denny?"

"Sure. Before we do, though, what is a dean from Pomponio University doing here in Finny? Isn't that down near Pescadero?"

"Yes. Ms. Sawyer was working with me on an exhibit of her students' work here in my gallery."

"Was?"

"Well"—Napoleon looked apologetic—"actually, it was a favor for a friend of mine who is on the board of directors there. It is a fine university. I did some undergraduate work there myself, and of course, I have contributed to their efforts to beautify the campus. Have you heard of the Prinn Gardens at the student commons?"

"I'm afraid I haven't."

"No matter. One of the chancellors asked me to feature some of the work from their school of art at my dedication. I agreed, to help promote the university."

And it wouldn't hurt your reputation to be a benefactor to a prestigious college, either, Jack thought.

"To make a long story short, the pieces that Ms. Sawyer brought me were simply abysmal. I couldn't accept such juvenile work at my gallery. I have a reputation to protect, and I had to tell Ms. Sawyer to cancel her participation in the dedication."

More likely, Jack thought, she had voiced an opinion like the one he heard today, questioning Prinn's judgment. "And I imagine she found that uncomfortable to explain to her superiors?"

"I imagine, since she came back today to try to change my mind. I do feel badly for her; she is so intent on being a trustee there someday; this probably set her back a rung or two. I really didn't have a choice, you know. The integrity of my gallery must come first." He looked for affirmation from March, who became suddenly busy looking through her notebook.

"But I'm sure you have more important things on your mind. Shall we take care of your other questions?"

Jack flattened himself into the brocade chair as best he could. "All right. I understand Crew Donnelly was an employee of yours. How long did he work for you?"

"A matter of six months or so. I hired him for maintenance of the grounds, sometimes a delivery or two. That sort of thing."

"What do you know about him?"

"Not much. We didn't chat often."

Jack eyed the immaculate suit and manicured nails. He imagined the curator didn't speak to any of the hired help, except perhaps to the pretty lady seated next to him. "Ms. Browning, isn't it?"

She glanced nervously at Prinn before nodding.

"What do you know about the victim?"

"He did some work around town, at the library and such. When Mr. Prinn asked me to find a gardener, I asked Ellen Foots about him. She said he hadn't been in town long. He was checking out books one afternoon, and he heard her talking about landscaping the breezeway. He offered his services and told her if she didn't like the results, she didn't have to pay him. The results were fabulous, as you can see for yourself, so we hired him after the library project was finished."

"Was his work here satisfactory?"

March glanced again at Prinn. "I believe the grounds were very well maintained."

"He was rather free with advice at times," Prinn interjected. "To be perfectly honest, Detective, I intended to let him go at the end of the summer."

"Did he know that?"

"No. I just decided a few days ago when I caught him in the greenhouse for the second time."

"Gardeners aren't allowed in the greenhouse?"

"Not in my greenhouse. My plants are extremely sensitive, and I will not have people tramping in and out uninvited. I explained this several times to Mr. Donnelly, but he nonetheless intruded on at least two occasions."

"So you decided to fire him?"

"I was intending to let him go, yes."

"Where did he live?" Jack knew exactly where the gardener lived, having been to the place several times since the murder. He wondered how well the curator knew his employees.

"He rented a bungalow on the beach, I think. That small place that the inland people rent in the off-season."

"The inland people" was the local term for everyone living outside of Finny to the eastern seaboard. "I guess I'll take a trip to the beach, then." He struggled loose from the brocade. "I don't suppose you know who wanted Crew Donnelly dead?"

Prinn stiffened and March blanched. "No, Detective, I'm afraid we don't," Prinn said.

"Oh, one more thing. Do you think I could get a peek at your greenhouse? I'll be careful not to trample anything."

"Of course. March will show you around on your way out."

"Thank you. I'll be seeing you soon." The door closed softly behind him.

15

*H*er arm throbbed. The bulky silver and blue splint the doctor had welded to her two broken middle fingers made her feel as though she were continually committing an obscene gesture. She would have, should have, gone straight home to a pint of Chunky Monkey, but now the cop was asking to see her.

She pushed open the heavy door, knocking softly as she entered the room. He was lying with his eyes closed. Asleep, she thought. Poor guy. Everywhere she could see seemed to be either scratched or blue, except for his face. That looked drawn and pinched. Maybe he always looked drawn and pinched. She'd only seen him unconscious and passing out. Benjamina cleared her throat delicately.

Nothing.

She coughed slightly.

Not a flinch.

"Hello!"

She intended to murmur a greeting, but it must have come out more forcefully than she meant, because his eyes shot open and he half jerked upright like a jack-in-the-box with lumbar problems.

He blinked several times. "Afternoon, ma'am. Are you looking for someone?"

Why does saying "ma'am" make everyone sound like they come from Mayberry? "Actually, I was told you asked to see me."

He looked totally befuddled. Probably the medicine, she surmised.

"Do I know you, ma'am?"

"We've met briefly. You were more or less unconscious at the time."

"Unconscious?"

She heaved an impatient sigh. Medicine aside, there was a pint of Chunky Monkey and a prescription for Vicodin at home with her name on it. "I am the gal that found you on the side of the road."

"Gal?" A moment's hesitation. "Did you help the fella out?"

"What fella?"

"The man who was at the scene. Ben, I think he went by."

The clouds parted. "Oh, I see. You were expecting someone else. I'm afraid you'll have to settle for me. I am Benjamina Pena. Most people call me Ben."

"You? I can't believe. . ." he stammered.

The turmoil of the day finally caught up with her. Annoyance crept in underneath the throbbing. "You can't believe what? That you were rescued, for lack of a better

63

word, by a woman? Is that just a little too much for your macho mystique to handle? Well, there weren't any other manly rescuers around, so I did the best I could."

The man's face became distinctly pink under the fatigue. He passed a hand over his eyes briefly. "They told me there were shots fired, that someone scared off the guys who jumped me. I just. . ."

"You just assumed it was a man. Of course. I can't believe this. Here I am driving along, minding my own business, and there you are in the middle of the road, not even having the decency to remain conscious long enough to radio for help. Do I look like a person who enjoys radioing dispatch and shooting armed thugs? Do I?" Her voice rose.

He lay watching her, mouth agape.

Her tone edged up another few notches. "And you just had to get up after I TOLD you not to and fall down on me. Do you see these fingers? They were perfectly good this morning. Do you know what I do? I am an art teacher. I PAINT! How do you suppose I am going to do that without my fingers?"

The man cleared his throat. "I sincerely apologize, Ms. Pena. I am very grateful for your help."

Benjamina gathered herself. "Well. All right then. I may have been a little harsh. It has been a very strange day, Mr.—Officer? Is Roper your first or last name, anyway?"

"First. My name is Roper Mackey. Just call me Rope."

"Okay, Rope. Listen, I think I'd better be going. I'm sure you need to rest, and I need carbohydrates."

"Thank you again, Ms. Pena." He extended a dry, calloused hand for her to grasp. "By the way, there is one thing I really need to ask you."

"What's that?"

"What exactly is a troglodyte?"

A smart tap on the door sounded like a gunshot in the perfect silence of the house. Ruth dropped the manuscript in a heap on the floor. In a fit of cowardice she had left a message on Monk's machine when she knew he was at work. Her headache was back, she had said; she would have to miss Sunday service. With a quiver of guilt she knew it was not her head that was sick, but her spirit. Maybe Monk had decided to come check on her on his way to church. For a moment, she stayed in the chair, frozen.

"Hallo? Anybody home?" called a voice attached to the face peering through the wire mesh.

Ruth rubbed sweaty palms on her pants and unlatched the screen. "Well, hello, Red. It's so nice to see you. Come in."

"Thanks. I don't usually barge in on people, but I got bored just walking up and down the beach talking to myself, so I thought I'd just visit the only person

I know in this town. A guy named Monk told me where you lived. I hope you don't mind the intrusion." Her voice was low.

"Not at all," Ruth said. It took a supreme effort to summon up charm, to stir up the silence she was steeped in. "I'm happy to have the company of an unfeathered friend. Would you like some tea or ice water? Lemonade?"

"Water would be great."

Ruth bustled off into the kitchen and returned with two yellow glasses. As she returned to her guest, she was dumbfounded to see Red skimming through the pages of her husband's writing.

"I hope you don't mind," said Red, taking the glass. "It was on the floor. Are you a writer?"

"Uh, no. No. My late husband was, I think," she stammered lamely.

"Well, how does it end?"

Ruth stared at her blankly. "What?"

"The story. What happens to the girl who saved the cop? How does it end?"

After an endless pause, she answered. "I don't know. I haven't gotten that far. I'm not sure it was ever finished."

"Wow." She nodded her head thoughtfully for a moment. "Are you going to do it?"

"Do what?"

"You know. Finish it."

Ruth's mouth dropped. She managed a weak "Me?"

"Why not? You've got the beginning, don't you?"

"Well, yes. I guess I do, but I really have no idea how he was going to end it or, uh, anything like that."

"Hmmm. You didn't discuss it with him?"

"No." Her stomach did a sudden flip-flop. "No, not really."

"Oh." Her brows knitted together like copper-colored springs. "That means you get to make it up on your own. You know, write your own fantasy ending."

"I am not a writer by any stretch of the imagination. I am just an amateur photographer in an itty-bitty town. Speaking of towns, how do you like ours, anyway?" She felt desperate to change the subject.

"It's very quaint, I suppose. In a sleepy fishing village sort of way."

Ruth sipped, watching the amber eyes that watched her. Tendrils of hair floated around Red's face like an unraveling hem. Ruth found herself warming to this vibrant girl. Red's eyes wandered to the rusty hydrangeas outside, spots of color in the gathering mist. "So how can you stand it here every day, with the awful fog?"

"You get used to it, I guess."

"Yeah. How does that poem go? The one about the neighbor holding the lamp until her friend's eyes adjust to the dark?"

"Oh, gee. I haven't heard that one in years. It's Dickinson, I think. Something about being accustomed to the dark. I can only recall the line 'as when the neighbor holds the lamp to witness her good-bye.' I know there is something about evenings of the brain, too. I've had one or two of those myself," she said ruefully.

"I hear you."

A feeble knock rattled against the door. "I'm sorry," Red said, struggling out of the overstuffed recliner, "I didn't know you were expecting company."

"No need to leave. It's Solomon. He stops by almost every day for a snack and helps me with the birds."

She ushered in a tiny child with enormous cocoa eyes and a dangerous-looking mop of black hair. He had his Giants cap wrung between his fingers, one foot hooked behind the other. The cocoa eyes were immediately fixed on the tile floor.

"Solomon, I'd like you to meet Ms. Finchley. She works for a big art gallery in New York City."

The boy mumbled something to the tiles.

"Solomon is in third grade. He is a tremendous help to me, and the birds just love him, don't they, Sol?"

More mumbling.

"I am glad to meet you," Red said, smiling. "I would love for you to show me how you take care of the birds."

Ruth led the way to the kitchen.

"Let's have our snack now, Sol, then you can give Ms. Finchley a demonstration."

With a relieved sigh, the boy clambered up onto a red stool as Ruth poured lemonade and handed around a plate of chocolate chip cookies. Wordlessly, he began wolfing them down.

Red and Ruth watched the boy surreptitiously fill his jacket pockets with two cookies he had secreted in his lap. It gave Ruth tremendous satisfaction to watch the little boy enjoy her cookies. How many batches had she made for her own son? At times it seemed like the only thing he would take from her, the only way she could show him love.

When the last of the chocolate was licked off Sol's fingers, he carefully carried the plate to the sink and rinsed out the glass.

"Go on out, Sol. We'll be right behind you." The door slammed shut before she finished the sentence. "He's a sweetheart, but he's had a rough road. His mother is an alcoholic and vanishes every few months or so. Dad is out of the picture. I think he's hungry for more than cookies. He stores them up like he's collecting them in case the well runs dry."

Noting the concerned look on the younger woman's face, Ruth added, "He's been unofficially adopted by an absolutely stalwart woman in town. She has five children of her own, but she always has room for Sol. I'm sure Mrs. Brody supplies him with treats often; she's a wonderful baker."

"Poor guy," Red said.

"Do you have children, Red?"

"Me? No. No siblings, either. Probably a good thing from all the stories I hear about other people's family dysfunctions. I grew up with a dog, a sort of schnauzer-type concoction by the name of Hubbard."

"Named after the old mother with the empty cupboard?"

"Nope, the squash. He was built like a solid little squash with legs. What about you? Do you have family in Finny?"

"I have a son," Ruth said quietly. "He's grown now, with a wife. He lives in Chicago where his wife's family owns a trucking company. He keeps the books for them."

"Do you see him often?"

"No. No. I really just get my information from the annual Christmas letter." She laughed ruefully. "We were never very close, I guess."

From the moment he was born, Bryce seemed detached from his mother, indifferent even. She remembered him scooting to the far corner of his crib, staring at her with those serious black eyes. As a toddler he was so independent, so intolerant of the physical attention she tried to shower him with. He answered her offers of help with a stern "By myself!"

When she was very tired, she wondered if she had only imagined being a mother. No, she concluded, she would have imagined it better. She would imagine her boy growing up to be a gentle, kind man, a man like Jack.

"Let's go outside. Sol really does want to show off for you, even if he doesn't have the right words to say it."

The birds were hopping from foot to foot, madly trying to snatch the stale popcorn from Solomon's hands as he stood on a chair. He conducted a wild orchestra of feathers and webbed feet, leading them from one side to the other with flying trails of popcorn.

The boy plopped onto the ground, and the birds, finally convinced that the food was gone, settled themselves around his legs, pecking each other nastily as they jockeyed for position.

"Do they actually show affection?" Red asked in amazement.

"I don't know if I would go so far as to say affection, but they tolerate humans, some more than others."

Solomon drew his finger back quickly as Rutherford bit him. He stuck it in his mouth and began stroking Zachary instead.

"You see? They will even bite the hand that feeds them." An odd smell tickled Ruth's nostrils.

TROUBLE UP FINNY'S NOSE

A sudden darkening of the sky made them all look upward.

"What in the world is that?" Red asked, watching the drifting plume of black smoke.

"I don't know," Ruth answered. Scanning the sky, she gasped. Finny's Nose was smoking.

16

J ack thought of Lacey every time he saw barbed wire.

They had met when he visited the Funshine Travel Agency to plead for a donation for the police charity auction. She was newly transplanted to Finny from the Midwest and happy to donate a weekend trip to Half Moon Bay on behalf of Funshine. He bought her lunch to thank her. Tuna salad on wheat, no mayo.

They went out a few times. He couldn't think of anything but her most of the time, but he didn't call it love. He wasn't sure he would recognize love if it came delivered by a fat boy in a diaper with a quiver of arrows on his back.

One afternoon he got a call from her neighbor, Louella Parsons, asking him to come right away. Not red-lights-and-sirens right away, but immediately would be good.

He arrived to find Lacey straddling the top of a six-foot fence, completely tangled in the barbed wire that ran across the top of the redwood planks. She was imprisoned by a cotton sock and at intermittent intervals along her blue checked sweater. Strands of her blond hair were interwoven in the sharp prongs.

He cleared his throat, and she turned her head.

"Oh, hi, Jack. How is your day going?"

He stood there, completely unable to respond. Finally he managed a weak greeting. "Just fine, Lacey. Uh, are you having some trouble?"

"As a matter of fact, yes. I was trying to put a baby bird back in the nest, and somehow I got all tangled up. The bird seems comfortable, though." She laughed, and he thought he had never seen anything more beautiful than this crazy woman hanging from the barbed wire.

Eventually, he got her untangled. "I'm sorry to have bothered you," she said. "I'm sure you have more important stuff to do than detangling."

She chuckled and looked at him, waiting. He just stood there. Then he couldn't stand it anymore. He grabbed her shoulders and kissed her until they both ran out of breath.

He could still feel that kiss. He could still feel everything about her: the soft skin behind her neck; her cold feet pressed against him at night; the bump on her collarbone, a souvenir of a fall from a ladder in the fourth grade. He hadn't really savored those things when she was alive, fool that he was.

He wondered when the feelings would fade. Alcohol expedited the forgetting process for a while, and though he knew it was stupid, he turned to it more and more in the months following Lacey's death. Then one night he woke after one too many to find Mr. Boo-Boo and Paul looking at him reproachfully. He had not heard Paul struggling with the bathroom door. Jack threw the soiled Batman underwear and the remaining bottles in the trash and hadn't touched another drop.

The last year was a frenetic blur, a jumble of long hours at work, psychologist appointments for Paul, frantic calls to babysitters when things came up. Lacey always told him never to leave clothes sitting in the dryer too long or they would wrinkle. That's how he was living his life, tumbling through it to avoid the damage that comes from stillness. At odd moments, memories of his past sometimes poked their way into the present. Like the amazing woman trapped in barbed wire, a woman he had taken for granted.

"Get a grip," he said, shoving the emotions back into their dark ventricle. He balled his hands into fists and squeezed his eyelids together to shut out the memories.

Work.

Stepping under the yellow tape, he entered Crew Donnelly's cottage to see if he had missed anything the last two times he'd been there.

It was hot, dank. He left the door open as he walked slowly around the tiny area. A small bed, made up neatly. A semi-enclosed kitchen with a microwave and a dorm-sized fridge. The microwave smelled like baked potatoes. The fridge held a half can of black olives, an opened Coke, and a slice of pizza on a greasy paper napkin.

The bathroom was bare; the only decoration was a dried-up plug-in air freshener shaped like a shell. Nothing in the medicine cabinet but some aspirin and toothpaste. The toothbrush was glued to the counter in a crusty plop of toothpaste.

Wandering back out into the main room, he paused. His officers had leaned the Zimmerman seascape against the back wall during their search of the place. It was gorgeous; even he could see that. Roughly textured, waves of blue-green crashing on a foggy coastline.

Gorgeous. In a room entirely void of any beauty. So what in the world was it doing here?

A huge dark figure hurled itself into the room and knocked the detective to his knees. "Get off, Boo-Boo. How do you always find me? You're supposed to be in the backyard protecting the property, you big idiot!"

The dog slobbered joyfully into Jack's ear, washing him in drool and a pungent cloud of dog aroma. "All right, you mongrel. All right." He scratched behind a ragged ear until the dog's hind leg began to keep time with the scratching.

Abruptly, the animal stood rigidly still, both ears zinging upward like radar dishes. Whirling around, he started nosing wildly at the painting, sending sprays of saliva down the surface.

"Stop it, Boo-Boo! Stop!" Jack grabbed Boo-Boo's collar and hauled him out the door, slamming it quickly. The dog started to whine and paw at the door, his nails scrabbling on the metal threshold.

Jack looked at the moist painting. Carefully he wiggled his pocketknife between the thin wooden backing and the pseudo frame holding the canvas in place. The backing soon came away, and he shined a penlight into the opening.

"Would you look at that," he said. "Maybe Lacey was right about the crazy dog after all."

That's when the acrid scent of smoke finally permeated his consciousness.

Ruth immediately sent Solomon home, and she and Red raced down the slope behind Ruth's cottage and up the wooded hillside. It seemed as though the fog was working against them, thrusting out chilled hands to prevent them from reaching the plateau. Ruth scrambled to the top minutes before her panting partner. At the apex, they were able to see clearly the orange glow coming from Prinn's greenhouse.

Clouds of black smoke swirled inside, and pockets of orange flame sprouted up here and there like a crazed monarch butterfly beating itself against the glass windows. They ran closer until they could feel waves of heat enveloping them.

"Oh no!" gasped Ruth. "I hope no one—" The sound of exploding glass flattened them to the ground; they shielded their faces. Shards imbedded themselves into the long grass around them, and Ruth felt a prick on the back of her neck.

Several more people crested the top of the hill, and Ruth could make out Napoleon through the swirling smoke. He went from an all-out sprint to a dead stop as his greenhouse came into view.

"Those thugs!" Prinn shouted, throwing a vicious punch at no one.

He began to move toward the blazing structure. Ruth saw March put out a restraining hand. He shook her off angrily and took two more steps before a thunderous crash stopped everyone in their tracks.

Ruth and the others watched, mesmerized, as the peaked ceiling imploded with a shriek of protesting metal, raining glass down into the hellish fire.

March stared at the sight in horror, her face starkly white in the gloom. Again she reached out a trembling hand toward Napoleon, but it stayed frozen in the air, never making contact.

Randy and two men in speckled white overalls with paintbrushes still clutched in their hands jogged up to join them.

"I called 911. They should be here any minute." Randy's face looked oddly greenish in the glow. "I think we should move back in case the side walls blow out completely."

He put a hand on March's elbow and guided her away. Ruth, Red, and the painters followed. They all huddled near a stone bench, watching Napoleon silhouetted against the bonfire.

Randy looked uncertain. After a moment's hesitation he returned to his brother and spoke quietly to him from behind.

"Get away from me!" Prinn said loudly enough for all of them to hear.

The whine of a fire truck announced the arrival of the volunteer fire department. Setting up a hose line well back from the falling glass, they began a relatively futile effort to extinguish the fire. Streams of water seemed to anger it into hissing and bellowing with renewed vigor. Even Ruth's untrained eye could see there was no hope of saving the structure.

Captain Ernie Gonzalez approached Napoleon. "Mr. Prinn, is there a possibility that anyone was inside?"

Napoleon's voice was so low, Ruth almost didn't hear his reply. "I don't think so," he said dully. "Just my plants."

"Okay. I'm afraid it's pretty much a loss. We'll keep the water on it and watch the surrounding area to make sure it doesn't spread. You need to move away for your own safety." He took hold of Prinn's sleeve and gently pushed him over to a bench. "You'd better sit here until the cops arrive."

"Cops?"

"Well, clearly the thing didn't burst into flames on its own. That fire spread like butter in the sun. Some sort of accelerant. Just sit tight and wait for PD. They'll be here soon."

Ruth waited until the captain had left before she sat down next to Napoleon. She noticed a thin line of blood trickling down his forehead like a tiny wandering worm.

"You're cut. Above your eye. Do you have a handkerchief or something?"

He ignored her, staring into space.

"I am so sorry. I know how important your greenhouse was to you." She waited, her conscience battling with her curiosity, curiosity finally winning out.

"You said 'those thugs.' Do you know who set this fire, Napoleon?"

His head snapped around to fix her with an intense stare. "No. No. Of course not. I didn't say that. I must have been spouting some expletive, Ruth. You misunderstood me."

She looked at him as his gaze returned to his greenhouse, the flames dancing in the dark pools of his eyes. He looked so lost, so utterly defeated, that for a moment she had a strong urge to put her arms around him.

The strobing red and blue lights of the Finny Police Department caused them all to look up and see Jack Denny arriving, code three.

All except Napoleon Prinn, who sat and watched his greenhouse burn. Ruth had a strange feeling he wasn't thinking about his incinerated plants.

*S*he was halfway through. Twenty-six more pages to go. Not a bad attempt for a first-year graduate student. She was starting to add another comment in the margin when a sudden clearing of the throat nearby caused her to launch the papers into the air.

Through the blizzard of papers floating slowly to the floor, she saw a very embarrassed uniformed man, holding a white paper bag with one hand and a cowboy hat in the other, standing in the open doorway.

"I didn't mean to startle you, Professor Pena. Let me help you pick these up."

Roper Mackey dropped to his knees and began retrieving papers. She met him on the floor halfway under her desk.

"Don't worry about it. The pages are numbered," she said, pushing heavy black hair out of the way. "We only have to find the last twenty-six."

A few minutes later they both stood up. Roper banged his head as he tried to extricate his wide shoulders from underneath her desk. Sheepishly he handed her a tousled stack of papers.

"I am really sorry about that. I guess I'm about as helpful as long underwear in the desert." He paused, looking totally self-conscious, like a kid at the opera. "So, er, what are you reading about?"

"Manet," she said, plopping down into the chair again. "If you want the whole enchilada, it's 'The Function of the Picture Surface as Redefined by Edouard Manet,' but that's a mouthful."

"Er, yeah. I guess so." He cleared his throat again, softly. "I just wanted to tell you, to say, to apologize again for my comments in the hospital. I didn't mean to sound like a chauvinist pig, but I guess that's how it came out of my big mouth. Anyway, I'm sorry for being rude."

"And for breaking my finger," she added helpfully.

"Especially for breaking your finger." He cleared his throat again. "You must be new in town. I would remember seeing you around, I think."

"I just started here two weeks ago."

"How do you like it? Georgia, I mean."

"I liked it just fine until I got mixed up in a homicide in progress."

His eyes wandered until they rested on the bag in his hand. "Oh. I brought you some carbohydrates."

She laughed and took the bag. "Mmm. Chocolate chip cookies. I may just have to forgive you after all. Thank you, Officer Mackey."

TROUBLE UP FINNY'S NOSE

"Well now, why don't you call me Rope?"

"Okay. And you can call me Ben." Noting the strangled look on his face, she added, *"Or Benjamina. That's good, too."*

"That's great. I see you've got a lot of reading to do about the picture thing. I'd better let you get back to it." He hesitated, looking down at his worn boots.

"Is there anything else, Rope?"

"Well, I sort of figured, since you are new in town and all, maybe you haven't seen any of the sights. Maybe I could. . ." His voice trailed off.

She regarded him thoughtfully, the huge macho cowboy, looking remarkably like a nervous little boy. *"Sure."*

He looked up. *"Sure?"*

"Sure. I'd love to see the sights with you."

"You would? Well. You would. How about I pick you up on Saturday? Around 1:00?"

"I have a class until 1:30."

"All right. How about two, then?" His relief was obvious as he replaced his hat and turned to leave.

"Don't you want my address?"

He paused. *"Oh, right. What is your address?"*

"You already know it, don't you? Along with all my other vital statistics."

He grinned. *"Just one or two. See you on Saturday, Ms. Pena."* She didn't correct him as he walked out the door.

◄━━━►

This chapter was not in the notebook. At first, Ruth assumed Phillip had merely skipped a number, but she found it while cleaning out an old receipts file in the study. She sat down to read it, but her mind kept straying back to yesterday's greenhouse disaster.

She had stayed at the fire scene well into the afternoon, questioned first by Captain Gonzalez and then by Jack. The details got blurry after the fire was contained and the witnesses bustled off.

Somewhere in the midst of it all, the Finny Ladies' Organization for Preparedness arrived. Regrettably known as FLOP gals, the ladies of Finny felt it their duty and calling to provide comfort and aid of all kinds in cases of catastrophe or stress. Mrs. Florence Hodges was the figurehead of the organization, and Ruth knew her to be a woman of steely nerves. Flo believed that every catastrophe in life could be eased by a cup of steaming coffee and a triple-fudge brownie. She had shown up with both at the hospital the night Phillip had the heart attack.

The FLOP ladies arrived on scene in the middle of the melee at the greenhouse bearing coffee and treats for those watching the blazing mess. They all sat, huddled together in disbelief, munching on brownies. Napoleon stood apart, as if he were daring the fog to touch him.

Monk was there, too. He came charging up the path, puffing like a freight train. Ruth saw him seek her out, his face creased with worry. She assured him she was fine, but he put his arm around her anyway. For a few moments, she let him.

For now she put that out of her mind. The person who kept surfacing was Napoleon Prinn. "*Those thugs,*" he had said, his face a mask of rage. Why rage? Certainly shock, grief, disbelief. The one emotion that was missing was surprise.

Napoleon Prinn did not seem surprised to find his beloved greenhouse burning to the ground.

18

The greenhouse looked like a hideous black spider lying on its back with charred legs poking up into the air. Though it was two days after the fire, the air was still heavy with the acrid smell of old smoke. Shards of glass lent a sparkle to the scorched grass.

Inside the burned-out shell, Ernie Gonzalez was on his hands and knees, avoiding the glass as best he could. In spite of the brisk morning air, his black curly hair was dripping with sweat as he heaved his heavy torso along the ground. Behind him, in a borrowed pair of turnouts, Jack held a silver paint can in one gloved hand and a camera in the other.

"Why can't we use plastic bags, Ernie? These paint cans are a pain in the neck."

"That's why you're carrying them." Ernie stopped to peer closely at a blackened pile. "The hydrocarbons would eat right through plastic bags. Didn't you pay attention in your fire science class?"

"I must have missed that one. Are you sure about this?"

"I'd bet my new reel on it."

They peered in silence for a few minutes. "What are we looking for again?"

"You'll know it when you see it. Something out of place. Some sort of—*Aha!* What did I tell you?" He pointed to a spot just beyond a tangle of broken pots. "Get a couple of shots of that. Be sure to get a few wide shots so we can see it in relation to the windows."

Dutifully, the detective took digital pictures of the spot Ernie was pointing to like an eager hunting dog. Gonzalez waited for Jack to finish and gingerly picked up the broken sooty bottle. There was still a fragment of blackened cloth stuffed into the mouth.

Ernie beamed like a man who had just found the Hope Diamond. He lowered it reverently into a paint can and tamped down the lid with his thumbs.

"That's it?" Jack was expecting something more dramatic.

"Whaddya mean, that's it? It's a Molotov cocktail. Pretty crude. You grab an old bottle, fill it with some sort of flammable liquid like gasoline, and add a shot of diesel. Stuff a handkerchief into the mouth, light it, and chuck it through the window. Whoosh!"

"Which window did it come through?"

"That one, I'm thinking." He pointed to what used to be the west window.

"Lots of shrubs around the perimeter. Wouldn't be hard to do the deed without being seen."

They walked outside and took a few more pictures. The ground crunched underfoot as if they were walking over a bowl of Grape-Nuts.

"How long from the time it was thrown to the time you guys got here?"

"Hard to say. When we arrived it was fully involved. I'd say maybe fifteen minutes or so."

"So whoever it was had plenty of time to wander casually away. You don't think it was kids out for some fun?"

"No way to tell for sure, but doesn't feel like kids. Too much prep work involved to make a cocktail. Gotta bring the gas, rags, and stuff. Kids do dumb spur-of-the-moment stuff. This isn't where they usually come to hang out, either. If it was kids, I'll hear about it real soon. Never met a teen who could keep their mouth shut about a thing like this for very long."

The radio on the captain's belt began to sputter.

"I gotta go. Old Mr. Deenish says there's a cobra in his backyard. I've told him a thousand times we don't have cobras here, but he couldn't tell a snake from his own garden hose. Call me if you need anything else."

He clambered into the beat-up Bronco and started the engine. Then he stopped.

"Gee whiz," Ernie said thoughtfully, "I just thought of something. This being an arson fire and all, I guess you'll be writing up the report. See you around." He drove away laughing.

Jack headed off for the gallery in search of the curator. As he entered the building, he caught sight of his face reflected in the glass. He wiped the soot off of his nose as best he could before walking to the rear of the building in search of Prinn's secretary.

"Hello, Ms. Browning."

March looked up from her papers nervously, a wave of blond hair falling into her face. "Hello, Detective." She shoved the hair back behind one ear. "What can I do for you?"

"I'd like to talk to Mr. Prinn. Is he around?"

"Well, yes. He's very busy, though. You know, dealing with the fire and the opening and everything."

He nodded pleasantly. "I'm sure he's not too busy to spare a few moments for the police, now, is he?" His casual demeanor did not hide the intensity in his eyes. He was sweaty, tired, and in no mood to be trifled with.

"Yes. I mean no. I'll see if I can get him for you." She scurried away.

The curator was sitting at his desk, thumbing through files marked COLONIAL HOME INSURANCE. He looked up at the detective and smiled politely.

"Detective. How nice to see you. What can I do for you?"

TROUBLE UP FINNY'S NOSE

Jack seated himself once again in the torturous brocade chair. He decided on the direct approach. "You have had a few misfortunes lately. I'm beginning to think your string of bad luck is more than a coincidence."

"Bad luck?"

"I'd say the murder of your gardener was pretty unfortunate."

"Oh yes. I expect he fell in with the wrong crowd."

"Then there's the torching of your greenhouse."

"That could have been accidental. The wiring in that place was quite old."

"More likely it was the Molotov cocktail that did it."

Prinn was silent for a while. "I can't imagine why anyone would destroy my greenhouse. It must have been vandals."

"Is the greenhouse insured?"

"As a matter of fact, no. Only the gallery proper is insured, not the greenhouse, because it was an outlying structure. No matter; it won't be that costly to replace." He spoke cheerfully.

"Who would want to burn down your greenhouse?"

"I've no idea."

"Do you have any idea why Donnelly had one of your Zimmerman paintings in his cottage before he was murdered?"

"No. I can't imagine why he would have one."

"Didn't you notice one was missing?"

"All of the artwork has been removed from the walls and put in the storage room. I had no idea any was missing. I'll take an inventory immediately." He scribbled a note on the desktop blotter. "I didn't realize Mr. Donnelly was an art lover."

Jack smiled. "Maybe he just loved the marijuana."

Prinn started, eyes round, mouth open. "What? What did you say?"

"I said marijuana. Dried, pressed, and packaged beneath the canvas. Waiting to be shipped out, I would guess."

Prinn closed his mouth and swallowed. "Surely you aren't implying that I have anything to do with drug smuggling?"

"You housed the painting. You hired the handyman. Your greenhouse is torched. Like I said, you seem to have a really bad string of luck working here."

Napoleon sat up straight in his chair. "I house lots of paintings, Detective. That's my business. I hired Donnelly purely by chance, and as for my greenhouse, I don't know what happened to it. That is your department."

"Did you know Donnelly before you hired him?"

"No."

"Did you make several trips to New York last year?"

"Yes."

"Did you meet anyone there?"

78

"Of course. I met lots of people there," he snapped.

"Did you meet anyone there who was involved in the drug smuggling business?"

"Not that I'm aware of."

"Did you have any knowledge that your paintings were being used to smuggle marijuana?"

"Absolutely not."

Jack stood. "A team is on its way down here to search your storage rooms and files." He noted the belligerent look on the curator's face. "Yes, I do have a warrant."

Prinn rose and leaned over his desk, his hands like spiders on the desktop. "You see to it that they don't ruin any of my artwork," he hissed, the calm façade breaking apart like fractured glass, "—or dirty my gallery. I have an event here on Friday, and I won't let anything jeopardize that."

Jack felt the perverse thrill that often came when people pushed, mistaking his good nature for pliability. When the situation called for it, he could be as pliable as quick-drying cement.

"They will be careful, Mr. Prinn." He fixed the curator with an unblinking gaze. "And you will stay out of their way."

At the threshold he paused. "One more thing. Someone has decided to incinerate something very important to you. Seems like they're trying to send you a message. I'd listen if I were you."

❦

On his way down the hall, Jack headed for March's office. As he approached, he heard voices coming from behind the open door.

"What did he do to make them angry?" a woman's voice said.

"I don't think it takes much to make them angry."

"What are we going to do?"

"Nothing. We just wait, like we planned. See what happens."

"Randy, I feel like this is spinning out of control. I don't want to get caught up in something bad."

"Don't worry, honey. Everything will be fine. I'm going to take care of you. I promise."

Jack walked into the office. On the other side of her desk, March and Randy stiffened, electrified.

"Detective! I didn't hear you come in. How long—what did you want?" March's face was white.

Randy regained his composure more quickly, the easy smile back in place. "Did you finish your investigation of the fire?" he asked. His hands were thrust into the pockets of his wrinkled khakis, and he leaned casually against the desk.

"Not yet. We're broadening the scope a bit. To include other things."

"Like what?" he asked. "Or is it top secret?"

"Like marijuana smuggling. You wouldn't know anything about that, would you?"

Their mouths dropped almost in unison.

"Marijuana?" March stammered. "What? In the greenhouse?"

"No. In the artwork displayed in this gallery. Did you know anything about that?"

"In the artwork? Are you kidding me? Who? Are you saying our paintings have been used to smuggle drugs?"

If she was faking complete shock, she was doing a great job of it. "Mr. Prinn denies any involvement. What do you say?"

Randy squared his shoulders. "What exactly are you accusing her of, Detective?"

"I'm not accusing her, or you, of anything. Yet. I just want to know what she knows."

"I had no idea there was any marijuana in this gallery." Her blue eyes looked straight into his, chin raised defiantly.

"How about you?" Jack gazed at Randy.

"Hey, I just came into town to write up a story on a gallery opening. If I had known illegal substances were involved, I would be writing a much better piece, believe me."

"I see. How did you and Ms. Browning happen to meet?"

Randy gave him a knowing look. "It was entirely coincidental, you'll be disappointed to learn. We hooked up at an art convention in Mendocino last year. I had no idea she worked at my brother's gallery when I met her." He looked at her slyly. "She wasn't wearing a name tag or anything."

March's face went from white to a deep red before it settled into a rosy shade of pink. "Do you have to tell him?" she mumbled.

Randy went on. "I was there covering the event for the *Coastal Times*, and she was there scouting some new talent for my brother. Incredibly, we booked rooms right next to each other at a bed-and-breakfast. I heard a cry for help from next door and I responded code three, I think you would say in the police world. Fortunately, the door was unlocked, and I found this lovely lady in distress." He laughed.

"Well, you might as well tell him now," March said, exasperated. "I was doing some yoga in my pajamas, and I had a terrible back spasm. I couldn't even get up off the floor to grab the phone and call for help. I was stuck right in the middle of a downward dog."

She began to giggle. "He was really nice about the whole thing. He helped me up and put some ice on my back until the spasm went away. We were both surprised to learn that I worked for his brother, and I made him swear under pain of losing his liver that he would never breathe a word of our meeting, or the relationship in general, to his brother."

"Why did you want your relationship with Randy kept quiet?" Jack asked around a grin.

"I knew Napoleon couldn't stand his brother, and I figured it would only make it harder for me here."

"Right. So who were you talking about? Before I came in. Who do you think torched the greenhouse?"

March swallowed convulsively. "He is my boss, Detective." She folded her arms across her silk blouse, twining them together like wicker.

"Whatever you say to me will stay between us for the time being." He sighed and rubbed his sooty jaw. "You don't really have much choice here."

Randy and March exchanged glances. March went to the door and closed it. "I don't know what is going on. We worked so hard to build this gallery. Now what happens? The gardener is dead. Marijuana in the paintings."

She looked angry. "I have made this idiot gallery my life. I poured my heart and soul into it and not for the money, I can tell you that. And not for the gratitude, because there isn't any. We were finally getting there. Getting some recognition for quality work and the gallery itself."

She slammed both hands flat on the desk with a crack. "My parents didn't send me to college so I could wind up wasting my entire life."

Jack let her breathe heavily for a minute, while Randy gently massaged her shoulder.

"You knew something around here wasn't right. When did you realize there was a problem?"

She sank slowly back into her chair. "Look. All I know is there have been weird phone messages coming in every once in a while. They're from men. They never leave names. They just want Napoleon to call. Every time he gets a message, it scares the stuffing out of him. They don't sound like they're interested in art, you know?"

"Where do the calls originate?"

"The East Coast. New York."

"What do you think is going on?"

She shot Randy a quick look. "I thought maybe he borrowed money from the wrong people. Something like that."

"Did he come into some money recently?"

"Well, the gallery renovation wasn't cheap, and the new piece from New York was pricey. I don't keep the books, so I can't tell you how much money was involved or where it came from."

"So you figured he borrowed from the wrong guys and they've been hassling him to collect. Got it. I need to get things going. I'll be back to talk to you both again, I'm sure." He turned to go.

"Are we still going to be able to have our gallery dedication on Friday?"

"There will be a team arriving to search the gallery and offices momentarily. If they don't find anything too spicy, you can have your dedication as planned."

She sighed and nodded.

"Is there anything else you need to tell me, Ms. Browning?"

"No. What else could I tell you?"

He looked into her blue eyes and wondered the exact same thing.

19

Ruth sucked in the savory aromas that circled around Monk's shop. She came to deliver some brochures she had done for him, complete with photos of some of his more mouthwatering dishes. Monk wasn't there, but there was a scatter of tiny pasta on the floor. She was on her way to fetch the broom to sweep up when the bell on the door tinkled.

Ruth called out from the back storage room as soon as she heard the front door open. "Monk, is that you?" She heard scrabbling noises followed by a muffled crash as a body hit the floor.

"Oh no," Ruth cried, running to the front. "Are you hurt?" She ran over to assist the young man who was sprawled on the floor.

Monk had raced through the door just in time to see him fall. His arms were full of paper grocery sacks. Panting, he dropped the bags on the counter and knelt beside the prone figure. "Oh, for the love of lasagna. Are you all right there, fella?"

"Should I call 911?" Ruth asked.

"No need." Randy extended a shaky hand from his uncomfortable position on his back.

"Monk, this is Randy Prinn, Napoleon's brother."

"Pleased to meet you," Monk said. "Let me help you up. I should have swept that up before I left." He looked up. "Hello, Ruth. You look lovely today. I got you some onions at the Wednesday sale."

She blushed as they each took a hand and hauled Randy to his feet. "I'm really sorry, Randy," Ruth said. "I was just going to get the broom when I heard you come in."

"That's quite an alarm system you got there. What is it?"

"Couscous," Monk explained. "One of the bags split and sent the buggers everywhere. I just went to get some more. You sure you aren't hurt?"

"Not hurt." He brushed the tiny pasta balls from his denim jacket and released another shower from his pant cuff. "I was taking a stroll around the main drag here and I smelled the heavenly aroma of coffee. I was wondering if you dabbled in the retail java business. I could really use a fix."

"Sure thing. It's on the house."

"Better than on the floor."

Monk went to prepare a pot of coffee, pointing to some fresh muffins for

83

Ruth to pile on a plate.

Randy sat at a scarred table looking out at the shore. Monk plunked a steaming cup of coffee in front of him and squeezed around the other side of the table, holding his own mug. They sipped quietly for a minute, warming their hands on the mugs.

"Do you want to join us, Ruth?" Monk asked.

"No, no," she said. "I'm just going to clean up this coffee mess." The cleaning allowed her to be within comfortable earshot of the conversation.

"So you are Prinn's brother," Monk said. "If you don't mind me saying so, you're not a lot alike."

"What? I don't strike you as an obnoxious egotist? I'll take that as a compliment."

Ruth smiled to herself.

"Well, I wasn't going to insult your kin, but he does come across that way now and again."

"I know. Believe me. I grew up with him."

"Round here?"

"Down south. My father had a dental practice. Boney stayed there until he graduated, and I stayed until my parents died."

"Oh. Sorry to hear that. Accident?"

"I guess you could say that. Dad had a few too many at the club and gassed an old lady during a gum-planing procedure. She died. The malpractice suit pretty much ruined them both."

He stretched his long legs under the table. "Dad had a heart attack, and Mother died six months later of a stroke. I think it was more from shame than arteries. Her socialite friends cut her out like a patch of Ebola."

"No wonder Napoleon has such an unusual personality, with that family life," Ruth muttered to herself.

"Well, that is a spot of bad luck," Monk said. "Must have broken you up pretty good."

Randy shrugged. "Actually, it wasn't too bad for me. Took away some of the pressure."

"How do you mean?"

"Oh, I was the proverbial black sheep for reasons too numerous to mention, so I felt compelled to try and find something I was really good at. You know, unloved kid tries to win parents' approval."

Randy put down his mug and shoved his thumbs into the belt loops of his worn jeans. "Maybe it's because we're twins: Boney and I did everything more or less at the same time, in the same location. I was a flop in school. I decided to become an athlete, but as it turns out, you actually have to be good at sports to succeed in that career. Then I decided my real talent must be writing. What about you? You have family here?"

"Not here. Mom and Pop live in Kansas. Both in their nineties and still running a ranch, although my brother does most of the heavy stuff now."

"And you didn't get the ranching bug?"

"Nah. You ever been to Kansas? All it is, is a lot of flat surrounded by a lot more flat. I couldn't wait to get out. The navy was the perfect answer for me."

"Did you retire?"

"I took an early retirement." Monk folded his hands across his rounded belly and stared absently up at the overhead lights. "The navy has changed a lot since the dark ages when I enlisted. Now the newbies are young bucks with college and computers under their belts. And then they started letting women aboard." He shot a quick look at Ruth.

"Don't worry, Monk," she said, "I know you are a closet chauvinist."

Randy laughed. "It's a whole new world, my friend, especially where women are concerned."

"You attached?"

"Nope. I hardly know a soul in town."

Hmmm. He seemed to know March pretty well, Ruth thought.

"Say, that was some fire the other night," Monk said. "What's the scuttlebutt around the gallery?"

Randy took a swig of coffee before answering. "The detective on the case is sure it's arson, but no word about any suspects that I know of. Arson's not as bad as the Mary Jane, I guess."

"Who's Mary Jane?" Ruth could not resist asking.

"That's marijuana. Apparently someone has been smuggling it in Napoleon's paintings."

Ruth's jaw hit her clavicles. "You're kidding."

"There's quite a scheme afoot, according to Detective Denny." He drained the rest of his mug. "I guess I have to go face the big bad world, but it's a lot less bad with a cup of joe under my belt. Thanks."

"No problem," Monk said. "I'd better get to it, too. I've got crab cakes to fry, and crab waits for no man."

"I'll take your word for it. Thanks for the coffee and chitchat. I'll come back for some couscous when you cook up a batch."

Randy left. Though Monk seemed composed, Ruth could tell he was as shocked by the information as she was.

"Can you imagine Napoleon involved in smuggling?" he asked.

"No," she said slowly, remembering Randy and March together in whispered conversation, "but I wouldn't rule out his brother."

20

The door to Jack's office opened and a tired-looking Nathan Katz entered. Nathan's permanently somnolent demeanor was largely due to the fact that he had five children, including triplet girls entering their threes. Sometimes tired gave way to completely exasperated, but today tired was winning.

"Give me some good news, Nate."

"The hole in the ozone layer seems to be stabilizing."

"Funny. Try again."

"It's almost Friday?"

"That's not very encouraging to a guy who works weekends." He paused for half a minute before adding, "Do you know your mustache is sparkling?"

The officer slumped dejectedly into a chair, huffing into his bushy mustache. "I know. It's Glitter 'n' Go cheek powder. The stuff is there forever; I've even tried paint thinner. I think it's the same glop they use to glue 747s together."

"You fell asleep in front of the TV again, didn't you?"

"Yeah. Iva Marie got me. Pretty stealthy for a three-year-old—I didn't feel a thing. I'm pretty sure she's got a good pick-pocketing career ahead of her."

Jack laughed. "Okay, Tinkerbell. Talk to me."

"We combed the place, Jack. Nothing. No drugs, no drying or packaging materials. The paintings are clean, and so is the gallery from what we can tell."

"Phone records?"

Nate looked at his notes. "In the past six months the gallery received four New York calls from public phones. He didn't return any of them, at least not from a gallery phone. He made several calls to the Shaum Gallery, and they returned them. No reason to believe it wasn't legit business."

"What about the books?"

"Everything looks fine, but we made copies. No unusual deposits of money or regular withdrawals of significant sums. Of course, if he is getting some cash from an unsavory source, it isn't likely he's going to keep a record of it."

Jack sighed and leaned back in his chair. "So we have nothing to tie him to the dope."

"What about Donnelly? You get anything on him?" Katz cracked open a bottle of water that the detective handed him.

"Nothing new. Busted for possession. Small-time stuff. He only did a couple of months. He seems to have stayed out of trouble, at least until he landed in our quiet little hamlet."

"Maybe he planted the dope." Nate swigged down some water.

"It's possible. But why use a Zimmerman painting? And where did he get such a quality stash? That is some excellent weed, to quote the lab boys. Why can't we find the connection here?"

Nate drained the water bottle and slam-dunked it in the trash can. "Oh yeah. One more thing. Mary accidentally knocked an ashtray thingy over when we were searching the storeroom. Only it wasn't an ashtray; it was some work of art or something. Prinn says you owe him eight hundred bucks."

"I should have been an orthodontist," Jack said to the closing door.

———

When Ruth arrived at the door of the gallery Friday evening, she was impressed at the immaculate paint and the burnished brass doorknobs, highlighted by the footlights at each side of the cement steps. No one would ever guess there had been a fire only two hundred yards away now that the setting sun concealed the blackened greenhouse beams.

A tall teenage girl greeted her warmly. "Hi, Mrs. B. How are those birds?"

Lizzie Putney was a high school student who had worked for a while at Phillip's veterinary clinic. Ruth eyed the row of hoops twining down the girl's left ear and connecting via a delicate chain to a hoop in her nostril.

"Hi, Lizzie." She wrapped the girl in a hug. "You look. . .great," said Ruth, shifting her camera bag to the other shoulder.

"I'm helping out Monk tonight with the food. Don't I look the part?" She minced along for a few steps. "I'll show you to the dining hall, my lady."

Ruth gave her a squeeze. "Thank you. And how is your menagerie?" The girl had, at last count, four turtles, six cats, a one-eyed frog named Nelson, and an ancient guinea pig fondly referred to as "the old geezer." As a much younger child, she had soberly lugged each unfortunate critter to Dr. Budge for medical advice.

"Oh, they're all fine." She giggled. "But my dad says I had better come up with a plan before I go away to college. He says he isn't Dr. Doolittle." She giggled again as she led the way into the large foyer. "See you later, Mrs. B. I gotta go be couth!"

Ruth wondered if couth and nose rings were compatible.

The room was sparkling with white linens and candles twined with garlands of white roses and ivy. Prinn had class, no doubt about it. She took out her camera and snapped a few shots of the pristine dining tables. A few people were milling about, and she took their pictures, too.

Maude Stone was standing with Flo Hodges, pointing at a watercolor. She wore navy blue from head to toe with a matching feathered hat. Flo burst into loud peals of laughter at some comment from Maude.

Nestled in an inconspicuous corner of the foyer was the catering headquarters, and looking supremely conspicuous in a chef's white togs was Monk. He snapped off a jaunty salute with his slotted spoon and plunged it into a steaming stockpot. Her heart beat faster as she approached.

"That smells divine, Monk."

"Thankee, ma'am." He lowered his voice conspiratorially. "The little weasel ordered me not to associate with the guests, but I won't turn down a compliment from such a gorgeous lady. Is this place duded up or what?"

She blushed, looking around the foyer and beyond, into the adjoining corridor. There was a movement of shuffling people. More guests were arriving. Bubby Dean looked uncomfortable in a too-tight blazer. He waved at her, and she waved back. She guessed Alva had not been invited since he was not standing at the hors d'oeuvres table stuffing his pockets.

She whispered a good-bye to Monk and made her way past cushioned chairs to the displays of art. Her eyes were drawn to the soft watercolors. Foamy waves, peaceful gulls bobbing gracefully on gray water. Ha! Nothing like her family of squabbling children, fighting to the death over a stale muffin.

Farther down the hallway were reproductions of various well-known paintings and sculptures. The rest of the gallery was devoted to watercolors, oils, and the occasional sculpture, all done by coastal artists. Ruth knew enough to recognize that Napoleon had an exceptional eye.

She spotted Randy's curly head bent in deep conversation with someone she did not at first recognize. As the lady threw back her head to laugh, Ruth identified Summer Sawyer. She was wearing a very tight, very black sheath dress with enough of a plunge to display plenty of skin.

Summer laid a hand on Randy's arm and caressed it.

"I wouldn't know about that," Randy was saying. "I'm only a lowly reporter with no ambition to be anything else."

A rapid staccato of high heels announced March Browning's approach. She looked so different that Ruth had to glance again to be sure. March had quite literally let her hair down, and the cascade of blond waves settled around her face like a sigh. Her blue eyes mirrored the deep cobalt of her satin dress. She was lovely, and Ruth was surprised she had not noticed it before.

"Hello, Ms. Sawyer," March said icily, pushing past her to take Randy's arm. "I see you've met my fiancé, Randy. And this is our resident photographer, Ruth Budge."

If Summer was surprised to hear about Randy's premarital status, she gave not the slightest indication of it. She nodded casually and tossed the hair back out of her face.

"Yes. We were just getting acquainted. We're both twins, so we have a lot in common." Her black eyes rested completely on him without a glance at March. "My brother is a doctor."

"Does he practice in the area?" March asked.

"No. He moved to Arizona to be nearer to my mother after my father left. Doug works on an Indian reservation somewhere in the desert. He is the great protector to his adoring tribe, my mother included."

Summer shrugged her slender shoulders. "Don't mind me. I'm just being catty. My brother really is a doll; I've worshipped him my whole life. He says it's his calling to heal people. The amazing thing is, he really believes that." She addressed her next comment to Randy. "So I guess we have something in common. We both have high-achieving brothers."

March spoke through gritted teeth. "How nice of you to come tonight, Ms. Sawyer, even though Mr. Prinn wasn't able to show your students' work."

A glint of anger surfaced in Summer's eyes. "It wasn't a problem. I know Mr. Prinn will come around eventually."

"I'm sure. Randy, I need to discuss a few things with you. Excuse us, won't you, Ms. Sawyer?"

Summer nodded smoothly. "Of course. I was just going to find another Perrier anyway. I'll be seeing you soon." She walked gracefully toward the bar. Ruth was just about to edge away as quietly as she had come when Randy took her arm.

"Mrs. Budge, you look fabulous. The eyebrows are coming along."

March said acidly, "He inherited some of the Prinn charm, don't you think, Ruth? All the lovely ladies seem to think so." She stiffly pulled away from him.

"Are you going to unveil the new piece for us?" Ruth asked.

"I think Mr. Prinn would not appreciate me stealing his thunder."

"If you don't mind my asking, why didn't Napoleon want to show the work from Summer's college?"

March grimaced. "He said the work was fine at first, but then he changed his mind. He said it was juvenile."

"Was it?"

"As much as I hate to admit it, I thought the work was quite good." She lowered her voice and leaned closer. "I think what it really came down to is that she told him his "new addition" wasn't worth the price he paid for it. He doesn't like to be made a fool of. He ruined her chances of moving up in the university, I think." There was a tiny smile of satisfaction on March's face.

"She's definitely a woman who knows what she wants," Randy said thoughtfully.

"I have some things to check on. I will talk to you later." March gathered her skirts and walked away in an angry hiss of satin.

TROUBLE UP FINNY'S NOSE

"If you'll excuse me, I think I'd better go smooth some ruffled feathers." He started off after her.

"Ah, there you are, Mrs. Budge. I was afraid you had gotten a better invitation."

"Hello, Napoleon."

He took her elbow and steered her toward a small cluster of people. "Come over here and mingle. You'll have a perfect view. I will get started shortly."

Ruth kept her head low in an effort to avoid Maude. She found herself standing next to the rumpled Buster Dent and his daughter. Dimple looked like a little woodland elf in a green silk shift. Her hair was twisted in a loose braid, and tendrils floated down her full cheeks. Buster appeared to be a shade short of furious, his weathered skin pulled into angry puckers around his eyes.

"Hello, Mr. Dent. Are you here to admire the new acquisition?"

"I've already seen the ugly thing. It surely ain't worth thirty grand," he growled. Beads of sweat shone on his upper lip. He had made an honest attempt to spruce up for the evening, plastering his white hair into a sort of hirsute halo and changing his flannel shirt and jeans for polyester pants and a wide striped tie.

"So you've seen it, then?" Ruth pried.

"Seen it? I practically bought the piece of junk."

"Why don't you like it?"

He glowered at her for a moment, his face so close to hers she could smell the shrimp puffs on his breath. "I guess it doesn't matter, now, does it? He doesn't need my approval, just my money."

A nasally voice crept into the conversation. Wanda stood close by with arms crossed, a shiny-headed man slightly behind her.

"I just cannot fathom what is happening to our gallery. What will become of our local artists if we begin importing talent?"

"I don't know, Wanda. Have your paintings been displaced?" Ruth asked.

Her face flushed. "Of course not. They are displayed on the north wall, there. They have to be grouped thematically, you know, since the focal point of this room is apparently sculpture now."

"Apparently. Where is Bun tonight?"

"Oh, she can't make it to these evening functions. It's way too tiring for her."

Ruth nodded as she watched Napoleon mount the dais and clear his throat.

"Welcome. I am so pleased to see you all here this evening to witness a triumph for the Finny Art Gallery. As you well know, it has been my mission since the inception of this gallery ten years ago to represent the finest artists in the region. I believe I can say, with all modesty, that that mission has been accomplished."

As the curator droned on, Ruth edged to the side and aimed her camera at the crowd. Randy lounged indolently against an oak beam, a pencil projecting from behind his ear. March drummed nervously on a glass in her hand.

The man Ruth remembered as Buck Pinkey positively shone as he sipped Perrier.

"The new addition marks a turning point for this gallery. Instead of limiting our works to coastal artists, we will now be representing important works from all over the country. The first is a sculpture from the artist Carmine.

"Somewhat of a mysterious fellow, he has never attended any showing of his work and remains elusive, preferring to stay in the shadows. His work is praised for its luminous quality and perfect balance of line and contour. He is a sculptor in the purest sense. His works are few and highly sought after, and it is with great pride that I present to you the new addition to our gallery, entitled *Broken Bird*."

With a flourish, he whisked the white canvas from the shoulder-high statue. The room was buried in complete silence.

Gradually, low murmurs and the hum of quiet conversation filled the void. Wielding her camera and elbows, Ruth made her way to the platform, squeaking past Red. Her breath caught in her throat.

The raw emotion of the piece stunned her. The figure was a young child. A naked girl, crouching, crumpled in agony. In her outstretched hands a lifeless bird lay, limp wings draping over her slender fingers.

The statue was marble, and the girl's face seemed almost to shine with the bitter tears coursing down her cheeks. Amazed at the captured emotion, she managed to get one shot of the piece before she tore her eyes away.

"Oh brother," Wanda said. "This is it? The great gift to our local art world? How completely maudlin." Spotting Red nearby, she went on. "This is the great work from the Shaum Gallery? Really, I've seen better in park fountains."

"Yeah?" Bubby said, stuffing a shrimp into his mouth. "Looks okay to me. I kinda like it."

"You would," Maude said.

Red narrowed her eyes as Wanda continued.

"Art isn't your business, Bubby. Tourists are not going to come to Finny and take home a thing like that in their suitcases."

"Do you sell to a lot of out-of-towners?" It was Buck.

"I sure do. I've sold six just this month. People come here especially to find my work. They don't need to have a fancy piece from New York to impress the neighbors. My clients have good sense."

Ruth could see Red stiffen.

"I suppose it would be possible for me to care less, but I'd really have to work at it," Red said quietly.

Wanda stared at her, unable to comprehend what she had just heard. *"What?"*

TROUBLE UP FINNY'S NOSE

Bubby must have sensed a storm brewing. "I'm going to get some more of those crab thingies." He moved away.

Red replied slowly, fiercely. "What gives you the right to pass judgment on this sculpture—or any other piece for that matter? What do you actually know about art, anyway? Or do you just parrot the ignorance around you?"

"Who are you calling ignorant?" Buster's face was starting to mottle. His calloused hands were balled. "Just because you work for some fancy city art gallery don't make you the skin on the cream, lady."

Napoleon, who was across the room talking to Maude and Flo, looked over at the raised voices.

"Spare me the country witticisms," ordered Red. "None of you knows the most infinitesimal thing about art." She folded her arms and regarded the oils on the far side of the room.

"You should be careful about those generalities, you know." Summer looked over the rim of her glass as she settled gracefully onto a padded bench.

March hurried over, a worried crease in her brow. "Ms. Finchley, would you care to pose for a picture in front of *Broken Bird* since you brought it to our gallery?"

Ruth readied her camera. Unfortunately, the intervention didn't distract Wanda. "How dare you!" she spat. "I happen to be an artist. My work brings in thousands. I haven't seen any of your work on the walls, you cretin."

"Wanda, why don't we go and get you a drink?" March said more desperately.

Red replied coolly, "I haven't seen any of yours, either. Why don't you just fess up? Tell them the truth."

"What truth?" Wanda spat.

"Tell them that you aren't the person who painted these pictures."

21

If ever there was a palpable silence, Ruth thought, this was it. You could probably suck it up with a straw. Napoleon finally disengaged himself from Maude and hurried over to the brewing crisis.

All eyes were focused on Wanda, who stood with her mouth so far ajar that her silver fillings winked in the overhead lighting. When nothing commenced from her mouth, four sets of eyes shifted to her accuser.

"I hope everyone is enjoying the evening," Napoleon said.

"I'm enjoying it a lot more now," Maude said.

Mr. Pinkey masticated a piece of ice in little staccato bursts. "Wanda didn't paint these pictures? That's a pretty strong statement, Ms. Finchley." He pulverized some more before swallowing. "Got anything to back it up?"

She strode to a huge oil framed in silvered wood. Sweeping her hand from side to side, she said, "Just look closely at the impasto."

Ruth had a fleeting thought about an hors d'oeuvre she had seen demonstrated on the cooking channel. "What exactly is—?"

Red snorted. "Impasto. Thickly applied paint. It can be done with a brush or applied right out of the tube." She looked at the blank faces. "Like Van Gogh. Stand up close and you can see the ridges and channels in the paint. This oil was done with lots of tube application and minimal brushwork. Look at the sweeping arcs from the bottom up and to the right."

"I don't think this is the time. . ." Napoleon began.

The group leaned forward and collectively wrinkled their noses, Magoo-like, at the canvas. Summer stayed where she was, unruffled.

"I see what you mean, but I don't know why that proves Wanda didn't paint them," Randy said.

"Because she's left-handed. This paint has been applied by a right-handed person. Follow the channels in the paint from the darker spot where it was squeezed from the tube upwards as the artist smoothed it with his fingers. They all flow from bottom left to top corner right. Besides, sculptured nails? There's no way you can do impasto from the tube and have Barbie doll nails like hers." She rounded on Wanda. "I'll give you credit, though. You did sign the painting. That's your signature, isn't it? At least you contributed something."

Wanda made a sound akin to the air leaking slowly from a balloon as she slid to the floor at the foot of the painting.

TROUBLE UP FINNY'S NOSE

The small group of people progressed from stunned immobility to comic book action. March rushed to the dais and asked the guests to gather for another round of thank-yous and small talk before they had a chance to notice the chaos brewing in the corner. She successfully drew the majority of the people away from the stricken woman. Ruth and Buster raised Wanda's head and patted her hands until her eyelids fluttered open. Her mouth opened and closed like a grounded fish gasping for air.

Red laughed harshly and left, followed by Summer Sawyer.

"Wanda, can you hear me? It's Ruth."

"I think she's out of it," Buster commented gruffly.

"Maude, Flo, please go get some water," Ruth said.

Though Maude looked dismayed at having to leave the scene of the drama, she followed Flo out of the room.

"Imagine that," Buck Pinkey said, peering closely at the painting and ignoring the body underneath it. Napoleon grasped him by the arm and, with a backward glance at Wanda, drew him away down the hall. "I'll be right back," he called over his shoulder.

Wanda was the color of Wonder Bread. "I can't believe it. Who would say such things? All lies. Slander. I hope you all realize. . ." With Randy struggling under one arm and Buster under the other, Wanda was deposited on a padded bench, her body propped against a nearby ficus.

A half hour later the company straggled toward the tingling dinner bell. The ambiance was romantic, soft candlelight playing over the pristine linens. The scent of roses hung in the air and mingled with the tantalizing aroma of seafood and garlic. Everything from salad forks to sugar tongs was arranged with meticulous attention.

The dining hall should have been a gentle billow of people sipping beverages and chatting as they settled into plush chairs.

It wasn't.

Ruth was seated at a corner of the rectangular table, between Buster and Wanda. The sound of Buster's teeth grinding set hers on edge. Wanda sat silently in her place, staring at the goblet in front of her, a ficus leaf spinning crazily from a strand of hair.

"Are you sure you're feeling all right, Wanda?" Ruth asked. "I'd be happy to drive you home."

"I am fine, and no two-bit tramp from the big city is going to push me out of this party," she hissed.

Across the table was an empty chair. Ruth tried to appear inconspicuous as she eavesdropped on Randy and March, their heads bent close together. It seemed like a fairly serious conversation, and she couldn't make out a single word of it. After a moment, March excused herself and glided away.

No sign of Napoleon or Buck Pinkey. Dimple was missing, as well.

Bubby shoved a napkin down the front of his shirt and looked around hopefully for food. Maude rolled her eyes and turned her back on him.

Red sat down with arms folded and leaned back in her chair, watching Summer talk into a cell phone the size of a pack of Juicy Fruit, the hint of a smile playing over her glossy lips.

A metallic crash caused those seated at the table nearest the catering station to jump. "I can't hold dinner interminably!" Monk growled, each syllable rising in volume. "This crab bisque is ready *now*."

Another crack with the now-dented ladle sent Bert Penny hurrying to deliver steaming plates to the guests. Lizzie ran from place to place, refilling water glasses. The strained conversations gave way to contented munching as the diners enjoyed warm, pillowy sourdough rolls.

As the last bits of crusts were being devoured, March stepped to the middle of the room and tapped on a water glass. "Um, ladies and gentlemen. Er, thank you for coming tonight. Enjoy your dinner." She retreated quickly to her chair and sat down.

"Wow. Do you think she writes her own material?" Summer asked.

"I liked it," Bubby said, his mouth full of bread. "Short and sweet."

"Typical." Maude snorted.

Ruth glanced at the clock. Eight thirty-five. Tardiness was definitely not a Napoleonic trait. She dipped her spoon into the creamy saucer and inhaled deeply. She was amazed to discover that her appetite had returned. Was it the delicious food or the simmering intrigue that whetted her hunger?

Heavenly. The soup was creamy and peppered throughout with succulent chunks of crab. Ruth thought Monk had to have some divine powers lurking in that sturdy body. Wait a minute though. There was definitely a shell of some sort grating against her spoon.

No, not a shell. Gingerly, she fished around and carefully removed the foreign object. A bisquey set of keys dangled from her spoon.

She momentarily froze, watching the bisque dripping off of the keys into her bowl. Buster and Wanda both stared at her, their own spoons suspended in midair.

"Well, it's better than finding a thumb," Maude said.

Several things happened simultaneously. The keys continued to drip as they dangled from her spoon. March shot to her feet as if her knees were spring loaded. Red began to laugh, and Dimple entered the dining hall and began to warble.

The warbling soon eclipsed the other details as it escalated into a shriek and resolved itself into a spectacular keening that echoed off the overhead lighting and bounced from goblet to goblet.

It ended abruptly as Dimple's head sagged forward and she fell to the floor, her head coming to rest squarely on Wanda's foot.

Wanda reflexively jerked her foot away as if she had encountered dog excrement, causing Dimple's head to thunk on the hardwood floor. "Hey! What is going on here?"

Randy knocked over his chair as he ran to the fallen woman and gently felt for a pulse. "I think she's fainted. I'm sure she wasn't aiming for your shoes, Ms. Zimmerman." He muttered, "Another one bites the dust."

Wanda backed nervously away as Monk joined Randy to examine the fallen girl. Buster pushed through the group to pat the back of her hand awkwardly. "She's never fainted before. Musta got too overheated."

"It seems to be going around tonight," Maude said.

Dimple's eyelids began to flutter, and the keening started again.

"Heee'ss—heee's—"

"I think she's saying something about cheese," Bubby stage-whispered.

"Not cheese, you moron. Why would she be talking about cheese?" Buster shouted.

"Heeee's—bleeding—I—" Her head thunked to the floor again.

"Oh, for goodness' sake, will someone keep her head from hitting the floor every two minutes?" March stood at Dimple's feet, her fingers twisted together in an intricate fleshy pretzel. "What is she talking about?"

"I don't think she's coherent," Summer said, peering over the huddled shoulders in front of her. "She sounds delusional, or does she always sound like that?"

"March, call 911," Randy ordered, wiping the sweat off his forehead. "She doesn't seem to be coming around."

"You could put her on the bench near the ficus," Red piped up. "I think it's still warm."

"I don't know why," Randy said slowly, catching Monk's eye, "but I've got a strange feeling we ought to have a look down the hallway she just visited."

Monk nodded. "I think you may be right. Let's go."

Randy handed the cloth to March, and she and Buster knelt beside the tiny bundle on the floor. Ladle in hand, Monk led the way like a drum major marching through a firing range.

After depositing the keys in a napkin and stuffing them in her pocket, Ruth trailed behind them. Her head did not want to know what lay at the end of the hallway, but apparently her feet did, because they followed along in spite of some intellectual objections.

TROUBLE UP FINNY'S NOSE

The hallway had doors opening on each side, leading to two storage rooms on the left and offices on the right. They headed immediately for the only door that was ajar, Prinn's office.

Being a step or two behind the men, Ruth did not hear their synchronized gasps. She added her own seconds later.

Napoleon was indeed in his office, and he had a very good excuse for being late for dinner.

He was wearing the remains of a ceramic pot on his head, the broken rim hanging crazily over one eyebrow. His upper body leaned against the front of the mahogany desk, and his legs were twisted under him.

Ruth was awed by the sheer amount of blood that covered Napoleon Prinn in a satiny sheet and saturated the plush mauve carpeting, creating a fantastic black whorled pattern spreading out from underneath him. Here and there tendrils of a delicate flowering plant dotted his tuxedo, and plops of soil made grainy islands in the mess.

His eyes were open and staring, seemingly fixed on the branch that appeared to spring directly from between his eyes. Still trapped in her out-of-body mode, Ruth's brain registered the comic quality to the situation, but her stomach was less than amused.

She bent over the nearby Persian throw rug and threw up.

22

Ruth had never noticed before that her shoes needed polishing. Now that she was sitting on a chair in the gallery foyer with her head between her knees, the scuffs on her genuine imitation leather pumps cried out for attention. She felt as though she might be screaming, but she realized the shrieks were only in her mind.

When she thought her head was whirling less aggressively, Ruth ventured to poke her head upward, turtle-like.

Things were strange. Surreal.

Two medics were loading Dimple onto a stretcher, Buster bobbing up and down behind it. She could see the top of Dimple's curly head and one of her pale hands peeking out from under the yellow blanket.

Another stretcher was lying idle in the hall, a black zippered bag neatly folded on top, waiting for another passenger. Ruth swallowed hard, blinking against the memory of Napoleon lying in a wash of blood and plant.

She noticed Detective Denny, which made her feel more secure. He was listening intently to a seated March, whose hands were clutched. Randy stood across the room watching her. They both looked wild-eyed.

The two young participants, Lizzie and Bert, were huddled together, eagerly awaiting their brush with law enforcement.

"What are you saying? Are you saying he was killed? Murdered?" Wanda sprang up from her seat across from Officer Katz so suddenly she knocked the notebook out of his hand. "I know. It was that Finchley woman. She did it."

Nate urged Wanda back into her seat. "What makes you say that, Ms. Zimmerman?"

Her glance darted around the room. "She is a troublemaker. Coming here from New York, spreading lies about my work and bragging about her high-end gallery in New York. I bet she was having an affair with him or something."

The word "affair" caused everyone to stop their conversations and look up.

Red entered the room just then, accompanied by a uniformed Mary Derisi. She glanced at Wanda. "Would you like me to write out a confession and then you can sign your name to it? You could take credit for that, too."

Before Wanda could launch herself off the bench, Nate grabbed her arm and replanted her while Mary steered Red to a seat in the far corner of the room.

A hand squeezed Ruth's shoulder, startling her. Monk bent over her, his eyes crinkled in concern. "Are you all right? I didn't realize you were behind us. It was a terrible thing to come upon."

"Yes. I think I'm better now. Did I really throw up all over the crime scene?"

"Well, yes. But I'm sure it's happened before. Got a little queasy myself. Haven't felt that way since the boiler blew on our ship and took two of our boys with it. What a thing." He sat down next to her, still holding the dented ladle.

Jack exchanged a few words with Officer Katz before approaching Ruth and Monk. "Quite an evening for you," he said. "I need to ask you a few questions before you can get out of here, I'm afraid. Feeling better?"

She nodded, blushing.

"What exactly made you two go looking for Mr. Prinn in the first place?"

Monk tapped the ladle thoughtfully on his leg. "First off, I was waiting for him to get his behind seated so we could serve dinner. We had agreed on eight o' clock sharp, and that's when the food was ready. You know when you're dealing with a bisque you can't just let it sit around for a couple of hours. If the cream boils—"

Jack interrupted the culinary tangent. "Okay, you needed to get dinner rolling—what next?"

"I sent Bert to look for Prinn out in the gallery, but he couldn't find him. Then Dimple came in and started screaming. We figured something was up."

"She entered from the rear door?"

"Yes. Saying something about blood."

"Is that what you heard, Ruth?"

"Yes, something like 'He's bleeding.' I don't know why I followed along behind Randy and Monk. I wish I hadn't now." She closed her eyes and shuddered, bile rising in her throat.

"We're almost done here. I understand there was a confrontation between Wanda Zimmerman and Red Finchley. Can you tell me what you heard?"

She retold the ugly argument. "Have you talked to Wanda about it?"

"Sure have. She denies any wrongdoing, says Ms. Finchley is some kind of, what did she say? White trash. According to the interviews I've done so far, the argument was witnessed by you, Randy, Buster, and Summer Sawyer."

"And Mr. Pinkey," Ruth added.

He looked up sharply. "Who?"

"Buck Pinkey. He's visiting here from—somewhere. I ran into him as he left the gallery one day. He asked me about renting Crew Donnelly's place. Did you meet him, Monk?"

"No. I can't recall anyone by that name."

Jack was speaking quietly into a radio. "What does he look like?"

"Nicely dressed. Thick around the middle. Short, about my height. His eyes are. . .dark. Mostly I noticed his bald head. It's sort of speckled like a gull's egg. And shiny." She felt foolish.

He murmured into the radio again. "Where did everyone go after the argument?"

"I don't know really. We all just kind of wandered away. March tried to lure most folks at the other end of the room. Wanda said she wanted us to leave her alone. Napoleon and Buck went off somewhere, I think. I didn't keep track of everyone."

"Was anyone missing from the table after the dining hall was seated?"

"Well, Napoleon of course. Dimple. March entered a few minutes after I sat down. Red and Buster were seated when I got there. Come to think of it, I never did see Mr. Pinkey sit down. I wonder what happened to him?"

"I wonder," Jack said. Officer Katz approached, looking deadly serious, though the tract lighting encouraged a definite sparkle in his mustache. He mumbled a few words into the detective's ear.

"Okay," he sighed, "I'm going to release these folks now. Make sure we've got everyone's contact info and send them home. Meet me at the ER in twenty." The officer nodded and left.

"Monk, we're still printing and photographing everything, so I'm going to have to send you home without your equipment. It's a shame, too. The soup smells excellent. What is it? Chowder?"

"Bisque. Crab bisque."

Bisque! She stood up with a jerk and patted her pockets. "Here. I completely forgot I found these in my bowl of bisque." She handed the detective a wadded-up napkin with the keys bunched inside.

"What is that?" Monk's jaw fell open in shock. "How did those get in my bisque?"

She shrugged helplessly, feeling somehow responsible for the offending hardware.

Monk's outraged grunting overlapped the detective's chuckle. "This story gets weirder by the minute," Jack said, poking at the sticky keys with a ballpoint pen.

"If it was a novel, I wouldn't pay a nickel for it." Ruth shouldered her camera bag and heaved herself homeward, hoping the chilly walk would clear her mind.

~

Eden Hospital was a very familiar place to Ruth Budge. There was Phillip's fishhook-in-the-thumb trip. Her fall off the porch steps after tripping over a greedy bird. The birth of her son and the death of her husband. Everything seemed to culminate here.

She hadn't even made it home after the gallery fiasco. Something pulled her to the hospital. Concern for Dimple? Perhaps an unwillingness to face her empty house after the horrific evening, to spend the long hours listening to nothing. She knew that one word from her and Monk would hold sentry on her couch, but she just couldn't ask another man into Phillip's house. Yet.

Choosing not to dwell on motivation, Ruth headed toward the emergency room only to learn that Dimple was already scanned, medicated, and bundled off to a room on the second floor.

She padded down the tiled hallway, following the green arrows directing her to the even-numbered rooms. The door to room 214 was open. In the doorway was a doctor, Jack, and Buster. The doctor was speaking in the quiet, measured way professional people do when they are speaking to hysterical people. She inched closer, unsure whether to retreat or announce her presence with a timely cough.

"She's going to be fine, Mr. Dent; they both are. There is no evidence of a concussion, just a nasty bang to the head. She is resting comfortably now."

Both? Who else was injured at the gallery? She lost the next few sentences until Buster's voice worked its way up to shouting level.

". . . is going on? You must be wrong. Those tests are wrong!"

The detective raised a calming hand and ushered the threesome into the hallway. "Mr. Dent, just calm down."

"You calm down! I can't believe what he's saying about my daughter. I ought to crack you a new—"

Jack's calming hand became a restraining one. "That's enough. I know this is hard for you to hear. Facts are facts, and doing something stupid is not going to change anything." He turned to the doctor. "Can I talk to her now?"

"I don't think that is advisable. She's been through some trauma, and the best thing for her and the baby is rest. Come back in the morning, Detective."

Not wanting to be caught eavesdropping, Ruth scurried away, taking the stairs two at a time.

Out in the parking lot, she sat down on a cement planter to assimilate. So Dimple was pregnant. It wasn't a disaster of epic proportions; the girl was in her twenties, not a teenager. All the same, she felt terrible for her. The prayer came out before she thought about it. "God, please watch over Dimple and her baby. Help them know they are not alone." It felt good to pray for someone else. It eased her heart for a moment. She wondered why her prayers hadn't lessened her own sense of loss.

Then her mind filled with questions again.

Who was the father? She had never seen Dimple with anyone at all.

Wait a minute. She flashed back to Dimple sitting on the steps of the gallery. Then again to the scent of roses that clung to Napoleon as he passed her on the path to the greenhouse.

"He can be temperamental, you know," she had said.

101

TROUBLE UP FINNY'S NOSE

Ruth clapped a hand to her forehead.

The gunning of a motor made her jump. A car peeled out of a parking space, running up onto the curb before correcting itself. The driver stopped for a second and glared into the rearview mirror before roaring off in search of the exit.

An overwhelming feeling of déjà vu swept over Ruth. That day in the woods, when Ruth and Dimple had almost been run down.

It was the same car and the same furious driver.

Buster Dent.

23

Ruth watched the waves crash angrily against the shore, sending spray in every direction. She saw Alva amble his way along the foam at the edge of surf and shore, waving his metal detector in graceful arcs in front of him like an orchestra conductor. Now and again he would stop to dig a small hole with his yellow plastic shovel and sequester the contents in one of his pockets. Avoiding the Saturday morning joggers, he carefully spread the *Finny Times* out on the dry sand and sat on it. He continued to pat his pockets as the birds stabbed nosily through his belongings. "Do you have any candy, Ruth? I'm out."

"Hi, Alva. Let me see." She began poking around in her backpack, at the same time shooing the birds away from his treasures. "I'm sorry about the birds. Did they ruin anything?"

"No way, nothing to ruin. Just a few bottle caps and a watch. Cheap Timex, no good."

Ruth victoriously held up two sticks of sugar-free gum and a mauled Snickers bar. He took the chocolate.

"Shouldn't eat that sugar-free stuff, sweet cheeks. Gives people cancer." He took out his teeth and began gumming the candy bar. "I heard about Neopolitan. Got his lights smashed out. He had it coming, I'd say."

"Why do you think someone wanted to kill Neopolitan, er, Napoleon?"

"I think it was mainly because he was an idiot."

She nodded.

"And the lizard."

"The what?"

"The iguana. I was picking up cans from the recycle bin behind the gallery, and I heard him and a lady having an awful row. Regarding the iguana."

"An argument? When?"

"Last week. Day before the fire."

"Who was the lady?"

"Don't know. Shades was down. She smelled real pretty, though. Flowery. It reminded me of my Aunt Noony's flower beds. Always so nice. Except when they had the big molasses flood. Stunk up the whole town, flowers and all."

Ruth tried to usher him back to the subject at hand. "It was a lady who smelled nice."

"Real nice. Flowery. Like Aunt Noony's garden."

"What did she sound like?"

"She had a soft voice, but it got louder and louder. Then it sounded like she commenced to cryin'. Now that's a real bugger of a man, makes ladies cry. Worse than Georgie Porgie." He shook his head disgustedly, white clusters of hair dancing around his face like tufts of cotton.

"But, Alva, why were they talking about lizards?"

"Don't know. She said something about she didn't want to raise no lizard no more, and he said she would jolly well raise it until he said he wanted it back. I left after that on account of I didn't want any trouble."

"Why in the world would they be talking about iguanas?"

"Can't say. Never thought much about lizards myself. Always seemed kind of standoffish to me. Maybe they make okay pets, though. They said it was a cheerful sort. Happy."

Ruth was beginning to feel like she was trapped in a Laurel and Hardy movie. "Happy iguanas?"

"Don't that just beat it?" He stood up and shooed the birds away from his remaining candy bar. "Well, thanks for the candy, sweet cheeks. See you around." He shuffled on down the beach.

She collapsed on her back in the gravelly sand. The birds clambered over to check her pockets. If Alva was to be believed, the sweet-smelling woman with the soft voice sounded an awful lot like Dimple. Arguing with Napoleon. The day before a fire wiped out his greenhouse and a week before a fuchsia wiped out his life. Arguing. About lizards?

Did I really just have a ten-minute conversation about happy iguanas? Which one of them was the crazy one, anyway?

Chocolate-chip-fudge-death-by-triglyceride brownies.

They smelled obscenely good. That was surprising considering how long it had been since Ruth baked anything other than a frozen dinner. The afternoon culinary project gave her an excuse to put off looking for the rest of Phillip's novel. She piled the squares neatly on a Chinet plate. They provided an excuse to visit Dimple, anyway. And maybe, just maybe, a few left over for Monk.

She checked on the birds huddled on the gravel in the backyard. Grumpy. She decided to fix them their treats later when the sun came out. They always perked up on sunny afternoons.

October along the coast was the best time of year. The weather was mild after the early morning fog burned away. The fruit and vegetable stands were brimming with squash, potatoes, and artichokes. There was a smell in the air of rich loamy soil—and expectation. She wished the smells and colors would touch her the way they used to. She wished anything would.

Her thoughts rambled bumpily along, reviewing the recent chapter of Phillip's story. She found herself thinking about it often, the dark-haired Benjamina Pena and the country cop. She would conjure up images of the people she knew, whom they had grown up with, trying to find the sources of Philip's inspiration. So far, the quest remained completely frustrating.

Breathing heavily, she crested the top of Finny's Nose and worked her way down a shaded side street past a dilapidated barn and a phlegmatic billy goat. The Dent household was quite lovely and not at all dilapidated. It was a large three-story house with gables over the upper-floor windows and a slate walkway. The front was luxurious, with purple bougainvillea and hydrangeas working diligently to try to squeeze out one last bloom of the season. There was Dimple's rescued fuchsia on the front porch. Ruth shuddered and rang the bell. When there was no answer, she continued on to the guest house. She knocked gently on the front door.

No answer. She tried the bell. Still no answer. She tried knocking again and just about rapped Dimple right on the nose.

"Oh, Dimple. I hope I'm not bothering you. Is this a bad time?"

The woman looked well enough. Good color, nicely brushed hair, a pretty blue dress tied at her slender waist. About the only sign of the recent trauma were dark shadows under her eyes.

"It is always a good time to greet a neighbor." Dimple ushered her into the sitting room. The floors and wainscoting were washed pine, and sunshine flooded through the puffy flowered drapes. It was light and airy, definitely a woman's house.

"What a lovely cottage. Did you decorate it yourself?"

"My mother and I did. She loved beautiful things."

Ruth sat on a puffy loveseat while Dimple unwrapped the brownies and started filling glasses with ice.

"Are you feeling okay?" Ruth began hesitantly.

Dimple returned with two glasses of iced tea. "Yes, thank you. I am feeling well. Just a little sad. About—him."

Ruth looked at the serious face nibbling a corner of a brownie. "Dimple, I know you and Napoleon were close. It must have been a terrible shock to find him. . .like that."

She nodded, lips trembling. "We were going to get married. Later. After the gallery was more established. We didn't tell anyone, mostly because of Daddy. He wouldn't approve, and you know what his temper is like."

Ruth knew all too well. Try as she might, she just couldn't get a mental picture of Dimple as Napoleon's wife. They were more than just opposites; rather like species from two completely different planets that did not share the same galaxy.

Dimple gazed at the glass in her hands. "Love is a thing from which all pleasures flow."

"Er, yes, it is. Does." She took a sip of tea and choked. It tasted like potpourri. "Wow. What an interesting blend. What is it?"

"My own creation. Dandelions, mint, rose hips, and ginger. It cleanses the circulatory system."

She set the glass down, fearful of any further cleansing. "What sort of man would your father choose for you?"

Dimple stared at Ruth, looking suddenly much older. "My father has hated my mother for twenty years since she ran away. He looks upon me as a reminder of her." She nibbled on her brownie. "I live out here to get away from the angry energy that envelops him. He can only contain it for a while, and then it explodes. Anger is just helplessness disguised." She looked down at the ice swirling around in her glass.

Ruth felt a trickle of fear. "Dimple, he doesn't hurt you, does he?"

"He did when I was younger. Only a few times. Then I showed him the error in hurting another living soul."

"How did you do that?"

"I left my senior project on his pillow one morning. He was impressed."

Her brain zinged. Dimple Dent? A student? She tried not to sound too incredulous. "You were working on a degree?"

Dimple smiled. "I studied at UCLA. Botany and herbology. I love plants. I even have my own secret greenhouse in the knoll." She giggled. "Nobody ever bothers me there."

UCLA? Ruth hoped her chin had not hit her chest. Dimple Dent a college student? Or any kind of student for that matter? It really was true that still waters run deep. Or maybe cloudy waters. Uh-oh. She was beginning to think in fortunes, too.

"Did you earn a degree?" she asked.

"No. I came home for spring break three years ago and did some odd jobs at the gallery. I got to know Napoleon." Her eyes grew misty. "He was so intelligent, so refined. He made me feel like I was, well, a beautiful woman. I never felt that way before."

She shook her head slowly from side to side. "We fell in love. At least, I fell in love." She squeezed her lids tightly together. "I never went back to school." She passed a hand over her eyes. "I have to tell you something. I—I am going to—I have become—"

"I know. I know about the baby. It's Napoleon's, isn't it?"

She didn't ask how Ruth knew. Ruth reached over and patted her hand. She could not seem to think of any sage advice, any words of wisdom that would help in such a predicament. Where were those perfect Hallmark verses when you needed them?

"Somehow it will all work out, Dimple. God will make sure of it." The hypocrisy of her own words stuck in her throat. She used to believe them until her own world splintered apart.

They sat for a few moments in silence. Dimple looked so forlorn, so childlike, that Ruth could not bring herself to ask about the altercation in Napoleon's office.

"I'd better go now. I'm sure you would like to lie down."

"Thank you for coming. And for the chocolate."

"You're welcome." The sunshine felt warm upon her face as she turned down the gravel path, but inside she felt chilled. She stopped after a few paces.

"Dimple, what was your project about? The one that you put on your father's pillow?"

"It was called 'Deadly Poison in Your Backyard: A Gardener's Guide to Lethal Flowers.' I got an A on that paper."

Ruth turned the knob gently and closed the door.

24

Thank you for coming, Ms. Finchley." The office was quiet on Saturdays. Jack led her through the empty front room to his office and gestured to the seat in front of his desk. He opened a battered spiral-bound notebook. "I just have a few detail questions. You said that you moved to New York by way of California. Did you grow up in the area?"

Red folded her hands in her lap. "My mother was from Miramar actually, so I lived on the coast until I was three or so. Then we gradually made our way across the U.S. until we wound up in New York."

"You are an artist?"

"Yeah." She laughed, a toothy grin lighting her face. "In my dreams. Actually, I really want to be a painter, but the only audience that appreciates my work is me. I work for the Shaum Gallery, so I can sort of say I'm a part of the art world."

"What do you do exactly for the gallery?"

"A little bit of everything. Press releases, community outreach, arranging exhibits, stuff like that."

He nodded. "We talked the other night about Napoleon Prinn. Tell me again how you two met."

"Last year my curator decided to do an exhibit on the ocean. All seascapes using different mediums and interpretations. It was my job to arrange a traveling exhibit from the other coast. Yours."

"And you happened upon our Finny Gallery?"

Red gazed at him intently before answering. "You aren't much of an art lover, are you?"

"Not exactly. Is that relevant?"

"Well, believe it or not, your Finny Gallery has quite a good reputation for featuring innovative, quality art. It also has an awesome Web site. I did some research over the Internet and decided to give it a shot. Mr. Prinn was excited to provide a few pieces, and he even flew out himself for the exhibit opening."

"Did you strike up a friendship with him?"

"I did my job. That's what I'm paid to do. Just like you." Her green eyes narrowed, the lashes translucent against her skin.

"How did he come to purchase a sculpture from your gallery?"

"I talked him into it. He really wanted something new and dynamic to set his gallery apart. The Carmine was a logical choice. Say what you will about the guy—he knew art, and he knew a good piece when he saw it. All I had to do was work on him. Get him to swallow the price tag."

"Which was?"

"Thirty thousand dollars."

Jack took a breath. "Quite a price tag."

"Worth every penny. The piece is awesome. I arranged for it to be flown here, and I picked it up at the airport and delivered it myself."

"Have you received payment?"

"The Shaum got half when Prinn purchased. Upon delivery we were supposed to get the other fifteen grand. He agreed to pay the other half after the gallery shindig." She paused. "I guess that's going to take awhile now, isn't it?"

"I would tend to think so. What are you going to do now?"

"I'm not sure. He didn't fulfill the monetary obligation, so I guess the Carmine goes back to the Shaum. I'll have to talk to my curator and see what he says." Red straightened her shoulders. "Are we done here? I've got some things to do."

"Sure." Jack stood behind his desk, feeling as though he knew her only slightly better than he had a half hour ago. "By the way, do your people still live in New York?"

She grabbed her denim knapsack. "Let's just cut the small talk, shall we? You already know all the facts about my life. I'm sure you've run my particulars and have it all in that notebook. If there's anything you didn't find out, you can with a phone call or two."

He eyed her freckled face closely, surprised at her reaction. She was right, of course. He knew her mother was a New York resident, as well as the fact that she attended an art school and dropped out her senior year. She had received excellent evaluations from the Shaum Gallery, and the curator trusted her implicitly. He wasn't sure why he had asked the question. He had no reason to.

"Thank you for coming in, Ms. Finchley. We would appreciate it if you could stay in town a few more days until we get some loose ends tied up."

"All right. I've got a few days of vacation coming. Might as well spend it at the beach, even though it's so ridiculously cold here." She turned at the doorway. "By the way, Detective, I thought Napoleon Prinn was a complete jerk, but killing him would be like killing the goose that lays the golden eggs, now, wouldn't it? Why would I want to do that?"

Jack had to admit he had no idea.

~

The next person to enter the detective's office arrived in a cloud of Chanel No. 5. Summer Sawyer wore tight leather pants and a silk tunic, all in a sizzling shade of red. Her shoes were high, strappy, and filled with little red-painted toes.

TROUBLE UP FINNY'S NOSE

"Hello, Ms. Sawyer. Thank you for coming," Jack began again. "I just have a few questions for you about the Napoleon Prinn murder."

She leaned back in the chair and crossed her legs. "Fire away, Detective."

"You knew Prinn through his connection to your university. He was going to show some of your students' work at the dedication of the gallery, but at the last minute he decided it wasn't up to snuff. Is that about the size of it?"

"Yes." The small silver hoops flashed against her black hair as she nodded thoughtfully. "I guess that's about it."

He looked at her for a beat or two. So much for helping the police. "And how did you take that decision?"

"Take it? I took it to be a really lousy decision. There is nothing substandard about that art. He was just bent out of shape because I criticized his choice of sculpture."

"How exactly did you criticize it?"

"I told him he paid too much for it. He really doesn't, didn't, know much about sculpture. The piece is lovely and well executed, but he would have done better with some advice from people who specialize in sculpted works."

"You, for instance?"

"I could have directed him." She clasped her hands over one knee, lacing the French-manicured fingers together.

He decided to be blunt. "How has Prinn's rejection affected your career?"

She raised an eyebrow. "Negatively. That's pretty obvious, isn't it?"

"How negatively?"

"If you weren't so handsome, Detective, I might not find you charming. His rejection set me back in the eyes of the trustees, which will delay my plans for promotion for a while." She smiled and folded her arms. "He slowed me down, that's all. I'll get what I want in the long run. I always do."

He didn't doubt that for a second. "What do you know about Prinn's death?"

"Only that he was clobbered in his study. I was out in the gardens getting some air after the, uh, entertainment portion of the evening. The nasty scene between Wanda and Red. Did you hear about that?"

He nodded. "Go ahead and tell me your impression."

She thought for a moment. "It seemed like a good old-fashioned catfight to me, although I don't know what the cause of their animosity is. They're not in love with the same man or anything conventional like that." She laughed.

"And after your stroll?"

"We all assembled in the dining room to wait for Napoleon. March gave that ridiculous toast, and then the little fainting girl showed up."

"Do you have any idea who would want to kill Napoleon?"

"Anyone who knew him would be my guess."

"Ms. Sawyer, did you have a physical relationship with Mr. Prinn?"

She laughed, white teeth gleaming against satiny red lipstick. "No, Detective. He just isn't my type." She looked at him through lowered lashes. "I can't resist a man with a badge."

He blinked several times, trying to unfog his retinas before continuing. Jack was accustomed to interviewing old ladies with lost cats or farm laborers with property disputes. Maybe an addict here or there and occasionally a homicide or two would crop up, usually the result of drugs or jilted lovers. It had been awhile since he encountered a piranha woman.

"You have been staying at the Finny Hotel since the day before the murder. Did you meet any of the other guests?"

"Hmmm. I met the redheaded freckly girl. She kept to herself. And a middle-aged man, bald. Really nice clothes. What was his name? I think it began with a *B*."

"Buck Pinkey?"

She snapped her fingers. "That's it. He was a real smooth talker."

"What did you talk about?"

"Oh, nothing much. He bought me an iced tea. Come to think of it, he didn't say much about his business."

"That doesn't surprise me."

"Why?"

"He works for a drug cartel."

Her eyebrows went up. "Incredible. I should have had him buy me lobster, too."

"You didn't pick up on any details about his comings and goings?"

"No. He got a call on his cell phone while we noshed. He didn't talk long, just said he was going to be staying for a few more days."

"That's it?"

"Yes. I think so."

"You didn't overhear any names?"

"No. He hung up and we went our separate ways."

"Anyone else from the hotel that you. . .became acquainted with?"

"Not really," Summer said.

"Okay. I think I've got pretty much all I need. Thanks for coming down here. I'd appreciate you staying in town a few more days. I hope you're enjoying Finny."

"I'd enjoy it a lot more with some company. It's so quiet in Finny. What do you do for fun?"

Jack was not sure how to answer this one. "Well. . ." He cleared his throat as he opened the office door for her. "There's always the library."

25

Ruth had fallen asleep in the rocker, dreaming of maneating flowers, when a noise startled her awake. She sat up, disoriented and unsure why she had awakened until the knock repeated itself. Glancing at the clock, she wondered who would come to call at nine forty-five on a Saturday evening, or any evening for that matter, as she padded quietly to the door and squinted through the peephole. Astonished, she let in the detective and his boy.

The child was asleep, cheeks flushed, hair tousled. He was wearing footed Batman pajamas and clutching a blanket under his chin. The detective looked sheepish.

"I am so sorry to bother you this late. I just have to ask you something. It's been driving me crazy, and I can't sleep until I get an answer. I called, but you didn't pick up. I know this is really way too late to be dropping in."

She guided him into the sitting room, and he gingerly lowered himself into a bentwood rocker without waking the child in his arms.

"Would you like some coffee?"

"No, no. Don't go to that trouble. I'm bothering you enough already."

"Forgive my forthrightness, but I am a pretty good judge of faces. Your mouth said, 'No coffee, thanks,' but your eyes said, *I would commit heinous crimes for just one cup.*'"

He laughed quietly, continuing to rock the boy. "Is it that transparent? So much for my stony detective face. The coffeemaker at work is on the fritz, so I am way behind on my caffeine intake."

She vanished into the kitchen. As she brewed a pot, she thought how ridiculously pleasant it was to serve someone again. She poured the strong brew into one of the nice mugs.

He took it gingerly, holding it well away from the boy's body.

"He is darling," she said quietly. "I haven't seen him for a while." *He looks exactly like his mother*, she thought. "So precious."

"Thanks. I've gotta be a really bad parent to drag him out of bed, but he can sleep through a train wreck, so I was hoping it wouldn't mess up his schedule too much. Louella watches him when I'm at work. She's so great about coming over when I get a call, even in the wee hours, I just didn't want to ask any more of her today." He rubbed the boy's fleecy back in little circles. "Sometimes I think she's more of a parent to him than I am," he said.

112

"I think Paul knows who his daddy is. Has he shown any progress?"

He closed his eyes and sighed. "No, not really. He hasn't spoken since Lacey died. Even when he cries he does it silently. I've tried everything his therapist has recommended. I even bought him a mynah bird. Can you believe that? I thought Paul would be interested in teaching it to talk. It doesn't say a word either. Anyway, I should get to the point, Ruth, after barging in at this late hour. I came over after your near miss and we talked awhile. Why do I know the name Heston Blue? Did we discuss him?"

"Not him. It."

"Huh?"

"It. Heston Blue is a plant. The fuchsia that I, er, took from the garbage pile at the gallery, remember?"

"A plant," he repeated dully. "What is going on in this town?" He glanced down sharply to see if he had woken the child.

She waited, watching the wheels spinning in Jack's mind. His eyes darted back and forth as if he were reading a message graffitied inside his skull.

"Ruth, you are not going to believe this, but Napoleon Prinn's next of kin is a son. The name on the birth certificate is Heston Blue."

A quarter of an hour later, Ruth was trailing behind Jack as he walked back out to his car. He deposited Paul, gently strapping him into the car seat. They were both quiet for a moment, trying to put the bizarre pieces together. Could it be coincidence that a mysterious person delivered a plant to Napoleon Prinn called Heston Blue? The name of his son? And he had thrown it away, furious.

Jack said they had tracked down the woman believed to be Heston Blue's mother to Seaview Sanitarium, a mere fifty miles away; he secured permission from her doctors to interview her.

Ruth's head was whirling by the time she noticed the noise. Uh-oh. It sounded like a feathery prison break. Before she could dash to the side yard and shove the gate shut again, the inmates had made a break for it, flapping and squabbling all over the front yard.

After a moment of motionless surprise, she began running, snatching up the birds and holding their angry beaks shut while she shoved them into the backyard and slammed the gate. Grover scooted under the bushes, and Rutherford headed across the street with the speed of a fully fueled rocket, Ulysses right behind him.

"Come here, you crazy birds," she bellowed. Grover hunkered down and snapped at her hands when she tried to extricate him. She finally managed to grasp the beak and drag him from under his bunker. Flinging him in the backyard none too gently, she ran across the street for Rutherford. He was in the neighbors' herb garden, a strand of basil quivering from his beak. She returned him to the yard and joined Jack in the chase for Ulysses.

Jack finished strapping in his son before he jumped into the melee. He cornered the bird, who divided his attention between the tender grass shoots and the man attempting to capture him. Jack approached slowly, step by step, talking soothingly. "It's okay, fella. I'm not going to hurt you."

"Watch out, Jack! He has issues," Ruth hollered. Too late. She watched, hands over her mouth, as the detective grabbed Ulysses around the chest. The bird flapped furiously and paddled his yellow legs until Jack lost his grip. Not to be outdone by a bird, he careened after Ulysses as the gull galloped down the lawn and up onto the hood of his Chevy.

He pounced on Ulysses' neck, fighting off the pointy beak, panting and swiping at the blood running down from a scratch above his eye. Jack and Ulysses glared at each other, tired brown eyes staring into villainous yellow ones.

Ruth ran up to take the bird from his conqueror. "I am so sorry, Jack. How can I make it up to you?"

Jack's eyes suddenly opened wide as he turned his head to peer into the front car window.

Paul was awake, his little laugh bubbling out through the open car window and echoing down the quiet street.

26

Ruth had taken on the monumental task of cleaning Phillip's study while she avoided church yet again. She told herself the cleaning was long overdue, that it was a disgrace to leave it in such dishabille and it would be wrong to subject the congregation to her emerging case of sniffles.

The truth of the matter was, she was desperate to find the rest of Phillip's novel. There were so many pieces left to discover. Lately, she had only been able to locate short segments, none chronologically coherent. If she could be honest with herself, she was afraid to discover that there was no more, that she would never know where Phillip's story had taken him, would take them both.

From the file cabinet, she extracted a bulging, unlabeled file and sank with it to the floor, trying to keep the contents from sliding everywhere. It was filled with greeting cards of every variety, for every occasion. They both had been unable to throw the sentimental things away. A card he had given her on their silver anniversary brought a deep ache to the pit of her stomach. Inside on the fancy foil thing he had written, *Who would have thought we could make it from the tinfoil anniversary to the silver one? Let's go for the gold. I love you, Phillip.*

They hadn't made it to gold.

She didn't cry. There wasn't enough grief left anymore, just an overwhelming sadness.

Among the colorful collection, a brilliant red card caught her eye. It had a tremendously ugly lizard on the front wearing a plush red Santa hat. She could almost hear Phillip's voice reading the punch line inside. Iguana wish you a merry Christmas! Sheesh. So corny. So Phillip.

Snatches of the weird conversation with Alva on the beach played back in her mind. Happy lizards. Iguanas. Merry iguanas. Dimple said she didn't want to raise it anymore, and Prinn told her she would do it until he said so.

A merry iguana. Merry iguana. *Marijuana.*

It couldn't be. It was just too bizarre, too much like a funky Nancy Drew mystery. It must be a product of her depressed neuropathways.

"I even have my own secret greenhouse in the knoll," Dimple had said. *"Nobody ever bothers me there."*

It was time to bake another batch of brownies.

Ruth decided on a decoy if the brownie ploy didn't work. Herbert could use some extra attention, and there was nothing he liked more than an adventure in the countryside, a Sunday stroll to put the pep in his step. Her plan was to drop the brownies off at Dimple Dent's cottage and then take the scenic walk home.

Ruth practically had to chase Herbert until they got halfway up Finny's Nose. By then the small tern was so tired he could barely plop one bandy leg in front of the other. About a half mile before they reached the Dents' property, she hoisted him up and tucked him inside her sweat jacket with his head poking out of the top like a pop-up lawn sprinkler.

She knocked softly on Dimple's door. No answer. She knocked again louder and listened for signs of life. Nothing. She tried the bell and shouted hello.

She left the plate of brownies on the doorstep. *Well, I guess it wouldn't hurt to take a walk around the property. I don't think they have any signs posted,* she thought. She casually meandered back down the walkway, heading for the dense cluster of twisted cypress trees. As she crossed the driveway to the main house, Buster pulled up in a shower of dust.

"What are you doing here?" he asked, shoving his car keys into his pocket. He was dressed as he always was, in a faded flannel shirt and cowboy boots, a baseball cap pulled down to his bushy eyebrows.

She was suddenly furious. "What am I doing here? Are you surprised I'm still up and around after you almost ran me down?"

"You are a crackpot. And what is the matter with your stomach?"

Looking down, she realized that Herbert had rolled himself up like an armadillo when the screaming started and was quietly squawking. She looked like that scene from Sigourney Weaver's *Alien* movie right before the guy explodes.

"It's a bird. And if you can't admit what you did to me, maybe you would like to explain it to the police." She was trying to sound dignified and keep the bird still at the same time.

Buster narrowed his eyes and shoved both hands into his pockets. He grunted. "It was an accident. I didn't see you both there. I was driving too fast. I was mad about something."

Big surprise. "And you didn't think to stop and help us? Your own daughter?"

"I did stop," he said defiantly, "and you were movin' around, so I figured there was no harm done."

She shook her head in disbelief. "You almost ran down your own daughter. Doesn't that scare you at all? You could have killed her."

The red began around the flannel collar and worked its way slowly up to his neck and the stubbled chin. "I could have killed her, all right. And him, too." He smashed a fist onto the hood of the car. "I didn't raise my daughter to be like her mother. She knows better." Buster looked at her uncomfortably for a minute before examining the tops of his boots. "Never mind. That's dirty linen.

116

Shouldn't be aired in public. Look, I am sorry for scaring you. I woulda stopped if you, either of you, was hurt." He looked suddenly old as he shuffled up the walkway, deflated, like a helium balloon on a bitterly cold day.

Before he reached the door, she called out, "What's done is done, Mr. Dent. She is still your daughter." He didn't turn around. She waited until she was sure he wasn't coming back out before she continued as surreptitiously as a person could with a bird stuffed up her clothing.

Buster was a man cruelly disappointed by life. First by his wife's betrayal, then by his daughter's liaison with a man whom he despised. Jack had told Ruth unofficially that Napoleon was killed by someone who crashed a potted plant over his head with such force that shards of the terra-cotta had been driven deep into his scalp. Prinn had to have been facing the person, so it was likely someone he knew. Someone strong, someone angry, with no regard for the sanctity of life, plant or human.

Her thoughts carried her into the woods until the path became no more than a barely discernible thread. Feeling as though she should have left a trail of bread crumbs, she worked her way gradually downward, into a tiny hollow screened by trees and dense shrubbery. She came upon it suddenly, a small greenhouse, glass paned, glinting in the sunlight pouring in through the gap in the tree line.

"I can't believe I really found it."

The huge dog that suddenly materialized at her feet began to growl, showing a very white set of pointy teeth. The growl caused Herbert to shoot up her jacket like a champagne cork and flail wildly in the vicinity of her head.

"Stop, Herbert," she hissed. "You're not supposed to move around. They can sense fear. Nice poochy. Nice doggy. I'm sure we wouldn't taste good at all. I'm old and stringy, and Herbert here would probably be pretty gamey."

The dog continued to growl, waving his head back and forth as he matched his pursuing steps to their retreating ones, saliva dripping from his jowls in frothy tendrils.

"Oh no. I think we're kibble."

"I thought I heard voices." Dimple emerged from the greenhouse and patted the slavering dog on the head. "It's okay, Pepper. This is my friend Ruth. And her friend, er—?"

"Herbert." She was too relieved to feel idiotic about introducing her bird to a vicious dog.

"Herbert. Hello, Ruth. Why don't you come in and see my greenhouse? I have never had a visitor before. The warmth of a hearth comes from the friends who sit beside it." Dimple held open the door and led them inside.

Ruth's heart gradually began to resume its duty, along with her deprived lungs. Long rectangular trays were filled with water, holding up brown pots with varying stages of plant growth. The plants closest to the wall were tiny seedlings, the ones in the center were a full five inches tall, and those bordering the walls were fully grown.

Lush, spiky, fully grown marijuana plants. Just like those pictured on the bulletin board at the police station.

Ruth turned to face Dimple, staring at her with bulging eyes. "Dimple. Do you—? Don't you—? Hasn't anyone—?"

Dimple continued to gaze patiently.

"Do you have any idea? There are laws. You just can't— What are you growing?"

"Would you like some tea? I know you've had a shock."

"Yes. No! No, I don't want any tea. I want you to tell me about this." She gestured wildly around the greenhouse.

"Well, as you can see, the plants are all fed hydroponically. That way the nutrients are controlled and you avoid brackish water and root rot. I use a water filtration system to reduce the sulphur, which can build up in the plants if you're not careful."

Ruth stared at her.

"Of course, I am not a marijuana user myself, but I believe every plant has a right to reach its full potential. Don't you?"

This time, Ruth collected herself enough to recover her powers of speech.

"Dimple," she said quietly, only a hint of hysteria in her voice, "you do know you are growing a crop of drugs in this greenhouse?"

"Well, of course, Ruth. I'm not dense, you know. But Napoleon sold these strictly for medical use. Would you like to see my gardens outside? I have some beautiful cyclamen and a patch of lemon geranium."

"Why are you doing this? Don't you know you could be arrested? It is against the law to grow crops of marijuana! Marijuana is an illegal substance in the state of California for practically everyone!" She realized she was yelling because Herbert made another retreat into her jacket. She took a steadying breath.

Dimple's green eyes clouded in confusion. "Napoleon asked me to. He knows, he knew, I am very gifted in the nurturing of plants, so he asked me to grow some for him. He supplied the seedlings and helped me outfit the greenhouse. It goes to reputable pharmacies for research purposes. It's all legal, I'm sure."

Ruth felt as if she were in a scene from a bad movie. "What do you do when the plants are ready?"

"I dry and package them and deliver them to Napoleon. At least that's what I used to do. He sold them to research firms and doctors for treating patients. Towards the end, things became anxious, though." She lowered her eyes and continued faintly, "He would get really angry and yell if the plants weren't ready when he wanted them."

She wiped her eyes with the back of her hand. "I didn't want to grow them anymore. They just seemed to cause tension, and I wanted to plant something more inspiring. I thought perhaps peonies. Have you ever grown peonies?"

Intent on avoiding another conversation derailment, Ruth said quickly, "You must know that this is not the best thing for you."

She looked sad. "Ruth, I am not a stupid woman. Not completely, anyway. My IQ approaches the genius level, actually. I loved him, and when I did well, when it was a really good crop, he was happy with me. I believed him. About everything." The words tumbled out, like birds fledging from their nest. "He loved me. He was going to marry me." Her voice trailed away.

Ruth took her hand gently, feeling her grief, brittle as glass, wishing desperately she had some comfort to give the girl. "It's okay. I understand."

Silently, she said a prayer that Detective Denny would, too.

27

Napoleon Prinn was cremated, reduced to ashes like his greenhouse.

March orchestrated the memorial service at the gallery gardens. Monday was, miraculously, a warm day, almost balmy, and the white chairs stood out sharply against the deep green of the lawns and shrubbery. A glossy portrait of the gallery owner was displayed on an easel, and baskets of fantastically colored hydrangeas were scattered around.

The town had turned out in force. Maude and Flo perused the program. Flo already had a handkerchief handy to cry for the man she hardly knew. She fluttered it in Ruth's direction.

Wanda steered Bun's wheelchair off to the side of the second row of chairs and sat down next to her, arms crossed over her shantung-silked bosom. Her mouth was set in a grim line, eyes focused straight ahead. Bun shot frequent worried glances at her daughter as if she were sitting next to a vibrating hive of hornets.

Dimple sat in the front row, next to Monk and Randy. Ruth arrived a few minutes behind Red, who looked warm in her gabardine skirt and jacket. The guests seemed anxious to seat themselves quickly, avoiding social give-and-take.

Alva had taken the time to iron his overalls and squash a brown derby of questionable heritage over his grizzled head. He parked himself next to the table of cold cuts and finger sandwiches and eyed the spread carefully. Jack stood inconspicuously under the overhang, eyeing Summer as she glided in on three-inch heels and sat gracefully in the back.

Luis Puzan hastily moved over to offer her a seat next to him.

March had called upon Henny Novato, pastor of the First United Methodist Church, to deliver the eulogy. Pastor Novato was in his seventies, a plump, ruddy-looking man who resembled a well-dressed Tweedledee.

"And in his drive to create something beautiful and lasting, Mr. Prinn worked tirelessly to improve and strengthen the bond between Finny and the larger world of art." He then asked if anyone had anything to share about the dearly beloved.

No one did.

Eventually, the group adjourned to sample the buffet.

Ruth noted that the unappetizing spread was most definitely not Monk's work.

"The yellow stuff is deviled egg, and the brown stuff is some hammy sort of thing," Alva announced to the group milling around the table as he poked suspiciously at the molded salad. "Don't know about that stuff. Looks like snot." March took hold of Alva's elbow and steered him away from the food table.

"That was a nice service," Monk said to Randy, who was standing near Red and the pastor. "I'm real sorry about your brother."

"Thank you. I'm still sort of in shock about the whole thing. I never thought I wouldn't have Boney around. Even though we hated each other most of our lives, it just seems strange not to have him in my life."

Red edged next to Randy, her plate full of crackers and salami. She cleared her throat nervously, "Yeah, me, too. I'm sorry about your brother. He had a great eye for art."

Unfortunately, Wanda was just then walking by.

"A great eye? Maybe he just had a great eye for the ladies. Maybe he was buying more than art from you." Wanda elbowed past the pastor and leaned into Red's face. Her hair was wound on top of her head in an elaborate chignon, and she bobbed slightly from side to side like a dashboard hula dancer. "Why are you here, anyway? What are you to Napoleon?"

"I represent the gallery he was working with in New York," Red snapped. "I think they call it paying your respects. Isn't that why you're here?"

"What respects? He didn't respect me enough to give my work the place it deserved." She gestured wildly toward the gallery and shifted her weight quickly to prevent herself from toppling. "And you had better not say one single word about my work." Her cheeks burned an unhealthy red against her normally sallow skin.

The level of conversation had now become so loud that it had captured the attention of the entire gathering. Ruth helped Bun clear a path toward her enraged daughter, Summer clicking along behind them.

"She'll blow. She's been drinking," Bun whispered to Ruth as they dodged chairs on their way to the buffet table.

"I wouldn't dream of bad-mouthing your work, Wanda." Red smiled slowly. "I wouldn't talk about something I've never seen before. When do you think you'll start painting something besides your signature?"

Wanda stood motionless for a moment like a building before it is demolished. Slowly, she balled her hands into fists, trembling with rage.

"Hold your temper," Bun hissed.

"Now, ladies," Henny Novato began, "I really don't think this is the place for—"

Wanda launched herself at Red, knocking Henny into the buffet table and taking out the nearest row of white chairs. Ruth quickly rolled Bun a safe distance from the melee. The old lady covered her mouth with her hands.

The two women rolled around, fingers entwined in each other's hair, screaming. The onlookers dodged here and there, toppling chairs in their efforts to stay out of the way of the rolling women. A flying plate landed on the exact center of Summer's cashmere sweater, and her arms flew up into the air reflexively as if she had been shot.

Alva carefully carried his plate to a chair directly in front of the fracas and sat down to watch.

Jack emerged from the wings, grabbed a handful of Red's copper hair, and held her still, while Monk seized Wanda by the ankles. Both women stopped struggling and released their holds.

Pastor Henny knelt next to the women, deviled egg sandwich in his hair. "Ladies, let us take a moment to—"

Wanda took that moment to kick viciously, catching Monk by surprise and knocking him backward into the pastor. They both crashed into the chair immediately next to Alva, who was eating cheese sticks and nodding.

"Yep. Always gotta look out for the southern end," Alva said.

All Ruth could think to do was pat Bun on the shoulder. "Oh no. This is terrible."

Bun did not answer. She sat in wide-eyed horror.

The women were back on top of each other with Jack and Monk in pursuit once again.

"I will kill you!" Wanda screamed, eyes dilated.

From underneath the pile Red grunted, "You couldn't come close, you stupid cow."

Jack hauled Red to her feet, and Monk did the same to Wanda. "Take Wanda to the parking lot so she can calm down. I'll call someone to take her home. I'll make sure Red stays here until things cool off."

Ruth handed Bun over to Maude, who rolled her away toward her daughter. She noticed Summer, who was peeling the plate covered with mustard off her black sweater, which left her looking like the hind end of a giant bumblebee.

"Are you all right?" she asked.

The woman's mouth hung open, and her eyes were wide in disbelief. "This is a cashmere sweater!" she screamed. Then much to Ruth's surprise, she started to cry, tears streaming down her flawless skin.

"Well, maybe we can get it off. Do you use club soda on cashmere?"

Summer looked at her as if she had suggested trying sulfuric acid. The tears were carrying trickles of mascara down her cheeks. "This is a nightmare."

Ruth led her away from the group to a quiet bench and sat down with her.

"This whole thing has been an absolute nightmare."

"What thing, Summer?" Ruth asked gently.

"Everything was going so well. Do you know I am the youngest person to be a dean at Pomponio? Not to mention, a female dean. That's even more incredible. Don't you think so?" She turned her watery gaze on Ruth.

"Yes. That is something to be proud of. I'm sure your parents are delighted."

"Sure. Delighted. Mom anyway. It doesn't compare to being a doctor to the teaming masses, but it wasn't bad for a girl who got herself kicked out of two high schools. That stupid jerk had to ruin my chances for the chancellor's appointment, just because I wounded his pride by telling him he paid too much for his sculpture. The old geezers at the university weren't exactly jumping at the chance to appoint a young woman anyway, but I brought so much positive attention and funding to the art department, they were really going to do it, until Napoleon bent their ears, that is."

"Will they consider you again in the future?"

"I doubt it. Universities don't like scandals. I may have to go elsewhere to get another chance." Summer reached into her tiny purse and extracted a compact. Snapping it open, she examined her face. "I must look terrible."

Ruth watched her powder and plump up her face and thought it must be a burden to be beautiful; it required such a lot of maintenance. She had never been bothered by it, so time's merciless march across her eyelids and under her chin did not cause her undue trauma. The gorgeous ones must have such a difficult time watching the tiny changes that creep in from year to year.

"Listen, I don't know why I'm blabbing all of this stuff to you. I guess you just have one of those nice listening faces."

Summer got up, smoothing her skirt. "I suppose I'd better go find another sweater." She walked a few paces before adding, "Um, thanks for, you know, listening."

Ruth returned to the garden to find the remaining guests attempting to repair the damage. Nathan was just driving away, Bun and Wanda in the backseat of his car. The pathetic sight of the ruined service deepened her own growing gloom. The buffet lay squashed and trampled in the grass. Dimple retrieved Napoleon's portrait from the muddy ground, looking sadly at a big hole where his left eye should have been. She was trying to wipe away some of the grime with a pink Kleenex.

The unfortunate Pastor Novato was sitting down with his fingers pinching the bridge of his nose to staunch the flow of blood.

"I'm so sorry, Pastor. I never dreamed in a million years it would turn into a brawl," March lamented, handing him another Kleenex.

"Are you holding up okay?" Ruth asked Randy as he wandered around righting overturned chairs. Randy didn't answer.

Alva remained in his chair in the middle of the devastation, licking deviled egg from his fingers. "Yup," he said, nodding, "never bet against a redhead."

28

Ruth sprawled on the sofa in the afternoon sun, recalling bits and pieces from the morning's disastrous memorial service. The pastor covered in deviled egg, two women flailing at each other for all they were worth, and Napoleon's portrait with its painted eye stomped out.

It was sad, really, Ruth thought as she brewed a cup of Earl Grey. All those people at his memorial service and none of them cared for Napoleon except Dimple, a woman who had been used and exploited, left in disgrace to have Prinn's baby. Maybe Randy held on to some feelings from childhood, though he seemed more lost than grieved. The whole situation was just bizarre. It would make a great television drama.

Ruth settled on the sofa on her favorite end trying not to listen to the ticking of the grandfather clock. Opening the tattered red folder, she began to read.

The lighting was soft, like the music, wrapping around the linen-covered tables and glinting off the brass quartet in the corner. Roper looked out of place in his uniform, camped behind the beverage table as inconspicuously as a six-foot-four, two-hundred-pound man can be in a ballroom.

She walked in. He stopped breathing along with several other men in the vicinity. Her hair was twisted into a loose pile on her head, a few long black tendrils floating around her face. The dress was long, backless. It was green, the perfect shade.

Catching sight of him, she walked over to the beverage table.

"Hi, Rope." She looked anxious. "Is my dress zipped in the back?" she whispered to him. "Everyone is staring. Is my skirt tucked into my underwear or something?" Casually, she turned her back to him, pretending to scan the room.

He squelched a grin. "No, ma'am. Everything is zipped and tucked properly."

"Hmmm. Then why is everyone staring at me?"

He cleared his throat. "I think, Ms. Pena, it's because you are the most beautiful woman they've ever seen. At least, that's why I'm staring."

She looked at him for a minute. Then she laughed. "You have that Southern charm thing down to a science. Why don't you just dance with me, you nut?"

"I would love to, ma'am, but I'm on duty." The university had been receiving bomb threats with more and more frequency in the last semester, causing the evacuation of the campus on two separate occasions.

"No dancing on duty, huh? Okay. I can accept that, but you really need to call me Benjamina. I mean, we've been out on a date, haven't we? Doesn't that count for something?"

It counted for a truckload, at least for him. He wasn't sure it had been quite so meaningful for her. He was trying to get up the courage to ask her out for a second time when John Toulouse, the district attorney, put his hand on her shoulder.

"Hello, Ms. Pena. It is such a pleasure to see you again. You look absolutely beautiful, as usual. Come with me so I can introduce you to some people." He steered her away. She tried to twist out of his grasp.

"Actually, I was talking to Officer Mackey."

"I'm sure you'll see him again in the parking lot. You are babysitting cars tonight, aren't you, Mackey?" He laughed as he led her away, a flash of perfectly capped white teeth.

"Troglodyte," Roper muttered under his breath.

⁘

It was almost eleven when Roper finished his umpteenth round of checking the parking lot. The only critters up to no good were the rats foraging around the Dumpster. He climbed back up the sixteen steps to the foyer and leaned against the wall, waiting to begin the umpteenth-and-one check of the lot. What a way to spend a shift.

He heard the whisper of silk before he heard the sniffling. He could only make out her silhouette in the moonlight, but he recognized the perfume. She was bent over, her forehead resting against the handrail. He cleared his throat gently to avoid scaring her.

She leaped upright, hands clutched together over her chest. "Oh, Roper. You scared me!"

"I'm very sorry about that. Are you. . .all right?" He could see the glint of tears in her eyes, her chest heaving rapidly.

Her voice shook slightly. "I—yes. I'm fine."

Another voice behind them startled them both. It was Toulouse.

"Well, here you are. I was wondering where you'd gotten to." He took a step toward her with an outstretched hand, and she jerked backward, directly into Roper's unyielding front.

"Your bracelet." The gold bangle glittered between his fingers in the moonlight. "It must have come unfastened while we talked. Why don't you come back inside and I'll help you put it on?"

Roper could feel her tight against him, trembling. "No. I—need some air."

"Wonderful idea. Let's go for a walk, shall we?"

"No. I want to talk to Rope, to Officer Mackey."

"Surely you don't want to miss out on that amazing brass group?"

"I'll be there in a minute."

The attorney's eyes narrowed slightly. "All right. I'll be looking for you inside *shortly, then." He turned on his heel and strode back toward the soft strains of trumpet and trombone.*

She waited until the door closed silently before she turned to face Roper.

"I want to go home. I'm not feeling well. Could you call me a cab? Please?"

"I'll do better than that. I'll take you home myself." He spoke quietly into the radio on his shoulder.

"I don't want you to get in trouble."

"Don't worry about that. My partner can cover the next few rounds."

Two minutes later he was walking her to the car, sandwiching her among the radio and computer console. The only noise was the static from the radio and the calm, intermittent voice of the dispatcher.

He wasn't sure what to do. Something had upset her, but she didn't want to talk about it, and he wasn't sure he should push. He walked her to her door and unlocked it.

"Thank you for driving me home. It was really kind of you." She smiled wanly. "I guess it's better riding in the front of a cop car than the back."

"I suppose so. Are you sure you don't want to talk about it?"

Suddenly she wrapped her arms around his neck, pressing her face into the bare skin under his chin. "I wish you could stay here with me," she said in a voice so muffled by uniform that he almost didn't hear her.

Gently, he raised her chin to look into her face. "Why don't you tell me what happened? Did someone bother you? Was it Toulouse?" His face hardened as he spoke the name.

"No. No one. I think I'm just catching something." She tried to smile brightly.

He looked unconvinced. "I'm off at one. I'm going to come by and check on you."

"I'll be asleep."

"I'll call you from my car."

"I'll be asleep. I won't hear the phone ring."

"Then you'll hear me break down the front door."

She stared at him. "I'll answer the phone."

"Good." He brushed the hair out of her eyes and leaned down to kiss her forehead.

"Thank you."

He reluctantly let her go. "Good night, Benjamina."

Ruth put the folder down and sighed. Benjamina should just level with the cop; he seemed like a good man who adored her. How often does a girl run into that sort of thing? What was the problem? Was it a skeleton from the past flying out of her closet or just a case of modern-day woman trying to juggle more than one man? And why was this novel consuming all her energy? Angrily, she began flipping through the folder, trying to find the next section in the mish-mash of papers, when the phone rang.

"Hello?"

"It's Ellen, at the library."

As if there could be another Ellen Foots lurking somewhere other than the library. "Oh, hi. What can I do for you?"

"You could return your library books on time. You have a copy of *Fuchsias: A Plant for All Seasons.* It was due back yesterday. There is a ten-cent-per-day fine, you know."

She had completely forgotten about the book. It was sitting on the coffee table buried under a pile of catalogues. She hadn't even opened it.

"Oh brother. I forgot all about it. I'll bring it in today. I promise."

"That would be helpful. Mr. Donnelly returned it on time. I was surprised; he didn't seem like the type that would respect library rules particularly, but I guess you can't judge a book by its cover." She laughed at her joke.

Ruth rolled her eyes upward. *Just what this town of Finny needs: murder, mayhem, and a comic Nazi librarian.*

"Thanks for the call. I'm sorry to have forgotten."

"Remember the library closes at 4:00 on Mondays, so finish your book and get it back here before we lock up."

"Sure thing, Ellen." Ruth hung up and rummaged through the stack on the table. Plopping down on the sofa, she flipped through the beginning chapters.

There were many glossy pictures and all sorts of advice for growing fuchsias using salt-free cocoa fiber, plant hormones, and antioxidants. She wondered how the things ever managed in the wild, as she figured they must have at one time or another.

She was about to close the book when she noticed that the bottom right-hand corner of a page had been dog-eared and then folded flat again. It was a photo of a lush, bushy fuchsia covered with gaudy orange and purple paper lantern blossoms. The common name printed in italics was *Payoff*.

Hmmm. She began going page by page, searching for telltale creases. There were only two other pages in the entire three-hundred-page volume that had been folded. One photo showed a plant completely covered with tiny blue flowers, common name *Mary Jane*.

Mary Jane. Tiny blue blossoms. "*This particular variety can have red or blue blooms.*" Ruth smacked a hand to her forehead. "That's the plant Dimple was holding outside the gallery. The plant Napoleon had told her to take."

Frantically, she looked at the remaining page. White flowers edged in pink. The same plant she had in her kitchen, the one she had rescued from the gallery compost pile. The same variety she watched Prinn heave out the greenhouse door in a fit of rage. A Heston Blue.

The name of Napoleon Prinn's son.

29

March yelped as she opened her office door to find a detective seated on the settee. "You scared me."

"Sorry," Jack said.

"Don't you people ever call before you barge on in?" Her face shifted from shocked to annoyed. "I have a million things to take care of. Is there something in particular you want?"

"I'd like to know what you want."

"What?"

"What do you want, March? What are you looking to get out of this life?"

"You've got to be kidding me. This sounds like a talk show. What does it matter what I want?"

"I know what your parents wanted for you."

She started and then looked away, taking off her wool blazer and hanging it on the hook behind the door. "What do you know about my parents?"

"I know they raised two kids. They both worked two jobs to send you to college, but it wasn't enough to cover it."

"So?" Her eyes were hard, narrowed.

"So your dad took out a second mortgage on the house."

"Uh-huh. Lots of people do that, Detective. What does that have to do with the price of eggs in China?"

He paused for a moment and looked into her eyes. "He has a balloon payment due by the end of the year, and it looks like he's going to lose the house."

She was swallowing convulsively now. "Yes. Well. He invested a lot of money in my career, and it looks like my life's work is going up in smoke. I guess you know all about me, don't you?" Her voice rose with every word. "I'll tell you what, Detective, you don't know anything about me."

He waited a moment before answering quietly, "I know your parents had a son."

March spat, "My brother? So you know all about my brother, huh? Then I guess you know he's dead. I guess you know that Chili was supposed to pick me up at school. Charles was his name, but we all called him Chili. I was sixteen and waiting for him to pick me up, but he forgot. I stood on the school steps for an hour until the gym teacher gave me a ride.

"I was furious when I got home, furious at being embarrassed in front of my friends. I let him have it, all right, and my parents agreed with me. They said he was grounded for the weekend. All of a sudden he was furious, too, shouting at me for getting him grounded." She glared at the detective. "I guess you know what I said to him? No? I told him I wished I didn't have a brother. Well, he got in his car and forty-five minutes later I didn't."

Tears were streaming down her face, her mascara running into shadowy pools under her eyes. "Do you know what that's like, Detective? To always regret the idiotic last words you said to someone?"

"Actually, I do. The last words I said to my wife were 'Don't forget to pick up my uniform at the dry cleaners.' She died before my shift was over."

The silence dragged on as she stared at him. He could see the anger melting away, leaving undiluted grief in its wake.

"I am sorry. I really am." She wiped a Kleenex under her eyes and blew her nose. "How do you live with it? Does it ever go away?"

"No. I just try to remember the nice things I said to her when I wasn't being a moron."

"Why did you come here to talk about my family? What does my father's financial trouble have to do with anything that's happened?"

"Because I think you had a plan to bail him out. A plan that involved this gallery and the keys you took from Napoleon's study the night he was murdered."

Her face was white and rigid. She opened her mouth, but nothing came out.

"Let me tell you what I think. I think that you took the keys from Prinn's office. I think you used them to unlock the file cabinet that had the safe access codes, which he changed weekly. I think you were going to remove a sum of money from the safe and get out of Dodge. How am I doing?"

"How do you know these things?" she whispered.

"Only two sets of fingerprints on the keys, yours and his." He was fudging here. The crab bisque pretty much rendered the prints inconclusive. "You mentioned he had come into some money recently." He paused before adding, "You purchased two plane tickets on a red eye to Seattle for the night of the dedication. The folks are from Seattle, aren't they?"

He leaned forward. "Look, Ms. Browning. I have spent a lifetime dealing with bad people. Crooks, dealers, extortionists, murderers, pedophiles, you name it. I know bad people. You are not bad people."

She looked up at him, desperation spilling from every pore. "Napoleon had all these grand plans for this place. A total renovation, traveling exhibits, maybe even opening up a sister gallery on the East Coast. I was totally caught up in it, of course. I thought we were going to make it big after all these years." She shook her head. "I mean, it was really the chance of a lifetime. A chance to get in on the ground floor, to build a gallery from the bottom up. Who could pass that up?

"Anyway, we were really starting to get some acclaim, features in regional papers and even some notice from the big boys back East. Napoleon decided to begin the renovation of the building and buy a few significant pieces from the Shaum.

"Last December, I began to notice that something was wrong; Napoleon was acting strangely, getting weird phone calls, disappearing for periods of time. He would show up at the beginning of each month with a satchel that went immediately into the safe. I knew it was money, but I didn't know it was from drugs. I thought he was gambling or borrowing from loan sharks or something."

She began gnawing on a fingernail that was already bitten to the quick.

"Was it your idea? To take the money?"

"No. Well, I can't say I hadn't thought of it. Napoleon treated me like a farmhand. Oh, I know he probably hired me because I don't look bad in a skirt and I played the pretty office girl to the public. But I got all the menial jobs and he cut me out of the good stuff, the buying and marketing decisions, I mean."

He steered her back to the topic, which was on the top of his list. "He deserved to get taken. Is that what Randy said?"

She removed the bitten fingernail and started on another. "I told Randy about the money that Napoleon put in the safe on the first of every month. I knew it was a lot, maybe thousands. It would definitely be something to help my parents and enough maybe for Randy to start a theater. I told him that Napoleon was into something shady and I wanted out before I got taken down along with him. We worked out the plan together."

"Go on."

"My part was to get the keys from his office and find the safe codes. We would wait until the dedication was over and things were locked up for the night. I have a key to the building and the alarm codes, so getting in wouldn't be a problem. We were going to come back, take the money, and then get to the airport."

"How did the keys wind up in Ruth Budge's soup?"

She blushed. "I can't believe it, but I dropped them in Monk's soup pot."

"How?"

"I took the keys from the office, and I was going to open the filing cabinet when I heard some people coming. I didn't have time to replace them, so I went out the back door and walked around to the dining room. My dress didn't have any pockets, and when I snuck through the French doors to join the dinner, Monk swooped down on me demanding that I give the toast. He wanted to get the dinner served before it was ruined, I guess. I panicked and the keys slipped from my hand into the bisque before he reached me."

Jack smiled, picturing the enraged navy officer bellowing about his crab chowder or whatever it was. "You said you heard voices, people coming into

Prinn's office. Could you recognize the voices?"

"No. One could have been a woman's; I'm not sure."

"Did they sound angry?"

"Not that I could tell." She took a breath and stared at him. "Detective, are you going to arrest me? Us?"

He returned her gaze. "At the present time, it doesn't appear that you and Randy actually committed any crimes. Lucky for you, your plans were derailed."

"Yeah," she breathed, relieved, "but not so lucky for Napoleon."

Ruth caught up with March in Napoleon's office, shortly after Jack drove out of the parking lot. He waved cheerfully at her, but she could see that he looked tired. The secretary was talking on the phone and gestured for Ruth to sit down. Since the gallery was officially closed, she was dressed casually in jeans and a lily pad–green sweater.

Ruth avoided the discolored splotches on the carpet and made her way to a chair in the corner, under the coatrack.

"All right. Thank you." She slammed the phone down.

"Never mind there's been a murder here and our gallery is closed down. This guy just has to have that painting to go over his sofa. I don't know why I feel compelled to stay on and sort this mess out. Let's go to my office. This place gives me the creeps."

They settled in next door.

"What can I do for you? Please don't tell me you bought a painting from us recently."

"No, no. Nothing like that. I wanted to ask you about a plant."

She looked amused. "A plant?"

"Yes. The plant that was used to kill Napoleon."

March closed her eyes and sighed gustily. "I've already been through this with the police! But I guess I could stand a few more questions."

"Where did it come from? The plant, I mean."

"I don't know. It just sort of appeared in his office right before the dedication. He seemed really ticked about it. He grilled me about where it came from, who delivered it, et cetera. The fact of the matter is, I don't have a clue. He asked me to get rid of it, but I didn't have time before the ceremony started."

"What did it look like?"

"You saw it, didn't you?"

"Yes," Ruth said slowly, "but I was sort of, distracted, by what was underneath it."

March nodded, crinkling up her nose. "Yes, well, I'm not much of a plant person, but I know it was a fuchsia. Lots of green leaves, white flowers with pink edges."

"Payoff."

"What?"

"Oh, nothing. I was just thinking aloud. Thanks for your help. I'll let you get back to your job."

She laughed bitterly. "Some job. See you later, Ruth."

―――

Outside, Ruth sat down on a wrought iron bench, her head whirling.

"This has got to be more than a coincidence." Napoleon had at least four fuchsias delivered to him by a mystery person. She had one in her kitchen. Dimple had another. One got smashed to bits on the sidewalk outside the greenhouse, and the fourth killed Napoleon at the gallery soiree. The Heston Blues, a Mary Jane, and a Payoff. Presumably Donnelly had caught on to this. What did it mean?

Was someone delivering messages to Napoleon in plant language? What was the message?

The Mary Jane must refer to the marijuana that Prinn was busily smuggling out sandwiched in paintings. Someone must have found out and began blackmailing him, hence the Payoff. Heston Blue?

She sat upright, remembering a whispered conversation in the library. "*I knew someone who was involved with a plant freak—even named a child after one.*"

She set off for the Zimmerman house.

―――

Ruth rang the doorbell twice before she heard the humming of a motor approaching the front door.

"Who is it?" rasped a voice.

"It's Ruth Budge."

The door opened and Bun peeked out, looking surprised. She was dressed in a paisley smock and orthopedic sandals, her hair oozing out of its braid like smoke.

"Wanda is out now. She went to talk to some other galleries in San Gregorio. Won't be back until late."

Ruth breathed a silent prayer of thanks. "Actually, I need to talk to you."

The old woman blinked watery eyes. "Oh. Well, okay. Could you go around back and meet me there? The place is a mess. There's a gazebo out there. I'll bring tea or something."

She picked her way to the gate and threw her entire body weight against it to force it open. The yard was overgrown, tall brown grass bent gracefully over the slate walkway.

She walked to the rickety gazebo. Looking around the dingy yard, she noticed a white terrier sitting in a doggy igloo watching her. He was so intense, so still.

Bun's voice in her ear startled her. "He's stuffed. Name was Poppet. Wanda loved him like a child, goofy old thing." Ruth wasn't sure if she was describing the dog or the owner.

"He was her whole life after that boozing bum of a husband left her. She was much better off with just the dog." Bun considered the stuffed creature. "Broke her heart when he died, though. She cried for months. You wouldn't believe it, but she still comes out here every night and talks to him. Covers him up with a blanket if it's cold."

She slowly followed Bun up the ramp to the gazebo. The thought of a grown woman, a woman who seemed confident to a fault, sitting outside in the rain seeking comfort from a stuffed dog was pitiful. It made her own life look positively cheerful.

Bun rolled up the ramp to the gazebo, a tray with two sodas and a box of Fig Newtons balanced on her lap.

She waited while Bun slowly tore the box of cookies open, pinching the carton between her left elbow and side and ripping it open with her right hand. Ruth opened the sodas and they sipped for a minute.

"I was remembering a conversation we had at the library earlier. Something you said stuck in my mind, and I wanted to ask you about it."

Bun regarded her under bushy brows and over the rim of her soda can. "So ask."

She took a deep breath. "I was looking at a book about fuchsias. You said that you knew someone who named their child after a plant. I'd like to hear more about that."

"Why?"

"Call me curious, Bun. I'd really like to know."

"It was a long time ago."

"When you were a nurse?" She corrected hastily, "When you worked for the hospital?"

"Mmm-hmm. I did a lot of home care in those days. For people who couldn't afford the hospital trip or just didn't trust organized health care. Nobody makes house calls anymore."

"That's true. So this was a patient of yours? The one who liked plants?"

"Oh, she didn't like plants. It was the boyfriend, if you could call him that. She was totally infatuated with him. He was a sharp one, smooth. Told her what she wanted to hear to get what he wanted."

"What was that?"

Bun gave her a look.

"Oh," Ruth said, blushing, "that."

"Yeah, that. Jenny was a real looker. Gorgeous, but pathetic. She wanted that man to marry her, and she'd have done just about anything to get him."

"He wasn't interested? In the marriage thing, I mean?"

"No. She wasn't his type, no wealthy family connections, no social ambition." Bun leaned back in her chair, her eyes distant and pained. "She was just a real sweet girl. A sweet, misguided girl."

"Please tell me what happened. I really need to know."

"Same thing that always happens: She got pregnant. I was there at the birth. He wasn't, of course. He dumped her early on, even before she knew she was expecting. Why can't these girls wait for the marriage license like the good Lord intended?

"She wrote to him, begged him to come back. Said she wanted them to be a family, said the child needed a father. Told him she named the kid after one of his plants. Can you imagine? Naming a child after a plant? Heston something or other. I had to ask twice to get it right on the birth certificate."

"The man was Napoleon Prinn, wasn't he?"

She looked at Ruth with ill-concealed disgust. "Yes."

"And the woman?"

"I don't see how that pertains." Her words were slurred.

"Please, Bun."

The woman watched her for a long moment. "All right. I guess it's all water under the bridge now. Jenny Tibbets. She's in a mental hospital now. After he abandoned her, she sort of lost her mind. She kept it together for a while, for the child. Then she packed up and moved somewhere. I lost track of both of them."

"How long ago was that?"

"Twenty-three, twenty-four years ago, maybe."

"Did you know the boy well?"

"Not at all. I was there at the birth and a few times afterwards. That's all. Why are you so interested in all this, Ruth?"

"I think Heston Blue was blackmailing Napoleon before he was killed."

"The gossip is that it was a stranger. Got in and killed him for the money in the safe."

"I don't think so."

"You should stay out of it, Ruth. It's for the police to solve."

"I just stumbled across some things."

"Well, don't you pay any mind to it. I know it wasn't Heston. He's long gone."

"How do you know? Would you even recognize the man if he was here in Finny?"

"Just leave it alone." Bun leaned forward, eyes intense. "It's not your business."

Ruth felt a twinge of fear. "Maybe you're right. Thanks for your time." She brushed Fig Newton crumbs off her lap as she rose.

Bun reached over the peeling table to return the cans and cookie box to the tray. As she did so, Ruth got a glimpse of her right hand. The fingers were strong, muscular, stained with smears of green and rust-colored paint. They both looked up and stared at each other for a long moment.

"It's you," Ruth whispered before she had a chance to think better of it. "Why do you let her take credit for your work?"

The old woman was silent for a moment. "All I need is to paint. Wanda needs to be famous. We don't always wind up with the talent that goes along with our dream. It's nobody's business but ours. You see?"

Ruth nodded. It was not her place to judge this strange symbiosis between mother and daughter. "I see. Thank you, Bun."

31

The sun finally burned its way through the fog that hugged Finny's Nose, leaving only a wispy mustache of white behind. Exactly five days after Napoleon Prinn's murder, Jack stood squinting perplexedly in the sunlight at the front door of Dimple Dent's house. He rang the doorbell.

Ruth opened the door. "Hi, Jack. Thanks for meeting me here. I know it seems weird, but I need to show you a few things." She tried to organize all the details that emerged from her meeting with Bun.

He scanned the room quickly before plopping in an overstuffed paisley chair with his back to the wall. Cop habit. Dimple was nowhere.

"So how have you been? How is Paul?"

"We've both been fine, Ruth, and you?"

"I've been fine. I mean, things have been strange lately, but really, when you consider all the things that could—"

He waited patiently until she ran out of words. "You have got my undivided attention for the time being. I assume these 'things' you need to discuss involve Dimple?"

"First of all, I need to tell you some wild theories that I've been cooking up about Napoleon's murder. It may concern Crew's, too." She began her elaborate story, starting from her library book discovery and ending with her theory that Heston Blue was a killer. "I think it couldn't be a coincidence that Donnelly was researching the same exact plants that were being delivered mysteriously to Napoleon."

Jack's eyes had gotten progressively wider.

She related her conversation with Bun, omitting the detail about the painting. "So you see, Bun nursed Heston Blue's mother, it seems, the woman you found in the sanitarium."

It was very quiet in the cottage when she finished, the only sound coming from the occasional *kerplunk* of the ice maker in the kitchen.

"Ruth, I have got to say you are the most efficient busybody I have ever met in my life."

She looked down, chewing on her bottom lip.

"And I am totally impressed. We've been looking for this Heston Blue since the night Ulysses wiped me out in your front yard, and we've gotten zip. The guy was a phantom. No marriage certificate, no DMV record or credit history, not even a voter registration. I have to say, though, we never even came close to the fuchsia clues. I didn't even know a fuchsia was a plant until you told me." He shook his head.

"Napoleon was a bad boy before he was killed," Jack continued. "He was smuggling drugs for the Mexican cartel, and Donnelly's murder put him off schedule. The cartel does not like to be put off schedule. We think one of their guys torched the greenhouse as a warning. We have a warrant out for the man you know as Buck Pinkey, but so far, he's smoke. Forgive the pun."

"Well then, maybe it was the cartel that killed Prinn?" For some reason, Ruth did not want Napoleon's son to have murdered his own father.

"Too messy. They don't generally do the murder-by-plant thing. Profit is their number one priority, and they figured out it's easier to grow the stuff in the States than trying to smuggle it across the border. That's why we started taking a look around for the plant boy, Napoleon's next of kin."

"Did you talk to Heston's mother?"

He nodded. "Yes. She wasn't much help, though. She's pretty out there. Mostly she just sang songs and brushed her hair when we talked to her. The staff has never heard her mention a son, and she's never had a visitor that they know of. Oh. Here's something an aide found in an old book on her shelf."

He handed her a copy of a worn photo. It was a black-and-white, though the colors had faded enough that everything was a darker or lighter patch of gray. A baby, propped up on fat little hands and tummy, peered out from the picture; a knit cap obscured the hair, and two tiny teeth poked out from a gummy, wet grin.

"Heston Blue?"

"Hard to say. It was the only photo they found."

She peered into the picture, mesmerized by the thought that this small innocent had grown up to be a killer. "Poor woman. Maybe it's a blessing she has checked out of the real world. Could I get a copy of this?"

"Keep that one. It's scanned. We have the original."

She stood up and moved uneasily to the window, looking out on the lush lawn and pots of flowers. "What about the keys? In the bisque? Do you think it was another message from Heston before he killed Napoleon?"

"No. I think we've got the key thing straightened out. It was a misunderstanding." He folded his arms across his flannel shirt. "Okay. Now tell me the part I don't want to hear," he said.

She looked up guiltily. "Huh?"

"The part that concerns Dimple, the part that you're scared to tell me. Let me have it, Ruth."

"I think we'd better talk on the way."

He threw out a hand and sighed. "Onward, Mrs. Budge."

She told him many of the pertinent details as they picked their way along the twisting path. Crossing her fingers, she related the bits she had been agonizing about since the day she wandered into the greenhouse.

"Wait just a minute." Jack stopped abruptly on the path. "Run that one by me again. You are telling me that Napoleon used Dimple and her greenhouse to grow marijuana?"

"Er, yes. That's what I'm telling you."

"How could she allow that in her own greenhouse?"

"He told her it was legal, for medicinal purposes only."

His eyebrows shot up. "And she believed that?"

"People ignore what they don't want to see, don't they? Oh, one other thing—there's a dog."

"A dog?"

The detective reached for his gun just as the huge creature came charging out of the greenhouse in front of Dimple.

"Hello, Detective Denny. This is Pepper. He's really a sweet dog; you don't need to shoot him. He keeps me company on my walks."

He looked unconvinced but holstered the weapon anyway. "Hello, Ms. Dent. I understand you are having some concerns about your greenhouse."

She shoved her hands into the pocket of her overalls. "Yes. You'll never believe it."

"I bet I won't," he muttered as he stepped past her into the greenhouse. He surveyed the array of equipment and plants. The most mature plants were enormous now, towering over his head in spiky green confusion. It was as if they were in some gorgeous illicit tropical jungle, and Ruth wouldn't have been surprised if a parrot or spider monkey swooped down to scold them.

Slowly, he turned and stared at the two women standing behind him. He rubbed his hands over his stubbled chin and breathed deeply before he continued. "Ms. Dent, you had no idea that it was illegal to farm marijuana? Is that correct?"

She raised her chin. "Yes. I mean, no. Well, he told me it was legal to grow as long as it was sold to sick people. He said they were researching ways to make it into a medicine for asthma. That sounded very helpful. My cousin Alice has asthma, and she never could make it through a full season of lacrosse. She was an excellent player, too."

Jack's eyes widened as he tried to follow the conversational segue.

"Uh, Dimple," Ruth interjected, "why did you keep it a secret?"

She bowed her head sadly, the fringe of hair covering her face, her baggy denim stretched over the tiny bulb of a tummy. A tear trickled down her face and plopped onto one of her high-top sneakers. "He told me to keep it quiet to discourage the curious, and I did. He left the cultivation entirely to me."

Jack cleared his throat and continued in a gentler tone. "And you weren't the least bit suspicious that it wasn't being used the way he told you?"

"No," she said, raising her chin. "I'm very good at following directions, not so good at asking questions."

"And when we sweep this place for prints, yours will be all over these flats, but not his, I take it?"

Dimple nodded silently.

His gaze swept over the greenery one last time. "Orthodontists never run into this stuff."

"What?" Ruth and Dimple asked at once.

"Nothing. I'm going to need to talk to you some more about this, ladies. For the time being, let's just step outside and close the door."

They walked into the cool outside air.

"So," he said incredulously, "there's a nice marijuana plantation right up Finny's Nose. The plants are pretty lush. Must be the climate," he mused.

"No, it all depends on the nutrient additives," Dimple corrected soberly.

The detective sighed again, and Ruth patted him on the shoulder.

32

W hen he arrived, she was applying paint in short, angry strokes to the naked canvas. Her smock was covered with speckles of every color, and her cheek was smudged with orange.

"Hello, Meena." He had shortened her name because Benjamina was too many syllables, and he just couldn't call a woman whom he had kissed Ben.

"Hi."

"You're angry about something."

"Why would you say something like that?" she snapped.

"Because you're painting the entire thing in red."

"I am not. For your information, Officer, this is vermilion, dusty carmine, and glossy ocher. Not a single red."

"A red by any other name." He wedged himself in a student desk and stuck his legs out in front of him, one scuffed boot crossed over the other. "Since you're not mad, I guess these roses on the floor must have been dropped by accident."

"I guess so."

He was slouching casually, trying desperately to see the print on the white card sticking out of the crumpled blossoms.

She whirled around to face him, paintbrush pointing from her hand like a dagger. "If I was mad, I would be mad at me. Do you know why?"

He was pretty sure this was a rhetorical question, so he decided not to hazard an answer.

"Because I am a strong woman. I should be able to take care of myself, shouldn't I? If someone is harassing me, I can take care of it without the help of a brawny man."

"Is someone harassing you?" He spoke very calmly.

"No. I said if someone did. And anyway, what would you do if someone was?"

"I'd take care of it for you."

"Exactly. That's exactly what I'm talking about. Do you see? I can take care of myself."

He paused for a moment before answering. "I don't understand your viewpoint, but I can empathize with your feelings of frustration."

She narrowed her eyes. "You went to one of those sensitivity training things for work, didn't you?"

"Is this when I am supposed to send an 'I' message or mirror your feelings? I always get that mixed up."

She collapsed into a chair and banged her head on the top of the desk.

"So," he resumed, "is someone harassing you?"

"What would you do about it? Never mind, I know. You'd punch his lights out, right?"

"Of course not. I'm a cop," he said, rubbing his chin, smiling. "You never go for the face; it leaves too many bruises."

She stared at him, openmouthed. Then she got up, took off her smock, and grabbed a shoulder bag from her desk drawer.

"Where are you going?"

"To find some chocolate."

"Mind if I go along?"

"Only if you don't give me any more idiotic 'I' messages."

"I understand your feelings completely," he said, ducking the flying shoulder bag.

Ruth was fairly sure she was going to be incarcerated momentarily. She couldn't think of any other reason Jack would summon her to the police station on this Wednesday, the day after their field trip to Dimple's greenhouse. She felt so tired, so very tired, as she shifted uneasily on the waiting room bench. It was ironic that a person who never even got a speeding ticket was going to jail for befriending a strange woman who concealed drug cultivation from the police.

Dejectedly she shoved her hands into her pockets. Her fingers closed around a paper. The baby picture. She slipped it from the envelope and squinted at it.

"Who is that? She's cute."

Her head jerked up so quickly her neck cracked. "Oh, hello, Red. Actually, it's a he. I'm not positive, but I think it's Napoleon Prinn's son."

Red looked at the photo, her face a picture of surprise. "Wow. A son. I didn't know he had one. How did you find it?"

"It belonged to the baby's mother. She's in a mental hospital in Miramar." She returned the photo to her pocket. "What are you doing here?"

Red hiked up the legs of her overalls and plopped onto the bench next to Ruth. "Oh, I just wanted to ask the coppers if I can get out of this town. I'm tired of fog and gravel. I want to go home."

"What did he say?"

"He asked me to stay until the end of the week." She yawned widely enough for Ruth to see her tonsils. "I guess I'm stuck here for two more days."

"What is going to happen to the statue? Of Broken Bird."

"It's going to stay right here in the heart of Finny until all this investigation stuff is over. Then, who knows? Maybe it will go back to the Shaum. I'm not really sure." Her tone was bitter. "I just want to go home, at this point, and put Finny and Napoleon far behind me."

"You must miss New York, being cooped up in this small town for so long."

"The town's okay. It's the people; they all know everything about everything. There is no privacy here. And the fog is so depressing."

The door to Jack's office opened and the detective came out.

"Hi, Mrs. Budge. I've been waiting for you." She couldn't read his face. "Thanks for coming by, Ms. Finchley."

Walking into his cluttered office, Ruth extended her hands and closed her eyes as she plopped into a chair. "I'm turning myself in," she said. After a few seconds of no wrist shackling, she opened an eye. "Aren't you going to arrest me? Isn't that why you hauled me in?"

He was grinning widely, shaking his head from side to side. "You watch way too much television." He laughed aloud. "I just need you to sign your statement about finding the body in the fountain. But now that I'm thinking of it, I'm going to pay a visit to K and K Nursery in Half Moon Bay. We think that's where the fuchsias were purchased. Maybe you could come along, since you know more about these plant suckers than I do."

"Oh. Well. Sure. Okay. Sure. When did you want to go?" Relief flooded through her, restoring oxygen flow to the deprived muscles.

"Are you free tomorrow?" He leaned forward, scowling ferociously. "I think you'd better say yes, or I'll have to bust you for interfering with a murder investigation."

"Well, when you put it that way. . ."

*R*oper Mackey was four yards away from Benjamina's office door when he stopped. It was hard not to eavesdrop on the shouting.

"It's not arrogance, Benjamina. I can tell when a woman is interested. I can tell when a woman is enjoying a kiss," Toulouse said.

"Enjoying? I could press assault charges for your behavior the night of the ball."

"No one would believe you."

There was incredulous silence for a moment.

The man continued, "You are a beautiful, cultured woman. You need a man with education and ambition. Someone who is going places, not some redneck cop who can open a beer bottle with his teeth."

Roper grimaced, leaning one shoulder against the wall.

"What I need and who I see is none of your business. The only thing you need to know is, I do not want to see you, talk to you, smell you, or otherwise share the same air you breathe in this lifetime!" She was practically shrieking by now.

Roper ducked back into a corner as he heard footsteps.

"You'll change your mind, Ms. Pena. I'll be waiting."

Roper watched the man's navy blue back with disgust.

Benjamina's voice reverberated in the close hallway. "And for your information, I've gotten better kisses from my springer spaniel!" A coffee cup crashed into bits against the office door, sending rivulets of brown liquid dribbling to the floor.

Roper waited a few moments until he was sure there were no other porcelain projectiles coming before approaching Benjamina's office.

"I didn't know you had a springer spaniel," he said.

She sat rigidly upright at the desk, hands clenched into fists, cheeks pink with rage, lips parted. "I always wanted one."

He nodded, walking behind the desk to take her in his arms.

34

The drive to Half Moon Bay would have been breathtaking if she had remembered her Dramamine. As it was, the route along Highway 1 was just winding enough to tint the cliff sides and thundering surf a faint shade of vomit green. Philip had always tried to plan vacations on very straight roads to very flat places with frequent stops for saltines and tepid water.

Jack glanced over occasionally on the straighter patches of road. "Are you okay? You look green around the gills."

She nodded. "Fine. I forgot to tell you I get seasick, airsick, carsick, and elevator sick. I don't travel well. But I never leave home without a plastic bag, so you don't need to worry about the upholstery."

He laughed. "I wasn't worried. You just let me know if I need to stop."

"Okay."

They traveled in relative silence until they began a gradual decent into the fertile valley colored with acres of young Christmas trees and rusty-hued mums. Jack drummed his thumbs on the steering wheel and shifted in his seat.

"There's something I've been meaning to talk to you about." He noted her uneasy glance. "Not related to manufacturing of an illegal substance. A personal thing."

She relaxed. "Fire away."

"Well, you remember the night I barged in on you to talk about the Heston Blue thing?" He waited for her nod. "After Ulysses and I finished our knock-down-drag-out on the hood of my car, you remember what happened? With Paul?"

"Of course I do. I'll never forget that giggle. Has he begun to talk at all?"

"No," he said, slowing for a sharp bend in the road, "that was it, just the giggle. Anyway, I was thinking that somehow he seems to connect with your birds. At least, he did then."

He turned to look at her, his eyes crinkled in frustration and despair. "I have to reach him, Ruth. I have to find the happy boy I had before Lacey died. I know he's in there somewhere. I'm not much good at this daddy thing, but I'm the best he's got."

She nodded gently. "You bring him over anytime, as much as you want. They aren't the most loving of companions, but if we fill Paul's pockets with onion rings, they'll follow him to the ends of the earth."

He laughed heartily and thanked her.

In spite of her uncooperative stomach, she enjoyed the conversation and the lush view as they headed away from the coastline. The valley was green and peppered with purple and yellow wildflowers. Ranch land suddenly shifted to a packed gravel path, which led the way to a split-rail fence that separated the nursery from the surrounding pasture. She opened the window to breathe in the scent of damp soil.

They pulled into the gravel lot of K and K Nursery. The building that greeted them was wooden and leaned somewhat starboard, with long, low windows and a peeling door trying desperately to part ways with its hinges. This was the office building. The entire property sprawled over twenty loamy acres and housed the most advanced greenhouses money could buy.

"The K and K stands for Kermit and Kermit. They are known for growing rare and exotic types of flowering plants. Four fuchsias matching the types delivered to Prinn the week before his murder were sold from this nursery to an out-of-towner."

"How did you find that out?"

"Exceptional police work."

She raised a newly sprouted eyebrow.

"Blind, stupid luck didn't hurt, either. Nate found a piece of the fancy foil stuff they use to dress up the plastic pots stuck inside Dimple's Mary Jane fuchsia. It was just a scrap, but he remembered seeing something like it, so he took it home to his wife. She used to work for a nursery wholesale supplier when she was in college. She recognized the swirly designs on the foil. It's a type used by only a few nurseries because it's apparently expensive and comes on big rolls that you cut yourself. Most places buy the cheaper stuff that's precut. Then it was just a matter of making some phone calls."

The interior of the shop was dark and cool. Kermit was not at all what Ruth had expected. Mentally slapping herself, she realized she had been expecting green flippers and ping-pong-ball eyes. Actually, the old man's eyes did look a little ping-pongish as he scrutinized them from behind lenses rivaling the Hubble telescope's.

His skin was as leathery. The hair standing straight out from the top of his head looked like new straw, and his eyes were a startling Play-Doh blue. He looked at them over the top of his glasses.

"You must be the cop. And—?" He pointed a crusty finger at Ruth.

"Yes, Detective Denny, and this is Ruth Budge. You are Mr. Narvik, Senior?"

"Uh-huh. You wanted to know about some fuchsias."

"Yes." Jack consulted his notebook. "Common names Heston Blue, Mary Jane, and Payoff."

"Mmmm. Some fella called in the orders. Saturday was the first two."

"The first two? They weren't ordered at the same time?"

"No. Fella ordered the Heston Blues. Said he couldn't pick it up until late 'cause he was coming in from out of town. Dropped his payment in the mail slot, and we left 'em on the porch for him after closing time."

"That was a week ago Saturday?"

"Yes, Saturday the eighth."

That must have been the plant she saw Donnelly taking to the trash heap, Ruth thought. The other came sailing out of the greenhouse door.

"How did he pay for it?"

"Cash. It wasn't cheap, either. We charge extra for special orders. It isn't easy to come by some of these fuchsias. I had to call around for Payoff. Not many people ask for that one."

Jack was scribbling furiously. "What about the other two orders?"

"Two days after he picked up the first batch—that'd be Tuesday the eleventh, I guess—he called again, asking for Mary Jane and Payoff. I told him I couldn't have Payoff until Friday but he could pick up the Mary Jane the next day. He dropped the cash in the slot Wednesday evening, sometime after seven o'clock. That's closing time. We did the same thing with the last plant on Thursday night. Put it out on the porch after quitting time."

Ruth did some quick mental math. Last Friday was the fourteenth, the day Prinn was killed.

"Did this person contact you again after he picked up the plant Thursday night?"

"No. Only saw him the once."

Ruth looked at Jack, whose lips had parted in astonishment. "You saw him?" she said.

Kermit was enjoying the drama he had created. He rubbed his nose thoughtfully and stretched his shoulders before answering. "Sure. I stuck around late one night, doing some book work, and I heard him on the porch. I poked my head out to be neighborly."

They both stared at him, and she thought surely her own eyes must be the size of ping pong balls. "Did you folks want some coffee or something?"

"No. What did he look like?"

Ruth could feel Jack's agitation increasing.

"Hard to say. It was almost dark and real foggy."

Kermit's comments were interrupted by the phone on his desk. He picked up the ancient receiver. "Yeah? Oh man, I already told you. Uh-huh, well, I guess I could. Got a pencil?" He covered the mouthpiece and gestured for them to sit in the Naugahyde chairs.

Ruth sat; Jack didn't move.

TROUBLE UP FINNY'S NOSE

Though she could only see the detective's back, she noticed a distinct flush creeping up his neck from under the collar.

"Well, that's because you are an idiot." Kermit covered the mouthpiece again. "My brother can't keep a recipe straight to save his soul."

By the time he hung up, Jack looked as if he were going to explode into millions of frustrated bits. "You said you saw him." His words were clipped and low. "What did he look like, Mr. Narvik?"

"Who?"

"The man who picked up the plants!"

"Oh, him. Well, it's hard to say. He was all muffled up, long coat, knit cap. Strong guy, though, hauled those plants up in no time, and they ain't feathers, either, when they just been watered."

"Did you talk to him?"

"Not much. I asked him what he wanted the plants for. He said it was for a collector friend. Said he was just visiting the coast, never been here before. I asked him what he thought about our coastal fog. He said he was getting accustomed to the dark. He was taller than me by a head. I think that was about it."

"Was there anything unusual about his voice?"

"No. Kinda gravelly, I guess. Like he had a cold. Spoke real quiet."

"Did you notice anything else? Eye color? Hair color? Age? Any distinguishing marks?"

"Mmmm. No. As I said, it was dark. He was all covered up. That's all I noticed."

Jack pocketed his notebook. "Thank you, Mr. Narvik. Here's my card. Please call me if you think of anything else."

"You're welcome. Come again."

Back in the car, Ruth and Jack were quiet for a while. Finally, Jack cleared his throat and twisted the key in the ignition.

"Well, Ruth? Do you have any thoughts worth sharing?"

She hesitated for a fraction of a second. "No. I don't think so."

He eyed her sharply. "There's something. What is it?"

"Oh, it's nothing. Just something about the conversation struck a familiar chord with me, but I can't think what it is. Maybe if I just stew on it for a while, something will come to me."

As the miles wound by, nothing came but queasiness.

35

It wasn't the crash of Alva's newspaper that woke her up Friday morning but rather the tense murmuring voices wafting up from her front porch to her open bedroom window. Wrapping a nubby purple robe around her, she padded down the stairs and peered through the peephole, directly at a very large person's chin. It was attached to the grave-looking face of Monk. Standing next to him nervously zipping and unzipping his jacket was Alva.

"It's a terrible thing, Ruth. Terrible." Alva's eyes began to tear up, and his lips trembled. "I can't feature who coulda done it."

Monk patted him gently on the shoulder. "It's okay, Alva. You did the right thing coming to get me. I can take it from here. Why don't you go along now?" He spoke gently, as if talking to a confused child.

Alva wiped a sleeve under his bulbous nose. "Okay. I just can't feature it." He shuffled off down the driveway, muttering to himself.

She was beginning to feel a rising tide of panic. "Monk. What is going on? What has happened?"

Monk shifted his weight uneasily from one huge foot to the other. He was wearing an apron stained with brown streaks and smelling of bouillabaisse, and a slotted spoon was shoved in the back pocket of his jeans. "Something bad has happened. I have to believe it was some crackpot, probably last night I think, or it could have been early this morning. . ."

"What?" she practically shrieked. "Just tell me already. I'm going to jump out of my skin."

"You'd better come with me."

He led her to the side of the house. It took her a few minutes to spot anything unusual. She saw something white lying at the bottom of the gate. At first she thought it looked like a bundle of laundry or maybe a pillowcase. As she got closer she stopped dead in her tracks, and her hands flew to her mouth.

"Oh no," she whispered, her stomach convulsing.

"He's not dead, just hurt. Alva saw him on his route. He didn't know what to do, so he came to get me."

Ulysses was sprawled on the ground, feathers draped in disarray like a white handkerchief flung on the ground. His eyes were open, little feet sticking up in the air. The muscles around his throat thrummed weakly.

She knelt down beside him, stroking his wing feathers gently. "It's okay, my friend. You're going to be okay." She noticed the piece of cardboard sticking out from under his body. Sliding it out, she read the one-word scrawl.

STOP.

"Stop? Stop what? Who could have done this?" She felt like crying, but no tears would come: Her eyes burned instead.

Monk looked at her helplessly. "I don't know. Do you suppose it has something to do with all the strangeness around here lately?"

The world was spinning, drowning her again and again.

She looked up abruptly, gazing at him without seeing. "I think someone wants me to stop looking for him. And I know who that someone is."

"I'll help you. Whatever you need. Let me help you, please." He opened his arms to fold her inside. This time, she did not push him away.

⸺

It was nearly two hours before she returned to her kitchen, still wearing the fuzzy purple robe. Nathan Katz had arrived to take her statement, followed a few minutes later by Jack. Ulysses had been delivered to the vet, who promised to do what she could for him. Monk said he would stay for a while at the vet's office.

Jack told her they would find the person who did it, but she didn't think that bird assault was probably very high on the Finny Police Department priority list. Unless, of course, the attacker of birds and gallery owners was one and the same. The police would be doing a drive-by check of her house every hour or two until they knew for sure.

The rest of the day passed in a blur of confusion. She did her chores robotically, feeding, cleaning, and trying to comfort herself and the birds. Afternoon morphed into evening, and still she could not shake her state of shock.

She could picture in her mind's eye how it was done. The perpetrator had gone to the gate, probably with some food treat, and the birds had come running. Ulysses was the most aggressive, and he had, no doubt, pushed his way to the front. It would have been an easy thing then to open the gate a crack and grab the bird as he edged through. She wondered if he had been surprised when the hands began hurting him. Quickly she shook her head to dislodge the disturbing mental picture.

She knew in her heart that it was Heston Blue. She could feel the anger and fear in that one simple word. *Stop*. He knew she had been to see Bun, maybe even knew she found out his secrets from the library book. What else did he know? He was close, watching. Maybe even right now.

Shivering, she checked the locks for the fourth time, then went upstairs to bed. Monk called again to check on her. The vet was hopeful about Ulysses' recovery, he reported. She thanked him and told him she was fine. As much as she didn't want to admit it, she looked forward to his frequent phone calls.

She lay down on the bed and folded her hands. Lately her prayers had begun to sound different. Maybe it was just a deeper level of desperation. Or maybe it was the fact that she had been drawn inextricably into the lives of the people around her for a brief moment. She wanted to feel again. Something, anything. Even the current turmoil was better than the awful numbness.

"Lord, I am not sure You're listening. I'm not sure of anything anymore. But I am going to ask You one more time. Help me, Lord. Help me crawl out of this dark hole. Help me turn my face to the light and feel Your loving embrace again. I am so tired, Lord. I am so tired of this life. Please show me a better one."

Pulling the covers over her head, she cried bitterly until she drifted off to sleep.

In her dreams she was running, chased by a dark figure in a trench coat with a bird in each pocket. Just as he reached her, grabbing at her hair, she awoke, dripping with sweat and breathing raggedly. It took a split second for her to remember. Even squeezing her eyes shut did not erase the picture of her maimed bird.

Ruth hauled herself out of bed and waited until the hammering in her chest subsided. Her glance wandered over the familiar items on her dresser. The fat bristled hairbrush, a beautiful bottle of eau de something that she never used, and the photo Jack had given her of Heston Blue.

The baby gazed out at her from the gray background, eyes wide and round. She fished around in her top drawer and found a magnifying glass. Squinting, she examined the figure closely. The dotted pajamas hugged the baby's plump arms, flexed with the effort of holding his body up. How did such a tiny thing become a cold-blooded killer? She looked more closely.

Her breath froze in her lungs as she peered through the lens.

The tiny dots weren't dots. They were hearts. Hearts, with a tiny flower inside each one.

Hearts? On a baby boy?

She stood there with the magnifying glass gripped tightly between her fingers. It seemed as if she were at the top of a high cliff, looking down. The thought of looking over the edge terrified her.

She thought of Benjamina; the strong, beautiful woman who was not afraid of challenges, of life. Ruth was not strong, not beautiful, not accomplished, but she felt something new welling up inside her; a feeling of strength that started at her cold bare feet and grew as it rose until she felt as though it would explode out of her. She was not strong, not beautiful, but maybe she could be that other woman, make her real for one moment in time. Maybe God would give her a chance.

She put the magnifying glass down very carefully.

Tomorrow morning she would finish her conversation with Bun Zimmerman.

36

By the time she reached the Zimmerman cottage, it was almost eight o'clock, and the morning chill froze her to the bone. Her knock sounded loud, echoing down the quiet street.

It was completely silent, so she banged again. Finally, she heard soft scuffling noises of someone heaving herself up to the peephole.

The door opened a crack and Wanda peeked out. "Ruth?" She opened the door wider, hand on her hip, flipping her ponytail in irritation. "What are you doing whacking on my door?"

"I need to see your mother."

She heard the sound of Bun's wheelchair bumping up to the front door.

"What is it, Ruth? I thought we were finished."

"I want to know about Heston Blue. The truth this time. I'm not leaving until you tell me."

Bun's eyes widened for a split second before she said, "I see. Come inside, then."

Wanda, in a state of bewilderment, opened the door and led her into a stale-smelling front room. The walls were marred with wheelchair scuffs; a candy dish on the table was filled with stony-looking pretzels. It had the musty smell of an attic or trunk that has finally been opened after years of neglect.

"You need to go, Wanda. This is a private matter," Bun said quietly to her daughter.

"What do you mean, a private matter? This is my house, too. I have a right to know what goes on under my own roof."

"Who pays the mortgage? Do you want to talk about that right now? Right here?"

Wanda ground her teeth and grunted angrily before she turned on her heel and stalked out.

"Now. What do you want to know?"

"I want to know the truth. It's incredibly important."

"I don't see why it matters now."

"It matters. You've got to tell me." Ruth realized her voice was getting louder.

The old woman took a deep breath and sat ramrod straight in her wheelchair. "All right, then. What do you want to know?"

"Heston Blue is a girl, isn't she?"

Bun exhaled dejectedly. "Yes."

"You helped deliver the baby. You were there. Why the lies? To me, and on the birth certificate?"

"I didn't think it could hurt anyone. Jenny was so desperate to keep Napoleon. She thought he would stay if she had his son. When the baby was born, she was heartbroken; she thought sure it was a boy." Bun plucked absently at a hair protruding from under her chin. "She figured if he would just come back, meet the baby, he would decide to stay and be a father for her. Poor, stupid girl."

"So you falsified the birth certificate, didn't you?"

"She wanted to send him a copy of the birth certificate. To prove she'd had a baby, a son. I figured that once her harebrained scheme failed, I could slip into the records office and change the document. Or maybe at the baby's first checkup the doctor would notice and think it was a mistake. A typo. She was just so desperate."

Bun gazed out the window. "I wanted to help her somehow. She had a really terrible life, always got the short end of the stick. Anyway, the whole mess didn't accomplish a thing because he never came back. When I went back to do the three-week checkup, they were gone. Jenny, Heston, and all their worldly belongings. I never heard from them again. I figured it was best to leave well enough alone."

Bun sat still, looking at the floor. Then, "Do you know where Jenny is? Is she still alive?"

"Yes. She's alive, living in a mental hospital not far from here." She tried to be gentle. "She's pretty confused. The doctors say she's happy, but not aware of the real world."

Tears gathered in the old woman's eyes, and she looked down into her lap. She wiped a sleeve across her lips. "Do you think Heston killed her father?"

"All I know is someone with a connection to Heston Blue is involved in two murders." She thought for a split second about Ulysses and shuddered, hoping she was not destined to be the third. "I've got to go." She reached out to grasp the woman's hand. "You did the right thing."

She glanced back and saw Bun watching her run down the street, into the gathering fog.

37

Ruth paced up and down her hallway and in and out of her kitchen, trying to unmuddle the muddle in her head. Her lunch lay untouched on the table. It was a case of way too much information for some compromised neuropathways, she thought. Heston Blue was not a man. Then who picked up the fuchsias from Kermit Narvik at his nursery? Something about the nursery owner's conversation was jiggling at the corner of her mind. Something familiar.

After a quarter mile more of hallway pacing, she gave up, placing one phone call before she went outside to gather her flock. They were nervous, vibrating with anxiety. As she let them out the gate and onto the sidewalk, they darted forward and then fell back in a confused acrobatic frenzy. They all needed a good walk to clear their bird brains, hers included.

She waved a hello to Alva as he pedaled a dilapidated purple bicycle complete with a wicker basket attached to the handlebars.

"Takin' a walk, sweet cheeks?" he croaked.

"Just trying to clear my mind. I think I'll head up to the gallery."

"Okey dokey," he called, wobbling away down the slope.

The air was cool, on the way to cold, heavy with moisture from the increasing fog as the day wound its way to a close. Her steps took her up the gentle slope out of town.

The gallery was quiet and very closed looking, but the front doors were unlocked. She walked into the front foyer and listened: no sounds of human habitation, so she wandered down the hallway toward the west wing and slowly pulled open the double doors and entered the showroom. It took a few seconds of blinking to accustom her eyes to the dimly lit space.

It hit her like a backhanded slap.

Snatches of a conversation in her own living room came back to her from the far reaches of her memory.

"How does that poem go? The one about the neighbor holding the lamp until her friend's eyes adjust to the dark?"

She had been unable to recall the exact lines of Dickinson's poem before, but now they echoed in her head.

"We grow accustomed to the Dark, when Light is put away. . ."

Kermit said that the person who picked up the plants that night was strong, rough voiced.

"I asked him what he thought about our coastal fog. He said he was getting accustomed to the dark."

The person who picked up the plants that night was Heston Blue all right, only Heston was a woman. A strong woman, with a gravelly voice, who knew Emily Dickinson poetry. The same woman who had sat in her house, reading Phillip's story.

Red Finchley.

Ruth was so completely stunned by her discovery that she did not hear the sound of the doors opening behind her.

"What are you doing here? I saw your birds outside when I was loading up some stuff."

"Oh, I—was—out for a walk." Her mind was racing. " I wanted to see the piece again. *Broken Bird.*" She walked quickly over to the statue, hoping her hammering heart wasn't visible on the skin side. There was an emergency exit door about five yards away.

Red followed along behind her. "What do you think of it?"

"I think it's just wonderful. Really. Wonderful."

Red looked at her closely, cocking her head slowly to one side. "You know, don't you?"

"Know what?" Ruth's mouth went dry.

Red lifted her chin, the kinks of red hair falling around her face like tangled snakes. "You know about me. I can see it in your face; you know it's mine."

Mine? She watched Red's face gazing in almost maternal admiration at the anguished figure of the young girl. Of course. She remembered a fictional scene between Benjamina and Roper.

"You're painting the entire thing in red.". . .

"For your information, Officer, this is vermilion, dusty carmine, and glossy ocher.". . .

"A red by any other name."

A red by any other name would be—a Carmine. Red was that Carmine.

"You're the sculptor?"

She folded her freckled arms. "That surprised you. So that isn't why you look so spooked." Her eyes bored into Ruth's face.

Ruth was suddenly aware of how strong Red looked.

"I see. You figured out the other little detail, too," Red said. "That I am really Heston Blue, Prinn's would-be son."

"I don't know what you are talking about. I'd better go check on the birds."

Red/Heston took a step closer, her lips pressed into a thin line. "You know exactly what I'm talking about. You've been hustling all over this jerkwater town trying to find out about me, haven't you? You had to go digging around Bun Zimmerman. She told you, didn't she? Then I saw you with that photo, and I knew that you were getting close."

"Is that why you hurt my bird? You got scared?"

Red licked her lips uneasily. "I didn't want to hurt him, Ruth. I just wanted to send you a message. It got out of control when he started fighting me."

Ruth took a giant leap. "Is that what happened to Crew Donnelly? Did he find out about you, too?" She edged one step closer to the exit door.

"He was greedy. He saw me delivering a plant to darling Daddy's office and he wanted to know why. He said he would go right to Prinn if I didn't come clean, so I arranged to meet him in town at some ridiculously late hour.

"Do you know what he let slip? That Daddy was smuggling marijuana in the paintings. Can you believe that? The great art curator, a common smuggler. Donnelly figured that I was blackmailing Prinn for a share of the profits. I told him I didn't have a clue about any drugs. I was here on a personal matter. He didn't believe me because I wouldn't tell him who I was. He said he was going to go to Prinn anyway.

"Then he turned his back on me. I can't stand having someone turn their back on me."

Red shook her head slowly from side to side.

"I slammed him on the head with a chisel I had brought for protection. I didn't mean to kill him. At least I hadn't planned to. After I knocked him out, I just slid him into the fountain."

"You murdered him."

"Yeah." She looked surprised. "I guess I did."

"Why did you come to Finny, anyway? Why these mysterious plant deliveries?"

Red pushed a wad of hair away from her freckled cheek. Her eyelashes were so fair they seemed invisible. "I wanted to get back at him. To show him who I really was."

Her words were bitter. "He left before I was born. He never wanted anything to do with us. Even after my mother tried so hard to get him back, telling him I was a boy and all that. He turned his back on us and it drove my mother crazy." The last few words were almost unintelligible. "She doesn't even know who I am now."

"He came to New York. Is that when you saw him for the first time?" Ruth prodded, trying to keep the woman talking as she sidled another step toward the door.

"Yeah. I was floored. Mother told me about him before she completely lost it, so I sort of followed his career. Then one day, out of the blue, he walks into the Shaum. And what's more, my curator assigns me to give him the grand tour and help him select a piece.

"I couldn't get over it. My own father walks right into my life and doesn't have a clue who I am." She laughed harshly. "It was just so bizarre. That's when

I got the idea. I was going to sell him my own work, then confront him at his gallery dedication and force him to admit that I am a pretty awesome sculptor for someone from such pitiful stock. My curator dedicated part of an exhibit to local talent, and my piece was already there, waiting. It was so easy to fabricate some press releases about the great Carmine to pique his interest. He was such a raging egomaniac, I just flattered him about his wonderful eye, and he bought everything I told him.

"It worked flawlessly until I got here. Then I had to go and get fancy." She snorted, rolling her eyes toward the ceiling. "I wanted to torture him. To send those plants to let him know his "son" was sniffing around. Just to see him squirm with guilt. It was stupid, I know."

She was lost in thought. "I was totally floored when Donnelly told me about the weed. I guess I was sort of disappointed in a way at first. I know that sounds weird. I always thought my father was scum, but I figured he really was a great curator, building his own gallery and everything. Then I find out he was padding his bottom line with drugs. I went ballistic. When I calmed down, I figured I would blackmail him into giving me a share in the gallery. I mean, what could he say? His own child an accomplished sculptor who just happens to know Daddy's little sideline?"

"So you ordered two more plants to scare him before you revealed yourself. Mary Jane and Payoff, wasn't it?"

"Yeah. Kind of clever, don't you think? I knew the plant nut would get the message." She paused. "I should have left town, but I had to finish my business with Daddy."

Ruth had only a few more steps to go to reach the door. She swallowed convulsively and continued. "What went wrong? Why did you kill him?"

There was silence for a moment. "I went to tell him. The night of the dedication." Her gaze became unfocused, her hands stroking the wooden rail. "I went to his office on some pretense of a last bit of paperwork. I had put the last fuchsia there earlier. He was so mad when he saw it, his face turned completely red." She giggled. "Anyway, I told him who I was. I told him that I was his daughter. I was the sculptor of his grand 'new addition.'

"Do you know what he did?"

Her eyes riveted on Ruth's, and the older woman could see years of pain and rejection there mingled with a profound rage.

"He laughed. He laughed so hard tears ran down his face. He said my pitiful attempts to get his attention had failed. He said he didn't care if I was his flesh and blood; he would never give me any part in his gallery."

Ruth was silent, imagining the awful scene. A grown woman trying to blackmail her father into acknowledging her existence.

"And things got out of hand again?"

"Yeah. I smashed the plant on that arrogant head. Then I left and ate crab bisque." She began a chuckling that gradually increased in strength and hysteria. "So I guess that means I've killed two people."

She stopped giggling and wiped her eyes. "And I guess that means I have to kill you, too. It's a funny thing about killing people. After you get over the novelty of it, it really isn't all that significant."

Ruth was no longer listening. Her body was taken over by a need that overcame her other five senses. She realized she desperately, unwaveringly, ferociously wanted to stay alive. Her body seemed suddenly bursting with all the feelings she had drowned out for the past two years.

In one brief moment of clarity, she knew that the life God had given her was precious, more than precious. She was more than a widow. More than a lonely person caring for homeless birds. She was loved and she mattered, with or without a husband. God had been there all along, even when she shut Him out. He gave her Jack, He gave her Monk, and she knew He would give her the strength to save herself.

Before Red finished with the last syllable, she flung herself at the panic bar on the door and made it outside. The girl pursued her in a flash.

Ruth was no match in strength or speed for the younger woman. Just before Red reached her, Ruth remembered the crumpled foil package in her pocket. Fingers scrabbling wildly, she tore open the bag of stale Fritos and hurled them into the air, shouting, "Treat!" with all the volume she could muster.

The birds reacted immediately, swarming around her, swallowing up the woman in their greedy haste.

Red tottered for a few seconds, yelping, before she fell over, grunting as she hit the ground. She scrambled to her feet again, but before she could resume her sprint, a voice halted her.

"Stop, Ms. Blue! Just stay right there, hands in front of you." Jack, gun drawn, stood between Ruth, the swarm of birds zinging crazily between the path, and the panting red-haired woman. Right behind him was a frantic Monk. Without taking his eyes off his quarry, Jack addressed a question over his shoulder to Ruth.

"Are you okay?"

Dragging herself upright, Ruth tried several times before the word "yes" actually came out.

"It's a good thing you called the station and told Nate that Heston and Red were one and the same." Jack circled around and cuffed Red's hands behind her back.

The look Red leveled at Ruth was filled with fury.

"How did you know to look for me here?" Ruth gasped, tearing her eyes away.

"A sweet old guy told me you were on your way to the gallery. Right before he asked me for candy," Jack said.

Monk enveloped her in a colossal hug. "Thank God." Tears shone in his eyes. "I could have lost you. Praise God, you're okay."

"Yes," she said, looking into his kind blue eyes. "Praise God."

38

The waves played a taunting game of tag with the birds, beckoning them with foamy fingers as the flock ran back and forth with undisguised zeal. Ruth watched without seeing them, her mind running amok through images of Red's anguish and her own mind-numbing fear the day before at the gallery.

Oddly, she could sympathize with the girl. Red had been dealt only rejection and pain in her life. She could relate to the feeling of betrayal. No, that was unfair to Phillip. It was not betrayal, not really. Just a shock, and maybe a way to know him again for a short while.

Her Sunday headache was gone by the time Monk picked her up for church that morning. It was his suggestion to spend some time at the beach later that day to "clear out her noggin." She watched him chasing after an errant bird. He looked up from his pursuit and waved at her. Praise God for this second chance at life. And perhaps a special man to live it with.

"I just can't imagine what this world is coming to," Ellen exclaimed, stalking up with her boxer at her side. The dog edged menacingly toward the birds until he got a good look at six pairs of hostile yellow eyes glaring at him. He wisely backed away, cowering behind her legs.

"It certainly is a tragedy."

"Here I am, trying to be friendly, giving that terrible woman a visitor's library card. What does it get me? Do you know that little felon checked out three items before she got busted? Goodness knows where they are now. We'll probably never see them again. That's a crime, I'll have you know. And she owes two dollars and sixty-five cents in fines."

Ellen marched off down the beach, mumbling to herself, leaving Ruth shaking her head and chuckling in disbelief. As she wiped her eyes, a blur of running feet sent her birds scattering in every direction.

Jack caught Paul up in his arms. "I thought you might be here."

"Hi, Jack. Hello, Paul." The boy buried his head in his father's jacket.

"Are you doing okay?" he asked.

"I think so. I was just sitting here thinking about Red. You know, I really don't think she meant it personally, trying to murder me, I mean."

"That's a healthy way to look at it, I guess. I'm just glad you are here to talk about it."

She smiled. "Me, too." She looked at the tiny boy in Jack's arms.

Paul began to squirm and contort himself until his father plopped him onto the sand. He ran directly for the gaggle.

Jack yelled over the crashing waves, "Don't chase the birds, buddy. You'll scare them."

Paul had already soaked his sweatpants up to the knees and grimed one elbow when he fell in the soggy sand. He turned to look at his father. Ruth gasped. His cheeks were flushed and eyes dancing as he flapped his own arms in wild delight.

Tears glistened in Jack's eyes.

Gently she squeezed his shoulder. "Let them play," she said.

39

*H*e was rolling code three seconds after the call came in to dispatch. A woman, being assaulted by three males, begging for help before the call was cut off.

Why hadn't he been more conscious of the danger? He'd been so focused on Toulouse that he hadn't anticipated that the thugs who laid him out that day with the bat might come back for Benjamina.

His tires squealed in her driveway, and he pounded up to the front door, his partner Greeney right behind him.

They were just in time to see a man vaulting out the open kitchen window. Greeney took off through the window, and Roper went room by room.

He found her in the guest room. She was lying facedown on the floor in a puddle of blood—her long black hair fanned out around her head and shoulders.

He knelt down.

"It's me, Meena. Roper. Can you hear me, baby?" His fingers were clammy and trembling as he pushed her hair aside and felt for a pulse. "Please let her be alive."

That was it. Ruth had searched every nook and cranny, checked every file on his computer. Nothing. Not a single sentence more. She pulled off the sweater she had not bothered to remove after the beach outing.

She felt an unreasonable anger rising in her chest, and this time she didn't try to stop it. How could he leave her with this unfinished story? This unfinished life? She would never know how it was supposed to end.

Red's words came back to her. *"Why don't you finish it?"*

Why?

Because it wasn't her dream.

Because she hadn't even known it was his.

The loose threads would torment her forever.

Unless.

She sat motionless for a very long time.

As if watching another person, she saw herself reach out and turn on the computer. It glowed a comforting blue, cursor blinking blandly.

How would it end? Would the woman bleed to death on the guest room floor?

Why not? Why not?

People died. Husbands, fathers, lovers. They left suddenly, with no tender good-byes or finishing of dreams. They left behind little children and empty houses. Quiet empty houses for quiet empty people.

The cursor blinked insistently. Why shouldn't Benjamina die and leave him alone?

Ruth thought for a long minute, weighting the scales with sorrow and sweetness. She was filled with a long-forgotten peace, and she knew how blessed she was to be there to make the decision.

She began to type.

He stilled every nerve, every breath, feeling for a pulse. Nothing. He moved fingers slippery with blood ever so slightly. There it was, a ragged, unsteady fluttering, like the beating of tiny wings.

Dimple sat on the rugged boulder alongside the path, studying her toes in the late Sunday sun. She looked almost childlike, except for the swelling around her middle. The noisy squabble was almost upon her before she looked up.

"Hello, Ruth," she said over the cacophony.

Reading lips more than hearing the words, Ruth replied, "Hi. How are you?"

She considered this as the feathery flood swept past her on the way to the pond. "I am well. I wanted to ask you something. I knew you would be walking the birds today here, so I've been waiting for you."

That surprised her.

"I need to go to the hospital for a check of the baby. The doctor is going to take a picture of it. I forget what he said it was called."

"A sonogram, I think."

"Yes, that's it. A sonogram. Don't you think that's amazing? A picture, a portrait, inside. The doctor says you can even see a tiny heart beating."

"That is amazing. A miracle, in fact." Ruth looked sadly at the woman. Amazing—a child within a child. All the same, perhaps it was better to be the product of a mind untouched by cynicism and doubt. But not untouched by grief, she thought, remembering Dimple's wail when Napoleon's body was discovered.

"The doctor said to bring a friend to the appointment and later to go to the classes with me, the birthing classes. Will you?"

"Me?" She was flabbergasted. "But surely you have other friends, other people who. . .your father, maybe?"

"My father says he is not my father anymore. I think that means I must be an orphan with living parents. Can you be that? An orphan with living parents?"

She stared at her, thinking of another young woman whose parents had left her orphaned, too.

"I am alone, Ruth."

She looked at the little round face, capped with curls. It was ridiculous to consider. The woman was a stranger. There was no way she could do what Dimple asked.

A soft whisper of warmth spread inside her. The words of Dickinson's poem came to her again.

"*We grow accustomed to the Dark—when Light is put away—As when the Neighbor holds the Lamp to witness her Good-bye.*"

She thought about the wild set of circumstances that had brought her to this place, this moment. She thought about Dimple's baby. About Red. About Philip. About Monk. About the precious love that never left her.

Either the darkness alters—or something in the sight adjusts itself to Midnight—and Life steps almost straight.

After a long while, she said quietly, "We will go together, Dimple."

With a deep sigh, Dimple stood and straightened her trailing skirt. "Tomorrow, then. We will go tomorrow."

Ruth watched her drift away, the late afternoon sun catching the colors on her dress.

"Yes," she murmured, "tomorrow."

Turning her face toward the sun, she gathered her flock and started on the path for home.

FOG OVER FINNY'S NOSE

1

I t's a toe." Ruth peered into the glass jar on the counter of the Plymouth Frock Dress Shop.

It was one day before the Finny Fog Festival kickoff, and Ruth found herself enduring another fitting for her costume.

Maude snorted. "How would a toe find its way to the middle of the golf course?"

"It's not a golf course—it's a putting green; and Alva says that's where he found it. He brought it here because he didn't know what else to do." Looking into the gargantuan mirror on the shop wall, Ruth added testily, "I know a toe when I see one."

"Hold still, Ruth honey," said Flo from her position on the floor as she pinned some fluttery silver gauze to the back of Ruth's tunic.

Ruth grimaced. The silver tights were giving her a wedgie. Moreover, the putty-gray disks that sandwiched her in between did nothing to complement her pasty complexion, wide shoulders, and robust bottom.

"Has anyone filed a report with the police?"

"You mean a missing-toe report?" Ruth peered at the gray bulb in the jar. The nail was longish and yellow, and a sprig of black hair sprouted just above the severed end.

"I presume that the toe belongs to someone who wasn't thrilled to lose it. Maybe there's a body around somewhere to match," Maude said. "That's what Alva has been blabbering about anyway, and for once I agree with the nutcase."

"Don't even kid about that." The village of Finny, California, might appear to be a tranquil beach getaway, but underneath, Ruth knew, all kinds of passions simmered in a vigorously bubbling broth. "Jack is on his way here. He said to leave it where it is and keep our hands off." The Jack in question was Jack Denny, Finny police detective.

"As if we would take the disgusting thing out of the jar." Maude sniffed. She rubbed the mole on her temple thoughtfully. "I can't believe Alva brought it here anyway. What in the world gets into him?"

Maude's four-foot-eight frame stood ramrod straight, her vertebrae as steely as her constitution. Even her hair was determined, defiantly maintaining its black color in the face of five decades of living. Ruth was again amazed that someone so unyielding had been a contortionist for the circus. Ruth had actually seen photos

167

FOG OVER FINNY'S NOSE

of the mighty Maude Stone neatly folded in half and stuffed into a vegetable crate.

Florence Hodges rose from her kneeling position and rolled up her tape measure. "He said he thought a squirrel might eat it and whoever lost it would need to get an artificial toe. It was thoughtful, actually." She unfurled a pink Kleenex to wipe the patina of sweat that sparkled on her round face and dampened her red hair. The rest of Flo was round, too, and as pliable as a jelly doughnut.

"That man wouldn't know thoughtful if it ran him over," Maude huffed.

"Just because you have issues with Alva doesn't make him a bad person." Flo pointed to the toe. "Looks a bit rough. Could have used some moisturizer, I'd say. By the way, have you tried the new hydrating lotion at Puzan's? It really soothed my skin after I dug up my potatoes."

"I told you it was too early to dig them up," Maude said. "They're going to be bitter."

"Mr. Hodges seems to like them just fine." Flo calmly pulled her hiked-up pants back down over her meaty calves.

"Mr. Hodges would eat anything you put in front of him, including the tablecloth."

"That's because he loves me and appreciates my cooking," Flo said mildly. "And he's never eaten a tablecloth. Once he swallowed a pink birthday candle, but that was purely by mistake." She attempted to gently cram a circle of tinsel onto Ruth's flyaway hair.

Tearing her gaze from the orphaned toe and her ears from the arguing women, Ruth surveyed her appearance in the mirror again. "I look like a giant silver hubcap," she said.

The huge cardboard disks she wore on her front and rear were spray-painted silver and festooned with shiny swaths of metallic satin. Her legs were squeezed into silver tights. She continued to look at her reflection, convinced that a nearly forty-eight-year-old woman had no business being within spitting distance of spandex.

Maude paced like a nervous tiger around the front lobby of the dress shop. "Don't be ridiculous," she directed around a mouthful of pins. "You look exactly like a fog bank, doesn't she, Flo?"

Flo was the unflappable leader of the Finny Ladies Organization for Preparedness, which lent itself to the unfortunate acronym FLOP. She had long ago cultivated a poker face to deal with disasters that visited the seaside town of Finny from time to time. She assisted in crises of all kinds, including the death of Ruth's husband four years ago, and ironically, she'd made the cake for Ruth's wedding to Monk six months ago. She looked solemnly at Ruth in her shroud of silver and remarked, "Maybe we ought to revisit this mascot concept, Maude."

"I agree," Ruth piped in. She had begun to rethink the idea almost as soon as she had been roped into being the character mascot for the first ever Finny Fog Festival. Finny could not boast any luxury hotels or quaint shopping districts, but *fog* the town had in abundance. Maude was the publicity chairperson for the festival and a hard woman to refuse. She had planned a full three days of foggy fun and frolicking. "Why do we need a mascot anyway?"

Maude's bun bobbed indignantly. "Why? Because we need this festival to be a success, that's why. We need something to bring people to Finny. Something to make visitors forget that people have recently begun to get murdered here." Her voice bounced off the racks of hangers. For a tiny woman, she was gifted with the lungs of a longshoreman. "And now with this toe business, we need all the positive press we can get."

Ruth had to admit Maude had a point. The whole mess two years ago had certainly not encouraged much tourist activity for the tiny town. Something about homicidal maniacs on the loose and the fact that Finny had nothing remotely resembling a mall kept people away. Visitors to the California coast seemed more inclined than ever to bypass Finny on their way to better-known stops, like neighboring Half Moon Bay.

"I think the Fog Festival will be enough of an attraction. People will come for the food and the crafts and music. They don't need a walking fog bank." Ruth heard a hint of desperation in her own voice.

"The kids will love it, getting their picture taken with Mrs. Fog. Speaking of pictures, have you taken those shots for the photo display posters?" Maude continued with the tenacity of an aggrieved pit bull. "You've just got to—"

A horrendous crash caused Maude to drop her pins on the shop floor. The three women ran out the front door to investigate.

They were met by a tangle of bicycle parts, human limbs, and little balls bouncing in multihued confusion in every direction. Delicate puffs of feathers floated lazily in the morning air.

"Alva! Are you all right?" Ruth raced to the fallen octogenarian, who lay upside down on top of a battered bike. Underneath the Alva layer was another human figure lying prone on the sidewalk.

"Yep. Right as rain." He clambered to his feet. "I was going faster than a greased pig when Martha flapped right out in front of me, crazy bird. I couldn't see, and I hit that guy. I dropped my bag of gum balls, too."

Alva Hernandez straightened slowly, cramming his fuzzy hat back over the equally fuzzy strands of white hair. After surveying the scene for a minute, he dropped to his knees and started scooping up the gum balls, shoving them in his pockets.

Ruth groaned. Most of her flock of crippled seabirds collected by her late veterinarian husband were content to stay in the backyard while she was away, but after one of the flock was maimed two years ago, Martha had become Ruth's shadow. Martha threw up such a squawk and a holler that Ruth had taken her along to the dress shop. The bird sat contentedly, sunning herself on a bench outside the shop. At least, that was where Ruth had left her, figuring a bird with a missing wing and a partial right foot could not get too terribly far.

Maude and Flo were already gingerly prodding the figure on the cement.

"Alva," Ruth said as she walked carefully between the skittering gum balls to join them, "why were you in such a hurry?"

The man lying on the ground began to grunt and mumble. He was egg shaped, bluntly round at the top, widening to a gentle oval in the middle where his black leather belt was cinched around his jeans. She was mesmerized by his head, completely bald and shining like the glistening flesh of an onion after the dry skin has been removed.

Maude assisted the man in rolling over and sitting up. The front of his head was every bit as dazzlingly white as the back. He might have been an albino except for the pale blueness of his eyes and a faint blush of color in his eyebrows. His glasses sat crookedly upon his nose.

"Wh–what happened?" he said, blinking furiously.

"We are so sorry," Flo spoke up. "It was an accident."

"Yes," Maude said, glaring at Alva. "Some people should not be allowed to operate moving vehicles. Especially *old* people."

A resident of Whist Street, Maude had earned her nickname of the Wicked Witch of Whist. She funneled her wrath to Alva, whom she accused of stomping on her primroses, and to the police, who refused to incarcerate him for the crime. Ruth had witnessed her leap onto the desk of a Finny police lieutenant, where she remained for an hour protesting Alva's mistreatment of her flowers.

"I don't think it was Alva's fault, exactly," Ruth said and then looked down at the stranger's gaze. "I'm awfully sorry. My bird walked in front of him and he swerved into you, I'm afraid."

He blinked translucent eyelashes again. His face was smooth and unlined, round and full like the rest of him. The man was much younger than his bald scalp first suggested.

"Can we help you up, Mr.—?" Flo asked.

Two more blinks. "Honeysill. Ed Honeysill." He offered his hands, and the three women grabbed onto his arms and hauled him to his feet.

"It's a pleasure to meet you," Maude said, pumping Ed's hand vigorously. "I am Maude Stone, chairperson of the Finny Fog Festival, and this is Flo Hodges and Ruth Budge, my assistants."

Ruth felt the bit of discomfort that commonly arose at her continued use of her late husband's last name. It seemed disloyal, somehow, to Monk. They both agreed, however, that no one in Finny would ever get used to a new name for Ruth, and Monk's last name presented certain problems. Duluth. Ruth Duluth, they both agreed, sounded like some kind of carnival ride.

Ed nodded, still dazed.

"Are you sure you're all right?" Ruth asked.

"I think so, yes. I'm fine." He straightened his glasses and blinked before gesturing to Alva. "Is he okay?"

Maude eyed Alva with disgust. The old man's pockets were bulging with gum balls. "He's fine. Alva, you know those can't be sold in the store after you dumped them all over creation. They're contaminated."

"I know. Goin' to keep 'em. Shame to let 'em go to waste."

"You can't chew them," Maude continued ruthlessly. "You don't have any teeth."

Alva's grizzled eyebrows drew together obstinately. "Do so." He removed his upper bridge and plopped it on the bench. It sat on the wooden plank, grinning in ridiculous pink gumminess. "See?"

Ruth suddenly remembered her previous train of thought. "Oh, Alva. You were going to tell us why you were going in such a hurry."

"It's on account of the proctologists."

"The what?" Flo said.

"Them radical proctologists. Saw them up nose, looking to cause trouble. They hate people. Probably searching for one to sacrifice. Maybe a mechanic or a UPS driver or something. Probably where that toe came from."

The three women stared at him.

"What in the blue blazes are you talking about?" Maude hissed.

"A bunch of proctologists. Weird people with lots of gear, heading up nose. One of 'em had a knife. I saw it plain as day." He popped a scuffed purple gum ball into his cheek.

"Proctologists?" Ruth repeated.

The shiny-headed man spoke up. "Er, I think he might be talking about ecologists. I did see a group of people I recognized this morning. They are some sort of ecological gang dedicated to the liberation of the earth or some such thing." He regarded the confused group before him. "They are pretty radical, I understand."

"Oh yeah," Alva said around the gum ball. "Maybe they did say ecologists. Anyway, I'm fixin' to get to the cops afore they off anyone around here."

Maude shook her head. "Pay no attention to him, Mr. Honeysill. He's an idiot, but a harmless one. What brings you to Finny? Did you come for the Fog Festival?"

"In a way. You're featuring some local produce at your festival, and I'm in fungus."

All three women looked at him blankly.

"I market edible fungus to restaurants along the coast. Mushrooms, truffles, and the like. I have a few things to check out here in Finny, one of which is the Pistol Bang Mushroom Farm. I hear they have a booth at the festival."

Alva's head shot up. "That was my granddaddy's outfit," he lisped.

"Oh, really? Are you in the mushroom business?"

"Not anymore. Newspapers now."

"You publish a newspaper?" Ed looked impressed.

"Not publish, deliver." Alva put his teeth back in and mounted his bike. "Gotta go to the store and tell 'em about the gum ball mess before I file my report with the coppers."

"Don't you need to apologize to this gentleman?" Maude demanded.

"Sure. Sorry, Mr. Honeypot. See you around." Alva wobbled away.

Ruth, jumping into the pause that followed Alva's shaky departure, decided to try to make amends for the melee Martha had caused. "Actually, I know the woman who runs the business now. She bought it a few months ago. I could take you there, if you'd like."

"Really?" Ed's eyebrows moved up on his bare forehead like wiggly blond caterpillars. "How about this afternoon? I'm only here for the first weekend of the festival, so I'd like to cover as much ground as possible."

"Okay." She caught a glimpse of a feathery bottom scooting under the bench. "I'll meet you here, say around three? Will that work?"

He nodded. "Is it far?"

"A couple of miles. Straight up Finny's Nose." She bent over and plunged under the bench. The feathery bottom scooted out the other side. Upright again, she noticed that Ed's caterpillar eyebrows had crawled upward again in confusion.

"The big hill. We call it Finny's Nose," she explained.

"It's all part of the colorful history of our quaint little hamlet," Maude interjected. "Ruth is doing a historical booklet on the history of Finny, complete with pictures. She's our photographer, when she's not busy with her other career."

Ed nodded politely. "What business are you in, Mrs. Budge?"

"She's a vermiculturist," Flo said.

Ruth noted the blank look on his face. She would have been surprised to see any other kind of look. "A worm farmer. I operate Phillip's Worm Emporium."

He smiled. "A worm farmer? Now I've never heard of that one before. How do you plant worms?"

"No planting required, just lots of hard work."

"I imagine living on the coast like this generates a good business from fishermen types looking for their bucket of night crawlers."

"Night crawlers reproduce too slowly to do well in a commercial venture. My husband and I farm red worms."

"Incredible," Ed said. "What do you do with them?"

"Most are sold for bait-and-tackle purposes, but I also sell the castings to organic farms like Pistol Bang's, and a few florist shops. The smaller ones I sell to local pet shops. I even supply high schools for their composting program, if you can believe it."

She dove with as much grace as she could muster behind a ceramic pot full of rosemary. Her fingers grazed Martha's wing, but the bird wriggled out of her grasp.

"I'd better get checked in at the hotel," Ed said.

Florence executed a sneaky end-around maneuver and caught the unsuspecting Martha. The disgruntled bird flapped her pewter and white feathers. Flo dusted off the naughty gull before handing her back to Ruth.

"You would never pass an obedience class, you bad thing." The bird tucked her head under Ruth's chin and fell asleep. "Okay, Mr. Honeysill. Three o'clock it is." There was some hesitation in the man's expression. "Is there something else?"

"Er, I was just wondering."

"Yes?" she prodded.

"Why are you dressed like a hubcap?"

Ruth sighed. "It's a long story."

⸺

Ed was as blindingly luminous in the afternoon sun as he had been in the morning. The light shone off his bald head like the coronas that surrounded the saints in old religious paintings. It was startling to see such display of scalp on a man still in his thirties.

Standing with him, arms crossed, was a tall woman with skin the color of the crystallized top on a crème brûlée. Ruth could not decide if she was African American or perhaps of Indian descent. She wore a cropped yellow shirt and low-slung jeans. Ruth didn't think her own stomach could ever be that flat, short of extreme liposuction and an industrial iron.

"Hello, Mr. Honeysill. Did you get settled into the hotel okay?" It was not a luxury hotel by any stretch of the imagination, but on weekday mornings, the nearby Buns Up Bakery whipped up a batch of their delectable apple fritters and the hotel patrons were treated to an onslaught of delirium-producing fragrance. Other than that, an extra roll of toilet paper and a free copy of the *Finny Times* were about the only amenities.

"We're all checked in. Ruth, this is my wife, Candace. She decided to join me on this trip to spend some time on the beach. We live in Arizona, so beaches aren't easy to come by."

The woman smiled and pushed a fringe of long straight hair from her eyes with a French-tipped fingernail. "Pleased to meet you. Where is the beach, by the way? All I've seen so far is fog."

FOG OVER FINNY'S NOSE

"It dissipates in the afternoon usually. The fog, I mean," Ruth said. "I'm afraid our beaches might not be what you're expecting. They're mostly gravel, and the water is only suited for the supremely committed." She had to admit gleaning a certain perverse amusement from the tourists who came to this tiny corner of California expecting to bask in sunshine but instead immediately dashing off to buy sweatshirts. "You have to go farther south to find tanning rays and sunny beaches."

Candace nodded. "I guess I should have checked my AAA manual before I packed my bathing suit."

Ed kissed Candace on the neck and pulled the shirt up around her shoulders. "I'll make sure my next business trip puts us around Pismo Beach."

Ruth noticed a faint look of annoyance steal over the woman's face.

"Well, shouldn't we be getting to the top of this nose thing?" Candace asked.

As they walked, the sun gradually emerged until only faint whispers of fog remained. The slope was graveled and muddy in places. Wild mustard blanketed the hills between clusters of twisted oak and cedar trees. A sweet smell of new blossoms greeted them. Ruth paused occasionally to act as tour director.

"Frederick Finny settled here after his ship ran aground trying to deliver a load of bootleg Canadian liquor. He tried dumping the rum into the water to lighten the load, but that only resulted in drunken crabs."

They continued on until they reached a flat, grassy plateau buzzing with activity. On the perimeter of the area, people were constructing booths and tacking up signs. Farther away, a group of men wrestled what appeared to be a giant sleeping bag. One man fought with a green fabric mountain, while another tinkered with an enormous wicker basket.

Ruth saw Maude deep in conversation with a third man who stood away from the group. Her mouth fell open as she watched her friend finger her hair and giggle. Yes, it was definitely a girlish giggle, emanating from the mouth of the Wicked Witch of Whist.

Maude looked less than thrilled when she noticed the group of three approaching. Eyes narrowed, she asked, "What are you doing here?"

Ruth said sweetly, "Don't you remember? I'm giving Mr. Honeysill a tour of our wonderful hamlet. We're heading up nose. This is his wife, Candace. Candace, this is Maude Stone, chairwoman of our festival. Would you like to introduce us to your friend?"

The man standing next to Maude was, Ruth had to admit, very pleasing to the eye. He had close-cropped blond hair, wide shoulders, and muscled arms straining against the confines of his T-shirt. She thought he looked like Superman, only slightly less inflated.

"Hello. I'm Bing Mitchell. I'm the owner of this balloon company, Phineas Phogg Hot Air Adventures. I'm here to do a few demonstrations for your festival."

Ruth introduced her two traveling companions. Bing took Ed's hand and then his wife's. "I've had the pleasure of meeting Candace before." He gave her a warm smile.

Ruth thought for a moment that it was a shade too warm.

"Are you both here for the festival, too?" Bing asked.

Ed nodded. "Sure are. Just checking out the local fungus. You do look familiar to me. I think we saw you when we were up in Oregon. Isn't that right, hon?"

Candace nodded. "Yes. I got to watch him inflate the balloons while you were networking," she said.

Ruth noticed a tiny stroke of sarcasm in the woman's tone. "Is this where you launch the balloons and land them?"

Maude piped up. "Oh, that's not how it works. It's practically impossible to land a balloon in the same spot it was launched from on account of the wind and all. Isn't that right, Bing?"

He smiled, dimpling. "It's largely improvisation and luck. We can generally land in the right vicinity. Don't worry, we won't take your visitors to Kansas or anything. We're just going to anchor the balloon and send it up so people can get a bird's-eye view of Finny and the ocean."

"Sounds like a popular attraction to me," Ruth said. "We're on our way to tour Pistol Bang's."

He laughed. "I just love this place. It's a slice of life, all right. I really need to shoot some video. It's a hobby of mine." He looked toward the open field where two men in Phineas Phogg T-shirts were starting the long process of inflating the balloons. "Well, I need to get back to work. It was a pleasure meeting you all, and seeing you again, Candace."

Ruth watched Maude follow Bing's departing form, a dreamy expression on her face. Then she realized that the Honeysills had continued meandering their way up nose. She left Maude to her ogling and hurried to catch up with the Honeysills, nearing them just in time to catch the hint of anger in their conversation.

"—just saying maybe there is a way to be in the black without threatening your high moral fiber." Candace snapped out the words like rubber bands.

"Quality and integrity—that's how to build a business, Candy; you know that," Ed said.

"Didn't you ever just do something without thinking of the morality or sensibility of it? Just do it because it feels right?"

He stopped and turned to face her. "As a matter of fact, yes. I married you. Just because I love you, and it feels right." He reached out a hand to her.

Ruth saw her fold her arms across her chest. She almost didn't catch her response.

"Maybe it doesn't feel right to me anymore," the young woman whispered.

Ruth cleared her throat as she caught up. "Well, that was interesting. I've never met a balloonist before. This fog festival is really opening up our world."

Candace nodded faintly, and they resumed their walk.

"How far up nose are we headed, Mrs. Budge?" Ed asked.

"Call me Ruth. It's just another mile or so, but it's an easy walk. I take the birds up here all the time because there's a pond where they can get their water fix."

"You have more than one bird?" he asked.

"Yes, currently I've got seven of the feathery monsters. One was delivered to me from the animal clinic just last week, minus a gangrenous leg and an eye that he lost tangling with a cat. Milton is doing well, but he's going to have to toughen up a bit to get anything to eat in my backyard."

Candace slowed to walk next to her. "Where did you come up with that name?"

"My first husband, Phillip, named all our birds after the presidents. I decided to carry on the family tradition."

"Ed told me that you have a business—Phillip's Farm or something like that?" Candace said.

"Phillip's Worm Emporium. My husband, Monk, and I raise worms for commercial sale."

Candace looked at her as though she were speaking in another language.

Ruth felt the strange intermingled pride and sadness that came when she told people about the farm. The ridiculous name emerged from one of their running jokes. At the same time, she embraced the strength that began to grow when she dove into the silly idea and made it a profitable business. Phillip would be proud of her, and it felt good. She knew he also would be happy she had found a good man to share it with, an amazing man of tireless strength who rubbed her feet and knitted sweaters. She enjoyed, too, the knowledge that she and Monk were partners, each helping the other's business to succeed. Monk embraced his worm-tending duties as cheerfully as she did her work at his catering business.

"I hear you've got someone in the truffle business here," Ed said. "That's a specialty of mine."

"Hugh Lemmon. He's just starting a new venture." Ruth paused for a moment. "How does a truffle grow, anyway? I only know about mushrooms and worms."

"They live in symbiosis with the roots of specific trees. The truffle passes nutrients and water to the tree and in exchange absorbs sugars for itself. The rarity comes in because there are many fungi that can provide the same service to the tree, so they all compete for space in the root system." He scratched his shiny scalp. "The truffle fungus doesn't win out all that often."

"So it's a truffle-eat-truffle world out there?"

"If you're lucky. You can't really weed out competing fungus species, so the only two choices are trying to provide hospitable conditions for the truffle fungus to take hold, or finding them in the wild."

"That's where the pigs come in?"

Ed laughed. "Actually, dogs do better because they don't gobble up the prize."

They emerged from a copse of trees onto the driveway of the Pistol Bang Mushroom Farm. The first building to greet them was a stone structure, with two small panes of glass serving as windows and a thick wooden door. The shingles were covered with a veneer of grizzly moss. A mushroom-shaped mailbox stood on a post off to one side, flowering clematis vines doing their best to smother it.

"Dimple must be in the back. Let's go around and see." She led the way into a burgeoning garden area. An irregular stone pathway ambled hither and yon through a collection of flowering shrubs and spiky grass mounds. The newly emerged sun bathed the whole mélange in dazzling light.

"Oh, it's gorgeous," Candace said. She stooped to finger the lacy white hydrangeas twined over a rough pine bench.

"Dimple is an amazing gardener. She studied botany in college." Ruth was surprised to hear an almost maternal tone in her own words. "She took over the property two years ago and began a complete overhaul, starting with building the tunnel. It's quite an astonishing place, really. Those logs over there standing next to each other are oak, waiting to be inoculated."

The logs stood close together but not touching, like miniature sentries alongside the ten-foot-tall polytunnel. A delicious smell of sawdust and hot wax hung in the air as the threesome made their way to a small workshop on the far side of the garden.

Two heads were bent over the rough workbench, Dimple's long blond curly hair obscuring most of Hugh Lemmon's unruly black mop.

"Hello," Ruth called. "We're here for the tour."

Dimple and Hugh lifted their heads in unison.

"Greetings," Dimple said. "You must be Mr. Honeysill. I'm Dimple. We've spoken on the phone."

"Yes indeed, and this is my wife, Candace. Thank you for giving us the grand tour."

"You are very welcome. This is Hugh Lemmon, a dear friend of mine."

Hugh shook Ed's hand.

"I've heard about you," Ed said over the handshake. "You've got a line on some imported truffles. I'd love to see them. They're sort of a specialty of mine, and I'm always looking for new sources."

"That would be great." Hugh put down the metal gadgets cradled in his long fingers.

Candace spoke up. "What are you two working on in all this sawdust? I thought mushrooms grew in soil."

"Actually, my mushrooms grow on logs. Hugh is helping me with the inoculator." Dimple held up a metal contraption that looked like the leftover parts from a bicycle overhaul.

"Amazing." Ed's eyes shone with excitement.

"Yes. Hugh can do anything related to plants. Do you know he almost produced a blue geranium for his senior high project?"

Candace blinked. "Is that hard to do?"

"Have you ever seen a blue geranium?" Hugh wiped sawdust off of his long neck.

"Uh, no. Come to think of it, I never have."

"Well, Hugh almost did it," Dimple continued.

"What happened?"

"Cutworms," Hugh said shortly.

"What a bummer," Ed said. He picked up the inoculator from the table. "This is excellent, a real work of genius."

"We use it to drill holes into the log and impregnate the wood with mycelium. Then we cap it with hot wax," Dimple said.

Ruth struggled through her winding corridors of memory to recall what exactly mycelium was. Candace came to her rescue. "What's mycelium?"

"Mycelium? Don't you remember, honey?" Ed regarded her with surprise. "It's the mass of microscopic threads, the body, if you will, of the mushroom."

Candace raised her delicate eyebrows. "Now how could I have forgotten that?"

"Most edible fungi are saprophytic." He looked up and noted his wife's narrowed eyes. "Er, they get their nutrients from decaying matter." He fingered the inoculator gently and examined it from all angles. "You know, this is really something. Where did you come up with it?"

Dimple smiled, patting Hugh on the shoulder. "It's his design. He is a whiz at anything mechanical."

A blush crept over the young man's face.

It was not unusual to find Hugh at Pistol Bang's, though his efforts were purely voluntary. Ruth had not noticed before the level of intimacy between Dimple and the young man. Well, why couldn't there be? They were the same age, more or less, and what were the odds of finding a partner with a common passion for fungus?

"I learned a few things to help out my dad. He can grow anything green, but when it comes to machines, he can't figure out how to plug in a toaster." He wiped the sawdust off of his T-shirt. "I'd better be going. It was nice to meet you folks."

Ed called out to his rapidly vanishing back, "Hey, don't forget, I'd like to see your truffles."

Hugh did not turn around as he strode away down the garden path.

"He is very shy, Mr. Honeysill. I'm sure he'd love to show you the truffles," Dimple said.

"No problem. How about you show me some of your operation here and maybe we can talk about some sort of mutually beneficial arrangement?"

She gracefully shook the sawdust from the folds of her skirt and led them to the door. "Let's begin in the polytunnel."

~~~~

Ruth was often struck by a strangely surreal feeling when she entered the polytunnel, like Dorothy landing in the middle of Munchkin country. It was dark and warm inside, the air moist and smelling of verdant forest. She could swear that in the total silence of the tunnel, you could hear the mushrooms multiplying, stealthily adding followers to their fleshy minions.

"Wow," Candace said. She craned her neck upward to see the top of the neatly stacked log towers, all bristling with tiny soft buttons, like millions of infant fingertips. "How many different types of mushrooms do you grow?"

"Just two. Oyster and shiitake. I have the greatest affinity for these two varieties. We understand each other," she answered dreamily.

Candace shot Ruth a questioning look. Ruth whispered in her ear, "She has an unusually close relationship with her plants."

"Incredible specimens," Ed said, poking his round head near the closest log. "So you age the logs outside after you inoculate them, close together but not touching to prevent any foreign mold from taking up residence, I would guess?"

Dimple nodded. "Yes. The mycelia colonize the wood for about two years. Then we shock the colonies by submerging the logs in cold water."

"Shock them?" Candace said.

"It is really very necessary, and not at all unpleasant as it would be to us. In the trials of today are written the fruits of tomorrow."

Ruth laughed, watching Candace try to decide if she had heard Dimple Dent right.

"They begin to pin shortly afterward." She glanced at Candace. "That means sprout, and in about seven days they are just about mature."

Ruth marveled anew at the silky caps of the plump shiitake and the fragile splayed fans of oyster mushrooms. It struck her as magic, growing edible treasure in near darkness. "How many crops can you get out of one log?"

"I am not positive, as this is a new venture for me. These are on their fourth pinning, and I think they have one more burst in them before they decompose."

She expected to hear another wisdom-of-the-ages comment, but Dimple's mental train was derailed by Candace.

"Thanks for the tour. I'm going to admire the garden a little more if you don't mind."

Leaving Ed and Dimple to talk fungal facts, Ruth followed her out.

Both women stood blinking in the sunlight, appreciating the cool breeze on their faces.

"She's an original, isn't she?" Candace said, gesturing to the polytunnel.

"Dimple? Yes indeed, she's one of a kind."

"Is she a local girl?"

"Yes. Her father was a pumpkin farmer in Finny for years before he sold his land to developers."

"What about her mother?"

She hesitated, not wanting to betray anything too personal. "She left when Dimple was a girl. Her father raised her." *More like maintained than raised,* she added to herself.

"Oh. That's too bad. Maybe that kind of explains her, er, originality. Does she ever see her mother?"

"Not since she left Finny twenty years ago." Ruth had to admit that when Dimple asked Ruth to assume the role of grandma to Dimple's daughter, Cootchie, a lot of maternal feelings grew for Dimple, as well. Ruth knew she couldn't fill the hole Dimple's mother had left, but she liked to think she made an adequate stab as substitute mom. A lizard scuttled over the walkway under a clump of yellow lupine. She noticed a slightly bored expression on Candace's face. "Are you enjoying your stay here?"

Candace twisted her long black hair into a rope and coiled it on top of her head, letting the breeze caress her neck. "I guess. To be honest, I'm a city girl. I'm from Miami, so this place is a tad slow for me." She sighed, letting the hair fall around her face. "I think this life is a tad slow for me."

"Do you travel with Ed often?"

"As little as possible. I can't think of anything more boring than visiting mushroom growers and trucking companies all day. Sometimes I come if it's a slow time at the office."

"What do you do?"

"I work for a real estate company," she said, and a spark kindled in her brown eyes. "I'm a receptionist now, but I'm working on getting my license. The man I work for specializes in finding getaways for celebrities. Private places where they have all the luxuries but away from the paparazzi and all that. He's got some really big clients." She rattled off a couple of names.

Ruth tried to cover her blank stare with an interested nod.

"You've never heard of any of them, have you?" Candace laughed ruefully. "I'm not surprised. It seems like this entire stretch of coast is stuck in some kind of time warp."

"Not true. We have running water and the Internet."

"Oh, I'm sorry. That probably sounded condescending. I really enjoy the coast; I guess I just need a faster pace."

And a faster husband? "If you don't mind my asking, how did you and your husband meet?" Ruth found one of the benefits to escaping a murderer a while back was that the experience seemed to remove some of her timidity. She didn't feel the need to restrain her nosy parker tendencies as much since the trauma.

"My father introduced us—can you believe it?" She rolled her eyes. "Mom died when I was eleven, and Daddy believed in the shelter-in-place method of child rearing. He sent me to private schools and kept me away from pretty near anyone except a few family friends until I went off to college."

She bent to pluck a mint leaf. "I went a little crazy with all the freedom. I guess it scared Daddy, because he cut off my tuition and brought me home. I am sure he considered finding me a nice room at the top of a lighthouse on some remote rocky island." She laughed. "Anyway, one of his dear old chums had a son—a nice, responsible sort, good provider, honest, true, a solid fellow. That's Ed. He seemed like a match made in heaven. To Daddy, anyway."

She dropped the leaf and brushed off her hands. "I'm not being fair. Ed is a good man, and he loves me very much. I should remind myself of that more often."

Ruth saw the wistfulness in the young woman's eyes, and she wondered if Ed ever saw it there.

The tunnel door opened, and Dimple popped out holding a double handful of mocha-colored mushrooms. "Ruth, would you mind cooking these up for us so Ed and Candace can have a taste?" She glanced at her guests. "Ruth is the best chef in Finny. She cooks lunch for us at least once a week if we're lucky."

"Thanks for the compliment," Ruth said, taking the velvety bundle. "I'll be right back." She heard Ed asking Dimple for Hugh's address as she headed for the kitchenette in the back of the office building.

As she heated the olive oil and sliced the mushrooms, she thought about what an unlikely pair Candace and Ed were. She was lovely, hip, and craved a fast lifestyle. He seemed more at home with fungus than females. As the oil reached the sizzling point, she slid in the chunks of shiitake and minced garlic. In went a hefty tablespoon of butter, and the mouthwatering aroma soon drove thoughts of the Honeysills out of her mind. She couldn't resist taking a taste as she slid them onto paper plates and put the plates on a tray. Heaven. The mushrooms were meaty with a delectable smoky flavor.

Tray in hand, she marched back out to the polytunnel just as Ed and Dimple emerged, stepping from darkness to day. Candace settled onto a bench, and they joined her.

Dimple's smile vanished as she looked over Ruth's shoulder, and a bewildered look crossed her face. Ruth turned. There stood a well-manicured woman with perfectly coiffed hair.

"Everyone," Dimple said with a quiver in her voice, "this is Meg Sooner. She's my mother."

2

At the stroke of seven o'clock, both halves of the Finny marching band stepped off to begin the Fog Festival parade with a rousing march. However, due to a series of miscommunications and the thick blanket of fog, the brass and percussion sections started at the Save Mart, marching in a southern direction. At the other end of town, the drum major led the wind instruments and flag bearers northward from the town square after he tired of waiting for the missing brass and percussionists. The musical hordes met up at the Buns Up Bakery, where half the group about-faced to resume a more unified advance down Main Street.

Ruth and Cootchie sat in lawn chairs that Ruth had parked on the sidewalk just after sunup. Early birds get the best parade seating. Actually, she awoke well before the birds with a vague sense of unease. She tossed and turned for some time before medicating her anxiety with strong coffee and a fat cinnamon roll. Even after the cholesterol slam, she couldn't shake the strange unsettled feeling as she kissed her sleeping husband and headed out.

The source of her unease didn't hit her until she saw the fire engine rumbling down the street behind Lou Fennerman's Cub Scout troop. The strobing lights, the plaintive wail of the siren. Today was Friday, March second, the five-year anniversary of Phillip's death.

At first she had counted the loss in weeks and months. She remembered past springs with a vague sense that she was a different person with each passing year. After Phillip died, she felt as if she were aging in dog years, growing exponentially older with every change of the calendar. She was a stranger even to herself, drowning in a profound grief. Until God threw her a flotation device.

It came in the form of a wafty woman named Dimple Dent. Somehow Ruth had managed to keep everyone else out with polite refusals and business. Jack Denny found his way in briefly, the night he asked for her help finding the dog that was the only link to his bereaved son. But no one else. No one until Dimple fell into her life.

Imagine a bizarre, fluttery woman asking a stranger to help raise her child.

Imagine a forty-something stranger saying yes.

And then came Monk, another answer to a prayer she didn't even know she'd prayed. Perhaps it was odd to house feelings of loss for a dead husband and love for a new one at the same time, but life was full of bittersweets. It had taken her

182

many decades to learn that.

Now that Dimple's mother was back, she wondered if it was time for more bitter. The woman had appeared out of nowhere to upset the precarious balance of her life. Ruth shook the thought away. Now was not the time for melodramatics.

The copper-haired Cootchie squealed when she saw her mother and flapped her little hand in a greeting. Dimple carried a tray laden with glistening white mushrooms of every size and shape and sported a felt fedora with PISTOL BANG MUSHROOM FARM on the brim. She handed the parade goers samples of mushrooms in white paper cups. Most of the recipients gazed suspiciously at the tidbits.

Ruth laughed as Dimple kissed Cootchie and handed them both cups of satiny oyster mushrooms before continuing on her way. Only Dimple would think of passing out mushrooms like party favors. She had even gone so far as to suggest that Ruth pass around pouches of worms to advertise Phillip's Worm Emporium.

Ruth had politely declined.

"Bye-bye, Mommy!" Cootchie shouted.

Dimple blew her another kiss.

It was a short parade. The fire engine followed the Cub Scouts. The Daisy troop trailed behind the engine. Interspersed here and there were some locals on horseback and representatives from FLOP dressed in matching yellow slickers. Ruth would have to inquire about the significance of the rain gear. It seemed to her more appropriate for monsoon season than a fog celebration.

The pageant ended with towering librarian Ellen Foots leading a small brigade of tiny tots dressed as puffy gray clouds. Most of them carried a book in their chilled hands, and two carried a banner proclaiming "READING IS FOR EVERYONE!"

Ellen peered out from underneath her wild maelstrom of dark hair and fixed her glance on Ruth. "You'd better get up nose. You're supposed to be changed and ready for photos in thirty minutes." She marched on by. The young children struggled to keep up.

"Okay, Cootchie. Looks like Nana's not going to get out of this. Let's find your mommy so I can keep my appointment with humiliation."

Before they left, she turned and looked down the street at the departing parade. The thick blanket of fog swallowed up the sparkling costumes and cheerfully obnoxious music, sucking them into a clammy void. It was odd how the fog could absorb life, surround it and smother it as though it had never existed.

How strange that she had never noticed it before.

Fifteen minutes later, Ruth tugged vigorously at the silver tights riding up into uncharted territory. She waddled her way to the open field where most of the festival activities were grouped. She stopped for a minute to watch the Coastal Comet Acrobats juggle fruits from their perches on the shoulders of the less fortunate Comets. A voice of doom cut through the hubbub.

"Ruth, it's about time." Maude still wore her yellow slicker and rain hat. She looked like a homicidal Gorton's Fisherman. "I've got a line of kids here waiting to have their picture taken with Mrs. Fog." They had decided after several pointed comments from informal focus groups, notably the children enrolled at library story time, that Ruth would not pass for a Mr. Fog.

"I'm here, with my best cheesy smile," she said, waving gamely to the children.

"Where's your hat?" Maude demanded, stabbing a short finger at the top of Ruth's head.

"If you mean that silver tinsel stuff, I can't wear it because it tangles up in my hair." She felt she had presented her case very well.

Apparently there was no room for a soldier's opinion in this woman's army. "Fortunately," Maude said firmly, "I brought some extra. That first trailer over there is the festival headquarters. Go get some tinsel and I'll put it on you. Hurry."

Thinking how nice it would be to throw a bucket of water on the Wicked Witch of Whist, Ruth trudged over to the long rows of trailers parked on the periphery of the field.

She yanked open the door and shoved her disks inside. It took a minute for her eyes to adjust to the dimness. The small trailer was crowded on one side with a full bed and on the other with a tiny sink and microwave. Several empty bottles of Perrier were lined up neatly on the top of the microwave.

"Well, I guess the festival staff have been enjoying themselves," she murmured grumpily.

As she scanned the room looking for anything tinsel-like, she noticed a man's athletic shoes standing neatly in the bottom of an open closet. They were the expensive kind, with cushions of air in the transparent heels and no visible laces.

"Who in the world would be wearing those?" She just managed to finish the sentence when she heard voices outside the door. They didn't sound like Maude or Flo or Ellen or any of the other Finny Fog Festival soldiers.

"Oh!" Her hands flew to her mouth as it dawned on her that she was in the wrong trailer. In a moment of panic, she squeezed herself into the closet with the athletic shoes and pulled the door closed. A conversation floated through the gap, voices muffled but slightly familiar

"This is wrong, Bing. I shouldn't be here." The woman's voice was deep and trembling.

"Just relax, hon."

Ruth heard the sound of liquid pouring.

"Here," the man said above the clinking of glasses. "We both know why you came."

"We can't see each other anymore," the woman said quietly.

Ruth felt her calves cramp up, courtesy of her bent-over position. She tried to figure out where she'd heard the female voice before.

"How am I going to get out of this mess?"

From Ruth's closet vantage point, she could see only the sandaled foot of a woman with shell pink toenails. A still-functioning lobe of her brain registered that the sandals were quite lovely, turquoise leather with tiny silver and black beads threaded onto the slender straps.

The voices continued to escalate. *This is not my business,* Ruth thought to herself. Normally she didn't mind eavesdropping, but doing so from someone else's closet was unforgivable. She stuck her fingers in her ears and tried to recite the Girl Scout pledge in her head.

On my honor, she thought frantically, *I will try—*

"We can't do this," the woman's voice shrilled.

To serve God—

The volume got more intense until it eclipsed the pledge altogether.

My country and mankind—

"Why can't you take no for an answer?" The shell pink toes stamped the floor.

—And to live by the Girl Scout law, she thought as loudly as she could.

Just then the door slammed.

As she attempted to silently stretch out her leg muscles, she could see a sliver of the window next to the front door. The top of a woman's head disappeared down the front steps.

"Women," the man muttered.

The door slammed again, leaving her in silence.

After an eternity, Ruth extricated herself from the closet. Her knees were shaking, and she made her way from the trailer area as quickly as her voluminous fog costume would allow.

Cheeks burning, she reached the open field at the edge of the foggy activities. This time she felt grateful for the heavy mist that shrouded her from prying eyes until she could stop trembling.

Maude greeted her with a camera in her hand and outrage in her eyes. "Where in the world have you been? And where is your hat?"

"Er, I couldn't find it."

"Oh, for crying out loud. Never mind, we'll take the pictures without it." She bustled the waiting crowd of three into a tidy line. "Are you catching something, Ruth? Your face is flushed."

"Must be all the excitement." Several yards away, a hot air balloon was fully inflated.

FOG OVER FINNY'S NOSE

Thanks to Maude's ruthless management, the children were all photographed in under an hour. By then, the Phineas Phogg balloon was aloft, floating upward with graceful ease, the rainbow stripes vivid against the blue sky. Ruth could see the propane flame strengthen as a man fired the burner. At first she thought it was Bing, but the hair color was wrong.

Ed Honeysill's wide face peered over the side of the basket as he waved to the crowd gathered below. Then he straightened and shaded his eyes with his hands, taking in the view.

As they drifted farther aloft, three men below monitored the ropes anchoring the balloon to the ground.

Ruth craned her neck to watch until her sinews began to protest. Suddenly a terrific bang cut through the crowd noise.

A dark spot raced its way through the sky, trailed by a stream of light and smoke. It ripped into the side of the balloon and tore a hole in one of the bright green stripes before exiting out a red one.

The balloon rocked violently to one side and then the other before the nylon burst into flames. The men on the ground stood in dumb surprise, holding the ropes slack for a moment before they snapped into action, desperately trying to haul the balloon earthward. One of the two figures in the basket leaped, falling directly on top of the inflated jump house and rolling off onto the grass.

Suddenly the burning side of the balloon disintegrated. The basket rocketed to one side. The second man flew out of the basket and flailed to the ground, landing with a thud at the edge of the clearing.

Ruth closed her mouth with a snap. "Call 911!" she yelled. She yanked the giant disks off her torso and started to run.

Maude struggled to dial and run at the same time.

They reached the spot and wheezed to a halt, panting and uncertain. The second man's limbs were splayed out in a windmill fashion around his body. The back of his head lay exposed, like a shiny white mushroom emerging from the soil.

It became sickeningly clear that there was no life in Ed's body, but Ruth forced herself to check for a pulse on the wrist closest to her.

Maude clicked off the phone and looked at her. "Is he dead?"

She nodded, swallowing her revulsion. Maude nodded back. "Okay. We'll keep people away until the authorities arrive." Though Maude's voice was steady, Ruth could feel a shock and horror radiating out of her that mirrored her own feelings.

A woman with stylish and familiar turquoise sandals came flying up to them. She stopped short when they moved closely together to prevent her from seeing beyond them.

"Candace," Ruth said gently, "I think you'd better sit down."

J ack rode with Nate and Mary to a hole-in-the-wall up the coast called Wings
and Things. Not the classiest ambience, but free nachos during the pre-lunch
hours. He went with reluctance. It didn't seem particularly important for
the Finny police detective to celebrate his thirty-fifth birthday. The night before,
the babysitter helped his almost-four-year-old son, Paul, bake a lopsided cake,
decorated with sugar letters spelling out HAPPY BIRTHDAY ADDY since Paul had
consumed one too many *d*'s.

Jack didn't make much fuss about his birthday, maybe because his wife had
died two days before his thirty-third. The sweater she intended to give him hung
unworn in the closet next to his dress uniform. He remembered her holding it
against herself when she didn't know he was looking, checking it for size. For
some reason, he couldn't wear it or give it away. But sometimes, very late at night,
he would smell the fabric, trying to catch the faintest whisper of her scent that
had long ago evaporated.

It seemed important to his colleagues to buy him lunch on his birthday, so
he plastered a smile on his face and allowed himself to be shanghaied. Besides, it
gave them a chance to skip town for a few hours after the parade took place. Yolo,
the newest officer, was left to maintain a police presence at the precinct.

The place smelled like wet carpet and stale cologne. Jack nursed a club soda,
not only because they technically were still on duty, but because he'd long ago
decided that drinking and raising toddlers did not complement each other. Mary
Dirisi was trying to teach fellow officer Nathan Katz how to throw darts. Nate's
throws wound up rattling to the floor, or they got stuck in the plant next to the
men's room door. Jack wondered how anyone with that kind of aim passed the
qualifications on the police firing range. Nevertheless, although Nathan couldn't
throw a dart worth a hoot, he was one of the few people Jack would trust with
his life.

Jack's thoughts strayed to the toe. The lab could contribute nothing more
than to confirm that yes, it was indeed a toe from an adult male human, and
it had been severed within the past two days. So far no one hobbled forward to
claim it, and the rest of the body formerly attached to the toe had not been found,
either. It was weird, but in Finny, weird was not uncommon. As a matter of fact,
since the festival had begun to attract people from everywhere, weird was getting
positively commonplace.

FOG OVER FINNY'S NOSE

Jack had spent the morning listening to Alva Hernandez spouting a tale about a bunch of murderous proctologists. Alva was convinced there was some sort of plot brewing at the top of Finny's Nose. The last time he filed a report with the Finny police, it had to do with the Loch Ness monster, which he was dead sure had holed up in Tookie Newsome's trout pond for the winter.

In the name of community outreach, Jack had driven upslope with Alva and examined the area. There was nothing much to find, only a few bits of wire on a grassy plateau bordered by an army of cedar and sycamore trees. Nothing much, but something did bother the detective about it. It didn't seem like the doings of the local kids looking for a place to make trouble. Something about Alva's story felt foreign, alien to the seaside town.

His thoughts wandered back to the present. With his back to the wall, he noticed a small woman a couple of tables over, sipping a glass of water. She was interesting—short dark hair, the tiniest hands he had ever seen, a dreamy look on her freckled face. She was not beautiful in the magazine-cover sense, too strong a chin, too round a face. Her sandal bobbed up and down over her crossed knee, as if she was tired of waiting for someone. A man in cowboy clothes sauntered up to her.

"Come on, Jack. Relax already. This is supposed to be a celebration, remember?" Mary plopped down next to him with a plate of steaming nachos. "I've given up on this idiot." She gestured to an approaching Nate. "He's the worst dart player on the planet."

Nate huffed into his mustache. "Yeah, well, I play a mean game of Candyland."

As the father of five girls, including five-year-old triplets, Nathan Katz was a man of infinite patience and an absolute whiz at dressing Barbie dolls, tiny stiletto heels and all.

"You've got to start beefing up your testosterone. You spend too much time surrounded by women," Mary said. She flipped her braid over her shoulder for emphasis.

"It's true," Nate agreed. "I'm pretty sure even our goldfish is a female. It's got kind of girly flippers."

"Goldfish don't have flippers," she said as she reached for a gooey nacho.

"Spoken like someone who needs a pet in their life."

"I'm considering getting one."

"I hear spider monkeys like strong female companionship," Nate said. A slug of melted cheese dropped onto his shirtfront.

"I was thinking more along the lines of canine, you toad."

Jack listened to their banter with one ear and simultaneously eavesdropped on the conversation at another table. The cowboy was making himself friendly.

"Actually, I'm waiting for someone, but thanks anyway," the small woman said, putting down her glass.

The guy, complete with pointy boots and enormous belt buckle, laid a smooth hand on her table. The creases in his plaid shirt labeled him more familiar with department stores than the wide-open range.

"You're much too good-looking to be left alone here," he breathed. "Some guy doesn't know what he's doin' leaving you by yourself."

"Thanks for the attention, really, but I am not interested in company. Why don't you go find another 'gal' to talk to, okay?" She smiled as she said the words.

"Awww, you don't really mean that, darling."

Jack put down his club soda and pushed out his chair a fraction. Mary and Nate grew quiet as they picked up on his tension.

The cowboy grabbed hold of her slender wrist. "Come on, honey, I'll show you how to loosen up." He pulled her out of her chair and yanked her to his chest.

By the time Jack and the others made it to their feet, the woman had kneed the drunken man in the groin, whacked the back of his head as he bent over in pain, and shoved him to the ground. Then she stood with a sandal planted firmly above his collar, her little painted toenails bright against the man's sweaty neck.

Bending down close to his face, she said calmly, "The next time a woman says no, maybe you should consider the possibility that she really means it." She picked up her purse, dropped a few bills on the table, and walked out of the bar.

Jack, Nate, and Mary stood in openmouthed astonishment.

"Man," Nate said.

"Man, oh man," Mary echoed.

Jack's legs seemed to work of their own accord. He was on his way to the door, following the woman, when his pager began to vibrate. Checking the screen, he muttered under his breath and took out his cell phone.

After a minute he said, "We've gotta go. Problem at the festival. Thanks for the birthday lunch, guys. Time to get back to work."

They paid the check and headed out the door as the humiliated cowboy slunk back to his buddies.

Out in the parking lot, there was no sign of her in the swirling fog.

4

If Cootchie was born under an unlucky star, it certainly didn't show on the surface.

She was a wild-haired, button-nosed preschooler, with chubby legs constantly engaged in a gallop. She would have been born into a privileged life if her wealthy grandfather had accepted her paternity. She should have been the object of adoration of her maternal grandmother if the woman hadn't abandoned her own child decades before. As it was, she was the daughter of a man who had been murdered before she showed up on a sonogram, the child of a mother prone to speaking in fortune cookie vernacular.

It was still a subject of wonder to Ruth that she had ever become part of this odd woman's life. She finally concluded that it was due to a stark vulnerability both women experienced at the same time, the murder of Dimple's lover, and Ruth's complete loss of identity and purpose after her beloved husband's death.

That and the murderer running rampant in Finny. Somehow, out of the chaos, God brought them together.

And now the chaos had returned, or so it seemed. Ruth's muscles ached from the wild sprint to the crash site the previous day. Poor, poor Ed. She felt queasy just thinking about the way his life abruptly ended. She had not slept well, tossing and turning, even after Monk prepared her a middle-of-the-night cup of tea.

The early morning was cold, heavy with fog. Cootchie twirled madly in Ruth's backyard, hands up in the air as the gulls circled around her and stabbed orange beaks into her pockets, looking for goldfish crackers. "Whee! Whee!" she squealed.

Somewhere in mid-twirl, one of the gulls succeeded in knocking the girl over, causing her to scrape her knee. She put her chubby fists to her eyes and whimpered. Ruth shooed the birds away and sat down with Cootchie on the porch steps.

"Did those mean birds knock you over, Cootchie? Let Nana Ruth see that scrape." She found the knee free from blood and gave her a hug, relishing her sweet-smelling hair and the chubby arms around her neck. The child's cheeks were cold from the morning chill.

She flashed back to the day Cootchie was born. It had been a frantic drive to Eden Hospital in the middle of the night; at the hospital, Dimple was stuck in a nonproductive labor that lasted three days. By the time the baby was finally coaxed into the world, poor Dimple was mentally and physically depleted. A chipper nurse handed the new mother a form to fill out for the birth certificate. Ruth could still see the nurse's frown as she handed it back to Dimple after scanning the paper.

"Are you sure the name is, er, spelled correctly and everything? That's just the way you want it?" the nurse had asked.

Dimple nodded wearily and fell asleep.

It wasn't until several hours later that baby Cootchie was returned to her mother's room and Ruth learned the infant's name.

"Dimple, uh, is Cootchie a family name?"

"No, it just came to me," Dimple said before falling asleep again.

Ruth joggled the baby for an hour, walking her in circles around the room, before she noticed the package of Cootchie Coo diapers on the counter at the foot of Dimple's bed.

It's a good thing they weren't Poopy Poo diapers.

She pulled her mind away from the fond memories. The girl was asleep with her first two fingers jammed into her mouth. Her hair collected in wild, sweaty spirals the color of a rusty nail.

Could anything be more soothing than holding a sleeping child? Ruth could vaguely remember rocking her only son when he was an infant. Bryce had been a crabby infant, colicky, the doctors said; but he'd put up with her tentative mothering skills just fine. As he grew, his independent personality was a source of confusion to her. Most of the memories from his early school years were of him pushing her away, rejecting her affection, physical and otherwise. She did not understand why their relationship was so distant, why it had always been that way. At this point, she was pretty sure she never would.

"He needs to go his own way," Phillip had said many times. "Some people are like that."

Bryce had finally landed in Chicago and now lived a separate life, married to Roslyn, with no children. Except for the obligatory phone call on her birthday, she never heard from him. Bryce had revered his father, but even at Phillip's funeral he was unable to express his feelings of loss to her. They stayed safe, discussing practical matters and the weather until he flew back home after the memorial service.

Cootchie stirred and blinked her eyes. "Where's Papa Monk?"

"He's at work, sweet pea. We'll see him later." She wished he were home. They had stayed up late into the night discussing the disaster. The police said it was a flare gun that took the balloon down, and Ed along with it.

She still had the images burned into her retinas: a haggard-faced Candace collapsed on the ground, Bing bent over her. The whole scene replayed itself in her mind.

She recalled Alva watching the proceedings with a puff of blue cotton candy clutched in his fist, and a wide-eyed Hugh arriving posthaste to the crash site with a host of other festivalgoers.

Then there was an infiltration of police and fire personnel that seemed to drift in and out of focus. They were focused intently on their individual duties, unaffected by the horror around them. Jack Denny talked into a radio as Nathan and Mary staked an area around the gore with yellow tape.

Jack had spoken to his officers in a low tone. "Check out the insurance situation—beneficiaries and such."

Monk materialized next to Ruth and wrapped her in a massive hug. "Are you okay? I heard a horrendous bang, so I locked up the store and came running." He looked into her eyes. "Is that a body over there? What happened? Are you hurt, honey?"

"No." The worry in his gray eyes filled her heart. She leaned her head for a moment into his garlic-scented embrace. Her words trickled out, faltering, uncertain. "There was a flash of something across the sky. A shot of some sort, and then the balloon caught fire and just sort of dissolved. They tried to get it down, but they couldn't do it in time. Ed Honeysill, he—fell out of the basket." She watched the paramedics load Candace up in the ambulance. "He's dead, I'm pretty sure. I can't believe it. It happened in a blink."

His embrace tightened. "What a thing for you to see. I never should have let you out the door this morning." He rested his cheek on the top of her head.

Bing approached then, his muscular arms folded against his broad chest. "It was a flare gun."

"How do you know?" Monk asked.

"I know a flare when I see it," he snapped. "It was fired at pretty close range, too. Maybe a couple hundred feet, I'd say." Bing shook his head. "That's an eight-thousand-dollar balloon. Just look at it."

"Yes," Monk said, "and a pretty big inconvenience to the passengers, not to mention the witnesses."

Bing looked at him sharply. "I almost lost one of my guys, too. He landed on the jump house. Just sprained an ankle and didn't flatten any kids in the process."

Jack had joined them at that point. "Mr. Mitchell, we're going to need to talk to you about what happened. Would you mind giving some information to Officer Katz over there?"

Bing strode off.

"Are you two doing all right?" Jack asked. When they nodded, he added, "I'm afraid this means a trip down to the office, Ruth. Can I schedule you for an interview tomorrow, maybe?" His brown eyes were soft.

She nodded.

Nathan walked up with two plastic bags in his rubber-gloved hands. "That's all we've got."

One bag held a bulky gun with a wide barrel and the other a twisted metal eyeglass frame.

Jack asked Monk to escort Ruth home.

Tucked into Monk's strong arm, she had made her way downslope. As they walked, a thought froze in her brain. If the flare was indeed fired at close range, then someone in Finny's swirling fog was a murderer.

And he was close.

Very close.

The thought made her shiver once again.

Now, as Ruth sat on the porch step trying to puzzle out who would have wanted to kill Ed Honeysill, Cootchie awakened and interrupted her reverie.

"Go park? With Paul?"

"We can go to the park, honey, but Mr. Denny said Paul has to go to the doctor today. Maybe we can play with him tomorrow. We can go for a little while before I take you home. Can you help me feed the worms first?"

Ruth took a minute to slide the solar panels off the eight-foot-long concrete beds, ignoring the ache in her left calf. Phillip had come up with the vermiculture idea, figuring it would be a unique business venture and a good supplement to the birds' diet of protein pellets and whatever they could lay their beaks on. He'd finished constructing the beds and ordered a starter supply of worms before he came across the fact that worms need to be kept in a cozy sixty-to-seventy-degree range. Hence the construction of the solar panels, which served not only to keep the worms happy but to keep the birds out. Worms were pretty easygoing critters unless the temperature got too hot. Only once did Ruth have to worry about the wigglers overheating. The weather in Finny topped one hundred about as often as Comet Hale-Bopp whizzed overhead.

Cootchie held the box of litmus strips while Ruth did a quick reading and found the pH to be a healthy 7.1. She shoveled a modest quantity of bird manure onto the top of the beds, and the child danced along beside her sprinkling the top with shredded paper.

She replaced the solar panels and grabbed her travel kit. The cameras and extra film it used to contain had given way to boxes of organic carrot juice, edamame, and toddler-sized overalls. She laughed to herself. "What a difference a year makes."

Beams of light made ghostly patches of sun and shadow but did nothing to dispel the chill from their fingers and toes as they walked. It was a gentle downhill trudge from Ruth's cottage to the park in the center of town. The sun was trying to burrow its way through the fog when they arrived. Along the way, they were treated to the sight of rolling seas of yellow mustard flower and patches of spiky artichokes that grew wild along the walking trail. Ruth was once again grateful for the rippled foothills that formed an uneven border almost completely around the rear of the mountain called Finny's Nose. They were just too topographically uncooperative to allow for much building development in the shadow of the nose.

She could hear the faraway strains of festival music. Finny Park was a small grassy area plopped without much planning or forethought in the town square. Blowing on her hands to warm them, she led Cootchie to the steps of a rickety slide. The girl climbed to the top of the steps and shouted, "Mara!" pointing to a spot behind Ruth.

It was indeed Martha, the escape artist bird, hobbling up behind her, quick in spite of the missing wing. "How do you *do* that?" Ruth muttered.

Martha had been given to Ruth's husband with a plastic six-pack ring embedded in her neck feathers, which had no doubt made her easy prey for the cat that maimed her. Phillip surmised that she had gotten tangled up in it as a very young bird and it began to slowly strangle her as she grew, leaving her, if not brain damaged, then certainly with a heavy dose of goofiness. It was theoretically possible that Martha could fly if she had the gumption to try. In her five years with Ruth, she never had.

Martha darted around the bench, attempting to rifle through the travel kit, when Hugh Lemmon approached carrying a cardboard box. The shy, gangly man nodded his head in a hello; then in mid-nod, he tripped over the leg of the park bench. He caught himself, but not before the contents of the box tumbled to the ground.

"Are you okay, Hugh?"

His eyes widened in alarm as Martha scuttled around, chasing the rolling black objects.

"Stop!" he yelled, leaping after her. "Don't let her eat those." He made it to the bird before Ruth did, grabbing her around the neck and prying the blob from her mouth. "Hold on to her until I pick them up," he said.

He poked around in the grass and under the bench, gently retrieving the items from where they had landed. Hugh had an impressive beaklike nose and looked not a little birdlike himself as he bobbed up and down on skinny legs. His chin and forehead sloped away from his prodigious schnoz as though to escape to lower altitudes. When he finished, he walked back over to Ruth, cradling the box in his arms.

"I was thinking about the balloon crash instead of watching where I was going," he said.

"Did any of your, er, whatever those are, get broken?"

He held up one of the black lumps and inspected it. "No, doesn't look like it. No harm done, I think."

"Hugh, I've just got to ask. What is that? It looks kind of like—"

"Poo poo!" Cootchie screamed gleefully from her perch at the top of the slide.

Ruth reddened, but she could see the child's point. Resting between his long fingers was a warty, lopsided wad, the color of the chocolate pudding she would never admit she'd eaten for breakfast.

Hugh laughed. His prominent teeth winked in the sunlight. "I know it's not that attractive to most people, but to many it's more mesmerizing than gold. It's a *Tuber melanosporum*. Otherwise known as a black truffle."

"Really? I've never actually seen one. I only recently learned on the Food Channel that the underground ones are different from the chocolate ones."

"The candy variety got their name because their small round shape resembled the tuberous ones."

"Tuffles, muffles, muffins, tuffets," Cootchie sang from the top of the slide.

"Where did you get them?" Ruth asked.

He gazed at the truffle fondly. "These beauties came from southwestern France."

"That's a long way to go for a little morsel."

"That's true. Oh, they've begun to farm truffles here and there, Texas and Oregon, but they are not of the same quality. Wild truffles go for up to four hundred fifty dollars a pound."

Ruth's jaw dropped. "A *pound*?"

Hugh nodded. "You betcha. I'm working out a deal with a supplier in France. He sends me as many pounds as he can find, and I sell them to the West Coast market. They're starving for the really good truffles here."

"Is that profitable?" Ruth asked after recovering use of her mandible.

"It will be. People here are willing to pay an extra fee for not having to deal with buying and shipping the truffles themselves. This is going to be a real moneymaker. I've even got a deal pending with a small charter plane company to fly them up and down the coast for me, and I've almost got my Web site up and running."

"That's really great. What exactly does a truffle taste like?"

"It's unlike anything you've ever experienced." Hugh pushed his glasses farther up his nose. "It's kind of musky, with a taste of nuts and ozone."

Ruth failed in her attempt to imagine what a nutty ozone flavor would be like. "Your father must be excited about it."

Hugh lived with his father, Royland Lemmon, who operated a very successful organic farm on the outskirts of Finny, specializing in field greens. Ruth had met him years before when she'd gone with Phillip to assist his examination of Royland's pig, Noodles. Noodles tipped the scales at eight hundred twenty-three pounds. Prior to the veterinary exam, she cocked her piggish snout, widened beady brown eyes, and fell deeply in love with Phillip. She dogged his every step, snuffling at the back of his hands when he left them within range and generally showering him with enough piggy adoration to bring a blush to Phillip's cheeks.

Hugh placed the truffle back into the box. "Dad's not involved. He doesn't understand moving with the times. He'll be growing arugula for the rest of his life."

"His arugula is wonderful, though," she said. It was, too. Pungent and crisp with a peppery bite. Nothing ozonish about it.

"Yes, it is. I can't argue with that. Dad's offering free tours of the farm for Fog Festival attendees this weekend. If there are any."

"Hopefully there will be a good crowd, in spite of the, er, accident."

Hugh nodded. "Yeah. Who would have imagined that happening in Finny? A guy killed right in front of everybody."

"I know." Ruth shook her head. "I still can't get over it. One minute Ed is alive, and the next. . ."

"He's spread all over."

She swallowed hard and nodded.

"Down, peese." Cootchie could never quite be convinced to slide down the slide once she got to the top.

"I've got to get this young lady home to her mother. I'm glad my feathered friend didn't cause any damage. I'll be eager to see your Web site when it's on its feet. Give my love to your father. And Noodles, of course."

Ruth lifted Cootchie down. "And good luck with your truffle business."

Hugh waved and continued on his way.

As Ruth packed up the child and her belongings, she noticed a stray black lump nestled at the edge of grass and sand. "Looks like he missed one."

Martha looked disappointed as Ruth slid the truffle into the pocket of her sweater. "At four hundred fifty dollars a pound," she said to the bird, "you're sticking to onion rings."

The twosome made their way from the park to Dimple's house. It was still chilly, but sunlight stabbed through pockets in the fog, dazzling their eyes as it bounced off the white stucco buildings of downtown. Ruth loved the intensely green leaves of the old trees that poked up in between the buildings. The sweet smell from the far-off fields of ornamental flowers drifted in and out of her consciousness. She gazed at Vern Rosario's stand of trees on the distant horizon. Sad to think that he would be cutting them down soon to accommodate his new barn.

A half hour later, Ruth and Cootchie were walking past the Dent mansion on their way to Dimple's cottage. Though the cantankerous Buster Dent refused to acknowledge his daughter and granddaughter, he allowed them to remain in the small home that Dimple's mother had decorated before she ran off with a visiting investment banker. Buster could not forgive Dimple for her affair with Finny's curator anymore than he could forgive his own cheating wife.

He was a hard man. Ruth had a feeling he had been that way even before his wife's desertion. Now he was wealthy from selling his vast acres of pumpkin farm to a developer. But despite his wealth, he was alone, as far as anyone could tell. Occasionally, though, as she herded Cootchie home, she had the uncanny feeling that someone was watching through the upstairs window of the patriarch's home. Someone who watched the little girl as she trotted happily along, filling her pockets with feathers and pebbles. This feeling kept Ruth from despising Buster completely. She knew what it was like to watch life from the outside in, to see love and warmth through an unforgiving pane of separation. She reminded herself to add him to her prayers.

And Meg. She should pray for Meg. Why did the thought of Dimple's estranged mother make her stomach knot?

After a deep breath, she knocked gently and ushered Cootchie into the bright kitchen. "Dimple," she called. "We're home. Are you here?" She waited, fearing she would hear Meg's voice. After a moment, she relaxed. Dimple's mother wasn't there.

She heard Dimple call from somewhere in the back.

"Just a minute," Ruth called back. "I can't hear you. Let me get Cootchie her snack and I'll be right there."

She poured a glass of pomegranate juice for the child. Once again the thought occurred to her that Cootchie must be the only almost-two-year-old in the world to have pomegranate juice and soybeans for a snack.

Ruth walked down the hall and through the sitting room, stepping over boxes of dusty books and papers stacked dizzily on the Persian rug.

"Where are you, Dimple?" she called again. A faint voice answered, but she could not make out the words. "What?" she yelled.

Cootchie trotted out into the sitting room, lugging a tattered copy of her favorite book. "Read, peese."

"Oh, all right. I guess your mommy is busy with something. Climb aboard." Ruth hauled Dimple into her lap. A few muscles complained as she did so.

The girl settled in her lap and opened the slim volume.

"So from the mould, Scarlet and Gold,
Many a Bulb will rise
Hidden away, cunningly, from sagacious eyes."

Cootchie's unusual reading habits began almost from birth. It had simply never occurred to Dimple that a young child might prefer hearing about a large purple dinosaur or a cat in a striped hat rather than the great works of the romantic poets. When the pediatrician advised her to read quality books to her baby, she took the suggestion to heart, immediately setting out to the bookstore and returning with *The Norton Anthology of Poetry,* as well as the *Iliad* and the

Odyssey and *The Mill on the Floss* for good measure. Ruth was hoping they could delay the George Eliot novel until Cootchie was at least four. That would give her time to read the CliffsNotes.

After a few more verses, Cootchie noticed the stacked boxes and toddled off to the pile and returned momentarily with a dingy leather-bound journal.

"Read, peese."

"What is this? I'm not sure Mommy meant for us to read this, honey. How about some Frost?"

Undeterred, the girl continued to hold the book out. "Read, peese."

She sighed. "All right, but if this is Faust, I'm out of here."

The writing was a lovely, loopy script, faded in places but for the most part legible.

> *August the 3rd, 1923*
> *Trouble tonight. A big bear of a man came in from San Francisco, one of Slats' boys. He said someone jumped him and stole the cash bag. No good will come of this, I know. Anyone who crosses Slats, does so at his own peril.*

Ruth's voice trailed off after the first sentence, leaving Cootchie disgusted enough to hop off her lap and sit down to play with blocks.

> *I got a new piano man for the dining hall. He does some nice ragtime tunes. The showgirls like his playing and folks enjoy the music, which gives me a chance to sell more Apple Bettys.*

"What in the world is this?" Ruth said aloud. Was it really a journal from 1923?

Suddenly a head popped out of the ceiling.

"Greetings, Ruth."

Ruth launched the journal into the air and yelped. The upside-down face trailed a blond curtain of hair. "What are you doing up there?"

"I'm sorry," Dimple said from the attic opening. "You said you wanted some old pictures of Finny, so I ventured into the attic. Do you want some iced tea?"

"Do you have any up there?"

"No. I would need to come down to find the tea."

Humor was hit or miss with Dimple. "Don't bother."

"No bother. A friend is a raft over the troubled waters of life."

"Er, yes. Well, don't launch the raft; I'll just get some myself."

Ruth chuckled as she headed toward the kitchen, pondering the wisdom of a woman who used to write fortunes for a living. She filled a glass half full of dark brown tea and added water. Dimple's homemade tea blends produced a liquid that could only be likened to drinking potpourri. Extra water and lots of ice made it more palatable.

Dimple materialized in the kitchen. She brushed her hands on the front of her long skirt. "Tell me about your day, Ruth dear," she said.

"Maude called to tell me crowds are really thin today at the festival. Probably due to the accident."

Dimple nodded. "What a tragic thing. Grief is a heavy weight to bear."

Ruth wondered how heavy it would be for the widowed Candace. "I managed to avoid any morning festival duties, so Cootchie and I played with the birds, and then we went to the park. We saw Hugh there. Did you know he's going to distribute his truffles all along the coast?"

She blinked. "Yes."

I discovered that Martha has a taste for them, too. But about this journal." She held the volume up for inspection. "What is this? Where did you get it?"

"From the attic. You said you wanted some authentic Finny historical documents for the booklet you're creating. I think these are authentic. They were in amongst some old photos that belonged to Grandpa Dent. I've never looked at the things before."

Ruth opened the book again. "The date is 1923, and the name on the 'Belongs to' page is Pickles Peckenpaugh. Does that name ring a bell?"

Dimple shook her head. "What is the book about?"

"From what I gather in the first entry, the woman runs a restaurant."

"That wasn't uncommon during Prohibition. Many were run by women. It was one of the few ways they could achieve economic empowerment."

"How do you know all that?"

"I know a few things besides how to grow mushrooms."

"Do you mind if I borrow this journal for a while? Ellen Foots gives presentations on Finny history to the schoolkids. Maybe I can ask her about it."

Dimple rubbed her nose. "Be my guest. Thank you for watching Cootchie for me today."

"My pleasure." Ruth watched the child peering at the carpet fibers through a magnifying glass.

"We're going to go pick some nettles for stewing after her nap."

Stewed nettles. Ruth nodded, wondering how Cootchie would be accepted in life by other children who didn't know nettles from noodles. By now, Ruth had learned not to ask.

"Okeydokey. Do you need anything else for Monday's birthday party?" It seemed strange to be celebrating anything on the heels of Ed's death, but Cootchie was looking forward to her special day.

"No, thank you. We're going to make the cake together tomorrow. Jack has volunteered to barbecue. It's his birthday celebration, too."

It remained to be seen if Jack would appreciate a hefty piece of carrot cake with tofu frosting, or even if he'd be able to spare any time away from work to eat it. "I can't believe she is going to be two. Where did the time go?"

Dimple smiled dreamily. "Time is our most patient friend and restive enemy."

When would Dimple run out of fortunes? She'd been away from the fortune cookie business for two years, and so far no sign that the stream of Zen wisdom was drying up. Ruth tried to figure out a way to bring up the subject she had been dreading. "It was a surprise to see your mother."

"For me, too," Dimple said.

"So are you—? How are things going? Between you?"

Dimple cocked her head to the side, green eyes thoughtful. "About as well as they should, I think."

"Oh." Ruth wanted to ask questions, to clarify, to ease her mind. Instead, she waited to see if she would add any more pertinent details.

"Would you mind bringing a bucket of castings if you've got any? My zinnia bed needs coddling now," Dimple said.

There was to be no mind-easing at this time. "Sure thing. Chips and dip and worm castings. I'll be here around six on Monday." She looked at her watch. "Oh boy. I've gotta get to the shop to help Monk."

Ruth kissed Cootchie and hurried down the walkway, eager to get home. She had a feeling Pickles Peckenpaugh had a lot more story to tell.

5

Monk whistled cheerfully as he hauled a twenty-pound sack of risotto rice over the threshold of Monk's Coffee and Catering. Ruth admired the easy way her new husband lifted the heavy bundle. An ex-navy man, he was built like a walk-in freezer. Everything from his head down to his booted feet was roughly squarish as opposed to her rectangular form.

He had a temper, and definite opinions where patriotism and morality were concerned. He was so very strong, yet so completely tender with her. He treated her like a delicate crystal glass that might chip at any moment. His devotion still amazed her.

At the moment, his cheeks were flushed with exertion. "You look like an angel," he said.

She laughed and kissed him before wiping up the puddle of milk on the stainless steel counter. "Are you sure you aren't just saying that to keep me on for the afternoon shift?" She manned the counter for a few hours to provide assistance for the caffeine-deprived folks arriving late in the day to participate in the festival.

"No way, ma'am. I never could resist a woman wearing an apron."

She blushed, feeling like a silly schoolgirl. Or maybe, she thought, like a newlywed. "You know that sort of remark can get you into trouble now. Women don't like to be seen in aprons these days. It's not very politically correct."

He nodded forlornly. "Don't I know it. They all want to be toting pistols or pagers. It's a strange world."

She knew that he did not comprehend the whims of the younger generation, particularly the female members. He was sometimes rendered speechless by the teen girls who came into the shop with belly rings exposed and profanity spilling from their glossed lips. She wondered what Monk would think of Candace.

"And getting stranger all the time." She shuddered, thinking about the balloon crash.

He took hold of her hand. "How are you doing with, you know, the crash? Feel any better?"

"I was hoping I would snap out of it and find it was all a terrible dream." She shook her head. "I still can't believe it."

"Me neither. I can't believe we're still going forward with this nutty festival after what happened."

FOG OVER FINNY'S NOSE

"Nothing short of nuclear war would keep Maude from fulfilling her festival dreams," Ruth said as she refilled a thermos with cream. "I just hope nothing else happens. I'm still wondering how come no one has found the rest of—you know—what was attached to the toe." The thought made Ruth feel squirmy.

"Can't begin to guess. I hear the police have had the dogs out sniffing down nose, but they haven't found any more digits to speak of." He put a tray of scones into the oven.

"Have you heard anything about a gang?"

"No." He closed the oven door with a bang. "Only what Alva has been going on about. Of course, I've been preoccupied thinking about Bobby."

She smiled. He was so excited that his niece was coming to visit. It had been all he could talk about recently.

The bell over the door tinkled as Detective Jack Denny entered.

"Morning, Monk. Hello, Ruth," Jack said before plopping into a scarred wooden chair. His face was stained with fatigue, and there was a sprinkling of dark stubble on his chin.

"Long day?" she asked.

"Uh–huh, and it's not over yet."

Ruth wanted to tell Jack about what she had overheard in the trailer before Ed's death, but she didn't want to be a gossip. *It's not gossip,* she reminded herself, *when a murder is involved.* Perhaps Candace had already told him. No, she didn't think that was likely. She decided she would tell the detective. She was ready to grill him right then about any further developments relating to the balloon crash, but the exhaustion on his face took the wind out of her nosy sails.

He looked as tired as she felt.

Aside from Ed's horrible death, another kernel of unease settled into her stomach, refusing to be dislodged. The feeling, Ruth was forced to acknowledge, was jealousy, pure and simple. She had spent a restless night contemplating the sudden arrival of Dimple's long-absent mother. The most irritating thing about Meg Sooner was that she appeared to be a genuinely nice person, from the few bits she'd gleaned from Dimple since the woman arrived. The feelings that rose in her own heart were far from nice. Those "deeds of the flesh" seemed to unroll in her mind, starting with jealousy and working through strife, disputes, and the illustrious envy.

The Post-it in her pocket bore her scribbled reminder: *Fruit of the Spirit.*

Love. Joy. Peace. Patience. Kindness. Goodness. Faithfulness. Gentleness. Self-control. Since Meg had showed up, Ruth didn't feel as though she was bearing much fruit at all, especially in the kindness and goodness department. She pushed the image of the small, well-manicured woman out of her mind.

"I've always maintained these long days would be so much easier for people if they didn't start so early," she said.

"Amen to that," Jack said. "It doesn't help that the coffee machine at the station is on the fritz again. I'm beginning to think the thing goes out every time someone sneezes."

"Well, if you don't want any latte, frappé, mocha thingy, I can help you with that," she said, grabbing a styrofoam cup. "I only know how to pour it straight from the pot."

"Perfect. Straight from the pot, to go, please."

Monk called over her shoulder, "How about a side of banana muffin? I made some fresh this morning. There are still a few left, I think."

Jack closed his eyes. "Coffee and carbohydrates. Sounds like a balanced meal to me. You don't have a pound of sausage to round it out, do you?"

"I'm afraid not," Ruth laughed as she prepared his order. "Paul and Cootchie had a blast last week. The birds are still lying around the yard this morning, too pooped to function."

"I hope he didn't hurt any of them."

"You know very well my birds are the toughest pets on the block." She poured out some steaming coffee. "All the neighborhood dogs and cats are petrified of them."

"Yes." Jack's brown eyes sparkled. "I remember having a knock-down-drag-out with one of them on your front lawn. I'm still not sure which one of us won."

Jack and Ruth had become friends after the sudden death of his young wife, Lacey. Following the tragedy, his two-year-old son had become selectively mute, refusing to communicate with anyone except their wild, rambunctious dog Mr. Boo Boo. Somehow Paul made a sort of connection with Ruth's flock of gulls that had begun to draw him out of his shell. Paul was not verbose by any means, but at the age of four, he was beginning to string a few words together. Either Jack or Louella, Paul's nanny, brought Paul by as often as possible to play with the birds and with Cootchie Dent. What with a yard full of gimpy birds, vats full of worms, and a little girl to play with, the Budge backyard was better than Disneyland.

As Jack inhaled coffee vapors, Monk finished unloading the last of his deliveries.

"Wonderful. She's here," he said, glancing out the window. "I wanted both of you to meet my niece. She's going to be helping me out for a while until these two weeks of Fog Festival stuff are over." He held the door open for a tiny dark-haired woman.

Jack knocked his cup of coffee onto the floor. He stood up, a dark patch of coffee soaked into the knee of his pants.

Monk planted a kiss on the woman's cheek and enveloped her in a smothering hug. "This is my favorite niece, Bobby Walker."

"I'm your only niece, Uncle Monk."

"No matter. You'd be my favorite even if I had a passel of them. I'd like you to meet Ruth, my amazing wife and the woman who is keeping me afloat."

Ruth clasped Bobby's hands in her own. "It's so wonderful to finally meet you."

"And you, Ruth." Bobby smiled back.

"And this fella with the coffee all over himself is Jack Denny, one of Finny's finest," Monk finished.

The woman turned her curious black gaze on him.

Jack recovered himself enough to reply. "Actually, we almost met before."

Bobby tilted her head. "We did?"

"Yes. I was at a place up the coast, Wings and Things. You were there waiting for someone, I think, and a fellow with a cowboy hat wanted to get chummy."

She thought for a minute. "Oh, right. I was waiting for this big lug, as a matter of fact." She stabbed a thumb at Monk.

Monk frowned. "That's the day my van had a flat. I couldn't reach you on your cell. I must have called fifty times and it said 'not in service.' " His eyes rounded in horror. "Did some guy harass you?"

"I don't think you've got anything to worry about," Jack said. "The lady seems to be able to handle herself."

"I'm a park ranger, and I've driven a school bus in east LA, among other things. I'm pretty hard to scare. I don't remember noticing you. Oh, wait a minute. Were you watching a man play darts? A guy who couldn't hit the broad side of a barn?"

"That would be my buddy Nate Katz. His incompetence with darts is legendary." He took some paper napkins from the counter and knelt to mop up the spilled coffee. "Are you vacationing here?"

"Sort of an imposed one. The park service is insisting we take our vacation days whether we like it or not. It seemed like a good time to hit the beach. Besides, I love the coast this time of year. Lots of fog and everything coming back to life."

"Where are you staying?" Jack asked.

"At the hotel. Uncle Monk wanted me to stay at the cottage, but three's a crowd."

The front doorbell tinkled, and a crowd of workmen came in. They were noisily discussing the plans to tape off a field for festival parking purposes. Bobby laughed, taking an apron from a peg on the wall. "So much for vacation. Okay, Mrs. Budge, you'd better show me the ropes posthaste."

"Please call me Ruth," she said.

Jack grabbed his refilled cup, thanked Ruth, and left the store.

Bobby joined Ruth behind the counter and readied the insulated cups while Ruth patiently explained to the customers why they couldn't have their gourmet coffee concoctions.

"I'm sorry, but we don't have anything that requires steamed milk or organic tea leaves. We've just got coffee, decaf, and coffee, caf. Oh, and there's cream and sugar, if you like."

A young man was the last in line. He wore a green bandanna and baggy brown trousers that ended before they could provide any warmth to his ankles. A slender braided ponytail snaked down his back. "So I can't get a chai tea here?" A coiled silver ring winked on the finger he used to shove thick glasses farther up his nose.

"No, but you can have a chocolate dipped éclair that will really toot your horn," Ruth suggested.

"Does it have animal products in it?"

"Uh, well, eggs, butter, and milk, among other things. No lard, right, honey?" Monk nodded at her over his steaming pot of what would become soup.

"Are the eggs from free-range chickens?"

"They're from Tookie Newman's farm," Monk called out. "They've got a chicken coop, but most of the time he just chases them all over creation when they squeeze through the fencing. Does that count as free range?"

"Never mind," he said. "I'll just have some hot water and a tea bag," he said. "Here's my mug." He slid a dented tin cup across the counter.

Bobby shot him a raised eyebrow.

"I'm not into polluting the earth with polystyrene," he said.

"Okay," Ruth said as she gingerly filled the cup with hot water while Bobby grabbed a tea bag. "Are you in town for the Fog Festival?"

He counted out a handful of coins. "Sure am. I'm one of the vendors, art and crystals, mostly. My name's Rocky Bippo." Ruth noticed a heavy silver chain looped around his neck under his smock.

"Fantastic," Ruth said, marveling that the festival was attracting exotic people from all over, people who drank chai tea and traveled.

"Have you gone to many festivals this year?"

"Yeah, this is our fifth this season. See ya around." Rocky took his tea and left.

Bobby picked up a box of chocolates lying on the counter behind the cash register. "Afternoon snack?" she asked, smiling.

Ruth chuckled. "Though I have been known to consider chocolate a meal unto itself, this is actually to serve as someone's salary. Have you met Alva Hernandez?"

"No. I don't think so."

"Well, you will, if you stay for any length of time. He's the town newspaper boy. He's helping me exercise my birds the days I'm working a long shift here."

Bobby nodded. "Actually, Uncle Monk told me about the birds. And the worms." She added slyly, "He told me about you, too. I've never heard him sound so happy."

Ruth blushed. "Oh, well, anyway, Alva lives with Mrs. Hodges."

Bobby looked confused. "Why doesn't he live with his parents?"

FOG OVER FINNY'S NOSE

"His parents? Oh, Alva is eighty-five years old. I forgot to mention he's the only senior citizen newspaper boy in Finny. He lives with Mrs. Hodges in exchange for fixing anything electrical. He's a genius that way. His family used to own the Pistol Bang Mushroom Farm." She restacked a pile of paper napkins. "Alva doesn't have much use for money, but he has a completely insatiable sweet tooth. He drives a hard bargain, too. This week it was a box of soft-centered chocolates, no nuts, no caramels."

Bobby laughed and looked out the front window. "Uh, Ruth? I think that might be your bird sitter running up the sidewalk right now."

Sure enough, Alva was racing along the walkway holding on to his baseball cap, with a cluster of honking birds at his heels.

"Incoming!" he shouted as the swarm of birds overtook him, careening in round-eyed terror to escape two dogs slobbering on their flippered heels.

Running along behind them was a gangly woman holding their unattached leashes in one hand and desperately trying to grab the slowest dog's collar with the other. "Stop, Maxie!" she panted, frantically shaking strands of silvering hair out of her face.

Bobby and Ruth ran out of Monk's Coffee and Catering trailing behind the leash lady, looking, Ruth imagined, like the parade of characters from some Brothers Grimm fable.

They all came to a confused stop at the fenced back lot of Luis Puzan's grocery store. All of the birds except Rutherford managed to squeeze under the chain link fence, leaving their feathered companion attempting to squeeze his wide bottom underneath the rail to join them.

Alva clung to the fence about three feet above the sidewalk, looking down anxiously on the two dogs that growled below him. His denim-covered seat hovered a fraction above the dental range of the snarling animals.

The lady stopped. She spoke in hushed tones to the dogs. Deftly she clipped the leash onto the wiry-haired one and edged her way toward the enormous white dog who was inching up to Rutherford, teeth bared.

Ruth reached out to stop the dog, fearing that Rutherford would have a complete cardiac incident any second.

"Stop!" the woman hissed. "Don't touch him." Her pale eyes glittered with unguarded emotion.

Ruth backed up.

The woman continued to talk soothingly to the dog. She touched him gently on the rear end and worked her way upward until she snapped the leash on his collar. The huge creature turned to face the woman and buried his bony head between her knees, whimpering.

"I'm sorry," the woman said, straightening and turning to Ruth. "I didn't mean to yell at you. Peanut has been through a lot, and he has to be handled carefully. I was just getting them out of their crate when the birds went by, and they took off before I could leash them."

Ruth nodded, her heart still pounding. She picked Rutherford up and handed him to Bobby. "Alva, are you okay? I think you can come down now."

The man grinned and hunkered down from the fence. "What a thing. I haven't moved that fast since old Pauley's bull took a liking to me."

She helped him climb down from the fence. "I am Ruth, and this is Alva Hernandez and Bobby Walker. Alva was walking my birds for me. None of them can fly, so they have to have their daily gadabout."

"I'm Evelyn Bippo. I'm with the Dog House group. We're showing our adoptable dogs at the Fog Festival." There was a faded Dog House logo on the front of her stained sweatshirt.

"Bippo? I think we just met another Bippo," Bobby added.

"Rocky? He's my brother; he's a vendor. Actually, we just finished the Sand and Surf festival down south. There are three or four of the vendors that travel together year-round. I'm always looking for a gathering to show the dogs, so I go to as many as I can."

Bobby looked at the dog, who continued to cower between Evelyn's legs. "What's his story?"

Evelyn shook her head. "Peanut is a wonderful, gentle dog," she said, a sharp edge in her voice. "He was adopted by a terrible jerk who tried to make him a guard dog by beating and starving him. Now he's completely broken, and he only listens to me."

Bobby's eyes filled with anger. "That's awful."

"Yes, it is. Just look at his ears." She widened her legs slightly so they could see the pink stumpy edges where the ears should have been. "The awful man thought since Peanut is part pit bull, he would look fiercer with cropped ears. Whoever did it nearly chopped them off."

Ruth felt sickened.

"I'm sorry," Evelyn said. "I am really not the militant type, but I just can't believe someone could do that to a gentle boy like Peanut."

She scratched her nose with a long, calloused finger. "Anyway, I am really sorry my dogs gave you a fright." She nodded apologetically to Alva. "And are your birds okay?" she asked Ruth.

"They seem to be fine, just winded." Rutherford had recovered enough to poke through Bobby's apron pockets.

"Okay. Well, I'd better get these guys back to camp. It was nice to meet you. I'll see you again, I'm sure."

They watched Evelyn gently lead the dogs away. Peanut stayed so close to her leg that she stumbled every few feet.

"Well, sweet cheeks," Alva said to Ruth, "I'm afraid this adventure is gonna cost you. Next week, I'm raising my fees to fudge."

Ruth stopped on her way to Royland's, the package of worm castings tucked under one arm and a bucket of her finest wigglers clasped in her cold fingers. The empty lot where Ed Honeysill died was quiet in the predusk. The hot air balloons were packed away except for the one taken as evidence. The rest had vanished along with the fog. In their place was a towering stack of Coastal Comets in street clothes, practicing for their performance that would commence in the morning. Canvas-covered booths lined the rectangular field, sporting signs advertising various culinary delights, from fried artichoke hearts to falafel. The scent of popcorn lingered in the air. It seemed incomprehensible that a man had plunged to his death in that very field. A few stragglers were milling about, bags clutched in their hands, and there was still a line at the baked potato booth.

Ruth plodded along past the swaying tower of Coastal Comets until she noticed Maude in the far corner of the field, banging hard on a black metal box.

Alva stood next to the woman, a purple container in his hands. "Yer just going to bust it," he said.

"Give me the fog juice, you old geezer," Maude snapped.

Ruth approached reluctantly. "What in the world are you two up to?"

"Hi, Ruth," Alva said as he wiped his nose with a piece of fabric that looked suspiciously like a necktie. "I was on my way to the bakery to see if they got any leftovers when this nutzo started banging on that thing. She's going to bust it."

"What is it?" Ruth asked before Maude could explode.

"It's a fog machine, for your information. I've just got to put in the juice and it will work perfectly. I'm testing it out for tomorrow."

"A fog machine?" Ruth was incredulous. "Maude, why do we need a fog machine? This is Finny, remember?"

"Our naturally occurring variety is a little sparse, if you haven't noticed. The rotten stuff has been thick as pea soup the entire week, and now it has deserted us in our hour of need. I want to make sure this thing works. It will enhance the atmosphere," she said, pouring liquid into a spout. "Where are you going? The crowds might pick up any minute now."

"I think it's pretty much done for the day, Maude, but in any case I've just got to run a quick errand. I'll be around if you need me." Ruth watched in wonder as Maude connected the machine to an extension cord and pressed the button.

Nothing happened.

Maude rattled the cord.

Still nothing.

Grumbling, she knelt down in front of the black box and pressed again.

A burst of white smoke fired out of the machine, and Maude fell over backward, her skirt flying over her head and baring her Vanity Fairs for all the Coastal Comets to see.

The most airborne of the Comets laughed so vigorously that he slipped, causing a domino effect until all eight of them landed in the soft dirt.

Alva roared with glee as he trotted away.

Ruth saw the wisdom in a hasty getaway as well, once she saw that Maude was not hurt, and she continued on her way to Royland's farm.

As she walked onto his property, it saddened her to see the sign indicating that a portion of Royland's beloved farm was for sale. She knew it killed him to part with even an inch of his land, but it had become too much for one man and an unenthusiastic son to manage. Royland was one of her best customers. She supplied him with five buckets of worm castings a month to enrich the soils on his farm.

Ruth easily could have had one of the local teens run the bucket of worms and castings up to Royland's place. They would do anything for pocket money. But the trip was a way to escape the chaos of the festival and a means to delay her inevitably uncomfortable conversation with Candace. She walked past cottages and small fenced pastures, a small white bucket in each hand, trying to think of ways to break her news to the woman.

She arrived at her first stop to find a gaggle of young adults seated on a rickety picnic bench in front of Lemmon's Organic Greens. At harvesttime Royland hired extra help to handpick his precious crop of arugula, spinach, and endive. She recognized Bert Penny and a few of his compatriots from the junior college, and Lizzie Putney, a twenty-year-old local girl whom Ruth had known for years. They were enthusiastically discussing the recent murder.

"Oh man," Bert said. "I heard it was gruesome. The guy fell out of the basket and hung from the edge, all screaming and everything, until he fell. Splat!"

"Gross, Bert," said Lizzie. "Did you actually see it?"

"Nah, I was helping with the parking," he said. "But I heard all about it from Dan."

"Hi, Mrs. Budge," Lizzie called, jumping up to give her a hug. "What brings you here?"

"I'll be busy at the festival tomorrow, so I have to get my errands done today. I see you all have been putting in a hard day's work." She motioned to their hands, stained green from nails to knuckles.

"Yeah," said Bert. "But Mr. Lemmon pays us okay, and we get dinner, too."

"Sounds like a good deal to me."

Royland and Hugh approached carrying shallow wooden crates. Royland greeted her warmly, putting down his load to take the two buckets from her hands. His voice was lightly peppered with an Argentinean accent.

"My supplies. Wonderful. I'm working on something new. Come and see."

He led the way to a greenhouse filled with tiny seedlings in peat pots and complex networks of irrigation tubing. On a workbench nearby was an empty basket and piles of loamy soil. She breathed in the wonderful scent of well-tended earth.

"I'm going to try hanging herb baskets. Thought the city folks might be interested in something they could keep in a small patio area. I was thinking thyme, maybe some arugula, and chervil. I want to make sure the whole thing is organic. You think your worms are up to the challenge?"

"I think they'll help your pots out tremendously as long as you don't overwater them."

"No problem. Easy on the water."

They left the humid space and walked back outside. Nestled next to the greenhouse was a split-rail pen containing a gargantuan, spotted pig.

"Hello, Noodles," she called out.

The pig dashed excitedly to the fence to sniff her hand. About six inches away from the fence line, she stopped, cocked her head, and wheeled around in retreat.

"I know. You thought Phillip was with me, didn't you? When are you going to stop looking for him?"

Ruth had the sudden realization that she had stopped thinking about Phillip every day. When had that happened? It had come so gradually she hadn't noticed. She felt a strange pang of guilt, but it vanished quickly. Thoughts of Phillip did not crowd her mind, because she was busy with her life with Monk. One did not replace the other, she thought with wonder. Both men occupied different places in her psyche. *Our God is an awesome God,* she thought.

Ruth and Royland chatted for a bit about the recent events as they walked.

"My helpers are having a tough time keeping their mind on their work. All this talk about the murder."

They watched the group on the picnic bench. Hugh stood apart from the rest, fiddling with some tubing. "I wish he'd try a little harder to fit in," Royland said. "I think that Lizzie would treat him okay if he would just talk to her. He's just not much for social things."

Ruth nodded, thinking that Hugh looked mighty comfortable clanking around Pistol Bang's. "Maybe he hasn't found the right girl yet." Apparently Hugh's father had no idea his son had developed quite a relationship with Dimple.

"At twenty-two I don't know what he's waiting for," he said, retrieving his crate. "I was married by then and working toward buying my place here."

"I think it was an accident, someone shooting as a joke or something," Lizzie was saying. "What do you think, Hugh?"

"Oh, I dunno." Ruth saw him duck his head.

"Did you see it happen, Hugh?" Bert asked, eagerness painted all over his face.

"I saw the balloon crash, but I didn't see the guy fall out," Hugh said.

Bert sighed with disappointment. "Bummer."

"Okay, you slackers," Royland announced, "back to work."

Yes, Ruth thought, there's no more avoiding it. Time to visit the grieving widow.

⌇⌇⌇⌇

A short while later, Ruth was just about to tap on the door of room number 7 when she heard voices from inside.

"Look, I know it's been rough on you, but you're free now."

"How can you do this to me?" Candace's voice cracked. "He's dead, for pity's sake."

"You didn't love him, Candace. It's not like you lost the great love of your life. Just cut the sentimental routine. You can do what you want now. We can be together."

"It's not that easy, Bing."

"It's exactly that easy. Your husband is dead. Time to move on."

"Get out!"

"Okay, hon," Bing said, "but think about it. It's a win/win. We were made for each other. You know we could have the time of our lives."

At that moment, the door swung open, and Ruth was wishing she had thought to retreat when she first realized whom she was overhearing. Bing did not seem at all nonplussed to find Ruth on the other side. "Hello, Mrs. Budge." He showed a dazzling white smile. "See you later."

Candace came to the door in a pink satin robe and slippers. Her face was gaunt.

"Hello, Candace. I'm terribly sorry to intrude right now, but I need to talk to you about something." She hesitated. "I didn't mean to interrupt your conversation with Bing."

"Don't worry about it. He was just leaving anyway."

"Is everything okay? I couldn't help but overhear—," she prodded. She wondered what Candace must be feeling, knowing that she betrayed her adoring husband before he was murdered.

"There's nothing between us two." She walked to the window. "I can't believe I ever saw anything in him. I must have been insane." She pressed her fingers to the glass.

"How did you meet?"

"I met him in Oregon, at some festival that Ed dragged me to. Bing is a spoiled, egocentric child. If anyone tells him no, all he hears is 'Keep asking until it's yes.' His parents sent him off to boarding school after he drove his motorcycle through a flower shop window. I guess it was easier than actually attempting to discipline him. Anyway, we were attracted to each other at the beginning, but then I saw him for what he was. I kept away for a long time." Her voice trailed off. "Not long enough, though."

Ruth sat still on the sofa, afraid to startle Candace away from her narrative.

"It happened after I lost the baby," Candace continued. "I got pregnant, and Ed was so excited. Then I miscarried early on. Ed was devastated, but he was more worried about me. He smothered me, hovering over me every moment. I couldn't stand it. He was driving me nuts with all his mothering. I just wanted to get away from him, and everything." She stopped talking and closed her eyes. "Bing is gorgeous, spontaneous, exciting. Everything my husband wasn't."

Ruth looked around the small room, buying time. She noticed a neat row of nail polish bottles on the coffee table. Electric blue, turquoise. Shell pink. It made her shudder.

"I am so sorry about your husband. I know how hard it is to lose a spouse."

"You do?" she said, turning. "Thank you. This feels like a nightmare. I'm really tired. What did you want to talk to me about?"

"I need to talk to Detective Denny about the—accident. He wants to ask me a few more questions."

Candace stared at her. "Uh-huh."

"I, er, I need to tell him the truth about everything. He's a good officer and a personal friend, like a son, actually."

"Okay. Why did you need to tell me that?"

Ruth felt the words burning in her mouth. "I know you were with Bing Mitchell just before the accident. Did you tell the police about that?"

Candace stared long enough that Ruth feared she didn't hear the question.

"You know? How do you know?" she whispered.

"Let's just say I was in the vicinity and I, er, overheard some things. I wanted you to know that I have to tell the detective. I certainly don't want to cause you any embarrassment, but he needs to know. I'm sure he will be discreet."

"Why?" Candace's pitch rose nearly an octave. "Why does he have to be told?"

"Because he needs to figure out who may have had a motive to kill your husband."

The young woman's lips moved, but no words came out.

"Candace, it's possible that after your argument with Bing, he shot the flare at the balloon himself."

"Why on earth would he do that?"

"He was jealous of your husband? He's in love with you, maybe?"

"Bing never loved me, not like Ed did."

But he seems intent on possessing you, Ruth thought. "I heard some talk. That Bing was supposed to go up with Ed in the balloon but he was late, so one of his people went up instead." She looked at Candace's stark face. "I'm really so sorry. Please forgive me for causing you any more pain." She glanced at her watch. "I'd better go now." She rose to leave.

Candace wrinkled her brows and pressed a ragged fingernail against her lips. "I can't believe this. Nothing like this should have happened to him."

"Did Ed ever get into any trouble?"

"Trouble? I don't think so. He had some financial strain when we first got married. Then things seemed to even out. Do you think someone had a grudge against him?" she asked, blinking through tears.

"I don't know. I'm not sure what to think."

"I will talk to the police, tell them what happened."

"I think that would be best. Good-bye, Candace."

As Ruth walked down the quiet hallway, she was struck by an awful thought. Candace had insinuated that she was bored with her life with Ed. She felt the union was forced on her by her father.

If Bing wanted to, he had plenty of time after his assignation to fire a shot at Ed Honeysill's balloon.

But so, too, did Candace.

6

The morning church service was subdued. The pastor spoke about death as a new beginning. Ruth knew it was true, that this life was only a stopover on a journey to a much better place with God. But all the same, she wondered what He thought about it all. How did He feel when His precious gift of life was taken away before it was meant to be?

In her mind it was a terrible thing to disrespect a divine gift in such a brutal, callous way. For some reason, Pickles Peckenpaugh surfaced in her mind. She thought about the journal, the fantastic characters who were once flesh and blood and now faded to memories. Hopefully she would have time later to read more about their escapades.

After church she kissed Monk good-bye and shouldered her camera bag on her way to a fenced area in the middle of the festival grounds. Ruth thought it looked much like a canine United Nations convention as she wandered around the fence line taking pictures to appease her ferocious publicity chairwoman. She was not sure if she had the patience to put up with Maude for one day plus another whole weekend of Festival activities, but she was determined to try.

The large penned area housed five smaller pens with yelping, napping, panting, and sniffing doggy delegates. A litter of wiry terrier puppies were jumbled together in a collective nap, gushed over by a pair of heart-warmed humans.

"Oh, Jeff. Aren't they adorable?" the young woman said, holding her long hair out of her face as she bent over the enclosure. Jeff agreed aloud that they were definitely precious.

Ruth saw Evelyn Bippo, the lady who had saved Alva from her enthusiastic dogs, hurry over to talk to them about the rigors of puppy adoption. The huge, earless white dog—Peanut, Ruth recalled—followed immediately behind her. Evelyn told them of the fees involved, mandatory obedience training, and the various annoying stages of dog maturation ranging from indoor accidents to the occasional dog neurosis that can result in the animal chewing the siding off the house.

Ruth listened intently. Birds and worms she knew about, but dogs were not in her menagerie.

She glanced to the left and saw Rocky Bippo, Evelyn's chai tea-loving brother, watching from outside the enclosure, his elbows resting on the fence just above a banner reading The Dog House. He nodded at her. Gesturing to the young couple, he said, "They're going home with a puppy. I've seen that look many times before, and no amount of warnings will make a dent."

"Your sister works hard for those dogs, doesn't she?"

He nodded, and a tiny silver moon sparkled in his earlobe. "Yeah, she feels more in tune with animals than people sometimes. We both do, but she's a softy for anything with whiskers."

Evelyn walked with the couple to the exit, smiling as they left. Then she came over to Rocky, nodding to Ruth.

"They're going to buy a leash and dog bed." Evelyn beamed. "That's the second adoption today."

"Great, Ev. Anyone for the older guys?"

Her smile faded as she contemplated the cages on the far side of the gated oval. "No. You know how it goes with the older ones." She reached down to stroke the neck of the earless giant with his head between her legs. "What will happen to our friends, Peanut?" The lines on her forehead deepened.

"Maybe things will look up. We've got two more days of festival to go next weekend."

Ruth moved away to take pictures of the Dog House banner, but she remained close enough to hear Evelyn and her brother.

Evelyn stroked the dog in her arms absently. "There was a guy here earlier," she said to Rocky in a whisper loud enough for Ruth's eavesdropping. "A rough-looking sort. He was asking me about Cliffy." She pointed to a muscular spotted dog that looked as though it had started out to be a shepherd until its genes reconsidered. "I didn't like the looks of him. I told him he was taken already." She bit her lip nervously. "I know it's getting really expensive to keep them all, but I just couldn't risk it."

"I know. Don't worry about it. We've been through a bad patch, but it's going to be better now. When the festival wraps, we'll take care of our business and be gone before anyone is the wiser."

"You know, I didn't think *he* would be here," Evelyn breathed.

"You're bound to run into him every so often. It's okay—he'll stay away. And if he doesn't, I'll get rid of him." There was an undertone of menace in his voice.

"Pretty tough talk."

He touched her shoulder gently. "You know I mean it, sis."

Ruth looked at the tight line of his lips and the glitter behind his dark eyes. She shivered.

"Yes, I do," the woman said.

❦

An hour later, after stopping at Puzan's for a life-sustaining chocolate bar, Ruth headed for home thinking about Rocky and Evelyn. They were very close. Whom was he talking about getting rid of? And what was the "business" he referred to?

FOG OVER FINNY'S NOSE

There was certainly a lot of tension circling the pair.

The gravel crunched under Ruth's feet. She had turned down the wooded pathway that was a shortcut from the open field upslope to the residential area clustered along the nostrils of Finny's Nose. The air was musky, spiced with azalea and cedar. Afternoon sun penetrated the canopy of branches here and there, dappling the wooded path with streaks of light.

She looked up, admiring the play of sun and shadow farther upslope. There was a sudden glint, a harsh reflected light from the top of Finny's Nose, as if someone was watching the festival below through binoculars. Now who would be doing that?

Ruth felt a prickle of fear on the back of her neck. She quickened her pace and made a beeline for home.

Unfortunately, Maude was standing on her doorstep when she arrived. "You've got to fix this," she commanded, thrusting a stack of papers out in front of her. "Just look at these flyers. That Len Brewster at the print shop is an idiot."

Ruth scanned the paper advertising the Fig Festival. "Well, Bubby Dean has a pretty robust fig tree on his property."

"This is no time for levity. You've got to go and have them reprinted. They need to be ready for the distribution team."

The team consisted of Flo who was already heavily burdened with managing the bake sale and manning the information booth. "Okay," Ruth said with a sigh. "I'll go talk to Len."

She didn't add, "As soon as I eat lunch."

Len proved to be fairly agreeable about changing the focus of the festival from figs to fog, once he had ascertained that Maude had not accompanied her. Even with his cheerful cooperation, it took an hour plus to make the changes and reprint the flyers.

She heard the ominous sound of the phone ringing when she finally heaved her body home again. "It's okay, Ruth," she said to herself. "Maybe it's a telemarketer."

"Ruth? It's Maude."

Her heart sank. "The flyers are fixed," she said. "Len said there was no charge as long as you stay out of his shop."

"Good. Now you need to bake a dozen treats of some sort. Something sweet that fits in with the fog theme. I'll pick them up tomorrow morning on my way to headquarters."

"The bake sale isn't until the last day of the festival. Why do I need to bake treats now?" She could not keep a whiny edge out of her voice.

"The tasting committee meets tomorrow to decide on the final choices for the bake sale next weekend. We need a variety of treats represented."

"And what are you baking?"

"My famous Cloudy Cashew Chewies."

Maude's Cashew Chewies were indeed famous. They made their debut at the Christmas cookie exchange. No fat, no sugar, and quite definitely no taste whatsoever. "All right," Ruth said heavily. "What am I supposed to bake?"

"Whatever you want. Just make sure it's sweet, doesn't require utensils, will keep well unrefrigerated, and fits the fog theme." Maude hung up.

Ruth slammed the phone down. "That woman has got to have some fascist relatives somewhere in her family tree." It would have been easy to call down to Monk's shop and ask him to rustle up a treat. He would be happy to do it, but she didn't want to add to his heavy workload. She scanned her cupboards, looking for inspiration. Chocolate chips, flour, sugar, espresso powder. Aha! Chocolate chip espresso muffins!

After the muffins were happily packed into the oven, she plopped down on the sofa with the journal.

August the 12th, 1923

Dan was here again tonight. They call him Soapy Dan because he always comes in clean and smelling of spice. I think he has his eye on one of my new dancing girls. I know he didn't come for the hash as he hardly touched a bite.

August the 16th

Slats came today to give us a once-over. We are to expect a group of his friends later on in the month. He wants them to get the royal treatment. The girls came to the dining room to meet him, dressed in their best and looking well. Except for Hazel. If I haven't told her a thousand times to lay off the chocolates! And to boot, she wore that robe de style in a luminous green which made her resemble nothing so much as an acorn squash! Far too plump to be on stage with the others.

I could tell from the way his bushy eyebrows came together that Hazel wasn't going to meet the mark. Sure enough, Slats said the girls were fine but Hazel had to go. But how could the Pickle Jar survive without Hazel? She's been here since we started. In a bit of daring, I told Slats she was the best cook this side of the Rockies and we needed her in the kitchen for those nights when we were to feed his associates. He was doubtful, but he is a businessman first, gangster second. He agreed to keep her on, for cooking duty only.

Fortunately he liked our new Janey. She is a wonderful dancer, I must admit. The customers love to watch her as they eat.

Hazel (along with Bertha, our real chef) made a chicken-fried steak and mashed potatoes. I was impressed. Slats gave his full approval to the fare. He even tried a few of the greens, though things of the vegetable persuasion are against his ways. Even I have to admit the rhubarb compote was a marvel.

He fell asleep in a chair by the fire. He looked kind of boyish, with his dark patch of hair thrown over his eyes. I'm not fooled by that little-boy-lost look. I know he'd murder us all if he thought we double-crossed him. I shudder just to think about it. I long for the day when I can buy the Pickle Jar outright and am no longer beholden to this man. Soon, maybe next spring, it will be mine to do with as I please.

In spite of the fires which we keep burning constantly, a cursed fog has settled over our town like a layer of poisonous fumes. I am worried more than ever about what will happen when Slats finds out who stole his bag of cash. I fear what will come of it, something awful. There are many desperate people in town who would do anything to feed their little ones. I just hope whoever did it runs far away from this gloomy place. I am not certain, though, if anywhere is far enough to escape Slats, even in this cloud of darkness.

Only time will tell what wickedness is buried in this evil fog.

The kitchen timer startled Ruth. She put the muffins on a rack to cool and piled the dishes on the counter. The clock chimed—9:30 p.m. and there were still critters to be tended to. It was Monk's late night, and he wouldn't be home for another half hour.

She grabbed a bag of Cheerios and protein pellets and headed out to the yard. After making sure the worm bins were covered, she made her way to the far corner of the grassy space.

"Dinner," she yelled to the undulating swarm of gulls. They followed her to the pen, pushing and pecking at each other. She threw in handfuls of food, and the birds fought their way into the enclosure. Not the sharpest crayons in the box but cooperative where food was concerned. She closed the gate and took one last look into the pen. In the corner, Franklin rested on his bottom. He was missing an eye and a foot after he got tangled in a fishing line and mauled by a dog. The red pucker where his eyeball used to be and the dark gray feathers on his white back gave him the look of a depressed, feathery Eeyore. She generally took Franklin for a hobble along the beach by himself, as it was too hard for him to keep up with the rest of the flock. He looked mournfully up at her.

"Oh, Franklin. I know I promised to take you to the beach, but it's late and I've got a headache."

The bird cocked his head.

"I'm so tired," she said. "I'll take you tomorrow."

He bowed his neck. If he had lips, she swore they would be trembling.

"Good grief," she said as she lifted him up. "How can you lay a guilt trip on me when you can't even talk?" The bird snuggled his satiny head under her chin as she retrieved the slim plastic tube the veterinarian had made to protect his stump of a leg.

"Let's go, Franklin. There are miles to go before we sleep."

～

The beach was dreamlike. The almost-full moon painted the fog in silvery tones and the gravel in tints of ebony and charcoal. It looked like an old black-and-white photograph. She walked along behind Franklin. Waves scurried back and forth to grab handfuls of loose stones, and the air was heavy with moisture and the scent of brine.

The cold was good for her husband's business. People lined up to purchase vats of his clam chowder on days like this. She smiled when she thought of him. They had only been married for six months. She had been married for twenty-five years the time before, until a heart attack stole her husband away. Their life as husband and wife was still so new, so uncertain, but by the grace of God, she was enjoying every minute.

At the moment, though, Ruth was far from enjoying things. Her indigestion was back, perhaps courtesy of her chocolate bar lunch, and a headache pounded the back of her eyes as she trudged along. Her thoughts were scattered, swirling around like the fog that seeped over the hillside to bury Finny once again. One image came to the forefront. Meg Sooner.

Dimple's mother was back, all right, and presumably assuming her role of beloved grandmother.

No one had seen hide nor hair of the woman for twenty years and then she blows into town like Mary Poppins. No, more like Glinda, Ruth thought with hostility. Meg was a delicate woman, well tailored and graceful to boot. Even her voice sounded tinkly and sweet when Ruth had spoken to her on the phone while trying to reach Dimple.

Ruth felt her stomach clench as she recalled that Dimple confessed to speaking with Meg several times in the past few months. From what she'd gathered, it was a near-fatal car accident that galvanized Meg into reconnecting with her estranged daughter. It stung a bit to know that Dimple had been in contact with her mother and Ruth had not known. Somehow it felt like a betrayal. She wasn't sure why. She was still Cootchie's nana. Their lives were inevitably intertwined since the day Dimple had asked her to help her through the pregnancy. A biological grandmother couldn't change that.

Could she?

A twist of uncertainty filled her heart.

She wished fervently that Grandma Meg would not be there for the birthday celebration. Ruth's agitated breaths fogged the cold air. Enough about Meg.

Ruth looked up at the moon and thought about the namesake of the town. In this ethereal moment, it was easy to believe that decades ago rumrunners like Frederick Finny would anchor in the choppy water and use smaller boats to ferry their precious Canadian whiskey to shore. It was a simple plan that worked like a charm.

Franklin stumped ahead and vanished around an outcropping of slimy rocks. Ruth hurried to catch up. Rounding the corner, she stopped abruptly.

It wasn't gangsters waiting on the beach this night.

Three small bonfires burned brightly. Around them sat three figures, clothed in black with hoods up or bandannas tied around their heads. In the center of the group was a woman.

They stopped their talking and leaped up to face Ruth.

Ruth remembered Alva's warning about the proctologists in search of a sacrificial victim. Her breath froze in her lungs. She could not make out their faces, only the glitter of narrowed eyes. They did not speak, but the biggest one took a step toward her.

"Uh," she began, her heart hammering with the force of a pneumatic drill. "Uh, well. I see you've found the beach."

The big man took another step and reached inside his vest.

"Uh, what a—a lovely night for a bonfire." Ruth's voice trembled.

Now all three figures began to move slowly in Ruth's direction.

"I'll just run and get some marshmallows!" she shrieked. Ruth scooped up Franklin and ran as fast as her middle-aged legs would carry her, reciting the Lord's Prayer all the way home.

Monk immediately began to rifle through the closet when she told him.

"What are you doing?"

He didn't answer her. Finally, he whirled around with a bat in his hand. "I'm going to go down there and teach those young punks a lesson."

"You can't do that," she gasped. "They might be some sort of gang. I called Jack before I got home, and he said he'd go right over and check it out."

"I don't care if they're Attila the Hun's army; they got no right to scare you like that."

It took several minutes of cajoling and pleading to dissuade him from his plan. "Please, honey. They didn't hurt me. They didn't even say a word."

Finally, he reluctantly agreed to suspend his baseball bat mission. They lay down to sleep, but several hours later her eyes were still wide open. She went downstairs and booted up the computer, typing in "ecoterrorists."

The deluge of information surprised her.

Millions of dollars of property damage. Intimidation. Harassment. Arson.

So there really were cells of people who orchestrated attacks against ranchers, loggers, miners, the government, et cetera.

Maybe Alva was right. Maybe the green bandanna folks were planning to carry out some action in Finny.

One line in the news article she was reading jumped out.

"One group even distributes manuals on how to infiltrate a target area and escape without being caught."

With cold fingers, she turned off the computer.

7

"You must be Detective Denny," Meg said to Jack. "It's so good to see you." She looked poised and calm in her green sweater set and slacks. "We're so glad you could come for dinner, even if you have to cook it."

"Hello. We're glad to be here. Mondays are usually quiet around the office, but today has been nuts. It's good to get out of there for a while." He handed her a bowl of potato salad. "We're in luck. Louella made this, which saves everyone from having to eat mine."

She laughed and took the bowl. "Is this your son?" she asked, trying to see around Jack's leg to the boy who clung there, his head under his father's flannel shirt.

"Yes, this is Paul. Can you say hello, Paul?" Jack patted the boy's head through the fabric. "He isn't much of a conversationalist."

"No problem. Cootchie is in the backyard, I think."

They excused themselves and headed outside.

Dimple greeted him with a hug.

In no time Cootchie and Paul were busy digging a hole. Dimple set Jack to work firing up the barbecue and handed him a platter of something.

He looked up from his study of the foodstuffs as Ruth joined him. "Hey, Ruth." He lowered his voice and looked suspiciously at the slender brown cylinders on the grill. "What in the world is a meatless hot dog made out of anyway?"

"Probably the same thing the cake frosting is made out of. In my experience, it's best just to go with the flow and not ask too many questions."

He laughed and wiped his long fingers on a Kiss the Cook apron. "I think you're right. Where's your hubby tonight?"

"He's got a catering gig in Half Moon Bay."

"You look tired," he said as he slid the food onto the grill.

"I couldn't sleep last night. I tried to nap today, but Maude has always got me doing something or other. I spent the entire morning and early afternoon bagging beads to use at the craft table. Do you think we can expect two hundred kids to attend next weekend?"

He laughed. "Not unless Disneyland suddenly packs up and moves here." He glanced back at the kitchen. "I wonder if Meg is enjoying her stay." He could see a question in Ruth's eyes. The same question that was no doubt hovering in the back of his own. Why had Meg Sooner come back to

Finny? Neither had a chance to vocalize their thoughts, as Meg and Dimple emerged, carrying presents to the lighted patio.

"Cootchie," Dimple called. "Why don't you open your presents before Mr. Denny has our dinner ready?"

They all gathered around the birthday girl, and Paul helped Cootchie open the gifts.

The girl squealed at the set of magnifying glasses from Jack and Paul and the fossil excavation kit from Ruth. Everyone leaned forward a little closer to see Cootchie unwrap the glittering package from Meg Sooner. It was a porcelain doll, dressed in pink velvet with delicate orange curls and painted eyelashes. The doll was gorgeous and expensive.

Jack saw the tiny gleam of satisfaction on Ruth's face when Cootchie tossed the doll onto the grass and hauled Paul away to start an archaeological dig.

"Oh dear. I thought all girls liked dolls," Meg said.

"I'm sure she'll love playing dolls after she gets the digging out of her system," Ruth said.

"Maybe you're right. I think I've got a lot to learn about my granddaughter. And my daughter." Meg looked at Dimple as she gathered up the crumpled paper.

After potato salad and meatless hot dogs smothered in organic mustard, Dimple and Meg set to work on the dishes. Jack and Ruth walked outside to watch the children digging by porch light in the yard. The sky was heavy with a wet blanket of fog. Pockets of brilliant star-speckled velvet poked through here and there. The round moon escaped its foggy mantle from time to time to bathe the yard in white light.

"Have you come to any conclusions about Ed's death?" Ruth asked.

"Only that we don't know who did it. There are so many people in town right now." He had one visitor pulling his mind away from work matters. The tiny dark-haired woman who had turned out to be Monk's niece. "So, er, is Bobby finding time to enjoy the festival?"

Ruth nodded. "Yes, but I think she would like Finny better without the crowds. She is always out on a hike or a run. She seems to thrive in the chill."

He wanted to ask how long Bobby was going to stay, but he couldn't think of a graceful way to do so.

After a while, the group assembled again on the porch to choke down carrot cake with tofu frosting. Even Meg seemed to require a lot of iced tea to get the stuff headed in the right direction.

Cootchie put down her paper plate and threw her head back to look at the sky. "It's de worm moon," she said, pointing upward.

"The what, dear?" Meg leaned down.

"She said it's the worm moon," Dimple repeated.

They all looked up at the almost full moon, outlined by a frame of ghostly fog.

"What does that mean, exactly?" Meg asked, her brow wrinkled.

"It's a Native American name to describe the full moon that occurs in March. As the temperature begins to warm, earthworm casts appear, trumpeting the return of the robins."

"Nana has worms," Cootchie said. She hugged Ruth around the knees. "She has a worm farm."

"Oh boy. I'm sure your, er, Mrs. Sooner doesn't want to hear about that."

"About what? I'd love to know more about you. You've been so good to my granddaughter."

Ruth was saved from having to answer when an explosion lit the sky with a bright orange fireball. The partygoers all stood openmouthed for a moment.

Jack reacted first. "Dimple, can you keep Paul here for a while? I've gotta go."

Dimple and Meg ushered the two children into the house. Ruth jogged along behind him. "Can I come with you?" she asked.

He hesitated only a moment. "Sure. I take it fire and catastrophe are preferable to the present awkward situation?"

"Exactly."

As they roared down the rock walkway and onto the main road, the dispatcher filled Jack in on the location of the explosion. He radioed for a fire engine as gravel shot out from under the speeding tires.

Jack enjoyed the frantic drive to the makeshift trailer park, all the while being careful of his passenger. Sometimes driving code three was the only perk of the job.

They arrived to find a fire blazing and people either running or clumped together in shocked groups. Jack made Ruth promise to stay out of the way of anything flaming and strode off toward the chaos.

The small trailer was burning fiercely, the flames licking at the striped awning. The interior was a swirl of fire and heavy smoke, punctuated by loud cracks and whooshing noises. A man in baggy clothes with a bandanna wrapped around his head squirted a lackluster stream of foam on the blaze with a fire extinguisher.

Seconds later a woman ran up to the trailer. She clutched a quilted robe around her tall frame. "Oh no, Rocky. Your trailer. Is anyone inside? Are you hurt?"

"No," he snarled, continuing to wave the extinguisher in erratic arcs in front of him, wiping at the sweat on his stubbled face. "Go back to your trailer. I'll come and get you when it's over."

Several men ran up to assist Rocky. They all wore green bandannas. The other fair vendors just watched the melee; some drank coffee, one ate a hot dog, and two still clutched their playing cards in front of them.

Jack worked to keep the bystanders back a safe distance from the fire. The trailer door next to him opened. Bing Mitchell stood there wearing a blue sweat suit. His feet were bare, and even his toes looked well muscled. He surveyed the scene with amusement.

"Hey there, Detective. Did you come for the campfire? This town is definitely a hot spot. I just can't get over it." His face glowed oddly in the moonlight. "What is that idiot doing?"

"Which idiot?"

"Rocky Bippo, the idiot with the fire extinguisher. And his sister, the dog lady. She's nuttier than he is. They're into some gang that goes around wreaking havoc on the general population. What is it about those two? Trouble follows them everywhere."

Before Jack could follow up on the strange comments, a fire engine careened into the area and disgorged several young volunteers who leaped off the rig with undisguised exuberance. The two seasoned firefighters exited the vehicle in a more sedate manner. One of them was the chief of the Finny Fire Department, Ernie Gonzalez.

"Hey, Jack," Ernie said as the others donned helmets and unrolled hose. "Nice little bonfire." A lush mustache draped over his plump cheeks. "What do you make of it?"

A deafening blast followed by a rocketing arc of fire caused them all to duck.

Jack straightened up tentatively. "Propane tank?"

Ernie guffawed. "You're getting good, J.D. Maybe there's hope for you yet. Let's get some wet stuff on the red stuff and we'll debrief in a while." He turned his attention to the blaze. "Now get everybody out of the way," he said over his shoulder.

Jack followed directions as he moved back and persuaded Rocky Bippo to follow him. Ruth hurried over.

"Can you tell me what happened?" Jack pierced Rocky with a steady gaze.

Rocky shook his head. His long hair flowed out of the bottom of his bandanna like an oil slick. "I don't know. I was reading in my trailer, and all of a sudden I heard a sound. Like a hissing or something. I was just opening the front door to check it out when—boom—the trailer tank exploded. Pretty soon the whole side of the trailer was on fire. I grabbed an extinguisher out of the truck and tried to put it out. A couple of the guys ran to get theirs, too, but it was too big by then. Then the other tanks went up."

"Were they your tanks?"

"Yeah. I use them to make the mushrooms."

Jack blinked, nodding to Mary Dirisi as she arrived on the scene.

Rocky tore his gaze from the fire. "I heat up PVC pipe with a propane torch. When it starts to burn, you can shape it and it gets stippled and discolored. Looks just like mushrooms. I sell them as garden art."

"Have you had any problems with the tanks before?"

"No. They're just small handheld jobs. I've never had a lick of trouble." He caught sight of Bing standing with his arms folded watching the blaze. "Never trouble with the tanks, anyway."

Evelyn Bippo was dressed in jeans and a worn T-shirt when she ran up to her brother. "Rocky, I can't find Edmund. I've looked everywhere."

Jack put a hand on his radio. "Who's Edmund?"

Rocky sighed. "Don't worry, Detective. He's a dog. A crazy beagle." He turned to Evelyn. "Is everybody else accounted for?"

She nodded, tears filling her eyes. "Just Edmund. I think the explosions scared him and he jumped over the enclosure." The fingernail she pressed to her lips was bitten to the quick. The firelight accentuated the creases in her forehead and cast eerie shadows on her face.

Rocky hugged her tightly and walked her away to a quiet corner, offering consolation as he went. "It's okay, Ev. We'll find him."

A sweaty Chief Gonzalez approached.

"Hey, Ruth. Those wigglers you got me really did the trick. I caught a ten-pound trout that was a thing of beauty."

"I'm glad, Ernie."

"Me, too. The wife's always on me about spending a whole day catching nothing but a cold." He snorted. "Okay, Jack. Here's the deal. Someone set fire to the stack of newspapers under the trailer's propane tank."

"How do you know?"

"Because I'm a stud," Ernie answered. He held up a half-melted lighter. "And we found this a few yards away in the grass."

With a grin, Jack scribbled notes on a pad. "Uh-huh. That's what set the trailer on fire?"

"Yup. The fire caused the propane to expand until the release valve failed and then—*kablam!*" He jerked his meaty thumbs toward the night sky. "That set the smaller tanks off, too."

"Does anybody know where this guy belongs?" Mary stood with a shivering dog cradled in her arms. The animal was panting heavily, leaving rivulets of drool on her pants.

Evelyn appeared at her elbow. "It's Edmund. He's mine." She gently took the dog and inspected him. The worry in her eyes turned to profound relief. "Where did you find him, Officer?"

"I was getting out of my car and he practically knocked me over." She looked fondly at the dog. "He didn't want to come at first, but I persuaded him with some peanut butter crackers I had with me."

"Is he okay, Evelyn?" Ruth asked.

She nodded as she massaged the dog behind his ears. "I think so. Just scared mostly. He's not used to being on his own. I only got him a few months ago."

"She runs a dog adoption service," Ruth said.

"Really?" Mary's eyebrows lifted. "So this guy needs a home?"

Evelyn, Rocky, and Ruth all nodded vigorously. Jack looked on in amusement.

"Maybe it's meant to be. When I'm done here, you can tell me more about Edmund," she said. "I've been thinking I need a dog in my life."

"Come over to my trailer. I've got his history, at least as much as we know."

"I certainly don't want this fire scene to get in the way of a good matchmaking session," Jack said, "but would you mind getting some statements, Mary?"

"Sure thing, boss. I'll come by your trailer later," she said to Evelyn, giving Edmund a final pat.

Rocky lingered behind, his eyes narrowed. He seemed to come to some internal decision. "I'm going to give Ev a hand. I'll be at her trailer if you need me."

Jack nodded as Rocky walked away.

"I'm going to be here awhile, Ruth. Let me arrange a ride for you back to Dimple's. Tell her I'll be by for Paul as soon as I can."

"Okay, though I know Cootchie will be thrilled to tuck him into her trundle bed. Poor kid, he'll be eating soybeans for breakfast."

8

The contestants in the Fog Festival cook-off were serious about their endeavors. Ruth picked up on the vibes even before she began taking pictures of the cooking enthusiasts packed into the courtyard of the Finny Hotel. It was the only weekday event. The dishes would be prepared and judged that evening, and the prizes awarded on the last day of the festival. Ruth thought it ironic that the big payola for first prize was an overnight stay at a bed-and-breakfast in neighboring Half Moon Bay. Second prize was a free ticket to the church spaghetti feed and a new spatula.

Outside of the cooking chaos, a giant white tent trembled in the cool breeze. It had been erected in a vacant lot to accommodate the Fog Festival staff and visitors. A half dozen people bustled back and forth from the tent, staggering under the weight of produce crates. Others sat on picnic benches outside soaking up the newly arrived sunshine. The scent of cypress and woody azalea mingled with aromas of garlic and tangy feta. A slight smell of smoke still hung in the air from the fire the previous evening.

Ruth saw the Sassie sisters, Lena and Anne, huddling in conference over a steaming pot of split pea soup, wearing matching green shirts almost the same color as their entry. Several people Ruth did not know tended their portable ovens and microwaves. A smoked salmon contingent poked at their specimen with all the precision of a neurosurgery team.

Royland Lemmon wheeled a squeaky dolly in front of him. It was so loaded with crates of arugula and radicchio that only his head was visible over the top. Squealing to a stop, he pushed back his worn cowboy hat with a thumb.

"Ruth," he said as his face crumpled into wrinkles. "It's nice to see you." His chipped front tooth lent him a comical look.

"It's nice to see you, too. Are you supplying the greens today?"

"Yes, ma'am. I've got six more crates of goodness in the truck. Fresh picked this morning." His brown eyes shone with pride. "You want a bunch to take with you?"

"I'd love a bunch," she said, taking the greens from his calloused hands. She buried her face in the tender green leaves and inhaled a lungful of spicy contentment. "Monk can make an amazing salad with this."

"My pleasure. I know you both appreciate my greens. Say, have you seen my son around here anywhere? I need him to help me unload these crates." Royland shook his head. "He's always off somewhere."

"He told me about his truffle business. What an interesting idea."

The man shook his head again. "Is that what it is now? Truffles? I thought he was still in the ergonomic bicycle seat racket. It's always something new."

Royland gazed off toward the coastline and sighed. "He's desperate to escape the life I've made here. Ever since his mother divorced me when he was twelve. The kids in school have always been rough on him, too." His shoulders sagged. "He just can't wait to get away from here. And me."

"I'm sorry, Royland. I do know how it feels." She thought about her own son who had moved to a different state to get away. Then she caught sight of Hugh. "Oh, he's over there, talking to the balloon man, Bing. I'm on my way to that side; I'll tell him you need his help at the truck."

"Thank you, ma'am. You enjoy that arugula now."

"I certainly will." She made her way past the clam chowder team to the two men. They were deep in conversation. Hugh's young face was rapt with interest.

"I'll bet you've been all over. How long have you been in the business?" she heard Hugh ask.

"Forever, it seems like. I know everything there is to know about it." Bing slouched against a freezer. "Ballooning has been around for generations. Many people don't know that the Japanese actually used balloons as makeshift bombs to terrorize our mainland during the war."

"No way." Hugh stared at his companion.

"It's absolutely true. They called them Fugo balloons." Bing scanned the crowd as he talked. "The Japs made crude balloons, just rubberized silk envelopes really, and filled them with hydrogen. They launched them into the Gulf Stream and let the air currents take them across the Pacific to the United States."

"Awesome. Did any of them make it?"

"Not many. Most didn't survive the weather. The Fugos only killed one person, a woman picnicking with her kids in Maryland."

"Unbelievable," Hugh said, his Adam's apple bobbing excitedly. "All that work and it didn't even make a difference."

It made quite a difference to the woman in Maryland, Ruth thought. Out loud she said, "Hi, Hugh. Hello, Bing."

Bing dazzled her with a perfect smile. "Hello, Mrs. Budge. How are the Fog Festival preparations getting on?"

"Fairly well, I'd say. Hugh, your father needs help unloading the truck."

Hugh nodded, consulting a watch bristling with knobs and dials. "Okay. I'll see you around, Bing. Is Dimple here yet, Ruth? I've got something for her."

"I think she said she'd be here around ten."

He nodded again. "See you later."

"I understand you're in the bait business," Bing said. "I'd love to get some

229

fishing in while I'm here."

"Come on by. I can supply all the bait you could ever need. I live in a cottage down below. Just follow the squawking bird sounds."

Ruth said good-bye and continued working her way through the room. Several contest officials were roaming around making notes on clipboards. It seemed that Maude didn't have to twist any arms to round up judges. Officer Katz looked thrilled to be wearing a Fog Cook-off Judge T-shirt as he poked his nose into various bubbling pots. Ruth snapped a shot of him frowning at the clipboard.

"Hello, Nate. How did you get roped into judging?"

"Oh, I volunteered when Mrs. Stone said you needed another judge. What could be a better job than judging a food contest?" He inhaled. "Do you smell that? I can't figure out what it is, but it smells awesome."

Her nostrils were working overtime trying not to let the amazing scents distract her mental processes. "I don't know, but I'm going to find out. See you later."

Her heart quickened when she caught sight of her husband behind his cooking station.

"Hello, honey," Monk bellowed. He left his spot behind the portable stove and planted a big kiss on her lips. "I've missed you today."

She melted into his embrace. "I've missed you, too." Looking over his shoulder, she added, "I didn't know you had decided on a recipe."

"You betcha. Are you here to get a shot of the winning dish?" He grinned. "Then come on over and take a look."

"A little confident, aren't we? What are you cooking?"

"It's truffled new potatoes. Very simple recipe, but guaranteed to knock you into another dimension." His close-cropped gray hair was stippled with sweat, and his face shone with enthusiasm.

It pleased her to watch him cook. She found it amazing that such huge, calloused hands could hold the kitchen instruments so delicately, like a jeweler setting precious stones. But he was a man full of surprising contradictions.

"Do you mind if I taste?"

"Nah, go right ahead. Those are the very best French black truffles. They oughta be, for what I paid for them."

Ruth looked at the pot and then back at her husband. "Black truffles?"

She flashed back to the boxful that Hugh had shown her at the park, and their conversation about the price they brought. They were so strange and exotic. Ed Honeysill would have enjoyed this, she thought with a pang. "Where did you get them?"

"From Hugh. He got them for me at a discount, if you can call one hundred fifty dollars a discount. I don't usually cook with truffles, so the price kind of hit me by surprise. I figured it would be a shoo-in recipe for the contest."

Ruth shook her head and sipped the spoonful. It was indeed scrumptious. "Are you looking to win that trip to Half Moon Bay?" she asked.

"Sure. But only if my lovely bride goes with me."

She smiled and busied herself with her camera, wondering when the thrill of being adored by this wonderful man would wear off. God loved her without a doubt to have blessed her with two amazing husbands in one lifetime.

"Did Hugh tell you who his source is?"

"No. Trade secret, I think."

Ruth caught sight of Dimple lugging a crate of luminous mushrooms to the supply table in the back of the room.

"Gotta go, Monk. I'll talk to you later."

Dimple heaved her box onto the table and stood there. Her fingers absently stroked the smooth mushroom caps.

Ruth hesitated. "Are you okay?"

She looked up, unfocused for a moment. "Oh, Ruth. Hello. I am okay, just thinking. It's so strange, having her back."

"Your mother?" she asked gently.

"Yes. For so many years I imagined where she was, what she looked like." Dimple thought for a moment. "I thought she would be taller."

Ruth smiled. "Did she say anything—about why she came back, I mean?"

"She said she wrote me several notes over the years, saying she regretted leaving me, and that she tried to keep in touch with calls, but Daddy threw away the cards and wouldn't allow me to talk to her."

Ruth could easily see that happening with a hardened man like Buster.

"Then she found out that I had a baby. She said she booked a flight twice to come and see me but each time she canceled." Dimple took a soft bristled brush from her pocket and gently whisked it over the mushroom caps. "Fear drains the vigor of intention."

"Uh, yes. I am sure that's true."

"She had the car accident, and it changed her priorities, she said."

"Does your mother—" Ruth stopped. "Is she going to stay in Finny?"

"I don't think so. She has a beautiful house in Arizona and a husband who dotes on her, she says. Not like Daddy at all. I just think she wants to get to know me, us."

Ruth felt guilty for the relief that flooded through her. The woman was going home! Ruth refocused her thoughts. "How are you feeling about it all? About your mother coming back?"

Dimple gathered her long blond ringlets into a bundle, loosely braiding it, and draped it over one shoulder. "I am not sure. It is so strange to have a mother again, after being an orphan for so long."

Ruth knew that Buster had all but washed his hands of his daughter when she became pregnant, leaving her, for all intents and purposes, parentless. "I'm no expert or anything, but I'm sure it's just fine to feel confused and unsure. It may take some time for you two to get acquainted again." She was pleased with her advice. Sometimes spending an afternoon watching Oprah paid off.

Ruth noticed a slim metallic cylinder on the table. "What's this?"

"It's a digital recorder for recording my observations as I check the polytunnel. Hugh gave it to me. Wasn't that nice?"

Ruth nodded. "It looks expensive." Maybe Hugh had finally come up with a moneymaking idea after all.

"Ruth," Dimple began, gazing absently out the window.

"Yes?"

"Why do you suppose a barbecued chicken just came flying out the opening of that tent?"

Ruth stared out the window into the lot next door. She was unable to fathom a reasonable explanation as a plate of jelly doughnuts followed the chicken.

9

Jack's car squealed to a stop, followed closely by Nate's and Mary's vehicles. They could see the sides of the tent undulating and the sound of screaming.

Alva came trotting out of the tent opening, a red stickiness dripping from his hair down the front of his plaid shirt.

"You're bleeding!" Jack said. He grabbed the old man and pushed him away from the tent.

"Nah, just hot sauce. I got off ten shots with the squeeze bottle before I took any." His face was wreathed in a huge grin. "It's a frenzy in there. Ain't seen anything like it since Korea."

Jack handed him to Mary, who steered Alva out of harm's way. The two uniformed officers then stood ready at one side of the tent opening, and Jack, in jeans with a badge clipped to his belt, moved to the other side. They did a slow count to three and plunged into the craziness.

Bodies were flying everywhere. Some launched food at each other; others hid behind overturned tables. Hugh stood on top of the long rectangular serving table shouting something at the top of his lungs, whopping anybody he could reach with a soup ladle. Jack could just make out Bing crouched under the table next to him.

"What in the world—?" Mary shouted as a square of lasagna hurtled through the air and hit the side of her head. "Who did that?" She grabbed the nearest human form, which turned out to be a dark-haired youth, one of the Coastal Comets acrobatic troupe. Hauling him to a nearby table, she cuffed him to the metal legs.

Nathan was attempting to intervene between the Sassie sisters and the giant of a man they were bouncing up and down upon.

"Get off me, you sacks of lard. I ain't even from this jerkwater town," the man wheezed.

"Sacks of lard?" one of the gray-haired women said in between bounces. "Just who do you think you are?"

"Ladies, let's just take it easy here," Nate began. "I'm sure the guy can apologize if you let him get some oxygen in his lungs."

Jack saw Evelyn crawl under tables along the perimeter of the tent, trying to feel her way to the exit. "Oh yuck," she muttered. "I can't believe this is happening."

FOG OVER FINNY'S NOSE

Jack jumped over puddles of chili and smears of barbecued chicken carnage as he made his way over toward the only fully upright people in the tent. He slipped on a ketchup-dampened patch of grass and slid on his belly, coming to a stop at the feet of Maude Stone and Bubby Dean.

"My fault?" Maude shouted over the din. "How is this my fault?"

"Because," Bubby shouted back, "this was your crazy idea to put up a tent for these lunatics. Some of them aren't Finny people, Maude. You can't predict what these nutcases will do in our town." A glob of custard quivered on the edge of his left eyebrow.

"Alva saw a bunch of them wackos headed up nose last night. Wearing bandannas and all. He says they think people are ruining the earth, and they're looking for a sacrificial victim to make an example of. I'm beginning to think he's right," Bubby bellowed. Then he added, "Maybe we should offer you up."

She ignored the last comment. "That's a load of hogwash. Alva is a crazy old geezer, and you are, too, for believing him." Maude ducked to avoid an airborne biscuit. "And what about you? It was your idea to host a luncheon in a tent, for Pete's sake. What about that cockamamy idea?"

"That's enough, you two," Jack said, clambering up from his prone position. Neither one looked down.

"That was a great idea. The council approved it. Don't try to shift this fiasco to my door." Bubby ducked too slowly to avoid the chicken thigh that followed the biscuit. It splatted on the back of his neck and slid forlornly down his T-shirt.

Maude finally noticed Jack. "Jack? It's about time. Just what in the world are you going to do about this mess?" Maude said. She flicked some spaghetti off her shoulder. "Is this the sort of behavior we tolerate in this town?"

"That's pretty highfalutin of you to say," Bubby yelled to the top of her head. "Finny was doing just fine before this idiot festival."

Jack slid back down to a kneeling position as he temporarily lost his footing again. "Just simmer down."

"Fine? You call finding a toe fine?" Her voice rose to a spine-tingling screech. "It's only a matter of time before they find the body that goes with it, you knucklehead. Then we'll have two murders on our hands."

"Knucklehead?" His face turned crimson. "You are the most—"

Jack made it to his feet. "Enough already!" he exploded. "Take it outside and sit down until I get there!"

Bubby and Maude started, looking at the detective. Without a word they both made their way out of the tent.

Jack put his fingers into his mouth and blew. Hard. The blast pierced through the din. The entire congregation froze in various awkward positions as if they were engaged in a violent Twister game.

"Listen up. I'm Detective Jack Denny from the Finny Police Department.

You will all remove your hands from each other and walk out of this tent. When you exit this area, sit yourselves down outside on the field and wait until an officer tells you to go. Now move it!"

The sticky horde ambled out of the tent until only the officers and the young acrobat handcuffed to the table remained.

Jack's T-shirt and jeans were soaked and grass stained. Mary Dirisi was trying in vain to push the stringy cheese out of her face. Nathan was covered from forehead to boots with a combination of cherry cola and potato salad.

"And they say nothing ever happens in Finny," Nathan said. A drop of soda collected in his mustache before it fell onto his shirtfront.

"Yeah, well," Jack said, "I'll take murder and mayhem over a food fight any day." As the words came out of his mouth, he felt a quiver of unease deep in his gut.

He slogged after the greasy crowd streaming out of the tent. Mary and Nate plopped the messy people into groups and wrote down pertinent information in their slightly sticky notebooks.

Jack noticed Evelyn and Rocky standing away from the group, talking quietly with their heads together. He edged closer when he noticed Ruth sidle up to them. He stopped to help a teen with noodles in his hair pick up several plates off of the ground. All the while Jack kept his ears tuned in to Ruth's conversation.

"Are you all right?" Ruth asked.

Evelyn looked up, her face smeared with a tomato-based product. "I can't believe it. I didn't mean to start a brawl. I just got so mad, I threw a dinner roll at him and it smacked some other guy instead. Before I knew it, there was food flying everywhere."

"Who were you angry with?"

Rocky answered first. "That jerk, Mitchell," Rocky barked. "He deserves a lot more than a dinner roll in the face." He swiped at a strand of spaghetti hanging from his narrow chin. "Where is he? He needs to be taught a lesson."

"Never mind, Rocky. It's over for now." Evelyn took a steadying breath. "I told you about the man who mutilated Peanut. Bing is the one. I was going to file a complaint with animal services, but he threatened to report me for having too many animals on my property."

"And he did anyway, Evelyn. You know it was him." He glared through the smear of mustard on the lenses of his glasses.

"I'm pretty sure, but there's no way to prove it," she said, wiping her eyes.

"If it wasn't for that low-down slimeball, I'd still have my car, too."

Jack finished stuffing the paper plates into the kid's plastic bag and came closer. "Well, it looks like we're all going to need some dry cleaning services. I couldn't help overhearing. How did Bing get your car, Rocky?"

Evelyn and Rocky looked at each other.

"Oh, it's a long story. Bing, uh, had something of ours that we wanted back, and we had to sell the car." She cleared her throat. "Anyway, it's water under the bridge now." The silver strands in her dark hair shimmered in the waning sunlight. "He's just so arrogant, so cruel. He asked me about my 'crippled mongrel' as if he had nothing to do with it. I just couldn't stand it."

"It's all right, Ev." Rocky put his arm around her shoulder. "Nothing awful happened, just a food fight." Rocky took several deep breaths. "Let's center ourselves."

Jack looked at the mottled flush on Rocky's face and figured he would require much more than deep breathing to center anything. They moved away and sat down on a log to wait for their turn with the police.

"Not bad," Jack said.

Ruth looked at the sticky detective. "What's not bad?"

He brushed a lettuce leaf out of his hair. "You are a pretty good snoop, I must admit. I don't think they'll be inclined to share that much information with law enforcement."

"Maybe not when you're dressed like a salad."

"Funny. I think they'd clam up even without the garnish."

"It's the motherly aura I exude," she said with a grin. "For some reason, people share their secrets with me."

"Let me know if you need some contract work with the Finny police." He smiled and walked back into the throng, wondering what Bing could have taken from the Bippos that would require them to sell a car to buy it back. He took another glance at the chaos. The misty air seemed to envelop the group, leaving Rocky and Evelyn framed against the foggy backdrop. Rocky reached to hug her and his shirt rode up in the back. Jack made a note to find out why Mr. Rocky Bippo had a knife tucked in his waistband.

As he turned away, his heart skidded to a stop. Bobby stood there, looking very clean in a white T-shirt and sweat pants. She flashed him a wide smile.

"Hello, Detective. I was just going for a run, but I couldn't resist poking my nose in all this mayhem." Her eyes traveled across his splattered shirt. "Looks like you've been right in the thick of it."

He felt a sudden shortness of breath. "It's been an interesting morning." He looked at her bob of silky hair and remembered the goo that was no doubt coating him from head to toe at the moment. *Conversation. Make some conversation,* he told himself.

"So, uh, running, eh?" He shoved his hands into his pockets, ignoring the avalanche of noodles that fell to the grass as he did so. "Running is good, yeah." *That was smooth, Denny.*

She laughed. The sound was high and musical. "It's good, yeah. Do you run?"

"Me?" He tried to remember the last time he went jogging. It might have been the fitness test at the police academy. "Running. Yes, I do running. I mean,

I jog. Yes." It was only when he needed to chase down a suspect, but that was running, wasn't it? He tried hard to think of a way to extend the conversation.

"Maybe we could go running this week. On your day off or something," she said.

His heart began to jackhammer again. "Yes," he said too loudly. "Yes, let's run this week."

She nodded. Then she leaned forward and raised a hand to his hair. He held his breath as her fingers brushed his cheek. She smelled like vanilla.

"Okay. But maybe you should leave the pickles at home." She handed him the slice of dill and jogged off, her laughter trailing behind her.

10

The morning shower was as hot as Ruth could stand it. As she watched the suds swirl around her toes, she could not get the memory of the crumpled balloon out of her mind. It was Wednesday, a scant five days after the balloon accident, and she could still hear the awful *thump* as the basket hit the ground. She had seen Ed so very much alive a few hours before the launch that she could not reconcile the picture of the congenial bald man with the twisted mass of flesh imbedded in Finny's Nose.

The food fight the day before did nothing to ease the atmosphere. She didn't know whether to laugh or cry at the thought of all those grown-ups hurling food at each other like a bunch of preschoolers.

Idly she wondered what the cultured Meg Sooner had made of the whole sticky mess.

Ruth stayed in the shower until the water became tepid, but she still could not focus her mind on anything but the current string of worries. She wished Monk was home, but the catering business demanded plenty of hours. Determined to snap out of her funk, she prepared a cup of near-scalding coffee and sat down at the table with the decrepit journal.

> *August the 25th, 1923*
>
> *It's all coming back to me now. It was two months ago when the old lady showed up. No one remembered letting her in, but there she was, a wizened old China lady. Her front teeth were gone and most of her hair. She was dressed from head to toe in a dreadful black shift with a huge crocheted shawl that seemed to swallow her up. She pointed a bony finger at me and croaked, "Where is she? Where is my Ling?"*
>
> *I told her Ling was gone. Slats sent her away a month ago because she wasn't able to keep up with the dance steps. Ling wasn't much of a looker to start with, and she just kept getting thinner and thinner until there wasn't anything left to do the kicks and turns. Her dance costumes hung on her like rags. I felt bad for Ling, but she took it well. Just packed her bags and left.*
>
> *"You get her back!" the old lady shrieked, still jabbing her finger in the air.*
>
> *By then all the girls were crowded around on account of the screaming.*

*I told the old gal that Ling was gone, and I didn't know where, but
she continued to scream in a most unholy way. Finally, my piano man
grabbed hold of her arms and drug her out. The screams echoed throughout
the restaurant.*

*I don't know why it's come into my mind again. Maybe it's this evil
fog that has been smothering us in darkness for weeks. I can't get her
screams out of my mind.*

Ruth read the passage twice, struggling against the loops and curves of the
penned script. It was a fantastic tale so far. A Finny woman, working for a gangster,
watching the developing loves and lives of her dancing girls. It had all the makings
of a tragic soap opera.

Reading the journal was an attempt to distract herself, but it had only stirred
her mind even further. Could the woman's story be true? Ruth knew that in the
early twenties there was indeed an eating establishment on the outskirts of Finny.
And it was certainly true that Finny was named after an unsuccessful rumrunner.
Ruth needed to find out if the journal was fact or fancy. She remembered her
earlier idea to visit Ellen Foots.

Picking up the phone, she dialed the Finny Public Library and made
arrangements to sit in on Ellen's next presentation later in the afternoon.

After hanging up, she waded through her birds in the backyard. "All right,
everyone. Here's breakfast." She heaved a tray full of bread scraps and vegetable
chunks onto the patio and left the birds to their squabbling. While they were
distracted, she turned her attention to her business demands.

The worms in the fattening bed were in wiggly ecstasy as she fed them their
mash. She tried to keep her mind fully engrossed in the task at hand as she moved
from feeding to harvesting. The standing orders for worm castings needed to be
filled regardless of the latest Finny catastrophe.

The regular beds were moist but not sticky. Just right, she thought with pride.
With a flathead shovel she carefully removed the first five inches of soil where
most of the worms congregated. She placed the shovelfuls on a plywood sheet
covered with plastic and switched on the halogen light that dangled just above
the wood. As the worms sought to escape the brightness, they began burrowing
down nearer the bottom.

Ruth whisked away the top two inches of soil with a small broom and
dustpan, emptying the contents into gallon drums. She waited patiently for
worms to burrow down deeper and repeated her whisking. Eventually she had
the required amount of worm compost for the latest orders and a solid mass of
grumpy worms on her plywood.

"Go away, Teddy," she said, shoving a plump gray gull away with her shoe.
She slid the worms back into the concrete bins and covered them with bird

manure, topsoil, and garden compost. The cleaning up was not quite finished when the phone rang. The voice on the other end came through the receiver with piercing decibels.

"You've got to get to the tent. The Bippo woman is doing a presentation for the natives, and you have to get a few pictures."

"Maude, are you sure? The last event turned into a culinary brawl. Maybe we should cancel the rest of the festival activities."

"Ruth Marilyn Budge. If you think for one minute we are canceling the rest of the festival, you've gone around the bend. We've spent big bucks on that tent, and the booths, not to mention the cotton candy and popcorn machines, and that jumpy house thing—which now needs to be repaired."

Ruth held the phone away from her ear to lessen the screech. "I see your point. I was just thinking about propriety."

"Who cares about propriety? Ed Honeysill is past caring, and we've got craftspeople from up and down the coast who paid for two full weekends of festival. We will carry on as planned until we wrap up Sunday at 5:00 p.m. Besides, the next batch of visitors won't even know there's been a murder unless we make a big deal about it."

Ruth found that hard to believe. "Okay, Maude. I can stop by the tent on the way to snap a few pictures." She hung up hurriedly before Maude had time to ask her to wear the Mrs. Fog costume.

Evelyn stood at the podium in front of the sparse crowd. It was a quiet, dazed-looking group that gathered in the tent, mostly silent except for the occasional furtive whisper regarding the previous day's culinary brawl. Behind Evelyn hung a banner announcing THE DOG HOUSE in red felt letters. As she spoke, she stroked a raggedy bundle under her arm. Occasionally the bundle poked a wet nose into the air and sniffed.

Ruth waved to Mary Dirisi. With all that had been happening lately, the more police around the better, even if they were out of uniform and on their day off. She turned on the camera.

She didn't even have time to raise it to her eye before Bing strode into the tent, taking a position near the entrance. Just as quickly, Ruth saw Rocky in jeans and a sweatshirt march down the aisle to him.

"You've got some nerve showing up here like you're some sort of dog lover," Rocky snarled in a not-so-soft whisper. His face was mottled, and his eyes flashed through the thick lenses of his glasses.

"I can show up anywhere I want," Bing barked. "And I am a lover of dogs. Normal dogs, not mental cases."

Ruth tensed and glanced at Mary. Evelyn continued to speak, her eyes fastened on the two men at the back of the tent. The dogs peered curiously from behind the short fences fastened together in makeshift kennels.

"Rudy, for instance, would be an excellent dog for a house with older children." Her words seemed as though they came out on autopilot. "He's an energetic fellow, but with training he would become a loyal family friend."

Heads began to turn toward the ruckus in the back. Mary frowned. "Did you say the dogs are fixed before they are adopted out?" she asked loudly, perhaps to assert her presence, Ruth thought.

"Yes, that's a requirement to ensure we don't increase the number of unwanted animals in the world."

"What are you, some kind of stalker?" Rocky snapped.

"The only person stalking anyone is you, you freak," Bing said with a laugh.

"Do you do any consulting on dog training?" Bubby asked between nervous slugs of coffee. "My dachshund, Inky, has the worst habit of trying to eat the mailman. I have to pick up my mail at the post office now. It's a real pain in the caboose."

Evelyn was just opening her mouth to reply when Rocky threw a punch that caught Bing under the chin and sent him over backward. With blood oozing from his mouth, Bing recovered and dove for him.

They both went over in a heap.

Evelyn raced down the center aisle. The three penned dogs in front of the podium leaped over their enclosure and followed, their barks deafening the audience.

"Man," Mary said. She got calmly to her feet and joined the fracas.

"Stop! Rocky! Stop!" Evelyn screamed, trying to grab hold of Rocky's arm. Her brother continued to slam his fist into Bing's ribs.

"Get off me, you psychopath!" Bing shouted with a kick that sent Rocky's glasses spiraling through the air. "Don't you have any more buildings to blow up?"

Ruth put her camera on a folding chair and joined Bubby and a few others trying to corral the yapping dogs.

Mary grabbed hold of Rocky's ponytail where it connected to the scalp and yanked him upward. He came with a grunted obscenity and fists raised to strike his new assailant. Catching sight of the look on her face, he reconsidered.

"Sit there," she commanded, pointing to a chair. To Bing she said, "You, get up. Step outside." Bing also followed directions and walked out of the tent. "I'll be back to talk to you in a minute," she said to Rocky. "If you move, I'm going to have to come after you, and I'm already irritated."

He watched her go while Evelyn held a handkerchief against a cut on his eyebrow.

Ruth finally managed to grab hold of the smallest of the canine escapees. She took a leisurely pace back toward the pen, giving her plenty of time to eavesdrop on the conversation developing just outside the tent opening.

"What's the problem between you two?" Mary demanded.

"There's no—" Bing began.

"Can the nonsense. It's my day off, and this is the last thing I want to be doing, so get to it."

"All right. We had a disagreement last year. Rocky blames me for abusing a dog I adopted from Evelyn."

Bing saw Mary's eyebrows rise in disgust and added, "I didn't do anything to the dog. I gave him back because he was nuts."

"And?"

"And Rocky blames me for reporting Evelyn to the authorities for having too many dogs on her property."

"And?"

"And I didn't do it. Rocky's as nuts as the dog. The guy is a few eggs short of a dozen, you know what I mean?" Bing smiled warmly. "You should run a check on him. He's been linked to some of that ecoterrorism stuff, you know."

Ruth thought about her late-night Internet research as she lingered near the tent opening.

"Go home," Mary said. "I'll come and get you if I need to haul either of your butts in." She turned back into the tent.

Ruth busied herself making sure the dog's collar was securely fastened.

Rocky pushed Evelyn's hand away from his eye and stood. "Officer, Mitchell is harassing me and my sister," he said.

"Sit down. He says you're mad over the dog thing last year. What's the deal?" Mary zipped her windbreaker against a breeze that wafted into the now-empty tent.

"He beat our dog last year and mutilated him," Rocky snarled. He blinked nearsightedly up at the officer.

"Did you press charges?"

Evelyn and Rocky looked at each other. "No," she mumbled.

"Why not?"

"Because he said he'd turn Ev in to animal control for housing too many dogs." Rocky wiped the blood away from his eye with his sleeve. "Funny how animal control got an anonymous tip a month later anyway."

"Okay, so we've got your word and his word. What happened just now to make you two lose your minds and start swinging?"

"He was leering at my sister, smiling in that playboy arrogant way. He doesn't have any business here. There's no way he's coming near my sister or her dogs again."

"He has as much business here as any other member of the public. What do you have to do with ecoterrorism?"

Rocky's mouth opened and closed. After a moment he said, "Nothing. I don't know anything about that."

Mary eyed him closely. "Okay, for the moment. Now since you jokers have disrupted your sister's presentation for the day, go home and cool off. Next time you go to jail."

Rocky shoved his bent glasses into his pants pocket and stalked off.

Mary turned to Evelyn. "Has he always been a loose cannon?"

Evelyn sighed, her thin shoulders hunched. "I guess so." She looked down at her worn loafers. "It's just because he loves me. He's really protective. My parents died when we were young. Rocky has taken care of me since I was seven."

"Has he been in trouble before?"

She hesitated. "No. Not since we were teenagers. He, uh, beat up someone years ago, a boy he thought was no good for me." Evelyn cleared her throat. "He loves me, that's all." She added softly, "He's the only one who ever has."

Mary Dirisi nodded. "Yeah, well, you know what they say, Ms. Bippo. Sometimes love hurts."

Ruth thought about the hatred in Rocky's face when he looked at Bing. She knew that Bing had something of the Bippos that they desperately wanted back.

Sometimes love hurts.

Ruth wondered if it could hurt enough to kill.

11

It turned into a ridiculously sunny afternoon as Ruth hurried to the Finny Public Library. She imagined Maude hard at work with her fog machine.

Ruth found the presentation commencing in the back room. It consisted of a fatigued-looking teacher by the name of Mrs. Finkelstein and a group of twenty-one exceptionally well-behaved third graders. The model behavior was due not to the efforts of the weary Finklestein but to the aura of aggressive energy emanating from the six-foot-four librarian.

Ellen sat in a straight-backed chair, hiking boots planted firmly on the ground, her hair a whirly confusion of black frizz that hovered around her face.

"Well then," she announced, "let's move on to the Roaring Twenties in Finny. Does anyone know why they are called the Roaring Twenties?"

No third grader had the internal fortitude to attempt an answer.

"Hmm," Ellen sniffed. "Disappointing. It was due to the exuberance and, I might add, moral degradation that accompanied the constitutional amendment which outlawed the sale or purchase of alcoholic beverages. It was a dangerous time to live here. Plenty of lawlessness and chaos."

Ruth noticed the children's eyes beginning to glaze over and roll back into their youthful heads as the librarian continued her historical diatribe. The glaze seemed to have infected Ruth's own eyes until a particular word caused her to start upright.

"—*murder*," Ellen said.

Mrs. Finkelstein sat up straight also, as though someone had slapped her. She adjusted her wire-rimmed glasses and swept the short bangs out of her eyes to get a better look at the speaker.

"I'm sure your teacher has told you about the Pickle Jar, which used to stand just below the tip of Finny's Nose. It was run by a woman named Pickles Peckenpaugh who came to Finny from San Francisco in 1922."

A tiny voice ventured out from a boy in the front row. "Who got murdered? Was there bodies and everything?"

Ruth looked over the children's heads to see Mrs. Finklestein gesturing wildly with a slashing motion across her throat and violent head shaking.

"Well, for goodness' sake, they're old enough to know the truth. It was a pretty brutal way to die, I'll admit."

The children were warming to the subject, encouraged by the fact that their classmate had not been slain. A chubby girl with a complicated array of braids spoke up. "How did it happen?"

"Oh, it was a mysterious case. Two terrible crimes occurred on Finny's Nose in 1923."

Crimes? Ruth leaned forward.

"The first was a young girl, tied to a tree and nearly burned to death in September of 1923, if I recall correctly. She was a dancing girl at the Pickle Jar. Rescued just in time. Terrible thing having someone try to set you on fire. Seems like shooting or strangling would be more humane."

Ruth noted Mrs. Finkelstein squinching her eyes together as she slipped down in her chair. There was a buzz of excitement from the kids.

"Then exactly one week later, there was a body found in the very same spot. A man, with his neck broken. He was believed to be the ringleader of a gang. The killer was never caught. What have I told you about gangs, children? A sure way to get your throat slit."

For the next fifteen minutes, they looked at grainy slides that Ellen projected onto the wall.

Ellen slapped her hands on her thighs. "Well then, that concludes my presentation, and it's time to check out a book before you leave. Except for you, Hugo." She pointed an accusing finger at a gangly boy in the back row. "You will not check out another thing from this library until you return *The Ultimate Adventures of Spider-Man*."

Since the teacher appeared to be out of commission, no doubt mentally reworking her résumé, the librarian rallied the troops and had them line up at the door to leave. Ruth joined her caboose to the end of the line. "What happened to the Pickle Jar?" she asked over the gabble of voices.

"It closed down after the murder and fell into disrepair. All that's left is a pile of foundation stones halfway up nose." She turned her attention to the hapless Hugo as the class began to file out of the meeting room. "You, young man, will have to dust the shelves while the others are checking out books. And there's a bulletin board that needs the staples removed." Then the ferocious librarian was gone, leaving a wiggly bunch of lined-up third graders and a dazed-looking woman feebly trying to rise from her chair.

~

Over a cup of coffee with extra cream and sugar, Ruth opened the diary again.

August the 27th, 1923
    Received a letter from Slats today. He is on his way to Finny and I am to expect him tomorrow. He says he knows who pinched his money and he's coming to settle the score. My blood runs cold and I haven't been able to

swallow a morsel. I must get word to Soapy Dan somehow. He must take to his heels before Slats arrives. I simply must reach him before Slats does.

August the 28th, 1923

Slats arrived this morning with two of his thugs. He asked Janey most politely if she knew of Dan's whereabouts. Janey told him things had ended between them before Dan skipped town. Slats spoke to all of us calmly as though he hadn't a care in the world. Maybe things will be all right if Soapy Dan does indeed disappear for a while. Perhaps things will be all right after all.

September the 7th, 1923

I cannot even force my horror into words. What I saw last night is burned into my brain and will stay there forever. I came down to open the doors in the morning, and Hazel met me in the kitchen.

"She's gone, Pickles!"

I threw on some clothes and woke Roscoe. By then most of the other girls were there and we headed up Finny's Nose, following the awful shrieking. We were almost to the top when we saw her there, tied to a pine. She looked so small and white in the midst of that poisonous fog. I almost didn't see her at first until the needles under her feet caught.

As I live and breathe, I will never forget the sound of that whooshing flame, or the look in her eyes as she watched her skirt begin to burn.

Roscoe and I ran forward to try to undo the ropes. We managed to drag her away just before the fire exploded everywhere. Her face was untouched, but her arms and legs were burned. I could see terror and anguish in her eyes. We could all feel the terrible evil settling into the air around us. Only God can mend the horror in our hearts.

This place will forever echo with the screams of that poor girl.

The ruins of the Pickle Jar could have been passed over completely unnoticed by the casual observer. As it was, Ruth almost missed them. The charred beams were nearly covered by a scalp of brilliant green grass, a tint of green found only in rare tropical frogs and play dough. Here and there a pile of crumbling bricks dotted the small plateau, and a fallen tree surrendered to the onslaught of decay.

Ruth and Cootchie trudged almost to the top of Finny's Nose for their pre-dinner outing in order to get a more aerial view of what used to be Finny's most infamous eating establishment. Ruth planted her bottom on a spongy trunk and hoisted Cootchie up next to her.

"Juice?" the little girl inquired.

"Okay, sweet pea." Ruth fished around in her backpack and found a sippy cup full of pomegranate juice. She handed it to the child along with a handful of soybeans. Cootchie slurped away, picking long stalks of grass with her free hand.

Looking downslope, she saw that the plateau ambled along for several hundred yards before it dropped away gradually into a wooded depression with a creek running through it. In the spring, the creek swelled to a respectable width until summer came and reduced it to a series of shallow puddles. Now it barely burbled along. Cootchie hopped off her perch and put down her juice cup before beginning to further excavate a gopher hole nearby.

Ruth's thoughts turned to a diary entry she had read earlier. She had not yet finished reading it, but the horrendous description of Janey's attack stayed in her mind, along with Ellen's retelling of the murder. A cluster of pines above her head made her wonder if this might have been the spot where the unfortunate girl had been tied.

"Enough of this. Let's go home, Cootchie."

There was no answer.

Ruth jumped up. She looked behind the log and scanned the slope in all directions for the child. "Cootchie, where are you?" she called.

The only sound was the wind against the leaves.

She continued to call out with increasing volume and intensity until she was screaming louder than she ever had in her life.

A paralyzing panic squeezed her heart and lungs. "Cootchie! Cootchie, where are you? Cootchie, answer Nana Ruth!" she shouted. Her frantic cries echoed among the trees.

"Dear God, please let me find her." Her legs pounded over rocks and branches as she ran down the slope to the spot where she left her backpack. Grabbing her cell phone with shaking hands, she dialed 911.

"Please help me. It's Ruth Budge. I'm at the top of Finny's Nose and Cootchie has disappeared." Her shaking fingers almost lost their grip on the phone. "Please, please help me. I can't find her anywhere."

As she stood with the phone pressed to her ear, her eyes scanned desperately for a glimpse of the girl's blue checked shirt.

The only splash of color was the tiny cup, sitting on the log, the juice gleaming blood red in the sun.

~

The next several hours passed in an agonizingly slow creep. There were lights and sirens, people in uniform and one in an apron. They asked her questions, came and left with radios and phones. Someone made her sit down once again on the spongy log. The aproned person with a ladle in his pocket sat next to her. It took her a minute to realize it was her husband.

"It's going to be okay," Monk said, putting a beefy arm around her shoulders.

FOG OVER FINNY'S NOSE

"They're going to find her."

His voice seemed to come from a long way off.

The sun was behind the trees, and a chill fog rose to meet it.

A car wheezed up the slope and came to rest in a cloud of dust several yards from the log. Dimple and her mother stepped out.

Meg held Dimple by the arm, leading her as one would an elderly person. Dimple's face was very white.

As the two women approached, Ruth rose to her feet like a marionette controlled by some unseen hand. She looked into Dimple's eyes and saw a horror that took the words out of her mouth. There was no anger there, but a look of such profound fear that it made Ruth's throat go dry.

They stood there for a tortured moment of silence.

Meg clutched Dimple's arm more tightly. "We understand you took Cootchie up here."

Ruth nodded. Tears welled up and spilled down her face.

"Cootchie must have wandered away while Ruth's back was turned," Monk said.

Meg regarded him for a moment, her gray eyes narrowed. "Her back shouldn't have been turned."

Somewhere down deep Ruth registered surprise at the anger she heard in Meg's voice.

"Now wait just a minute, ma'am. Ruth has taken excellent care of Cootchie since the day she was born," he said.

"She didn't take very good care of her today, did she?" Her voice was shrill and hovered oddly in the rising fog.

"That's not fair, ma'am. You haven't been here to see how well Ruth cares for Cootchie."

Before Meg had a chance to respond, Jack approached and cleared his throat. "Ladies, I have something to tell you. It may be nothing at all, but I think you should know a witness saw a pickup driving down the fire trail on the far side of Finny's Nose."

They all stared at the detective.

Monk spoke first. "Who was the witness? Did he see a child in the truck?"

"It was one of the Coastal Comets, a guy named Hector Rodriguez. He was hiking and says he saw a pickup headed downslope about an hour ago. He has no details about the driver." Jack looked down at the faded knees of his jeans. "We found these on the ground near the fire trail." Slowly he held up a plastic bag. Inside were three soybeans.

Dimple buried her face in her mother's shoulder, and Ruth slid to the hard ground of Finny's Nose.

12

Jack collapsed in his squeaky chair at his desk, convinced that if the coffee machine wasn't repaired soon, he would have to shoot someone. The desperation he felt at not being able to find Cootchie only deepened when the pair from the FBI showed up to take over the search. It was now well into Thursday and still no progress. He thought constantly about his own young son. It was all he could do not to pick up the phone and call Louella to check on him again.

His stomach growled, reminding him he had not eaten lunch.

The phone rang, and he snatched it up. His face warmed when he heard the voice on the other end. "Oh, hey, Bobby."

"Hi, Jack. Is there any news?"

"No." He hoped his helplessness didn't seep into his voice. "It's pretty much the FBI's show now."

"I bet that really ticks you off."

He smiled. How did she know that? "Yeah, I guess it does. Are Monk and Ruth okay?"

"I don't think so. They won't be okay until there is word, I think."

"Me neither."

"Well," Bobby said, "I just wanted to tell you that I hope you're holding up. I know this is hard for you. Maybe we can go for that run after everything is settled and Cootchie is back safe and sound."

His heart jumped. "Oh sure. I would love that."

"When do you get to come home?"

He groaned. "Who knows."

"Okay. I'll fix you a frittata and leave it at your house. Do you like fritattas?"

He had no clue what a frittata was, but that didn't stifle the warm feeling in his gut. "Sure, that sounds great."

Nathan entered the office with a coffee cup in his hand.

"I've gotta get back to work. Thank you for checking in. I'm sure the frittata will be great." He hung up and looked at his friend. "If that's coffee, you are promoted to admiral."

"It's orange juice, and we don't have an admiral."

"Okay." He noted lines of exhaustion on Nate's face that he was sure matched his own. He struggled to pull his mind to the Honeysill investigation. "Did you catch anything from the Candace interview that I missed?"

"Nothing in particular. She came across pretty sincerely ignorant about the life insurance policy."

"It gives her a motive for killing him," Jack said.

"Two hundred fifty thousand motives, I'd say. Do you want the background on Rocky Bippo that Mary dug up?"

"Sure," he said wearily. "Let me have it."

Nate consulted a sheaf of papers. "He's a GOP."

"A Republican?"

"A Guardian of the Planet. Some sort of gang that goes around trying to keep people from cutting down trees and stuff like that."

"Legal or not?"

"He's been connected with blockading a logging road and dumping sawdust and a three-hundred-pound stump in the middle of an Oregon city council office. No charges filed due to lack of evidence. Oh, here's a good one. He was in the vicinity of the Elegant Tree Farm when it was torched."

"I thought they liked trees."

"Apparently these trees were propagated from genetically modified stock."

"And that's a bad thing?" Jack asked.

"I'll bet the GOPs think so."

He rubbed his face. "That's all we need. A bunch of environmental wackos on the loose in Finny."

Jack looked at his phone again, willing it to ring with news about Cootchie. "Who's next?"

"Bing the balloon guy again. He was supposed to be the one to take Honeysill up in the balloon, but he was AWOL at launch time. We got his basic story already, but he's back for round two."

They walked to the interview room and settled into hard chairs.

The door opened, and Bing stepped into the room. He looked like a man entering a country club rather than a squad room. His hair was spiked with gel, and his muscled arms were tanned under his blue polo shirt. To top it off, the man was carrying a styrofoam cup of coffee.

"How are you?" he said to the officers, extending a hand to both. "Good to see you again. Pretty nuts around here. I bet you guys are wishing this whole festival deal would pack up and leave town."

"Something like that. You remember Officer Katz. Have a seat, Mr. Mitchell."

"Great." He slid into a chair. "I've been on my feet all day. You can call me Bing. Sounds like you people are busy these days. I understand there's a kid missing."

"We're managing. Why don't you tell us again about the day your balloon crashed, Mr. Mitchell."

"Well, let's see." He took a sip of coffee. "Like I told you before, I got up around five or so—I'm an early riser. I went for a jog on the beach before I checked in with my guys to make sure they had everything under control. Then off I went in search of Starbucks. Never did find any. Had to buy this at a catering place. Can you really survive in a town without a Starbucks?" He chuckled.

"Barely," Nate commented.

Jack tried to block out the enticing aroma of coffee. "Where were you at launch time? The balloon was scheduled to go up at one o'clock. It left without you."

"Hey, I was just seeing the sights in this little burg. It's great here, just like Mayberry or something. I'm thinking of buying a piece of property. I think this would be a great place to set up shop. Folks would pay well to see the coastline from a hot air balloon."

"What sights were you seeing, exactly?"

"I can't recall minute by minute. I spent some time on the beach, searching for the sun. Then I went for a walk. I lost all track of time—that's why I was late for the launch." He put the cup on Jack's desk and laced his fingers across his abdomen.

"Come on, gentlemen. What motive would I have for shooting down my own balloon? The things are eight grand a piece, just for the nylon skin. That would be a poor business move on my part, don't you think? Plus my best guy was up there with him. It was just a stroke of luck that he got out of it with only a broken ankle."

"We're just putting the pieces together, Mr. Mitchell. How well did you know Ed Honeysill?"

Bing looked up at the ceiling, frowning. "Let's see. I met him about two years ago at a festival in Oregon. I've seen him a couple times since; we seem to frequent the same events. I know he sold fungus or something, didn't he?"

"And how well did you know his wife?" Jack pressed.

Bing looked startled, the easy smile still in place. "Why? What did she tell you?"

"That she knows you."

"We've become friends recently. Nothing too interesting. I'm just someone she talks to when Ed is—was—networking."

"Were you with her before the launch?"

"Oh yeah. I think we talked for a while in my trailer. I don't remember what time it was or anything. I forgot about it."

"You talked?"

Bing raised an eyebrow. "Among other things. We didn't break any laws, Detective. Maybe a few commandments, but no laws." After a moment he added, "Look. I know what you're thinking, but I've got no motive to kill Honeysill. I was getting all I wanted from Candace with him alive. You know what I mean."

Jack masked his disgust by swallowing a sip of orange juice. "Okay, Mr. Mitchell. Just one more topic. We've talked about your relationship with the Bippos. Run through it once more, if you don't mind."

"Oh boy." Bing sighed. He shook his head. "I don't really have much of a relationship with them. I adopted a dog from Evelyn, trying to be a Good Samaritan, you know? It didn't work out, so I gave him back. That's about it. I don't mix with them."

"Evelyn is pretty adamant that you abused the dog," Jack said.

"Come on, guys. Do I look like the kind of guy who tortures animals?"

Jack wanted to say that Bing looked about as nice as many of the psychotics he'd met over the years. "She says when she threatened to press charges, you reported her to animal control for having too many dogs on the property."

"That's not true. I just gave back the dog; that's all."

"She seems to think you're a real hard-hearted slimeball," Nathan spoke up. "So does her brother."

Bing twitched before his smile returned. "Just between us guys, women sometimes get a little more interested in me than I do in them."

"Are you saying Evelyn Bippo wanted a relationship with you?" Jack asked.

"She would have jumped at the chance, but she just isn't my type. Rocky is crazy, by the way. He's one of those wackos who eat wheatgrass and refuse to use plastic shopping bags. He loves trees more than people."

Jack digested the info as best he could with no coffee in his lower GI tract. "All right, Mr. Mitchell. One more thing. You own a ninety-nine Dodge Ram pickup truck?"

"Sure do. But it's back home in Oregon. I drove my Hummer here. The gas mileage is lousy, but it's worth it knowing you can roll over any moron that gets in your way."

"All right." He stood to signal the end of the interview. "Thank you for coming in. We'll be in touch. By the way, is there anyone else, besides the Bippos, that has a problem with you?"

"I'm a very likable guy, Detective—ask anyone. I really can't think of any enemies. Why do you ask?"

"It could be that Honeysill wasn't the intended target." Jack slam-dunked the coffee cup. "Maybe you were."

Jack watched Bing leave the office, a slight look of unease on the man's face.

Nate's phone rang. Jack could feel the tension before his friend spoke a word.

"Right," Nate said, eyes wide. "We're on our way."

13

The knock on the door sounded like a gunshot. Ruth leaped to her feet, hands covering her mouth, eyes staring wildly. Monk set the cup of newly steeped tea carefully on the mantel. He nodded calmly as he said, "I'll get that, honey. It's going to be fine."

Seemingly in slow motion, the door opened, and there was Jack, standing on the doormat with his hands jammed into his pockets. "Sorry to come by so late."

"Come in." Monk ushered the man inside.

"Ruth, I've got news," he said.

She stared at him like a half-wit. A terrible smothering blanket of terror pushed at her from all sides. In her mind she heard herself screaming, but no sound came out of her mouth.

"We've found her."

Monk cleared his throat and stood up straight. He gripped Ruth around the shoulders and pulled her close. "Tell us, Jack."

"She's fine, perfectly fine. Apparently whoever took Cootchie drove up the coast to Half Moon Bay and left her on the steps of the public library. She curled up in the nonfiction section under a bench and fell asleep. The custodian found her this morning. She told him she was from Finny and wanted a book about hydroponic gardening." He smiled.

"Did Cootchie say who took her?" Monk asked.

"She didn't tell us much of anything that wasn't about poetry or rocks. She said it was a man with glasses, though she can't say if they're reading or sunglasses. As for the vehicle, she says it was a spaceship."

"Was she—? Did he—?" Ruth stammered.

"The doctor at Eden Hospital did a thorough exam, and he said she's in mint condition. No sign of, er, injury or anything." He looked closely at her. "It's all over, Ruth. Cootchie is absolutely fine, and we're going to find the person who did this." When she did not respond, Jack added, "It wasn't your fault. No one blames you."

Ruth turned away from the two men and stared out the window at the lengthening shadows.

"Okay, Jack, thanks for coming over," Monk said.

"No problem. If there is anything you need, anything at all. . ."

"We know where to find you. I've got a pot of clam chowder simmering on the stove and a loaf of bread in the oven." Monk added more quietly, "We'll get through it."

"Maybe you could take her over to Dimple's. In a few days, I mean. Let things settle awhile."

Monk nodded. "I was thinking the same thing."

Ruth walked outside. The moist air surrounded her with an outer coldness that matched her inner chill. The fog deadened the sounds. Even the birds that rustled in the corner of the yard seemed as though they were in another world. She felt moisture on her chin from the tears coursing unnoticed down her face. In the middle of the horror came a realization that she'd been given a miracle. For a moment, the agony lessened. "Thank You, sweet Jesus," she said as she sank to the ground and gave her tears to the fog.

She didn't know how long she stayed on the cold ground. Vaguely she recalled the birds poking at her hair. Monk lifted her and brought her back into the house. She knew he talked to her for a while before he hoisted her in his arms, but she could not remember any of the words. Somehow she came to be deposited in a chair in front of the glowing pellet stove with a mug of steaming Earl Grey at her elbow.

Monk gave up trying to talk after a while. He sat in a rocking chair across the area rug from her and began knitting. The soft clacking of his needles and the shushing of the yarn through his fingers kept time with the rocking. That and the clock were the only sounds.

"What are you knitting?" she finally asked. A ludicrous question, but it was all her mouth could manage.

"A sweater. Cable knit, for you," he answered. He continued to watch her, his fingers working unsupervised. "You need a new one."

"The last one you gave me is still fine."

"I know," he said. "Can I get you anything?"

"No thanks." They lapsed into relative silence again.

Ruth watched the yarn loop and curl as it transformed from skein to sleeve. It was magical almost. She watched him pull a thread and unravel a row. Suddenly her heart clenched in one aching desire. If only she could undo that minute, that one second when she had turned her back on the person she loved so dearly. The moment when she let Cootchie down. Let Dimple down. The moment when she almost destroyed them all.

The sobs returned, but there were no tears left to accompany them.

Monk put down his knitting. He handed her a box of tissues and rubbed comforting circles into her back. "It's okay, Ruth. She's fine. She's just fine."

When her sobs relented, he excused himself to tend to dinner. She watched him add cream to the clam chowder and stir it slowly. The brown bread came out of the oven and perfumed the whole house with fragrance. He set glasses of iced tea on the table along with bowls of chowder and thick slabs of bread.

Ruth was too wrung out to protest as Monk took her hand and led her to the table. "Heavenly Father, thank You for this food. Thank You for bringing Cootchie back. Thank You for your boundless love that will help us through anything. Amen." He lit a bayberry candle. "Eat something. It will help."

She struggled to get the spoon to her mouth. In spite of her emotional condition, Ruth's taste buds found the chowder delectable. She managed several spoonfuls before she gave up. Monk finished his dinner and sat back, sipping the tea and watching her.

"Why don't you tell me what you're thinking?" he said.

"I was thinking," she said word by painful word, "that Cootchie saved my life. Or maybe it was Dimple. I'm not sure."

He nodded.

"I felt like my life was over because Phillip was gone. I thought I couldn't survive another day. Not one more day." She stared at the liquid that swirled in her glass. "I wanted to walk out the door and keep walking until I fell off the edge of the earth. Dimple found me somehow. She asked me to go with her to her first ultrasound." Ruth shook her head. "I didn't know her well, and from what I did know about her, I thought she was crazy. I mean, a woman who brews her own perfume and writes fortunes for a living?"

"Dimple is one of a kind," he agreed.

"I thought she was nuts. But she asked me to go with her. And for some reason, I did. I went because I felt God was urging me to. Just for the ultrasound. Then it was just for the Lamaze classes. And then only to see her through the delivery. Then I met Cootchie, and she became the reason for me to live." Tears began to roll down her face again. "God sent her to me so I wouldn't be alone. And then He brought me to you when I was able to love again."

Monk looked at her with an exquisitely gentle expression in his blue eyes. "Cootchie was the instrument. God showed you that you were not meant to waste all the amazing gifts you've been given."

She stared at him. "There is absolutely nothing amazing about me. I have ruined the one amazing thing in my life."

"It's going to be difficult, to overcome this. But you will, because it isn't right to waste those gifts any more now than it was then. You're too young for that. God has given you strength because He knows you will use it to His glory."

Ruth continued to stare at him.

He sighed, "Or as my father says, life is hard, but it beats the alternative."

She began to laugh.

FOG OVER FINNY'S NOSE

It was midnight before they got up from the table. She talked until there were no words or tears left. He listened to it all, commenting occasionally but mostly just nodding. He helped her up from the table and walked with her to the pellet stove to warm themselves against the evening chill.

She awakened an hour later, snuggled up against his wide back. She knew the morning would bring back the horrible trauma. But for now, she relished the warmth against her cheek and the quiet snoring that enclosed her in a comforting basket of sound.

14

The police station door crashed open early Friday morning. Jack watched from his office, a phone pressed to his ear, as Alva and Hector Rodriquez, the Coastal Comet, careened in. Mary looked up from her paperwork and walked to the front counter.

"What's up?" she asked with a suspicious look at Alva's companion.

"Me and Hector was up nose, lookin' for clues. To help find Cootchie," the old man said, breathing hard. "Hector wanted to be a private eye before he went into the acrobat business."

Hector smiled, his silver front tooth winking in the overhead lights.

"Alva," Mary began.

"Don't worry; we didn't mess up any police scenes or anything."

Hector nodded.

"Alva, I guess you didn't hear. We've already—"

"We found something," he continued. "It's a clue." With that, he heaved the mass onto the counter with a terrible crash.

Jack almost dropped the phone.

Mary shot backward in surprise. Her sudden movement knocked over the nearly empty watercooler, causing her to skid to the tile floor behind the counter. He hung up and went to assist.

Alva forged ahead. "We found it about half a mile from the top of the nose. It's a clue for sure. First that toe shows up without a foot, and now we come upon this. Don't that seem like a pattern or something?" His watery eyes grew to Oreo size. "I know it was that gang. I seem 'em with my own eyes skulking around up there."

From behind the counter, Jack heard words and water begin to flow as he headed into the front office.

"Would you just shut up for a minute, Alva?" Mary continued grunting as she tried to regain her footing, water soaking into her pants.

Jack took his eyes off the mayhem to see Hugh push through the door. "Hey, Alva. I heard they found Cootchie. Did you. . ." He caught sight of the mass on the counter. "Oh man."

"It's a clue." Alva nodded. "What do you mean they found her? Is she okay?"

"Yes, she's fine," Jack said, trying to grab Mary's slippery wrist.

FOG OVER FINNY'S NOSE

"I came here to get the word firsthand," Hugh said. "It didn't seem right to go bother Dimple about it just now. Why is there water pouring all over the floor? You got a broken pipe or something?"

"It's not a broken pipe." Mary's voice came from behind the counter as Jack tried to help her up.

"Who said that?" Hugh asked.

"The gal on the floor," Alva said. "Who you figure took the little girl, Jack? Maybe they was fixin' to get some ransom." His shaggy white eyebrows flew upwards. "Maybe one of them gangsters. What do you figure?"

"I don't know, but we'll find out," Jack said.

Nathan walked out of the back office and slipped on the growing lake of drinking water. He grabbed hold of the counter to steady himself and, in doing so, knocked a file tray full of papers, a half empty coffee cup, and the business end of Mary's phone onto the floor with a crash.

As he clung to the counter, he asked, "Mary, what are you doing on the floor?"

She finally succeeded in grasping the counter and hauling herself to her knees with Jack's help. Only her head showed above the Formica. "I'm just having my nails done, Nate. What does it look like?"

"Okeydokey," he said. "Hey, Alva. Did you hear we found Cootchie up the coast? She's not hurt or anything."

The old man's face wreathed in a wrinkly grin. "Well, that's just fine, ain't it?"

"Do they know who took her yet?" Hugh asked.

"Not yet, but we'll get him."

Hugh nodded. "Did Cootchie give you any details about the kidnapper?"

"We're still sorting through all that," Nate said.

Jack's heart sank as Maude slammed the door open and squelched into the room. She whisked her knit cap off her head. "What is all this water on the floor?"

"They got a broken pipe or something," Alva piped up.

"It's not a broken pipe!" Mary yelled over the top of the counter.

"Well," Maude said in a tone of profound disgust, "if this isn't the most unprofessional police force I've ever seen. I just came to verify that Cootchie Dent is safe and sound—if it isn't too much to ask. Is that information accurate?"

All four people in the damp waiting room shouted in unison. *"Yes!"*

"Fine then. I'll just be on my way." She whirled on her heel and marched to the door, talking over her shoulder. "Would anyone like to explain why there is a bear trap dripping gore all over the reception desk?"

No one had an answer.

Jack was halfway done with yet another check up nose when his cell phone rang.

"Hey, Jack."

"Nate, is that mess all taken care of?" He didn't want any more visitors walking into the police station to find water on the floor and bloody animal traps on the counter.

"Clean as a whistle. Say, if you're not in the middle of something, I think you'd better meet me. I'm at Vern's place."

"What's going on?"

"Uh, well, you'd better come see for yourself. Now, would be good."

"I'm on my way. Do you need backup?"

"Nah. Just you should do it."

"Okay." He shoved the paperwork into his car and climbed in. "Be there in five."

"Make it four."

Jack sped along the winding frontage road as it bumped and twisted its way to Vern Rosario's ranch. He couldn't imagine a situation that Nate couldn't handle with his unique combination of brawn and humor.

When Jack reached the gravel driveway, he saw the amber lights of Nate's cruiser. The big man stood, thumbs tucked into his belt, talking to someone perched on a rock underneath a spreading walnut tree. The figure looked familiar.

"What's going on, Nate?" Jack caught sight of two interesting details simultaneously. The figure poised on the rock was Bobby Walker, and a denim-clad leg ending in a heavy leather work boot was hanging out of the tree.

Officer Katz stepped away from the tree and spoke to Jack, keeping his peripheral vision on Bobby and the dangling leg. "It appears to me," he said, the corners of his mustache fighting against a smile, "that this little woman treed Vern Rosario."

He stared at him. "What are you talking about?"

Still smiling, Nate continued. "Ms. Walker was out for a long hike and happened upon a Mr. Rosario putting an animal of the feline persuasion into a sack, along with a rock. As he was getting ready to carry the sack in question to the pond, Ms. Walker came onto the property to discourage Mr. Rosario from engaging in said activity."

"Uh-oh." He remembered her performance at the restaurant. "How bad?"

"The cat is fine. Vern doesn't seem any worse for wear to me, but all I've seen of him is the bottom of his boots. The vocal chords seem to be in good working order."

"Is that you, Jack?" a voice called from the tree. "It's about time. This crazy woman comes onto my property and attacks me, and you take your sweet time getting over here. Did you have to stop for a doughnut or something? Did we interrupt your nap time?"

Jack approached the tree. "Mr. Rosario, why don't you come down here, and we can sort this thing out."

"I'm not coming down until you take that nut to jail. She's guilty of trespassing and assault."

Jack left the man shouting with gusto and sat down next to Bobby.

She sat with her hands clasped under her chin, regarding him with sober brown eyes. He wished his stomach wouldn't start spiraling every time she tilted her head to one side like that.

"Hi," he said.

"Hi."

"Why don't you tell me what happened?"

She sat for a moment in silence. "I guess he's about got everything. I did trespass and assault him."

"Why exactly, Bobby?"

"He was going to drown the cat. This cat." She gestured to a cat that sat curled around her ankles. "He can't do that. Drown a cat." She spoke very calmly.

He nodded for her to continue.

"I tried to reason with him. I told him I would take the cat. He wouldn't listen; he just kept screaming and telling me to get off his property."

That did not surprise him. Vern was capable of many things, but reasoning was not way up on the list. "And?"

"And I took the bag out of his hands. He grabbed a handful of my hair, so I clobbered him. Not real hard, just enough to get him off of me."

"Anything else?"

She wrinkled a freckled nose thoughtfully. "He climbs a tree pretty good for an old guy."

"So it would seem," he said, stifling a smile.

Bobby turned to look at him. "I don't want to get in the way of what you have to do, but I won't let him drown this cat."

There was dead-on determination in her eyes. "Just sit tight for a minute." He headed over to the man Nathan had just talked down out of the tree.

Vern was a large rectangular man with a deeply lined face and wispy hair. "Well?" he demanded. "I don't see any handcuffs here. What are you waiting for? I want her arrested, and I want it done now. Bad enough I had to chase some gang off my property last night. Now I got to defend myself in the daytime."

"I think you need to calm down, Mr. Rosario. Back up a minute. Who was here last night?"

"How should I know who they were? Bunch of men and one woman, tramping around my property in the night."

"Where?"

Vern stabbed a finger eastward. "There. On the plot I'm clearing out this summer. I fired a shot and told them to get lost, whoever they were. Now today I got to deal with that girl."

"She offered to take the cat, Vern. Why didn't you let her?"

"I don't have to answer to anyone what I do with my property," he shouted around Jack's shoulder to the woman. "Not to no gang, and definitely not to no woman."

"You could have just given the cat to her and been done with it." Jack wanted to add, "you arrogant blowhard," but he restrained himself.

Vern suddenly pushed past Jack and strode toward Bobby. "I can do whatever I jolly well please with that cat," he said, spittle flying. "As a matter of fact, as soon as your scrawny carcass gets taken to the tank, I think I'm going to bash it a couple of times with a shovel before I throw it in the pond!"

She sprang from the rock and knocked the man to the ground, expertly flopping him over and planting her knee between his shoulder blades. She grabbed an ear with each hand and smashed his head into the ground. "You—will—not—kill—that—*cat*!" She punctuated each word with a smash.

Jack grabbed her around the waist and lifted her off of Vern, pulling her arms together behind her back. Nathan restrained the now-upright rancher.

"You see? Did you see that crazy broad attack me?" Vern screamed. "Put her away. Take her to the station and throw her in the clink."

Jack frog-marched Bobby several yards away and stood behind her, pinioning her arms until her breathing slowed. He spoke soothingly into her ear. "Okay, okay. Calm down. You need to get it together. Take a deep breath." He turned her around to face him. "Are you in control?"

She gazed past him, nostrils flared. "I will not let him kill that animal," she hissed through gritted teeth. "If you need to arrest me, go ahead, but I'm not leaving him with the cat."

"I know. I need you to let me handle it. Will you trust me to do that?" He gently tipped her chin so she had to look at him.

After a minute, she nodded.

"Stay here," he commanded. "Do not move from this spot."

He returned to the two men. "Okay, Mr. Rosario. Here's what you're going to do. You are going to let the lady have the cat, and we will remove them both from your property. No charges will be filed."

The man stared incredulously. "What? Are you insane? Why would I do that? I am the victim here."

"Because," he said, leaning forward until his face was very close to the other man's, "if you don't, I am going to tell every one of your bowling buddies that a woman the size of Minnie Mouse chased you up a tree and then kicked your sorry behind into the dirt."

Vern's eyes narrowed into vicious slits. "You can't do that."

"I sure as shootin' can. Now go back into your house and forget this ever happened."

Jack watched as the man grudgingly plodded back toward the house. Vern hesitated, and Jack added, "Hey, Vern? I think Ellen Foots is going to get a little tip about animal cruelty at this address. She might want to check things out."

The man groaned and stalked into the house.

Bobby walked to the car, cradling the cat. "Who is Ellen Foots?"

"The Finny librarian and an amateur animal protection officer. She's six foot four inches of tempered steel without a shred of humor."

"I think I'd like to meet her."

He glanced at her and shuddered at the thought. "Get in the car, Bobby."

The ride back from Vern's was a very quiet one. Jack did not know quite what to say to the puzzling woman beside him. Bobby sat with the cat in her lap and watched the fog roll in over the top of Finny's Nose.

"Are those Douglas firs there?" she asked, squinting through the side window. "Just over the top of the nose? See that really big one right next to the smaller group?"

"You'll need to ask someone else, I'm afraid. I wouldn't know a Douglas fir from a Christmas tree," he said.

Bobby laughed. "They are Christmas trees. I just wondered how they got up there." She looked over at him. "Vern really shouldn't cut down that stand of trees. It's a crime to cut old-growth redwoods."

"It's his land. He can do what he wants." He cleared his throat. "Bobby, you don't happen to be the woman Vern saw on his property last night, do you?"

"No, I reserve all my lawbreaking for the daylight hours."

"Good," he said with relief then suddenly checked his watch. "Uh-oh. I just realized what time it is. I promised Louella under pain of losing important parts of myself that I would be home by six sharp." He checked his watch again. "Five minutes to six. Would you be okay coming to my house for a minute before I take you home?"

She regarded him with the head-tilted glance. "Sure. Uncle Monk told me about Paul. Said he's a great kid. I'd love to meet him."

He nodded, swallowing hard. Visitors to the Denny household had been reduced to a trickle since Lacey died, except for an occasional colleague. He couldn't remember the last time he had invited someone into the house who wasn't wearing a badge. It might have been the cable guy.

They drove up to the small ranch-style home and pulled in along the street. Jack had not been able to park in the driveway next to the mailbox where Lacey died. Even now he waited until dark to retrieve the mail, whistling vigorously to prevent his mind from straying too far back to the past.

"I think maybe you ought to put your cat friend in the garage. I'm not sure Mr. Boo Boo will take to him."

Louella was waiting for them at the door. He introduced the two women. Louella didn't hide the surprise on her round face as she eagerly grasped Bobby's hands and patted them. "Well, isn't it just a pleasure to meet you?" She beamed as she tucked flyaway strands of white hair behind her ears. "It's been an age since we've had company." She narrowed her eyes at Jack. "How come you didn't phone me to say you were bringing a visitor? I could have cooked something for you."

"It just sort of came up, Louella," he muttered. "Don't let us make you late for your meeting. Let me carry your bag to the car." He grabbed her canvas tote and headed to the front door.

"And this is Paul," Louella said. She stroked the blond hair of the boy who had suddenly materialized behind her leg.

The boy peeked around her ample flowered hip. "He's a good boy, so handsome and kind." She added slyly, "Just like his father."

He walked Louella to her car while she peppered him with questions about Cootchie and then Bobby. After he finally stowed her safely in the front seat, Jack returned to the house to find the front hallway empty. Following the sound of murmuring voices, he wandered into the family room.

He stopped dead in his tracks.

Bobby was lying on her stomach on the carpet, concentrating on a colorful pile of Legos. Paul was draped over her back, chin on top of her head, watching in breathless wonder.

He expected his son to hide in his room, or at the most ignore the guest as he typically did new people. "Wow," was all he could manage.

They both looked up. "It's better than wow. It's a rocket ship," Bobby said. "I'm a whiz at Legos, don't you think, Paul?"

The child nodded and rolled off of her to go search for his astronaut action figures.

She stood up. "Louella is nice. I get the feeling she thinks it's about time you brought a girl home."

He blushed and raked his fingers through his close-cropped hair. "Uh, yeah. I'm sorry she kind of put you on the spot."

"Not a problem," she said, walking to the back door and looking out into the yard.

A huge shadowy blur hurled itself against the sliding door. She leaped backward.

"Sorry. That's Mr. Boo Boo. He only knows a few tricks, and polite greetings are not one of them."

She looked at the dog with his tongue lolling out, one ear standing up and the other at right angles to it. "Does he have two different-colored eyes?"

"Yup. I think he was sort of assembled from leftover parts." He looked around distractedly, trying to remember how to engineer polite conversation.

"Hey, if I'm intruding here, I'll just head for home," she said.

"No, no." Suddenly he wanted her to stay, to keep standing there, looking at him from under the fringe of black hair that fell into her eyes. "I'm going to make Paul some dinner. Why don't you join us?"

"It might be less complicated if I didn't."

"How's that?"

"I'm a vegetarian."

He looked at her blankly. "A vegetarian?"

"Mm-hmm. You know, no meat."

"No meat?" he repeated.

"No meat. Chicken, beef, nothing that had a face. Maybe I'd better go home. Uncle Monk is used to my strange eating habits."

"No. No problem. Nothing with a face." Jack went to the kitchen and studied the contents of the fridge. Leftover meat loaf, Louella's. One chicken pot pie, Louella's. Some macaroni and cheese. Mustard. Black olives. Finger Jell-O. Eggs. He grabbed the egg carton and removed one. Eggs didn't have faces, he thought triumphantly. But they came from animals with faces. Hostile faces with beady yellow eyes and sharp beaks like Ruth's cranky birds, he remembered.

Bobby poked her head into the kitchen and startled him from his confused remunerations. "Jack?"

He whirled to face her, egg still in hand. "Yeah?"

"Eggs will work."

"Eggs will work," he repeated. "Okay then."

Thirty minutes later he had produced two pretty decent cheese omelets and sliced some ripe tomatoes from Louella's garden. Paul's plate was piled high with scrambled eggs and finger Jell-O.

The kitchen echoed with the sounds of Bobby's laughter and Paul blowing bubbles in his milk. After dinner, the boy sat down with a Thomas the Train video while Bobby helped clean up.

There was an intimacy in cleaning dishes together. Washing away the remnants of a shared meal. Drying the dishes and disclosing their secret resting places in the cupboard. Standing side by side in front of a chipped porcelain sink. It made him feel uneasy and foolishly pleased at the same time.

"So how are all your investigations going? Aren't you up to three now? Toes, Cootchie, and Ed Honeysill?"

"We're busy, all right. Things are going slowly, but the FBI is helping out with the Dent kidnapping."

"Thank God she's all right."

"I'll second that. I know you won't believe this, but life in Finny is generally quiet and uneventful." He thought about the strange path his day had taken since the call from Nathan summoning him to the Rosario farm. He smiled.

"What's funny?"

"Oh, I was just recalling the look on Vern's face after you steamrolled him."

"I only steamrolled him a little. You do think he deserved it, don't you?"

"Absolutely. I didn't think I'd ever meet the person who could put him in his place, though. You are the most fearless woman I have ever met."

She frowned, rubbing a dish. "I don't think I would describe myself as fearless."

"No? In the short time I've known you, you've trounced a guy in the bar and treed a cranky old codger who outweighs you by about one hundred fifty pounds. And you didn't even flinch at meeting my four-year-old. That isn't fearless?"

"I've been plenty afraid in my life. Everyone has fears, don't they?" She looked at her reflection in the ceramic dish. "When I was sixteen my mother got ovarian cancer. I was terrified that she would die. I skipped school constantly to stay home with her. I kept a four-leaf clover inside my bra and slept in the hallway outside her door for months, I was so afraid of losing her. I prayed until my fingers were numb. You know what?" Bobby put the dish into the cupboard. "She died anyway. I guess I just figured then that fear doesn't really change things much."

He nodded, remembering how the bottom had fallen out of his stomach when he got the phone call about Lacey. "But it sure is something you remember."

She looked at him closely. "Are you thinking about your wife?"

"Yes." He continued rinsing the omelet pan as he spoke. "It never occurred to me that I should worry about losing her. I never even entertained a thought about her dying until I got the call that she was gone. She died of a brain hemorrhage on her way to get the mail."

"That's when Paul stopped talking?"

"Yeah. He saw her die, I think. He didn't say a single word for two years." He closed his eyes to shut the pain back into place.

"How did you cope with it all?"

"Not very well. Day by day, like we're coping now. Lots of people helped out as much as they could, like Louella and Ruth. I get down on my knees and thank God for them every day. Things are better now that Paul is talking some."

He exhaled with a groan. "Now what really scares me is that he will forget his mother ever existed." The water gurgled quietly as it trickled down the drain. "I still can't really accept it. People tell me that God wouldn't give me more than I can bear, so I guess I need to toughen up."

She fished the rest of the silverware from the dregs of soapy water. "In my expert opinion, Jack, your conclusion is a bit off."

His eyebrows shot up. "What?"

FOG OVER FINNY'S NOSE

"Of course God gives us more than we, alone, can bear. Who can bear losing a wife while a child watches? Who can bear having a child kidnapped, for that matter? What about the parents who never get their kids back? No one can bear that, not alone. So He gives us people to lean on. People who shoulder the load when we can't do it one more minute." She looked him straight in the eye. "He gives us the miracle of a life and the tools to deal with all the junk that comes up in the course of living it."

He looked into her eyes, seeing the glimmer of earnestness that was so very rare in his experience. "You are unlike anyone I've ever known," he said softly.

Bobby chuckled and finished putting the silverware away. She peeked into the family room, where Paul slept in his train pajamas in front of the television.

"I've got to get going. Thanks for dinner, and tell Paul I want to show him how to make a Lego space shuttle sometime. It will knock his socks off."

"Just a minute and I'll pop him into the car and drive you to the hotel."

"Don't bother. It's not far, and I like to walk at night." She noted the look of concern that stole across his face. "I think we've established that I can take care of myself."

"I know that, but I'd feel better if I took you home."

"I'll be fine." She picked up the box he'd found for her and headed to the garage to fetch the cat. "Besides, this is Finny. What could possibly happen?"

15

Ruth put her back into whipping cookie dough batter within an inch of its life. The muffins she'd made were already baked and cooled. Now she tossed handfuls of pecans and chocolate chips into the vanquished cookie dough.

Monk sat in a chair with a cup of coffee in one hand and a cookie in the other. "Ruth," he said between bites. "We're going to have to talk about this sometime."

"Talk about what?"

"You know what. You're avoiding the issue. You are upset about what happened to Cootchie, and I think you need to talk about it some more." There were lines of frustration on his face. "I love you. Let me help you with this."

"I am not avoiding the issue," she said. She added a teaspoon of vanilla. "I have to get these things baked for the sale tomorrow. Why do you say I'm avoiding the issue?"

"Because every time I try to talk to you about it, you bake another batch of cookies. So far you've made oatmeal raisin, snickerdoodles, and now chocolate chip."

"Chocolate pecan chunk."

"I stand corrected." He put the coffee down and stood, trying to catch her eye.

"I don't want to talk about anything." She couldn't understand the anger in her own voice. She wanted to wake up and find the whole mess over, forgotten, her carelessness erased like chalk from a blackboard. "I've got lots to do. It's the last festival weekend, and you know how Maude is."

"Okay. I can see this isn't going to get us anywhere." He rubbed his forehead above his massive eyebrows. "I'm new to this marriage stuff, Ruth. Plus I'm an old guy and I never got a chance to practice on anyone. I just want to say again that I love you and anytime you want to talk, I'm here."

She didn't know what to say. She knew she was being unfair to him, but she didn't know how to cope with his kindness on top of her own emotional maelstrom. It was a relief when the phone rang. "Yes?" she answered with a tremor in her voice. "Sure, Dimple. Okay. I can meet you there." She hung up. "I've got to go now."

She didn't dare to look at Monk's face as she took off her apron and scurried out the door.

FOG OVER FINNY'S NOSE

Her feet took her to the door of the bungalow, though her mind screamed a protest every inch of the way. How could she face Dimple? What would she see in the woman's eyes? Anger? Disgust? Hatred, even? She knew it could not be put off for one more minute.

Her hand trembled as she knocked.

Dimple opened the door. She looked well, Ruth thought. There was color in her cheeks, and her eyes had lost their halos of misery.

"Hello, Ruth. Please come in. I have been thinking about you," she said.

She stepped through the door and stood facing the woman. Her whole body began to shake. "Dimple," she began, "how can I ever tell you how sorry I am? How terribly, terribly sorry I am?" She was terrified to see a look of recrimination on the young woman's face.

Dimple stopped her with a hug. "You have always been a blessing to me and my daughter. We love you just as we always have."

Ruth clung to her for a moment, until she noticed the objects stacked on the coffee table over Dimple's shoulder. "What are the suitcases for?" The question gave her mouth something to do, though she already knew the answer.

Dimple looked at her with somber green eyes. "I am going to send Cootchie to be with my—with Meg for a while. She has a big place in Phoenix and lots of room for Cootchie to run. I'll go visit them in a few days when I can get away." She squeezed Ruth's shoulder. "I just think it would be safer, until the villain is caught. It won't be for long, I promise."

Ruth nodded. She knew speaking would result in a torrent of tears. Already a chilling pain was mounting in the pit of her stomach, as though she had swallowed a frozen lump of granite.

"I'll go get her. She'll want to say good-bye." Dimple glided off toward the back of the house.

Slumped on the sofa, Ruth bit down hard on her index finger to keep from screaming aloud. She felt a weight on the couch next to her. Meg sat there in a fetching coral pantsuit. Tiny luminescent pearls dotted her earlobes, and her lipstick matched her outfit to a tee.

"I'd like to apologize for the things I said to you after Cootchie disappeared." She looked into Ruth's eyes. "I was upset, but that was no excuse to blame you for what happened." She took hold of her hands. "The fact of the matter is, you have taken excellent care of my daughter and granddaughter when I didn't have the courage to. I am in your debt, and I hope you can forgive me for what I said that day. I can only say again how truly sorry I am."

Ruth looked down at their clasped hands. Meg's skin was soft and unwrinkled. The fingernails were filed in graceful crescents and painted with a subtle creamy taupe. Her own hands were calloused, rough from dishwashing, and the nails were chewed off. She withdrew them from Meg's grasp.

"There's nothing to forgive. You didn't say anything out loud that I wasn't saying to myself. I won't ever forgive myself for what happened."

Meg was about to respond when Cootchie bounded into the room and jumped into Ruth's lap.

"Hi, Nana. I am goin' on a plane tomorrow," she said.

Ruth cleared her throat. "Yes, I heard you were going to stay with, ah, your grandma. That will be fun, won't it?"

"Yes, Nana." The girl played with the strings on Ruth's sweat jacket.

She smoothed the girl's flyaway curls, savoring the silkiness with her fingertips.

"Cootchie, Nana is very sorry. I should have been watching you more closely. So the—the man couldn't have taken you. Nana made a terrible mistake." The words burned her mouth.

Cootchie fixed her heavily lashed eyes on Ruth. "It's okay, Nana. I went to de library. I got a book on rocks. When I come back, we can hunt for rocks together. Okay?"

Ruth could not answer. She hugged Cootchie and buried her face in the mounds of curly hair. "I love you, Cootchie," she whispered. "I love you."

"I love you, too, Nana." Cootchie danced away to find her magnifying glass to add to the collection of things in her suitcase.

Somehow Ruth made her way to the door and said her good-byes to Dimple and Meg. The door closed behind her, and she staggered down the walkway to the trees at the end of the drive.

Monk stood there with his hands in his pockets. "I thought maybe you could use a shoulder."

Ruth began to cry bitter tears. He folded her in his arms and held her.

Maude called almost hourly to add more afternoon Mrs. Fog appearances for the final weekend of the festival. Ruth appreciated Maude's intention—to keep her mind and heart busy. Monk plied her constantly with containers of soup and homemade bread.

She was in a fog, shrouded by the horrible "what if" feelings that swirled inside her head. As much as she struggled against it, she felt herself sliding back into the black depression that had gripped her soul after her first husband's death. She'd lived in that darkness for years, but since she'd started her new life with Monk, it had disappeared. Now it was back with a vengeance.

A steely resolve crept up inside her. No. She would not allow the darkness to overtake her again. She had fought too hard, too long to let it take away her soul a second time. She gripped her hands together and prayed until her fingers were numb.

When she opened her eyes, she was filled with a need to do something. Anything. In a blink, she knew where she had to go. If Monk was right and God gave her courage because He knew she would use it, then it was time to face her demons. Maybe there was something there, some infinitesimal clue that would reveal who had taken Cootchie on that terrible day. It was all she could think to do.

Monk offered to accompany her up nose, but Ruth knew she had to do it alone. At least, almost alone. She took an eager Martha along with her for feathery moral support. The bird felt warm against her chest, soft feathers silky under her chin.

As she passed the Buns Up Bakery, she noticed a familiar face. It was Candace, sitting at a corner table, talking on her cell phone. Judging from the woman's expression, it was not a pleasant conversation. Suffering from an acute case of nosiness and procrastination, Ruth walked inside the store, tucking Martha into her jacket.

The delectable smell of apple fritters filled the small space.

Al, the owner, greeted her cheerfully. "Ruth. It's so great, isn't it? Cootchie is back and no worse for the wear."

Ruth nodded, unable to find words for a moment.

Al continued to ramble on as Ruth eavesdropped on Candace's conversation in the corner.

"I don't think so," Candace muttered. "Nothing has changed."

Al put two fritters in a bag. "I been thinking about that toe. Where do you think it came from?" he asked. "Do you think it is related to the kidnapping or to Honeysill's murder?"

Ruth shot a quick glance at Candace. "I don't know." Ruth took the bag and paid for the treats. "It's a mystery to me."

He leaned toward her. "Plenty of strangers in town. Some of them up to no good. I saw a guy in here yesterday. He talked like a New Yorker. Wore real fancy clothes and all."

"Who was he with?"

"He came in alone, but then he struck up quite a conversation with that balloon guy." Al wiped down the counter as he whispered. "Ask Hugh. He was here. He can tell you about it."

She thanked Al and turned to leave just as Candace finished her conversation.

"No. That's it. I don't have anything else to say to you."

She punched off the phone and met Ruth at the door.

"Hello, Candace. How are you holding up?" Now that the woman was close, Ruth could see the lines etched into her dusky skin.

"I am okay, but I can't wait to leave this town."

Ruth nodded. "I can imagine there aren't many good memories for you here." Martha poked her head out of the jacket to peck at the paper bag.

"I've got to stay until the end of the week," Candace said. "The insurance company is sending someone out, so I've got to answer more questions." Her eyes were dull.

"Oh?" She pulled the bag out of the bird's beak.

"Ed had a pretty substantial life insurance policy, and I'm the beneficiary, so I guess that makes me look pretty suspicious."

Ruth wondered if Bing had known about the policy before the crash, but she didn't dare ask.

Candace said good-bye.

"All right, Martha," she said. "Let's get this over with." Without a word to anyone else, she headed up nose.

It took her a very long time to reach the spot where Cootchie had disappeared and a very short time to pass through it. As she approached the horribly familiar ground, Ruth felt herself in the grip of a terrible guilt; a feeling that somehow she had changed things forever with one moment of carelessness.

There was nothing here to fill in the blanks, no answers lying in the weeds, just trampled grass and a rotten log.

Cootchie was gone with Meg. When and if Cootchie and Dimple returned, Ruth was not sure they would slip back into the easy life they enjoyed before. She didn't know if Dimple could ever trust her fully again. She wasn't sure she would ever trust herself.

"Oh God, please help me." She wanted to ask for forgiveness again. To ask Him to take away the curiosity that distracted her from her duty that day. For the strength to face what could have happened. The words would not come out. He had already forgiven her anyway, she knew. She had to find a way to forgive herself.

She had to do something, anything to help Dimple, to make amends. There were the daily chores at Dimple's farm that needed doing and had no doubt been neglected for days. The thoughts churned through her mind faster and faster until her feet picked up the frenzy. She scooped up the tern, who squawked in protest, and began running. She didn't stop until she staggered across the threshold of the Pistol Bang Mushroom Farm.

The place was as lush as ever, she noticed through the searing cramp in her side. It seemed to have a Brigadoonesque ability to thrive no matter what wintry blight the world outside was struggling with. As she deposited a writhing Martha on the ground, Ruth was surprised to see Hugh exiting the polytunnel.

"I didn't expect to see you here."

The young man looked up abruptly. "Oh, hi, Ruth. I came by to check on the shiitakes. They are pretty close to harvesting. Do you think Dimple will be back soon? I can handle the harvest if she isn't. I know the ropes."

"I can't really say. Why don't you give her a call? I'm sure she would appreciate talking to you."

Hugh became engrossed in his boots. "Oh, I don't want to bug her or anything. She's really had it rough lately."

She felt her heart give a painful twist. "Yes, she has, I'm afraid."

"Cootchie is all right, isn't she?"

"She handled the whole thing better than all of us."

"It turned out okay, then. Lucky for everyone."

Ah, the wonderful optimism of youth. "I thought I would check the office while I'm here."

"Yeah. Good idea. I gotta go. If you see Dimple, tell her, uh, I'll be talking to her soon, okay?"

"Okay." He plodded down the gravel walkway like a stork waddling through a muddy marsh.

Ruth spent the next hour emptying wastebaskets, sweeping the office floor, and taking messages off the answering machine. Typically Ruth did these chores for Dimple on a weekly basis, but now the duties seemed imbued with a new importance. When she could think of nothing else to do, she locked up and walked into the garden.

She felt exhausted. As much as she wanted to collapse on the wooden bench, she knew if she didn't get home in a timely fashion, Monk would come puffing up nose to find her.

As she heaved herself downslope, Martha in tow, a small figure approached. She recognized Bobby, pink cheeked, consulting a piece of paper taken from her denim jacket.

"Hi. Where are you headed?"

"Hey, Ruth." She closed the gap between them and bent to scratch Martha's head. "I'm off to the top of Finny's Nose. I want to check something out. How are you doing? I haven't seen you in the coffee shop." She brushed dark hair out of her eyes. "Uncle Monk said you've been kind of down about everything."

"I'm trying to hold myself together. It's been hard." She was dismayed to feel tears stinging her eyes. "To think what could have happened."

"Could haves can kill you."

Ruth looked at her curiously. "You sound like you have some experience with catastrophes."

She laughed. "Hasn't everyone? By the way, Ruth, is Finny's Nose private or public property?"

"It belonged to the Dent family for many generations, but Buster gave it to the city to keep in preserve. I guess you'd call it a regional open space."

"Hmm." Bobby's brow furrowed. "Okay, thanks. I've gotta get going before I lose the daylight. I want to drag Jack up here to show him something, and I need to do my homework."

"Jack? Jack Denny? He doesn't seem like the nature-loving type."

"He isn't. Hence the verb 'drag.' "

"What do you think about these mysterious people parading around at night?"

"I think they're ecoterrorists."

"I read something about that on the Internet. I can't believe people would go to such lengths to further a cause."

"They believe they have a moral imperative to protect the earth," Bobby said, "even if it means breaking the law."

Ruth thought about Rocky's earlier comment. *"We'll be gone before anyone is the wiser."*

"What does Jack think about that?" she asked.

"I haven't gotten that far with him. We've been working on other issues."

Ruth was secretly thrilled to imagine Jack spending time with this interesting young woman. As far as she knew, he hadn't seen anyone since Lacey died.

"I have forgotten how long Monk said you were staying in town," Ruth said. The Fog Festival would be finished in the next two days. She was hoping the girl was planning to hang around for a while after the festival limped to a close. It would give Jack a little more time with her.

"I'm here at least through the festival. The park I work at has closed for flood cleanup for two months, so I've got some time. Maybe if Uncle Monk is still really busy, I'll hang out here for a few more months."

Ruth made a mental note to inform Monk that he needed to be very busy for the next few months.

"Are you going to make it home all right? You look tired."

"Oh sure. I've got my attack bird here to look out for me."

They both looked at Martha, who sat on the ground at Ruth's feet. The slender bird had closed her tiny eyes and tucked her beak into her downy chest. "Yup. I'm sure no one will pester you with that critter on duty. See you later."

The young woman walked briskly upslope, leaving Ruth to wonder what sort of homework could be done by a determined woman all alone at the top of a mountain.

That night Ruth could not sleep, even after her sprint up to the mushroom farm. Perhaps it was the lingering terror from the abduction, or the emotional discussion

273

with Dimple, or the persistent heartburn that nagged her stomach. Maybe it was just the continuing trauma of knowing that Cootchie was in Arizona that kept Ruth wide awake at 1:45 on Sunday morning. Determined not to watch the hands of her bedside clock tick off another hour, she wrapped herself in a worn flannel robe, slid quietly out of bed without disturbing Monk, and retreated to her place of refuge. The kitchen.

She knew the best thing for crisis control was chocolate, but for some reason she could not drum up an appetite for it. Even the piles of plastic-wrapped cookies on the counter did not tempt her.

Everything had been going so well. Her small family, weird though it was, was happy and content. Then it had all gone directly downhill. Ed's murder, Meg Sooner's arrival, Cootchie's kidnapping. And the strain the whole event had put on her new marriage. She loved Monk without reservation, but this was the first real trauma in their relationship. Was it the brevity of their marriage or the fact that she had weathered many crises alone that kept her from fully unburdening herself to him? She had never entertained the foggiest notion of relating to anyone of the male species after her husband died. Firmly she propelled the thoughts from her head. She had gotten past that hurdle, and she would get through this one, too, with God's help. It was time to start using the strength He gave her to face problems, relationship or otherwise, head-on.

A metallic crash from outside made her jump.

Her heart beat wildly as she turned on the porch light and squinted into the backyard. The weak light picked up millions of tiny water droplets, thick as snow. It did not illuminate anything else.

Rats, she thought, *the birds have probably gotten out again.* She put a hand on the dead bolt and stopped.

A ripple of terror crept through her, as if some part of her mind could see farther into the darkened yard.

And what it saw scared her.

She pulled her hand away from the locked door and cried out.

Monk got downstairs in a flash. He was wearing a frayed sweat suit emblazoned with the word NAVY. There was a baseball bat in his hand. His eyes were still sleep glazed. "I heard you call out my name, or did I dream that?"

"I'm sorry. Maybe I'm just being dramatic," she said, her cheeks warm. "There might be nothing out there. My imagination has been in overdrive these past few days."

"You did the right thing. I'm not sure if an old chef like me can protect you from anything other than a marauding head of garlic, but I'll give it my able best."

She handed him a flashlight.

A blast of cold air hit them both as Monk opened the sliding door. "Stay here

274

and keep the phone handy." He vanished into the fog.

Several minutes later he was back. "Well, the birds are still penned and safe. There's nothing that I can see out of order, although your side gate is unlatched. Any chance you left it open?"

She shook her head. "I always double-check at night in case the birds make it over the wall. It was definitely closed before."

They looked at each other for a minute. "Come outside with me. Maybe you'll notice something that I didn't."

She checked first on the birds to reassure herself of their well-being, though she needn't have bothered. Seven pairs of yellow eyes glared balefully at her from behind their chain link enclosure. They had the "You'd better be carrying a bag of Fritos" look on their hostile faces. Her flashlight illuminated the rest of the area a slice at a time.

It took her two passes around the yard before she noticed.

"I can't believe it," she said.

"What?"

"My castings. Three buckets of worm castings for Royland. They were right here on the porch. They're gone."

"Worm castings." Monk shook his head in confusion. "Doesn't seem like they are worth the trouble."

"Not really. Twenty dollars apiece, unless you have to spring for the eighteen-dollar shipping and handling fee."

"Let's go back in and see if we can unmuddle this mess."

Safely inside with mugs of hot decaf coffee, they plopped down on the sofa.

"Why would someone want your castings?"

Ruth couldn't see why someone would want to steal them. They were the by-product of the worm after it swallowed soil and plant litter. The material mixed in the digestive tract and came out as casts. "As far as I know, it's only used by organic farmers as a fertilizer. That's what Royland uses it for. Some florists use it for ornamental plants grown in baskets, I suppose."

"I can't picture a nefarious florist heisting your castings in the dead of night," he said thoughtfully.

"Me neither. Maybe someone mistook the buckets for something else."

"Were they labeled?"

"Just with the Phillip's Worm Emporium sticker on them."

They mulled it over for an hour more before he carried his mug to the sink. "I'm going to sleep down here tonight. Just in case whoever it was comes back." He looked at her open mouth. "If anything is going to come through that door, it will have to get by this old battleship."

"Thank you." She swallowed the emotion rising in her throat. "I'm sorry I've been acting strange lately." Her eyes glistened with tears. "I love you."

At half past 2:00 a.m. on Saturday, Jack was driving down the dark frontage road after checking the parking lot where most of the festival vendor trailers were situated. All was quiet on the western front. God willing, it would stay that way for the last two days of the festival craziness. He had enough ongoing investigations to last for months.

A light drizzle speckled his windshield, and he turned up the heater to fight off the wet chill. Finny was closed up tight, like a vacuum-sealed jar. The only place open for business was Eden Hospital. It crossed his mind to stop there to see if they could give him an IV coffee drip.

Maybe he could get Alva to take a look at the evil Mr. Coffee. If he promised him a bag of jelly beans, the old man would do it. If he threw in some candy corns, Alva would no doubt have a crack at the ancient pencil sharpener, too. Jack was trying to figure out how early was too early to call on Alva when he noticed a slender woman walking along the shoulder, hunched inside a waterproof jacket. Pulling up alongside the pedestrian, he rolled down his window.

"Isn't it kind of late for a walk?" he asked.

"A little early, I'd say." Bobby stuck her head in his passenger window. "I'm involved in an investigation. Don't hassle me, copper."

He laughed. "Why don't you get in and tell me about it?"

She hopped into the car and wiped the moisture from her face. "Okay, but don't go blabbing it around. I'm investigating some strange doings up nose."

"Really?"

"Really. Drive to the trailhead and I'll show you."

He looked into her brown eyes, and for a split second he would have rolled himself in bacon grease and walked into a lion's den if she suggested it. Mentally he shook himself back to the rational world. "Let's go."

After a mile he pulled off the main road and they got out of the car. The rain had stopped, and the moon shone between the clouds.

"Look," she commanded, pointing up nose.

Jack squinted. "I don't see anything but the end of your finger."

"Come on, Detective. Be patient and keep looking."

Then he saw it.

A pocket of light flickered unsteadily halfway up the steep wooded hill.

276

"Huh. I wonder what in the world is going on up there."

"That's exactly what I was going to find out."

"Alone? In the dark? After all the murder and mayhem that's been going on around here?"

Her lips curled in a crooked smile. "What's the matter? You don't think I can handle it?"

"Oh, I'm fairly certain you can handle anything. Why don't I come along anyway and you can protect me?" He waited for her nod and contacted the police dispatcher to fill her in on his plans. He grabbed his radio and clipped it to his belt.

"Onward and upward," he said.

They walked easily for the first mile. The slope was mild and speckled with enough trees to screen them from whatever was at the top. The full moon shone just enough for them to pick their way up the uneven trail. When Bobby stumbled, he instinctively reached an arm around her waist to steady her. He found her scent tantalizing.

"Are you sniffing me?"

Jack felt his face warm, and he was grateful for the darkness. "Uh, well, actually. . . Sorry about that. I think my brain is scrambled, but you smell just like a strong cup of French roast coffee." He felt like an idiot for saying the words out loud.

Her laugh echoed softly. "I think I did splash a little on my shirt during my shift at Uncle Monk's. I take it your coffee machine is still on the fritz?"

"Yup," he said. "We're getting close to declaring a national emergency."

"So next time I'm out scouting for a man, I'll pass up the Chanel No. 5 and rub some coffee grounds on my wrists." She tucked dark hair behind her ears.

"That would definitely get my attention."

They lapsed into silence as the slope became steeper. Their breath came out as white puffs in the cold air. They stopped now and then to look up at the moon. It was round and full as a ripe melon. As he began to pant, he noticed Bobby's breathing was not labored in the slightest. "So how do you like the park ranger gig? Better than bus driver?"

"Definitely. I started out as an interpreter, leading tours and stuff like that. It was fun, but the real excitement started when I got into the law enforcement end of it." She stopped to shake a rock out of her boot. "It's still blows me away that I get to work in some of the most gorgeous places on earth, and I get paid for it."

"Sounds perfect."

"Not perfect. Wide-open spaces are very freeing to people. On the one hand, it lets them escape from the status stuff—cars, clothes, Starbucks. It kind of puts everyone on a level playing field. The downside is sometimes people misuse the freedom. Think they can get away from the rules that apply in the civilized world."

"What kind of stuff do you have to deal with?" He pushed aside a low-hanging branch.

"Drinking, drug use. Small-time, mostly, but sometimes it gets to be dicey when it's time to arrest someone. And in the past few years, we've got bigger problems. Drug rings starting up plantations on the outskirts of the park."

"I've heard about that. How do you handle it?'"

"You pray you don't stumble into a crop when you're alone. And you really hope they aren't packing a bigger weapon than you are." Her teeth gleamed in the moonlight. "You can relate, I bet."

"Sure can." He could relate completely, and it astonished him. This woman was so different from Lacey, yet he connected with her easily. It was a connection that had been missing from his life for years.

She frowned. "You know, I saw Ed Honeysill headed up here just before his balloon crashed. He said he was out for a walk, and I didn't question it at the time, but I wonder if I should have mentioned it before."

Jack tried to figure a reason other than exercise why Ed would climb up nose. He couldn't think of one.

As they neared the plateau at the top of Finny's Nose, they slowed their pace to avoid twigs and pockets of leaves. In the clearing just ahead, they could hear voices. Orange flames danced in the distance.

They came within several yards of the clearing before they crouched down behind some scrubby bushes.

Five figures, dressed in dark clothes with bandannas on their heads, sat in a circle. One of the group stood in the approximate center of the clearing bent over a campfire. The light caught her for a second, revealing a woman with long silvered hair. A pile of duffel bags and rope lay nearby, as well as a pile of metal rods.

"It's Evelyn Bippo," Bobby breathed in Jack's ear, sending tingles down his back. "I don't recognize the others."

"The tall one, there. I think that's Rocky. It looks like his ponytail hanging out, anyway," Jack said. "What are they saying?"

They strained to make out the words. "Somehow I don't think it's 'Rah rah ree, kick 'em in the knee.'" She giggled.

Without warning, one of the figures pulled a knife from his pocket.

Jack grunted as he reached to draw his gun.

"Wait," she whispered, squeezing his arm. "They're not going to hurt him."

Rocky stood up and took the knife. He raised his voice to a near shout. "Today we recognize Dan as a member of the GOPs for his role in planning our next act of liberation." Then he turned the knife and presented it, handle first, to the man seated next to him.

More conversation followed, but it was too low for Jack to make out.

Bobby grabbed Jack's free hand and leaned close. "Let's go. I'll fill you in after we get out of here."

The sun was just beginning to pry feebly at the foggy night when they made it back to the car. Jack fired up the engine and cranked the heater to megablast. They bumped along until they reached the main road.

"All right. Let's have it," Jack said.

She clamped her teeth together to stop the chattering and looked at her watch. "Well, since it's almost morning, why don't you take me back to the coffee shop. I have a key. I'll make us some breakfast. I think I've got some 'splaining to do."

He couldn't have agreed more.

17

Ruth hung up the phone for the fifth time.

Monk sat bleary eyed at the kitchen table, coffee mug in hand.

"Just call her already," he said. "You're driving yourself nuts."

"I don't know. Maybe it's a bad idea. What if she doesn't want me to speak to her? What if she hangs up? Besides, it's really early."

"She won't hang up, and it's an hour ahead in Phoenix. That makes it a leisurely 8:05 there, and she's taking care of a kid. We're talking Cootchie here. That woman has been up since the first beam of dawn."

He was right. Cootchie was always up before the roosters finished their cock-a-doodling. She greeted each morning as if it was made just for her and she didn't want to miss a minute. Ruth dialed with a trembling finger. She watched Monk as the phone rang for the third time. He sat there drinking coffee and eating chocolate chip cookies as if he had always belonged there as much as her ancient beloved blender.

"These are great, honey, really great," he said around a mouthful of cookie. "The perfect breakfast food. You should give me the recipe. No, never mind, you should make them for me on a regular basis. That's a better idea."

She smiled at him around the phone mouthpiece. "I'll think about it. Oh no, someone is answering. What should I say? Hello, uh, Mrs. Sooner? Uh, it's me, Ruth. Ruth Budge. I hope I'm not calling too early. Uh, I wanted to call before the festival activities get under way."

He started on his second cup of coffee while she waited for the polite small talk to subside.

"Er, I was wondering. I've been missing Cootchie so much. I just was thinking maybe I could talk to her. That is, if you think it's okay. I know you just got settled in there and all, but I wanted to hear her voice. It's silly."

"I think that would be fine. Cootchie mentions you all the time," Meg said.

"Oh really?" Ruth tried to hide the ecstasy in her voice.

"Yes. She's also been saying things that I just don't understand. I think it's something to do with squirrels."

"Squirrels?" She laughed. "Well, you never really know what's going on in that brain."

"I certainly don't." Meg's voice dropped a notch. "She's been talking about the man who took her."

Ruth could feel her heart begin to pound with the force of a jackhammer. "What did she say? Is it anything that could be helpful to the police?"

"I'm not sure. Why don't you talk to her? Here she is."

There was a second delay while Meg handed the phone to Cootchie.

"Hi, Nana Ruth."

"H–hi, Cootchie." She fought the tears that suddenly flooded her eyes. "Are you having fun with your grandma?"

"Yes, Nana. We find rocks. I saw a rabbit with big ears but no squirrels here, Nana. De muffin man says good squirrels is dead squirrels."

"The muffin man?" Ruth gave Monk a baffled look. "Who is the muffin man?"

"De man who took me to de library. De muffin man."

"Uh, the muffin man, like the 'Do you know the muffin man?' rhyme?"

"What rhyme?"

She gave herself a mental whack. Of course Cootchie would have no idea about nursery rhymes. The child was more familiar with Molière than Mother Goose. "Never mind, Cootchie. The man, the muffin man. Did he stop at the store to get muffins when you, er, went to the library?"

"No, Nana. He grewed them."

"He grewed, grew them? He grew the muffins?"

"Yes. I have to go find rocks. Today I will dig a well to make wishes in. Good-bye. I love you, Nana."

Ruth whispered, "I love you, too," as the phone line went dead.

Monk insisted that a morning walk along the beach would be just the ticket for Ruth's dark mood. She was not sure that taking a flock of seven crabby gulls along was the ticket to anything but a bleeding ulcer, but it seemed like a good way to avoid the Saturday festival crowds. She thought that speaking to Cootchie would help ease her heart, but it seemed to stir up the emptiness even more.

The waves clawed angry foamy fingers against the gravel. The birds waddled in obvious bliss, poking around for bits of plants and unsuspecting pale crabs. A low-lying fog layer diminished as the birds watched, leaving only a cold wind behind. Maude would not be pleased.

Monk reached in between Teddy and Grover to separate them when they came to blows over a dropped pretzel that lay on the beach. "All right, you nasty critters," he said. "Enough of that squabbling. Did you bring anything to help round them up?"

She pointed at her pocket. "Fritos. Don't leave home without them."

He sidled closer and closer until he draped a huge arm over her shoulders. "I need body heat," he said. "I'm freezing."

"I could remind you that it was your idea to come here," she said.

"It seemed like a sound, husbandly suggestion at the time."

A man in a jogging suit trotted into view. It was Bing Mitchell, with hardly a bead of sweat on his brow.

"Hey there. So the kid's been found," he called as he jogged up to them.

"Yes, she has," Ruth said. "How did you hear about it?"

"Hugh told me."

"She's just fine," Monk said. "Safe and sound."

"That's good. Say, I understand Hugh's old man is looking to unload some property. Have there been any offers made on it?"

"I really couldn't say," Ruth said. "You'll have to talk to Royland about that. Why do you ask?"

"Just looking to expand the business. Are you folks going to make the Fog Festival an annual thing?"

She exchanged a look with Monk.

"I sincerely hope not," she said.

"You really should think twice. It brings people here from all over."

Monk shot him a look. "Exactly," he said.

The young man laughed and stretched his arms in a wide arc. "I'd better get back to my run. See you soon." He ran on down the beach, passing another figure running in the opposite direction.

Alva careened awkwardly toward them, his knobby knees pasty white above striped crew socks.

"Hey," Monk said. "What are you doing? Bicycles are better for exercise than jogging, my man."

Alva staggered to a halt. He panted heavily and held the canvas fishing hat on his head with both hands. "I ain't exercising. I found it. I finally found it. Come on!" With that he turned his back on them and galloped back to the lichen covered boulders lying in reckless confusion several yards away.

Ruth and Monk looked at each other and followed him as fast as the shifting sand would allow. When they got to the rock pile, Alva stabbed a finger under the eroded side of the granite that made a shelf a few feet above the ground.

They ducked their heads to get a better look.

Ruth screamed and covered her hands with her mouth.

18

N ot bad for a vegetarian," Jack said around a mouthful of blueberry pancakes.

"Just because I don't eat meat doesn't mean I can't cook," Bobby said. She took off her apron and walked around from behind the counter of Monk's Coffee and Catering. "Coffee?"

His smile was blissful. "I haven't had a good cup of coffee in—"

"Hours?"

"Feels like years." He noticed the way her hair curled from the wet hike down the hill, framing her flushed cheeks. He cleared his throat. "Okay, spill it. What's the deal with the knife people?"

She pushed the damp bangs out of her face. "I can't speak for all people, but this group looked a lot like some that descend on the national parks every time some deforesting needs to be done."

"Deforesting?"

"Yeah. Controlled burns, cutting to quarantine disease, that sort of stuff."

"Uh-huh. Does that have to be done often?"

"Thankfully, no. Certain strategic sites need to be thinned sometimes to control runaway wildfires. The gap in the understory, the plant growth under the big trees, creates kind of a speed bump that slows the fire. Some level of fire is good for the ecology. It burns off duff, the low-lying stuff on the ground, and clears the way for new growth."

"Makes sense."

"It's the runaway fires that are bad, and those happen most often in the dense areas. If you've got a real thick tree cover, it creates kind of a ladder effect."

She noted his furrowed brow. "Fire can climb from the ground to the treetops. Then the flares carry it from tree to tree when it's really windy. When you get crown fires like that, you're in trouble. They burn hot, fast, and high. Not much can stop them at that point."

He watched her while he sipped, admiring the play of early morning light on her face.

"Then there's the disease factor," she said. "In my park we have huge numbers of old-growth oaks. There have been years when we had a real problem with oak wilt, and the only way you can effectively control that is to clear out the sick trees before it spreads."

FOG OVER FINNY'S NOSE

"I'm not clear on why people would oppose these techniques," he said between bites.

"No one likes to cut down a tree, especially not a park ranger," she said, fixing her intense black eyes on his, "but sometimes it is necessary to prevent a bigger loss. Most people don't have a problem with that, but there's a radical element that feels any tree cutting is wrong."

"And you think that's what we've got here, with Rocky Bippo and company? Have you ever heard of a group called the GOPs?"

"No, but I get the feeling the Bippos are involved in something along those lines. Traveling the festival circuit gives them an opportunity to visit plenty of different locales. The vending business provides a livelihood of sorts."

He took a swallow of coffee. "The sister seems to be legit with the dog thing."

"She probably is. I think most conservation groups have pure motives. It's when they become above the law that you've got a problem. Evelyn may be sucked into the whole thing because of her brother, too. You never know."

"He's a hothead."

Bobby ate a bite of pancake. "Last season we had to cut a stand of trees to prevent the spread of wilt, and we had protesters coming out of the woodwork, claiming it was being done for profit or some such thing. Most of the people were harmless enough, but there were five arrests out of that whole episode, and my partner got his jaw broken when his Jeep ran into a blockade they put on the trail."

Jack shook his head. "What's up with the knife?"

"I think it's some sort of hazing ritual. You're only a trusted member after you've plotted some sort of protest crime. It's easier to trust each other when you've all done something illegal together. Doesn't pay to squeal on a buddy when you'll go to the slammer right along with him."

"So Rocky and his gang are working on some mischief while they're here. Any guesses?"

"Remember the metal rods we saw? Next to the rope? I'm betting they're planning on spiking Vern's trees to make it impossible for him to chop them down." She smiled wickedly. "It's wrong, though I would enjoy seeing the look on his face when his plans went south."

"Me, too, but I'm going to have to put a damper on that scheme anyway. The Finny PD does not have the time or resources for any more investigations at the present time. We're full up."

Bobby refilled his mug and her own. "Who would think Finny could be such a hotbed of discontent?"

"Who indeed? At least I've got enough information to put a monkey wrench in the evil plan." He looked down at the pager on his belt. "I have to take a call."

Bobby poured more syrup on her pancake.

"Jack Denny," he said into the cell phone. After a minute his eyes widened, and he said, "I'm on my way."

"I've gotta go. That was Mary—she's on her way to the beach." He drained the coffee cup in one gulp. "It sounds like Alva finally found the body he's been looking for."

〜〜〜

The sand-covered lump behind Alva was indeed a body. Idly Jack thought how disappointed Bobby was when she had to stay to open Monk's shop instead of accompanying him. He refocused on his duty.

Mary was already on scene, talking into her radio.

Jack could discern the denim-covered legs on one end with knees curled up close to the torso. One hand covered the face. The hand was coated with a layer of blood and grit.

"See?" Alva stage-whispered, his eyes popping. "I told ya there was a body around to go with that toe."

Jack felt slightly sheepish recalling the way he'd dismissed Alva's ramblings after they'd failed to find any body to match the toe.

"All right. Stand back there with Ruth and Monk, okay?" He and Mary squatted gingerly beside the body, and Jack reached out two fingers to check the wrist for a pulse.

The body sat up.

Jack stood abruptly. Mary fell in the sand. Ruth, Monk, and Alva shouted simultaneously and leaped back.

The face that presented itself to them was covered in mud and grime. One of the eyes was swollen shut, and a wide smear of blood leaked from a grotesquely swollen upper lip. A pair of smashed glasses lay on the sand.

"Oh no! It's Hugh," Ruth gasped.

"Aw, gee, Detective," Alva said. "It ain't a dead body. Only a live one."

"That's okay, Alva. Better luck next time." He knelt next to Hugh. "Are you okay, son? The ambulance is on its way."

Hugh coughed and groaned.

"Monk, there's a bottle of water on the front seat of my car. Do you mind?" Jack said, handing him the keys.

" 'Course not." Monk lumbered off.

Ruth extracted a tissue from her pocket and tried to brush some of the dirt out of Hugh's eyes.

"Can you tell me what happened?" Jack asked.

He mumbled and coughed several more times. "Those gang people."

"Who?" Mary said.

"The bandanna gang. They were here on the beach early this morning." He

285

began to groan again, holding his side.

"Oh my gosh," Ruth gasped. "I saw them, too, Sunday night."

Jack looked up sharply. "You told me about that, but you said you weren't sure they meant any harm. Did they threaten you directly?"

"They didn't say a word to me, I just ran as soon as I came upon them."

"Okay." Jack turned to the boy. "You were here at the beach this morning and you saw them? What time was that?"

"Around five. I woke up early and decided to take a walk. They were here. They saw me watching them, and they—" He squeezed his eyes shut. "They beat me up. They said they would kill me for spying on them."

Monk returned and handed over an opened water bottle to Hugh. "Well, you sure took a lickin' there, young fella," he said.

The fire chief and another firefighter arrived carrying a medical supply box. They knelt beside Hugh and began to check his pulse and pupils.

Jack looked over their shoulder. "Did you know any of your attackers, Hugh? Could you identify them?"

He shook his head. "I didn't see their faces. It was still dark."

"Could you recognize their voices?"

"No. It didn't sound like anyone I'd met before." He winced as Ernie prodded his ribs. "I just saw the bandannas."

"Can we have some space here, Detective?" Ernie said.

Jack, Ruth, and Monk moved away. Mary stayed with Ernie and snapped pictures of the crime scene. They watched as the firefighters bandaged various cuts and abrasions. Hugh stood unsteadily amid a shower of gravel.

"What's going on?" Jack asked. "He needs to go to the hospital."

"I know." Ernie removed his latex gloves with an annoyed snap. "You can lead an idiot to water, but you can't make him go to the hospital."

"Hugh," Ruth said, "you've got to go. I'm sure you've got broken ribs and maybe a concussion. It's best if you go to the hospital."

"No," he croaked. "I'll be fine. I just need a ride home."

Jack sighed. "How about I take you home and we'll talk more about who attacked you."

"No way," Hugh said, swiping at a trickle of blood under his eye. "Forget about the whole thing. There's no way I'm identifying anybody or pressing charges. I just want to go home." He stood and limped his way up the beach.

Jack took him home.

<hr>

The officers ducked under the beaded curtain that served as a doorway to Rocky's booth at the edge of the field. Nate swatted at a blue crystal bead that clung to his hair. Waist-high wooden cases housed baskets of polished agate stones, tie-dyed shirts, and porcelain fairies. Dozens of tree ornaments made of metal, glass, and ceramic hung overhead. They twirled in the early morning breeze. A few stalwart shoppers meandered along the row of craft booths, but none had made it into Rocky's stall.

Rocky looked up from the box he was rummaging through. His long braid twisted over one shoulder. "What can I do for you?"

"Hello, Mr. Bippo," Jack said. "You remember Officer Katz. We'd like to talk with you for a minute."

Rocky regarded them through slitted eyes. "What about?"

"About an attack that happened last night."

"An attack?"

"Yes," Jack said, "a young man was beaten severely."

"Beaten?" Rocky whistled. "Wow, beatings, explosions, murder. This is a dangerous town."

"It seems to be getting that way," Nate chimed in.

"Yeah," Jack said. "What was it that Alva was saying, Nate? Something about a gang on the beach?"

Nate bobbed his chin. "Yup. A bunch of folks in bandannas, carrying knives and such."

"All right, officers," Rocky snorted. "I can see the local busybodies have been sniffing around. I'm one of the bunch, as you put it. We like to hang out on the beach. What of it?"

"Who is in your, er, group?" Nate asked.

"Just me; my sister, Evelyn; and Dale Palmer, Rudy Anderson, and Dan Finch. They work the popcorn booth and run the jump house. Sometimes a few other festival roadies join in, but they're not here this time."

They stared at him in silence.

"We're friends, not felons. I'm sure you've checked. No arrests on my record."

"That's true. Maybe you just have really bad timing. Maybe you just happen to be around when tree farms burn and logging trails are blocked."

"And tree stumps are dumped," Nate added. "Don't forget the tree stumps."

Rocky threw the box down and kicked it into the corner. "I'm an ecologist. I'm interested in anything that threatens the natural balance of the earth. That doesn't make me a criminal."

"How about assault and battery? Does your group go in for that?"

"None of that, either."

"Were you on the beach last night?"

Rocky nodded. "Yeah. Some friends and I hiked up to the top of Finny's Nose. Then we stopped at the beach before we went back to our trailers for the night."

"What time, exactly?"

"We hit the beach about four o'clock, I'd say. But we didn't see another soul the entire time. We didn't see anybody, and we certainly didn't beat anyone up."

Jack tried to ignore his growling stomach. He wished he had made it through a few more of Bobby's pancakes before he was summoned to the beach. "I understand you have some difficulties with Bing Mitchell. You two have been mixing it up since you blew into town."

"My only difficulty with him is that he's a pig. Other than that, I got no problem with him." Rocky swiped at the crystal moon that hung from the tent. "Why? Was he the beaten-up guy?"

"No," Jack said.

"Too bad."

"Are you sure you don't want to tell us anything else? Like what does Bing have that your sister had to sell her car to pay for?" Jack decided it was the right moment to use the interesting tidbit that Ruth uncovered after the food fight.

Rocky's mouth opened and closed.

Jack remained silent, staring at him.

"Okay." Rocky looked at the ground. "The creep taped one of our protests. He got us doing something that might be considered questionable."

"Go on," Jack prodded.

"The stump thing. He videotaped us breaking into the city council offices with the stump."

Nate huffed into his mustache. "Definitely qualifies as questionable."

"I don't know how he found out about it, but he said if we didn't give him five thousand dollars, he would send the tape to the cops. I said go ahead, but my sister was upset. I couldn't let her get into any trouble, so I sold the car and paid the guy off."

"Did he give back the tape?"

He fixed them with a glare. "No, he did not. Now is there anything else you want? I've gotta get to work."

"Just one more thing. If, during your stay in Finny, you happen to trespass on Vern Rosario's property with or without spikes in your possession, you will be arrested."

Rocky's eyes widened, and his mouth gaped.

"We'll talk to the other people in your group to see if they have anything to add," Jack said.

"Go right ahead." Rocky took a step toward them. His eyes glittered behind the thick lenses. "Just see that you don't harass my sister."

Jack locked eyes with him. "We're not in the business of harassing people, Mr. Bippo." He zipped his denim jacket against the chill outside the booth. "You ought to be careful, though. That almost sounded like a threat."

19

September the 13th, 1923

The weather is miserable, cold. Just ripe enough for a nasty drizzle. We returned to the awful spot to pray. There we stood, under the great fir tree. It was so terribly lonely. Just this one blackened tree and no others to stand near. What we need is a good downpour to wash away the horrible stain of evil.

Janey has been completely incoherent since the fire. She just rocks back and forth in a daze. I wonder if she will survive the week. Dan came to see her, but she didn't seem to know who he was. He looked like a dead man, just enough life in him to pump his lungs, not enough to reach his broken heart. He wouldn't take a bite or even a drop of coffee to warm himself.

There is a terrible anger burning deep down in his eyes. I think he has in mind an act of vengeance. As much as I would like to see Slats punished for the terrible thing he did to that poor girl, I tremble to think of Dan going after that heartless monster on his own. I fear he will not live to enjoy his revenge.

Ruth finished reading the journal passage a minute before the doorbell rang. She turned the knob with a sweaty palm. She expected it to be Maude with a terse reminder that she was supposed to photograph the winner at the sand sculpture competition and closing ceremonies. Or maybe Flo coming by to pick up the brownies she'd made to include in a care package for Hugh.

Instead, Jack stood hand in hand with his son, Paul. He held out a bag of apples in greeting. "Hello. Maybe you'll know what to do with some of these apples. So far Boo-Boo is the only one eating them, and I don't think dogs are supposed to have that much fiber."

"How nice," she said. "They sort of scream apple pie with big globs of ice cream to me." She knew perfectly well the fruit provided an excuse for the detective to check up on her, and she appreciated it.

"As long as I get a piece, I think that's an excellent idea."

"Come in. Hi, Paul. How are you doing today, little man?"

Paul nodded, looking around. "Cootchie?"

Ruth felt a pain stab through her like an electric shock. "I'm sorry, Paul. Cootchie has gone away for a while. We'll have to find things to do without her."

He toddled off toward the backyard, leaving Ruth and Jack alone.

She swallowed hard. "Jack, I know you wouldn't ever want to hurt my feelings. But really, I—I would understand if you—didn't want me to watch Paul next week."

He looked at her for a moment, his dark eyes warm. "I am perfectly comfortable that you will take excellent care of Paul as you always have. What happened up nose happened because of some sicko who, for whatever reason, wanted to scare all of us. It did not happen because you were negligent."

"Thank you." She tried to blink back tears as they followed Paul into the yard. When she could trust her voice again, she went on. "How is the investigation going? Both Cootchie's and Ed Honeysill's, I mean."

They watched as Paul stalked Grover, who danced out of the boy's path.

"Well, I gotta tell you. This is stretching our resources a bit. We haven't had one bit of info about the owner of the missing toe, and as for the kidnapper, all we've got is Cootchie's description of a man with glasses and a hat driving a pickup, or maybe a snowplow, depending on what she's been reading before we ask her."

Ruth laughed.

"As for the Honeysill case, plenty of people with the means to fire a flare gun and dump it in the grass at the edge of the parking area. No prints. No witnesses as everyone seemed to be looking up at the time. There were plenty of men wearing glasses of one type or another in the crowd. Plenty of strangers in town, even a loan shark from New York that we've got our eyes on. We don't figure he came into town for the fog."

"You know, Al at the bakery was telling me about a city type who came in. He said the man didn't exactly blend in with the surroundings."

"It's possible Honeysill got himself in some financial trouble and somebody was settling a score. Or maybe he wasn't the target. The killer might have assumed Bing was in the balloon. It seems a few people have it in for him, too."

"Do you think. . ." Her voiced trailed off.

"On the surface it doesn't seem like the murder and Cootchie's kidnapping were related," he said softly, "but we're going to check out every possibility."

She swallowed. "And now Hugh Lemmon is attacked. What is going on in this town?"

"I've been wondering that myself."

He walked over to the concrete bins. "I still think it's amazing that you can farm worms. Does that make you a wormologist?"

"A vermiculturist, actually." They both laughed. "I should tell you that I talked to Cootchie on the phone and she said the 'muffin man' took her."

He frowned. "What does that mean, exactly?"

"I don't know. The only Muffin Man I know is that character in the Mother Goose rhyme."

"Hmm. I'll run that by Nate. He's a master of all things Mother Goose. I've got to get going now. Louella is waiting for Paul, and in the middle of all this chaos, Bobby seems to think I need to go for a nature walk." His smile was eager, and she noticed a faint whisper of cologne.

She smiled back at the detective. "Okay. Thanks for coming by, and give my love to Bobby."

Jack collected Paul and left.

When they were gone, she plopped onto the sofa and breathed in the quiet.

Wait a minute. She sat up abruptly.

What had Jack said about the Honeysill investigation?

"Plenty of men wearing glasses of one type or another in the crowd."

And Cootchie's kidnapper wore glasses, too.

She felt suddenly sick to her stomach. It was possible that the person who murdered Ed Honeysill and the kidnapper were one and the same in spite of Jack's reassurance.

She shivered and went to lock the door.

The sand sculpture competition was set to commence at 11:00 a.m. after the tide went out and with plenty of time to wrap everything up before it returned. Ironically, the weather was once again magnificent with not a wisp of fog anywhere to be seen.

Most of the coastline that snuggled against the nostril portion of Finny's Nose was gravel strewn and rugged. Treacherous riptides had been known to snatch unsuspecting beachcombers from the sharp rocks where they delved for treasure. There was really only one stretch of beach suitable for a sand sculpture contest.

The gentle inlet had been known as Honey Beach since the early thirties when it was used to land boats carrying crates of sweet clover honey. On this day, Finny natives were working hard to take full advantage of the waning hours of the festival, and the tiny beach was crammed with people.

Ruth waved to Bubby, who stood next to a trailer that housed his boat, *The Stinky Limpet*. The Sassie sisters were haggling with him about the price of a charter fishing excursion. They gripped a set of fishing poles menacingly, both iron-gray heads wagged in unison. Judging by the disgruntled look on their faces, they had not fully recovered from losing the previous week's cooking contest to the salmon smokers. She hoped for Bubby's sake the day would not end in a mutinous uprising aboard his vessel.

Bobby stood with Monk behind a plywood table. Their sign boasted cold drinks, coffee, and homemade cookies. "Hey, Ruth," she called. "How come you aren't working behind the counter today?"

"I've got to attend to my photography duties. I did contribute a couple dozen cookies, however. Chocolate chip and oatmeal raisin."

"You did?" She lifted a layer of tinfoil from the top of a paper plate. "I only see oatmeal raisin."

Monk became suddenly busy counting out stacks of napkins and fiddling with the thermos of coffee.

"Uncle Monk?" Bobby said accusingly.

"Hmmm? Oh. Well, I thought they were for me." He reddened. "I love those chocolate chip pecan ones. It isn't fair to tempt me. It's like putting a rabbit in front of a greyhound."

The three of them laughed.

"I just saw Candace in front of the hotel," Bobby said. "She said they've given her the go-ahead to fly home for Ed's funeral."

"Oh." Ruth's thoughts flashed momentarily back to Phillip's funeral. Though she couldn't remember most of it, she hoped Candace would salvage some peace of mind by laying her own husband to rest. Thinking about Candace's betrayal of her spouse, Ruth wondered if guilt would be a part of the woman's life for the rest of her days.

"It's a good thing the Fog Festival is about over," Monk said. "I don't think this town can handle much more drama."

"That reminds me. How is Hugh doing?" Bobby asked.

"Flo stopped by to see him, and she says he's doing well. Sore and bruised but nothing permanently damaged. He'll be back in action by the time we harvest the next set of mushrooms for Dimple." Saying her name gave Ruth a pang of sadness.

"And no arrests?" Bobby asked, pouring sugar packets into a bowl.

"Not that I've heard of."

Maude marched by with a roll of fluorescent pink string and a handful of wooden stakes.

"You looking for a vampire or something?" Monk called out.

"Funny," she said, glaring from under her fringe of bangs. "For your information, we have a last-minute entry to the contest. That makes twelve spots we've sold at ten dollars apiece."

"That's wonderful," said Ruth. "What's the winning prize?"

"A twenty-pound wheel of cheese."

"Cheese?"

"It's very good cheese," she said, her thimble of a nose pointed aloft. "Aged and extra sharp." She stalked off toward Bubby.

"Describes Maude to a tee." Monk chortled.

Ruth wished Monk and Bobby luck and went in search of the perfect Kodak moment.

True to her word, Maude had staked out twelve five-foot-square sections of beach for each contestant. Each square was filled with a collection of buckets, shovels, water bottles, and spatulas. A teenage boy was hard at work in one square sculpting a fighter plane. His face was fixed in concentration as he smoothed the wings with a Popsicle stick. Ruth took his picture, thinking he must be a real cheese lover to go to such lengths on a sunny Sunday morning.

The next contestant wore a fuzzy knit hat over his equally fuzzy hair. He was on hands and knees working a trowel over the perfect rectangle he had created.

"Hi, Alva. I didn't know you entered the sand sculpture contest."

The old man smiled broadly. "I want to win that cheese. Extra sharp and aged."

"So I've heard." She watched him for a few minutes as he fussed and fidgeted over the rectangle. As far as she could see, he was not making any attempt to transform the angular sand pile into anything recognizable. "What exactly—I mean, what type of sculpture are you working on?"

"Cancha tell?"

She peered at the rectangle again. "I give up. What is it?"

"It's a sandwich," he said with glee.

"Ahhh," she said. "Now I can see it. Good luck, Alva."

"Thanks, sweet cheeks."

She took his picture as she moved on.

There were a few other notable sculptures. Ruth was impressed with the mermaid rising from square number six. Her hair spread around her, and a giant tail curled above the sand. Many spectators shared words of encouragement with the sculptor.

Ellen towered over the men with arms crossed across her own much less impressive cleavage. "Ridiculous," she said as Ruth took a picture. "All this work for a wheel of cheese. They could have at least thrown in a magazine subscription or something."

Ruth left the librarian to her glowering and walked to the edge of ocean and sand. A woman stood several yards away, framed by the turbulent ocean.

Evelyn appeared to be watching the foaming scallops wash over her toes. She wore tomato-colored pants and a stained jacket. Her long hair whipped around in the breeze. A tiny dog was tucked under her arm.

"Hi, Evelyn. Did you come to see the sand sculptures?"

"Yes. Did you bring your birds?"

"Maude wanted me to bring them as some sort of tourist attraction, but they don't get along well with the able-bodied of the species." She gestured to the mob of birds, wings outstretched, undulating around the children with food in their hands. "I see you've got a friend there."

She stroked the tiny dog carefully. "His name is Gulliver. He's eleven years old. Nobody wants a dog that old." Her voice was stained with melancholy.

"Then I guess he's really lucky to have you."

Evelyn stared at her. "Sometimes," she said softly, "I feel as alone as they do."

The wind blew the hair away from her face, and Ruth could see the sadness nestled in her eyes. "I think everyone feels that way at one time or another."

"There doesn't seem to be a point to things anymore. I just move from one place to the next, but I don't feel like a part of any of it." She looked a Ruth with desperate eyes. "It feels more like existing than living. Have you ever felt like that?"

"Oh yes," Ruth said quietly. "I have felt exactly like that."

Evelyn opened her mouth then closed it, but the question remained on her face.

For a moment there was only the sound of the waves. Ruth felt a surge of courage in her heart. Before her brain had a chance to stifle it, she spoke. "There is Someone who can help you, who will be there to love you when the world lets you down. Someone who will never betray you."

They locked eyes for a moment. Ruth wondered if she had offended the woman. Evelyn stayed silent.

"If you ever want to talk, about Him, we can do that."

The tiny dog licked Evelyn's chin. "Thank you. Maybe—maybe we could talk, sometime."

"I would like that."

Evelyn gave Ruth a weary smile and left.

She watched Evelyn leave, each step etching a stamp in the sand. Ruth hoped fervently that those steps would lead her home.

Though her heart was light, her head was pounding when she made it back to her cottage. The strange home she had made with a flock of crippled birds and a pasture full of worms seemed pretty tame compared to the wild world outside. *Well,* she thought, *today is the last day of this awful festival. Maybe things will return to normal again.*

She thought about the toe and the murder and the terrifying disappearance of Cootchie Dent. The dark musings consumed her until she recalled the strange wondering look on the face of Evelyn Bippo. Suddenly a distant crack made her jump. Could it be a gunshot? No, probably a firecracker tossed by an errant festivalgoer. Jack would probably be more relieved than she when the Fog Festival staggered to a close. It would be heavenly to have things return to normal.

She thought of the growing closeness between Bobby and Jack.

Then again, maybe a few changes might be in order.

20

Jack couldn't see her from his position on his stomach behind a rock. Though it was irrational to blame all his trouble on the ridiculous festival, he couldn't wait for the event to be over. Things were not safe, he tried to explain to Bobby on the phone, and he didn't want her charging up Finny's Nose unescorted. She hadn't listened, of course.

Now, as he sheltered himself behind the rock pile, he prayed she wasn't going to pay a terrible price for her impatience. His heart refused to let him consider a tragic outcome. Not now, not Bobby.

The afternoon sun temporarily blinded him. He could hear the shots whacking into the dirt and trees just in front of him. He thrust his head above the granite edge, trying to get a shot off, but the sting of flying rock chips caused him to recoil. It would be another five minutes until backup arrived, even with Mary Dirisi at the wheel. Heart pounding, muscles tensed, he made a decision.

"We're going to have to do this the hard way." Scuttling on his belly around the outcropping, praying he wasn't stirring up any dust, he did a slow count to ten before he launched himself into the clearing and dove behind a twisted clump of trees.

Two shots zinged over his head, and then there was silence.

He crouched in as small a ball as he could manage and listened.

Nothing.

Ten seconds later he heard a small crack and the quiet crunch of leaves.

Creeping forward, both hands around the gun barrel, he poked his head around the pile of rock obscuring his sight.

"Hey there," she said, her voice weak. "I thought you decided to go for coffee." She was sitting hunched over, back against the rocks, blood dripping down the side of her face.

He took a steadying breath, noting the tightly controlled look of pain on her face. "No coffee. How badly are you hurt?"

"I'm not sure yet. How many of you are there?"

He swallowed. "Just one, I'm afraid."

"Hmmm. Then I think I may have some sort of head injury."

"Okay," he said, holstering his gun and feeling her arms and legs. "Any bullet holes I should know about?"

"No, and don't think this is going to get you out of going for a run with me," she said.

"Never crossed my mind." She winced as he passed a hand over her bloodied head. "Good thing you have excellent reflexes."

"Yeah. I felt the shot graze my hair and I dove. Unfortunately, I think I was a tad anxious and I rolled headfirst into a boulder. Who is shooting at us, by the way?"

He continued his examination, running fingers along the back of her neck. "I don't know, but we need to move. Are you up to it?"

"Sure."

He helped her up and then caught her as she collapsed again, vomiting on his shoes. He lowered her back to the ground, brushed the hair out of her eyes, and wiped her mouth with his shirtsleeve.

"I'm really sorry about that," she said.

"No problem. I've been through worse. Let's try it again, this time more slowly."

He raised her to her feet. She stood, clinging to his arm, her face pasty white.

"Okay?" he whispered.

She nodded.

"We're going to have to run for it, back to the trees. It's not far." He forced his voice to sound light, encouraging. He tried to ignore the quantity of blood staining her shirtfront and the glazed expression beginning to creep into her eyes. She was going into shock.

He counted softly to three, and then they ran, stumbling along to the tree line until he threw himself down on top of her, covering her head as best he could. Shots drilled into the trunks above, speckling them with splintered wood.

After a few minutes, the shooting stopped, replaced by the wail of sirens and running boots. Nathan hurled himself to the ground next to Jack, panting, eyes wide.

"You okay?" he asked.

"Yeah. She's hurt. Did you get him?"

"No. Mary and Yolo drove up the access road. Nothing yet. You think it's a single shooter?"

He nodded. "Reloaded twice. I think I heard him running downhill."

Nate eyed the pale form between them. "Ambulance won't start. They're sending a rig up, but it won't do the slope very fast."

While they exchanged information, Jack rolled Bobby over, peeling the blood-soaked hair off her face.

She was still and drained of color.

"Where is the engine?" he shouted. "Never mind, we're taking her now."

He lifted the woman in his arms and carried her to Nate's squad car.

Her blood tattooed a trail on the slope of Finny's Nose.

He was on his fourth cup of coffee in the Eden Hospital waiting room when Ruth found him.

"Hi, Jack. How is Bobby doing?"

"She's going to be okay. She got a fairly good concussion, and she's been pretty out of it since we made it here. Doctor says she needs to stay quiet until tomorrow, and then they'll do another CAT scan."

She was glad to see only a shade of worry in his eyes. Monk had told her he was on the verge of panic when they met at the hospital earlier. "Any leads on the shooter?"

He grinned at her. "You're beginning to sound almost coplike, Ruth. Must be from your frequent brushes with the law. We don't have any leads yet, other than it was someone who knows the area real well. Lots of empty shell casings sent to the lab, but that's about it."

"Hmmm." Ruth nodded. "Would you mind telling me what Bobby was going to show you up nose? I saw her up there as I was on my way down from Pistol Bang's a few days ago, and she said she was doing homework so she could show you something. What was it?"

"Let's see—it kind of slipped my mind, what with everything that followed. She called me about two thirty or so and asked me to meet her at the top. What did she say?" His eyes searched the ceiling for an answer. "She said something about trees, fir trees, something weird about the cluster of trees at the top." He chuckled. "Frankly, I didn't really get where she was coming from, but that's not unusual for me when it concerns Bobby."

"You really like her, don't you?"

He looked down at his work boots. "Yeah. I really do."

"Well, when she wakes up, you tell her I'm bringing her an éclair. Her uncle has been busily baking batches of them for her. I know those things have mystical healing powers in addition to the five thousand calories and a bushel of fat."

"Excellent." Jack smiled at her. "What intriguing thoughts are going on in that head of yours? What's up with the tree thing?"

"I'm not sure. I was considering about taking a walk up nose before dark. Do you think it's safe?"

"We've still got people up there, so it's pretty quiet." He stretched and resettled himself in the chair. "Take Monk with you anyway."

21

"Why are we climbing up this infernal hill again?" Monk's cheeks were ruddy, and he was panting.

"I don't know exactly. It's just that Bobby was interested in something about the trees up here, and I just can't get it out of my mind. There is something up here that is the key to this whole mess." Ruth stopped as they crested the nose. "Let's sit down for a minute and cogitate."

He settled his large frame on a rock. "I'll give it a try, but my cogitator is low on fuel. Seeing Bobby hurt and all that just really took it out of me." He cleared his throat.

She joined him and patted his leg, saying another silent thank-you prayer for Bobby's safety. The late afternoon sun silhouetted an enormous Douglas fir against the sky. Ruth studied the tree standing sentinel over the younger trees nearby. She thought about Pickles Peckenpaugh's journal recounting the horrible tragedy that had taken place atop Finny's Nose. Could this be the very same tree? There was no outward sign of the crime; the charred bark would have grown over long ago in any case. Was it under these same boughs that the young girl Janey was found and later the body of Slats the gangster, who undoubtedly died at the hands of Soapy Dan?

Restlessly Ruth clambered down off the rock and walked under the spreading branches. The ground was damp and sticky, speckled with uneven patches where something, presumably squirrels, had been at work. Looking down from her vantage point, she counted four more fir trees, evenly spaced on each side of the parent. Standing where she imagined the women of the Pickle Jar had gathered, she could hear echoes of voices from decades past.

"There we stood, under the great fir tree. It was so terribly lonely. Just this one blackened tree and no others to stand near."

A lone fir. No others to stand near.

Yet as Ruth stood there in the gathering fog, she was yards away from four other fir trees. Younger trees, but still with many decades of growth to their credit. Perfectly spaced, equidistant from the giant fir.

Ruth looked down at the dark soil beneath her feet. Something looked familiar about the surface. The nubbly, tubular trails of earth that poked out here and there amid the rocks and needles.

Of course! Her worm castings. They were so plentiful around the base of the tree that she knew they had to have been placed there. Dug in here and there with a trowel or rake. Those had to be her castings. But why bring them up here? Why steal them at all for that matter?

She continued to walk under the scented branches, lost in thought, until she felt her foot sink into something soft and pliable. Looking down, she screamed.

Monk made it to her side with remarkable speed for a man of his bulk. "What is it? Are you hurt?" he yelled.

She could only point to the mass at her feet.

"Leaping lentils," he said, kneeling to examine the heap.

The squirrel's leg was trapped by the metal jaws. Its eyes were closed, breath coming in pants.

"Man. That's an awful way to catch something. These bear traps have been illegal forever. Alva said he found one this week and brought it to the police. What kind of an idiot would use a bear trap to catch a squirrel?"

"Good squirrels is dead squirrels," Ruth whispered, feeling the bile rise in her throat. "Can you free him?"

Monk didn't seem to hear her as he knelt closer. Carefully he wrapped a handkerchief around the squirrel's head to protect from getting bitten. With a supreme effort he managed to open the trap wide enough for her to remove the injured animal. "We'll take him up to the doc. She may be able to fix him up."

She took off her sweater and wrapped the poor shivering animal inside the soft folds. "You'll be okay. The doctor will take care of you." Turning to Monk, she asked, "Who would do such a terrible thing?"

He poked at the hinge with a stick. "Look at this. There's some white leather caught in here. Like the kind they make sneakers with. You don't suppose this trap caught more than a rodent, do you? Kinda brings to mind a certain toe we've got floating around Finny, don't you think? Ruth?"

She was staring into Monk's face, a look of horror frozen onto her own. "Monk. I know who the muffin man is."

He looked at her as though she were speaking in another language. "Huh?"

She felt a fierce tide of protectiveness swelling inside of her. The muffin man had taken her little family, the family she'd worked so hard to build, and brought it to the edge of disaster. Life had taken her first husband without so much as a warning. God had blessed her with another family, strange as it was, and she knew that it was in grave danger. A strength swirled inside her that she'd never felt before. In a blink, Ruth was suddenly concretely positive that no earthly being could be allowed to take Dimple and Cootchie away, too. She knew what she had to do. With God's help, it was time to make things right.

"Monk, we need to find Jack and Dimple right away."

22

Ruth read lots of mysteries. She knew how confronting a killer was supposed to work. Not that she expected to encounter the murderer at Dimple's farm. She'd frantically called everywhere looking for Dimple as they raced to town with no success. The phone at Pistol Bang's gave her an endless busy tone, which made her heart beat a panicked staccato.

Monk clicked off his cell phone, panting slightly. "Jack's just returning from a meeting. I left him a message to meet us up nose."

"We can't wait. We've got to get to Pistol Bang's and warn Dimple, if she's there. I just can't stand the thought that she might be in trouble."

"I've got your back, Ruth. Let's go."

It took them another twenty minutes to make it from the vet's office back to the top of Finny's Nose. The farm was quiet, without a sign of movement anywhere, until a noise from the polytunnel made them jump.

Monk lowered his voice to a whisper. "Probably just a squirrel on the roof, but I'm going to check it out. You stay here, Ruth."

She waited with her stomach in knots while Monk disappeared around the corner of the tunnel. Unable to remain still, she tiptoed to the office to peek in the window. A muffled noise made her whirl back in the direction of the tunnel. She heard Monk holler and bang against the door, which was now wedged with a piece of metal pipe.

She took a halting step to free her husband from his impromptu prison when she saw him.

Ruth recalled those satisfying literary conclusions in which the hero confronted the villain in the inevitable showdown, calmly laying out the facts in a careful, orderly fashion, while the police waited in the wings to apprehend him or her.

She reviewed these facts in her mind. Now that the moment had come and she was face-to-face with a killer, her mouth took an entirely different tack.

"What is the matter with you? Your father works hard for a living every day of his life, and you reward him by killing people? Why, Hugh?"

He looked at her calmly, hands tucked into the pockets of his corduroy pants. "I don't know what you're talking about."

"You jolly well do know what I'm talking about. I know you've been farming truffles at the top of Finny's Nose. I also know you killed Ed Honeysill and tried to kill Bobby Walker."

He sighed, wiping his nose on his sleeve. "I wouldn't expect you to understand. You're one of those complacent old-timers, content to live out your days on social security benefits until you die. You think too small to come up with a way out." There was a sullen glint in his prominent eyes behind the glasses.

"Ah yes, the brilliant plan. The plan where you inoculate the trees at the top of Finny's Nose with truffle spores and grow them yourself, selling them as French exports at triple your cost. Never mind that the land doesn't belong to you, you idiot."

"Who cares who it belongs to? Nobody uses it anyway."

"I see. So you cooked up the idea to farm the truffles. You transplanted new trees, I noticed. When, exactly, will the younger ones start producing truffles?"

"I don't know for sure. I moved them from another part of the nose. They're about fifteen years old, but I've already harvested some smaller truffles. It's all experimental. In five years or so, I will have some grade-A truffles. Until then, I have the crop from the mature tree. Soon I'll have enough socked away to go wherever I want to."

"When did you become a truffle expert?"

"While the others were out at dances and parties, I was working. I've always been working, since I was a kid. My high school agriculture class gave me the basic tools to learn about inoculation and hybridization. When my blue geranium project went up in smoke, I began working on introducing spores to the root system of host trees. It's not hard; it just takes patience. You just have to manage the pests, especially the squirrels. And then there are the human pests." Hugh spat out the words, shifting his weight off of his left leg.

Ruth's mind flashed to the toe. "That was your toe; you cut off your own toe with the bear trap, didn't you? Was that part of the plan?" Somehow the antagonistic tone of her voice did not fit with her literary image of the cool detective, but she could not stop the anger that was humming in her veins. A pain began to throb in her temples.

"I was trapping the vermin, and I stepped in my own trap," he replied, shifting his weight again. "While I was tying up my foot, a Steller's jay took off with the toe." A drop of spittle flew from his mouth.

Ruth suppressed a rift of laughter.

"That's the only thing that went wrong, anyway. My next crop is ready to harvest, and I have buyers all lined up. Then I can pay off the money I owe and it's all profit."

"What money?"

"I had to borrow some money for the spores, the Web site, a new truck, that kind of thing. My father certainly wouldn't cough up a penny to help me."

"Who loaned you the money?"

"Some people." He looked sullen.

A light flashed in her mind. "Oh, I get it. You borrowed money from a loan shark. Jack mentioned there was one in town." She thought back to the day Alva found Hugh on the beach. "So that's who beat you up and left you on the beach—not the bandanna gang."

"The truffles weren't ready as soon as I thought they would be. I couldn't pay off the loan on time." Hugh shook his head. "I tried to tell them I would have the money soon, but they wouldn't listen. That's the problem today." His voice rose in volume with each word. "No one listens!"

"Gee," she said, ignoring his raging, "crooks with no patience. Imagine. That's when you decided to blame your beating on Rocky and his group?"

"I saw them on the beach a couple of times, and they kept poking around my trees up nose. I figured accusing them would explain things. They're crazy anyway. I set fire to one guy's trailer to keep him from sniffing around near my truffles." He ran rigid fingers through his hair. "It's okay. It's all okay. My plan is working out in spite of everything."

Suddenly his face changed. The last trace of youthful enthusiasm melted away, leaving something crazed in its wake.

Ruth should have been terrified, but the fear did not succeed in uprooting the anger that vibrated in her gut. "So you don't figure murdering Ed was a tiny snafu in your plan? Why did you have to kill him?"

"Ed was suspicious; he knew my truffles weren't French. He kept pressuring me to see them, sample them. I saw him and the dark-haired girl up looking at my trees. He left a message at Dimple's asking to see me before he left town. I knew he figured it out, so I had to get rid of him."

Hugh's prominent Adam's apple bobbed up and down as he spoke. "I didn't really think he would die when I shot the balloon down. I thought he would get scared and go home. Then that girl came sniffing around, measuring the trees and examining the ground underneath. She was close to figuring out they were transplanted or seeing evidence of my cultivation. I should have killed her, too, but I'm not a good shot." The words tumbled out faster and faster, like cockroaches after filth.

She knew she should feel sorry for this young man. His mind had been fractured beyond repair. But her heart could not pity the man who had taken Cootchie away.

"Look on the bright side," she spat, "at least you didn't shoot off your other toe. And then the best part of your plan. You decided to kidnap Cootchie. That's right, isn't it? You were the man with the glasses who took her, weren't you?" The words snapped out of her mouth.

"Yeah, no big thing. I wore a wig and a fake mustache. She didn't even recognize me. I took her to Half Moon Bay and left her at the library. It got you all out of my hair for a while," he said, rooting around in his pocket. "It got all the festival nuts off my land while everyone looked for Cootchie, especially those tree freaks. They kept trampling my truffles." He sniffed. "I didn't think it would be such a big deal anyway. I wouldn't have done it if I had known Dimple would be so upset."

Ruth thought about Cootchie's phone conversation. It wasn't the muffin man she referred to, but the truffle man. The man she had seen at the park when he spilled the truffles on the ground. "She's smarter than you think, Hugh. As a matter of fact, I think she's smarter than you, period."

A deep flush mottled his cheeks. "That's where you're wrong. Where everyone has always been wrong. I'm not just a geek, some loser farm boy. You go ahead and laugh, but I'll have the last laugh in the end."

His eyes glittered in the afternoon sun. "Besides, how is this your business anyway? You didn't even know Ed, and Bobby Walker is fine. So I took Cootchie for a few hours. What's it to you? I didn't hurt her. There was no harm done."

Ruth felt as if his words came from far away. There was a rushing in her ears, and her temples pounded. She felt warm all over, as if her veins flowed with molten lava. "No harm done?"

By the time his hand emerged from his pocket with the switchblade, she had grabbed the log that stood upright near her feet. She did not feel the knife slice into her forearm as she swung the log like a baseball bat, smashing it down onto his injured foot.

He doubled over in pain but quickly straightened again and lunged with the knife. She swung again.

The log whacked into the side of his head with a satisfying *thud* and sent him crashing to his knees on the gravel path.

Not bad for someone who hasn't played baseball since the third grade, she thought. She hooked her hands under his armpits and dragged him to the sturdy oak post supporting the sign reading Pistol Bang Mushroom Farm.

As she looked around, she spied the metallic cylinders. Smiling, Ruth Budge set to work.

❦

Nine minutes later the detective was running up Pistol Bang's gravel walkway, gun drawn, with Nathan and Mary at his heels. Jack stopped short, almost causing his officers to plow into him from behind. Ruth sat on a wooden bench, tying up her bloody arm with the sleeve of her jacket.

Jack had to do a double take to realize that the silver cocoon under the signpost was Hugh Lemmon wrapped from waist to crown of head in multiple rolls of duct tape. The only spots showing on his upper body were two dazed-looking eyes and his prodigious nose. The rest of him was completely mummified in silver tape.

Nate succeeded in freeing Monk from the tunnel.

Monk puffed up, gasping and red faced.

"Ruth, are you all right?"

"Yes, I'm fine. He only cut my arm, and I have a tremendous headache, but that's about all the damage. To me anyway," she said, continuing to wrap her arm.

"Ambulance is on—" Nate stopped talking as he got a good look at Hugh. "Er, ambulance is on its way. Does he need, uh, medical attention?"

"Oh, he may have a concussion or something. I hit him with a log. Other than that, I think he's just fine." She smiled. "Until they have to remove the duct tape, that is."

All three officers grinned.

Mary listened to a message on the radio. "Dimple is fine. She was off picking lentils or nettles or something."

With a deep sigh, Ruth stood up and brushed off her hands before she collapsed.

23

Ruth was staring at her IV, wondering if she could request a chocolate flavor, when the door opened.

"Hello, Ruth," Dimple said. Her green eyes were puffy with fatigue. "How are you?"

"I'm okay. I had to have a few stitches, and apparently the doctor decided to have my oil changed and air filter replaced while he was at it."

"That sounds practical."

"I'll probably go home this afternoon when the test results are in." The silence dragged on. "How is Cootchie?"

"She is having a lovely time with, uh, Meg. She said it's fun to play in the yard and look for bones. I think she might be disrupting Meg's landscaping, though."

The silence stretched into the uncomfortable zone.

"Dimple, I am so sorry. For letting him take Cootchie." She choked out the words.

Dimple laid her tiny hand on Ruth's arm. "Ruth, dear, you did not know the evil around you. Neither did I." She blinked back tears. "He was with me all the time. I trusted him. I trusted him around my daughter."

"If it means anything, I really don't think he meant to kill anyone. He just didn't see the reality of it. It was like something out of a movie."

Dimple looked away from Ruth. A phone buzzed somewhere in a distant corridor.

"What is it?" Ruth asked. "Tell me."

She took a steadying breath. "I'm going away for a while. I'll close the farm for a few months and go to stay with Meg in Arizona."

"I thought you might." An iron weight settled over her heart. "I can understand that, after everything that has happened."

"I won't stay. Cootchie and I will come back. I just want to know what it's like. To have a mother."

She nodded. "I will miss you so much."

"I will miss you, too." Dimple's long hair tickled Ruth's cheek as she leaned over to hug her. "The heart will always find the path towards home."

Ruth wondered despairingly if the path would end in Arizona with Meg.

⁓

Dr. Ing strode quietly into Ruth's hospital room a few hours later. As she listened to his words, she recalled his quiet, soothing tones years earlier when he explained how her husband of twenty-five years had suddenly stopped living. He was just as quiet and soothing now.

"Ruth, I have some news for you. We've run tests, as you know. I always like to do that as a precaution in cases like this."

Tests? Her heart beat faster.

"As much as we know about the human body, it's still a mysterious, enigmatic thing. People who should be dead live on for years. Perfect babies die without explanation."

She stared at him with wild fear that filled every pore.

He returned her gaze with eyes full of compassion. "I am afraid this is going to be a shock to you, Ruth, but I have no doubt that you will be able to handle it."

Monk rushed into the shop. Ruth was seated at a scarred wooden table an hour before her morning coffee shift would start. She stared out the window at the hydrangeas wearing their cotton-candy colors. She didn't meet Monk's gaze. He sat down next to her, removing the ever-present ladle from his pocket and squeezing the smooth metal handle.

"Honey, I've been so worried," he began. "I tried to find you, but you'd already gone." He paused, tapping his ladle on the table. "I wanted to take you home. They said you insisted on being discharged. Are you sure that was a good idea?"

"It was what the doctor told me," she mumbled as she continued to stare out the window. "They did tests, you know."

His breath hissed through his lips. "So the doctor did. . .tests?" He inhaled again. "I understand if you don't want to talk about it." He chewed his lower lip. "Maybe it's better to wrangle with it for a while, until you figure out how to deal with it, or treat it, or whatever." He paused again.

She turned to him. "I'll be forty-nine soon. That's a long time to live, don't you think?"

Monk's eyes widened. "Yes, I guess so."

"I've lost a husband and become Nana to a stranger's child. I've even learned how to raise worms for a living and found another good man to love. Don't you think that's a full life?" She looked intensely at him now.

"Yes." He swallowed. "But whatever it is, it doesn't mean the end. We can fight it, or figure out how to live with it. People survive things all the time." His words tumbled out like tiny fish darting from a predator.

"That's what Dr. Ing said," Ruth said, her voice flat.

"I'll help you," he said. "We'll do it together. I will be here for you." His eyes were warm and filled with tears, radiating a tenderness that was at odds with his hulking stature and quick temper.

"I don't want to be a medical curiosity," she said, "some freak of nature."

He stood and put a huge hand on her shoulder. "Just tell me what to do, Ruth, how to help you. I'll do whatever I can."

"I know—" She suddenly realized that Monk thought she was dying of some disease.

What a precious man she'd married. She looked into his weathered face, reading the emotion flashing in his eyes. He had been there through it all. Steady and quiet. Ready to be asked about whatever she needed. She remembered his earlier words. God gave her strength because He wanted her to use it. She sat up straighter in the chair.

"Monk, it's not what you think. The doctor said I'm pregnant."

He jerked upward; the ladle flew out of his hand and shattered the window into millions of sparkling droplets.

The crash reverberated all the way to the top of Finny's Nose.

TREASURE UNDER FINNY'S NOSE

1

"Your ship went down in a violent storm. You've spent three days clinging to the wreckage, watching the people around you die from exposure and exhaustion. You finally struggle to shore and collapse there, unconscious until the sun warms your body, easing you back to life. What is the first thought that fills your head when you open your eyes?"

Ethan Ping leaned forward in anticipation.

Ruth Budge heaved a sigh. "I want Milk Duds." She felt only a sliver of guilt as Ethan, her director, slapped his clipboard against his thigh. The man couldn't be more than twenty-two and a college student to boot. How could he understand a forty-eight-year-old pregnant woman? Come to think about it, how could she? The only thing she knew for certain was if she didn't get some Milk Duds soon, she was going to have to put the director in a half nelson. Reenacting the life of the indomitable Indigo Orson could wait. She was a desperate woman.

Ethan continued to stare at her in exasperation, the leaves of the oak behind him silhouetting his dark hair in green. His slender eyebrows drew together in a single line above his almond-shaped eyes. "Mrs. Budge, I know you are having a bit of trouble concentrating."

He didn't know the half of it. She was pregnant and just months away from her forty-ninth, yes, forty-ninth, birthday. If her life were a novel it would be ridiculously improbable. She might very well be the oldest known mother in the Western Hemisphere. Then a kick from somewhere in the vicinity of her kidney reminded her that it was all too real. Ignoring the heartburn that plagued her regardless of what she ate, she tried to listen to the young filmmaker.

"We've got a deadline on this reenactment project, Mrs. Budge. It has to be finished by the end of June, or we're not going to make our deadline. I don't mean to pressure you or anything, but Reggie here needs to get the footage."

Reggie, a tall man with cocoa skin, waved at her. He rested the giant camera on his shoulder as if it weighed nothing at all.

She waved back and resisted the urge to curl up on the ground where she stood for a nap.

Sandra Marconi, a chubby blond with her arms full of binders, interrupted. "Maybe Mrs. Budge just needs a little break, Ethan. Ruth, why don't you go sit in the sun for a minute."

Ruth didn't need a second invitation. The spasm in her back was working its way up her spine and into her shoulder blades. She eased onto a lawn chair that sat in a precious spot of early summer sun and closed her eyes. The warmth lulled her into a comfortable haze until the sound of a bell startled her.

Alva Hernandez wobbled up the path. He rang the bicycle bell again before he dismounted and hobbled over, a red toolbox in his gnarled hand. "Hello, sweet cheeks. What's shakin'?"

"Hello, Alva. Did you help Monk load up?" Monk, her husband of almost one year, had reluctantly left on a trip to care for his ailing father. She hoped it was reluctantly, though with the state of their house and her propensity to burst into tears every five minutes, maybe he viewed it as a respite. He was a patient man, but she knew sometimes he was at a complete loss about how to handle her kaleidoscoping emotions. She really couldn't help him with it as she was confounded by her emotional state herself.

"Yup, I helped your hubby stow his gear." Alva shoved his wiry white hair out of his eyes. "He's off to the airport. He assigned me a mission 'fore he left, though. I ain't had a mission since Korea." His filmy eyes sparkled. "Ain't that something?"

Ruth smiled at the enthusiastic octogenarian. "What's the mission, Alva?"

He started. "Oh yeah. I'm to be your, what's it called again? Oh yeah. Your ninny."

"My what?"

"Ninny. No, that don't sound right." He scratched his chin. "Give me a second here. Oh, right. Nanny, not ninny. I'm to take care of you and the little bun in your oven until Monk gets back. I'm to help you with the birds and make sure you get enough food and all that. Help you tie your shoes iffen the baby swells you up too big and the like. Stuff like that."

Ruth suppressed a groan. Alva was indeed a help with her crabby flock of disabled seagulls, and he often lent a hand tracking down an AWOL bird. The man was half a bubble off plumb, but he was devoted to her. Still, she really just wanted to climb into a hole and disappear. The thought of having a personal attendant until Monk returned didn't appeal to her at all.

Alva set the toolbox on the ground and snapped open the lid. It was crammed to the brim with candy. "I put me together a survival kit. Whatcha want? Kisses? Chocolate bar? Tootsie Rolls? The peanut butter cups is squashed so they ain't good anymore. How about a package of gumdrops?"

Ruth's spirits picked up. "You don't possibly have any Milk Duds in there, do you?"

He foraged around in the bottom. "Aha. There you are, sweet cheeks. I said I'd take care of you, didn't I?"

Ruth mentally retracted any unenthusiastic thoughts about Alva's nannying. "Thank you, Alva. You are a lifesaver."

He cocked his head and began to rummage in the box again. "You want a

Lifesaver? I got them, too. Cherry, butterscotch, them purple-colored ones. . ."

"I'm fine with these, Alva." She tore open the package and ate greedily.

Sandra squeezed into the chair next to Ruth. "I'm sorry about Ethan. He's really a brilliant guy, but he's driven, so delays make him crazy."

Ruth sighed. "I don't mean to criticize, but why did you ask me to do this reenactment business anyway? I mean, for one thing I'm not Hispanic and I'm not an actor. I'm just a vermiculturist."

"What's that?"

"A worm farmer," Alva piped up. He offered a bag to the woman. "Candy corns?"

"Uh, no thanks. Well, as you know, this is the anniversary of the wreck of the *Triton* right off the coast there. At least that's what our research lends us to believe." She pointed down the slope to the foam-capped ocean. "Our project is to take a photographic record of the wreck, but Ethan thought adding a dramatic reenactment would punch up the human interest element."

"I agree," Ruth said, "but why don't you get a real actor?"

Sandra twiddled with the binder. "Because you have to pay real actors, and our budget is stretched as it is with the underwater photography gear. We've got every available dime invested in this project, believe me, and there's just no wiggle room. Besides, your public relations gal told us how versatile you were."

Ruth coughed. "My what?"

"Tiny lady with a loud voice. Maude something." Sandra snapped her fingers. "Maude Stone, I think it is. She found out we were coming to Finny and contacted us to see how she could be involved. We told us we needed an actor. She suggested herself at first, but we didn't think that would work since her leg is in a cast."

"As soon as I get hold of her, she's going to need a cast for the other leg," Ruth grumbled.

"Pardon?"

"Never mind."

A bird swooped overhead and headed toward the water. The women looked up into the brilliant blue sky over the ocean. A small boat bobbed in the water. Ruth could just make out the banana-yellow cap of Roxie Trotter, a relative newcomer to the town. The wind picked up, toying with the oak branches above their heads.

"Do you get many tourists in June?" Sandra asked.

"Some, but fall is better weather-wise because there is much less fog." Ruth pointed to Roxie's boat. "Roxie started up a fishing tour business a year ago. She said her business booms in the fall."

Sandra tipped her face to the sun. "It is beautiful in Finny right now. The vegetation is so lush, almost tropical. Once the fog burns off, everything sort of puts on these dazzling colors."

TREASURE UNDER FINNY'S NOSE

"Yes, it is nice here." Ruth inhaled the tang of salt air. "Even in the winter you can still find good weather in northern California. From the top of Finny's Nose, you can see all the way to the Farralon Islands when it's clear."

She had a sudden flashback to standing on top of the mountain three months back, when the pieces of a murderous puzzle fell into place. She shuddered, reburying the memories of that awful time back where they belonged.

Sandra laughed, gazing at the vibrant green outline of the tall peak. "I've never stood at the top of a nose before. You're right. The thing really does look just like a nose."

"If you look at it upside down, it's the spittin' image of Richard Nixon," Alva added, around a mouthful of candy.

Sandra gave him an incredulous look.

Ruth could only shrug at her.

Reggie took the camera off his shoulder and sauntered over. "Hey, ladies. We've lost the light for today. We'll have to pick it up tomorrow."

Ruth tried to look disappointed, but her feet were shouting a silent *yippee!*

Sandra handed her a binder. "Why don't you read up on Indigo tonight? I think you'll find her inspiring. I'll see you tomorrow, Mrs. Budge."

Ruth finished her candy and took her nanny's arm.

The comforting smell of furniture polish greeted her back at the cottage. In spite of the emptiness she felt at Monk's absence, she was relieved to be home. After making her way carefully around the piles of sheetrock left by Carson the contractor, Monk's crazy Italian bowling buddy, Ruth snuggled on the sofa with a cup of tea. She opened the binder and read the prologue.

> *Isabela Ortiz was a Mexican servant in the house of Mr. Edward Orson. She accompanied them on a steamship which departed from New York in 1851 en route to San Francisco. The ship was overloaded with coal, and only fifty passengers were on board when the ship collided with another steamer, which sustained only minor damage. There were twelve reported survivors of the* Triton *passengers and crew. Eleven were picked up six miles south when the tide carried them to a rocky outcropping. Isabela, separated from the other survivors, made it to shore in a different location. Fearing persecution from the white miners, she took the name Indigo Orson and lived as a man.*

Imagine, Ruth thought. *Surviving a wreck, washing ashore, and assuming a new identity.* She pictured the Finny shoreline, rugged, cold, inhospitable for much of the time. Isabel was indeed a force to be reckoned with to have carved out a life here. She skimmed the first few pages until a photocopied passage caught her eye. The script was loopy and hard to read even when she held it to the light.

Why am I alive? I can only think it to be the grace of God. He must have His own plan, to save me, a worthless servant, and let the others die. It is a miracle to have my tiny book and stub of pencil to write with. The ship broke like an old matchstick with a terrible groaning sound. Señor Orson was crushed by falling wood, lifted in a mighty wave. He looked surprised when the beam hit him. All his money couldn't do him any help then. Down he went, the waves swallowed him up as if he'd never existed.

Señora Orson and I clung to a piece of wreckage. She looked so lost, poor niña. I tried to comfort her, but she never had an idea how to take care of herself, that's why she had me along on the trip. She could not understand that her husband had been killed right before her very eyes.

I knew from the moment Señor Orson determined to sail to San Francisco with his precious box that we would be thrown into trouble. And so desperate he was to go that he booked passage on this coal-filled tub. Why oh why couldn't he have waited until a right proper ship was available? It was a doomed trip from the very start, and Señor paid a terrible price in more ways than one.

Poor Señora Orson. After the boat cracked into pieces, she just kept on asking if it was safe. When will we get home, she asked over and over. I looked out at the terrible wide ocean and all the poor dead folks floating like corks around us. I felt the tug of the current and the whack of the sea creatures that would touch my legs where they dangled in the water. What did it matter then? It was all in God's hands and He cares little for treasure.

Treasure? What kind of riches would have caused Orson to risk it all and take passage on the coal ship?

The phone rang. Ruth jumped.

"Hello, gorgeous. How are you?" Monk's voice boomed across the line.

"I'm not gorgeous. I'm big and fat, and I have eaten my body weight in candy today."

"Now, none of that kind of talk. You're always beautiful to me. Did Alva help you with the birds?"

"Yes. They're all fed and tucked in for the night."

"How's the drywall repair coming along?"

"I only know Carson's been here because there's a gaping hole in the baby's room and a pile of sheetrock in the middle of the living room floor."

He snorted. "Who would think termites could cause so much damage?"

"Carson could give them a run for their money. How is your father?"

"He's on the mend. Doctors say he'll be home in a few days. That means I will, too. I can't wait to get back to you."

She felt trembly inside. "Is that really true, Monk? Even though I am the oldest expectant mother on the planet?" *And the one child I had decades ago is a virtual stranger?* She pushed the thought away.

"Listen to me, Ruthy. You're my darling. I don't know why the good Lord decided to put us up to this parenting thing so late in the game, but He knows what He's doing. I love you and we'll face everything together."

She could picture him there, his giant hands cradling the phone, his eyes warm and gentle. "I love you, Monk," she said softly.

"I love you, too, Ruthy. You just give Junior a pat for me, and I'll call you again tomorrow."

"Okay. I'll pat somewhere around my pancreas. I think that's where Junior is wedged right now."

His laugh echoed in her ears as she hung up and headed for bed.

Though her body was steeped in fatigue, she could not get to sleep. Every time she found a comfortable position, she'd feel a strange flutter of movement. Maybe it was gas, as everyone seemed to believe. The infant was barely three months along, so how had it managed to expand her waistline and grow big enough for her to feel it so distinctly? She remembered an old black and white horror movie about a woman who had given birth to an octopus-like creature that immediately set out to conquer planet earth. She hoped this child would at least fix the sheetrock before he or she embarked on world domination.

Finally, somewhere after two a.m. she got up and fixed herself more tea. She looked out of the front window toward the inlet where Indigo's ship had foundered so many years ago. Was it a dark night like this when Isabel found herself in the sea? Was there only a sliver of moon to light the way to shore?

Ruth started to put down her cup to return to bed when she saw it.

A tiny flicker of light, dancing under the waves like a fallen star.

2

Ruth steeled her stomach as she sprinkled scraps on the worm bed. In the pre-dawn gloom she watched the surface of the soil undulate with happy wiggling bodies. She tried not to inhale the scent of vegetable peelings and loamy soil. The standing monthly order at Pete's Fish and Tackle had to be filled whether she was nauseated or not. The birds rustled and squawked from their pen in the corner of the yard. She counted seven beaks. It was always a relief to know that they were all present. Not too long ago poor Ulysses was mutilated by a deranged killer looking to send a message to Ruth. The bird had gone to live with a friend who didn't have so many other beaks to tend to, and she still looked for his fuzzy head in the gaggle.

The feathered brood was founded by her late husband, Philip, who just couldn't stand to euthanize the numerous avian victims brought to his veterinary office, and since they were unable to fly, there was no hope of releasing them. He named them all after U.S. presidents, except for Martha, who was the first lady of the bunch.

Grover pushed his way to the gate and inclined his pearly head for a scratch. He was knocked aside by the larger Milton, who flapped his white wings and gave her a "Where is my breakfast?" honk.

"You don't get your breakfast until I get mine, you greedy bird. Then we'll go for a walk, if you can behave." After a virtually sleepless night, she wondered how she would find the energy to walk.

Her breakfast, as it turned out, was dry toast and decaf coffee. She had doubts that even that simple meal would stay where she put it. With grim determination, she donned her warm jacket with the ever-present bag of corn chips in the pocket and went outside to gather the squadron.

The morning air was chilly, but the fog that huddled along the ground was scant. It would burn off by early afternoon. June really was a good time to come to Finny, she thought as she headed through town. After the cool of morning, the afternoon would no doubt shape up to be lovely. A glorious scent of cinnamon from the Buns Up Bakery signaled the start of Al's morning preparations. She waved a hello to Luis Puzan as he cleaned the windows of his grocery store. A light shone in the top floor of the Finny Hotel.

"I wonder if Ethan is up doing some work on his script?" It was a good place for creativity. The bougainvillea was vibrant against the peeling white paint of the old inn. In the distance, patrons could see the wild Pacific, wind tossed and shadowed by the enormous beds of kelp that undulated under the surface. The building was slightly ramshackle, but the view couldn't be beat.

She scooped Rutherford out of the fountain in the center of town square. Even over two years later she couldn't forget the day she and Alva pulled a slippery body from that bubbling water. The nausea returned with a vengeance. She took several deep breaths and sniffed the orange peel Flo Hodges insisted would drive away the worst morning sickness.

A cheerful bicycle bell announced the arrival of her erstwhile guardian. Alva coasted to a perilous stop, weaving his way in and out of birds, dinging his bicycle bell to startle them out of the way with very little effect. "Morning, sweet cheeks. Monk told me to check every day and see if you done ate your vitamins." He took a battered notebook and a pencil stub out of his jacket pocket.

"Yes, Alva, I did take my vitamins, and so far I haven't thrown them up."

He scribbled a note. "Saturday. Seven o'clock. Took pills. No throw up. Got it." The pencil stuck out at a jaunty angle after he put it behind his ear. "Where are we going today?"

She tucked the flyaway hair that was riddled with ever more gray strands behind her ears. "I thought I'd take the birds for a walk down to the beach before rehearsal. I saw a strange light in the water last night. I can't get it out of my mind."

His white eyebrows shot up. "Strange? You figure maybe it's a sea monster or something? You know I saw that Loch Ness creature swimmin' in Tookie Newsome's trout pond last spring. I betcha he relocated to the ocean on account of he needed more leg room."

Ruth suppressed a giggle. "Could be. Tookie's pond is a bit small for a sea monster. Did you finish your route?" Alva was probably the oldest newspaper delivery boy in the country, but he did his job with meticulous care.

"Sure. I got up extra early so's I could report for bird walking duty." He opened the tool box and handed her some Milk Duds.

She patted his arm. Ignoring the fact that her waist was expanding with every passing minute, she opened the package.

A tiny, black-haired woman with an ankle cast hobbled over, her arms full of grocery bags.

Ruth's eyes narrowed. "Good morning, Maude. I understand I've got you to thank for being roped into this acting job."

Maude shot a poisonous look at Alva before giving Ruth her full attention. "Well, I would have been happy to take on the role myself, but they said the cast was a problem. I really can't see why they couldn't shoot from the waist up. Of course, if somebody hadn't left their inflatable raft on the steps of Dr. Soloski's office, I never would have broken my foot in the first place."

Alva crossed his arms. "How many times do I gotta say it? I told you that tweren't my raft. I dunno how it got there. You can't pin that on me."

Alva and Maude had a long-standing feud that began when she accused Alva of stomping on her primroses while he delivered the newspaper. Though Maude tried everything, even videotaping, to catch Alva in the act, she had never found proof of intentional wrongdoing.

The wind whipped Maude's hair into a wild tangle. "Well, you were there for a cleaning, weren't you? Even though you don't have any real teeth left."

"I do so have teeth, lots of 'em, the real kind and the plastic kind. Fer yer information, Doc says I gotta have a cavity filled in my back mortar."

"That's molar, you idiot." Maude was distracted by the crinkle of Ruth's candy bag. "What are you doing eating candy at this hour?" Her glance shot to Alva. "Did you give her that?"

He straightened up. "It just so happens, I'm her nanny. It's my job."

"You're not a nanny, you're a nincompoop. A woman in her condition, especially at her age, should not be eating candy."

Alva folded his arms. "She's gonna have anything she wants while the bun is in the oven. Monk said so. I'm keeping a report for him. I'm in charge."

Ruth noticed the flush mounting across the woman's cheeks. She hastened to intervene. "Maude, what are all the bags for?"

"I'm making boxed lunches for the first tour group."

"What tour group?"

"I've sold twelve tickets to the Women's Literary League of Half Moon Bay. They're coming to visit the film site. You can meet them later. I'm providing lunch and a comprehensive informational tour. I've got another group lined up, too. A few more weeks of this and we might be able to buy that copy machine for FLOP."

FLOP was the Finny Ladies Organization for Preparedness. With Maude at the helm, they were prepared for anything, from quakes to quarantines. "You're giving tours of the film site? Did you run this by the director?"

"Oh, please. He doesn't dictate what goes on in Finny. He might be inspired to greater artistic heights, having a real audience there." She shifted the bags and leaned closer, peering at Ruth's face. "Why don't you ask the crew about some stage makeup? You look all waxy and there are some sun spots on your cheeks that could stand to be concealed. Do you have your lines memorized yet?"

Ruth moved her waxy, spotted face away from Maude. "Not yet. I'm working on it."

Alva wrote in his notebook.

"What are you doing?" Maude demanded.

"I'm adding to my report. Saturday. Seven thirty. Heading to the beach. Interrupted by old bat with a sack full of groceries."

Maude's lips parted in fury.

TREASURE UNDER FINNY'S NOSE

"Uh, we've really got to go walk the birds before rehearsal." Ruth grabbed Alva's arm. "Come on, let's hurry. Bye now." She moved off as fast as her thickened middle would allow. They headed down slope to the beach.

The morning chill held the fragrance of cypress and cedar. Gravel crunched underfoot as they walked, the birds milling in a noisy crowd around them. She felt a sudden onslaught of self-pity. "Alva, do you think I look waxy?"

He looked closely at her face. "Nah. You're a real looker, Ruth. Your face is all plump and shiny. The best women are like doughnuts, you know, round and glazed."

They lapsed into silence as Ruth tried to digest Alva's wisdom. Round and glazed. Neither sounded particularly attractive. She was overwhelmed by a pang of loneliness. Not just for Monk. She desperately missed her friend Dimple and Dimple's daughter, Cootchie. Cootchie had been a part of Ruth's soul since she had stepped in to raise her when Dimple's lover was killed. At times, when Ruth pleaded with God to help her be a good mother to her unborn child, He sent her a tender memory of Cootchie. It was as if He said, *"You love Cootchie, and you'll love this child, too."*

Another voice spoke up, with different words. *You loved Bryce with every ounce of your being, and he won't give you the time of day. And look what happened to Cootchie, kidnapped while in your care. Now she's living with her real grandma in Arizona.*

Ruth silenced the thoughts with a strengthening prayer. She might be waxy, round, and glazed, but she still had enough strength to pray.

They made it down to the rugged stretch of beach, the wind fighting them along the way. A crooked line of rocks dotted the gravelly sand and joined up to form a black cliff in the distance.

The birds swarmed back and forth, playing tag with the waves. They kept away from the few able-bodied birds that poked in the sand. It made her sad that her birds knew instinctively that they were not part of that wild flock anymore. She wondered if they felt a pang when they saw their uninjured brothers fly away on graceful wings. Did they realize they were forever earthbound?

She walked carefully around the slick boulders, keeping an eye on Franklin. He was her delicate bird, after losing an eye and a foot to a cat. The vet had fashioned him a little plastic tube that slipped on his leg to protect his stump and help with balance. He despised having the contraption put on, but it helped him keep up or at least out of the way of the others.

Looking back, she saw Alva with his plastic shovel, digging for treasure. The image brought back the words of Isabel Ortiz. As she watched the gray waves scour the sand, she wondered what it had been like for the servant woman to cling to the wreckage and watch the people die all around her. All those people and their possessions, lost to the arms of an angry ocean.

Franklin hobbled ahead and disappeared around yet another jagged rock.

"Don't go too far," Ruth scolded. "I'm in no position to attempt a water rescue."

She edged around the obstruction.

Franklin poked his slender beak in a pile of slippery black kelp.

Ruth took another glance at the oddly shaped mound of seaweed.

Her mouth went dry.

"Alva," she called in a shaky voice. "Can you come here for a second?"

He trotted over, still holding onto the bucket. "Good news. I found a can opener. Ain't that handy? You just never know when you're gonna need a can opener. It don't seem hardly rusted at all. Wonder why someone threw it away?"

She pointed. "Take a look over there, Alva. Is that what I think it is?"

The old man squinted, mashing a fist into his eyes before he peered again. "Well, would you look at that. It ain't no sea monster." He patted his pockets.

Ruth fought hard against the bile that rose in her throat. It took all her strength of will to contain the scream that coalesced inside her. After a moment, she got her vocal cords to cooperate. "Alva, I think you better call the police."

"Who, me? I ain't got a phone, sweet cheeks." He found the pencil and notebook. "I gotta add this to my report." He licked the pencil point and began to write with relish. "Saturday. Seven fifty-five. We found ourselves a body."

3

Jack Denny tried again to get out of the police car, and again he stopped with his hand on the door. There must be some paperwork to be done, an arrest report or neighbor complaint that needed to be addressed, that would take him away from this location. He stared down at the cell phone clipped to his belt. It remained stubbornly silent. The irony.

"Man, Jack," he mumbled to his stubbled chin in the rearview mirror, "you are losing it, fella." That was only partially true. He'd already lost it the moment he'd laid eyes on Bobby, right before she'd flattened an obnoxious assailant twice her size. She had been gone from Finny for two months but had returned to run her uncle Monk's business while he was away tending to his father.

Yes, Bobby was back, and Jack was alternately terrified and elated.

He stood outside Monk's Coffee and Catering with sweating palms and his stomach in knots. It was ridiculous. He could deal with homicides and mobsters, so why did this woman make his heart hop around like a wild rabbit? Jack took a gulp of air and headed toward the shop. He made it almost to the front door before he stopped again.

Maybe Bobby had met someone. She had been away long enough. She was an attractive, educated, intriguing woman, and a park ranger to boot. Maybe she'd met some outdoorsy type who wasn't afraid to take on a relationship, a man who didn't fear losing everything. The thought sent a stab of ice through his gut.

The windows were dim. Bobby must not be opening up the shop today. With a surge of relief, Jack reached for his keys to head back to the station.

"Are you admiring Uncle Monk's new paint?"

He whirled around and dropped the keys.

Bobby looked at him with her head cocked, black eyes sparkling under a fringe of bangs. She hardly came up to his chin, but her eyes had such power and strength.

"I, uh, no, not really, no." He picked up the keys and felt a flood of heat to his face. "I heard you were back."

"Word travels fast in Finny. I was taking out the trash and I saw your car. Do you want to come in for some coffee?"

He sighed. "I would love to."

They walked into the shop. Bobby prepared the coffee and filled heavy mugs. The two settled into battered chairs by the window. In the distance, the ocean performed acrobatics under a delicate layer of fog. Jack sipped the strong brew and tried to calm his pattering heart. "When did you get in?"

"Just this morning. I haven't even seen Aunt Ruth yet. Uncle Monk asked me to keep the coffee and muffin business open and take catering orders. He's hoping to be back next week. It killed him that he had to go."

"It's great that you could help out. Ruth has her hands full right now. Maude's already got her doing some photo documentary thing and an acting job." He cleared his throat. It was time to ask the question that kept him awake at night. "Have you decided on a job?"

"I've been looking at some positions in Arizona, and one in California, plus the spot that's up for grabs in Utah. They all have their good points, but I haven't made any decisions yet."

"I see." Jack's thoughts ran wild. *Pick the one in California. Stay here, close to me. Please.* He wasn't sure which scared him more, the thought of her leaving or the thought of her staying.

She put down her mug. "So how have you been? How's Paul?"

"He's great. The doctor is really pleased with his progress."

"Is he talking more then?"

"Not as much as he did when you were around."

Paul had been selectively mute since he saw his mother die suddenly when he was two. Now, at age five, he was just starting to string words together. Paul and Bobby spent hours building Lego spaceships, and Jack spent hours watching them, afraid to break the spell. "He misses Cootchie, too. We're all hoping she comes back this summer."

The conversation died away. He found himself watching her, staring at her as if he was trying to memorize every detail of her face. When the silence became awkward, he cleared his throat. "Nate told me to ask you how to get a Barbie shoe out of his pencil sharpener."

She laughed, high and musical. "Did the triplets get him again?"

He nodded. "I keep telling him not to fall asleep in the recliner. Cunning little stinkers. You'd think a cop wouldn't be so easy to ambush, but he sleeps like the dead."

"Well, I can't help with the Barbie thing, I never played with them. I was more of a Tinkertoy kind of gal."

He put down his empty cup and his fingers brushed her arm. Without thinking, he covered her hand with his. "I missed you."

She squeezed his hand before pulling away to gently straighten the collar of his plaid shirt.

His breath caught at the feel of her soft touch on his skin. He wanted nothing more than to pull her into his arms and never let her go.

She opened her mouth to speak when the chirp of his phone interrupted.

Suppressing a groan, he answered it. Bobby took their mugs to the kitchen while he talked. After a minute he hung up. "You are not going to believe this, but Ruth found a body on the beach."

Her eyes widened. "Oh no. Who is it? Is she okay?"

"I don't know, but maybe you'd better come along with me. She may need support."

"I got your back, Detective."

He should be so lucky.

⁓

Jack drove code three down the bumpy trail to the beach. Bobby didn't seem to mind the jostling. As a matter of fact, she looked as energized as he felt. Cold air rushed in through the open windows, and her cheeks pinked under her swirling cap of short black hair.

Alva met them at the top of the bluff. His eyes were enormous in his shrunken face. "Right down there, Detective. Howdy, Miss Walker. You come to check out the body? I been keeping the folks back. I sent Roxie away, but that busybody Ellen Foots is here with Dr. Soloski. I told 'em to keep off on account of they could smudge the evidence or something, but you can't tell Ellen nothing. She's as bad as Maude. You may just hafta arrest her for construction of justice or something."

Jack nodded. "Thanks, Alva. Let's go have a look."

They made their way down the windy path to the beach. Ruth sat on a boulder, amidst a swarm of seagulls. Ellen stood next to her, her six-foot-four frame towering over a slender man who completed the trio.

Officer Nathan Katz knelt next to a slick heap several yards away, taking pictures. He looked up and nodded. Jack and Bobby hastened over to the group.

Ruth looked up, her face the color of plaster. "Hello, Jack." When she saw Bobby, tears began to roll down her face. "Bobby, I'm so glad you're here." She jammed a tissue under her nose. "I'm so sorry. I can't believe I'm unraveling like a loose hem. It's just so awful. A body, another one."

"It's okay, Aunt Ruth." Bobby hugged her tightly. "You're having a bad morning. Cry all you want. No one will blame you a bit."

"Well, Detective," Ellen Foots boomed. "What is going to become of our little town? Another body. It hasn't even been four months since the Fog Festival murder. I think it's connected to the film crew. That's what happens when you let new people in." She turned wide eyes on the man next to her. "Oh, not you, of course, Gene. We are so lucky to have a dentist here." She squeezed his arm.

The sandy-haired man winced under the pressure of Ellen's assertive gesture. "Detective, I'm relieved you're here. I took a look to see if there was any need for resuscitation, but there, er, wasn't."

Jack thought the poor guy looked as green around the gills as Ruth, but that might be attributed to the attention of the ferocious librarian. "Thanks, Doctor. I'll need to talk to you both in a few minutes." He put a hand on Ruth's shoulder. "Are you all right?"

She nodded, balling up another Kleenex. "Yes. You'd think, seeing as how this is the second body Alva and I have happened upon, I wouldn't be such a mess. It must be the baby."

"Don't worry about it. Baby or no, finding a dead person is not something anybody takes in stride." He and Bobby exchanged a glance, and she sat down next to her aunt. "Sit tight. I'll be back in a minute."

Jack did a slow circle around the body. The stiff figure was sizable, clad in a dive suit, complete with air tanks that lay half buried in the sand. The body lay face up, eyes closed. Jack looked at the ocean for a moment to clear his brain.

Nate was down on one knee, taking a close-up of the dead man's head. The damp sand made a wet patch on his pants where he knelt.

"Whatcha got, Nate?"

"Ruth said his name was Reggie. He was a cameraman for the film crew. Big guy, good diving gear. He's been dead awhile." Nate huffed into his lush mustache. "His mask is missing, but I don't see much sign of trauma. Wasn't shark chow, I don't think. Coroner is on his way."

Jack raised an eyebrow. "You know you have the word *Daddy* written in magic marker on the side of your neck?"

He nodded. "I know. I told Maddie we need to send them to a convent, but she says they don't take six-year-olds, especially triplets."

"At least they can spell Daddy right. That's a good sign."

"Yeah." Nate stood up and brushed the sand from his hands. "Is that Bobby over there?"

"I was at Monk's when I got the call. She came along to give Ruth some help."

Nate shot him a sidelong glance. "Is she staying in Finny for a while this time?"

"Maybe. So what's your take on this? Diving accident?"

Nate sneezed and blew his nose on an enormous handkerchief he pulled from his pocket. "Could be. But why would the guy dive at night anyway?"

Jack watched a bird swoop down to investigate and flutter away again. "I know they've been filming the wreck. Do you suppose they decided to get some night footage?"

Nate shook his head. "In these waters? By himself? That's gotta break every rule in the safe diving handbook."

They stared for another few minutes. Jack sighed. "I'm going to talk to Ruth and Alva again."

Nate readied his camera and went back to work.

The old man was sitting by a red toolbox when Jack returned. "Tell me how you and Ruth found the body, Alva."

He scratched his wrinkled forehead. "We're walkin' the birds, ya see, me and Ruth. Then I find this here can opener in the sand. Don't that just beat it? That's a lucky find, I'll tell you, and hardly any rust."

"Okay, you were walking the birds and you found a can opener. What next?"

"Sweet cheeks calls me over to see the sea monster. Only it ain't no sea monster, it's a dead guy. I don't have no phone so I run back to town and Bubby calls it in." His face darkened. "Ellen heard me 'splaining it to Bubby and she and the doctor headed down. I been tryin' to lay low on account of the fact that I need to get my mortar drilled and filled. I'm not too keen on the idea." He continued to rummage in the toolbox.

Jack smiled. "Did you know the dead man, Alva?"

"Nah, never met him. Just saw him at the film site a couple of times. Never said more than a 'good morning' to him." He straightened up. "Aha! Here it is, Ruthy honey. I told you Alva was gonna take care of ya." He handed her a crumpled bag of Milk Duds.

Ruth gave him a wan smile. "Thank you, Alva. You are so good to me."

Jack waited until she ate a few candies. A tiny stain of color returned to her pale cheeks. "Did you want to add anything to Alva's statement?"

She closed her eyes for a moment. "Yes," she said, as she opened them. "The reason we came to the beach in the first place. Last night I got up around two, I think, and I looked out my front window. I saw a light, far out in the water. It almost seemed like it was under the water, but I couldn't be sure. Do you think I imagined it? I am under the influence of rampant hormones at the moment. I can't remember my name half the time."

He chuckled. "I don't think you imagined it. The victim was diving at night for some reason we can't figure right now. You might have seen his light. Two o'clock you say?"

"Somewhere around there."

Gene Soloski's forehead creased as he and Ellen approached. "Not my business, of course, but it seems pretty ridiculous to dive at night in these waters, especially alone."

"I agree." Ellen patted the dentist on the back. "Do you dive, Doctor?"

"No, ma'am. I'm a land creature all the way."

Ellen smiled coquettishly. "Except for your days as a tree doctor."

"I guess I traded in the bark for the bite."

Ellen exploded into loud guffaws. The librarian's wild mane of hair vibrated along with the laughter. "You're just a stitch, Gene."

"And they say dentists don't have a sense of humor." Dr. Soloski spotted Alva, crouched behind Ruth. "There you are. I've been leaving messages with Mrs. Hodges for you all week. Don't forget your appointment on Monday morning,

Mr. Hernandez. We've got to get that tooth fixed before you wind up with an abscess."

Alva's brows drew together. "I think I got me some other appointment on Monday. Could be I got a Boy Scout meeting that day."

"Cancel it." Ellen didn't take her eyes off the dentist.

Alva's face crimped. "I don't got a ride to the office, and this leg's been bothering me. Too far to walk."

"I can take you, Alva." Ruth patted his shoulder. "I'll stay with you, too. It will be okay."

"There, you see?" The doctor smiled. "It won't hurt a bit, I promise."

"Yeah, yeah," Alva grumbled. "I bet that's what they said to that Marie Antoinette broad, too."

Jack finished scribbling in his notebook. "Okay, I think we're done for now. I'll be talking to each of you again, soon."

"All right." Dr. Soloski took a last glance at the body and shuddered. "I don't think I'll ever see this beach the same way again." Ellen and Dr. Soloski made their way back up the path.

Alva closed his box. He took the corn chips from Ruth's pocket and sprinkled them on the ground. Seven birds came running to peck up the treat. "I'll help you get these critters home."

"I'll bring up the rear." Bobby gave Jack a smile. "Come by for a coffee refill when you get this mess under control."

King Kong couldn't prevent him from taking her up on that offer. "Thanks, Bobby, I will." He watched her small figure move up the path, her pace matched to Ruth's. Bobby reached out an arm and wrapped it around Ruth's shoulders. What he wouldn't give to have her arm wrapped around him. Nate's voice snapped him out of his reverie.

"Hey, boss?"

He returned to the grisly pile where his partner knelt. "What's up?"

Nate held back the neck of the man's wet suit with a pen. "What do you think about this?"

Jack squinted and then his eyes widened. "I think I should have been a dentist."

4

Ruth wasn't sure whether or not to report for filming on Monday morning. She spent the weekend reading about Indigo Orson. The past seemed much more attractive at the moment than remembering the awful present that included Reggie's untimely end. She grabbed her binder anyway and made her way to the plateau overlooking the sheltered cove. There was no one there. She sat on a card chair, snuggled farther into her jacket, and flipped through the pages.

> *A stranger life I could not imagine. Washed up on shore, all alone in an alien country was almost more than I could bear. I fancied I heard the words of my mother entreating me to keep going. Mama, who had taught me to read and write against the wishes of my father. Mama, who died from the same infection that killed him.*
>
> *They were gone. The Orsons, dead. I was completely alone. Yet in my terrible state, afloat on a plank of wood, He sent me a treasure. There it was, bobbing on the water, a small barrel, no bigger than a man's boot, but what it held would save me. I grabbed hold of it with all my strength and made for land. It was hard going, clawing against the waves which seemed determined to drag me out to sea.*
>
> *The sun beat down on my head though my fingers were numb with cold. The salt water stung my eyes and the sight of those poor souls adrift in the waves as I struggled through the water sickened me. I could not hold on for a moment longer. When I felt the gravel under my feet, my spirit was renewed, and I fell to my knees praising our Father in heaven for deliverance. I was alive. I was alive.*

The sound of a woman's voice startled Ruth. She looked up to find Ethan and Sandra, heads bent together, locked in intense conversation as they headed up the path toward the grassy clearing where she sat.

"But he's dead," Sandra said, choking back a sob. She turned her face toward the ocean below. "Reggie's dead."

Ethan held up a hand. "We couldn't have foreseen that. If he hadn't gone off on his own, this wouldn't have happened. You better believe he wouldn't hesitate to double-cross us."

"It doesn't matter what we did or didn't see coming. The man is dead. I. . ." Sandra jerked her head around as she caught sight of Ruth. "Oh, Mrs. Budge. I didn't think you would be here. I'm sure you've heard about. . .about Reggie."

"Yes. Alva and I found him on the beach, as a matter of fact. I'm very sorry."

"We are, too." Ethan's face was smooth, bare of emotion. "He was a great friend and colleague. It's a terrible tragedy."

A friend who would double-cross them about something? Ruth decided to indulge her nosiness. "Why was he diving at night?"

Ethan blinked. "At night? I don't know."

"Was he doing something for the film project?"

"No, definitely not. We would never have him do a night dive. That's much too dangerous."

Sandra tugged a strand of blond hair. "Maybe he was doing some recreational diving."

Ruth frowned. "That seems odd. What would he be able to see at night?"

"I'm sure the police will find out it was an accident. In any case, we're going to keep to the schedule as best we can. I'm going to see if I can get another cameraman out here, and if I can't, I'll take it over myself. Why don't you use the time today to read through the notebook and we'll start the filming as soon as possible. I'll let you know." Ethan turned his attention to an accordion file.

Sandra's mouth opened, but she didn't speak as Jack's police car pulled up the winding road.

Though Ruth would have liked nothing more than to eavesdrop on the conversation, she knew interfering in police business wasn't a good idea. Jack was a great friend, but first and foremost he was a cop. She waved good-bye and headed back to town to pick up the reluctant dental patient as promised.

Alva didn't answer when Ruth knocked. Finally Flo Hodges, who owned the small cottage where Alva rented a room, unlocked the door. Alva was under the bed.

Ruth peered into the dark space. "Please don't make me get down there, Alva. I'll be hard-pressed to get up again. Come on out. I'll take you over to Dr. Soloski's, and it will be over in no time. I promise."

"I don't wanna," came the plaintive voice.

"Tell you what. Why don't you come out, and I'll ask Bert Penny to give you a ride on his motorcycle after your tooth is fixed."

There was a moment of silence. "Really?"

"Really."

"Ya think he'd do it?"

"I'm sure he would if I asked him to."

There was movement from under the bed. "Well, all right then. I guess I can let the quack take a look."

"That's the spirit."

Ruth led the way as the two walked down the slope toward the town that squatted at the nostril end of Finny's Nose. Even with Alva's reluctant pace they arrived at the tidy office in less than twenty-five minutes. A nautical theme, right down to the rustic wood benches and abalone shell business-card holder, decorated the bright space. She had a mental picture of the dentist doing his work wearing a sailor's cap.

Dr. Soloski came out to greet them in the usual dentist garb. Alva hid behind Ruth.

"Good morning. How are you feeling, Ruth, after that awful thing on Saturday?"

"I'm all right, thanks. Trying not to think about it, mostly. I'm going to wait here for Alva, if that's okay." She stepped aside to reveal the cowering old man.

"Certainly. Come along, Mr. Hernandez." The doctor patted Alva on the shoulder. "We'll have you fixed up in no time."

Alva shot Ruth a desperate look as he was ushered into the back.

Ruth sighed. Her ankles felt puffy and swollen. How was it possible that a fragile three-month-old fetus could wreak havoc on a perfectly serviceable body? That must be why people had babies in their twenties. With a twinge she remembered she'd had a baby then, too—her son, Bryce, who didn't want to be within spitting distance of her. Where had she gone wrong with him? And would she repeat the same mistakes with this late-in-life baby?

She shut down that depressing line of thought and turned her thoughts to Isabel Ortiz and her mysterious treasure. The page was still dog-eared where she'd left off reading that morning.

This is wild country. The men here are rough without the civilizing influence of women. The rush for gold has brought hundreds to this shore. They have eyes filled with desperation and want, a reckless need to throw every caution away in search of that elusive gold nugget. There are no women here and that is both a blessing and a curse.

I decided from the earliest instance that I would be in great peril if these men found a helpless woman on their shore, a Mexican woman at that. They think anyone with skin of a different color is lower than a dog. When we were aboard the Triton, *I heard tell of a group of white miners calling themselves "the hounds" that chased Mexican miners off their claims and beat them near to death. What could I do to save myself?*

It was then I became Indigo Orson. With my ragged, unkempt appearance, they had no reason to suspect my secret. A pair of grizzled old miners took me in and let me sleep in a corner of their tent. They were most curious about my barrel. I slept with it under my head in the night.

With the first light of dawn, I opened my treasure trove and prayed that God would give me the courage to see it through. The barrel did its work, and the flour was dry as dry could be. I measured out a precious dip from inside. With a borrowed pan and a bit of grease, I cooked up a batch of biscuits, light as air and golden brown on top. At the first smell of baking bread, the miners emerged from their miserable hidey holes like gophers from their burrows. They lined up around my campfire to watch, mouths open, as I baked up the biscuits. Imagine my surprise when one man shouted, "I'll give ya five dollars for them biscuits." Five dollars? Such a fortune for a bit of bread? To these men who have been eating roots and berries for months, the flour was treasure indeed.

I settled for one dollar per biscuit, and only two per man. At the end of the morning I had a ten-dollar gold piece and a handful of other coins. God saved me with His white treasure. That night with my pocket full of coins, I thanked Him and said a prayer for Señor and Señora Orson, God rest their souls.

Ruth shook her head in amazement. Indigo Orson. A Mexican woman, impersonating a man, cooking for half-starved miners. She could imagine the fear that Indigo felt, but that stubborn will to survive that could only come from the Lord. The episode was better than fiction and certainly worthy of being documented on film. She hoped she would be able to do justice to the amazing lady.

With thoughts of Indigo swirling in her mind, Ruth dozed.

⌇

Less than an hour later, Alva stomped into the waiting room, shouting over his shoulder at the dentist, the plastic bib fluttering under his chin.

"You said it wasn't a-going to hurt. Whaddya call that needle poke, huh? A love pat?"

Dr. Soloski stiffened. "I guarantee you, Alva, no other dentist could have done a finer job on that tooth."

Alva's ears pinked as he continued his tirade. "How should I know what kinda job you did? Not like I could see yer work or anything. Maybe you left a tool in there or somethin'. Maybe I'm goin' to find a screwdriver in my mouth when I eat my snack today. Or maybe a chisel."

The dentist stared at him in openmouthed surprise. "There are no tools—"

Alva cut him off with a loud snort. "Never mind. It's all done and I'm still alive and kicking. Now where's my prize?"

Dr. Soloski's eyebrows furrowed. "Your prize?"

"Yeah. I talked to Ralphie over at the preschool and he says ya get a prize when yer finished at the dentist."

"Oh. Of course. I let the kids pick out a trinket. Help yourself." He pointed to a wooden chest filled with plastic toys and sugarless gum.

Alva turned to the reception desk and grabbed the abalone shell. He carefully unloaded the business cards on the counter. "I'll take this."

"Alva," Ruth began, "he meant—"

Dr. Soloksi waved his hand. "It's okay, Mrs. Budge. I can find something else to hold my business cards. He's welcome to it if that will make him feel better about his appointment today."

Ruth guided Alva to the door. "You wait outside. I'll just be a minute."

When they were alone, she attempted an apology. "I'm so sorry, Dr. Soloski. Alva is just terrified of dentists, or doctors of any kind for that matter. You wouldn't believe what we had to do to get him in for a physical. The doctor gave up after an hour and pronounced him healthy."

The dentist ran a hand through his thick brown hair. "I know I shouldn't take offense. I'm a perfectionist. I see dentistry as an art as much as a science." He chuckled. "I've had people weep with joy at being relieved of their dental problems. I think Alva is a long way from that kind of response."

They both laughed. The phone rang. He sighed. "I'll just let the machine pick it up."

"Have you hired a receptionist yet?"

"No. I've had several applicants, but I'm a perfectionist in that area, too, I guess."

The door crashed open and Ellen Foots strode in, a plate of plastic-wrapped muffins in her hands. "Hello, Dr. Soloski." Her face tightened when she saw Ruth. "Oh, hello, Ruth." She turned her attention back to the dentist. "I was just in the neighborhood, and I thought I'd bring you some breakfast. I just whipped these up this morning."

Ruth peeked at the plump muffins. Blueberry, topped with crumbs, and very familiar. They looked exactly like the kind sold at Monk's shop, a far cry from the hockey puck variety Ellen provided for the last library function. She watched the giantess smooth her frizzy hair.

Doctor Soloski patted his trim waist. "Oh. Why, thank you. I'll save them for later. Have to keep the body in shape and all."

"Of course. I'm a real fitness nut myself. I saw you out running one day, early. What time do you usually go?"

"Well, the time varies according to my schedule."

Ellen nodded. "Did you look over my application? I do have a dental health background, you know, and I could whip your schedule into shape in no time. If you don't take control of your schedule, it will take control of you, I always say."

Dr. Soloski's eyes widened a bit. Ruth gave him a sympathetic look and left the dentist with the formidable librarian.

Outside she found Alva stroking the pearlescent interior of the abalone. "It's a fine shell, ain't it?"

"Yes, Alva, but you weren't very polite to the dentist."

Alva blinked. "No?" His eyes narrowed with mischief. "I'll bet he'd rather have me in that there office than her." He pointed at Ellen Foots through the window. The woman seemed to have cornered the unfortunate dentist by the water cooler.

"I think you may be right about that."

She treated Alva to a chocolate milk, which he dribbled a bit due to his numb mouth, and herself to one of Al's black and white cookies. Thoroughly satiated with carbohydrates, she walked Alva home. It was close to one o'clock when she headed up the driveway to her small cottage. From the outside, it was impossible to detect the havoc Carson had created in his attempt to repair termite damage to an exterior wall. To the unsuspecting visitor, it was a cozy three-bedroom bungalow, surrounded by hydrangeas and a massive lemon tree.

She inhaled the delicate aroma of citrus as she approached the house. The scent always soothed her nerves. Before she could open the front door, an enormous man with close-cropped salt-and-pepper hair stepped out on the front step and wrapped her in a hug.

"Monk." Her eyes filled with tears. "I missed you. I feel like you've been gone forever."

He kissed the top of her head. "Me, too, baby. Me, too. Let me see you. How are you feeling? You look fantastic."

She laughed. "I've been told I look waxy and glazed. How is your father?"

"He's doing well. That stroke isn't going to slow him down for a minute. He's as determined as a freight train."

"Sounds like you came by your genes honestly."

"My mother is beside herself with excitement about this baby."

"I wish I could just be excited and leave all the other worries behind."

He rubbed her shoulders. "Don't you fret. We're going to work it out in good time. I'm just glad to be back home, with the crazy stuff that's going on here. Did they figure out what happened to that diver? I couldn't believe it when you called to tell me. The riptides must have gotten him."

"They're still investigating as far as I know. Let's go inside. I want to hear all about your trip."

He did a quick sidestep to prevent her from entering. "Well, honey, there's something I should tell you before you go in."

"Has Carson done something again? What else could he possibly have broken? We're already down one lamp and a picture frame. Is he aware that we're going to have to put a baby in that room in a matter of months?"

"No, no. It's not the house."

"It's not the house?" She took in his uneasy expression. "What's wrong, Monk?"

"Well, I wouldn't exactly say anything was wrong. It could be a real good thing, I mean, after you've got some time to think about it." He shifted his weight to the other foot.

"Monk."

"I know I should have called, and actually I tried, but you weren't home and I had to make a decision. I hope I did the right thing."

Her last shred of patience evaporated. "Monk, if you don't tell me what's going on right now I am going to start to howl at the top of my lungs."

Before he had time to answer, the door behind him opened.

Ruth's mouth fell open in shock.

5

Jack tightened the strap of his helmet. The bike wobbled as he pedaled, as if the wheels had a different direction in mind. After a few minutes he achieved the proper pedal to steer ratio and headed up slope, skirting the shadow of Finny's Nose.

This is ridiculous. I've got a murder to investigate. What am I doing on a bike right now?

In spite of his negative thoughts, he recognized the perfect beauty of the day. The Monday afternoon was warm, brilliant June sunshine broken by the thick canopy of eucalyptus and pine trees that bordered the trail. The scent of cedar mingled with the faint tang of the sea. Jack's cell phone chirped. He lurched to a stop and answered. He had to wait for Nate on the other end of the line to finish his sneezing fit. "God bless. When are you going to take some allergy medicine?"

"When they can make some that won't put me to sleep. You remember what happens when I fall asleep."

Jack smiled. Usually Nate's triplet girls attempted to paint his nails or use him as a Barbie dive platform when he slumbered at home. "What do you have from the lab?"

"Nothing yet," Nate said before he blew his nose. "And I'm still trying to find next of kin. Where are you? You sound winded."

"Uh, out. I'll be back in the office in a few hours."

Nate laughed. "Right. Tell Bobby I said hello."

Jack grunted and clicked off the phone just as Bobby coasted up. Her cheeks were flushed pink from the combination of exertion and the temperature.

"Hi," he said, feeling his stomach do the two-step.

"Hi."

He fiddled with the handgrips and ran a finger under his chin strap. "So, uh, here we are."

"Yes, here we are." She sipped out of a water bottle.

"Nice day for a bike ride."

She wiped her mouth. "Yes, it is, but I have to admit I'm surprised, Jack."

"About what?"

"Lots of things. You're not in the office the Monday after a murder, for one thing."

"I went in early this morning, so I'm due to have a break. The bike riding idea

335

was perfect." He took in her skeptical look. "I'm trying to find balance."

"Uh-huh. I didn't picture you as the bike-riding type."

He laughed. "Would you believe I'm a man of mystery?"

"No. Closemouthed, yes, but not really the mysterious type."

"Guilty as charged. I couldn't resist your invitation to go for a ride."

The wind picked up her black hair and tousled it across her eyes. "That's a surprise. Seems like you resist me plenty."

Jack stared at her, drinking in the pink of her cheeks, the wild sparkle in her dark eyes. Resist her? He couldn't get through one hour of the day without thinking about her, wondering where she was, wishing he could be there next to her. He tried to think of a safe way to put his feelings into words. Before he could answer, she stowed the bottle and pedaled off up the slope.

He gritted his teeth and followed.

The road was mostly gravel by the time they hit the top of Finny's Nose. Jack tried to control his gasping breaths as he dismounted and pressed a hand to the cramp in his side.

Bobby hiked past a cluster of manzanitas and sat on an outcropping of rock that provided an unobstructed view of the vast Pacific. A hummingbird zoomed in to check out the strange visitor to his territory, and she stayed still to put it at ease. The bird hovered for a moment, as if exchanging a greeting with her.

Jack watched her profile, the small nose, determined chin, short hair fluttering in the wind. For a moment, his breathing grew even more unsteady. He wanted to say so many things but found himself speechless.

"I always pictured California as having clear blue water and golden sand, until I came here." She regarded the gray waves that thundered onto the rocky beach below. He joined her, and they took in the gulls circling the beach in a great noisy cluster.

"I imagine that's what Frederick Finny was looking for when he wrecked his ship trying to smuggle rum along this coast. He was probably surprised about the beaches, too."

She giggled. "At least he got a mountain named after him."

"More of a big hill really."

Jack's eyes narrowed at the sight of a stranger picking his way along the sand. The man was tall, his gait purposeful. Jack wished they were closer so he could make out the face. Strangers were uncommon on this rough bit of coastline. Visitors tended to gravitate toward Honey Beach or the quaint shops and restaurants in town. Many made a beeline for Roxie Trotter and her fishing excursions.

And some visitors wound up murdered on Finny's unforgiving shore, he reminded himself. The cameraman was actually the third murder since last October.

Bobby handed him a thermos of coffee. Her fingers seemed to generate their own heat where they touched his hand.

"You brought coffee? How did you know I'd be ready for some?"

She smiled. "Because I've never known you not to be in the mood for some java."

He took a hefty slug of the brew, burning his tongue in the process. "When is Monk coming back?"

"He flew in this morning. Apparently he ran into Ruth's son at the airport."

"Bryce?"

She nodded. "Bryce is going to stay with them, I think."

Jack wondered how that would go over with the man's newly pregnant mother. Then his mind raced ahead to the implications of Monk's return. "But you're going to stay for a while? That's what you said, right?"

"Maybe until Ruth's baby comes. Or until I get a job offer. I'm not sure."

He watched the soft curve of her lip, so prone to break into a smile. It brought him back to another face, a face from his other life. The two faces were so alike, and so different.

Bobby fixed her black eyes on his. "What are you thinking about?"

"Me? Nothing."

Her brows knitted. "Here's an idea. How about you tell me the truth? Even if it's personal or you think it makes you look silly."

There was no anger in her words but a trace of sadness that he wanted to erase. He tried to breathe out the weight that settled in his chest. "I was thinking about Lacey."

"You miss her."

"Yes. She's been dead for almost three years, but it doesn't feel like that sometimes." It seemed like only a moment ago when he'd gotten the call. Lacey dead from a brain hemorrhage at the foot of their driveway, with their toddler son, Paul, watching it all from the window. Was it only a few years ago? Or a lifetime?

The stranger Jack had noticed before now disappeared around a rugged cliff. Jack cleared his throat. "She was always asking me to take time away from work. To go on picnics or bike rides, especially after Paul was born. She was a big one for taking nature walks."

Bobby's voice was low. "And you didn't go very often?"

"Not enough."

"She sounds like a very smart woman."

"She was. She had a lot of heart, like you do." He looked down at his scuffed shoes.

"Jack, do you feel guilty for having feelings for me?"

He swallowed. Hard. He wanted to deny it. Instead the words came out haltingly, like a deer trying to stand on newborn legs. "I. . .yes."

For a moment she was expressionless. Then her face lit with a smile. She leaned toward him and pressed her lips against his, soft and gentle. "Thank you for being honest. I guess you really do care about me."

When his breath returned, he wanted to crush her to him, to bury his face in her neck and shut out the world, and his guilt. Instead he whispered a prayer. "God help me."

Bobby gave him that sideways tilt of her head. "He is, Jack. He's helping you heal."

"How do you figure?"

"It's like being in the ocean and swimming back to shore. You've got to go through the rough surf sometimes, but it has to be done, no matter how uncomfortable. Otherwise, you're just—"

"Treading water?"

Her eyes sparkled. "Exactly, and sooner or later that doesn't work anymore."

His phone rang again. With clumsy fingers he answered, listening intently. "I'm on my way."

"I hope it's not another body."

"No, not this time, but I do have to get going."

Bobby laughed and checked her watch. "Well, that was one hour and forty-three minutes away from work. Not bad."

He sighed as they retrieved their bikes. "It's a start, anyway."

⁓

The station was in the usual state of chaos when he returned. Alva lay on his back on the front counter. His heavy black boots overlapped one side of the Formica, and his knit cap jutted over the other, a tiny blue pom-pom clearly visible. "I wanna report a theft. I got my rights to report a crime, ain't I? Look in here, just look why don'tcha?"

Jack tried to sneak past into his office, but he couldn't get by the angry lady in front of him.

Maude Stone stiffened her minuscule frame. "You are an idiot, Alva Hernandez. A moron of the highest degree. Why do you even pay attention to him, Mary?"

Officer Mary Dirisi reached over Alva's stomach for a pen. "Because he's lying on my workspace. Okay, Alva, I've got a report to do, so spill it. What's the deal?"

Alva shoved a finger into his mouth and angled his face in the officer's direction. "Aarrrgh uz iitttte ere."

"What?" she said, pencil poised.

"Arrggh us ittt—"

Jack squelched a smile.

"You imbecile, take your finger out of your mouth!" Maude yelled so loud it echoed through the office.

Alva removed his finger. "That quack dentist stole my tooth. I had one way in the back and now it's gone. I didn't notice until the Novocain wore off. He stole it, sure as shootin'. That's grand theft dentistry. He probably sells 'em on the black market to toothless people in Bangladesh."

"I don't think people even in Bangladesh are that desperate for teeth," Mary said, scribbling on a form.

Alva considered this. "Well, maybe he took 'em for some other reason. Could be he sells 'em as fake relics to churches. Now my tooth might be from St. Alva, Patron Saint of Molars."

Maude snorted. "Patron Saint of Fools is more like it. Alva, shut up and listen. Dr. Soloski probably explained everything to you, but you were too ding blasted stubborn to pay attention. I spoke to him earlier, and he told me that when he was putting in your filling, he noticed you had a chipped molar and he filed it. It's not gone, you nitwit, it's probably just smoothed down so it feels different."

The old man sat up. His eyebrows undulated as he explored the area with his tongue. Mary handed him a mirror from her purse.

He peered into his mouth, moving his head this way and that to get a better view. "Well, I'll be a smitten toad. There it is. I guess he ain't stoled my tooth. How about that?"

"No," Maude said, "but somebody stole your brain. Now quit maligning Dr. Soloksi. We need all the professional men we can get in this town."

Maude caught sight of Jack edging toward his office. "Oh, there you are, Detective. I've been trying to find you since Saturday. I want to know what's going on with this murder investigation. What exactly is the status? Do you have any suspects? Made any arrests? It's terrible for our Finny image. What will people say?"

Probably the same thing they said after the murder at the Finny Fog Festival in March, he thought. "Don't worry, Maude. People will still flock to Finny for the clean air and great fishing. Nothing will tarnish our quaint fishing village appeal."

Maude opened her mouth, but Jack cut her off. "I've got a meeting. Talk to Officer Dirisi if you have any more specific questions."

Mary shot him a poisonous look as he escaped into his office.

He eased into his chair and took the cup of coffee Nate handed him, feeling only a twinge of guilt at leaving Mary at Maude's mercy.

Nate blew his nose. "How's Bobby?"

"She's fine." He ignored the sly smile under Nate's bushy mustache. "What's the word?"

"Well, we notified next of kin, a mother in Des Moines. We got the sheets back on him and it seems as though Reggie was into some trouble, small stuff mostly. Petty theft, fencing stolen merchandise, anything to earn a quick buck."

"Funding a drug habit?"

"Nah, gambling debts."

"Okay, the guy needed quick cash." Jack tapped a pencil on the desk. "How does that put him in the ocean at night?"

"Could be unrelated. Maybe he dove for fun. He was into all that survival stuff."

Jack eyed the crease in Nate's forehead. "But you don't think so?"

"No. What are you going to see diving at night in those rough waters? Even Jacques Cousteau couldn't handle that in his little submarine thingy. And Reggie didn't have a camera that we can find anyway, just a real nice underwater flashlight and some light sticks. The guys from county also found his line with a full tank attached."

"Full?" Jack's mind raced. "He set up an extra tank, planning on doing some deep diving, but he never got the chance. Is this about that shipwreck?"

"Don't know. The college people insisted they are interested in it purely as a research project. Last group that dove the wreck years ago didn't find much of anything anyway. 'Course we had that killer storm awhile back. Maybe that stirred something up."

"Let's get Sandra and Ethan in here and apply some pressure."

"They'll be here at three o'clock."

"Okay."

Jack felt a vein pound behind his left eye along with tightness in his quads from the bike ride. "Pictures?"

Nate slid a set of digital photos over the desk and pointed. "No official word from the coroner yet, but I'm thinking this little baby did him in, not the ocean."

Jack squinted at the rope wrapped around the victim's neck in the picture. "I've never seen a knot like that."

"Me neither. Looks like some kind of sailor's knot. I wonder if Monk knows it. He's an old sea dog."

"I'll head over there later."

Mary poked her head into the office. "I got rid of Maude but only after promising someone will give her a call later today. That someone is not going to be me."

Jack sighed. "I don't get paid enough to endure Maude Stone."

Mary flipped her braid over her shoulder. "None of us do, but I just did my turn, remember? Coroner's office called. You were right, Nate. Guy was strangled."

Nate thumped his chest. "I am Ubercop, ruler of the police world. I am invincible."

Jack laughed. "Well, Ubercop, give my regards to Maude when you call her this afternoon."

6

The men are dirty. Rough and coarse, with long matted hair and hands hardened into claws. They treat me well, though, because I am the only one who can cook. Even so, I daren't tell them I'm a woman or all would be lost. It is a dangerous place here for all but intolerable for the female sex. I heard tell that the vaqueros ride among the Indian villages and drive out the young girls and sell them for 100 dollars each. How can it be true? With such tales, I have no choice but to remain Indigo Orson.

The day I went to town for supplies, I came upon a group of men standing next to their long tom, watching a pot on the fire, looking as if they had been knocked down. Come to be known, they were trying to figure out why their rice was not cooked properly. I told them in as gruff a way as I could manage, to add water to the pot! Imagine. They are without even the most basic skills. Probably they never gave a thought to how their women back home prepared the meals or mended the clothes. What they would give for their wives' home-cooked specialties or excellent laundering now. They say men are the stronger sex, but here they have been reduced to little children without the civilizing influence of women.

Children. Now there was a touchy subject. Ruth closed the binder and sipped from her thermos of hot tea. The Tuesday morning sun was barely approaching the horizon and her cheeks were cold. She'd left Monk snoring softly and tiptoed away down to the beach. Now her thoughts rolled like the waves that heaved along with her stomach.

Bryce was back.

The son she hadn't seen since her first husband's funeral greeted her with a "Hi, Mom," as he emerged from around Monk's back.

Hi, Mom, as if he was stopping in for his daily visit.

It would be more natural if he called her Ruth. That would fit the distant relationship they endured. He was twenty-six now, but he looked older. And different somehow. Ruth pulled her hood tighter as she remembered. He looked a trifle. . . uncertain. She did not recall seeing anything but a confident look on his face the last few times she'd encountered him.

Monk appeared and lowered his bulky frame onto the rock next to her. The shadows under his eyes marked a fitful sleep. "All right, let's get it out on the table. How much trouble am I in exactly? I'm here to take my medicine."

"No trouble. It took me by surprise, that's all." Surprise? More like total shock. They'd managed a few forced pleasantries before Bryce retreated to the guest room and her to the bathtub.

Monk sighed. "Honestly, he surprised the stuffing out of me, too. There I am, just getting off the plane at the San Francisco airport and this young fella comes up to me and says he thinks we know each other. I didn't even recognize him, but he whipped out our wedding picture. Doggone if the guy isn't your son. Imagine my surprise to find out he was on his way here. What are the odds of that happening at an international airport?"

Bryce carried around their wedding picture? She swallowed some now tepid chamomile, supposedly a cure for morning sickness. It left her watery and every bit as nauseated. "So you invited him to stay with us."

"Uh, well, yes." Monk pushed a pile of sand around with his shoe. "It didn't seem right sending him to the Finny Hotel, him being your son and all. I tried to call you, honey, really. I didn't want to spring it on you out of the blue."

She looked at the crinkles around his eyes. No, he couldn't have sent her son to the hotel. His big heart wouldn't have allowed that. It was clear how much agony the decision inflicted on him. She squeezed his hand. "You did the right thing, and I'm not mad about it. But why did Bryce come here, Monk? Now, I mean. He didn't even come for our wedding." His absence hurt her more than she could put into words.

"He didn't say, but I got the feeling he's had some trouble."

"What kind of trouble?"

"I don't know exactly. I expect he'll get around to telling you."

She wasn't so sure. The waves left ribbons of foam on the beach. Further down, an area of sand was blocked off with yellow tape. She shuddered and turned her eyes away.

A crunch of gravel made them both turn. Dr. Soloski, dressed in sweats, huffed up the trail. When he saw them he turned off his iPod and slowed to jog in place. "Morning again. How's Mr. Hernandez holding up?"

"Alva's fine, Dr. Soloski," Ruth said. *Once he figured out you didn't steal his tooth and send it to Bangladesh,* she thought with a smile. "I've never seen you take this path before."

He shot an uneasy look over his shoulder. "Oh, well, I thought I'd check out the view. I can't get enough of coastal living."

Monk chuckled. "You're a sucker for the fresh sea air?"

"You bet. Cities aren't for the likes of me. I avoid them like the plague." His eyebrows creased. "Did you hear something?"

They listened for a moment until they heard the sound of approaching feet.

TREASURE UNDER FINNY'S NOSE

The dentist turned on his music and waved. "I'm off then. Talk to you soon." He sprinted away.

"He's in an awful hurry," Monk said.

Five seconds later Ellen Foots careened down the trail. Her mane of hair was twisted into two stiff black ropes that protruded from the top of her scalp like the knobs on a giraffe's head. She was dressed from neck to ankle in shiny green spandex.

She pounded to a stop and looked around. "Where is he?"

"Who?" Ruth said.

"Dr. Soloski."

Monk beamed. "Why? Did you have a dental emergency, Ellen?"

"Of course not. My teeth are in excellent condition. I use an ultrasonic cleaner and fluoride rinse every day. I just happened to be out for a jog, and I thought I saw Dr. Soloski."

Through binoculars from her perch in the top of a tree, Ruth thought. "I didn't know you were a runner."

She shuffled a bit, the gravel crunching under her sneakers. "I decided to take it up. A person can never be too healthy. The body is the temple, after all." A flicker of movement in the distance caught her eye. "There he is."

Ellen darted off.

"I hope he runs fast. He's gonna need to break some sprinting records to outrun her." Monk helped Ruth to her feet. "Home again, my love?"

"Uh, no, er, I think I have a rehearsal."

His thick eyebrow lifted. "Really? In view of the murder, I didn't think there was anything to rehearse."

"I promised I'd check in again, anyway. Sandra and Ethan are meeting me at the hotel."

"I'll go with you."

"That's okay. You go on home and see if. . .if Bryce needs anything."

He wrapped her in a final hug. "I love you, Ruthy. It's going to be okay. You'll see."

She could feel his gaze as she headed toward the center of town.

※

Sandra and Ethan sat in the lobby of the Finny Hotel, papers strewn on the oak table. The place was dark, a sharp contrast to the vibrant bougainvillea that painted the outside of the building with fluorescent orange and pink. Ruth took a deep breath to settle her stomach. "Good morning. I thought I'd come by and check on the schedule."

Sandra looked up from her clipboard. "Oh, hi, Ruth. Um, I really appreciate you coming all the way here but, you know, I don't think we're going to rehearse today. We've got some work to do."

Ethan pushed the wire rim glasses up his nose. "Sandy and I need to retool a bit. We've only got a week left to wrap this up before the next term starts, so we'll start filming tomorrow maybe."

"Will that give you enough time to finish?"

Sandra blinked. "Finish? Oh sure, sure."

"Who is going to run the camera?"

"I will," Ethan said. "I'm not as good as Reggie but I get by. It's too much to find another guy at this point."

Ruth thought back to Indigo's scrawled passages. "I read that the *Triton* has been excavated before. Did they find anything interesting?"

Sandra gave her a sharp look. "Interesting? Not really. It was a coal transport so there wasn't much to find. Why?"

"I just wondered."

Ethan's eyes narrowed. "There's nothing on that boat but coal. Whatever artifacts there were have long since been removed or covered with barnacles."

Ruth wondered at his strong tone. "Are you going to take any more underwater footage? It seems so dangerous."

Ethan shook his head. "No, we're not filming anything else in the ocean. We'll work around it. Sandy will let you know when we're going to rehearse again." He turned back to his open laptop.

Sandra wiggled her fingers in a good-bye.

Ruth met Alva as she exited the hotel. "Howdy, sweet cheeks. Time for a snack. Want some candy?"

She took the can opener from him and then the dentist's shell while he searched his pockets and produced a bag of candy.

"Here you go. Did I tell you old Alva would take care of you? Say, I checked the beach this morning but there wasn't no more bodies." He looked disappointed as he rooted around in his pockets, emerging with another small bag.

"Thanks, Alva. You really are a gift from God." She admired the play of afternoon sunshine on the pearlescent interior of the shell as she handed it back along with the can opener. "Don't you think you should give this back to Dr. Soloski?"

"Why? He didn't have nothing to do with finding that can opener."

"Not the can opener, the shell."

"Give it back? Huh-uh. He told me to pick a prize. That there's mine now." He shoveled in a handful of candy corns. "Where are you headed?"

She sighed. "Back home, I guess. My son is here."

He looked with wild eyes from her head to her stomach. "What? How'd it get out that quick? How come you're still inflated?"

"No, no. Not this baby. My son, Bryce. He's a grown man now. You probably met him when he lived here a long time ago."

Alva screwed up his face. "Bryce, Bryce. Oh yeah. Serious little guy? Always playing by himself?"

Ruth cringed. "Yes, that's him."

"Does he still like to dig at the beach?"

She had a sudden memory of Bryce as a little boy, holding a small plastic pail and shovel, solemnly scooping out holes in the sand. "I don't know what he likes anymore, Alva. I guess it's time for me to go find out."

Ruth tiptoed into the quiet house. Her husband was gone, she knew, busy at Monk's Coffee and Catering. She listened for sounds of movement. Nothing but the *tick* of the grandfather clock. With a sigh of relief, she headed into the kitchen in search of orange juice.

Bryce sat at the table, reading the paper. He looked up with eyes that reminded her so much of Phillip's.

Her breath caught for a moment, heart pounding in her chest. "Hello, Bryce."

He nodded. "Morning. Not much news here in Finny, is there?"

"Not as much as Chicago, I imagine."

"There is an article about the man you found on the beach. It says the cause of death is under investigation. Is Jack handling the case?"

She nodded.

"I figured it was a diving accident. Those are rough waters, easy to lose your bearings."

"Yes. I sure wouldn't want to dive there." The kitchen melted into silence. "Um, do you want me to fix you some lunch?" It brought her back a couple of decades, when she was a doting mother, trying to do anything and everything for a spoiled little boy.

"No thanks. I'm not hungry. I made myself some coffee. Hope that was okay." He folded the newspaper into a precise rectangle.

She wasn't sure whether to sit at the table or take her juice to the other room. She settled for standing and sipping.

He looked at her, his face an unreadable mask. "I didn't know you were expecting."

Her face heated. "Oh, yes, I meant to tell you, but I just never managed to make the call. Things have been really crazy here." The excuse sounded lame to her own ears.

"When are you due?"

"December."

"Oh." He drummed his fingers on the table. "A baby, wow. That's unusual for someone. . .in your phase of life."

She flushed. At least he hadn't said *old*. "It is, but we're both happy about it."
Happy and terrified beyond all reason.

"Roslyn was pregnant, too."

The words startled her, as did the flood of emotion that they caused. "Bryce, that's—" Her flutter of excitement was fleeting. "Was?"

"She lost the baby at three months."

Ruth's heart twisted at the tremor in his voice. "I'm so sorry."

He shrugged. "The doctor says it happens and most of the time they never know the reason." He shook his head as if to clear the memory away. "Monk says you're doing all right. I guess that means I'm going to have a brother or sister."

"One or the other. We didn't want to know ahead." She gulped some juice. "Um, how do you, uh, feel about that?"

"I'm not sure. It doesn't really matter how I feel about it anyway, does it?"

She was not sure what to say in response so she settled on a change in topic. "So, what brings you to Finny?"

"Roslyn."

"Are you vacationing here together?"

"No. She left me."

Ruth coughed. "Roslyn left?"

"Yeah. She met someone. A florist, if you can call him that." He spat out the words. "The guy sells flowers out of a roadside shack. He rides a moped to work."

Her breath caught at the anger that was written in his clenched jaw and the deep crease in his forehead.

Bryce sat ramrod straight in the chair. "The business failed, too."

The business, too? Bryce had taken on his wife's family trucking company when they married. From the rare Christmas card, she gathered it had been doing well. Until now.

There was something about his face, a streak of small child vulnerability mixed in with the anger, that gave her the sudden urge to wrap her grown boy in a hug. She knew it would not do, just as it had not satisfied him twenty years ago. She could not fix this problem for him and he wouldn't want her to try.

Instead, she laid a hand lightly on his arm. "I'm so sorry, Bryce, about everything, especially the baby."

He did not look at her.

He did not move away.

"Yeah," he said, his voice awash in bitterness. "Me, too."

⁂

The sun mellowed its way into the hills. From her seat in the luscious pool of sunlight next to the worm beds, Ruth offered up a prayer of thanks. "Thank You, Lord, for this precious day. Thank You for letting this baby inside me have another day to grow and flourish. Please reach out Your healing hands to Bryce and help me to give him what he needs right now."

She hadn't finished the amen when Monk opened the sliding door and ushered Roxie into the backyard. The woman blinked and rubbed under her nose with a red handkerchief. "I came for my worms. I've got a couple booked for a fishing expedition tomorrow, and I promised to provide the bait."

"That's great." Ruth searched through the white plastic tubs for Roxie's. "How's business?"

She shrugged. "Not great. I've had a few folks book for this week and next, but it would be better if those collegiate types would leave."

Ruth found the container and handed it to Roxie. "Are they causing problems for you?"

"Nothing terrible. It just makes me nervous, them slipping in and out of the water. My customers like to think they're the only people allowed in the ocean at any given time. The happier they are, the better my business."

Ruth perked up. "You've seen Sandy and Ethan diving? When?"

"Last two nights, just after sundown."

After sundown? "Were they taking pictures, do you think?"

"I didn't see a camera, only flashlights. They're up to something. No one should be in the water late. That's insanity. They didn't learn a thing from their cameraman dying in those waters. People can be so stupid, especially when they're young."

The door opened again, and Bryce stuck his head out. "Monk said to tell you dinner's ready." He shot Roxie a curious look. "Hello."

Roxie waved a hand at him.

"Thanks, Bryce. I'll just be a minute." Ruth finished packaging up the worms.

"Who was that?"

"My son."

"I didn't know you had kids."

"He's visiting from Chicago."

"Crazy city." Roxie looked back at the door, an odd expression on her face.

"Do you have children, Roxie?"

"Me? No." Ruth almost didn't hear the second whispered comment. "Not anymore."

Ruth watched her pull at a hole in her knit cap. "Would you like to join us for dinner? Monk's making his famous meatballs, and there's always enough for an army. We'd love to have you."

"No. Thanks for the offer, but I've probably overstayed my welcome already. I'll take my worms and get out of your hair."

Ruth led her back through the cottage to the front door, watching until the woman was out of sight. She stood there for a moment, breathing in the evening air that had turned cool and the savory smells of oregano and browning meat from the kitchen.

So the college students were hiding something, busy making night dives in spite of their comments to the contrary. Roxie was right. No one should be in the water that late.

Then again, why was Roxie?

7

I'm mighty glad to have my niece home." Monk slid Jack a heavy mug filled with coffee. There was a lull in the Wednesday morning breakfast traffic so he untied his apron.

"Me, too. Bobby seems like she belongs in Finny." They walked to a table by the window. Jack tried to look casual as he peered around the coffee counter. "Is she here today?"

"She's visiting Ruth, but she'll be along later." He eyed the detective. "If you dillydally with that coffee long enough, you'll see her."

Jack felt his cheeks warm. He cleared his throat. "I actually came to see you. Official police business." He pushed a photograph toward the big man. "What do you make of this?"

Monk squinted at the paper. "Is this the knot tied around his—"

"Uh-huh."

"I've used many a knot in my day, but I've never seen one used like that on a person. I thought the man drowned."

"No. Coroner says he was strangled and then dumped in the water. I wondered if you could tell me anything about the knot."

Monk scratched his stubbled head and looked again. "It's a figure eight on a bight. Not too fancy, easy to do with some practice. I imagine plenty of folks use them but me; it's not my favorite."

"How so?"

"It would be difficult to untie after you had a heavy load on it, which is why the murderer didn't take the time to remove it, I'd imagine. Plus it's bulky, and it takes a lot of rope to make."

Jack sighed. "So you can't deduce that this knot was tied by a left-handed ex-sailor with brown eyes and a size 14 shoe?"

Monk drained his cup. "Sorry, no. I'm no Hercule Poirot. Ruth's the mystery solver in our family. I guess I didn't solve your case for you then."

"Afraid not but it was worth a try. How is Ruth getting on these days?"

Monk grinned sheepishly. "Fine as can be. 'Course having her grown son sprung on her was kind of a shock, especially after finding a body and all."

"Is Bryce staying with you two?"

"Uh-huh. One big happy family." He sipped some coffee. "Not that it's my business or anything, but Bobby and I were jawing last night and she says she might take a job out of state. Seems pretty serious about it, too, Jack."

Jack nodded, swallowing the odd feeling of panic that rose in his gut.

Monk raised an eyebrow. "I'd sure hate to see her leave, a great girl like that. Wouldn't you?"

Jack busied himself gulping coffee to avoid an answer.

A couple came in with cameras around their necks, cheeks flushed. "Excuse me," Monk said. "They look like they need some reviving."

"Don't we all," Jack muttered as he left the shop.

He opened the door and stepped through, just in time to stumble into Bobby, almost knocking her down the front step. He reached out and caught her, and his heart kicked into overdrive. "Good morning."

She regained her footing. "Good morning. Did you come for your coffee fix?"

"Yes, ma'am. How is Ruth feeling?"

"Sick, but otherwise okay." She eyed him closely. "How are you? You look tired."

He chuckled. "I think that's the look you get when you pin on a police badge. It's a perpetual part of the uniform."

She laughed. "Can I come over and play with Paul after I pick up Uncle Monk's supplies this afternoon? I bought him some more Legos so that we can make a pirate ship. It's really cool."

"You bet." He tried to sound casual, but his pulse began to pound at the prospect of sharing an evening with her. "Um. . .when. . .around what time will you come around?"

"I'm thinking four-ish. Louella will let me in, won't she?"

"Of course. She'll be thrilled. I'll call her and give her the heads-up."

"Don't do that. She'll start cooking up a storm."

"Yes, but you always put her in a panic, being a vegetarian and all. She's convinced if you tasted her pot roast, you'd become a meat eater on the spot."

Their laughter mingled as Bobby walked around him into the shop. "See you later, gator."

He inhaled the scent of strawberry shampoo as he jogged back to his car, with a new energy that had nothing to do with caffeine.

***

Sandra Marconi shifted in her chair in the conference room. "Are we almost done?"

Jack nodded. "Pretty much, but I want to know why you're here, and I don't think you've quite given me that yet."

She blinked, eyes wide above her full cheeks. "Why we're here? I thought I explained all that. It's a project for our thesis. Ethan and I are filming a documentary about the—"

"The wreck of the *Triton*, I know. You told me that before. But according to your college neither of you are enrolled at the moment."

"Oh, that. We had to take a semester off, is all."

"Why?"

Her gaze darted back and forth before returning to Jack's face. "Because we couldn't keep up with a full load of classes and still get this project done, among other things."

"What other things?"

"Money things. College isn't cheap, you know."

"So you had to drop for a term. Why not wait on the project?"

"The timing is right to do it now. It's the anniversary and—"

"Isn't it unusual for college sophomores to take on such a big project? Why wouldn't you want to wait until your senior year maybe?"

She straightened. "Sometimes you've just got to move on a gut feeling, you know?"

The words vibrated in his ears. "I understand that."

"But you still think I'm hiding something?"

"I've been a cop for a long time, Ms. Marconi. I've learned that when something strikes me as odd, it bears checking into. I find it odd, that's all. Risky, to leave school. Why not film later in the summer during break?"

"Then we'd be here along with the other tourists."

"That's not usually too much of a problem in Finny."

"If we can pull off this project, the university will be impressed, maybe even impressed enough to offer us a scholarship."

"Sounds pretty iffy."

She sighed. "I suppose it is. Call us optimists, I guess."

His stomach grumbled to remind him he'd skipped breakfast again. "Who's bankrolling the project then if it isn't the college?"

"We got a five-thousand-dollar grant."

"From whom?"

She picked at a thread on her shorts. "I'm not sure it's public information."

He waited a beat. "There's no such thing as private information during a murder investigation. Who is bankrolling you?"

"The Skylar Foundation."

"Tell me about them."

"I don't really know anything about them. You'll have to ask Ethan."

He made a note on his pad. "One more thing. How are you going to finish your project without a photographer?"

"Ethan's going to film it."

He saw a flicker of uncertainty in her blue eyes.

"Ethan? He's got quite a few talents. Okay. That'll do for a while. You're free to go."

When the door closed behind her he called to Nate, who was trying to unclog his pencil sharpener. "Ever heard of the Skylar Foundation?"

"Nope."

"They give grants to students."

"Do they provide financial assistance to precocious six-year-old triplets?"

"I don't know, but you can ask them when you call."

———

He made it back home a few minutes to four, in time to kiss Louella and usher her to the door.

"Why the rush, Jack?" She put her hands on her massive hips. "Don't you tell me. You're having a lady over." Her round face crinkled in alarm. "My stars, you didn't tell me again. I should have cooked. I could have whipped up a nice lasagna. There's hardly any meat in that. I can fix you some chicken. Does a chicken count as meat?" Her eyes rolled in thought. "They're mostly bones and beak."

He helped her pull on a sweater, ignoring the grin that expanded her face a few more inches. "No need to cook anything. I just thought I'd come home early."

Her eyebrow arched in disbelief.

"And Bobby might come by," he admitted.

She kissed Paul good-bye. "Well, if you ask me, it's about time. I saw Bobby chatting with a handsome young man yesterday. Fine girl like that won't wait around forever."

The word shot out like a cannonball. "Who?"

"Don't know," Louella said, gathering her purse. She leveled a serious look at him. "But maybe you ought to find out, Mr. Detective."

The door closed behind her and Paul peeked out around the corner, a chocolate milk mustache dark on his pale skin. "Scary Bear?"

For the hundredth time, Jack thanked God for letting Paul talk again. The period of selective mutism the boy suffered after watching Lacey die nearly put him over the edge. Every word, every syllable was precious now.

"You'd better run, little man. Big Scary Bear is coming." With a growl he took off running after the happily shrieking boy. He caught Paul on the back porch, throwing him over his shoulder and doing his loudest bear impression. "Now Big Scary Bear is going to eat you for dinner."

Paul hollered and laughed as Jack tickled him.

They both stopped short to see Bobby come through the side gate. She stooped to pet Mr. Boo-Boo, who promptly rolled over to give her access to his canine belly.

"Hi," she said. "I knocked but no one answered. I heard a bear on the rampage, so I let myself in the backyard. Hope that's okay." Her black eyes sparkled.

His stomach fluttered. "You bet. Sure. No problem."

"Hey, Paul." Bobby held up a Lego box and shook it. "I got some new ones so we can make that pirate ship."

"Daddy, down."

Jack righted the boy, who took off like an arrow toward Bobby, pulling her inside. "Let's go make our ship."

"Right, Captain Paul, but I get to be first mate." She laughed as Paul tugged her toward his room.

"Can you stay for dinner?" Jack called to her back.

"If it's no trouble," she said as she vanished down the hall.

"No trouble!"

He pumped his fist in a silent victory cheer and went to unpack the groceries he'd picked up on the way home. As he laid out the food, Louella's words intruded on his happiness. Bobby had been talking with a handsome man? Someone Louella didn't know? Must be an outsider. It wouldn't be hard to find out and he was going to. Soon.

He put the thought aside and went to work warming cheese quiche and slicing green beans to steam. Strawberries and melon and a side of hot dog for Paul. The hot dog made his mouth water, but he wasn't about to give in to his carnivorous instincts in front of vegetarian Bobby. *Best behavior, Jack.*

When he finally finished the dinner preparations, he went to find them. They weren't in Paul's room. Following the sound of laughter, he found them in the studio. For one second, he couldn't breathe.

It was a room he hadn't entered since the day he had buried his wife, a room that still smelled of her paints, though the tubes had long since dried out. Paul sat on Bobby's shoulders, pointing to an amateurish oil painting of a sunrise.

Jack had never understood Lacey's desire to paint, hours spent with brushes and palettes to produce a painting that would never be sold, or most likely even hung up. "What's the point?" he asked, after a particularly bad day at the office.

She looked at him, blond hair pulled back and green eyes much older than her twenty-eight years. "Because you never know when there's something beautiful right at your fingertips."

He'd been too much of a fool to see the beautiful thing he had until it was too late.

Bobby looked up. "Nice paintings. I'm a wreck at art. I can't even draw a stick man. Best I can do is a smiley face and even that turns out looking like a football most of the time."

He opened his mouth, but nothing came out.

She looked closely at his face and then lifted Paul down. He scampered down the hallway. "Um, I think maybe I wasn't supposed to come in here. I'm sorry. I should have asked first. I didn't realize it would upset you."

He managed a wan smile. "No, nothing like that. I, er, don't come in here much."

She slowly wrapped him in a tight hug. He burrowed his face into her neck, soaking in the satiny feeling of her skin. After a long moment he took her hand and led her out, carefully closing the door behind them.

"Paul said his mommy loved to paint."

Jack blinked some tears away. "Did he? He doesn't talk much about his mom. I wasn't sure he remembered that."

"I'm glad he does."

"Me, too." Jack held her hand as they returned to the kitchen.

Paul and Bobby hauled out the Lego creation they'd built and put it on the table. It made a fine centerpiece.

Jack raised his glass of tea. "To a couple of excellent construction workers and very accomplished pirates."

"Arrrgggh," Bobby said in reply.

They clinked glasses and dug in.

Paul looked pleased, Jack thought, as he wolfed down his hot dog. When he trotted off to find more Legos, Bobby chuckled. "He's talking quite a bit more now than he did when I first met him. Long sentences and everything. You must be happy."

"Beyond happy, I'd say. He still goes quiet when he's upset, and that gets my heart thumping, but so far we're weathering the storms pretty well. I. . .uh . . .notice he always seems to be extra chatty when you're around." His cell phone rang. He excused himself and answered, taking a few steps into the front room.

Nate gave him the report. "Cagey bunch, the Skylars. I've had to beat the phone bushes and cyber pavement to get anything on them."

"And what did you find on the elusive Skylar Foundation?"

"It's not much of a foundation. More like a salvage company, funded by a guy named Barnaby Skylar. He likes to provide the odd grant to folks involved in historical research."

"Well, that fits."

"Yeah."

Jack picked up the hesitation in Nate's voice. "So what's eating you?"

"There's very little info on his past projects. He's not affiliated with the university, I can tell you that much."

"So you don't think he's bankrolling Sandra and Ethan out of the goodness of his heart, or to get credit in their paper?"

"Not likely."

"Okay, Nate. Keep on it."

He hung up.

"Did I hear you say the Sklyar Foundation?" Bobby pushed her plate away as she joined him again.

"Yeah. It's the group that supposedly funded the film crew that's poking around here. You ever heard of it?"

"Yes." She frowned, twisting a strand of her straight black hair. "But I can't remember where. It will come to me. Of course, you could just ask Ethan."

Jack stilled. "Ethan? Do you know him?"

She nodded. "Actually, I met him in a geology class last year. I was surprised to see him in town."

"I didn't realize you two knew each other."

"Not well. We went out a few times. Nothing serious. I'm going diving with him tomorrow."

Jack put his fork down too loudly. The mystery of the handsome stranger was solved. "You're going to dive together? Is that a good idea?"

She frowned. "Why wouldn't it be?"

"He's a suspect in a murder investigation."

"A suspect? You don't really think he killed his camera guy."

"It's a possibility."

"I promise I'll always keep my guard up."

He didn't return her smile. "It's a bad idea, Bobby."

She folded her arms. "Let's put it on the table. This isn't about your investigation. This is because you don't like me hanging out with someone else, isn't it?"

He took a sip of water to stall for a moment. "I don't like you muddying the waters when I'm working on a case."

She snorted. "Muddying the waters? You make me sound like some sort of dog, playing around in your pond."

"That's not what I meant. I just think you should know who you're going to be gallivanting around with."

"Sometimes I'm not even sure I know you." Her eyes blazed as she stood and pushed her chair in. "Don't worry. I'll be very careful not to contaminate any evidence when I'm out in the ocean with Ethan. Thanks for dinner."

She grabbed her jacket. He heard her kiss Paul and wish him good night. The front door slammed. After a moment he followed, jogging down the front drive. "Bobby, wait. I'm sorry."

She was too far away to hear, or maybe too angry to turn around.

His gut told him Bobby should stay away from Ethan Ping. A stab of conscience made him wonder if it really was his gut. Or his heart.

8

Ruth's camera was cold in her hands as she took pictures of the sunrise over the wild Pacific. She told herself the extra money from the sale of the postcard photos would help with the ever-growing list of baby essentials. She was rationalizing, of course.

"What kind of mother is afraid to be around her own son? Lord, what kind of a mother will I be to this new child?" She whispered her prayer to the wind. The baby kicked, a fluttery butterfly feeling.

The minutes of this pregnancy ticked away in a blur. Was she really forty-eight and pregnant? Would she love the baby as she loved Bryce? Would it turn out the way it had with him? Monk would be there, by her side, but she knew from painful experience that nothing in life is a given.

Bryce was finding that out the hard way after losing his baby, his wife, and his job in the space of a year. He wasn't used to losing. She'd tried so hard to prevent him from feeling that sting as a child, she wasn't sure he would be able to weather it now.

The wind whipped her hair around into a frizzy ball. Through her camera lens the steel gray ocean was choppy, restless. A figure came into view along the cliff line. She could just make out the angular face of Dr. Soloski. His head was bent, shoulders hunched. She considered calling out to him, but the man was absorbed in his own thoughts, as engrossing as her own. He looked tired, perhaps from running away from Ellen Foots.

Her stomach rumbled, and she was suddenly ravenous. It was a cruel trick, as she knew the hunger would be replaced by morning sickness in a few hours. Morning sickness. What a misnomer. If it was confined to the morning hours she'd count herself lucky. In the past few months she hadn't dared leave home without an airsick bag in each pocket.

For the moment, she turned her thoughts to food. Her mind traveled back to Indigo Orson's cramped handwritten scrawls, and she picked up the binder she'd brought along, to read the next passage.

These men ate poorly, scavenging whatever they could and trying to turn it into something, anything edible, until God tossed me onto their shores. They told me of a cactus stew they had tried to make after a traveler traded them some for fresh water. Not a one of them gave a thought to removing the prickles before they boiled it. The traveler gave them dried tortoise, too. Most had never seen a tortoise, alive or dead, but that did not stop them from eating every speck of it.

It reminded me of the strange animals Señor Orson told of when he returned from Australia before our disastrous voyage on the Triton. *If there were kangaroos in California, they would be hopping for their lives to escape the stew pot.*

Mostly the men were used to beans and more beans, seasoned with only a bit of salt, so anything different was a joy to them. Once Old Severus brought me six abalone he'd pried off the rocks with an iron bar. What a sweet delight they made, fried up with a pat of butter.

With my precious remaining treasure, I baked a dozen biscuits and sold them. I earned enough to buy more flour, some dried chilies, and salt pork and a set of tin plates. There was a quantity of wild onion and garlic growing near our camp to which the men paid no mind, but I gathered as if it was manna. I even found a small patch of wild oregano, and happy I was to pick some, too. It will be a wonderful treat for the men to have their food with a dab of seasoning, though they would happily eat it plain.

They now regard me as a priceless addition to their camp and afford me whatever small luxuries they can, such as a bucket for hauling water and a woolen blanket. Patchy even provided me with a crude butter churn, though where he got it I shiver to consider. When I can lay my hands on some milk, the men will have their butter.

Before I finished soaking the beans and chilies they circled like hungry dogs.

"What is it?" a fellow by the name of Slack asked me. "Never mind," he said. "Don't care what it is. When can I eat it?"

By the time they returned from their long day at the river, the chili was done. At the risk of disclosing my gender, I made them wash their filthy hands before I served them.

It is an oddly exhilarating place here, in this wild land. The work is backbreaking, sure enough, but it's my work, fashioned with my own hands, planned in my own mind and brought about by the sweat of my brow. For the first time in my life, I am beholden to no one but myself and my God. I work to survive, sure enough, but I feel as though the compensation I receive goes beyond the coins I collect.

I know these are heathen men, rough and hardened. Ah, but it does my heart good to see them fill their stomachs. Perhaps if I can ease the ferocious hunger which gnaws at their bellies, God can fill their souls and take away the gold fever that reduces them to animals.

TREASURE UNDER FINNY'S NOSE

As she closed the binder, Ruth was seized with an overwhelming desire to cook. The supremely elemental need to nourish another person filled her. If she couldn't talk to Bryce, at least she could feed him. She stretched the light sweater over her belly and headed to town enjoying the sights and smells of early summer.

She stopped at Puzan's Grocery and filled her basket with onion, chili, sausage, and a bunch of Royland Lemmon's gorgeous herbs. She held the fragrant bunch of thyme to her nose and breathed in the smell of greenery and, she imagined, sorrow.

Though she knew it wasn't her fault Royland's son was a murderer, she had definitely had a hand in solving the crime, and it pained her to see the look of defeat in Royland's face since his child went to prison. She insisted on delivering the farmer's worm order personally once a month, and staying awhile on his farm to chat. She knew she would never think of Royland without feeling that odd mixture of pity and guilt.

As she shifted the binder of Indigo's writings to pull the grocery money out of her pocket, a slip of paper floated to the floor. The small blue note was cryptic: *P.max. 468c/470c.* With a confused frown, she pocketed the paper and headed home.

Monk waited in the kitchen with a cup of tea already steeping. After kissing her on her lips and both cheeks, he put out a roast beef sandwich for himself and a grilled cheese for her.

"I thought you'd be busy at the shop."

"Bobby's handling things for a while." His forehead creased. "Is something going on with her? She seems awfully quiet. Said she's going diving with that Ethan fellow after lunch."

"Ethan? I didn't know she knew him. I wonder what Jack thinks about that."

He raised an eyebrow. "I can imagine what he thinks. Ethan better not break any laws while he's in town, or he'll be thrown in the slammer with a life sentence."

They laughed.

"I hope they work things out," Ruth said. "They are good for each other."

"Just like us." Monk toasted her with a root beer. "I've been so busy since I got back we haven't talked much. So how are you doing, honey? With the baby and. . . everything?"

She took a deep breath and, seeing the sympathetic look on his kind face, burst into a shower of tears. He came around in front of her and squeezed her gently.

"What is it, Ruthy? What's wrong?"

"Everything," she wailed. "I'm fat and sick, and I didn't do a good job mothering the first time and I'm way too old to learn how to parent now."

He patted her back, her tears soaking his shirt front. "You are a good mother and you'll be a good mother to Junior, too. You're just going through a patch of worry now. The hormones aren't helping, I'll bet."

"But, Monk," she said, pulling away. "Bryce didn't want to be around me, ever. He always wanted to do things himself, and if he couldn't do something he asked Philip for help. I think I tried to do too much for him." Her voice dropped to a whisper. "I smothered him, spoiled him, and he's paying the price for it now."

Monk tipped her face to his and patted her tears away with a napkin. "Ruthy, there's one very important thing you're forgetting."

"What?"

"Where did he go when his life fell apart?"

She blinked. "He, he came—"

"Home to you," he finished.

She fed the worms their vegetable peelings and sprinkled the beds with a layer of hay. As usual, the gulls jostled around, their beaks poking into the dark soil, the fanning of their wings creating a breeze on her legs.

"No, you don't, Rutherford." She pushed him away, then sidestepped the eager Grover. "Here's your lunch." She tossed cubes of stale bread and bits of apples to the feathery swarm. Their loud squawks filled the cool afternoon air with discordant music. She couldn't help but smile at the greedy horde. The sight always brought back a fond memory of Phillip. For a long time, she'd pushed the memories away, but now she savored them, like looking at old photos in a scrapbook.

A laugh made her turn.

"Those are the strangest pets," Bryce said, arms folded across his chest. "Most people would choose a dog or cat."

"They are strange companions. They don't heel, they can't fetch, and only Martha comes when called. Weird is an understatement, but your father chose them for us, so that's that."

He nodded. "I was on my way to the beach and I ran into that blond lady, the filmmaker. What's her name?"

"Sandra Marconi."

"That's the one. She said she needs to talk to you. She'll come by later."

"I wonder what that's all about." Absently she fingered the paper in her pocket and pulled it out. "Bryce, does this note mean anything to you?"

He frowned at the scrap. "No. Not really. Looks like some kind of foreign language. Where did you get it?"

"I found it in the notebook Sandra gave me."

"Oh. Maybe she can tell you then." They lapsed into silence. Bryce shifted from one foot to the other, dark eyes fixed on the swarming birds as they finished up their meal.

"Who was that other lady? The one with the cap that came for worms last night?"

"Her name is Roxie Trotter. Why?"

"No particular reason. She looks familiar to me, but I don't know where from." He watched the birds bob and weave across the yard.

Ruth wondered as she looked at Bryce's thin face. Who was this grown man? What were his passions and dreams? He might be a total stranger who wandered in off the street, for all she knew about him. She wanted to talk, to free them from the distance that yawned between them, but she couldn't think of a way to do it.

Ruth brushed off her hands. She spoke before she had a chance to think about the logic of her plan. "I'm going to make chili."

Bryce raised an eyebrow. "Really? I figured spicy food would make you sick. Roslyn always had heartburn. I used to keep a roll of antacids in every jacket I owned so she'd have some when she needed them."

Her heart ached to see the flitter of pain on his face. "It does and it will, but for now, I'm making chili."

"Okay." He trailed behind her into the kitchen. "Maybe I could give you a hand."

Her heart skipped a beat, and she fought to keep her voice level as they entered the kitchen. "That would be great. Can you get out my chili pot from down there? Bending over makes my head spin like a top." Without a word he pulled the pot from the low cupboard. She handed him the dry beans. He sat at the table, his head bent, sorting them into precise piles and removing the occasional stone, like a miser poring over gold pieces.

She chopped an onion and peeled the garlic.

Bryce poured his sorted beans back into the pot and added water. It was quiet for a while except for the sound of her knife on the cutting board. Bryce retrieved the herbs from the fridge.

"Remember earthquake cake?"

She started, her mouth open in a momentary *O* of surprise. "Earthquake cake? That awful chocolate thing we spackled together with frosting for Dad's birthday?"

"Yeah. Dad said it was the best cake he ever had."

Against all reason, her eyes filled. Bryce remembered earthquake cake. "He would say that about every cake we ever made."

"Yeah. He was a natural-born optimist." Bryce fingered the leathery skin of the chilies. "I miss him."

"I miss him, too."

"Do you. . .ever visit his grave?"

"Of course, honey, often. Monk and I go together every now and then. We pray and leave flowers. Sometimes I take the birds. I think your father would have liked that."

TREASURE UNDER FINNY'S NOSE

"I think you're right."

Bryce's cell phone rang, and he went in the other room to answer it.

Ruth tried not to listen. His comments were short. The sound of the bubbling pot did not quite drown out the angry cadence of his words.

When he returned, his brow was furrowed, and he looked much older than he had a moment before. "Roslyn needs me to sign some papers so we can put the house on the market."

"Oh, I see. That's. . .sad. Isn't it?"

He shrugged. "Might as well sell it. It's not my home anymore. I need some air. I'm going for a walk."

Ruth watched him through the kitchen window as he left the house, studying the flagstone path beneath his feet as he headed to the street.

She looked around at her own small house, the scratched tile counter, the smooth wooden floor, drapes that fluttered in the breeze from the open window. Those walls had been home to two husbands and a little boy at one point. Sweet little Cootchie had listened to her read many a story here. Soon it would be home to another child. Through all the heartbreak of losing Phillip, and the struggle with Bryce, it had never stopped being home to her.

"How very blessed I am, Lord. Thank You for reminding me."

She made sure the beans were simmering, starting the process to fill their bellies, praying that God would fill Bryce's soul. As she hummed a tune, marveling that the scent of onions and garlic hadn't sent her stomach on a roller-coaster ride, Ruth didn't notice the small clink as her wedding ring slipped off the counter and into the sink. She started the disposal, and the horrible clanking noise made her slam off the switch.

She fished around in the drain and came up with the object.

The plain gold band was twisted and scarred.

With trembling fingers she held the band to her chest and cried.

An hour later Ruth ushered Sandra into the kitchen in the late afternoon. The fragrance of cooking chili filled every nook and cranny of the house.

"That smells wonderful," Sandra said.

"Thank you. I was inspired by Indigo Orson, only she made hers without the benefit of a sink or cutting boards. The miners didn't seem to mind."

Sandra laughed, making her eyes sparkle. "She was an amazing woman."

Ruth gestured for Sandra to sit. "How did you learn of her?"

"I was doing some research on steamships, and I came across her name on a passenger list. I was lucky enough to find her journal buried in the archives. It was a miracle really. The papers were mixed in with a pile of receipts and such, ready to be disposed of."

"Are you a history major then?"

Her face broke into a wide smile. "Not anymore, but I sure miss it. I love everything about it, the thrill of finding a new connection between the past and the present, poring over old maps. I even love the musty smell of old books. I'm a history geek for sure."

Ruth laughed. "You'll have to go visit Ellen Foots, our librarian. She's ferocious about her passion for research materials. I think she was a history major, too."

"Actually, when the project is done, I'm going to switch gears and work on a master's in business."

"Really? Why?"

Sandra tugged on a strand of her white blond hair. "Sadly, I learned that you really can't pay the bills too effectively with a history degree. I've had to look for other means. I've done everything from flipping burgers to stocking shelves." She flexed her knee. "I tore my ACL last year, and the surgery for that cost me a bundle, let me tell you. My surgeon sends me little pink notes every month reminding me I'm not finished paying for my bionic knee. They're not valentines, I can tell you."

"Was the surgery a success?"

She sighed, rubbing her knee thoughtfully. "I guess, but the body never really does recover from some things."

Ruth remembered the stretch marks that snaked like snail trails over her protruding belly after Bryce was born. What permanent marks would this later-in-life baby leave on her body? "I'm afraid you're right about that."

"Are you feeling okay? Is the pregnancy going okay and everything?" Sandra looked uneasy. "Oh, maybe that's too personal to ask. I'm sorry if I was rude."

"Not at all. I'm the topic of conversation at dinner tables all over Finny. As far as I can tell, everything is right on track," Ruth said. "I've got one of those big appointments coming up, the pregnancy milestones that make you stay up at night and worry."

Her smile was sympathetic. "I've never been pregnant, but I've had plenty of those nights, especially lately." Sandra glanced at her watch. "The reason I stopped by is I need the binder, with Indigo's notes."

"Oh, really? Are we going to quit filming?"

"No, no. In fact, we need to speed things up. The long-range weather gurus are forecasting a storm by week's end. I need to, um, make some notes. I'll give it back tomorrow. I promise." She held up three fingers in a Girl Scout salute.

"Sure. I'll go get it." Ruth passed the nursery on her way down the hall, wondering for the umpteenth time if it should be blue or pink. The day before, she'd decided on the palest of yellows, but that was yesterday. Maybe she should just ask the doctor and get it over with. Maybe it would help to make it all more real, somehow.

She retrieved the binder and remembered the cryptic piece of paper. On impulse, she jotted down the numbers on a pad before she replaced the note among other pages and returned to the kitchen.

Sandra looked up from the chili pot. She blushed and replaced the lid. "Oh, sorry. I hope you don't mind. It's been awhile since I smelled a good home-cooked chili. My dad makes a mean pot, but I haven't been home in a few years."

"Where is home?"

"Montana. He moved us up there after my mom took off."

"Oh. That's too bad. About your mother, I mean."

She shrugged and took the binder from Ruth. "It happens. I was only three so I don't remember her much. My brother was ten so it really threw him for a loop. He's dead now. Car wreck."

Ruth saw grief in the woman's face. "I'm so sorry."

"Me, too. He was a great big brother." Sandra turned to go. "I'd better go. Nice talking to you, Mrs. Budge."

"Call me Ruth. I'll save you some chili when it's done."

"That would be super." Sandra gazed into her face for a long moment. "You're going to be a good mother, I'll bet."

Ruth felt a warmth in her cheeks. "It's what I'm praying for."

❧

Just before midnight Ruth wandered into the kitchen, which still smelled of chili in spite of leaving the windows open for several hours. Though she had eaten two bowls earlier, the smell now made her stomach quiver. She held her breath and poured a glass of milk. It surprised her to find Indigo Orson's journal on the sideboard with a note.

> *Mom, Sandra saw me in town and asked me to return this to you. You were asleep when I got home, so I put it here. I ate more of the chili for a snack. It is good stuff. Bryce.*

Smiling, she sat on the sofa to sip her milk and thumb through the photocopied journal pages. There were no changes that she could detect. Then she checked the front inside flap.

"I take that back. There is one change," she muttered to herself.

The cryptic numbered note was gone.

9

Jack waited until ten thirty in the morning to go to the library. He knew Ellen Foots attended a Thursday People and Paws meeting at the high school gym on Fridays at that time so he figured he was safe from the prying giantess.

He made his way to the nonfiction section and hunted until he found it. *Beginning Scuba.* Perfect. Three hundred fifty pages of details that would open up a whole new undersea world or condemn him to a watery grave. As he went to the front desk, he wondered why anyone would choose to strap on a bottle of air and sink themselves on purpose. It was just an unnatural thing to do. Plenty of people did it, however, he thought with a grimace, including Ethan Ping, who he'd heard was escorting Bobby on another dive that very afternoon. He slapped his library card down on the front desk more forcefully than he intended.

Ellen emerged from the back, her hair poking out from a headband that struggled to hold it all in.

His heart sank a notch. "Ellen. I thought you were at your People and Paws meeting."

"Had to cancel. Maude had a dental emergency." Her heavy brows furrowed. "At least, that's what she says. I think she's just trying to get her claws into Dr. Soloski. She's on him like pudding skin."

The guy must feel like the last hunk of meat at a tiger convention. "That's too bad."

Ellen scanned the bar code. "You're going to learn how to scuba dive?"

"Uh, no. Just a little background for the investigation."

Her face grew thoughtful for a moment and then resolved into a scowl. "You know, I'm going over there right now to check on Maude. If she's got a cracked crown, I'm Nefertiti."

He hid a smile as he took the book.

An hour later the book remained on the front seat of his car and Maude was in his office. She still wore the paper bib from the dentist visit.

"It's stalking, I'm telling you. Or invasion of privacy. Imagine, bursting in on a patient's dental exam. Why, poor Dr. Soloski could have slipped and put his hook through my lip or something."

We couldn't be that lucky. "But it all ended well, didn't it? Dr. Soloski was able to fix your crown after all, wasn't he?"

"Crown? Oh, it wasn't cracked after all. Silly of me."

Jack looked at Maude's tight bun and her squared shoulders. The woman didn't have a silly molecule in her spindly body. He reined in an exasperated sigh. "I'm not going to arrest Ellen, Maude, so is there anything else I can do for you?"

Maude's cheeks colored. "Stalkers. Bodies washing up on beaches. People slinking around at night, and what does the Finny police department do about it? Nothing. Not a pinky lifted to help out the citizens of this town. Shocking. I tell you it's shocking."

Jack sifted through the rambling. "Who's slinking around at night?"

"Not that you'd be interested at all, but there's been a boat out the last two nights. Late. Around two o'clock in the morning. My insomnia has been troubling me so I happen to notice them. No one has legitimate business out on the water at that hour, now do they?"

"Who was it?"

"I don't know. My binoculars weren't strong enough, but the boat looked like Roxie's. Whoever it was had to be up to no good." Maude's black eyes widened under her pencil-drawn brows. "I know. I bet it was Ellen. She was probably dumping a body over the side."

Jack looked at her. "Whose body would she be dumping exactly?"

"Oh, I don't know. You're the police. Aren't you supposed to figure things like that out? You did go to investigator school, didn't you? I know she's got a motive somewhere in her shady past."

Nate poked his head in. "Hey, Maude. There's a group of women roaming the town looking for you. They say they're ready for their visit to the movie site."

Maude shot out of the chair so fast she knocked it over. "Oh my. Is it that time already? Business is hopping. I've got another tour group to lead. Excuse me, gentlemen."

Nate nodded. "You might want to take off the bib first."

She sniffed and swept out of the room, her cast thumping against the floor in a rapid staccato.

Jack slumped in relief. "Thanks for the rescue. I'm promoting you to the upstairs office."

Nate uprighted the chair and settled in. "Great. If we should ever build an upstairs, I'll remind you of that. Louella called."

His heart skipped a bit as it always did when Paul's babysitter called. "Is everything okay?"

"You bet. She said to remind you the butterfly tea party is this afternoon at the preschool and the pleasure of your attendance is required."

He felt a twinge of guilt because he had not remembered what the twelve thirty entry in his PDA was for. "Right. Butterfly tea. I'm on it."

"Do you have to bring your own butterflies?"

"Funny. You shouldn't be handing out grief here. I remember you making an Easter bonnet when Janet couldn't make it to the triplet's Sunday school party."

"It was a fine looking bonnet."

"Can't argue with that. I particularly liked the way you drew handcuffs on the side. What do you hear about Reggie?"

"He's still dead."

"Uh-huh. And?"

Nate pulled his mustache. "And he participated in some questionable treasure hunting."

"What kind?"

"The kind when you salvage artifacts off a historical wreck and sell them for profit."

Jack sat up straighter. "A historical wreck?"

"Mmhmm. Worked for a man last name of Skylar. Ring any bells?"

"My bells are ringing. Did he have an arrest record for this hunting?"

"Nope. Turns out maritime law is a bit foggy. According to the Abandoned Ship Act, the government owns all shipwrecks in state waters out to three miles on the Atlantic and Pacific coasts. The particular wreck in question was slightly over that distance so Skylar hired a crew to pick it clean. There wasn't much there worth salvaging, but they got themselves on the Coast Guard watch list."

"Strange coincidence that a man of the same name is funding this little voyage through history, right off our humble coast."

"Isn't it, though? Think the *Triton* was carrying any good cargo? Maybe there was something buried under all that coal."

"Might be interesting to find out."

Nate checked his watch. "Eleven thirty, boss. When do you have to report for butterfly duty?"

"Soon, but I've got something to do first."

Jack walked partway up the steep trail, stopping behind the gnarled cypress. Down below he could see them making their slow exit from the water. Bobby's figure was slight and smaller than Ethan's, the only way he could tell the two wet-suited people apart. On the beach they began to strip off their gear. He couldn't make out their words, but Bobby's peal of laughter came through loud and clear.

His stomach muscles clenched when Ethan held Bobby's arm while she removed her flippers. There had to be some reason this guy should be in jail. He'd make sure to find out what it was.

Ethan shouldered his gear and, with a wave, headed away toward town. Bobby pulled off her wet suit. She sat on the sand in her one-piece bathing suit, gazing out at the ocean. Jack watched her black hair dance in the breeze, and he unconsciously took a step forward, wishing he could join her on the warm beach. He thought better of it and leaned back. The rocky ground under his feet gave way, and he tumbled down the slope.

~

The sun was warm on his face. Fingers stroked his cheek, coaxing his eyes into opening. He blinked.

Bobby's eyes were wide, anxious. "Are you all right?"

He blinked again. "You smell nice."

She raised an eyebrow. "No, I don't. I smell like seaweed."

He was relieved to find no trace of anger on her face from their last meeting. "No, you smell like a great cup of coffee."

She laughed. "Okay. I know your nose is working. Did you hurt anything else?"

He shifted his limbs. Aside from dozens of pain pricks, all the parts seemed functional. He sat up and waited for the sparks to stop dancing in his head.

Bobby looked into his eyes. "Pupils look normal, but I'd better call an ambulance anyway."

He grabbed her wrist as she started to go. "No. I'm okay. Just, just stay here for a minute."

She settled back next to him. "Do you want to tell me why you were spying on me?"

"Spying? I wasn't spying. I was out for a walk, and I saw you down there with College Boy."

"His name is Ethan, and I don't buy that for a minute."

Jack bit back a sarcastic remark. He didn't want to make an idiot of himself again.

She gently brushed the gravel bits out of his hair and ran soft fingers along his head. The feel of her wrapped his insides in a flood of warmth.

He cleared his throat. "Did you enjoy your dive?"

"Sure." She continued to watch his face. "I love diving. Beautiful kelp beds out there."

"Yeah. I've been considering trying it out."

"Trying what out?"

"Diving."

"You?" She laughed. "That's a good one."

He sat up straighter. "What's so funny about that?"

"Nothing. Diving is great. You'll love it, but don't go alone."

"Does Ethan dive alone?"

"I don't think so. Why? Oh, I know. You think he's up to no good, right?"

"You said it, I didn't."

She stood, brushing sand from her legs. "Let's not have another argument here, shall we? You're not going to use me to dig up dirt on Ethan. He's a nice guy, Jack."

"Then why is he in partnership with a modern-day pirate?"

"What?"

"The guy funding his quote unquote research is a man who steals treasure from shipwrecks that belong to the state."

"Hard way to make a living." Her eyes narrowed. "Besides, there's one problem with your pat theory."

"What's that?"

"The *Triton* carried a giant boatload of coal. Not coins, jewelry, or even silver. It was a cargo ship with very few civilian passengers. So there isn't anything on that boat except maybe a few trinkets of interest to historians."

He looked out at the waves. "Maybe, maybe not."

"Let's get real here. Your case is weak and you know it. Ethan has nothing to gain from that wreck except historical information, which is exactly what he said he was after in the first place."

Jack sniffed and looked away. "My gut tells me he's not just here for the history."

"Sometimes people really are what they seem to be." She picked up her air tanks and wet suit. "I'm gonna go now. Are you sure you're all right?"

"Absolutely."

He heaved himself from the ground and stood upright before a wave of dizziness made him stagger. Bobby dropped her gear and grabbed him. "Absolutely, huh?" She tucked a shoulder under his arm and helped him walk.

Jack leaned on her. "Why are you helping? I thought you were mad at me."

"I am mad at you. And you know why I'm helping."

"I do?"

She stopped and sighed deeply. Her fingers wound around his neck, and she kissed him full on the mouth. "Because I love you, you idiot."

The kiss ended too soon. He was momentarily overwhelmed with joy, dizzy and not from the fall. She loved him. He should open his mouth and tell her how he felt. He should. He should.

She waited a fraction of a second longer and then dropped her gaze to the sand. "That's what I thought. Come on. Let's get you back to your car."

They reached the parking lot, and he brushed off his clothes, feeling her disappointment, heavy as his own. "Bobby—"

She shook her head. "Don't say a word. You'd better go home and take a shower."

"I wish I could, but I'm late for a party."

"What kind of party?"

"A butterfly tea party. We're making tissue flowers."

Though her face still wore the signs of sadness, Bobby tilted her face to the sun and laughed.

———

Paul wrinkled his nose in concentration as he folded the tissue into pleats. He poofed the delicate yellow paper and a smile lit his face as he held it up for his father. "See? It's a flower."

"Nice, buddy. Great job." Jack felt the curious glances from the room full of moms. He was scratched and bruised from his fall. The muscles in his back ached. The classroom was filled with mothers and children, expertly making tissue flower bouquets and pasting minute plastic butterflies on them.

"Now you." Paul slid the pipe cleaners and a handful of tissue at his father.

"Oh, Dad's not so good at this kind of thing. Why don't you make some more? Yours are super."

His face fell. "You're supposed to do it."

Jack couldn't stand that look for another second. "Well, I'll give it a try. Let's see, how did you fold it?" As he fiddled with the wads of tissue, Jack thought about Lacey. She would have made perfect flowers. *But she's not here*, he thought angrily, *she's dead, so I'm stuck making tissue flowers that look like someone chewed them and spit them out.*

The paper would not cooperate under his clumsy fingers. He produced a sad, crumpled mass, like a blossom trodden under the weight of many feet.

Paul looked at it. "That doesn't look good, Daddy."

I'm not good, Paul. I'm an idiot and a coward to boot. Why hadn't he told Bobby he loved her? He could feel love in every pore of his body, but he hadn't said the words to anyone besides Paul since Lacey died. He loved Lacey. And he loved Bobby, but he continued to let her down. No wonder she was scuba diving with other guys. "Sorry, son. I'll try again."

Someone took the pipe cleaner and tissue from his hands and slid into the chair next to him. Bobby folded the paper into the perfect tissue bloom. She smiled. "There you go, Paul. Isn't that the best flower you ever saw?"

"Oh yeah," the boy yelled. "That's great, Bobby."

She nodded. "Yes, it is. Get me a butterfly and more tissue, and we'll finish this bouquet." She lowered her voice to a whisper. "Ours will be the best one at this party."

With a giggle, Paul leaped out of the chair to fetch more supplies.

Jack looked at her. "I thought you were mad at me."

"I am mad at you. You're a jealous cretin who has no business telling me who I can and cannot see. And you are also a dismal failure at arts and crafts." She flipped her bobbed hair out of her face. "I, on the other hand, made six thousand tissue flowers for a Cinco de Mayo float so I'm a professional. I figured Paul could use a hand."

Jack looked into her black eyes and saw love shining there, love that he didn't deserve. "He sure could." *And so could I.*

10

God has sent me a soul even more wretched than I was the day I washed up on this shore. He's a Chinese boy, name of Hui, which means splendor, I have since discovered. I found him one day, hidden under a broken wagon. I wouldn't have noticed him at all if he hadn't sneezed.

His mother died of fever when he was born, and his father came to California to work the gold fields. Of course, being Chinese, they were forced to work the claims that had already been stripped clean. Hui was one of a group of fifty Chinese men and boys that came to Gold Country only to find themselves banned from the most current diggings. Gradually they dispersed, looking for meager leftovers from already bare land. The fortunate ones with some money to front were able to open laundries and restaurants and the occasional store in town.

Hui and his father were not so lucky. They camped in a cave halfway up the side of the mountain until some white men caught Hui's father panning in a forbidden place. They beat him to death. Hui buried him as best he could and survived by snitching food from the campsites at night. They caught him once, and he has a bruised face and a broken finger to show for his narrow escape. I am reminded that these men remain more animal than human sometimes.

I found him, one midnight, hiding under that wagon with scraps he'd taken from the rubbish heap, bone thin, black eyes huge with terror. I don't speak Chinese, but Hui speaks a good bit of English that he learned from listening on the ship voyage from China. He didn't need to say a word, though, for me to see the desperation on his young face. I don't suppose he's much older than ten years, though he isn't exactly certain of his birth date because the Chinese calendar is much different than ours. Somehow I persuaded him to come to my tent and eat some dried meat and berries. The food was meager, but he devoured it in a thrice before he ate the three biscuits I'd been saving for breakfast.

We made him sort of a bed out of a blanket and some burlap bags. Though the night was hot, he trembled in a miserable state until he finally fell into an exhausted slumber. That was three nights ago, and he still shivers when darkness comes, rolled into a ball on the floor of my tent.

He lives in terror of being killed, and goodness knows he has reason for his fear. Like the Mexicans, the Chinese are despised in the mining camps, lower than dogs. The first morning Hui peeked out of my tent, Slack saw him and came running with a shovel. I stood between them and raised my ladle like a sword.

"This boy is mine, Señor. Any one of you who lays a hand to him will never eat from my pot again. I'll see you starve first."

That made them temper their anger. Losing their chance at real food proved stronger than the need for foolish violence. They look at him with cruel eyes, but no one has dared to touch the boy. Nonetheless he stays at my side every minute and helps me with the cooking and cleaning up. He is very good at tending the fire, making sure it never goes out or burns too hot to scorch the soup. He gathered leaves from somewhere and brewed them into a sort of tea which we have both found to be of comfort on these cold mornings.

I believe Hui knows that I am a woman, but he will keep my secret, I am sure of it. We are both strangers here, and God has put us together for His good purpose. I hold His promise next to my heart for both our sakes: "For I know the thoughts I think toward you," saith the Lord, "thoughts of peace, and not of evil, to give you an expected end."

Ruth eased down onto the sofa, trying to keep down the glass of water she'd drunk. *The plans I have for you.* She groaned, clasping a hand to her aching back. A later-than-midlife pregnancy and a son whose world was crumbling sure seemed like the definition of calamity. What was the future going to look like? A decade ago she thought it was a life with Phillip, the man she adored, but that was not to be. And what should she hope for? For a long life with her husband and a new baby? She had already cherished that hope a lifetime ago. God's plan seemed as foggy to her as the Finny coastline in the spring. The terror of it all swept over her again.

Alva knocked, and she clambered to her feet to let him in. He fished the abalone shell from his cavernous pocket. "I need yer help, sweet cheeks. Can you keep it safe fer me? That thievin' dentist may aim to swipe it back."

Ruth squelched a smile. "I'm sure he's over the loss of his business card holder by now."

"Maybe, maybe not." Alva put the shell on the kitchen counter and filled it with apples from the fruit bowl. "There. Hidden in plain sight and all. I stowed my other treasures in separate locations so as to foil any criminal masterminds. Are you ready to go to town?"

"Yes, Alva. I've gone to the bathroom three times and managed to swallow those horrible prenatal pills. I'm ready to face the afternoon."

"Okeydokey. It's free sample day at the Buns Up Bakery. You and me can swipe a bunch of them sugar cookies. You got big pockets?"

The thought of food made her stomach heave. "I'll head to the jewelers. You can stop at Buns Up if you want to." Ruth took her mangled ring from the counter.

"Well, whaddja do to it anyway?" Alva squinted a rheumy eye at the squished band of gold. "It looks like ya done run it over or something."

Ruth pocketed the metal, feeling the tears threaten again. "I dropped it down the sink when the disposal was running. What a klutz."

Alva patted her hand. "Oh now, don't you pay it no never mind. One time I dropped Daddy's teeth in the dog food. Fluffers ate it up afore I could fish it out. We had to wait two days until it made an appearance again. Daddy twerent happy about it at all."

She pulled a sweater over her protruding stomach and gave up trying to button it. "I don't feel so bad about the ring then."

Ruth and Alva linked arms as they headed toward Main Street. The air was warm, full of the promise of a hot summer ahead. The potted hydrangeas that lined the sidewalks were dotted with blooms, and the bougainvillea climbing the cracked stucco walls of the hotel seemed to vibrate with a wave of color.

Alva handed her a bag of candy corn. "Vegetables, so the baby don't come out with two heads or anything."

She sucked on a sweet triangle.

"I've been reading this book that Petey Fisk loaned me about babies. What's this about them havin' a soft spot on their heads?"

"It's only for a while, until their skulls fuse together."

He looked alarmed. "Sakes. You think we ought to get the little dickens a helmet until the fusion thing is done?"

It felt so good to laugh. "Let's see how it goes, okay?"

Alva nodded. "Whatever you say, sweet cheeks." He stopped long enough at the bakery to load his pockets with cookie samples. Ruth stayed outside. They continued their stroll until they came to the shop. With a gallant flourish he opened the door of Finny Jewelers, and she headed inside.

Roxie stood at the glass counter with Stew Barnes, Finny's only jeweler. Stew looked up. "Hello, Ruth. Good to see you. Come on in, and I'll be with you in a minute."

Ruth nodded. She wandered around the cases and listened in with only a sliver of guilt.

"Last time you gave me ten per shell," Roxie said.

"Last time I needed them for a display. This time I'm just being nice." He piled the stack of three abalone shells on the counter and measured them with a ruler.

"They're legal," she snapped. "I know the rules. They're all bigger than seven inches."

Stew raised an eyebrow. "And you didn't harvest them using scuba gear?"

Roxie's cheeks reddened. "Of course I didn't. Now, are you going to pay me or not?"

Alva's eyebrows zinged up. "Pay her? You gonna pay her for the shells? Without the pearls in 'em?"

The jeweler put down his ruler. "Pearls don't come from abalone, Alva. They come from oysters. I use the shells for display because they're pretty and you can fit a whole necklace inside."

The old man's eyes darted around in thought. "I got me a sweet shell from the dentist. How much you give me fer it?"

Stew's eyebrow arched. "You got a shell from the dentist? What happened to lollipops?"

"He ain't that sort of a dentist. He said lollipops would give me the decay, so I picked the shell instead. What'll you give me?"

Stew scratched the bald patch on the top of his head. "As I was just saying, I have enough shells. I'm using them for a new pearl display, and I've got plenty. I'm not going to buy any more from Roxie, either."

Alva chuckled. "Oh, that's what you say now, but you wait till you see the beauty I've got. That shell is tops."

Roxie grabbed a black bag from the counter. "I guess we're finished here."

Alva tugged on her shirt. "Where'd you find them shells? I'd like to get me some sweet abalones for sure. A wad of butter and a smack of garlic." He licked his lips.

"Go find them yourself," she snarled, walking to the corner to repack her shells.

Alva didn't miss a beat. "Right then. Say, Mr. Barnes. You got any cardboard boxes out back? Bobby said she'd show me and Paul how to make a rocket."

"Sure thing. Help yourself to whatever is out there."

"Be back in a jiff. I need an extra strong one for the life support systems." The old man hobbled out the back door.

Stew opened his mouth to answer, but Alva was gone. "His elevator doesn't quite reach the penthouse, does it?"

Ruth laughed. "Probably not, but I'm not convinced mine does, either. Maybe sanity is overrated."

He shrugged. "What can I do for you, Ruth?"

She held out the mashed gold band. "Can it be saved? Tell me it can, Stew. Please."

He turned the ring around, squinting at it from all angles. "Might be easier just to get a new one."

"I can't. It's my wedding band." She swallowed hard.

"Well, let me take it in the back and have a closer look. Be back in a minute."

Ruth wandered over to the glass counters. The pearl display was lovely. Pastel colored orbs nestled on satin set against iridescent abalone shells. The colors winked and shimmered in the sunlight that streamed through the window. She looked at the placard standing on an easel in the case. There was a picture of an enormous, misshapen white blob. The tiny writing underneath read *Pinctada maxima*, 14 lbs. The thing was the size of a small dog she used to own.

A voice startled her. "Now that's a big pearl," Dr. Soloski said.

He wore yet another jogging suit.

She nodded, peering again at the picture of the massive pearl. "Wouldn't work too well in a ring."

They stared at the luminous spread. "I've always kind of admired oysters, though." Dr. Soloski peered through his wire-rimmed glasses. "They take something bad, an irritation really, and make it into something wonderful. That's what a pearl is, a protective coating around an annoying bit of sand or grit."

Ruth looked at a teardrop-shaped pink pearl. "I never thought of it that way. It's amazing that someone would dive down and get these things from the bottom of the ocean. I sure wouldn't go to such trouble, even for a fourteen-pound pearl."

"Me neither. Diving is not for me."

Ruth looked up to see Roxie peering closely at the dentist. "They didn't have to dive far for those. Most of them are cultured pearls, a thin layer of nacre around a manmade center."

Stew emerged from the back in time to hear Roxie's comment. "There's nothing wrong with cultured pearls. Hello, Dr. Soloski. I've got your order ready. Would you like that gift wrapped?"

"That would be nice." Dr. Soloski followed Stew back to the counter. Ruth casually eased closer to watch Stew package a gold heart locket in a small box.

Dr. Soloski was buying someone a nice gift. Was it a love token? Had he finally succumbed to the not-so-subtle charms of Ellen? Or Maude? Her thoughts were interrupted when Alva barreled back into the store, hauling two enormous cardboard boxes.

"These are going to make a fine rocket. Hey. Who's the locket for? My auntie Mim had a necklace like that. Carried a picture of her wart in it. Looked just like Gerald Ford. The wart, not Auntie Mim."

Alva caught sight of Dr. Soloski and shrank back behind his cargo.

"Hello, Alva. Are you going to come and see me again soon? We've still got that cracked filling to take care of."

"I hear the phone ringing. Gotta go." Alva pushed out the door, knocking

Roxie's bag out of her hands in the process.

Ruth halted a rolling abalone shell with her foot. She helped Roxie pick up the half dozen bumpy runaways. They felt oddly light in her hands, the outsides rough and ugly, the insides an iridescent rainbow of colors. She marveled that God could create such a perfect beauty and hide it in the roughest of exteriors.

"These are so interesting, Roxie. Too bad Stew can't use them all. Did you get them from around here?"

"Yeah. I'm done, though. I've met my limit for the year."

"Really?"

"It's three per day maximum, twenty-four per year."

"That's pretty strict."

"Abalone grows slowly, and it's been exploited for commercial harvest. In the past people basically decimated the population and didn't leave enough stock to regenerate. Some species are practically extinct now."

Ruth watched Roxie close the bag. A suspicion crowded into her mind. "I guess some restaurants would pay top dollar for good abalone. That might encourage people to bend the rules a bit."

Roxie straightened, eyes narrowed. "I guess it might. But some of us have principles, no matter how broke we are. There are things in this world more precious than money." She shoved the door open and left.

Dr. Soloski finished his purchase and said good-bye.

Stew wrote up an order slip. "The good news is I can fix it. The bad news is it's gonna cost you fifty dollars and it will take a few days."

Relief swept through her like an ocean current. "Oh, thank you so much. I'm not in a hurry. Call me when you're ready for me to pick it up."

Outside the shop, Ruth felt suddenly exhausted and sank down on a bench on the sidewalk. The first hurdle of the day was behind her. She checked her watch. In half an hour came another hurdle that took the very breath out of her. It was all she could do to heave herself to her feet when Monk showed up. He kissed her twice, leaving her breathless.

"Ready, Ruthy?"

Her insides went cold. "No. No, I'm not ready. I can't do it. What if—?" She could not give voice to the fear.

He squeezed her hand. "No, what ifs. We will eat anything dished out to us."

She managed a faint laugh. "Is that a bit of catering wisdom?"

His wide face split into a grin. "Nah. That's navy."

"Really, though. I mean, it wouldn't be totally unexpected if, you know, there was something, not right. At my age and all." She looked at the scuffed toes of her walking shoes.

Monk stopped and turned to face her. "Now you listen to me. I don't want to hear any more of this 'at your age' talk. There's a reason that God blessed us with this at this time in our lives. He knows what He's doing. We are going to operate on the notion that this baby is in tiptop condition until we are told otherwise. If there is anything unusual to face, we will do it with His help." He resumed their march to the clinic, tucking her arm in his.

On the way she studied the set to his chin, marveling at how very blessed she was to have such a truly good man to love. He didn't fool her, though. The worry line between his brows spoke volumes. He'd been on edge about this doctor's appointment, too. It hadn't occurred to her to wonder about his fears and misgivings in the face of her own constant emotional ebb and flow. She squeezed his hand as they entered.

They waited an interminable amount of time, it seemed to Ruth, sandwiched in the holding area between Monk on one side and a young expectant mother on the other. Though she tried not to stare, she couldn't help but notice the woman's smooth face and her hand that lay across her belly. It was soft, unspotted, nicely manicured, and decorated with two rings. She read a magazine called *Yoga and You.*

Ruth tucked her own hands under her thighs. She would not dream of encasing her body in spandex and setting foot in an exercise class. Her bladder felt like a tightly stretched balloon. She whispered to her husband, "I drank all the water I was supposed to, but I've just got to go to the bathroom or I'm going to explode right here in this waiting room."

"Go ahead. I'll cover for you," Monk whispered back. "If anybody asks, I'll say you stepped out for a breath of fresh air."

When she got back, a smock-covered lady named Mai ushered them into a waiting room and helped Ruth don her putty gray hospital gown. Ruth lay on her back while the woman applied warm goo to her stomach and pressed a wand gently against her abdomen.

"Don't press too hard," Ruth advised. "Even though I snuck in a trip to the bathroom, I'm so full of water we might have a breach in the dam."

Mai smiled. "Don't worry, Ruth. I've seen plenty in this exam room. Just try to relax. This won't take long." She swiveled the wand around the vicinity of Ruth's belly button. Her brows drew together in concentration.

A full minute passed.

She lifted the instrument away and then pressed it again to Ruth's skin.

The frown increased and another minute crept by.

"What—what is it?" Ruth felt a cold fear clamp down on her heart. "Is there something wrong?"

Monk rose from his seat by the video screen. He gripped Ruth's hand so hard, he squashed her fingers together. "Tell us."

Mai put the wand on a paper and held up a finger, a bright smile on her face. "I need to get the doctor for a quick consult. Don't worry. Be right back." Mai scurried out the door.

The silence closed around them in a smothering blanket of fear. "Oh, Monk. There's something wrong." Her hands went icy cold.

He brushed the hair out of her face. "We don't know that. She's a technician but she's not allowed to comment on the ultrasound results. Didn't you tell me that? Even if, well, in no circumstance is she supposed to give her two cents."

Her head was too muddled to speak. She thought inexplicably of Cootchie, her pseudo granddaughter, and the moment, the one horrific moment, when she looked around and Cootchie was gone, snatched right from under her nose. Tears crowded the corner of her eyes. She fought hard to keep breathing.

The door opened. Dr. Ing glided in on rubber-soled shoes. "Hello, folks. I can feel a hot summer ahead, can't you?"

All Ruth could feel was the gathering winds of a bitter winter. "Is the baby okay?"

Dr. Ing peered at the screen as he passed the wand from side to side. His eyes widened almost imperceptibly. He put the wand down and slid off his rubber gloves. "I can't believe we missed it."

His look was compassionate, but she could not see it clearly through her tears.

11

J une afternoons in Finny would be perfect, Jack thought, if people would
just take a break from sin and let the police have some time off. He sipped
coffee from a travel mug and appreciated the brilliant sunlight as he drove
toward Mrs. Hodges's house. Already since the butterfly tea ended, he'd corralled
a menacing dog and discouraged a resident from building an eight-foot brick wall
to keep nosy neighbors at bay.

His eyes wandered to the red tissue-paper flower that festooned the rearview
mirror, Bobby's little joke. He wondered again why he couldn't say those three
words she needed to hear. *Why is that so infernally hard for you, Jack? Let go of
Lacey. She's dead, and she would have wanted you and Paul to move on.*

His head told him it was true, but his heart, or his conscience, would not
sign on. So much for mind over matter. "God, help me, please. I'm making a mess
of things down here." His prayer was cut short as he pulled up to Mrs. Hodges's
cottage.

Alva met him at the front drive. His white hair stuck up from his scalp like
fluffy icebergs. "It's a heinous crime, a traverstine of justice. They coulda been
lying in wait. I coulda been murdered in my sleep or maybe tied up and smuggled
to Barbados to work as a slave."

Jack held up a calming hand. "Let's just slow down here, Alva. What's the
problem?"

"I done been burgled. Someone busted into my room and went through my
stuff."

"What was taken?"

"Nothin'. But that ain't the point."

Mrs. Hodges lumbered over, her round faced etched with concern. "Good
afternoon, Jack. Come in for some cookies. I just took some out of the oven. Alva,
would you go ahead and put some napkins on the table?"

With a grumble, the old man shuffled off.

She took Jack's arm as they headed into the house. "I thought Alva was just
off on one of his tangents, but this time I think he's right."

Jack raised an eyebrow. "You think someone broke in?"

She nodded, setting her jowls wobbling. "They tried to, anyway. Come and
have a look."

Jack forced himself to walk past the pan of still-warm cookies in the kitchen, the aroma making his mouth water. Mrs. Hodges escorted them into Alva's room, a small whitewashed space that looked out on her prodigious vegetable garden, jammed with clusters of tomatoes just beginning to show color, and several zucchini plants decorated with showy yellow blossoms.

Alva scuttled by them and sat on his tidy bed, arms folded.

Jack noted a small wooden writing desk stacked with newspaper clippings and comic books. A crate at the foot of the bed held the rusty can opener and a hodgepodge of other dubious treasures.

"So, er, how do you know someone's been in here, Alva?"

Alva glared at the detective. "It's obvious, ain't it? Them books on my shelf been moved, and the dust under the bed's been stirred around."

Mrs. Hodges pinked. "I promised Alva when he came to live here that I wouldn't intrude on his privacy so the cleaning is up to him." She fanned her cheeks with a hand. "I can tell you there's no dust under any of the other beds in this house."

"Right." Jack peeked under the bed frame and scrutinized the bookshelf. "Alva, are you sure you didn't, uh, just look at some books and maybe forget you'd done it? Or maybe Mr. Hodges—" His voice trailed off at the ire kindling in the old man's eyes.

"Number first, I ain't prone to forgetting things, and number second, I ain't touched one of them books in all the years I done lived here."

Mrs. Hodges nodded. "He prefers comic books. And Mr. Hodges is out of town on a fishing trip. He doesn't go into Alva's room anyway."

Jack went outside to peer at the window that was open halfway. Alva trotted along at his heels. There was no sign of a forced entry. "Did you have it locked?"

Alva snorted. "Locked? What fer?"

Jack sighed. Mrs. Hodges pointed to the ground. There was no imprint of a foot, but she directed his attention to an overturned pot, pressed down into the earth.

"Someone needed a boost. That pot was right side up yesterday, with a new pepper plant in it."

Jack continued to scan the ground and windowsill for any telltale marks. "The guy or gal was careful anyway. What time do you guess they had access?"

Alva spoke up. "They came when I was out digging for treasure, I'll bet. I was gone from about seven to ten thirty. Then I spent the night at Petey's cuz it was Boy Scout camping night, so I didn't notice it until just now when I got back from walkin' Ruth to the jewelry store."

Mrs. Hodges nodded. "I didn't notice it either, but late night seems most likely. I was at a FLOP meeting until around then. I know it definitely happened before eleven."

"Why?"

TREASURE UNDER FINNY'S NOSE

"I finished up watching the shopping network about then and let him into the garden."

"Who?"

"Pedro."

Jack couldn't restrain a nervous glance over his shoulder.

"It's okay." She patted the detective on the arm. "Pedro only has access to the yard during the night. He's in Mr. Peterman's field during the day doing weed control. Otherwise that goat would have mowed down any trespasser and chewed him into little bits."

Alva nodded, rubbing his knee thoughtfully. "I still got a piece missing from the last time Pedro waylaid me on my trip to the mail box."

Jack smiled. "Everyone who has ever met that goat has lost a part or two. It couldn't have been Pedro that upended the pot and ruined your pepper?"

Mrs. Hodges shook her head. "Pedro can't stand peppers."

Alva cackled. "Human flesh is more to his taste."

Jack nodded. "You're sure there's nothing missing?"

Alva shook his head. "Nah. Just some stuff moved around, kinda." His shaggy eyebrows drew together. "If I hadn'ta hidden my treasures, the burglar would have made off with a fortune."

Jack followed Mrs. Hodges and Alva into the kitchen. "What treasures are we talking about here, Alva?"

Alva settled himself into a chair and tucked a checked napkin around his neck. His voice dropped to a whisper.

"My jar of glass marbles is over at Bubby Dean's place. They'd be after that fer sure. And Ruth's got my baloney shell and a box of old coins I found on the beach. My collection of newspaper clippings is hidden in the fake potted plant at the library, but Big Foots don't know it. Good thing I spread 'em out, otherwise I'da lost it all."

Jack held up his coffee cup for Mrs. Hodges to fill. "Definitely a good thing. Has anyone been interested in your treasures lately? Asking questions, things like that?"

Alva jammed a cookie into his mouth, chewing carefully. "Nah, but I been pretty busy keeping track of Ruth and all. I'm her ninny, uh, nanny."

Jack and Mrs. Hodges exchanged a smile as the lady filled Jack's plate.

"Ya know," Alva said, eyes rolling around. "If I'da been home when he busted in, I might be dead now. He mighta conked me over the head and I'd be too dead to be eatin' these cookies now."

"Is anything disturbed in the rest of the house?" Jack tasted the gooey chocolate chip cookie. He would never take handouts or kickbacks, but it would be a sin to refuse a neighborly offer, especially from Mrs. Hodges, the best cook in the county.

"No, nothing else. I'm glad Mr. Hodges is going to be home today. I never would have thought someone would break into our house." She sat heavily in the chair, causing the floor to tremble. "Then again, I never would have thought someone would murder that poor cameraman, either."

Alva took a gulp of coffee. "Never say never."

~~~~~~~~

Jack drove Alva to the police station so he could give a statement. It wasn't strictly necessary, as Jack could take one just as well from the cottage, but Alva was not going to be cheated out of his experience. The old man made sure to fill his pockets with change to use the station's vending machine.

"Best M&M's in Finny in yer machine," he said. "It's on account of the patina of terror that paints this place. The air is plumb filled with the aura of desperation from all of these hardened criminal types."

Jack raised an eyebrow. "Have you been watching a lot of television lately?"

He nodded. "*Masterpiece Theater*. Oh, just looky there. A desperate citizen, right in front of our noses." He made straight for Maude, who sat on a chair in the reception area with her ankle cast propped on a chair.

"Hey, Maude. Whatcha doin?"

She looked up from the book she was reading. "Not that it's any of your business, but I'm here to ask Jack to execute an investigation."

Jack forced himself to ask. "What kind of investigation?"

"I think we should check into Ellen's past, see what sins she has buried under that self-righteous facade. The more I think about it, the more convinced I am that she's not who she says she is." Her black eyes gleamed in her tiny face.

"We don't investigate citizens unless there's a good reason, Maude. Now if you'll excuse me, I've got to go."

Maude shot to her feet. "There is a good reason. She's poking around in other people's business all the time, as if she was collecting information or spying."

Alva laughed. "Sounds just like you, Maude."

She shot him a look of pure acid. "Stay out of it, you old goat."

Alva folded his scrawny arms. "It's clear as icicles that yer jealous 'cuz Ellen is tryin' to get her hooks into that dentist fella."

Maude colored. "Oh, fiddlesticks. That's ridiculous."

"I ain't thinkin' so."

She snorted. "You don't waste any time thinking, do you?"

A sly look crossed Alva's face. "I'm all wet, huh? Then I guess you ain't interested in what the doctor was buyin' at the jewelry store 'round lunchtime today. A real pretty thing, he bought, a romantic type thing."

Jack barely suppressed a smile at the change on Maude's face. Hooked like a trout, he thought.

"I'm not interested, no." She grabbed her purse and took a step to the door.

"But Ellen probably already knows because she's a bigger snoop than you."

Alva chuckled. "Maybe. Or maybe she knows because he done gave the gold heart locket to her. Wouldn't that be something?"

Maude's expression kindled a surge of guilt in Jack. There was a sadness and vulnerability there that he had never seen before. For the first time he realized how lonely it might be for Maude. *Forgive me, Lord, for judging.* He summoned the words of Romans 14:10 in his mind. *"You, then, why do you judge your brother? Or why do you look down on your brother? For we will all stand before God's judgment seat."* And the Lord already knew he had plenty to answer for. "Maybe we can talk later, Maude, after I'm done with Alva."

She waved a hand at him as she stumped away. "You're wasting your time with that geezer. He won't help you catch anything but a cold."

Maude left and Alva toddled away to stock up on candy. Jack said a hello to Nate and Mary, who were both keeping company in the coffee room until Maude left.

Nate looked around Jack's shoulder. "Is it safe to come out now?"

"Yes. Maude's gone. Can you take Alva's statement?"

"I'll do it." Before Mary cleared the door she stopped. "Oh, I almost forgot to tell you something I found out about our cameraman."

"The dead one or the living one?"

"Reggie, not Ethan. He's got a local connection."

Jack waited for her to finish.

"He got busted for some petty theft stuff along with a kid named Eddie Seevers."

Jack's brow furrowed. "Okay. What's the connection?"

"Eddie Seevers was Roxie Trotter's son."

"Was?"

"Drug overdose five years ago."

Nate tapped his mustache. "Five years? Isn't that about the time Roxie came to Finny?"

Jack sighed. "I guess I'm on my way to visit Ms. Trotter, then." He headed back out to the car. *But I can spare a few minutes to stop by Monk's for a cup of coffee,* he thought, crossing his fingers that a certain lady would be there to pour it for him.

Bobby was there, but she was up to her elbows in dough. Even worse, Jack noticed, she was deep in conversation with Ethan Ping. He tried to tamp down the irritation that flared in his gut as he took his coffee to a table. Sandra Marconi sat nearby, soaking in the sunshine that poured through the glass window.

She gazed out at the glittering expanse of ocean that was visible down slope from the coffee shop.

"Hello, Ms. Marconi. How goes the filming?"

She jumped, almost spilling her tea. "Filming? Oh, er, fine. Thanks for asking."

"Are you finding it hard to work without your official cameraman?"

"No. Ethan is great with a camera."

"How is he with salvage work?"

She blinked. "What?"

"Underwater salvage, for historical artifacts and such."

"I, uh, I don't know. We've never done that before. Why do you ask?"

He let the silence linger for a moment. "Reggie did some questionable recovery work, so I wondered if Ethan was in on it."

She blanched. "No. He's here to direct a film for our project, that's all. I've got to go." She hopped out of her seat and went to the door.

Darting a quick look in Jack's direction, Ethan said good-bye to Bobby and followed Sandra out.

Jack approached the counter. Before he could speak, Bobby shot him a look.

"Scaring away our customers, Detective?"

"Not at all, just having a friendly conversation, like you were with him."

She opened her mouth to reply when the phone rang. "Monk's Coffee and Catering." After a second her eyes widened. "Okay. Okay, yes, I'll come over right now. Are you at home? Okay, I'll close up here this minute." She stood with the phone dangling from her fingers.

Jack took the receiver gently and hung it up. "What is it, Bobby? What's wrong?"

"That was Uncle Monk. They just met with the doctor. I need to go."

12

Monk went to find Ruth a drink of water while she pulled her clothes on with shaking fingers. She made it to the hallway and slid into a chair, chin on hands, and let the cool air bathe her heated face.

Her insides felt like the tiny seeds of a dandelion, blown in all directions by a careless wind.

"Hello, Ruth."

She looked up to find Roxie, emerging from a room a few doors down.

"Hi, Roxie." Her voice trembled only a little.

Roxie pulled on her knit cap and looked at Ruth for a minute, before sinking into a chair next to her. "Looks like you're having a bad day."

"I—" Ruth clamped her mouth shut to avoid bursting into tears.

Roxie sighed. "I've been there."

Ruth noticed a square of white tape on the woman's arm. She swallowed hard. "Are you okay?"

"Sure, sure. I get regular blood tests because my kidney is failing."

Ruth was temporarily jerked from her malaise. "Oh, I'm so sorry to hear that."

"It's okay. I've gotten used to the idea. Normally I go to a hospital in San Francisco. They've got a specialist there who is determined to keep me alive, in spite of all the given facts." She fingered the tape. "I had an appointment in the city yesterday. Saw Dr. Soloski there. I don't know what his problem is, but our paths cross a lot at that hospital."

Ruth pressed the balled-up tissue to her nose again.

Roxie gave her a sidelong look. "Say, if you'd rather be alone. . ."

"No, no. I–I've just had a shock, is all. It's—it's. . .twins." Saying the words aloud almost sent her into a shower of tears again.

"Twins?" Roxie smiled. "Oh boy. Double blessing, huh?"

"I know that's what I should be feeling. Twins are a miracle, an amazing special gift times two. I should be on my knees thanking God, but all I can think of is, how will I cope?"

The words gathered momentum and flew out in a steady stream. "I'm going to be forty-nine, and I didn't do a good job the first time I had a child. I spoiled him, sheltered him from disappointments so he never learned how to deal with them. And now—" She swallowed a tide of rising panic.

"Not me," Roxie said. "I was a perfect mother. I was patient, but firm. I had rules and plenty of structure with time left over for fun. As both the mother and dad I was great, even if I do say so." She handed Ruth another tissue. "You know what? My son turned out to be a screw-up, and eventually his choices got the better of him and they are getting the better of me an inch at a time. He couldn't keep away from trouble and it killed him, just like it killed Reggie."

Ruth straightened, wondering at the connection between Roxie's son and the dead cameraman.

Roxie gazed at the worn tiles on the floor. "It killed me, too, really, only my death is taking awhile longer." She shook her head. "Anyway, the thing is, Ruth, I couldn't have loved him more if he'd turned out to be the president of the United States instead of a deadbeat."

She stood. "Funny, isn't it? It doesn't really matter who they are or what they decide to be, or even how many in the batch. Mothers love their children in spite of everything. Where did we learn how to do that, I wonder?"

Roxie patted Ruth on the shoulder and left, as Monk arrived, puffing, with a bottle of water.

~~~

They walked back to the cottage in relative silence. Monk's expression changed alternately from wonder to abject fear. Several times he started to speak but sputtered into silence. He settled for gripping her hand firmly in his, as if she might fly away if he let go.

She couldn't keep her mind on any practical thought. It kept spinning back to the incredible truth: twins. The writhing bundle of kicks and pokes was the project of two babies. Two. She had to rest for a minute to stop the spinning in her head.

They'd made it several blocks when Alva caught up with them. "Oh sakes," he said, wringing his cap between his hands. "I was at the hospital getting me some of that free coffee when I done heard the news." He panted and pressed a hand over his heart. "Don't let it worry you none. Even if it comes out with scales and a tail we'll love it, you'll see."

Monk gaped at him. "What are you talking about?"

"The baby. I heard it's gonna have fins, but don't you pay it no mind. My cousin Swannie had webbed toes and we didn't respect her none the less. Besides she was an expert at the swimmin' pool. We'll love the little bun in Ruth's oven, fins or no fins."

Ruth felt a swell of laughter building. She managed a quick, "Twins, not fins," before she started to laugh.

Alva blinked. "Twins? Ain't that what they call a pair?" He pointed to her stomach. "Two of them in that compartment?"

She nodded, giggles escaping like spurts of steam. Monk began to guffaw, too, until all three of them roared with laughter.

Alva wiped his eyes. "Well, that's a relief, ain't it? I'll just go back to the hospital and tell 'em they made an error. Whew. I thought we was goin' to have to keep it in an aquarium."

Ruth and Monk got the hysterical laughter out of their systems by the time they made it home. Bobby and Jack were waiting on the front step when they arrived. Both shot to their feet and stood awkwardly. Then Bobby wrapped Ruth in an enormous hug, and Jack pumped Monk's hand vigorously before they all entered the sitting room.

"I can't believe it," Jack said. "Twins. Amazing."

"My sentiments exactly." Monk's wide face was still pale. "I don't believe there's a propensity for doubles in either of our families that we know of."

Ruth took the steaming cup of tea gratefully from Bobby's hand.

"Aunt Ruth, is everything. . .all right with the babies?"

She inhaled the herbal steam for a moment, willing it to sooth her jangled nerves. "Yes, they are perfectly fine, as far as Dr. Ing can tell. One is a little small, but not abnormally so." She read the question on Bobby's face. "We decided not to know the gender."

Jack smiled. "Going for the surprise finish. I like it."

Monk smiled back. "It seems like we've had a big enough surprise for one day."

The look Monk gave Ruth was so tender it made her want to start crying again. Instead she changed the subject. "Jack, how is the investigation going?"

"Nowhere fast. There is some question about the folks funding this historical project." He shot Bobby a look. "And Reggie was a man who lived on the fringes, that's for sure."

Ruth recalled the strange comment from Roxie. "Have you, er, found out if Reggie was working with anyone besides the college people?"

Jack gave her a sharp look. "Why?"

"Oh, just something Roxie said about her son, comparing him to Reggie. It just struck me as odd."

"Odd for sure. Her son, Eddie Seevers, was in trouble on and off. Some of it with Reggie. Small time, mostly."

"Jack, what happened to Eddie?"

"He died. Lost a kidney as a complication from drug use, and his mother gave him one of hers. Died of an OD."

Ruth sighed. The pain must be unbearable for poor Roxie. "At least she can breathe easy knowing Eddie wasn't responsible for what happened to Reggie."

"He's in the clear for sure." Jack jammed his hands into his pockets.

"You sound doubtful," Monk said.

Bobby laughed. "I think he's always a little doubtful."

"It's just a question of who knew whom. Eddie knew Reggie before the guy was strangled. So did Roxie, and she never mentioned it to me. That's a pretty big omission."

Monk nodded in agreement. "Yes, can't exactly blame that on forgetfulness. Any luck tracing that knot?"

Jack shook his head. "No."

In spite of the shiver in the pit of her stomach, Ruth could not suppress a yawn. "I'm so sorry. This day is catching up with me."

Jack and Bobby gave her a hug, and Bobby whispered in her ear, "It's going to be okay, Aunt Ruth. We'll be here with you every step of the way."

Too overcome with emotion to speak, Ruth squeezed her hand.

The house settled into quiet. Monk busied himself wiping down the kitchen counters, taking out the trash, and dusting until Ruth couldn't stand it anymore. "Monk. Stop. Please just stop and tell me this is going to be okay."

He stood frozen for a moment. Then he came over to the sofa where she sat and knelt next to her. "Ruthy, I'll be perfectly honest and tell you the idea of having a pair of babies gave me a turn. To think, two to hold and juggle around, and the bills—" His gaze became unfocused.

Her eyes started to fill. "I know. I can't believe it. At our age. What are we going to do?"

He blinked. "Do? We should take action to prepare."

"How do you prepare for this exactly?"

"We're going to start by making a list right now." He fetched a pencil and began writing. "Two cribs for sure." His brow crinkled. "Is it two cribs, Ruth? Or do you just kind of stack them in one?"

She gave him a look of complete exasperation. "I have no idea."

"Okay. I'll put a question mark next to that one. Two car seats and sets of bottles. How about strollers? Do they make two-seaters, or do you get singles and strap a couple of them together?"

She squeezed her eyes shut. "Lord, help us. We are in double trouble."

Monk grabbed his keys and gave her a peck on the cheek. "I better go buy a book about this twin stuff. I'll be back soon."

Ruth spent the evening fluttering from one thing to the next like a hyperactive bee, accomplishing nothing of consequence. She heard Bryce come home after eight, hair tousled from time spent at the beach. Monk was still gone, trying to catch up on the catering work he'd fallen behind on due to their doctor's appointment. She lay in the bed, too tired even to get up and see if her son needed anything. The slam of his bedroom door told her he was still brooding about things. She knew firsthand how difficult it was to disentangle two lives. Roslyn was removing herself from Bryce's life as effectively as Phillip's death had removed him from hers. She'd never thought of divorce in that light before. It was like a death, in a way.

Divorce. The word sent a shudder through her spine. What would she do if Monk left? How would she cope without him? Alone, with two babies. What if the strain of having an instant houseful sent him over the edge?

Desperate to take her mind off the future, she grabbed the notebook from the bed stand and flipped it open. Indigo's life was much more fun to think about than her own at the moment.

The spring has been a mild one, praise God. The twisted pear tree outside my tent has a promising collection of buds. I have tagged each blossom with the name of a miner who will pay two dollars and fifty cents for the chance to have his own pear when summer comes. It makes Hui laugh to see the paper tags dancing in the wind, festooning the branches like dozens of kites.

In the afternoons, sometimes, if the sun is shining, we hunt for mushrooms. Hui knows which ones can be eaten and he has shown me how to dry them along with some seaweed he collected. I do not know what we will concoct with these exotic ingredients, but it eases my mind to know that we have started to collect some bits of food against the harsher winter weather which will come.

Hui has shown me something that may help us save enough to buy a little shop someday. He told me about something called a Hangtown Fry. It was hard to understand him at first, but I surmised it to be a type of dish made of an egg scramble with bacon and oysters mixed in. They call it egg foo yung in his country, but here it is a delicacy. The men are quite willing to pay two dollars a plate for it. Two dollars! Hui swims like a minnow, so he dives along the edge of the surf and pries the oysters from the bottom. If he cannot reach the oysters, we use abalone instead and the men seem just as happy. Though it terrifies me to watch his dark head disappear under the water, he is thrilled beyond measure when he hands over the lumpy oysters and whatever abalone he can find.

We pry them open and he crushes the shells to add to the glittering walkway that leads from our tent to the beach. Twice now he has even found a pearl. They are irregularly shaped and oddly colored so there is no sense to sell them. It brings me greater joy to see how he likes to keep them in his pocket, taking them out now and then when the men aren't around to see them shine in the sun.

Hui sees treasure in things that other people take for rubbish. To think that Señor Orson worked so hard for his treasure and lost his life in

*the process while we reap riches tossed up from the ocean straight from the
fingers of God.*

*I have heard that we are lucky to have so many oysters and abalone to
make our Hangtown Fry. The miners in areas farther south have stripped
all the good-sized beds. All the better for us as the rare traveler to these
parts will pay handsomely for his supper, too.*

Ruth closed the notebook when the phone rang.

"Hello, Mrs. Budge?"

"Yes, hi, Sandra."

"Hi. Um, I was wondering if you could tell me if there's a convenience store
anywhere close by? Everything seems closed up tight."

She checked the clock to find it was almost nine. "That's Finny for you. We roll
up the sidewalks at six o'clock. You'd have to drive to the next town for a convenience
store open at this hour. Is there something I can help you with?"

"Oh, uh, no, not really. I just needed some disinfectant and gauze."

"Are you hurt?"

"No, no. Ethan is scraped a little."

"Scraped? What happened?"

"We were out walking, and he fell and cut himself on some metal."

"Really? Does he need stitches? There's a hospital right off Whist Street. They
can fix him up there."

"Ethan is kind of private. He doesn't want to make a big deal out of it. Never
mind, Ruth. It's not that important."

"Why don't you come over here? I've got bandages and gauze. Please. I'd be
happy to help out."

Sandra hesitantly agreed. Ruth threw on some clothes. When Sandra arrived
fifteen minutes later, her cheeks were pink from the walk.

Ruth looked around. "You didn't bring Ethan with you?"

"Ah, no. I told you he's really private. I'll just take the supplies back over and
clean him up."

"Are you sure he isn't going to need some stitches?"

"No, no. He's fine."

Bryce came into the kitchen and greeted them. Ruth explained the situation.

"Who would think taking a walk was so hazardous?" Sandra laughed nervously.

"What did he cut himself on?"

Sandra shrugged. "A drainpipe, I think. Sticking up from the ground. Can
you believe it?" She grabbed the supplies and thanked Ruth again before she
scurried out the door.

Bryce frowned. "You know, Mom, an hour ago I was walking down by the
cliffs."

She waited for him to continue.

"Funny thing, but I saw two people suiting up for a dive."

"A dive? At night? Who were they?"

"I couldn't see the guy real well, but I recognized the girl all right."

Her own face pulled into a puzzled frown. "Sandra Marconi?"

"Uh-huh, and I sure never heard of anyone taking a walk wearing a wet suit."

R uth spent Saturday in a blur of activity. She felt the urgent need to cook, clean, garden, whatever would help her prepare her mind and house for the arrival of the babies. She didn't remember eating, or the sporadic visits from her husband. There was only work and the eventual collapse into bed at an insanely early hour.

She woke the next morning in a mass of twisted sheets, her body covered with cold sweat. Her eyes flew open. Twins. It hadn't been a dream. She clamped her lids shut and tried to take a couple of deep breaths. When she opened them again, the frightening fact remained: She was still pregnant with not one baby but two.

How did one even birth two babies, let alone raise them? Maybe Monk had the right idea. She should start reading every book she could on this wild and scary topic. *No,* she thought firmly. With Bryce she'd read every book ever penned on the subject, and all that did was make her feel inferior. She was going to let God handle things this time and hope it all turned out better. What did God do with His children? He loved them unconditionally. He did not spare them from disappointment and sorrow, but He guided them through the pain. She thought about Roxie.

"Mothers love their children in spite of everything. Where did we learn how to do that, I wonder?" Ruth knew. There was only one model of perfect love.

She felt a surge of confidence. "I can do this," she said aloud. "I can raise two babies."

Climbing out of bed, she enjoyed the fleeting moment of peace. Then she went into the bathroom and threw up.

On her way to the kitchen, an iridescent flutter of color caught her eye. It was Alva's abalone shell, winking against the flood of morning light. She picked it up, thinking of Indigo and her glittering path of crushed oysters and abalone. The thought pleased her. Treasures tossed up from the fingers of God. Absently she stowed the shell into her purse to return it to Alva before the hapless Carson showed up to wreak more havoc on the house.

After a breakfast of dry toast and weak tea she composed herself enough to make it to church, where she slid into the seat Monk saved for her. "How are things at the restaurant?" she whispered in his ear.

"Fine, just fine." His eyes rolled in thought. "Say, Ruth, do you think we ought to consider having a bathroom added onto the house? I mean, aren't we going to need two of everything? Maybe we could squeeze in double sinks, but they'll just have to share a shower. No way we can fit in two of those."

The look she gave him must have blasted the idea away because he cleared his throat and patted her hand. "Um, never mind. We'll talk about that later."

The news had already spread throughout the congregation. Even Pastor Henny exclaimed over the miracle from his spot at the podium. The attendees cheered for Ruth and Monk as if they were rooting for a basketball team. Ruth's face flushed, and she tried to sneak out after the service.

She was waylaid by people offering their best wishes and folks reaching out to touch her stomach. Feeling more like a parade float than a parishioner, she finally made it to the parking lot. Monk kissed her and offered to drive her home before opening the shop.

"No thanks. I could use a walk to clear my head." Then she started to giggle.

"What's so funny?"

"I was just thinking it's a good thing Alva didn't persuade everyone the babies were going to come out with fins."

He chuckled as he drove away.

Ruth strolled along the tree-lined sidewalk, oblivious to the clumps of rhododendron that provided a shelter for dozens of small birds. Her thoughts ran in anxious circles. Twins. How many bottles would she need for two babies? Would their car be big enough for a pair of car seats? High chairs! They only had the old wooden one of Bryce's. Did they make double seater high chairs now?

She groaned. "I'm beginning to sound like Monk." To avoid driving herself completely crazy, Ruth turned her energy to Indigo's writing. One line in particular danced in her head. *Señor Orson worked so hard for his treasure and lost his life in the process.* What could the treasure be? It must have been some valuable treasure indeed that Orson was willing to book passage on an overloaded coal ship instead of waiting for a proper steamer.

Curiosity drove her to the library, with only a quick stop to snack on the ever-present crackers she carried in her purse. Sundays were the best day to visit the library, as Ellen wouldn't be in until afternoon, leaving more genial volunteers to run the place in her absence.

Ruth sat at the computer, removing the abalone shell from her purse when it poked her in the side, and did an Internet search on lost treasure. She found several entries about rock bands she'd never heard of, a perfume guaranteed to "turn the wearer into the queen of her destiny," and many articles about shipwrecks. With a sigh she turned her focus to Indigo's more practical treasure, typing in *Hangtown Fry*. The old computer was still stuck in think mode when a voice made her jump.

"As you can see, I run a tight ship here. No book out of place, no lights on unnecessarily. Every bit of paper recycled, and ink cartridges as well." Ellen stopped when she saw Ruth at the computer. "What are you doing here on a Sunday?"

A weary-looking Dr. Soloski stood just behind her, still wearing his suit from church. "Hello, Mrs. Budge."

"Hello, folks. I didn't expect to see you today, Ellen. I was just doing a little research."

Ellen fisted a hand on her hip. "I see. And what is the topic du jour? Anything you need help with?" She snatched up the shell. "What's this?"

Ruth felt suddenly embarrassed. "It's Alva's shell."

The doctor smiled. "Ah. I thought it looked familiar."

Ellen gave a ferocious snort. "You've seen one shell, you've seen them all." Her eyes swiveled back to Dr. Soloski.

He looked at Ruth as though he were a drowning man asking for a life preserver.

Ruth began to babble. "Oh, well, this shell is really nice. It's smaller than the other abalone, and it doesn't weigh very much." She decided to change the topic. "Dr. Soloski, Roxie said she saw you at the hospital in San Francisco. I hope everything is all right."

His eyebrows shot up. "Oh yes. Everything is fine, thank you for asking. I go there weekly to visit Jane."

Ellen's eyes narrowed. "Jane?"

"My sister. She's been disabled since birth. I became her caretaker when my mother died five years ago. I brought her a locket."

"Ohhh." Ellen patted his shoulder, relief shining across her face. "Such a good son. Jane is so lucky to have a brother like you." She returned her attention to Ruth. "You enjoy your research," she said, taking Dr. Soloski by the arm. "I'm sure you'll be an expert in no time. Just remember, you don't get pearls from abalone." She laughed again, the sound echoing through the quiet library.

Dr. Soloski shot her a rueful look as he was dragged away.

The computer finally finished its cyber cogitation and the screen popped up with several articles on the infamous Hangtown Fry. True to Indigo's description, the dish was indeed a scramble of eggs, bacon, and oysters. One tale about the recipe attributed it to a condemned man who requested the dish for his last meal, figuring the difficulty in acquiring the rare ingredients would provide him a stay of execution.

"I wonder if it worked for him," Ruth muttered. Sadly, she noted, the shellfish were such a hit, many of the oyster beds were depleted by 1851. Abalone suffered the same fate. Another case where humans had disrupted God's careful balance.

A kick from her belly button region spurred her to turn off the computer, pack up Alva's shell, and head to the stacks. She grabbed a couple of books on Pacific Coast ocean life and one about famous shipwrecks before she sat down to read. Settled in the sunny corner on a padded chair, Ruth made it all the way to page two before she fell asleep.

She awoke an hour later with just enough time to scurry home, unload the bulky shell from her purse, grab the relevant pages from Indigo's life story, and make it to the beach for rehearsal. As she hurried up the path to the film site, Maude waved from her position at the head of a half dozen gray-haired ladies. Ruth tried to dodge in the other direction, but it was no use.

"And this is Ruth Budge. She's a feature actor in the project." Maude beamed. "As you can see, she's expecting. Twins, can you believe it? At her age. Though she's sick all the time and obviously bloated, she shows up nonetheless. She's an inspiration to us all. Ruth, won't you share a few words with my tour group?"

Ruth wanted to share a few choice words all right, but she managed to control her temper. "It's been a very interesting project. Thanks so much for coming." She tried to edge by a disappointed-looking Maude.

"Oh, come now," Maude said. "No time for modesty. Ruth is also somewhat of a sleuth. I'm sure you heard about the murder at the Fog Festival? The balloon crash?"

The gaggle of women nodded, wide-eyed.

"Well, Ruth here was the one who solved the crime. With plenty of help, of course, not a little of which came from yours truly. Isn't that right, Ruth?"

She gave Maude a dark look. "I'd rather not relive it, thank you."

"And then there is the body of Reggie the cameraman tossed up on our gravelly shore only days ago. The police are very close lipped but there's no doubt it's"—Maude dropped her voice to a whisper—"murder."

The word elicited gasps from the ladies.

"And once again here is our Ruth Budge, deep in the thick of it. How does that make you feel, Ruth?"

She sighed. "The only thing I feel at the moment is queasy. Enjoy your visit." She dodged around Maude and headed to Ethan and Sandra, who sat at a card table going over some papers. "Who knew you'd have tour groups coming to see your project before it was even finished?"

Ethan sniffed. "Who indeed? I told them they had to stay back at the edge of the grassy area and so far they're following orders."

He wore long pants so Ruth could not see where he had been injured. "Ethan, are you okay? Sandra told me you cut yourself last night."

He nodded at her. "Yes, I'm fine. Thanks for asking."

"Great." She thought out her words before she dropped them. "You know, my son was out for a jog last night, and he saw you two ready to dive. Were you doing some photography for the project?"

Ethan's eyes widened and Sandra's mouth fell open. "No," he said firmly. "We weren't diving. Your son must have been mistaken."

"Hmm. Night diving is such a bad idea, nobody around here would try such a thing. Bryce was pretty convinced it was you two."

His dark eyes bored into hers. "Of course it wasn't us. Diving at night is ludicrous, as we learned the hard way with Reggie. Must have been some tourists or something." He shuffled his papers and smiled at her. "Let's get to work, shall we? We wouldn't want to disappoint our tour group." He gestured to the gaggle of women who smiled and waved at him.

Sandra walked her over to the shelter of some eucalyptus where they had erected a shack to represent Indigo's hideaway. She helped Ruth slip on a blousy tunic and rough boots. Ruth noticed Sandra's hands shaking. "So it really wasn't you and Ethan diving last night?"

Sandra jerked as if she'd been slapped. "No, no. Just what he said, we were walking. It's nice here for walking." She fiddled with the tie on Ruth's tunic. "A lovely town, even at night."

Ruth considered. "You know I've been reading my script and it seems Señor Orson had some kind of treasure on board the *Triton* when it went down." Ruth eyed her closely.

Sandra blinked several times. "Treasure? Oh yes, we caught that reference. Here's your hat."

"What do you think it was?"

"What?"

"Señor Orson's treasure. What do you think it was?"

Sandra attempted a smile. "Beats me. Could be figurative. Maybe he was referring to his wife. It could have been an heirloom that meant something only to him. You know what they say, one man's trash is another man's treasure. I'll go tell Ethan you're ready."

As Ruth waited for Sandra to return, she watched the afternoon sun catch bits of metallic sparkle in the crushed rock under her feet. She tried to picture the spot as it had looked in the 1800s, with the glittering pathway of broken oyster shells. Sandra was right, one man's trash was another man's treasure, but she was more and more convinced that Sandra and Ethan were in search of something more precious than a historical reenactment. She resolved to keep her ears open for more information.

They worked through the scene several times. At the end of the session, Sandra helped her remove the costume. "Good work today, Mrs. Budge. We should be able to wrap up in the next few days."

"Really? So soon?"

"Yes. We've decided to abridge the project a little." She fingered the costume's worn material. "Actually, we should probably get the script back from you so we can go over it and see if there's anything we missed."

"Don't you have a copy?"

"Oh, well, sure we do, but we've made notes on both and it's just good practice to be thorough. Right?"

"Of course. I'll bring the whole thing back tomorrow."

"I'm going to be out later today. I'd be happy to come by and get it."

Ruth smiled sweetly. "No need, Sandra. I'll bring it tomorrow." *Right after I read every word of it.*

Ruth met Monk and Bryce that evening for dinner. She hadn't had time that afternoon to finish the script since Carson arrived to replace the ravaged sheetrock. Though he was a small man with a wild mop of curly black hair, he made more noise than a high school football team.

A knock at the door just after six made her jump, but Monk only smiled. "Excellent. They really do deliver quick." A uniformed man stood on the doorway chomping on a wad of gum. He handed Monk a clipboard.

Monk scrawled his signature and the parade of packages began. A massive carton with a picture of two blissful babies sleeping side by side in a crib came first, followed by two car seats, two inflatable baby bathtubs, and a pair of bouncy seats.

Monk beamed as he arranged the wall of boxes in the middle of the sitting room. "Take a look at this, Ruthy. The bouncy seats vibrate. It's supposed to jiggle 'em around so they fall asleep. Quite an invention. Amazing, huh?"

"Sure, amazing," she answered weakly as the mountain of boxes grew.

Bryce lent a hand to carry in several unmarked cartons and an enormous package containing a changing table complete with a colorful clown mobile.

Ruth gasped. The pile of baby things grew along with the tension in her stomach. She felt closed in by a cardboard prison. "Where are we going to put all of this stuff?"

Monk whistled happily as he returned from the garage with a toolbox. "Don't worry, hon. I'll get it all assembled, and we'll put the nursery to rights."

Ruth stepped over a box boasting a set of teddy bears that made noises similar to a mother's heartbeat. If the thing was realistic, the heart would sound like a jackhammer right about now. "But, Monk, we haven't even painted the nursery yet. Carson hasn't finished the patching up yet. Don't you think we should do that first?"

That caused him to pause. "Oh. Well, no matter. We'll store the gear in the garage until he's done. How's that?"

"I can help you paint," Bryce offered.

The room continued to close in on her until she could stand it no longer. "Fine, fine. I'm going to take the birds out for their walk. I'll be back soon."

Monk didn't look up from the pile of screws and washers and an ominous-looking set of directions. "Okay, honey. Be careful. I've got this under control,

Bryce. You go on with your mother."

She got her coat and made sure there was a bag of Fritos in the pocket before she let herself out into the yards. The birds milled around, eager for their nightly stroll. Bryce joined her as she headed down the drive.

"Mind a little company?"

"Of course not." Truth be told, Ruth would have preferred to be alone with her dark thoughts. Her house, her life was being transformed into baby playland before her very eyes. She should be joyous, welcoming every tiny toy and tool. But she wasn't. God help her, she wasn't.

They walked in silence for a while, the only sound coming from the quiet scratch of the birds' feet on the earthy shoulder that ran next to the road. The sky was almost dark, the creeping cool of night whispering in as they strolled.

Bryce's phone rang, the sound harsh in the quiet of the evening. The conversation was short. "Yes. Yes, I'll look for it. Okay. Right." He hung up, his face a mask of rage. "That was Roslyn. She is faxing the papers for the sale of the house. Apparently we've got to make it snappy so she can start her new life with flower boy. I need to go meet with a lawyer."

Ruth sighed. "Where will you go after the house is sold?"

He shrugged.

The words came out straight from her heart before she had time to think better of them. "Maybe you should come out here." Seeing his face change, she regretted the comment as soon as she said it. *Meddling, Ruth, meddling.*

"Mom, that's just why I left," he snapped. "Don't tell me what to do. I don't like to have my life managed for me."

She felt like she'd been slapped. "I guess that wasn't my business. I apologize."

He didn't answer.

Suddenly her hurt changed to anger. "Bryce, what about your baby?"

"My baby?" His eyes shone in the gloom. "There is no baby. Roslyn miscarried, remember?"

"I know. And you're grieving about that, I can tell. So this baby, this life that you never even met, you felt something for, didn't you?"

He nodded. "Sure."

"So let yourself imagine for a minute, if you can, what you would feel for a child that has actually been born, Bryce. It's everything to you. It's your heart walking around outside your body and you try to keep it from getting hurt. I know I protected you too much. I managed you too much, but I did it because I love you, and I would think that creating a child of your own, you could understand that in some small way." Her voice quivered, her breath coming in pants. She clamped her lips tightly together.

He was quiet for a minute as they walked.

Now he will really be chomping at the bit to leave, she thought miserably.

Finally he spoke. "I guess you're right, Mom. I was out of line. I—I'm sorry."

Her eyes filled inexplicably with tears. "Me, too, Bryce. I wish I hadn't tried to keep disappointment away so much. Maybe it would be easier for you now." She reached out her hand for his.

He squeezed her fingers. "I think it would still hurt just as much." He cleared his throat. "I've got to go to San Francisco to finalize the divorce."

How sad he looked. How unutterably sad. She was so overwhelmed by the swirl of emotion she did not hear it at first.

The roar of an engine coming from behind.

There was no time to escape.

The last thing she saw was the startled look in her son's eyes as the car bore down on them both.

14

Jack's ears were still ringing as he pulled up to the Budge cottage. Monk had bellowed into the phone that someone had tried to run down his wife. It didn't matter that Jack was off duty for the evening. Cops were never really off duty in a small town. Not that it made a speck of difference. The thought of Ruth being in the path of a hit-and-run driver was more than enough to send him back into cop mode.

"Thanks, God, for Louella," he whispered, as he had many times before. The woman was sent directly by the Lord, he was sure, to pull his bacon out of the fire on a regular basis. Nonetheless he hoped Paul wouldn't wake up and find out he was gone again.

He pulled on a windbreaker against the night, which was thick with clouds that screened the pale moonlight. Hints of an early summer storm hung in the air. His fist didn't quite make it to the door to knock before it was yanked open and Monk ushered him inside.

The big man looked completely unglued, face flushed, brow sweaty. "I'm glad you're here, Jack. I can't believe it. I should have been with her, not doodling around with the crib. To think what could have happened. I'd never forgive myself, never."

Jack gripped his arm. "Let's not play any blame games now, Monk. I need to know what happened."

Monk led him to Ruth, who sat on the sofa with a blanket on her lap and an untouched cup of tea on the coffee table, holding a gauze bandage to her elbow. "Hello, Jack."

"Hi, Ruth. I thought I'd be visiting you at the hospital. Are you sure you don't want to go get checked out?"

She raised her chin a fraction. "No. I've been through this already with Monk and Bryce. Bryce pulled me out of the way and I landed on top of him, poor guy. I only scraped my elbow. He took the brunt of it. I wouldn't be surprised if he had some broken ribs or something."

"Are you hurt?" Jack asked.

Bryce shrugged from where he stood next to the fireplace. "No. Like she said, I pulled her to the side and we both went over backward, but no harm done. The birds managed to get out of the way, too. We couldn't see who was driving."

"Do you think it was intentional?"

Ruth shook her head. "I'm sure it wasn't. It was dark, we were near a turn. The driver probably didn't even see us. We shouldn't have been walking late, but there are never really any cars on the road there that I've ever encountered."

Bryce looked at her but didn't say anything.

Jack caught his eye. "Is that what you think, Bryce?"

"No. I think it was deliberate. Whoever it was turned off their headlights as they accelerated and drove onto the shoulder on purpose. Sorry, Mom." He shot a look at his mother, who blanched.

"This is intolerable." Monk's face flushed even darker. "Who would do such a thing? To Ruth. To the babies." His hands balled into fists. "If I ever get my hands on the driver—"

"Leave that to us. We'll find out who did it. Any impression about the car make and model? Color?" He looked from Ruth to Bryce and back again.

"It was small," Ruth said. "That's about all I can say."

"I agree with Mom. Some sort of compact model, dark color, is about all I picked up. We were too busy trying to get out of the way to pay much attention."

Jack fiddled with his pencil as he looked at Bryce. "Have you had any problems since you came to Finny?"

"Me? No. I left my problems behind in Chicago."

Ruth gave Monk a smile as he pressed her hand. "Why do you ask?"

Bryce gave his mother a dark look. "He's wondering if the guy who tried to run us down tonight might have been after me."

The room fell into an uneasy silence.

"Who would want to run you down?" Ruth's voice had a slight quaver.

"I don't know, Mom, but in a way, I'd rather somebody was after me than you."

Ruth's cheeks pinked and she blinked hard. "This is crazy but, maybe, I mean I'm not sure or anything, but I wonder—"

Jack waited patiently.

"Well, I have this feeling the college people are up to something. Bryce saw them suiting up for a night dive but they denied it, said they were out walking. That's odd, isn't it? Of course, it certainly doesn't mean they would try to run either of us down. I'm sure they wouldn't do that. They just don't look like the kind of people who could be capable of such a thing."

Jack smiled. "That's why I like you, Ruth. You never seem to think people are capable of the terrible things they do."

Monk kissed Ruth on the forehead. "I like that about her, too."

"Okay." Jack sighed. "It's not much to go on, but maybe somebody else saw something. I'll check with the locals along that strip of road."

Monk stood with him and lowered his voice. "I am going to keep a close eye on her, Jack. I'll take some time off."

"Oh no, you won't." Ruth put down the cup with a sharp *clank*. "You are not going to take time off to babysit me. I am perfectly fine. When I have to walk the birds, I'll take someone with me. Bryce, you'll go, won't you?"

He nodded. "Sure."

"And if he's not home, I'll take Alva."

Monk gave her a dubious look.

"Or Bobby," she added hastily.

"Nothing against your son or Bobby, Ruthy, but I think it would be better for me to stay with you."

Ruth stood awkwardly. "You need to work, Monk. Otherwise who will pay for all this?" She waved a hand at the mountain of boxes. "Besides, it will drive me crazy to have you hovering all the time, as much as I love you."

He huffed. "I still think—"

"Jack will look into this accident or whatever it was. Right, Jack?"

"Absolutely."

Monk put a hand on her shoulder. "But he may not have any luck, Ruthy. It's not going to be easy going, is it, Jack?"

"No, honestly it'll be another mountain to climb, but I'm used to that."

Bryce snapped his fingers. "A mountain to climb. That's what I've been trying to remember."

They all stared at him.

He shook his head. "Don't know why I didn't come up with that earlier. I remembered where I saw Roxie's picture before."

Jack frowned. "Roxie Trotter?"

"Yeah. She used to live in Chicago. She was some sort of professional person, I think. I remember reading about her in the local paper because she was into mountain climbing. Made it to the top of Mt. McKinley in record time."

"Roxie was a professional?" Ruth's face crinkled in confusion, thinking about Roxie's attempt to sell shells to the jeweler. "She seems to have fallen on hard times."

"What are you thinking, Jack?" Monk said.

Jack replayed a few facts from Reggie's murder in his mind. "I was just thinking that mountain climbing is an interesting sport. It requires lots of specialized equipment." He zipped his jacket and said under his breath, "I wonder how good Ms. Trotter is at tying knots."

<hr>

In the morning, Ms. Trotter seemed to be doing her best to tie Jack in knots. She sat, burrowed down in her ragged jacket, cap pulled to her eyebrows. The look she gave him was hostile at best. "Give it your best shot, Detective. Try to prove I killed Reggie. The guy probably drowned on his own, out doing a night dive. Stupid."

"He didn't drown."

She blinked, but her expression didn't change. "Not my business how he died. I don't really care anyway."

Jack continued. "I'm not trying to prove you killed anyone. I just want to ask a few questions about your relationship with the deceased."

"I think the deceased was nothing but trouble. I didn't want him around my son, but since Eddie is dead, that was no longer an issue for me."

"Why didn't you want him around your son?"

"The same reason you wouldn't want him around yours. Because he hung out with the wrong people, people who drove nice cars and carried wads of cash without doing an honest day's work. Bad kind of people."

"Can you give me any names?"

"No. That was back in Chicago, and it was a lifetime ago."

Jack gave Nate an exasperated look.

Nate cleared his throat. "Say, Mrs. Trotter. I read somewhere you were a chiropractor. Still practicing? I've got a permanent kink in my neck."

She raised a thick eyebrow. "Does it look like I'm still practicing? I lost my license, as you well know."

"That's a bummer. What happened?"

"Again, I'm sure you already know every minuscule fact about my life, so why go into it?"

Jack fixed her with a look. "Because it would be helping us out. Think of it as doing your civic duty."

She glared at him for a moment. "I stole from some of my clients. Broke into their homes while they were on vacation. They didn't press charges so I avoided doing time, but I lost my license to practice."

"Really?" Nate tapped a pencil on the desk. "Seems like you had a pretty good client list. Business must have been good. Why jeopardize things by stealing?"

Her eyes glinted. "There's never enough money to go around, is there?"

Nate nodded. "I guess not. Wonder why the cops didn't charge you."

Roxie heaved a sigh. "They thought I was trying to cover for someone. Seems somebody saw me at the time of the last robbery in the grocery store. Isn't that just something? An alibi when I didn't even want one."

"And why didn't you want one?" Jack said. "Folks aren't usually eager to do jail time. Most of the people we meet are more inclined to try to run away from a conviction than welcome it."

She shrugged. "I'm not most people."

Jack consulted his notes. "I see you left Chicago after your son died."

"I had nothing to keep me there. No business. No family. No reason to stay. I like the diving here, the fresh air, et cetera."

Jack consulted his notes again. "You catch abalone and sell the meat and shells?"

"Yes. I'm sorry to disappoint, but I do it the right way, keep to my limit and no scuba tanks. Believe it or not, I respect wildlife. I'm not about to deplete the ecosystem for my own profit."

Nate huffed into his mustache. "When did you take up mountain climbing?"

Roxie looked startled. "What?"

The easygoing smile never left Nate's face. "Mountain climbing. You made it to the top of Mt. McKinley in twelve days. That's awesome."

"You are thorough, I'll give you that. After my son died, I realized how quickly it can all go away so I decided to cut loose. I climbed in high school and college so it wasn't too huge a learning curve."

"But with one kidney," Jack said. "Amazing."

A brief smile lit her face. "Yes, it was amazing. It was the last amazing thing that's happened to me in a long while and probably ever will again. Sometimes I look at the pictures just to prove to myself I really did it."

"Do you know a lot about knot tying?"

"Some. Why?"

Jack showed her a picture of the knot.

She shrugged. "Sort of a figure eight knot. Not one I would use."

"Why?"

"It's bulky. Why do you ask?"

Jack waited a second. "It's the knot we found around Reggie's neck."

Her mouth fell open. "He was strangled?"

Nate nodded. "Yup."

"So he really was murdered?"

"Really," Nate repeated.

Her face settled back into its expressionless mask. "What do you know? All that trouble finally caught up to him. I guess there is justice for some people."

After a few more routine questions, Jack told Roxie she was free to leave.

She smiled at the detective and officer. "Well, I guess that means there's another murderer here in Finny. To think I moved here for some peace and quiet."

Nate watched her go. "Well, Reggie found his peace and quiet. Too bad it came at the end of a rope."

Jack suppressed a shudder as he picked up the phone. "Yeah, too bad."

~~~

His fingers trembled a little as he dialed.

Bobby, Bobby. She was embedded in his heart and thoughts.

Thinking about her on the other end of the line made his breath catch. She picked up after the third ring.

"Hello?"

"Good morning, Bobby, it's Jack."

"Hi, Jack."

"What's up?"

"I'm headed over for my shift at Uncle Monk's. What's up with you?"

"Working."

"Finding the guy who tried to run Aunt Ruth down, I hope."

"Trying as hard as I can."

She sighed, a soft, fluttery sound. "Good. I think that person needs to do hard time in a rock quarry or something."

"Well, we don't have a rock quarry that I'm aware of, but I'll see what I can do. So, uh, Bobby, I wanted to, to ask you—"

"Yes?"

"If you. . .wanted to show me some diving techniques."

She laughed and then grew quiet. "You're serious."

"Yes."

"Today?"

"Sure. We could grab some lunch after."

"No, Jack."

His heart fell. "Why not?"

"Two reasons. One, diving isn't something you learn on the fly. You need to take a class with a certified instructor. And two, I guess you've been inside all morning, but there's a storm coming in. Looks like a good one. Not diving weather."

He felt slightly relieved. No diving meant she wouldn't have a reason to hang out with Ethan, either. "That makes sense. How about lunch anyway?"

"I need to work that shift so Monk can check on Ruth. Maybe another time."

Her tone made it clear. There would not be another time. He'd blown it. "Look, Bobby—" The words tangled themselves up inside him, refusing to come out.

She finally broke the awkward silence. "I have a question for you."

"Fire away."

"Where is Ethan? You didn't arrest him, did you?"

"No. As a matter of fact I need to talk to him."

"Me, too."

Jack stifled the urge to slam a hand on the desk. "What about?"

"Nothing important. He was supposed to meet me last night, and he never showed up."

15

Ruth wasn't sure if it was the nightmare that awakened her in the predawn hours of Tuesday morning, or the strange flittering movement in her womb. Monk sat bolt upright at her soft moan. He listened and stroked her back as she told about the car bearing down on her and Bryce amidst a squabble of clamoring birds. He fetched a cool cloth for her sweaty brow and brought the glass of orange juice she craved.

She settled back in bed, his big hand laid protectively on her shoulder, and fell into a more restful sleep until the phone rang at seven a.m.

"Hi, Nana Ruth. Is the baby here?" Cootchie's breathing sounded loud across the phone lines.

Ruth sat up, a joy growing inside. She smiled, picturing the wild-haired little girl, and a happy warmth infused her.

"Hello, Cootchie. No, the baby isn't here yet, but guess what?"

"What?"

"It's two babies. I'm going to have twins." For the first time it felt a bit less like a curse and more like a blessing.

The girl let out a cry. "Two babies? How do they fit? Does Uncle Monk have one in his tummy?"

Ruth covered the phone and repeated the comment to Monk, who was up and dressed. He laughed.

"You tell her my stomach is all muscle, no baby."

Ruth chatted with her adopted granddaughter, feeling again the hole created by her absence. "How are you getting along in Arizona with Grandma Meg?"

"She's made me a sandbox, but there's no worms in the sandbox. Mommy wants to talk. Love you, Nana."

"Love you, too, angel." Ruth swallowed against the tears until Dimple came on the line.

"Hello, Ruth. Greetings of the morning."

"Greetings right back at you, Dimple." The woman had never seemed to give up her pattern of speaking in fortune cookie phrasing. Ruth filled her in on the twin situation.

"Twins? That will mean one for Cootchie to hold and one for me."

"Sort of a buy one, get one free bonus. How are things in Arizona?"

"Dry. I'm just about finished."

"Finished with what?"

"Packing. To come home."

Ruth's breath caught. "To—to come home? To Finny?"

"Yes. I am eager to get back to the mushroom farm."

Dimple was the owner of Pistol Bang's Mushroom Farm, which had lain idle since she left town after Cootchie's brief abduction. Ruth was almost too overwhelmed with emotion to speak. "I didn't think you'd be coming back so soon."

"Cootchie will start pre-school next fall. I should have the mushroom farm back up and running by then. Don't you think?"

Ruth tried not to squeal with glee. "Oh yes. That's very sensible."

"I hear there has been another murder in Finny. Are you involved this time, too, Ruth? It seems these things have a way of coming home to roost on your doorstep."

Thinking about the near accident two days before, she couldn't stifle the shiver that crept up her spine. "It doesn't involve me too much this time, I'm happy to say. When will you be back?"

"We will stay until after the surfing tournament at the end of the month."

Ruth wracked her brain, thinking about desert surfing. "Um, I didn't think there was much surfing in Arizona."

"It's Cootchie's idea. She's invited all the neighborhood kids to come for a party on Grandma Meg's lawn. She intends to set up a Slip 'N Slide and serve doughnuts and mung bean sprouts." Dimple paused for a moment. "I think perhaps the surfing part is an exercise in visualization."

Ruth laughed. "If anyone can make a bunch of desert dwellers visualize the ocean, it's Cootchie. I can't wait to see you both."

"We are anxious, too, especially to meet the babies. Have you thought of names?"

"Not yet."

"I will put my mind to it and share my thoughts next time we talk."

What would Monk think about a woman who christened her daughter Cootchie having a hand in picking his kids' names? She hung up with a lighter heart. "They're coming home," she told Monk with a rush of joy.

He hugged her. "I'm so glad. It's been far too long since we've seen our Cootchie, and Dimple, too. What can I fix my fine lady for breakfast?"

She glanced at the clock. "Nothing. You're supposed to be at work, remember? Earning the money to pay for this arsenal of baby supplies?"

"My job today is to take care of you since Bryce is out of town."

Bryce had left for his overnight trip to San Francisco to meet with a lawyer.

What followed was a fierce argument carried out in very civilized tones. It concluded with Ruth's final statement. "Well, if you need to have me in your line of sight all day, then I'm just going to go to the shop with you. At least that way you'll get some work done and maybe I can help in some way."

He sighed. "All right, you can come but no helping, just resting and relaxing."

Figuring that was the best she was going to get, she quickly dressed, rolled up the remaining pages of her script, and slipped them into her coat pocket before they headed off.

Monk conceded to at least let her stop at the Buns Up Bakery for a cinnamon roll, when the morning sickness let up. They ducked into the store and out of the light drizzle. As Al delivered his treasure along with a carton of milk, she noticed Monk casting anxious glances at the people waiting on the wet sidewalk outside his shop door for it to open.

She sat firmly at a table. "Go. I will eat my roll and walk carefully over to your shop after looking both directions twice. I promise."

He folded his arms, brow wrinkled in thought. "Well, I guess it would be okay for you to stay here for a few minutes, but I don't want you crossing by yourself. Call me when you're ready and I'll escort you." Half reluctantly, half eagerly, he went.

Feeling like a five-year-old, Ruth settled into munching with a sigh of relief. The clouds were gathering into a solid gray wall outside. She pulled the stretched and misshapen sweater around her and attacked her carbohydrate missile with vigor.

Dr. Soloski came in and ordered an herbal tea.

"Oh, good morning, Mrs. Budge. Your husband's shop was closed so I came here. Someone told me you had some trouble Sunday night. Are you okay?"

"Yes, I'm fine. Probably just a careless driver. No harm done."

"That's good." He cast a nervous glance out the window.

"Won't you sit down and join me?" Ruth pushed out a chair.

"No, I really should be getting back to work." A tall figure with wiry hair stalked past the window, in the direction of the dentist's office. He shrank a little as Ellen sailed by without noticing him. "On second thought, it wouldn't hurt to take a few minutes." He slid into the chair. "I've been meaning to ask you something anyway."

"Go ahead."

"Ellen says you're working with the college man. Ethan, I think his name is, on a project of some sort."

"Yes, he's filming a documentary."

"I just wondered—not my place to say really—"

"What is it?"

"Well, is he taking underwater footage?"

"He says he isn't. After Reggie, uh, died, he promised they wouldn't be attempting anything in the ocean."

"Odd. I've seen him in the water twice now, near sunset. Foolish, if you ask me. The waves are rough and visibility is poor with the thick kelp forest we've got here. It's purely suicide to think about a night dive."

"You're not the first person who has noticed him diving. Maybe it's recreational. Are you sure it was Ethan?"

"I guess it could have been someone else. Young, fairly trim male." He shook his head and straightened his glasses. "I shouldn't spend time on worrying about somebody else's problems."

Ruth noticed the shadows under his eyes and the pale cast to his thin face. "Forgive me for saying so, but you look tired. Is everything okay with your sister?"

He heaved a sigh. "As okay as it gets. She's been disabled since birth, a child in a grownup body. I go to see her as often as I can, but she's generally out of it most of the time. She has respiratory issues as well and a load of other complaints that I won't bore you with."

"Oh dear. How awful for you both."

"I've gotten used to it. Jane was sixteen when mother died, so I've been on duty since then."

Ruth couldn't hide her surprise. "Then your sister is quite young."

"She'll be twenty-one next month. Mother didn't think she could have any more children. Jane was her miracle child, disabled or not."

Ruth thought she detected a hint of jealousy in his voice. "It must have been quite a shock."

He sipped some tea. "Mmm. I was in my early twenties when she was born. My parents persuaded me to give up the tree business and start on something more respectable, so I changed directions and went to dental school."

"That's a big switch."

He gave a rueful smile. "I miss it, but it was a practical decision. Hospital bills aren't cheap and insurance will only take you so far." His face brightened. "Things will be better next month, though. Janey's trust fund kicks in when she's twenty-one." He laughed. "Maybe then I'll be able to take up tree climbing again."

He said good-bye and headed out, with a cautious look around first.

Tree climbing might be a big help with Ellen on the loose, Ruth thought as she wiped her sticky fingers and dutifully dialed Monk to escort her across the street.

The soothing smells of chowder and baking bread surrounded her in the cozy corner of Monk's shop. He had no catering job that day, so the lunchtime crowd would have to suffice. The late morning sky was thick with storm clouds, which she hoped would help spur any passersby to come in for soup. Ruth eased the window open a crack to let in the sharp tang of sea air and let out the rich aromas to attract some customers.

In spite of her husband's baleful looks, she had wiped down the counters, tidied the remaining tray of breakfast scones, and refilled all the jugs of milk and creamer before Monk propelled her into a chair, demanding that she "take a load off."

Though she didn't like to admit it, it did feel good to settle her girth into a chair and sip tea. Her lively onboard cargo had settled for the moment so she could concentrate on finishing Indigo's journal without distracting kicks to the midsection.

Though I never would have conceived of it, I am beginning to think of this windswept corner of the world as my home. Hui and I have labored long and hard with endless cooking and cleaning and our efforts have been rewarded. Though my back aches by day's end and Hui's hands are chapped and hardened, the work is a blessing. This is the only country in the world, I think, where a woman receives anything like just compensation for her work, even though they still believe me to be a man.

I learn new things from Hui every day. He has some queer customs from his homeland. Bathing, for one. He insists on cleaning himself in an old tin basin before every meal and changing his clothes. Though he has not much to wear, he will put on the cleanest of his tunics and sit down solemnly before we sup. This is certainly a wonder as most Americans I am told bathe only once or twice a year. I settle for washing my face and hands and a twice weekly dip in an isolated pond we've found in our explorations. Hui climbs a tree and keeps watch when I bathe, sounding a whistle at the approach of any strangers.

I bartered with some newcomers to the mining fields who agreed to assist us with our carpentry needs in exchange for two square meals a day and any mending they might require. They cut down pine trees and made shakes for a cabin. It's a bit drafty, but oh the bliss of sleeping at night with a roof to keep out the rain and animals. It is grander than any palace indeed. I've begun to put together a rag rug for the floor, and though I have not convinced Hui to sleep in a cot, he has strung a hammock for himself in the corner where he sleeps soundly.

Our typical day goes as follows: Before the sun comes up, Hui starts the water boiling for coffee and tends to the cooking fire. We take a minute to give our thanks to the Lord or "the sky Father" as Hui calls Him, and eat some bread and drink a cup of Hui's tea to break our fast. Then I begin with biscuits, fried potatoes, and pounds of broiled steak and liver. It seems like mountains of food until the miners plunk down their money, sit at our rough board tables, and gulp it down in minutes.

When the men have gone off to their duties, we start on dinner. I prepare six to eight loaves of bread, pies if there are berries to fill them, and whatever kind of meat there is to boil. This week I cooked a pot of chili seasoned with bear meat I bought from a trapper passing through. Abuela *would never believe her chili recipe would be feeding a score of rough-and-tumble miners. Though the pot was enormous, they ate every morsel and even sopped their bread in the vessel to soak up every last drop.*

The men seem to like their chili hot, spiced with jalapeños and onion the way Abuela *would have prepared it herself. After spending the day knee deep in icy water, I imagine they welcome anything that will bring them warmth. Never have I received so much joy from cooking for people. The Orsons enjoyed their meals but not with the relish and zeal of someone half starved. It is true there is no better seasoning than hunger.*

If the weather permits and he can find them, Hui and I enjoy some seasoned abalone. Ah, it is pure joy to eat the soft strips, bathed in garlic and butter. There are not many, as they grow so very slowly, so we keep this small treat for ourselves. The shells we use to hold our money, strapping two together and hiding them in the hollow space under the floor. Hui laughs, telling me our lowly abalone now hold pearls of great price like their fancy oyster cousins. I smile to think of it as I read to Hui from Matthew 13:45–46.

"Again, the kingdom of heaven is like unto a merchant man, seeking goodly pearls. Who, when he found one pearl of great price, went and sold all that he had, and bought it."

Our strange treasure abalones will soon be enough to start a little restaurant. I have been looking at a stove in town, and it will not be long before I can buy it outright. Then we shall have a proper kitchen for cooking, and I will know that Hui's future will be more secure. We are truly blessed, praise be to God and the Son. My only sadness comes when I look out on the great wide ocean and think of the Orsons. How I wish I could change the terrible moment when Señor and Señora Orson were sent to the bottom with no help from their   .

Ruth peered more closely at the paper. The words had been blacked out with ink. Were they like that all the time? She couldn't remember. She pulled the paper close until her nose almost touched the paper. What did it say? And more importantly, why would Sandra and Ethan want to conceal it?

16

The sound of clanking tools and muttered complaints woke her from her nap that afternoon. She wrapped up in a sweater against the sudden chill and found Monk, crouched next to a pile of parts that was supposed to somehow morph into a baby swing.

He looked up and gave her an aggravated smile. "We should have paid extra and had this thing put together for us. I'm a cook, not a mechanic."

She patted him, ignoring the swell of nausea in her stomach. "You've got a few more months, honey." The thought sent her into quivers of fear. In a few months she would be the proud parent of two babies. Two. Babies. At her age. The cacophony of fear and doubt started again in her head.

"Lord," she whispered, "help me. Help me to want this."

The phone rang, and she settled onto the sofa to try and relax. Monk's voice grew tense as he talked. Something was wrong. It was written all over his worried face. When he hung up, he came to sit down next to her.

"That was my brother Dave. It's Dad again."

Ruth reached for his hand. "Tell me what happened."

"He was behaving like a stubborn fool and went and climbed a ladder. Fell off and dislocated his shoulder." Monk rubbed a hand over his face. "They've got to get the first apple crop in this weekend, and my brother can't do it all by himself."

She didn't have to think twice. "Go. Go help your father."

Monk ignored her. "Dave tried to hire on some guys but everyone is hustling their crops in and he can't find any help."

Ruth gently turned his chin to face her. "Go help your brother, Monk. I'll be fine."

He frowned. "No. I can't. Wait a minute. Maybe I can. Why don't you come with me? I'll close up shop and we'll go for a while. It'll be a mini vacation."

Ruth smiled. "Honey, I love you, but I'm not up for a trip to Kansas right now. It's bad enough throwing up every few hours, but doing it on a plane is just too much for me. Besides, I need to make sure Carson finishes that nursery or we're going to have to put the babies in the kitchen sink."

His face clouded over. "Then I'm not going. I can't leave you, not with some nutcase on the loose. You could have been killed by that crazy driver."

"Tell you what. How about I ask Bobby to stay with me until Bryce gets

413

back? I can go to the shop with her in the daytime and help, and she'll be here at night to stay with me."

Monk looked anguished. "Ruth—"

"I know. You love me and I love you, too. I will be safe, and if I feel the least bit nervous, I will go to stay with Mrs. Hodges and Alva can stand in for bodyguard or I can sleep at the police station under Nate's desk. How's that?"

He looked unconvinced as she struggled to her feet. "Where are you going?"

"To make sure you've got enough clean clothes to pack."

True to her word, after Monk booked a last-minute flight and rushed to the airport, Ruth spent the late afternoon at the shop with Bobby. They chatted while they set things to rights for the next day. The air was heavy with the promise of the approaching storm as they headed home. Ruth filled Bobby in on the cryptic Indigo Orson passages.

Ruth let them into the house, and Bobby set to work making grilled cheese sandwiches for dinner.

"That's an incredible story. I've heard only bits and pieces from Ethan about it."

Ruth shot her a look. "Is he a close friend of yours?"

She laughed. "You sound like Jack. No, not a close friend. We dive together sometimes. Mind if I have a look at that script?"

"Not at all. Sandra is supposed to be picking it up soon, so you'd better look while you have the chance."

Bobby went over the pages while Ruth showered. Clean and wrapped in a warm robe, she found Bobby still peering closely at the inked-out words.

"I wish we could make them out." She held the paper close to the lamp.

Seeing Bobby silhouetted in lamplight sparked a thought in Ruth's brain. "I've got an idea." She took the paper and held it to the light, peering at it from the underside. Her pulse quickened. "The copied words are slightly lighter than the ink that was used to cover them up. From this angle I can make out a few of the letters. There's a *W* and later a—what is that?"

Bobby knelt on the floor. "It's two words, I think. The first three letters are *Whi* and the second begins with a *Q*."

They sat back and pondered. Bobby chewed her fingernail thoughtfully. "The first word has to be *while* or *white* or something like that. What about the second?"

"The *Q* has to be followed by a *U* to make sense in English, so what could that be? *Quite? Quack? Queer? Quince?*"

"Queens," Bobby said with a snap of her fingers. "I think it's queens."

Ruth nodded. "White Queens."

They both smiled. "So Señor Orson's precious cargo was a bunch of white queens?" Bobby giggled. "Sounds like something from Alice in Wonderland."

"Yes." Ruth sighed. "Just another mystery to solve."

She was just booting up the computer in the bedroom to do some cyber sleuthing when there was a knock at the door. It was a breathless Alva, wet from the rain. He clutched a hand to his heart. "Evening, ladies. I come to tell ya Paul's been hurt."

Ruth's heart dropped. "What? How? Is it bad?"

"Don't know. Louella said he done fall down the stairs. Jack's on his way back from Half Moon Bay, but his car's given out so Nate went to get 'im." Alva sucked in another deep breath. "Louella told me to go get Bobby."

Bobby was already pulling on a jacket. "Where's Paul?"

"At the hospital."

Bobby looked at Ruth. "Uncle Monk wouldn't want you to be here alone. Come with me."

"Never mind that. I'll stay with her." Alva hitched up his pants. "Don't you worry none. I'm on the case." He marched into the house and immediately checked all the kitchen windows to be sure they were locked before he opened the cupboards mumbling something about candy.

Bobby hugged Ruth. "I'll be back as soon as I can."

"Take care of Paul and call me as soon as you know anything."

She nodded and headed into the rainy night.

Alva made himself at home on the couch. Ruth fixed him some hot cocoa with extra marshmallows and turned on the TV to an old *Howdy Doody* show. Alva sipped happily.

Ruth's stomach was in knots thinking about Paul. She prowled the house for awhile, straightening pillows and rinsing a cup left in the sink. "Come on, Ruth," she muttered to herself. "It could be awhile before Bobby can call you."

She returned to the computer and typed in *white queens*. Nothing helpful emerged on the screen. She thumbed through the journal pages to find any tidbit that might help refine her search. Before the computer finished cogitating, there was another knock at the door.

Alva stared into the peephole. "Whatcha want? Do ya know the password?"

"No," Sandra's voice was muffled by the door.

Alva scrunched up his face. "Coming to think of it," he muttered, "I durnt know it either."

"It's okay, Alva. Sandra is here for her journal."

He returned to his show, and Ruth opened the door and invited Sandra in.

"No thanks, Mrs. Budge. I'm here for the binder, then I've got to go."

Ruth handed it over. "I wondered about something. What are the White Queens?"

Sandra dropped the binder and it snapped open, sending papers all over the floor. With much effort, Ruth helped her pick them up. She repeated her question.

Sandra shoveled up the pages in a sloppy pile. "White queens? I don't know. Never heard of them."

"Really? I thought they had something to do with Señor Orson."

Sandra gathered up an armful of untidy papers. "Señor Orson? Um, no, not that I know of. I've really got to go. Thanks so much." She darted down the walkway, leaving Ruth to slowly close the door.

"Jumpy little chicken," Alva called from the couch. "She could use a nap or something."

Ruth retrieved several sheets of the journal that had slipped under the kitchen table. After refilling Alva's cocoa cup and making sure the phone was in reach, she padded back to the computer. There was still nothing on the screen that shed any light on the mystery. She thumbed through the papers in her lap, looking for some unusual tidbit. One passage jumped out at her.

> *The traveler gave them dried tortoise, too. Most had never seen a tortoise, alive or dead, but that did not stop them from eating every speck of it.*
>
> *It reminded me of the strange animals Señor Orson told of when he returned from Australia before our disastrous voyage on the Triton. If there were kangaroos in California, they would be hopping for their lives to escape the stew pot.*

She added Australia to her search terms. The answer materialized in front of her eyes in a moment. The title of the article was "AUSTRALIA'S WHITE QUEENS: LOST TREASURE."

> *Australia's most precious treasures really are down under. The rare Pinctada maxima, or South Sea oyster pearl, must be dived for in a select number of deep ocean habitats, many of them off the coast of Australia. The work is extremely difficult and dangerous yet the rewards are enticing.*

Ruth sat up straighter and read on.

> *The most legendary set of South Sea pearls was dubbed the White Queens for their enormous size and glorious sheen, believed to weigh in at a whopping four hundred seventy carats each. Owned by merchant Wesley Marble, they were reportedly purchased by an unknown traveler in 1851 for an exorbitant sum and were never heard of again. Today's valuation would put the White Queens' worth at close to five million dollars.*

Ruth knocked over her teacup with a *clank*.

Alva sat up, his eyes wild. "Whatsa matter? Is it an invasion?"

She fetched some paper towels to mop up the spill. "No, Alva. I was just doing some research. It's okay."

Grumbling, he settled back on the sofa.

The phone rang, startling her again.

"It's me, Aunt Ruth."

She could hear the worry in Bobby's voice. "What is it? How is Paul?"

"They're taking him in for a CAT scan now to check for head injuries. He has a broken wrist. Jack hasn't made it here yet. I'm sorry, but it looks like I'm going to be staying for a while."

"Of course. Don't you worry about anything here. Alva is keeping me company." She pictured little Paul, scared and in pain, and her eyes filled with tears. Unconsciously, she pressed a hand to her abdomen. "Bobby, I'm going to pray for you all."

"Thank you. I'm praying here, too." There was a tremor in Bobby's voice as she said good night.

Ruth turned to give Alva the news, but he was snoring soundly. She covered him with a warm blanket and headed for the bedroom. Her thoughts were spinning in all directions. Worry about Paul warred with the strange information that had come to light from her research.

Señor Orson's treasure was a set of priceless pearls, the White Queens. She was sure of it just as she was equally sure Ethan and Sandra were trying to recover them. The note she'd found inside the binder proved it. *P. max, 468c and 470c* referred to the species name and carat weight. It could be nothing else.

She snuggled under the down comforter, all the while mulling it over. Reggie must have known what Ethan and Sandra were there for. Had he gotten too close to the treasure and they killed him? Or was there another party interested in the fantastic horde?

Monk called as she settled into bed. She told him about Paul.

"Oh sakes. Is the little guy going to be all right?"

"We'll know soon," Ruth said, hoping Monk wouldn't ask to speak to Bobby. There was no point in worrying Monk by telling him Alva was currently serving as her bodyguard.

Monk sounded exhausted. "I got in okay. We didn't get much done before sundown, but we'll hit it hard tomorrow morning. We're going to have the crop in by week's end."

"Take care of yourself, honey. I don't want you to hurt anything."

He laughed. "I should be saying that to you. Give yourself a hug for me and pat our little bundles, okay? I love you."

"I love you, too, Monk." She hung up and whispered a prayer for her soul mate in Kansas and the little boy in Finny's only hospital. In spite of her anxiety, the sound of the rain soothed her until her eyelids grew heavy, so heavy that her brain did not register the flash of headlights, quickly extinguished as a car pulled into the shadows outside.

17

Jack was about to explode. He'd gotten a frantic call from Louella about Paul falling down the stairs. He heard from the hospital that Paul's condition was uncertain. And that was it. The uncertainty was killing him. Again he pounded a fist on the roof of his car, water streaming down his windbreaker.

"Piece of junk," he bellowed to the empty, rain-slicked street, straining again to catch a glimpse of Nate's car.

A cab approached from the opposite direction. Jack reached for his badge, ready to commandeer the vehicle, just when Nate screeched up to the curb. Jack jumped in and they took off, as fast as was safe through the storm. He gave Nate a look.

"No word yet, man. They gave Louella a sedative. Bobby's there."

He felt a surge of relief. "Thank You, God," he whispered. At least Paul was not alone. There was someone there he knew and loved. He pulled out his cell and dialed Bobby's number.

She answered on the first ring. "Jack, I've been trying to call you, but the reception is bad here. Paul is having a CAT scan. We'll know more in a little while."

"Bobby—" His throat closed around the words.

"I haven't been able to see him yet. I'll stay right here until I do."

"Okay, thanks." He clicked the phone off.

They didn't speak as they flew back towards Finny. Nate drove like a man possessed and both were silent for most of the trip. Before the car fully stopped, Jack was out and pounding up the steps into the building. Bobby looked up from her pacing and ran to him until they were wrapped together in a wet, drippy hug. "Thank you for being here," he whispered in her ear.

She swallowed. "It's Paul. Where else would I be?"

He could see the tears in her eyes when he let her go and began to prowl the hallway. "How long could it take to do a CAT scan?"

"The doctor said he'd be done soon."

Nate joined them a few minutes later and handed Jack a dry shirt. "Mary's bringing you a change of clothes when she can, but this will have to do for now."

By the time Jack emerged wearing the shirt, Nate had three cups of steaming coffee for them. Though he didn't feel like drinking it, he did anyway, letting the liquid burn the reality into him.

TREASURE UNDER FINNY'S NOSE

Paul was hurt. The wrist was the least of their problems. Jack had seen enough accidents in his career to know what a head injury could mean. Paralysis. Brain damage. Death. What would he do if Paul died, too?

The thought made him shudder.

He got up again to pace the floor, willing the doctor to come out and tell him, tell him what they hadn't been able to when they'd brought Lacey in. Bobby and Nate sat in silence, watching him. They came to stand beside him when a surgeon in green scrubs approached.

Jack's mouth went dry. He tried to speak but nothing came out.

After what seemed like an interminable pause, the doctor spoke. "Paul has sustained a concussion, but not a major one. The wrist will have to be seen by an orthopedist, but it doesn't look like a complicated break. We'll keep him overnight, but I think he'll be just fine."

Jack gripped him by the hand so hard the surgeon winced. "Thank you. Thank you very much."

Bobby sighed loudly. "Is Louella going to be all right?"

The physician smiled. "Absolutely, but she can stay the night, too. She'll be fine once the sedative wears off. I don't think she's going to let Paul use the stairs anytime soon."

Jack felt light-headed with relief. "When can I see him?"

"Give the nurse a few minutes and then you can go in." He waved as he left them.

Jack flopped into a chair. Nate gripped his arm. "I've gotta go back to the shop. Mary's by herself." He gave a last squeeze and exhaled, the breath ruffling his mustache. "Good deal, man. Good deal."

Jack nodded, hearing the unspoken emotion in his partner's voice. "Thanks, Nate."

"You bet."

Jack checked on Louella, who was sleeping, fortunately. There would be an emotional storm when she woke up, he knew. He returned to the waiting chairs and sat down next to Bobby. The hallway settled into silence.

Bobby checked her watch. "It's so late. I hate to disturb Aunt Ruth, but I know she's waiting for my call." She dialed the number. "Busy signal. She must be talking to Uncle Monk. I think I'll wait to see Paul, if that's okay with you, and then I'll take off."

He reached out a hand to hers. "Of course it's okay. I wanted to say, to tell you, how much it means to Paul that you were here for him." *And to me. Say it, you idiot. Tell her what she means to you.* The emotion choked off his words.

Bobby nodded. "I know. You don't have to thank me."

He sighed. "I hate the smell of this place. It's like it's burned into my brain. Every time I come here I get a whiff of the cleaner or whatever it is they used the day my wife died. They probably don't even use that kind anymore, but it still smells the same to me."

"But this time you got good news. Your son is going to be fine."

He leaned against the wall and closed his eyes. He'd never been so completely exhausted in his entire life. "I don't know what I would have done if the news had been different. Losing Paul would be—" He couldn't finish.

Bobby took his hand and prayed out loud. "Father, thank You for watching over Paul. Thank You for keeping him in Your loving hands and delivering him safely from this accident. Bring Your peace down on all of us, Lord, and receive our deepest gratitude."

Jack spoke the amen along with her.

Soon the nurse ushered them in to see the boy. He looked pale and small in the big hospital bed, a purple bruise showing on his forehead. Jack stroked his hair. "Hi, buddy. I heard you took a fall. Does your wrist hurt?"

Paul shook his head, eyes half closed. "Uh-uh."

"That's good. I was worried there for a little bit." Jack blinked back the moisture in his eyes. "Miss Louella is sleeping here tonight in the room next door. Bobby is here to see you, too."

Bobby kissed Paul lightly on the cheek. "Hey, kiddo. You're supposed to wear a helmet if you're going to fall down the stairs."

Paul smiled and slipped into sleep. Jack and Bobby took up positions in the chairs. Jack tried to think of a line of conversation that would keep her there, near him, near them both.

"You were right about the wreck, by the way."

She blinked. "What?"

"That's why I went to Half Moon Bay. I talked to a salvage guy there who is also a history buff and he agrees with you. The *Triton* was a big bucket of coal, no treasure that would pique the interest of any profit seekers. I guess I owe you an apology."

"You might owe Ethan one, but I'm not so sure anymore."

It was his turn to blink. "Why?"

"Aunt Ruth's journal, the one Ethan and Sandy gave her. It refers to some sort of treasure called the White Queens, though the words were blacked out."

"What's a White Queen?"

"I don't know, but Aunt Ruth was on the case when I left to come here."

He laughed. "Leave it to my two favorite women to ferret out another mystery. Do you think that's what Ethan and Sandy are diving for?"

"I don't know. I would rather not think of Ethan as a liar, but it does seem suspicious."

He took a deep breath. "If it does turn out to be true, I'm sorry. I know Ethan is a friend of yours and I probably haven't given him a fair chance."

She shrugged. "I'm sure he's got reasons for what he's been up to. I'm going to step out into the hall and try Aunt Ruth again."

Jack watched the steady rise and fall of Paul's chest, more beautiful to him than the mesmerizing ebb and flow of the ocean waves. He was overwhelmed with an enormous sense of gratitude. God spared his son. He did not yet understand why the Lord took Lacey, and he probably never would. But Jack had Paul, and he would die to keep the boy safe and happy.

Bobby returned with a frown on her face. "Still busy. I think I'd better go home and check on things." She walked to Paul's bed and stroked a finger lightly down his cheek. "I am so glad you're safe, kiddo," she whispered.

The sight of them there, heads bent close together, filled up his soul. Jack's own voice came out in a whisper. "You really love him, don't you?"

She continued to gaze at the boy's face for a moment before she turned her attention to Jack. Sadness washed over her fine features. "I do love him, a little bit more every day." She looked Jack squarely in the eyes. "That's why I'm taking the job in Utah."

⟶

The lancing pain in Jack's chest did not go away, even after Bobby had headed off to Ruth's. She was leaving, for good. He should have run after her, but he didn't. He stayed, rooted to the dingy tile floor, watching her vanish through the doorway.

He felt a flare of anger. How could she leave? She loved Paul and he loved her. Was it fair to pick up and take off? The anger was quickly overtaken by despair. Why should she stay? Just to be a friend to somebody else's kid? She had given him everything: friendship, sympathy, support, and he had given her nothing in return.

He scrubbed a hand through his cropped hair. He'd thought the problem was the guilt he felt about committing to another woman after Lacey, but the revelation came to him in a flash. It wasn't guilt. He was afraid, gut-wrenchingly, spine-chillingly afraid to love someone else and lose her as he had his wife.

Paul stirred and mumbled in his sleep. Jack spread the covers more securely over him.

Jack continued to puzzle it over. To love meant, perhaps, to lose. It was a frightening burden to care about someone else so much. But not to love? If he had the choice, would he rather not have a son? This precious kid who kept him awake with worry and wrenched his gut with indecision?

Paul was the greatest thing in his life. To not risk, would mean to not have experienced that overwhelming connection. His head spun. What was he doing? His life was running by in a frenetic blur and the only moments worth savoring were the ones he spent with Paul. And with Bobby.

But could he risk that kind of pain again? For them both? He watched Paul's delicate profile. Could the child withstand losing another woman in his life?

Ruth's face flashed across his mind. She had buried her beloved husband and somehow, somewhere, she'd found the courage to start another life.

He knew he had to talk to her. He needed to find out if he had what it took to love again.

18

Ruth's eyes flew open. She lay there, disoriented. The sound of a fierce storm battered the cottage walls. The time on the bedroom clock read 2:15 a.m. She wondered why Bobby hadn't called. She lifted the receiver to dial the woman's cell.

No dial tone.

"The storm must be messing with the reception," she babbled to herself.

She heard a *thunk* from the bedroom next door.

Her stomach clenched. Maybe it was Alva looking for something. Or perhaps Bobby had returned. But why would she be in the nursery?

Ruth grabbed a robe and tiptoed out into the hallway, inching her way across the creaky wood floor. She listened. All was quiet. Feeling chilled to the bone, she padded into the living room. There was Alva, snoring on the couch. The door to Bryce's room where Bobby was bunked was open and dark. Again she heard a noise from the nursery.

She searched for her cell phone to call the police. Where was the silly thing? With a sense of rising panic, she went to the sofa and gently shook Alva awake.

"Whaaa?" he said, one eye open. "What's a-goin' on? Is it morning yet? I ain't done sleeping."

"No," Ruth whispered in his ear. "I think someone is breaking in, through the nursery window. The phone is dead, too."

Both of Alva's eyes shot open. "Whazzat? A burglar? I'll handle this." He leapt off the sofa and charged into the kitchen in search of a weapon. He grabbed the first thing he saw, a crusty baguette, before he began to tiptoe down the hallway.

Ruth tried to restrain him. "Alva, let's get out and call the police."

"You just stay put, sweet cheeks. I'm ex military. I tangled with communists. I can handle it. Whoever it is ain't got nothin' on a commie." He hitched up his baggy trousers and continued stalking toward the bedroom, his socks slipping slightly on the wood.

"This is crazy, Alva. We need to get the police," she hissed. "Come with me."

Alva ignored her. After a moment of deep breathing, he launched himself, shoulder first, at the nursery door.

"No!" Ruth's cry filled the hallway, but it was too late.

The impact of the collision sent Alva's spindly body rebounding back across the space. His head made a hollow *thwop* noise as he came to a stop against the far wall.

She ran to him. "Are you okay?"

He shook his head and pushed her away before he approached the door again, this time trying the knob. It turned easily in his hand.

Ruth's skin prickled all over with goose bumps and she struggled to breathe.

The old man pushed the door open a few inches and stopped, readying the baguette like Don Quixote's spear.

"Don't do it. Please." Ruth's voice rose on a tide of fear. "Alva, no!"

With a deafening howl, he careened through the doorway.

Ruth screamed.

There was a crash and a high-pitched yell.

She ran into the room and flipped on the light.

Bobby lay on her back, covered in bread fragments. Alva sat on his bottom across from her, blinking against the sudden light.

"It's you," they both said at once.

Ruth was too stunned to speak.

"Whatcha doin' in here, Miss Walker?" Alva picked up the ruined baguette and absentmindedly stuck a wad of it into his mouth. "How's Paul?"

Bobby picked herself up in a shower of breadcrumbs. "Paul's got a concussion, but he's going to be okay. Why did you poke me with a loaf of bread?"

"We thought you was a burglar. Heard someone breaking in. Why did ya come in through the window anyways? I wouldn't have mashed you if you used the door."

Ruth was relieved to hear about Paul. She sank down on top of a cardboard box theoretically filled with all the parts necessary to build a playpen. Her knees shook. "It's my fault, Bobby. I heard someone climbing in. I must have imagined it."

"No, you were right. There was someone trying to get in."

Ruth's mouth went dry. "There was?"

Bobby nodded. "I heard someone shout 'no!' from the house, and I figured the fastest way to get in was through the window. Before I could get there, someone jumped out and ran down the street. I saw a car pull out. Sorry if I scared you. Are you two all right?"

Ruth nodded. "I think so, but the thought of someone breaking in terrifies me. What could they want?"

Bobby shook her head as she helped Alva to his feet. "Something to do with your research maybe?"

A light dawned in Ruth's mind. "Could be. Maybe Sandra noticed the missing pages from her notebook and came back to retrieve them."

Alva snorted. "Woulda been a mite bit easier to ring the doorbell."

Ruth had to agree with him on that point.

She filled Bobby in on her White Queens discovery while they called the police department and waited for Nate to arrive. Ruth contemplated calling Monk, but she decided it would only make him crazy with worry. There was nothing to be done. She was safe, temporarily, with Bobby and Alva for company.

Nate came and left, after dusting for prints and promising to drive by several more times before his shift was over. Mary would take over in the morning. Ruth knew she should get to sleep, but her nerves were on edge. The babies must have been stimulated by her emotions because they kept up a rigorous rolling and tumbling match.

Bobby fixed them both some tea, and Alva fell to snoring on the sofa again.

Ruth watched her from over the rim of her mug, noting the fine crease between her brows. "Bobby, what's wrong? You look like something is bothering you, aside from all this, I mean. Is it Paul's accident?"

She shook the black hair out of her eyes. "Oh, it's nothing. I've—I've decided to take the job in Utah. I told Jack tonight."

Ruth tried to keep her expression neutral. "What did he say?"

"Nothing." The disappointment was evident on her face. "I knew he wouldn't, but still. . ."

"You wished he would have stopped you?"

She sighed. "Yes, but he didn't, and that tells me I'm making the right decision to go. I'm going to stay long enough to wrap things up here. I'll still come and visit as much as I can."

"Things will not be the same here without you. Your uncle will be sad to have you move out of state, and so will I."

Bobby nodded, toying with her mug. The grief and determination revealed themselves on her face.

Ruth measured her words carefully. "I will miss you so very much, but if that's what you think is best, Monk and I will support you."

"Thank you. I've got to make a new beginning. It's time for me to restart my career." She yawned. "I'm going to lie down for a while. It's been a long night. How about you?"

"Yes, I'll try to get some sleep, too." She wondered if Jack Denny would be getting any rest that night.

Bryce and Maude arrived at roughly the same time the next morning, only moments after Bobby left. Maude held a plate of wrapped cookies in her hands. Bryce stepped through the door and kissed his mother, said hello to Maude, and then disappeared.

Ruth did not comment on the angry cast to his face. *Don't pester,* she reminded herself. *Don't smother. He'll tell you when he's ready.* She pulled her robe more securely around her middle and offered Maude some coffee.

"No, thank you, Ruth. I'm not ingesting caffeine anymore and you shouldn't, either."

"It's decaf," Ruth said, too tired to defend herself properly. "Please sit down."

"Ahh. Well, I happened to be at the police department this morning and I heard about your burglar. What is the world coming to these days?" She drummed stubby fingers on the table top. "I brought you some cookies."

"Oh, thank you. How considerate. What kind?"

"No fat, high fiber, soy bran cookies."

Ruth tried to look enthusiastic as she put them on the kitchen counter. "Er, thank you. I'll have some later."

Maude looked around and picked at a scratch on the wood. "Ruth, um, I need to ask your advice."

She swallowed her surprise. In all the years she'd known Maude, the woman was vastly more experienced at giving advice than asking for it. "Sure. Go ahead."

"I was wondering, if, you know, I should dye my hair."

Ruth eyed Maude's black bun. "Whatever for?"

"Well, I've got a few grays, you see, and anyway, somebody told me blond is more flattering on an experienced face."

Experienced face? Ruth tried to hide her smile. "Maude, is there by any chance a certain dentist you are trying to impress?"

"Me? Trying to impress Dr. Soloski? Of course not." A pink stain crept into her face. "He's not the kind you could impress easily, anyway. He's old money."

"I thought he was a dentist."

"Funny, Ruth," Maude said with a face that indicated she didn't think it was at all amusing. "Dr. Soloski is from *the* Soloskis. His parents made a bundle in the oil business."

"If he's from wealthy stock, why did he settle here?"

She raised an eyebrow. "To be near his sister, of course. She's an invalid."

"Yes, he told me. He said it's expensive to care for her."

Maude snorted. "He's just being modest. I admire that in a person, don't you? Taking care not to make anyone feel inferior?"

"Oh yes." Ruth looked up to find Alva chomping a cookie he'd taken from Maude's platter.

"Blecccch," he said, spitting it into the sink. "Whaddya call these? Shoe leather cookies? You could use 'em for coasters."

Ruth intervened before Maude could get her hackles up. "Alva, thanks for staying with me. You were a big help last night."

He nodded. "No trouble at all, ma'am. Just doing my job. I'm gonna go home now. Mrs. Hodges will expect me for breakfast."

Alva and Maude exchanged a glare before he left.

"Well, anyway, Maude, I think your hair is fine. It suits you."

"I've always thought so, but everyone needs a change now and then, don't you think?"

"I suppose."

"Maybe auburn instead of blond."

Ruth tried to make her expression encouraging. "Maybe. So have you been spending much time with Dr. Soloski these days?"

"Oh, not really. We chat a little when we can. I heard from Gene, I mean Dr. Soloski, that Roxie has some sort of health problem. Kidneys or something?"

"Yes. I heard that, too."

Maude lowered her voice. "She's not exactly lily-white, you know. I heard her son was a thief and stole from her clients. She tried to take the fall for him and it ruined her. Sad, isn't it? Raising a no-goodnik?"

Ruth thought back to her earlier conversations with Roxie. "Her son died, Maude. I don't think anything he did while he was living would make that loss any easier."

She sniffed. "Maybe, but the whole thing certainly left her penniless. She's a renter, you know."

Maude said the word as if it was a profanity.

Bryce came hesitantly into the kitchen. "Just looking for some breakfast."

Ruth resisted the urge to jump up and make it for him. If she was ever going to get this mothering thing straight for the twins, she'd have to be strong with Bryce. *Don't smother.*

Maude excused herself with a parting shot. "Make sure you keep moisturizing your belly. The stretch marks will be insane with two in there."

Ruth sighed and saw Maude to the door.

Bryce did not seem inclined toward conversation as he fixed himself toast and two fried eggs. The smell drove her from the kitchen along with a sudden recollection that it was the first Wednesday of the month and she needed to take Royland his worm delivery. Burglars or no burglars, she had a business to run. She pulled on some clothes and waddled out into the backyard.

The birds were happy to be released from their fenced area and promptly swarmed around her as she scattered bread cubes and protein pellets onto the ground. That would keep them busy and away from the worms. She added a few of Maude's cookies for good measure, noticing that the birds scrupulously avoided the bits.

The mash she applied to the top of the worm beds sent them into wiggly ecstasy. When they crept to the surface to feed, she scooped up a generous quantity of the squirming soil and put it in the spinner. A few cranks and the drum whirled off most of the dirt, leaving a pile of disgruntled worms at the bottom. She packed them into a breathable plastic bag and covered them with a thin layer of soil to keep them happy on the journey.

Bryce was watching her with a cup of coffee in one hand and a corner of toast in the other. Milton stared at him, dancing up and down on impatient bird feet.

Bryce ignored him and finished the toast. "Making a delivery?"

"Yes, it's Royland's day."

"I'll go with you."

"You don't have to."

"Yes, I do. Monk wouldn't want you to go by yourself, and he's not a man I'd want to make unhappy."

She laughed. "Me neither. You should have seen what happened when our summer help decided Monk's chowder needed more pepper."

Bryce smiled. "I'll bet he's not your summer help anymore."

"Exactly." Ruth walked slowly through the gaggle of birds to the gate, and they began their walk.

The sun shone through pockets of clouds, the ground saturated by the storm the night before. Sunshine warmed her back as they strolled along. She wanted to ask how his trip to San Francisco had gone, but she wasn't sure he'd welcome the inquiry. Instead she filled him in on the burglary attempt.

"Wow, Mom. You sure are attracting someone's attention and not in a good way. What did Monk say about the latest problem?"

She flushed. "He doesn't know yet."

"Oh, I see. If he did, he'd be on the next flight out."

"Or rent a car and get all kinds of tickets driving home at breakneck speed."

"Nice to have somebody love you that much." Bryce kicked at a stone on the sidewalk as they headed out of town.

They both shot an occasional look over their shoulders for oncoming cars. A welcome coolness in the air made the temperature just right for walking. The long winding drive to Royland's farm was damp when they arrived, so they had to pick their way carefully to avoid the sticky spots.

The silence lengthened until she couldn't stand it anymore. "How was your trip to San Francisco?"

"Okay, I guess. I signed the papers Roslyn is so anxious to get. The house can be sold any time. She probably has it up on the market by now." He jammed his hands into his pockets. "I also spoke to an employment agency but that led nowhere. It's so blasted unfair. I ran a company, I don't need to work for somebody and take orders like a high school kid. I've got a degree."

She looked at the petulant jut of his chin. *Oh, Bryce. You've got so much to learn.*

He looked at her. "You think I'm being arrogant, don't you?"

Stay quiet, Ruth. Keep your opinions to yourself. "Yes, I do."

His mouth tightened. "I've got skills. I'm a smart guy. Why should I have to start out doing a bunch of grunt work? One trucking outfit wanted me to tidy the office in between assignments."

Now that she'd gone ahead and opened her big mouth, might as well finish it off. "These people don't know you, and they won't until you can prove yourself. Your father started out sweeping and cleaning clinic floors until he got his own office. Nothing is owed to you, Bryce, just because you're intelligent and college educated." She waited for the inevitable fallout of her criticism. Why couldn't she have kept her mouth firmly closed?

Bryce's look gradually changed. A smile crept onto his face. "I thought you were going to say I was so smart I should hold out for something better."

"I wanted to, but I thought the other advice was more helpful."

He laughed. "Sometimes bitter medicine works best, as Dad would have said."

She joined in the laughter until it struck her. "Bryce, are you looking for a job. . .around here? In California?" It couldn't be true after so many years of distance.

Bryce looked up at the ramshackle farm as they approached. "I've got no reason to stay in Chicago. I thought I might stick around for a while, get to know my new brother and sister, or brothers, or sisters."

"That sounds like a great idea to me." Ruth's heart felt lighter than it had in a very long time as they walked together in the sun.

Monk was more than perturbed. He about jumped through the phone line when Ruth told him late that afternoon about the break-in.

"What is going on there?" he roared. "You've got to go immediately to the police station and stay there until I get back. I'll book the earliest flight I can find."

She waited for his tirade to wind down. "Honey, I'm not going to go sit in the police station. Bryce is here and Jack is coming over later to talk to me about something. I'm perfectly fine, safe as can be."

"What about the babies? Are they okay? Did the shock of the break-in stunt their growth or anything?"

"Not that I can tell from the kicks to my kidneys. Did you get the crop in?"

"Most of it. Dave can finish it up. Look, Ruthy, I'm going to hang up now and call the airport. Don't go anywhere by yourself, not even out to get the newspaper from the driveway. Those college people are trying to do you in, I just know it. The whole thing makes my skin crawl."

"I'm going to tell Jack all about the White Queens and leave the whole thing up to him. How's that?"

"You promise to stay out of the investigation?"

"I will do my best to keep my nosy tendencies in check."

Monk grumbled. "Well, I guess that will have to do for now, but I'll feel much better when I'm back home."

Ruth hung up thinking the very same thing.

A scant half hour later, Jack arrived. Instead of staying for a visit, he took Ruth on a ride back toward town. "Nate's meeting me at the Finny Hotel. We're going to take Ethan and Sandra in for questioning. I wanted you to stick around and add your two cents on this White Queens thing Bobby told me you figured out. How does that sound?"

"Great, I'd be happy to help. Monk will be relieved that I've got a temporary police escort. He thinks I should be living at the station until he returns."

He laughed. "I wouldn't recommend it. The coffee is terrible. Can I buy you some dinner after?" He tapped his fingers on the steering wheel. "There's, er, something I want to talk to you about."

"Of course." Ruth took a moment to call Bryce and tell him about her plans.

"Okay," he said. "I'll fill Monk in when he calls every half hour. I'm going to go for a run on the beach, but I'll take the cell phone with me."

They pulled up to the Finny Hotel and she waited in the car while Jack and Nate headed inside. Jack returned a few minutes later, a frown on his face. "They checked out this morning."

Nate blew into his mustache. "Yeah, but the clerk said they were carrying dive gear, almost as if they were going to take one last dip before they skipped town."

Jack arched an eyebrow. "Surely they wouldn't do that. I called and told them to wait for me this morning. They know something is up. Why go diving?"

Nate considered. "Maybe they're desperate to find something. Desperate people do desperately stupid things, as we are daily reminded."

"Maybe," Jack said as he got into the car. "How about a quick trip to the beach, Ruth?"

⌇⌇⌇

Sandra and Ethan were just headed into the choppy water when Jack and Nate pulled up. They stood there, frozen for a moment, the waves lapping around their shins, before exchanging a hurried conversation as the officers approached. Ruth stayed a safe distance behind, but not so far that she couldn't hear every word.

Jack's tone was like iron. "I told you to wait at the hotel."

"Oh, uh, is that what you said? We weren't sure." Sandra's face was milk white where it was framed by the black of her wet suit. They shuffled up to dry ground to meet the officers.

Jack did not return Sandra's smile. "You need to come to the station now."

"Right now?" Ethan said.

"Right now," Jack assured them.

The young man straightened. "Why? What exactly is the reason for this? Are we being arrested?"

"Not yet." Jack smiled at them.

It didn't look like a friendly grin to Ruth.

"Just wanted to chat about a couple of Queens. You have time for that, don't you?"

Sandra and Ethan looked at each other again before they followed Nate to his car, Ruth and Jack a few steps behind.

⌇⌇⌇

They must have been granted time to change their clothes after they arrived at the station, Ruth noted, because Sandra joined them in the conference room wearing sweatpants and a long-sleeved shirt. She sat rigid in the chair, fingers laced, knees pressed together. Her throat worked convulsively as she darted a glance around the room. "Where's Ethan?"

Jack offered a cup of coffee, which the woman declined. "He's waiting with Mary. We thought it would be nice to chat with you both separately."

"Um, I'd rather not."

Though his tone was light, Jack's words left no room for compromise. "I think you don't have much choice. I can arrest you, if you'd like, and we can take it from there."

Her eyes rounded in terror. "No, no. I didn't do anything. I didn't commit any crime."

"I asked you before why you were here in Finny and you only told me half the truth. Now tell me the real reason." Jack stared at her from behind his desk. "All of it."

She didn't answer.

Nate gave her a smile. "You'd be better off going along with him, ma'am, otherwise he's going to be stuck to you like duct tape until you come clean. I've seen it before and it's not pretty."

Ruth held her breath to see if the woman would talk.

Sandra cleared her throat. "We didn't do anything wrong. Well, we maybe didn't exactly tell the whole truth, but that's it. We were following the clues from the journal."

"Are you sure Indigo's writing is factual?" Ruth said.

"All the details check out. The life of Indigo Orson is traceable, and believe me, we know because we spent months doing just that."

For some reason which she could not understand, Ruth was relieved that Indigo really did exist.

"Why are you here in Finny?" Jack repeated.

"We really did come to do a reenactment of Indigo's life, but we sort of had another goal in mind, too."

"The White Queens?" Ruth said.

She nodded. "I guess we didn't cover our tracks very well."

"So there really is a set of priceless pearls right under Finny's nose?"

"We believe so. I told you I stumbled on Indigo's journal in an old box in the university basement when we were researching for our project. We did some more checking and all the facts came together. Orson was carrying the pearls when he boarded the *Triton*, as far as we can ascertain."

Jack snorted. "But that was more than 150 years ago."

"As far as history records, the boat was supposedly only carrying coal so it hasn't had a whole lot of attention. Plus it settled at an awkward angle so the lower cabins, where the Orsons stayed, were pretty much inaccessible."

Jack stared at her, with his elbows on the table. "So you decided to recover the pearls yourselves?"

"It was a long shot, but Ethan is a great diver. He talked the Skylar Foundation into giving us some money up front, providing they got their cut of the treasure. They sent Reggie to help, but I really think it was more to keep an eye on us."

As little as she'd seen of Reggie, Ruth was not surprised to hear he was more than just a cameraman.

Jack nodded. "People dove that wreck before. How do you know they didn't recover the pearls and keep it on the lowdown?"

"They didn't know what to look for, for one thing, and the big storm you had last year caused the wreck to shift. According to Ethan's preliminary dive, the movement opened up the under decking for exploration." She toyed with a thread on her pants. "He was sure we would find the pearls."

"What made him so certain?"

Her face crumpled. "Desperation, I think, same as me. The university didn't renew his scholarship for next term, and his family couldn't help him with the tuition. He figured we'd give the research project a good effort and hopefully find the pearls, too. I never could snag a scholarship in the first place, so the idea of finding something that would fund my education seemed like a reasonable gamble."

Nate tapped a pencil on his knee. "Correct me here, but wouldn't the pearls belong to the state government since that wreck is within a three-mile distance of the coast?"

Sandra clamped her lips shut, her face coloring. "It doesn't matter anyway, does it? We didn't find the pearls."

"Did Reggie?"

She started. "Reggie?"

Jack cocked his head. "It would fit. Maybe he found the pearls and decided to take them for himself. One of you strangled him and dumped his body in the ocean."

A shiver rippled Sandra's shoulders. "That was horrible. We didn't kill him. As a matter of fact, we cautioned him against night diving, but Reggie was a, uh, determined person. Ethan tried to keep an eye on him, figuring he'd be happy to double-cross us. The night Reggie went out, Ethan kept watch for hours until he gave up. And anyway, why would we stick around if Reggie had already gotten the pearls and we'd killed him for them?"

Jack leveled a look at her. "Good question, Ms. Marconi. I'd love to hear your answer."

Sandra didn't seem to have an answer. She stuttered to a stop several times before bursting into tears. Nate went to fetch a glass of water. She was dismissed to the waiting room and told to stay in Finny for the next few days.

Ethan's interview was similar in content though much less emotional. "We haven't committed a crime. We should be allowed to go. You have no right to keep us here."

Jack drummed his fingers on the desk. "Did you try to run down Mrs. Budge?"

Ethan blinked but remained expressionless. "No. Why would I do that?"

"Because she figured out the secret of the treasure you're looking for."

He shot her a quick look. "I didn't know that possibility existed until Sandra told me there were missing pages. Frankly, no offense, Mrs. Budge, but I thought the journal was so generic that you wouldn't be smart enough to glean any info about the pearls from it."

Ruth sighed. Round, waxy, and dumb. She really had to work on how she presented herself.

"Did you try to break into her house to retrieve the papers?" Jack continued.

"No." He sighed. "We're probably idiots for thinking we could find those pearls, but we're not criminals, believe it or not."

Ruth believed him, but then again, she reminded herself, she believed everyone.

After another string of questions, Jack dismissed him with the same admonishment he'd given Sandra, along with one other piece of advice. "Stay out of the water."

Ethan gave him a cool look. "I will, but if someone murdered Reggie for those pearls, then we're not the only ones you need to be worrying about."

Jack slouched in the chair after Ethan left. Ruth noticed the tired shadows under his eyes. Paul's accident had taken a toll on him and she was sure Bobby's announcement had, too.

"Thanks for helping out, Ruth. Are you ready for dinner?"

~

He took her to a small café at the edge of town, one busy with locals and visitors. She wondered if he was looking for some background noise to discourage busy ears from listening in. They settled down over bowls of chicken chowder and chopped salads.

"Thanks for having dinner with me. Too bad it's not as good as Monk's soup."

She laughed. "Nothing's as good as Monk's soup."

"True. Monk is an amazing guy, and he's devoted to you."

"Yes. I am very blessed."

Jack looked around the room for the umpteenth time before he finally spoke. "In a way, that's kind of what I wanted to ask you about. You've heard that Bobby is leaving?"

"Yes."

He shifted, toying with the spoon in his hand. "I'll be honest here. I want her to stay, but I'm having trouble giving her a reason. I'm not sure if I can't let go of Lacey or if I'm just a coward about committing to Bobby." He sighed. "I'm a dismal failure in my personal life."

Her heart ached at his painful admission. He looked so confused, a vulnerability creeping over his face that she hadn't seen before. "No, you're not, Jack. If you were, Bobby wouldn't love you."

"I guess. Do you mind if I ask you something personal?"

"Fire away, Detective."

"I just wondered, you know, after Phillip died, how you found closure and everything. How did you put that behind you so you could start a new life with Monk?"

"That's the thing, Jack. I don't think it is a new life. It's just another phase of the one God gave me in the first place. But I admit that I spent years being mad, and devastated, and then a few more feeling guilty for not feeling that way."

He nodded slowly. "I've been trying real hard to figure it out. I loved my wife more than anything, but I know that she wouldn't want me and Paul to be alone. I think it's something else." His forehead creased. "I'm pretty sure that I feel more afraid than guilty."

She covered his hand with hers. "I know that kind of fear, Jack. I've been there, too, and now, at my advanced age, I'm going to bring two more lives into this world with all the worry and fear that entails. If that isn't enough to strike terror into the heart, I don't know what is."

He leaned forward. "So how do you do it? How do you accept that?"

She thought carefully before she answered. "I try to remember Jeremiah 29:11."

He squinted in recollection. " 'For I know the plans I have for you,' declares the Lord, 'plans to prosper you and not to harm you, plans to give you hope and a future.' "

She sat back. "Exactly, and I can tell what you're thinking. We've both already experienced a hefty dose of harm, haven't we? Your wife, my husband."

"That's right."

She took a breath, trying to put into words the sum of a lifetime of love and loss. "But we're still here, Jack. We still have joy and terror and fear, and more joy and bunches more fear. We still have the chance to laugh and hug and weep. We have the great privilege to get up every day and love someone, to show the tenderness to another that God has shown us. As long as we have that chance, we have to take it."

He didn't look convinced. "That's a hard thing to do."

She nodded. "Yes, but if we turned our back on the chance to love, then our lives would be a much greater calamity, a waste of our God-given purpose. There's a reason you are here, beyond your job and your duties. You are here to love other people, and that's just not a safe thing to do, is it?"

He looked at her for a long moment, as if he was solving a puzzle in his mind. Then he grinned, a wide, slow smile that spread over his face in degrees. "Nope, it's a crazy, risky, nutzo thing to do." He laughed. "How did you get so smart, Mrs. Budge?"

"Oh, believe me, Jack. Most of my days are spent in terror about the impending birth of two—count them—two babies. But now and again, God pokes me with a bit of joy and I know He's got my future in His hands and theirs, too." She thought of Bryce and his decision to stay close by, and Cootchie and Dimple's imminent return. An infant elbow, or perhaps a foot, made a tickle in her belly. "Watching Monk try to put together a baby crib provides enough laughter to fill me up for a long while."

Their chuckles were cut short by the chirp of his cell phone.

"Duty calls," he said as he answered it.

She watched his face change. The pleasure gave way to a professional mask, his voice morphed into clipped tones. "I'm on my way."

He clicked off the phone and looked at her. "I'm sorry, Ruth. It's Bryce."

20

Jack drove her to the hospital and supplied her with sketchy facts along the way. Bryce had been found on the beach with a serious head injury.

Ruth felt as though her head was spinning like a carousel. "Did he fall off the cliff?"

Jack gave her a sympathetic look. "I don't know the details, but we'll find out soon."

She sat in numb terror as they completed the drive.

The nurse met them in the waiting area. "There's a lot of swelling in his brain. The doctors are taking some images now to assess the situation."

Assess the situation. Did medical professionals have a book somewhere that taught them how to give information without really telling a person anything? She felt light-headed, and Jack led her to a chair. For the first time Ruth noticed Roxie in the corner, knit cap twisted in her hands.

Her eyes were bloodshot. "Ruth, I'm so sorry. I found your son on the rocks and called the ambulance. Is he going to be okay?"

"The rocks?" Jack came over. "How was he lying? Did you see anyone else around?"

She shook her head. "I was out checking the boat because I just had the motor adjusted and I wanted to see if I got my money's worth. Bryce was lying on his stomach on the bottom of the cliff, the one that the pelicans like to roost on. There was no one with him, but the tide was coming in fast, so I thought I'd better get him out of the water."

Jack's eyes narrowed. "So he was just on his stomach there? Alone? No one else was around?"

"No. Maybe I shouldn't have moved him, but the tide didn't give me much choice."

Ruth's stomach spasmed. "This is like some kind of horrible dream."

"So you didn't see him fall?" Jack pressed.

Roxie's eyes widened. "Look, Detective, I didn't do anything to this kid. I could have left him there to drown, but I didn't, so don't give me the third degree. It's called being a Good Samaritan, isn't it? I thought that was a good thing." She jammed her hands into her pockets. "Oh, I forgot about this."

She fished a small object from her pocket and gave it to Ruth. It was a fragment of shell about five inches long, pearly on the inside and the outer covering rough and dull colored. "It was in his hand when I found him. Weird."

"Why weird?" Ruth managed as she stared at the thing.

"He must have brought it with him or something because that's not from any kind of abalone I've ever seen."

Ruth squeezed the shard in her hand, too scared to speak, too overwhelmed to say anything. Visions of her boy swam before her eyes. Bryce, her baby, her son. "Please, God," she whispered. "Please help."

Jack pressed a hand to her shoulder. "Are you okay, Ruth?"

She shook her head. "I am going to be sick."

Jack ran to summon a nurse, and Roxie escorted Ruth to the bathroom, where she promptly threw up. Roxie helped her to the sink, and she got a good look at herself.

The terror had carved her face into an aged mask. She pressed a hand to her cheeks, wondering how much longer her legs would hold her up.

Roxie watched her in the mirror, her eyes bright with sympathy, her hands ready to catch Ruth if she faltered. "Can you make it back to the waiting room?"

"I'm not sure. My knees are awfully wobbly."

"Lean on me." Roxie put her shoulder under Ruth's and clasped a hand around her waist. She half escorted, half carried her out to a chair. The nurse went off to find a temporary room for Ruth. Jack brought her a cup of water. They stood, uncertain, watching her for a sign of what they should do next.

None of it seemed to touch Ruth. She was isolated, insulated, by a cloud of disbelief thick as Finny's springtime fog. The only sound that made a dent was the booming voice of Monk charging through Jack's phone line. The detective handed the cell over to her and moved a discreet distance away with Roxie.

"Ruthy? Jack told me. How is Bryce? I'm still stuck here because there's a whopper of a storm coming in. Oh, Ruthy, if I thought it would be any faster, I'd rent a car and drive, or even crawl on my hands and knees. Are you okay? I mean, health wise? Do you need to see a doctor?"

"I'm okay." Her voice sounded dull in her own ears. "Just sick. They're finding me a room to lie down."

"This is killing me, not being there with you. Is Bobby there? Is Jack staying with you?"

Ruth looked up to see Bobby just entering the building, a worried frown on her face. "She's here. They're all here. I'm perfectly fine. It's Bryce I'm not sure about. He's got a bad head injury." Her voice broke.

"I know, honey, but he's a strong young man. Comes from good stock. He'll make it. I just know it."

It was exactly what she needed to hear. They talked for a long while; the anguish in his voice was clear.

"I'll be home just as soon as I can, Ruthy. I'll pray for Bryce. Mom and Dad will, too, and Dave. We're all going to pray like crazy for him and for you. I love you. I love you so much."

"I love you, too, Monk. Come home soon."

The doctor emerged a moment later with discouraging news. "He was hit with something, I'm fairly certain. The wound is too precise to have come from falling against those rocks. He has a skull fracture and significant swelling. We'll keep him in a medically induced coma to allow his body to rest. When the swelling subsides a little, we'll see if we can bring him out of it."

"If you can bring him out of it?" Ruth repeated, stupidly. "What happens if you can't?"

The man raised a hand to quiet her. "He's had a severe head injury. Nothing is guaranteed here. We'll have to take things one day at a time. That's the best I can do for now."

It seemed to Ruth that she'd been taking things one day at a time since the day she'd discovered she was pregnant. *I ought to be better at it by now.*

Dr. Ing was summoned to check on her. Bobby sat with her through the doctor's gentle poking and prodding. The sound of the babies' heartbeats reassured Ruth. He told her to get some rest, keep hydrated, and try to relax.

"That's a good one," she told Jack and Bobby as they rode home in Jack's car. "How can I relax? Someone tried to run me down, Paul is hurt, our house is broken into, and now Bryce." Her eyes pricked with tears. "I should be there, in the hospital. I should stay with my son."

Bobby squeezed her hand. "The doctor insisted you go home until morning. They'll call if there's any change at all. I'm going to stay with you every minute, and we'll pray together. Jack, Mary, and Nate are going to take shifts watching the house at night. Uncle Monk will be home as soon as he can. You need to take care of yourself and the babies."

She nodded, but the feeling of dread in her gut did not lessen.

"And if that isn't enough," Bobby said with a smile, "we can always go get Alva. He's ferocious with a baguette."

In spite of herself, Ruth smiled. "I guess it will be okay to go home for a little while."

They bundled her into the house.

Jack lingered in the kitchen after checking the house and grounds. Ruth surmised he was hoping to talk to Bobby alone, so she made herself scarce.

Jack's plan apparently did not pan out as she heard Bobby say, "Let's talk later. Now isn't a good time."

It is a good time, she wanted to tell the girl. She felt the urge to scream it at the top of her lungs. *Grab hold of love because it can be gone in a moment.* Sobs choked her throat. She went into the bathroom and turned on the bathtub taps for a good long soak. The running water covered the sound of her weeping.

Tucked into bed an hour later, her dreams were troubled, vague images of cold water and suffocating darkness. Sleep eluded her for a long while until she did finally drop off into a fitful sleep.

The next morning she got up before dawn and quietly made tea, trying not to wake Bobby. She was halfway through her cup of decaf Earl Grey when she remembered the shell Roxie had given her. It was still in the pocket of her sweater. She laid it gently on the table, watching the play of colors in the fluorescent light. A picture of a sparkling walkway sprang into her mind. She could see them both in her imagination, Hui and Indigo feasting on Hangtown Fry, watching the sun electrify the treasures thrown up from the sea.

Bobby interrupted her thoughts, padding into the kitchen in a robe and slippers. "You're up early. Did you get any sleep?"

"Some." Ruth pushed the shell to her. It seemed so important somehow, to understand how the small piece wound up in her son's hand. Thinking of Bryce made her throat thicken, but she steeled herself against tears. She wouldn't do him any good if she turned into mush. "How could Roxie tell this abalone isn't from around here?"

Bobby peered at it. "It looks like a regular abalone shell to me. I'm better with land species than ocean life, I'm afraid. I was learning a lot from Ethan, but we didn't have a chance to complete our dives. Do you think it's a clue to who—" Her words trailed off.

"I don't know, but it's the only thing I can do to help him. Wait a minute." Ruth hurried to the shelf where she'd put the library books.

She grabbed the one entitled *Pacific Coast Ocean Life*. There was a section on abalone, oysters, and mussels. Ruth read aloud about the five major species of abalone along the California coast.

"Did you know abalone come in designer colors?" Ruth squinted at the small print. "Black, white, green, pink, and red."

"I've never seen most of those types."

She read on. "That's because abalone is such a slow grower and reproducer. Indigo was right when she said their numbers were falling, and apparently we haven't done much to fix that problem since 1850. Look at this."

Ruth pointed to a section in bold print. "In California currently, all five major species of abalone are depleted."

Bobby picked up the shell and looked at it closely while Ruth continued to read. "People can still harvest red abalone, but they have to follow strict rules. Roxie was telling me about that. It is illegal to harvest white, green, and pink and black at all. The white one is even on the endangered species list."

Bobby frowned. "You know, I've seen red abalone shells before and this one is different, now that I think about it." She turned it over and examined the other side. "Of course, we've only got a piece of it, but it's pretty high domed and small." She hefted it in her hand. "It's light, too, and the inside is silvery white rather than multicolored."

Ruth scanned down the page to a small picture. "Does it look like this one?"

They bent their heads together and held the fragment up to the tiny photo.

"Sure does to me." Bobby read the caption.

The both sat back in surprise.

Bobby was the first to break the silence. "The question is, considering they're nearly extinct, where did Bryce get a shell from a white abalone?"

~

They puzzled it over as they drove to the hospital for the second time that day. Bobby insisted that Ruth come home for a proper lunch and a nap after she sat with Bryce for several hours. Now her lunch sat precariously in her stomach as they returned. Ruth had an increasingly uneasy feeling. All of the frightening events from the past few months began to fit together. Who had an excellent knowledge of abalone, a connection to Reggie, and a definite need for money? She'd been so focused on the college people, she hadn't considered the other person who fit all the criteria: Roxie Trotter, the woman who found Bryce on the beach. She shared her thoughts with Bobby.

"It is mighty coincidental, but why did she bother bringing Bryce to the hospital? If she'd already murdered Reggie she couldn't have too much regard for the sanctity of life."

"Maybe she remembered how much it hurt to lose her son and she couldn't kill mine." The thought sent a ripple up Ruth's spine.

"And why bother running you down and breaking into the cottage? Doesn't seem like there's much for her to gain by that." Bobby drummed her fingers on the steering wheel. "I think we'd better talk to Jack about all this again. When is Uncle Monk coming back?"

"He finally got a three o'clock flight. Bubby Dean is going to pick him up at the airport at six." She felt a surge of relief even saying the words aloud. Monk would be home soon. They would pick up the pieces of their crazy life and move on. He would be right by her side until Bryce recovered and help her figure out the whole rotten mess. She held onto that thought firmly as Bobby drove her to visit her son.

Her eyes flooded with tears again at the sight of him. He was pale, so pale, against the white of the pillows, his face swollen in its white wrappings. An IV tube curled around his arm, and a monitor recorded the steady beat of his heart.

In her mind she heard the tiny beating of her twins' hearts, and she held Bryce's hand. Her three children, her three precious blessings from God. She had made mistakes, no doubt, but sitting there with one hand on her abdomen and the other in Bryce's limp fingers, she knew. No one on earth could love these three children like she did. She would embrace even the smallest moment God gave her with them, and with His good grace they would live or die knowing that they were loved.

Tears flowed freely down her face as she pressed her cheek to his hand. "Lord, if it is Your will, help my son to heal. Help him to wake up and be there to love his new siblings. Help me to keep them all safe."

She closed her eyes imagining the sound of their heartbeats outside and within.

—

Alva woke her some hours later when he clanked his toolbox down on the small table.

"Oh, sorry there," he stage whispered. "Didn't mean to startle ya. I figgered I'd just leave some candy for you and the buns in yer oven. The nurses said I shouldn't bring it in so I hadta hide it in a laundry bag. Nurses is kinda crabby sometimes. Must be from hanging out with all them sick people. Or maybe it's 'cuz they don't let 'em roller skate in the hallways. Hungry, sweet cheeks?"

"No, not really."

His forehead creased into a web of wrinkles. "Them babies might be up for a snack, though. You shouldn't deprive them of their sugar. They need to crystallize their bones and all that, otherwise they'll come out like rubber chickens."

She laughed. "You may be right about that. What do you have in your stash today?"

"Oh, the usual, only I scored some red licorice at the grocery. Can't chew it, though; sticks to my choppers."

She selected a crumpled bag of jelly beans and they sat down to nibble. Alva ate his chocolate bar with gusto while he stared at Bryce.

He tossed the wrapper in the trash and pointed a sticky finger toward the stricken man. "So, when you figger he's going to wake up?"

Tears crowded her eyes again. "He's been badly hurt, Alva. The doctor's aren't sure . . .if he is ever going to wake up."

Alva stared at her and then at Bryce. All at once he started to laugh. His chuckles grew louder and louder until tears ran down his face. "Those doctors is a hoot, ain't they? Of course he's a-goin' to wake up. Everybody wakes up, iffen not here then in heaven. The likes of them doctors. So many years in them fancy schools and they ain't learned a scootch." He wiped his eyes.

She looked in amazement at Alva, a nutty old man who in the oddest moments saw things with such clarity that it took her breath away. She found herself filled with happiness at sharing a moment with him. She reached a hand out to his. "You are a great friend, Alva, and a very wise man."

He grinned and tapped a finger to his temple. "That's on account of the preservatives in this candy. Keeps a brain sharp, you know."

A nurse poked her head in. "You aren't handing out candy, are you, Mr. Hernandez? I specifically told you not to do that."

He wiped a hand over his sticky mouth. "Who me? Nah. I'm just chatting is all." He winked at Ruth and lowered his voice as the nurse left. "I'd better go. Nurse Atilla there will take my treasures if I'm not careful." Alva dropped a kiss on Ruth's cheek and got up to leave.

An odd thought popped into Ruth's head. "Alva, will you do me a big favor?"

"Anything for you, sweet cheeks." He listened to her request and scuttled off, checking the hallway in both directions for the nurse before he ventured out.

21

Jack had an extra shot of coffee before he headed to the hospital for the second time that day. He was terrified and elated at the same time. He knew it was wrong, with Bryce struggling to stay alive, but he also knew with a certainty that didn't visit him often that he was meant to share his life with Bobby. He had to tell her that he loved her, he had to ask her to stay. He'd waited far too long already.

He found her in the third floor waiting room.

"Bryce's condition hasn't changed," she told him. "Ruth has been sitting with him for hours. I'm worried about her."

"Should she go home and lie down?"

"I think so. I basically carried her out of here at lunchtime, but she wasn't having any part of it this time. She's got her mind fixed on figuring out who did this to him. As a matter of fact, Ruth and I have been concocting some wild theories that we figured we better share with you."

Noting the intensity on her face, Jack decided personal matters could wait a few more minutes. "You've got my undivided attention."

They sat, and Bobby filled him in on all things abalone.

Jack raised an eyebrow. "So you think that shell is the key to whoever attacked him?"

"Yes, crazy as it sounds. You don't look convinced."

"Oh, it's not that. Any theory is worth investigating at this point, and Ruth has delivered up some oddball solutions to previous crimes that have proven to be spot on. I've got another angle I'm working on. As a matter of fact, I'm meeting someone later today who may shed some light on things."

"Good. We could use some light around here."

"That's for sure." He coughed and cleared his throat, shifting on the hard plastic chair.

She looked closely at him. "Are you okay? You look kind of pale."

"Yes, I'm fine." He took a deep breath and took her hand. "Bobby, I want to talk to you about something other than murder and mayhem."

Her black eyes were curious. "Shoot."

"I've had some time to think about what's important." His words died away as she waited. Again he sucked in a deep breath and exhaled to steady the spasms in his stomach. "It's been hard for me, after losing Lacey, to think about starting

445

over, but here goes."

He looked into her earnest face and his heart melted again, filled with a warmth he was hopeless to describe. "I love you, Bobby. I've loved you from the moment I saw you. There is something about you that completes me, that gives me a reason to get up in the morning and fills a place in my heart that I didn't know was empty."

Her lips parted slightly. He thought he saw a sheen of moisture in her eyes.

Gaining courage, he forged ahead. "You are a huge part of my life and Paul's life, and I want you to stay here, to make a life with me." He waited, holding his breath.

She blinked. "Wow. I know how hard that was for you to say, Jack. I'm kind of surprised. I mean, I really hoped to hear that for a long time, but I'd kind of decided I was never going to."

"I know. It shouldn't be a surprise, but I've been stupid, afraid to commit, afraid of investing in someone again. I'm sorry it took so long, Bobby, but I'm ready now."

"Oh, Jack. You are a wonderful man and a great father." She squeezed his hand for a long moment before she let it go. "But I can't stay."

His mouth fell open. "What? Why not? Because I've been such a clod?"

Her smile was wistful. "No, not that. Let me think how to say it."

She looked away for a moment, before her gaze returned to his face.

"It's because I don't think you're over your wife." She held up a hand when he started to protest. "I have to finish this. I think you convinced yourself you had a change of heart because I said I was leaving, not because you really wanted to commit."

She reached out a hand to stroke his cheek. "I love you, Jack. You are so special to me, and maybe someday we can start a life together if neither of us has gone in a different direction, but I'm not going to force you into that decision. That's not good grounds for a relationship."

He started to speak, but she cut him off.

"It's better this way, for both of us, and for your son. I'll be sure to say good-bye to him before I leave for Utah."

And she was gone.

Jack felt like he'd been hit with a two-by-four. He was too weak to get up from the chair and go after her. His grand realization was too little, too late. Bobby was going to walk out of his life and Paul's and leave him with an aching hole in his heart. He'd finally messed things up so badly they couldn't be repaired.

His PDA beeped, reminding him of his appointment. The sound seemed far away, but it brought him back, at least enough for him to get to his feet. The pain in his gut did not lessen as he headed to the car. Why had he been such a fool? Bobby thought he was committing out of guilt, not out of love.

Maybe she was right. Was he really over Lacey? Did anyone ever really get over losing a spouse? Maybe he hadn't gotten over it, but he'd been able to move beyond, he was sure. He was ready to start a new phase, as Ruth had put it. He believed that with all his heart. It didn't matter, though, because Bobby didn't believe it. She would move on, find someone else, and he would see her only when she came to visit Monk and Ruth. Darkness gripped his insides.

The road north to Pacifica seemed endless. The surf thundered along Highway 1, mirroring his own inner turbulence. Another storm was rolling in along the water, dark clouds massing on the horizon. He could not keep his thoughts from Bobby, with her easy laugh and gentle smile. Bobby falling in love with someone else, making a life with another man.

It was after four before he pulled up at the small stucco house set apart from the road by a scruffy patch of lawn. Mr. Glenn greeted him with a smile and a hearty hug. "Well, hello there, Detective. Come to work on another merit badge?" The man's blue eyes sparkled from under white shaggy brows.

"No, Mr. Glenn. You made me do enough of those to earn my Eagle Award. I just had a question."

"A question for your old scoutmaster? I can't imagine what information you don't have access to in your line of work. Come in, let's get out of this wind."

They settled into a tiny living room. Mr. Glenn brought Jack a cup of coffee. "If you don't mind my saying so, you look a little down. Everything okay at work?"

"Oh, crazy as usual. Work is fine."

"And Paul?"

"He broke his wrist falling down the stairs. He's okay, but Louella is exhausted because she insists on holding his hand every time he goes up or down. I think the woman is about pooped out."

Mr. Glenn laughed. "Louella can handle it. I recall her managing a den full of ten-year-old boys without breaking a sweat."

"She could still do it, I'll bet." Jack put down his cup. "Anyway, that isn't why I came. I remembered something you taught us a long time ago about knot tying. Do you recall that project?"

"Of course. I also recall you and Nate tying up Roger so thoroughly we had to cut him out with a knife."

Jack laughed. "I blocked that out, I guess. I wonder if Roger has forgiven me."

"Probably. What can I do to help you?"

Jack slid the photo of the knot over to him. "Do you recognize this type of knot?"

"Hmmm. Let me see. I'm thinking it's a figure eight on a bight."

"That's what Ruth's husband thought, too, but he said it isn't the kind of knot they used a lot on board his ship."

"I wouldn't think so. It's bulky and you need a lot of rope to tie it."

TREASURE UNDER FINNY'S NOSE

"Yes. That's why I came. I know it's a shot in the dark, but I wondered if you might know what kind of hobbyist or professional might use this knot?"

Mr. Glenn frowned. "Well, rock climbers, maybe." He winked at Jack. "Eagle Scouts, of course. That's about all I can think of."

Jack sat back feeling depleted. "We thought of the rock climbing angle, too. Nothing else comes to mind?"

"No, son, I surely wish I could be of more help, but the little gray cells aren't what they used to be."

"No problem." They chatted for a while until Jack excused himself. "It was good to see you. I guess I better be hitting the road before the rain comes in. Thanks, Mr. Glenn."

"Anytime, Jack." The man walked him to the car. Wind swirled the leaves of a nearby bank of eucalyptus. Jack started the car and was pulling away from the curb when he noticed Mr. Glenn waving at him.

He backed up and rolled down the window.

The man leaned down. "I just thought of something. There is one other type of person who might use a knot like that."

Jack's eyes widened as he listened. "Thanks so much, Mr. Glenn. I'll be in touch."

He hit the accelerator and took off for Finny.

✦

Nate was waiting for him when he returned, the printout in his hand. "You're right, but how did you figure it out?"

"I didn't. Mr. Glenn did."

"Scoutmaster Glenn? No way."

"Yes way."

"Did he make you whittle a spoon or something while you were there?"

"No." Jack's thoughts whirled. "It's the means, but what would the motive be?"

"That's the million-dollar question." Nate pulled on his mustache.

Jack's mind raced. "Could it have something to do with abalone?"

"What did you say?"

"Abalone."

The officer's face screwed up in confusion. "Why would somebody get murdered for abalone? They don't even make pearls."

"There are all kinds of treasure, my friend." Jack's thoughts turned to Bobby. He wondered if he'd lost his treasure forever.

22

Ruth held Bryce's hand, stroking it gently, willing the life back into it. The doctor explained that they were easing up on the medicine, hoping he would show signs of coming around. So far, she'd seen no movement but the rise and fall of his chest. Not the slightest hopeful twitch in the long hours she'd sat there. The clock read 6:15. Monk's plane would touch down soon.

She got up to stretch her back muscles, shuffling around the small room cluttered with IVs and equipment of all sorts. The shell she'd asked Alva to deliver caught her eye again. She picked up the thing he'd pirated from the dentist's office and held it to the light along with the shard that Roxie had given her. She rubbed her tired eyes, but the strange similarity remained.

How could it be? It was impossible. She twisted and turned them both until her hands ached.

Bobby arrived with a cup of decaf for her. "Looking at those shells again?"

"I'm telling you, Bobby, they both came from the same type of animal. Look here." She handed them over.

Bobby held them close to her face. "I see what you mean, but how did Bryce get hold of a white abalone?"

"And how did Dr. Soloski? He said he bought it at a garage sale."

"It's possible, I suppose. Weird, but possible." Bobby's eyes moved along with her thoughts. "Whatever is going on around here, it all keeps coming back to the ocean."

"Mmm hmm." Ruth prowled around the tiny room some more trying to calm her jittery nerves. "I need to go for a walk on the beach. The walls are closing in. Will you go with me?"

"I would love to get some fresh air, but I don't think Jack or Uncle Monk would approve."

"I'll leave a message at home for Monk, and you can call and leave word for Jack at the station. He can come along if he'd feel better about it." Ruth thought she saw a wistful look on Bobby's face for a moment.

Ruth called home and Bobby reported Jack was on the road, so she left a voice mail on his cell phone.

"Okay, Aunt Ruth. Let's hit the beach before the sun goes down."

Ruth kissed Bryce on the forehead, and they headed out.

The tang of salt air revived them both. It was still warm, but a wind blew the surf into puffs of white cotton and sent the few tourists scuttling back to town for hot coffee. They wouldn't find it at Monk's. He'd insisted they close the shop for a few days so Bobby would be free to babysit Ruth. She wondered how they were going to afford all the baby gear that currently crammed her house from floor to rafters. Only a supreme act of will kept her from opening their credit card bill to assess the damage.

They stopped in the shelter of some rocks and stared at the turbulent ocean. Waves dashed against the wall of rock that curved out into the water. It formed a sheltered cove for swimmers and divers, but not today. It was deserted save for a lone bird, poking for one last meal before the sun set.

Ruth shivered.

"Cold?" Bobby asked.

"No. I was just remembering finding Reggie here." Her mind flashed back to the awful moment. Alva, Ellen, Dr. Soloski, even Roxie had all been witness to the terrible sight. She pulled her collar up around her chin.

"Ruth, look." Bobby pointed to a figure in a wet suit, climbing along the top of the rocky cliff. The person was silhouetted against the waning sun. "Isn't that—"

"Yes, it is. What is Dr. Soloski doing out here at this hour? What is he wearing? It couldn't be a wet suit."

"I'm going to go find out."

Ruth put a hand on her arm. "Oh no, you don't. Those rocks are slippery, and Jack would most definitely not approve."

Bobby stiffened. "I'm just going to peek around the top and see where he's going, and I don't answer to Jack, by the way. I need to make a life without him." Her look softened and she kissed Ruth. "Stay here, and I'll be back in five minutes. Take my cell phone in case you need one."

Before Ruth could answer, Bobby was jogging up the beach toward the spot where Dr. Soloski had vanished over the top, after picking her way along the uneven path that led to the crest of the rock pile. Ruth tried to repress the anxious feeling in her gut by puzzling out the doctor's odd behavior.

Snatches of conversation played in her mind.

Ellen's grating voice. *"Do you dive, Doctor?"*

The doctor's reponse. *"No, ma'am. I'm a land creature all the way."*

So what was he doing heading into the surf wearing a wet suit? For a guy who was happiest in the trees, it didn't seem to fit.

The trees. A lightbulb flashed across her brain. He was an arborist, a person no doubt familiar with ropes—and all kinds of knots.

Take it easy, Ruth. The man is a dentist. He's from a wealthy family. Why would he want to kill Reggie? But he needed money. He'd told her how expensive the care was for his sister. Was he out looking for the White Queens, too? Had he encountered Reggie during the dive and murdered him?

It still made no sense, but Ruth's duty was clear. Even if it turned out to be her wild imagination at work, she had to get Bobby away from Dr. Soloski. With shaking fingers she dialed the police station, but the cliffs blocked the signal. She hastened a few steps onto higher ground with the same result. The cell phone was useless. There was no way to summon help except to return to town, and by that time it might be too late.

She peered once again at the black pile of rock. There was still no sign of Bobby. Ruth took off her hat and left the cell phone on a pile of rocks well away from the advancing tide. Then she set off for the cliff.

Jack listened again to the "signal unavailable" message on Bobby's cell phone before he clicked off his phone. His car engine idled outside the empty dentist office. He'd already checked the man's home with no luck. Ruth wasn't at the cottage or the hospital and neither was Bobby.

"Where is everybody?"

When his phone rang a second later he snatched it up. "Jack Denny."

"Where are they?" Monk bellowed. "Where are my wife and niece? The message on my machine says they went for a walk, but that was an hour ago. Do you have any ideas?"

Jack held the phone away from his ear. "I got the same message. Did she say where they went walking?"

"No, only that they went out for fresh air. Maude hasn't seen them, and Alva said they were at the hospital when Ruth asked him to bring his shell there, the one he boosted from the dentist. That's the last he's seen of her."

The shell? His suspicions were beginning to take on a more solid shade of black and white. "I'll check with the nurses and call you right back."

The nurse told him a minute later that they'd headed toward the beach. He dialed Monk again. "I'm going to pick you up. I think I know where they went."

Monk sighed. "Women. Why don't they ever stay where you tell 'em to?"

Jack didn't answer as he turned on the lights and siren and raced toward the cottage.

In five minutes Monk was strapping his big frame into the passenger seat. "What do you mean you think it was the dentist? Why would he kill Reggie? I thought the guy was well-to-do and all that. He's a professional man and all."

"I haven't figured out a motive yet. I may be totally wrong, but I did find out he is strapped for cash. His mother left everything in trust to the sick daughter and Soloski was left without a dime."

"Ouch."

"Yeah, but sister gets the bundle when she's twenty-one."

"Oh boy. I'll bet he's going to have her sign some papers on her birthday to give the wad to her loving brother, or—" Monk shot him a look. "Who gets the money if she dies?"

"Who do you think?"

"Uh-oh." Monk fisted his hands on his knees, his wide forehead bisected by creases of worry. "But really, Jack. What does it all have to do with Reggie?"

"I don't know, but Soloski needs plenty of income to pick up the tab on what insurance doesn't cover for his sister. His previous dental practice failed and left him near bankruptcy, but he's somehow been paying for her care all this time."

"So where's the cash coming from?"

"My question exactly."

Ruth watched the path carefully as she climbed the rocks. Inch by inch, the tide was filling in the cove far below. Getting past one more projection of rock should reveal Bobby's location. She carefully picked her way along and peeked around the black crag.

There was no one there. She looked in all directions for any sign of Dr. Soloski or Bobby. Where had they gone? If they'd climbed back down to the beach over the other side she would be able to see them on the ground below.

A sound made her turn.

"Hello, Ruth." Dr. Soloski's face was hard in the dusky light. His wet suit gave him an otherworldly appearance, as if he were a part of the rock from which he'd seemingly emerged.

Ruth tried to level her voice. "Oh, uh, Dr. Soloski. Where did you come from? I was, just, uh, looking for my niece."

He pointed to a crevice in the rock that she hadn't noticed before. It was virtually invisible, sheltered by a gnarled twist of black. "She's down there. Why don't you go join her?"

Ruth's breath grew shallow. Without taking her eyes off the dentist, she inched closer to the hole. "Bobby? Can you hear me?"

"She can't hear you." He smiled. "Too windy. Go on down and see her."

"I don't think—"

He grabbed her arm and propelled her toward the edge of the crevice. Her feet skidded on the wet rock. Soon she was forced down into the gap, scraping her elbows as she fought for balance. A rope ladder led down into blackness. Ruth looked at the man. "What will you do if I don't cooperate?"

His cruel smile told her the answer.

Feeling as though she'd stepped into a bad movie, she grasped the damp rope and climbed down.

Bobby lay at the bottom, bleeding from a cut on her head and chin. Ruth knelt next to her. "Oh, Bobby, did he hurt you?"

"He shoved me and I fell. I think I broke my collarbone. I'm sorry, Aunt Ruth. I'm sorry I got us into this mess with Dr. Scary here."

"Shut up," Soloski said as he stepped off the ladder and joined them. "You've caused me no end of trouble. I'll have to harvest early now, and that cuts into my cash flow."

Though the dark walls seemed to close around her in a black fist, Ruth decided the best course of action was to try to stay calm and keep him talking. "Harvest what?"

Bobby pointed into the dark water that was now lapping over her shoes. She peered into the inky surface. Glimmers of white shone in the weak light. It clicked. White treasure, only a different kind than Señor Orson's pearls. "White abalone. You found a stash of white abalone, and you're poaching them."

"I wasn't looking for them. It was dumb luck really. But there they were one day when I was out on a dive avoiding your monstrous librarian. There they were, a treasure trove right under everyone's noses. The best ones are the deepest, eighty feet or so."

"But they're an endangered species. You might drive them into extinction." Ruth realized the stupidity of her statement as soon as she said it. "You don't care, do you? You killed Reggie because he stumbled onto your little business?"

He shrugged. "A minor glitch. He was a nobody. I didn't figure anyone would be nuts enough to be in the ocean at night. That's when I harvest. The camera guy must have been a nut because there he was, swimming up from the lower vent. I suppose I should have handled it better, but I was so surprised I just dropped the rope over his neck and strangled him. More instinct than anything else. Your son was a bigger problem. He saw me heading out of my hidey hole. I tripped and one of the abalone fell out of the bag and smashed." He shook his head. "Such a waste. Anyway, your nosy son was right there to see it all, so I had to disable him."

Ruth was overwhelmed with rage. "Disable him? You could have killed him. All to make a few bucks."

"More than a few. My buyers will pay two hundred dollars each for these babies, the big ones anyway, plus a nice bonus for the trouble I take to smuggle them out of here. I've already sold almost five hundred of them and I figure I can scrape another five hundred or so before the lot is depleted. I ship the shells overseas and get a nice bit for those, too, before they're made into cheap jewelry or whatever."

He smiled in satisfaction. "All things considered it's enough to cover my expenses, at least until my beloved sister turns twenty-one next month. The abalone supply should hold out until then. When Mommy Dearest's trust fund kicks in, I won't ever need to sell another thing as long as I live."

Ruth's feet felt chilled to the bone as the water lapped her ankles. "Maude thought you were wealthy."

He laughed. "The old prune. She would believe anything, as long as it came from the mouth of an eligible man."

Bobby groaned. "Why did you come to Finny anyway?"

"I came to this nowhere town to escape some creditors. There isn't exactly a wealth of patients here so I had plenty of time to check out the beach. While I was diving one day, I noticed there is a vent along the cliff side about fifty feet down, so I dove to check it out, and bingo. I didn't know they were white abalone at first. I'd have been happy to poach any kind, really. Lucky they were a rare type. Restaurateurs will pay extra for them."

"And you said you didn't dive," Ruth said bitterly.

"I said a lot of things you bought, hook, line, and sinker."

"So why did you try to run her down and break into the house?" Bobby said, her voice thin. "Was there any particular reason for that?"

"I saw her at the library researching, and she had the shell that idiot Alva took from my office. I wanted to get it back, or discourage her from doing any more poking around."

"You are insane," Bobby said.

His smile shone white in the dark. "Insanely rich, soon. Rich people are forgiven all their little foibles." He glanced at the water. "The tide's coming in. I've got to go and be prepared to be suitably grieved when your bodies wash up on the beach."

Ruth fought a swell of panic. "You can't leave us here to die."

Dr. Soloski began to climb the rope ladder. "I could kill you first, if you'd like. I'm pretty good with knots." His laughter echoed through the cavern as he ascended and pulled the rope ladder up in his wake.

She could not restrain a shriek of abject terror as the ladder slithered upward and disappeared. The only sound was the rush of surf filling in the rock tunnel and then retreating, each time bringing the frigid water a few inches higher.

Ruth tried to move Bobby to a drier spot, but she resisted.

"Just help me up. We've got to get out of here."

Wondering how that was going to be possible, she hooked a shoulder under Bobby's arm and pulled her to a standing position.

The girl grimaced, leaning unsteadily against the rock, the water now up to their knees.

"Can we climb out?" Ruth peered upward into the circle of sky that was now a deep pearly gray, thick with clouds.

"I don't see how. The rocks are sheer and even if we did he might be waiting at the top. Did you call Jack before you came to get me?"

Her heart constricted. "Yes, but there was no signal."

Bobby put her arm around Ruth and chafed her shoulders. "It's not good for the babies to have your body temperature drop."

Ruth's smile was grim. "It's not going to be good for them when I drown, either."

The circle of freezing sea water had reached her waist. She tried to climb up higher on the rocks to keep her stomach out of the wet, but her feet couldn't get a purchase on the slippery rock. "You're right, there's no way to climb up and no one will hear us if we scream." The panic had now morphed into a numb blanket of terror that wrapped around her insides and seemed to squeeze the breath out of her.

Bobby looked into the dark expanse of water. "Then we'll have to go down."

Ruth wondered if perhaps Bobby hit her head in the fall. "What?"

"Aunt Ruth, listen to me carefully because we don't have much time. Dr. Soloski is right, there's a vent below us. I'd say it's probably twenty feet down from where we are standing. It connects this tunnel to the ocean. That's how the good doctor gets in and out at high tide."

"What are you saying, Bobby?" There was a frantic edge in Ruth's voice as the water crept toward her shoulders.

"We've got to dive down and swim to that opening and out into the cove. If it's big enough to fit the doctor in scuba gear, and Reggie, then we can fit, too."

Ruth's eyes widened. "I can't do that. I'm not even a good swimmer when there aren't waves and slippery rocks and two babies inside me."

"Stick close to me and I'll try to pull you along, but once we're out in the ocean you've got to make for shore. I'm going to be slow, so you just get out as fast as you can."

Her head whirled. "Bobby, you might drown. We both will probably drown. This is crazy. Maybe we should wait for help."

Bobby's black hair formed a helmet around her face. She pointed to the water that lapped her chest. "Aunt Ruth, we're going to drown right here, right now, or die of hypothermia. It's the only way out. Can you do it?"

No, her mind screamed. Dive into that freezing blackness and hope for a hole to squeeze through? She could not do that, it was too much. But how could she not give the babies that chance? How could she decide for them that they would all drown in this horrible cave and never see the precious light of day? How could she end their lives before they'd felt their father's caress or seen the love in their parents' eyes?

She thought about Monk, who would be mad with worry, and Bryce, who would have no one to wake up for if they died. She reached out a hand to Bobby. "Father God," she said, "give us the strength to fight for our lives. Help us to find our way back to the people who love us, if that is Your desire, and give us peace to accept Your will if it is not."

Bobby squeezed her frozen fingers. "I love you, Aunt Ruth. We're going to make it."

"I love you, too, Bobby." She took a shaky breath. "The babies are getting cold. Let's dive."

The dark feeling in Jack's stomach increased with each mile. He radioed the station to arrange for backup and a fire department response. Coast Guard, too, though they would not arrive for a half hour or so.

They'll be fine. We'll probably meet them walking back from the beach. Something told him it was not true. They pulled off as near the sand as they could get. Nate screamed in behind them, flashers still going. Half skidding, half jogging, they made it to the gravel trail.

"Look," Monk cried. He held up Ruth's hat and the phone. "She left them here for us to find. I know it."

Dr. Soloski emerged out of the darkness. He froze for a moment, his eyes taking in the three men. Then he took another step toward them.

"I was coming to get help. It's Bobby and Ruth. They were up walking along the rocks and the tide came it. I tried to get to them, but the surf is too rough."

Monk took one look at the man, and then he was on him like a mountain lion. His hands fastened around Soloski's throat over the rubberized wet suit. "My aunt Petunia's bonnet, you were trying to get help. What did you do with them?" His roar made the doctor flinch.

"I don't know what you're talking about," Dr. Soloski gasped. "I was trying to save them."

Jack and Nate tried to pull Monk's hands away.

Jack felt the desperation well up inside him. "We know you killed Reggie. Don't compound your crimes here by adding two more lives."

"Four," Monk said, savagely. "Don't forget Ruth's got twins on board."

The prone man gave Jack a look that showed for the briefest of seconds the wickedness under the veneer of gentility. "You've got no proof of anything, and if I were you, I wouldn't waste time with accusations when two women are probably drowning right this minute."

"Where are they?" Jack shouted.

Soloski only laughed.

Monk let go as if he'd been burned and ran on toward the surf. Jack followed, leaving Soloski for Nate to handcuff.

They raced along over the shifting pebbles. The outline of the rock pile was silhouetted against the last rays of sun. Waves crashed against the wall, sending arms of foam clear to the top.

Jack stared desperately, trying to pick out any sign of Bobby or Ruth. The narrow path that joined the beach to the cliffs was already underwater. "Bobby!" he shouted. "Ruth! Where are you?"

The wind flung the words back at him.

Monk's face was stark with terror. "I don't see them. Where are they?"

Both men turned their faces to the dark, heaving water. After a split second, Monk stripped off his shoes and Jack followed suit. The freezing water swirled around their knees. Then the sound of a motor cut through the night.

Roxie aimed a light at them from her motorboat. "Get in. I can take you close. I know these rocks."

Monk didn't hesitate. He splashed out to the boat and Roxie helped him in before they both gave Jack a hand up.

She steered the vessel out into the choppy surf. "I heard your call on my police radio. Where do you think they were?"

Jack pointed to the rocky crag. "Soloski said they were walking along the cliffs. He must have disabled them somehow."

Roxie shook her head as they boat chugged through the choppy waters. "I knew there was something wrong about him."

Jack wished with all his power that he had realized the truth earlier.

As the salt spray stung his eyes, he wondered if his error would cost four lives.

The ice-cold water swallowed Bobby in a moment. Ruth waited for one second more, sucking in as much precious air as she could before she let go of the jagged rocks and swam after her.

Her belly interfered with her downward progress, forcing her to grab onto rocks to pull herself farther into the abyss. Though her eyes burned, she didn't dare take them off Bobby for an instant. She knew it must be excruciating for the woman to make any progress with a broken collarbone.

Ruth's lungs ached as the darkness increased along with her panic. If they didn't reach the vent soon—

Something tugged at her pants, arresting her progress. She yanked the fabric loose from where it had snagged on a sharp rock. When she looked up again, Bobby was gone.

She frantically scanned in all directions, but there was nothing but black.

The facts settled around her like iron weights. She was going to die in darkness along with her babies. The only thing she could feel was the cold, settling into her very core. She couldn't move. Even the tiny kicks from inside had stilled.

God deliver us, she prayed as Indigo had so many years before in the grip of a violent ocean.

A glimmer of white caught her eye in the gloom. The abalone, clustered in a great wide band, lay like a pearl necklace against the rock. Knowing she had only seconds of air left, Ruth scooted along the trail of domed creatures, ignoring the cut of their barnacle-encrusted shells on her fingers.

Lungs screaming, eyes half closed, she saw it: an irregular circle cut into the rock.

The vent that led out to the sea.

"There," Monk shouted. He pointed to a bit of yellow on the swirling surf. He dove in. Roxie and Jack waited, bent over the side, until Monk dragged the bundle to the side.

Monk cradled Ruth in his arms on the bottom of the boat. Her eyes were closed, but she breathed. "She's alive." Monk's face was torn with emotion. "She's alive, praise the holy Father and His loving Son. She's alive."

Jack returned to the side and continued to scan.

Roxie played the light across the surface of the water.

Nothing.

Teeth clenched, every nerve on fire, he scanned left and right, left and right.

The tiniest flash of white caught his eye. He didn't think twice before he was in the water. The cold hit him like a slap, but he swam against the strong pull of the surf until he reached her.

Bobby floated facedown in the water, hair fanned out in the surf.

He flipped her over and started swimming with all his might toward the boat.

Waves pushed against him, crashing over his head.

He fought against the relentless power of the sea until he reached the pitching vessel.

Roxie and Monk lifted them back in.

Jack laid Bobby on the deck. Her face was deathly pale, tinged with blue. He held his cheek to her mouth.

"She's not breathing." He unzipped her jacket and tilted her chin back.

Roxie's face was grim. She took her fingers from the girl's neck. "No pulse. I know CPR. I'll do the compressions." She began to push on Bobby's chest in a steady rhythm that defied the rocking of the deck beneath them.

Vaguely Jack felt the boat move as Monk steered it back toward land.

He put his mouth onto Bobby's cold lips and blew, willing his life to mingle with hers and bring her back to him.

23

Ruth pulled the blankets around her, even though the hospital room was a toasty temperature. She felt as if she'd never be fully warm again. Monk opened the blinds to let in the morning sunshine. He kissed her on each cheek and her forehead.

"How are you feeling today?"

"Okay. How are you? Sleeping in a chair can't be too comfortable."

He rolled his big shoulders. "I didn't sleep much anyway. Mostly I just watched you."

Her cheeks warmed. "That must have made for a long night."

His eyes gleamed with moisture. "I could watch you every minute of every day and be a perfectly happy man."

She steadied her breath, luxuriating again at the simple blessing of being able to inhale and exhale. "How is Bryce?"

"The doctor says he's showing encouraging signs of coming around. We'll have to be patient and pray."

She laughed. "God has had an earful from me already."

"Me, too, but He's a great listener."

Jack knocked gently. "Mind if we come in?"

"Not at all." Monk moved to the other side of the bed to accommodate Bobby's wheelchair.

Ruth noted the pallor of Bobby's face and the sling holding her shoulder steady, but there was something else about her that made Ruth take notice: a calm and a contentment that she had not seen in the young woman before.

Jack kept his hand on Bobby's good shoulder as he talked. "How are you doing, Ruth? We were worried there for a while."

"So was I, but the doctor was able to stop the contractions. I'm on bed rest until further notice. What happened to the awful dentist?"

"He's been arrested for the murder of Reggie and the attempted murder of you two lovely ladies and your son. There will be more charges relating to poaching and such, but that will get us started."

Ruth watched the way Bobby reached up to cover Jack's hand with hers. She smiled. "Will you be postponing taking that job in Utah?"

"Yes. I think I'm going to stay here and hang out with this big lug. Almost drowning kinda put a new spin on things for me."

Ruth shivered. "I'll never swim in the ocean again."

Bobby laughed. "I don't have any choice. Jack needs to learn how to dive so he can keep the eyes of law enforcement on those abalone, or what's left of them."

They chatted for a while until Bobby showed signs of tiring and Jack wheeled her back to her room. Monk went off to fetch a cup of tea for his wife.

Ruth settled into the beam of sunlight that played across the bed. How very blessed she felt to be alive and warm and surrounded by people she loved. The babies kicked and rolled inside her. She knew they would be okay, growing and thriving with parents who loved them desperately.

From her window she could just make out the silvery rise and fall of the ocean. She marveled at all the treasures it contained.

God saved me with His white treasure, Indigo said of the small bit of flour that ensured her survival.

Had He done the same with Ruth? Provided a path of silvery white abalone to guide her home?

She smiled, feeling the babies rollicking inside her, and turned her face to the sun.

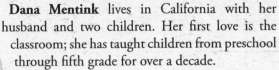

Dana Mentink lives in California with her husband and two children. Her first love is the classroom; she has taught children from preschool through fifth grade for over a decade.

Dana is perpetually in search of a great story, either through painfully expensive trips to the bookstore or via her own labors in front of the computer. She enjoys writing cozies for Heartsong Presents—MYSTERIES! as well as suspense stories.

In addition to her novels, Dana writes short articles, both fiction and nonfiction, for a wide variety of magazines. Dana enjoys mentoring other writers and finding new vehicles to provide her readers with a hefty dose of mystery, merriment, and make-believe. Contact Dana on her Web site: www.danamentink.com.

You may correspond with this author by writing:
Dana Mentink
Author Relations
PO Box 721
Uhrichsville, OH 44683

A Letter to Our Readers

Dear Reader:

In order to help us satisfy your quest for more great mystery stories, we would appreciate it if you would take a few minutes to respond to the following questions. We welcome your comments and read each form and letter we receive. When completed, please return to:

Fiction Editor
Heartsong Presents—MYSTERIES!
PO Box 721
Uhrichsville, Ohio 44683

Did you enjoy reading *California Capers* by Dana Mentink?

Very much! I would like to see more books like this! The one thing I particularly enjoyed about this story was:

_____

_____

_____

Moderately. I would have enjoyed it more if:

_____

_____

_____

Are you a member of the HP—MYSTERIES! Book Club?
Yes   No

If no, where did you purchase this book?

_____

Please rate the following elements using a scale of 1 (poor) to 10 (superior):

___ Main character/sleuth   ___ Romance elements

___ Inspirational theme   ___ Secondary characters

___ Setting   ___ Mystery plot

How would you rate the cover design on a scale of 1 (poor) to 5 (superior)? _____

What themes/settings would you like to see in future **Heartsong Presents—MYSTERIES!** selections? _____

_____

_____

_____

Please check your age range:
- ○ Under 18   ○ 18–24
- ○ 25–34   ○ 35–45
- ○ 46–55   ○ Over 55

Name: _____

Occupation: _____

Address: _____

E-mail address: _____